CW01391754

The
MX Book
of
New
Sherlock
Holmes
Stories

Part XX – 2020 Annual
(1891-1897)

THE MX BOOK OF NEW SHERLOCK HOLMES STORIES

STORIES

PART XX
2020 ANNUAL
(1891-1897)

SOUTHAMPTON
STREET

359

EDITED
BY
David
Marcum

OFFICES

TRADITIONAL HOLMES
ADVENTURES
COMPILED FOR THE
BENEFIT OF THE
RESTORATION OF
UNDERSHAW

First edition published in 2020
© Copyright 2020

The right of the individuals listed on the Copyright Information page to be identified as the authors of this work has been asserted by them in accordance with the Copyright, Designs, and Patents Act 1998.

All rights reserved. No reproduction, copy, or transmission of this publication may be made without express prior written permission. No paragraph of this publication may be reproduced, copied, or transmitted except with express prior written permission or in accordance with the provisions of the Copyright Act 1956 (as amended). Any person who commits any unauthorised act in relation to this publication may be liable to criminal prosecution and civil claims for damage.

All characters appearing in this work are fictitious or used fictitiously. Except for certain historical personages, any resemblance to real persons, living or dead, is purely coincidental. The opinions expressed herein are those of the authors and not of MX Publishing.

ISBN Hardback 978-1-78705-565-0
ISBN Paperback 978-1-78705-566-7
AUK ePub ISBN 978-1-78705-567-4
AUK PDF ISBN 978-1-78705-568-1

Published in the UK by
MX Publishing
335 Princess Park Manor, Royal Drive,
London, N11 3GX
www.mxpublishing.co.uk

David Marcum can be reached at:
thepapersofsherlockholmes@gmail.com

Cover design by Brian Belanger
www.belangerbooks.com and *www.redbubble.com/people/zhahadun*

CONTENTS

Forewords

Adventures

(Continued on the next page . . . .)

(Continued on the next page . . . .)

(Continued on the next page . . . .)

**These additional Sherlock Holmes adventures
can be found in the previous volumes of**
The MX Book of New Sherlock Holmes Stories

(Continued on the next page . . . .)

(Continued on the next page . . . .)

PART V – Christmas Adventures

(Continued on the next page . . . .)

PART VI – 2017 Annual

(Continued on the next page . . . .)

The Unwelcome Client – Keith Hann
The Tempest of Lyme – David Ruffle
The Problem of the Holy Oil – David Marcum
A Scandal in Serbia – Thomas A. Turley
The Curious Case of Mr. Marconi – Jan Edwards
Mr. Holmes and Dr. Watson Learn to Fly – C. Edward Davis
Die Weisse Frau – Tim Symonds
A Case of Mistaken Identity – Daniel D. Victor

PART VII – Eliminate the Impossible: 1880-1891

Foreword – Lee Child
Foreword – Rand B. Lee
Foreword – Michael Cox
Foreword – Roger Johnson
Foreword – Melissa Farnham
Foreword – David Marcum
No Ghosts Need Apply (A Poem) – Jacquelynn Morris
The Melancholy Methodist – Mark Mower
The Curious Case of the Sweated Horse – Jan Edwards
The Adventure of the Second William Wilson – Daniel D. Victor
The Adventure of the Marchindale Stiletto – James Lovegrove
The Case of the Cursed Clock – Gayle Lange Puhl
The Tranquility of the Morning – Mike Hogan
A Ghost from Christmas Past – Thomas A. Turley
The Blank Photograph – James Moffett
The Adventure of A Rat. – Adrian Middleton
The Adventure of Vanaprastha – Hugh Ashton
The Ghost of Lincoln – Geri Schear
The Manor House Ghost – S. Subramanian
The Case of the Unquiet Grave – John Hall
The Adventure of the Mortal Combat – Jayantika Ganguly
The Last Encore of Quentin Carol – S.F. Bennett
The Case of the Petty Curses – Steven Philip Jones
The Tuttman Gallery – Jim French
The Second Life of Jabez Salt – John Linwood Grant
The Mystery of the Scarab Earrings – Thomas Fortenberry
The Adventure of the Haunted Room – Mike Chinn
The Pharaoh's Curse – Robert V. Stapleton
The Vampire of the Lyceum – Charles Veley and Anna Elliott
The Adventure of the Mind's Eye – Shane Simmons

PART VIII – Eliminate the Impossible: 1892-1905

Foreword – Lee Child
Foreword – Rand B. Lee
Foreword – Michael Cox
Foreword – Roger Johnson
Foreword – Melissa Farnham

(Continued on the next page . . . .)

Part IX – 2018 Annual (1879-1895)

(Continued on the next page . . . .)

The Lambeth Poisoner Case – Stephen Gaspar
The Confession of Anna Jarrow – S. F. Bennett
The Adventure of the Disappearing Dictionary – Sonia Fetherston
The Fairy Hills Horror – Geri Schear
A Loathsome and Remarkable Adventure – Marcia Wilson
The Adventure of the Multiple Moriartys – David Friend
The Influence Machine – Mark Mower

Part X – 2018 Annual (1896-1916)
Foreword – Nicholas Meyer
Foreword – Roger Johnson
Foreword – Melissa Farnham
Foreword – Steve Emecz
Foreword – David Marcum
A Man of Twice Exceptions (A Poem) – Derrick Belanger
The Horned God – Kelvin Jones
The Coughing Man – Jim French
The Adventure of Canal Reach – Arthur Hall
A Simple Case of Abduction – Mike Hogan
A Case of Embezzlement – Steven Ehrman
The Adventure of the Vanishing Diplomat – Greg Hatcher
The Adventure of the Perfidious Partner – Jayantika Ganguly
A Brush With Death – Dick Gillman
A Revenge Served Cold – Maurice Barkley
The Case of the Anonymous Client – Paul A. Freeman
Capitol Murder – Daniel D. Victor
The Case of the Dead Detective – Martin Rosenstock
The Musician Who Spoke From the Grave – Peter Coe Verbica
The Adventure of the Future Funeral – Hugh Ashton
The Problem of the Bruised Tongues – Will Murray
The Mystery of the Change of Art – Robert Perret
The Parsimonious Peacekeeper – Thaddeus Tuffentsamer
The Case of the Dirty Hand – G.L. Schulze
The Mystery of the Missing Artefacts – Tim Symonds

Part XI: Some Untold Cases (1880-1891)
Foreword – Lyndsay Faye
Foreword – Roger Johnson
Foreword – Melissa Grigsby
Foreword – Steve Emecz
Foreword – David Marcum
Unrecorded Holmes Cases (*A Sonnet*) – Arlene Mantin Levy and Mark Levy
The Most Repellant Man – Jayantika Ganguly
The Singular Adventure of the Extinguished Wicks – Will Murray
Mrs. Forrester's Complication – Roger Riccard
The Adventure of Vittoria, the Circus Belle – Tracy Revels

(Continued on the next page . . . .)

Part XII: Some Untold Cases (1894-1902)

PART XIII: 2019 Annual (1881-1890)

(Continued on the next page . . . .)

PART XIV: 2019 Annual (1891 -1897)

(Continued on the next page . . . .)

(Continued on the next page . . . .)

(Continued on the next page . . . .)

The following contributions appear in this volume:
The MX Book of New Sherlock Holmes Stories
Part XX – 2020 Annual (1891-1897)

"The Adventure of the American Opera Singer" ©2019 by Deanna Baran. All Rights Reserved. First publication, original to this collection. Printed by permission of the author.

"The Tomorrow Man" ©2019 by S.F. Bennett. All Rights Reserved. First publication, original to this collection. Printed by permission of the author.

"Blood and Gunpowder" ©2019 by Thomas A. Burns. All Rights Reserved. First publication, original to this collection. Printed by permission of the author.

"A Word From Stepping Stones" ©2020 by Lizzy Butler. All Rights Reserved. First publication, original to this collection. Printed by permission of the author.

"The Atelier of Death" ©2019 by Harry DeMaio. All Rights Reserved. First publication, original to this collection. Printed by permission of the author.

"The Elusive Mr. Phillimore" ©2012, 2019 by Matthew J. Elliott. All Rights Reserved. First publication of text script in this collection. Originally broadcast on radio on May 27, 2012 as Episode No. 105 of *The Further Adventures of Sherlock Holmes*.

"Strength to Strength" ©2020 by Steve Emecz. All Rights Reserved. First publication, original to this collection. Printed by permission of the author.

"The Perplexing *X*'ing" ©2019 by Sonia Fetherston. All Rights Reserved. First publication, original to this collection. Printed by permission of the author.

"The Elusive Mr. Chester" ©2019 by Arthur Hall. All Rights Reserved. First publication, original to this collection. Printed by permission of the author.

"The Adventure at Dead Man's Hole" ©2019 by Stephen Herczeg. All Rights Reserved. First publication, original to this collection. Printed by permission of the author.

"What Could Be Better For the Purpose?" ©2020 by Roger Johnson. All Rights Reserved. First publication, original to this collection. Printed by permission of the author.

"A Case of Unfinished Business" ©2014, 2019 by Steven Philip Jones. All Rights Reserved. First publication of text script in this collection. Originally broadcast on radio on March 6, 2014 as Episode No. 114 of *The Further Adventures of Sherlock Holmes*. Printed by permission of the author.

"The Case of the Short-Sighted Clown" ©2019 by Susan Knight. All Rights Reserved. First publication, original to this collection. Printed by permission of the author.

"Foreword" ©2019 by John Lescroart. All Rights Reserved. First publication, original to this collection. Printed by permission of the author.

"Editor's Foreword: Not Just 'Always 1895' – A Hero for Now" and "The Keadby Cross" ©2019, 2020 by David Marcum. All Rights Reserved. First publication, original to this collection. Printed by permission of the author.

"The Sibling" ©2020, 2015 by Jacquelynn Morris. All Rights Reserved. The original version of this poem was presented as a toast on January 9, 2015 at the BSI Dinner, New York, and is now located the BSI Archives. Printed by permission of the author.

"The Case of the *S.S. Bokhara*" ©2019 by Mark Mower. All Rights Reserved. First publication, original to this collection. Printed by permission of the author.

"The Adventure of Old Black Duffel" ©2019 by Will Murray. All Rights Reserved. First publication, original to this collection. Printed by permission of the author.

"The Adventure of the Unkind Turn" ©2019 by Robert Perret. All Rights Reserved. First publication, original to this collection. Printed by permission of the author.

"The Blood-Spattered Bridge" ©2019 by Gayle Lange Puhl. All Rights Reserved. First publication, original to this collection. Printed by permission of the author.

"The Adventure of the Beauty Trap" ©2019 by Tracy Revels. All Rights Reserved. First publication, original to this collection. Printed by permission of the author.

"The Sweet Science of Bruising" ©2019 by Kevin P. Thornton. All Rights Reserved. First publication, original to this collection. Printed by permission of the author.

"The Mystery of Sherlock Holmes" ©2019 by Christopher Todd. All Rights Reserved. First publication, original to this collection. Printed by permission of the author.

"The Murders in the Maharajah's Railway Carriage" ©2019 by Charles Veley and Anna Elliott. All Rights Reserved. First publication, original to this collection. Printed by permission of the authors.

"The Ransomed Miracle" ©2019 by I.A. Watson. All Rights Reserved. First publication, original to this collection. Printed by permission of the author.

The following contributions appear in the companion volumes:
The MX Book of New Sherlock Holmes Stories
Part XIX – 2020 Annual (1882-1890)
Part XXI – 2020 Annual (1898-1923

"The Case of the Emerald Knife-Throwers" ©2019 by Ian Ableson. All Rights Reserved. First publication, original to this collection. Printed by permission of the author.

"The Adventure of the Chocolate Pot" ©2019 by Hugh Ashton and j-views Publishing. All Rights Reserved. Hugh Ashton appears by kind permission of j-views Publishing. First publication, original to this collection. Printed by permission of the author.

"The Adventure of the Wells Beach Ruffians" ©2019 by Derrick Belanger. All Rights Reserved. First publication, original to this collection. Printed by permission of the author.

"The Mahmudabad Result" and "The Impaled Man" ©2019 by Andrew Bryant. All Rights Reserved. First publication, original to this collection. Printed by permission of the author.

"The Case of the Rewrapped Presents" ©2000, 2019 by Bob Byrne. All Rights Reserved. This story originally appeared on-line in a slightly different form. Printed by permission of the author.

"The Scholar of Silchester Court" ©2020 by Nick Cardillo. All Rights Reserved. First publication, original to this collection. Printed by permission of the author.

"The Man in the Maroon Suit" ©2019 by Chris Chan. All Rights Reserved. First publication, original to this collection. Printed by permission of the author.

"The League of Unhappy Orphans" ©1944, 2019 by Leslie Charteris and Denis Green. First publication of text script in this collection. Originally broadcast on radio on October 23, 1944 as part of *The New Adventures of Sherlock Holmes* radio show, starring Basil Rathbone and Nigel Bruce. Introduction ©2019 by Ian Dickerson. First text publication of this revised version, original to this collection. Printed by permission of the Leslie Charteris Estate.

"The Adventure of the Tea-Stained Diamonds" ©2019 by Craig Stephen Copland. All Rights Reserved. First publication, original to this collection. Printed by permission of the author.

"Introduction – The League of Unhappy Orphans" ©2019 by Ian Dickerson. All Rights Reserved. First publication, original to this collection. Printed by permission of the author.

"The Prince of Pentonville Prison" ©2019 by David Friend. All Rights Reserved. First publication, original to this collection. Printed by permission of the author.

"The Sweetenbury Safe Affair" ©2020 by Tim Gambrell. All Rights Reserved. First publication, original to this collection. Printed by permission of the author.

"The Secret Admirer" ©2020 by Jayantika Ganguly. All Rights Reserved. First publication, original to this collection. Printed by permission of the author.

"The Tattooed Rose" and "The Enlightenment of Newton" and "The Cobbler's Treasure" ©2019 by Dick Gillman. All Rights Reserved. First publication, original to this collection. Printed by permission of the author.

"The Disappearing Prisoner" and "The Adventure of the Grand Vizier" and "The Adventure of the Incessant Workers" ©2019 by Arthur Hall. All Rights Reserved. First publication, original to this collection. Printed by permission of the author.

"The Bleeding Heart" ©2019 by Paula Hammond. All Rights Reserved. First publication, original to this collection. Printed by permission of the author.

"Holmes's Prayer" ©2020 by Christopher James. All Rights Reserved. First publication, original to this collection. Printed by permission of the author.

"The Case of the Purloined Talisman" ©2019 by John Lawrence. All Rights Reserved. First publication, original to this collection. Printed by permission of the author.

"The Fractured Freemason of Fitzrovia" ©2019 by David L. Leal. All Rights Reserved. First publication, original to this collection. Printed by permission of the author.

"The Adventure of the Doctor's Hand" ©2019 by Michael Mallory. All Rights Reserved. First publication, original to this collection. Printed by permission of the author.

"The Gordon Square Discovery" and "The Cat's Meat Lady of Cavendish Square" ©2019, 2020 by David Marcum. All Rights Reserved. First publication, original to this collection. Printed by permission of the author.

"When Best Served Cold" ©2019 by Steven Mason. All Rights Reserved. First publication, original to this collection. Printed by permission of the author.

"The Case of the Missing Pipe" ©2019 by James Moffett. All Rights Reserved. First publication, original to this collection. Printed by permission of the author.

"The Unveiled Lodger" ©2019 by Mark Mower. All Rights Reserved. First publication, original to this collection. Printed by permission of the author.

"The Indigo Impossibility" and "The Mystery of the Elusive Li Shen" ©2019 by Will Murray. All Rights Reserved. First publication, original to this collection. Printed by permission of the author.

"The Problem of the St. Francis Parish Robbery" ©2020 by R.K. Radek. All Rights Reserved. First publication, original to this collection. Printed by permission of the author.

"The Raspberry Tart" ©2019 by Roger Riccard. All Rights Reserved. First publication, original to this collection. Printed by permission of the author.

"The Adventure of the Three Fables" ©2019 by Jane Rubino. All Rights Reserved. First publication, original to this collection. Printed by permission of the author.

"The Invisible Assassin" ©2020 by Geri Schear. All Rights Reserved. First publication, original to this collection. Printed by permission of the author.

"The Nautch Night Case" ©2019 by Brenda Seabrooke. All Rights Reserved. First publication, original to this collection. Printed by permission of the author.

"The Adventure of the Changed Man" ©2019 by MJH Simmonds. All Rights Reserved. First publication, original to this collection. Printed by permission of the author.

"The Whitehaven Ransom" ©2019 by Robert Stapleton. All Rights Reserved. First publication, original to this collection. Printed by permission of the author.

"The Case of the Missing Rhyme (*A Poem*)" ©2019 by Joseph W. Svec III. All Rights Reserved. First publication, original to this collection. Printed by permission of the author.

"The Mystery of the Elusive Bard" ©2019 by Kevin P. Thornton. All Rights Reserved. First publication, original to this collection. Printed by permission of the author.

"A Game of Skittles" ©2019 by Thomas A Turley. All Rights Reserved. First publication, original to this collection. Printed by permission of the author.

"The Mummy's Curse" ©2019 by D.J. Tyrer. All Rights Reserved. First publication, original to this collection. Printed by permission of the author.

"The Adventure of the Matched Set" and "The Deceased Priest" ©2019 by Peter Coe Verbica. All Rights Reserved. First publication, original to this collection. Printed by permission of the author.

"A Case of Paternity" ©2019 by Matthew White. All Rights Reserved. First publication, original to this collection. Printed by permission of the author.

"When the Prince First Dined at the Diogenes Club" ©2019 by Sean M. Wright. All Rights Reserved. First publication, original to this collection. Printed by permission of the author.

Editor's Foreword
Not Just "Always 1895" – A Hero for *Now*
by David Marcum

In late 1887, Dr. John H. Watson finally accomplished what he'd been promising to do for years – to publish an account of the first case that he'd shared with Mr. Sherlock Holmes.

It had occurred back in early March 1881, when Watson had known Holmes for about nine weeks. They had first met a couple of months before that, in the laboratory of Barts Hospital on New Year's Day, a Saturday, after being introduced by a mutual acquaintance – simply because both had mentioned in this friend's hearing that they were in need of someone to split the cost of affordable lodgings.

The following day they examined the rooms at 221 Baker Street and, finding them acceptable, Watson moved his own possessions around that very night, with Holmes doing the same the next morning.

Watson's physical assets were limited. He'd only recently returned from Afghanistan, where he'd received a grievous and nearly fatal wound while serving at the Battle of Maiwand, only to further face the trials of enteric fever during his subsequent recovery. He states that after he and Holmes agreed to share the lodgings at 221b Baker Street, he was able to move his possessions from his hotel in a single night. Holmes's were a bit more extensive, consisting of several boxes and portmanteaus. No doubt these included materials for his scientific research, records of past cases, and his extensive commonplace books.

From early January to early March 1881, the two settled into a tolerable existence, mostly as adjacent strangers. Holmes turned twenty-seven a few days after they moved to Baker Street, and Watson was then around six months past his twenty-eighth birthday. However, in spite of this similarity in ages, they were vastly different individuals. Holmes, always brilliant, had been earning his bread and cheese as a consulting detective for a number of years, living in Montague Street by the British Museum while pursuing various studies to broaden and deepen his professional experience. Watson had trained as a doctor, and after receiving his degree in 1878, had eventually ended up in military service in India and Afghanistan, leading to his injuries and severance from the British Army.

In Baker Street, they each carried out their separate lives while trying not to bother the other. Watson was simply concerned with recovery, having neither the energy nor the inclination to do much more than stay around their rooms and wonder what his new flatmate was up to.

For Mr. Sherlock Holmes was something of a mystery to him. Watson, with nothing better to do, nowhere to go, and no other friends, began to try and learn more about this mysterious person. He wasn't very successful. In those early days, Holmes kept regular habits – early to bed, and gone before Watson rose in the morning. Holmes's trips away from Baker Street involved long walks through London, or to Barts. Some days he was energetic, and others found him lethargic, barely moving or speaking – just as he'd warned would happen when he and Watson first met and described themselves to one another.

Watson once made a list of Holmes's skills and limits, but after realizing that it wasn't really telling him anything, he threw it in frustration into the fire. He wanted to know more about this unusual person who seemed to be educating himself toward some specific but unknown goal, and who was visited by so many interesting people – for it wasn't long after they started sharing rooms that a curious collection of individuals began dropping by to consult with Holmes – although about what Watson didn't have a clue.

There was a young fashionably dressed girl, and an excited and grey-headed seedy visitor. And a slip-shod elderly woman. And an old white-haired gentleman and a railway porter. As Watson recalled, one of the visitors who came three or four times in a single week was a *"little sallow rat-faced, dark-eyed fellow"*, introduced simply as *"Mr. Lestrade"*. And every time that one of these callers arrived, Holmes would politely ask that Watson withdraw to his own bedroom so that he could use the sitting room as his *"place of business"* to see his *"clients"*. And Watson would climb the stairs for a while to his room – which was probably good therapeutic exercise for him – and then return a little while later, never quite willing to simply ask Holmes just what his business actually was.

This changed on March 4th, 1881, when the two flatmates had a discussion about a magazine article, written by Holmes, regarding observation and deduction. Watson was inclined to dismiss it as *"ineffable twaddle"* . . . although it was true that Holmes had demonstrated his skills at their first meeting when he'd stated that Watson had been in Afghanistan – an action that puzzled the doctor greatly.

That morning, Holmes had revealed to Watson that he was something called a *"consulting detective"*, so now Watson knew what and why Holmes did what he did – but he didn't really know anything at all. Not yet. Who can say what would have happened if this conversation had simply ended then and the two of them had gone about their normal daily business?

We are told that in a quantum universe, *all* possibilities exist. Schrödinger's cat is alive *and* dead. Every choice isn't an either/or proposition – rather, *both* happen . . . somehow. Somewhere there's a world where Holmes received a message from the police that morning of March 4th, 1881, in the midst of that conversation with Watson, and then he retrieved his hat and coat, departing to examine a murdered body on his own, while the invalid physician remained in the Baker Street sitting room, purposeless as he had been for the previous two months. Life in that universe continued along the same lines, with Holmes going out on his typical errands, and continuing to meet clients who came to obtain his armchair advice, while Watson continued to politely retreat upstairs. In a few months, Watson probably tired of this and sought another residence, while Holmes was likely making enough money from his consulting practice to no longer need anyone else to share expenses. After moving out, Watson might have continued to get better, or he might have slid into a life of profligacy and drunkenness. Holmes would certainly have continued to develop his skills, and to those that knew of him, he would have provided a great deal of help. But without anyone to make him known to a wider world, a lot less people would have known of him.

But in *our* universe, in the midst of their conversation about deduction and being a consulting detective, Holmes received the message from the police regarding a murder across the Thames in Lambeth, and instead of simply leaving, he curiously invited Watson to join him. Luckily we live in *that* universe where Holmes said, *"Get your hat."*

"You wish me to come?" asked a surprised Watson.

"Yes, if you have nothing better to do."

And so, after having been acquainted with Sherlock Holmes for sixty-three days, Watson finally actually *met* Sherlock Holmes – the *true* Holmes, and not just the random bits and pieces that he'd seen and tried to list over the previous couple of months – with just enough data jotted on a sheet to indicate that all the important questions were still unanswered. Finally, after seeing Holmes in action, Watson began to understand the *true* Holmes for the first time.

Of course this initial investigation was a success, and at the end Watson learned another thing – Holmes did this work for the sake of *the game*, and not for the public glory. Watson was amazed to see that the public records of the case gave credit for Holmes's work to the official force. Holmes didn't seem to care, but Watson felt otherwise. *"Your merits*

3

should be publicly recognized!" he cried. *"You should publish an account of the case. If you won't, I will for you."*

"You may do what you like, Doctor," Holmes replied. One wonders if he knew what he'd actually allowed with that one simple statement, for Watson – doctor and stalwart friend – was also an incipient writer. He faithfully recorded the facts of this case, and so many others that followed.

"I have all the facts in my journal," he told Holmes, *"and the public shall know them."*

Which brings us back to late 1887, when Watson, with the assistance of a literary agent, Dr. (and later Sir) Arthur Conan Doyle, finally published his version of that first investigation, initially relating his own personal history prior to January 1st, 1881 (in less than four-hundred words), and then telling of his meeting with Holmes, the empty days of January and February 1881, and finally the events connected with the murder in that empty house in the Brixton Road. But between early 1881 and late 1887, when *A Study in Scarlet* (as Watson's narrative was titled) was published, Holmes was involved in hundreds – nay *thousands* – of other investigations, many of which were shared with Watson. The good doctor kept notes about these, as well as additionally recording what he could learn concerning other adventures that took place without him, and also those that had occurred before he and Holmes were introduced. And thank heavens that he did make notes about these, and then find time to write them up, because one way or another, they've been finding their way into print by various paths ever since for those of us who want to know what else Mr. Holmes did besides what we're told those wonderful and yet pitifully few sixty stories that make up the official Holmesian Canon.

Initially there was a contemporary immediacy about the Holmes tales. When Watson first published *A Study in Scarlet*, he was narrating circumstances that had occurred less than seven years earlier. His next published volume, *The Sign of the Four*, appeared in early 1890, approximately seventeen months after that case took place. In June 1891, less than two months after Holmes was presumed to have perished at the Reichenbach Falls, further revelations of Holmes's adventures began appearing in *The Strand Magazine*, itself having been in business only since January of that year. Again, these records of Holmes's investigations were relatively immediate. "The Red-Headed League", published in August 1891, begins with Watson explaining that *"I had called upon my friend, Mr. Sherlock Holmes, one day in the autumn of last year . . ."* Further internal evidence places this narrative in October 1890 – less than one year before Watson's version of what happened appeared in print.

Imagine the thrill of Londoners reading these stories and finding out the complete facts in relation to what they may have already known, but without comprehending the full truth. For instance, "The Speckled Band" was published in February 1892 – not quite ten years after the business that it related. Certainly many who lived in the area of Stoke Moran still recalled the mysterious death of Dr. Grimesby Roylott in April 1883, but here was where many of them discovered for the first time – by way of Watson – what *really* happened on that terrifying night.

From the beginning, Watson's motive for recording the facts related to Holmes's investigations was to tell the public of this heroic figure. Of course, Holmes wasn't one-dimensional – he had faults, and uncertainty, and failures. But without a doubt he was a *hero*, which is certainly one of the most important reasons that he is still so well-known today, in the 2020's, decades after his death. And yet we are a great distance now from when Watson was writing of contemporary investigations for people who were aware of them as "current events". As of this writing, the investigation that made up *A Study in Scarlet* took place over 139 years ago.

When certain noted and legendary Sherlockians such as Christopher Morley and Vincent Starrett began assisting in the care and protection and promotion of Holmes's legacy and reputation in the 1920's and 1930's, Holmes and Watson were still with us, and Watson was still, with the assistance that same literary agent, publishing new accounts of Holmes's cases – right up until 1927, although they were no longer contemporary by that point. The last time that Watson released a narrative close to when the action actually occurred was when "His Last Bow" appeared in October 1917, telling what Holmes and Watson had done at the beginning of The Great War in early August 1914. After that, between 1921 and 1927, he wrote and published a further twelve Canonical cases (later collected in *The Casebook of Sherlock Holmes*) that occurred between 1896 and 1907, with most of them grouped around the turn of the century. And from the first published Canonical effort in 1887, *A Study in Scarlet*, to the last in 1927, "The Adventure of Shoscombe Olde Place", Holmes was presented as the hero that he truly was.

Too often of late, it has become fashionable to try and redefine Holmes as someone broken – from small instances to having him be a full-on sociopathic murderer. No doubt this is due to the need of some individuals to tear down heroes rather than admire them – For how can they who are not heroic themselves ever make a connection with someone that is? Better to replace the hero with someone damaged and with whom they can identify than have someone provide an example. With these motivations, some have tried to drag Holmes a long way from the hero that we first met in the publications of the late 1800's. And this is a mistake.

This can be blamed to a certain degree on the nature of the world in which we now live. Lately I've been seeing Vincent Starrett's poem *221b* referenced by Sherlockians quite a bit more than I usually do – often with a whiff of desperation. It's very familiar to those in the Sherlockian community, as it's often recited at the close of various Holmes-related gatherings as something of a benediction before returning to the responsibilities of daily modern life. Perhaps, with its nod toward times past, it provides a comfort as the world seems to be moving in an increasingly speedy express line in the proverbial hell-bound basket.

For those who don't know Vincent Starrett's well-known work:

221b

Here dwell together still two men of note
Who never lived and so can never die:
How very near they seem, yet how remote
That age before the world went all awry.
But still the game's afoot for those with ears
Attuned to catch the distant view-halloo:
England is England yet, for all our fears –
Only those things the heart believes are true.

A yellow fog swirls past the window-pane
As night descends upon this fabled street:
A lonely hansom splashes through the rain,
The ghostly gas lamps fail at twenty feet.
Here, though the world explode, these two survive,
And it is always eighteen ninety-five.

The concluding line – *And it is always eighteen ninety-five* – is often referenced amongst Sherlockians as if there is something particularly special about *that* year. As I've written elsewhere, (in the editor's foreword to Parts XI and XII of *The MX Book of New Sherlock Holmes Stories,*)1895 is definitely of Holmesian interest, as it's a year that falls squarely during those years that Holmes was in practice in Baker Street – but it certainly wasn't his busiest or most famous year. Canonical cases that occurred then – although agreement amongst Holmesian Chronologicists is by its very nature an impossibility – include "Wisteria Lodge", "The Three Students", "The Solitary Cyclist", "Black Peter", and "The Bruce-Partington Plans". But 1894 was a year that Watson specifically mentioned (in "The Golden

6

Pince-Nez") when discussing just how busy Holmes had been then, with three massive manuscript volumes required to contain both his and Holmes's work. And if one is looking for those cases that are often more remembered as reader's favorites, then one must examine the 1880's for all of those beloved tales recorded in *The Adventures* and *The Memoirs*. (For example, the highly revered "The Speckled Band" took place way back in 1883, when Holmes was only twenty-nine years old.) All four of the longer published Canonical works, *A Study in Scarlet*, *The Sign of the Four*, *The Valley of Fear*, and perhaps the most famous, *The Hound of the Baskervilles*, occur chronologically a number of years before 1895 – the first in 1881, and the other three in 1888.

And yet, 1895 is still the representative year most mentioned by Sherlockians – where *"it is always eighteen ninety-five"* . . . .

Vincent Starrett wrote these lines in 1942. While I cannot place myself in his mind, I can – as the holder of a Liberal Arts degree that involved numerous hours in English and Literature classes, teasing out various (and often ridiculous) themes and interpretations and speculations from honored literary works, and then going one step beyond to manufacture extensive entangling constructs from the vaguest of gossamer threads of guesswork and pretentious projection simply to impress teachers who became weak and giddy from being fed that kind of thing – be tempted to speculate that Starrett was looking around at the complicated and dark world of 1942 and wishing for the "simpler" times of 1895. Starrett himself was nine years old in 1895, so looking back, it probably represented a period that seemed less complex, less dangerous, and less depressing than what he was reading about in the 1942 newspapers. (And it didn't hurt that, as a poet, he'd found a year that rhymed with *"survive"*.)

In 1942, Starrett was fifty-six – just a year or so older than I am right now as I compose this essay. While our experiences were completely different – he was a Canadian born in the late 1800's who moved to Chicago as a small child, where he spent the rest of his life as a newspaper man, while I was born in the 1960's in the southern United States, where I still live and have ended up as a civil engineer – I can't help but think that there is some commonality among people of any historical period who reach a certain age and obtain any kind of earned wisdom. Thus, looking around now at the madness in today's world, I sense something of what Starrett felt when he expressed a wish for past days of the better and more innocent variety.

In 1942, Starrett must have thought that the world was falling apart. The Great Depression had started in 1929, and had continued throughout the 1930's – some say right up to the beginning of the World War in 1939, the event which forced the world economy to re-tool and get back to work for such a terrible reason. The war itself began in Europe in the fall of 1939 after a crazed period involving the unimaginable rise of vicious and evil nationalism across the world. While the war's initial spark might have started anywhere, in fact it was due to the actions of a diabolical madman, a seemingly unstoppable juggernaut of evil who had seized dictatorial power, inch by inch, in plain sight, and with the enthusiastic consent of both the ignorant cheering masses influenced by the dictator-controlled press and a group of equally evil, self-serving, and corrupt people within his own government who thought that they could control him, only to find that he was carrying out the Devil's own work with their assistance. How could such a thing happen?

1942 was the first full year that the United States had officially been involved in World War II, although support had been given to England and other allies for quite a while before then. The start of 1942 was just a few weeks after the events of Pearl Harbor, when America was suddenly in a race to bring its industrial machine to a war footing, and all over the country patriots rushed to volunteer for whatever service that they could provide. And sometime during this same year, as all around him America went to war, Starrett was prompted to write his famed poem, which is still referenced and recited at Sherlockian meetings across the U.S. – now seemingly more than ever.

But was 1895, particularly in Victorian England, really worthy of such idealization? Obviously not. 1895 was just seven years after the Ripper Murders, which had thrown London into a frenzy of panic while exposing the vast and disgusting gulf between haves and have-nots. It has been pointed out that The City in the center of London, which was probably the wealthiest place on the planet, was literally next door to the most vile and diseased part of London, where the Ripper rampaged amongst the poorest and most pathetic who existed in unimaginable conditions.

By 1895, England was still incredibly polarized in terms of politics and division of wealth. There was no diminishment of the fear of foreigners, and intolerance within the country took many other forms as well, as evidenced by the trial and imprisonment that year of Oscar Wilde. Additionally, the British were certainly aware of equally unpleasant conditions across the Channel, such as the ongoing miscarriage of justice against Alfred Dreyfus.

But as Starrett rightfully pointed out, there were two men of note living at 221b Baker Street during that time: One a detective, the other a doctor. Both were men of their times, but also enlightened and committed to seeking justice – which wasn't always defined by the actual law. As

8

Holmes remarked to Watson during a notable trip that they took to the Continent in late April and early May 1891:

> *I think that I may go so far as to say, Watson, that I have not lived wholly in vain. If my record were closed tonight I could still survey it with equanimity. The air of London is the sweeter for my presence. In over a thousand cases I am not aware that I have ever used my powers upon the wrong side.*

There are many casual Sherlockians who try to pigeon-hole Holmes and Watson into a specific era, while forgetting that they lived lives encompassing multiple decades. Both were born in the 1850's and lived well into the Twentieth Century. They saw the best and worst of those times – the continuing rise of industrialization and the various quality-of-life improvements that such could provide (for some), the increasing influence of Britain and its Empire upon the rest of the world, and advances in science with their theoretical benefits for mankind. But each of these had their substantial drawbacks, such as population displacement and the increased divisions between wealth and labor caused by new more efficient manufacturing methods, and the inevitable evils of greedy colonialism that went hand-in-hand with empire-building, and the losses of feeling toward humanity as cold science sometimes became the be-all and end-all goal of those in responsible positions.

Is it any wonder, then, that knowing Holmes and Watson were working on the side of *right* in 1895 – and for several decades on either side of that as well – that Vincent Starrett looked back from 1942 and a world at war and wished for what seemed to be a simpler time? And is it any wonder that we do the same now from our own snarled and grim days? For Watson wanted to let us know about a *hero* when he first published in the 1880's, and Vincent Starrett needed to *remind us* of that hero in the dark days of World War II. It's no mystery that, in today's inundation of daily spiraling disasters, we need to know about him too.

We live in an age of immediately available and constant information, which is forcing us to evolve as a species – whether we want to or not. I recently heard of a study that showed that the use of electronic maps through various online sources actually causes a part of the brain that affects one's sense of direction to atrophy – Why bother to try and keep track of where you are, or how to get from here to there, if you can simply look it up on your phone? Likewise, we don't have to memorize things anymore – We can simply look up a state capitol or a recipe. It's sad that human beings, who developed *reading* as a way to store information outside of our heads, have now reached the point where we store so much information that way (because there *is* so much information) that if we had to, it might be impossible to go back to the way things used to be.

While we used to have time to process information, we now have immediate news (as well as immediate opinions from countless scads of yapping heads to interpret it for us), and we can binge every episode of a television show, one episode after another, without ever going away and thinking about each separate piece and examining it this way and that to ponder and appreciate the development or the inherent puzzles. In the midst of this, our current world, there are people – some, but not all – that yearn for the simpler times. Maybe not 1895, but certainly a step back from the madness of today. And this can be found in the adventures of Mr. Sherlock Holmes.

Some are happy with the original sixty tales of The Canon. Others want more. I fall squarely in the latter camp. And while I complain about the crazed frenzy of the modern world, I can't argue that today's technology has allowed for more of Watson's narratives to be newly discovered than ever before.

When Watson first started publishing, *A Study in Scarlet* and *The Sign of the Four* appeared without much fanfare. It was only in mid-1891, when his efforts were placed in *The Strand*, that excitement spread. Over the next four decades, Holmes's adventures appeared at a very irregular rate. There were two-dozen in the initial *Strand* run from 1891 to 1893, and then nothing from Watson's pen (by way of the literary agent) until *The Hound of the Baskervilles* was serialized in 1901 and 1902. In September 1903, further short stories appeared in *The Strand*, beginning with "The Empty House", with thirty-two short stories and one novel appearing between then and 1927. And for those wishing to know more about Mr. Holmes, the pickings were slim – the Canonical stories appeared at a very uneven pace. Those seven collected in *His Last Bow* were published between 1908 and 1917, *The Valley of Fear* was serialized in 1914 and 1915, and the twelve in *The Casebook* between 1921 and 1927.

There were some other bits available for those who wanted more Holmes during these times, but not much. The countless parodies that appeared through these decades, as collected by such able scholars as Bill Peschel in his *223B Casebook Series*, don't really count as actual cases. A true early extra-Canonical story was William Gillette's 1899 play, *Sherlock Holmes*. Others were few and far between. In 1920, Vincent Starrett discovered "The Unique Hamlet", which he wisely brought forth years before his scholarly work *The Private Life of Sherlock Holmes* (1933) – showing that his skills at setting priorities are a shining example to us all.

In 1930, Edith Meiser brought Holmes to radio, correctly recognizing that the detective's cases were perfectly suited to that medium. But after several years of repeated adaptations of The Canon, she began to pull other tales form Watson's records, including an account of The Giant Rat of Sumatra, and another called "The Hindoo in the Wicker Basket" (broadcast January 7th, 1932). These narratives from beyond The Canon, both by Meiser, and later by Leslie Charteris, Denis Green, and Anthony Boucher, helped pave the way for easier acceptance of cases that didn't have to be presented by first crossing the literary agent's desk. But there were still far too few of them.

Through the 1930's and 1940's, extra-Canonical Holmes stories appeared in films starring actors such as Arthur Wontner, Basil Rathbone, and Reginald Owen. In 1948, the world was shocked to learn of a new Holmes story, apparently found in the literary agent's files, thus giving it some kind of supposed extra legitimacy. This story, "The Case of the Man Who Was Wanted", was actually determined to have been brought forth around the turn of the Twentieth Century by a man named Arthur Whitaker. The excitement that this one new story caused shows just how hungry the world was, even then, for new Holmes adventures.

In 1952 and 1953, twelve newly discovered chronicles, later collected as *The Exploits of Sherlock Holmes* (1954) were published in *Life* and *Collier's* magazines. These, as presented by the literary agent's son Adrian Conan Doyle and famed mystery author John Dickson Carr, were very authentic – although received with caustic hostility at the time in the Sherlockian community because of the well-earned animus directed toward Adrian by his past greed-directed actions in trying to "own" Sherlock Holmes.

In 1954-1955, the world was blessed with thirty-nine half-hour episodes – only a handful of which were based on Canonical tales – of the television show *Sherlock Holmes*, starring Ronald Howard. As is often the case with film presentations of Holmes and Watson, one must look past poor screen-writing or abysmal casting to see the Watsonian Truths underneath – but for 1950's television, and following those years when Watson's reputation was so terribly damaged by Nigel Bruce's portrayal, these are actually very good Holmes stories.

Scattered through the years were occasional stand-alone stories that kept the Holmes-fires burning. There were several films and early television broadcasts that presented new adaptations of Canonical stories. In 1965, something new arrived on the scene with the premiere of *A Study in Terror*, the first time that one of Holmes's many encounters with Jack the Ripper, a massively complex case from 1888, was widely revealed to the public. And then for the most part, except for the occasional appearance of a new and random Holmes short story, there was nothing until 1974, when Nicholas Meyer's *The Seven-Per-Cent Solution* was published, igniting a Sherlockian fire that has only grown ever since.

Meyer made people aware that Watson's manuscripts were out there – in attics and old trunks and stacks of family papers – just waiting to be found and presented to a public starving for more about Sherlock Holmes. Meyer found a few more, including his most-excellent 1895 exploit, *The West End Horror* (1976). In that same period, John Gardner uncovered some of Moriarty's journals – not those of the Professor, but instead his younger brother. In 1976, Nicholas Utechin and Austin Mitchelson discovered *The Earthquake Machine* and *Hellbirds*. Sean M. Wright and Michael P. Hodel found one of Mycroft Holmes's early investigations, *Enter the Lion* (1979).

Through the 1980's and 1990's, the flow of newly discovered Watsonian adventures continued, growing a little each year. Interest was fueled by the Granada television show (1984-1994), in spite of its steadily declining quality. (Sadly, except for a few stand-alone Holmes films, there have been no ongoing series about Sherlock Holmes on British or American television whatsoever since the end of the Granada series.) In the 2000's, the rise of the internet and the opportunities that it presented allowed for the dam to burst, and a very welcome surge of discovered Holmes history began to appear in the form of hundreds of online-stories, as well as books that could be prepared and sold without the strangling baggage that had been associated for so long with the publishing industry. A new paradigm washed away the old, where before a Holmes story might sit in limbo for a year or more before being published – if it were to be published at all. Now one of Watson's works could be found and brought to the public nearly immediately. And for someone like me, who has collected literally thousands of Watson's narratives for over forty years, the amount of Sherlock Holmes stories in the world was finally on the right track to being correct. But it isn't there yet, because truly *there can never be enough tales about the* true *Sherlock Holmes.*

And why? Because Holmes is a *hero*, and we need him now more than ever. As we're assailed by corruption, ignorance, intolerance, and pure evil at the highest levels – criminals and perverts and cheats and traitors of Biblical proportions – we need an essential example of someone who *thinks* and seeks knowledge instead of relying on superstition and ignorance and hunches and prejudice. We need someone who doesn't see facts as hoaxes, and someone who searches for the honorable path to justice, and not ways to subvert it. We need someone who *helps* rather than *destroys*, because of completely self-centered narcissistic greed, or simply for the warped and deviant joy of chaos. And like Vincent Starrett – who looked around in 1942 thinking that "*though the world explode*" and wished for a simpler time – we too need someplace where, though imperfect, we can look for inspiration – not finding Holmes as a broken criminal, the way that some now try to present him, but rather as the true heroic figure whom Watson wanted to honor in the 1880's, and whom Starrett wanted to remind us about in the dark depths of the early 1940's.

We may look back on Holmes where "*it is always eighteen-ninety-five*" – or several decades on either side of that – but in fact the *true* Holmes is a hero for *all* ages, and never more necessary now, and in as many stories about him as we can find.

* * * * *

As always when one of these sets is finished, I want to first thank with all my heart my incredible wonderful wife of nearly thirty-two years (as of this writing,) Rebecca, and our amazing son and my friend, Dan. I love you both, and you are everything to me!

Also, I can't ever express enough gratitude for all of the contributors who have donated their time and royalties to this ongoing project. I'm constantly amazed at the incredible stories that you send, and I'm so glad to have gotten to know all of you through this process. It's an undeniable fact that Sherlock Holmes authors are the *best* people!

The contributors of these stories have donated their royalties for this project to support the Stepping Stones School for special needs children, located at Undershaw, one of Sir Arthur Conan Doyle's former homes. As of this writing, these MX anthologies have raised over $60,000 for the school, and of even more importance, they have helped raise awareness about the school all over the world. These books are making a real difference to the school, and the participation of both contributors and purchasers is most appreciated.

Next is that group that exchanges emails with me when we have the time – and time is a valuable commodity for all of us these days! I don't get to write as often as I'd like, but I really enjoy catching up when we get the chance: Derrick Belanger, Bob Byrne, Mark Mower, Denis Smith, Tom Turley, Dan Victor, and Marcia Wilson.

There is a group of special people who have stepped up and supported this and a number of other projects over and over again with a lot of contributions. They are the best and I can't express how valued they are: Larry Albert, Hugh Ashton, Derrick Belanger, Deanna Baran, S.F. Bennett, Andrew Bryant, Thomas Burns, Nick Cardillo, Craig Stephen Copland, Matthew Elliott, David Friend, Tim Gambrell, Jayantika Ganguly, Paul Gilbert, Dick Gillman, Arthur Hall, Stephen Herczeg, Mike

13

Hogan, Craig Janacek, Steven Philip Jones, Michael Mallory, Mark Mower, Will Murray, Robert Perret, Tracy Revels, Roger Riccard, Geri Schear, Brenda Seabrooke, Shane Simmons, Robert Stapleton, Subbu Subramanian, Tim Symonds, Kevin Thornton, Charles Veley and Anna Elliott, Peter Coe Verbica, I.A. Watson, and Marcy Wilson.

I also want to thank the following:

- John Lescroart – While many know John as the best-selling author of the Dismas Hardy books (as well as a number of others also set in the Hardy Universe), I first encountered him by way of his novels relating adventures of young Nero Wolfe (although not quite under that name) during World War I – *Son of Holmes* (1986) and *Rasputin's Revenge* (1987). Holmes is very much a part of these books, and I later discovered that John had also written his own version of "The Giant Rat of Sumatra". It was only natural that I would ask him to write a foreword for these books, and he very graciously wrote a really good one. I've been a fan of his works – both Holmes-related and the highly-recommended chronicles of Dismas Hardy – for a very long time, and it's my personal thrill that he's a part of these volumes. Many thanks!

- Roger Johnson – I'm so grateful that I know Roger. His Sherlockian knowledge is exceptional, as is the work that he does to further the cause of The Master. But even more than that, both Roger and his wonderful wife, Jean Upton, are simply the finest kind of people, and I'm very lucky to know them – even though I don't get to see them nearly as often as I'd like! In so many ways, Roger, I can't thank you enough, and I can't imagine these books without you.

- Steve Emecz: I had the great good fortune to communicate with Steve way back in 2013, when I was interested in placing my previously first-published book with MX, the fast-rising superstar of the Sherlockian publishing world. It was an amazing life-changing event for me, and ever since, Steve has been one of the most positive and supportive people I've known, letting me explore various Sherlockian projects and opening up my own personal possibilities in ways that otherwise would have never been possible. Thank you Steve for every opportunity!

- Brian Belanger – In January 2020, I was able to attend – for the first time – the Holmes Birthday Celebration in New York. I met a number of wonderful people there in person after getting to know them through emails over the last several years, and I was especially glad to meet Brian, one of the nicest and most talented of people. He's amazingly great to work with, and once again I thank him for another incredible contribution.

And last but certainly *not* least, **Sir Arthur Conan Doyle**: Author, doctor, adventurer, and the Founder of the Sherlockian Feast. Present in spirit, and honored by all of us here.

As always, this collection has been a labor of love by both the participants and myself. As I've explained before, once again everyone did their sincerest best to produce an anthology that truly represents why Holmes and Watson have been so popular for so long. These are just more tiny threads woven into the ongoing Great Holmes Tapestry, continuing to grow and grow, for there can *never* be enough stories about the man whom Watson described as *"the best and wisest . . . whom I have ever known."*

David Marcum
March 4th, 2020
The 139th Anniversary of
Holmes telling Watson to
"Get your hat."

Questions, comments, or story submissions
may be addressed to David Marcum at

thepapersofsherlockholmes@gmail.com

Foreword
by John Lescroart

Ironically enough, Sherlock Holmes entered my life as a respite from literature. At the time, I was majoring in English at UC Berkeley, with an emphasis on *The Continental Novel In Translation*, immersed in the works of Tolstoy, Dostoevsky, Stendahl, Goethe, Flaubert, Camus, Thomas Mann, and many others of the all-time literary greats.

The problem was that they may have been superb stylists, but they were often not exactly easy to read. So, for example, I would have just spent five hours and three-hundred-and-fifty pages getting to the point in *Anna Karenina* where somebody's long-lost aunt dies (Not really, but you get the idea), and I found that I couldn't force myself to read another word of this high literature. Of course, in those days, I had neither a television set nor a computer – entertainment at my apartment came only in the form of more reading.

Fortunately, I had somewhere and somehow acquired the two-volume set of William S. Baring-Gould's *Annotated Sherlock Holmes*, and one day in the midst of my required reading of another of the classics, I couldn't take it anymore and, in despair, I reached over to my bookshelf to see what Dr. Arthur Conan Doyle was up to with this Sherlock Holmes fellow.

The answer was: Plenty.

I'd of course heard of Holmes, who after all is perhaps the most well-known fictional character in human history. But the discovery for which I was completely unprepared was the sheer accessibility of these stories. They were in many ways the polar opposite of the books I'd been laboring through. They were, in fact, eminently readable and plot driven – and yet there was an elegance and approachability in the writing itself that, in my opinion, stood up to the best of what my continental novels had to offer.

Beyond the "English Major" stuff, though, from the very first words of the very first book, *A Study In Scarlet*, Holmes (and Watson) come alive not just as interesting characters, but as fully realized human beings, imbued with depth, great intelligence, irony, humor, bravery, and sensitivity. These are wonderful people we come to know and yes, even to love. We want to spend more time with them, hang out with them, and be part of their lives, which are so familiar and yet so unique and remarkable.

Hence, this volume of new and original Sherlock Holmes stories.

One would be tempted to think that enough had already been written about Holmes and Watson and the world they inhabit. Surely, with Conan

Doyle's original sixty stories, with literally hundreds of pastiches published over the past century and more, the trove of Holmesiana must be close to exhausted.

But this is the miracle of Sherlock Holmes. It is not so.

Sherlock's appeal is so universal, Watson's language is so identifiable, the mysteries they encounter speak to all ages and to the human condition, that it is small wonder that writers, like the talented contributors to this latest volume, continue to be driven to visit and revisit Holmes and Watson, and to add their narrative voices to The Canon as nothing less than a universal tribute to the original.

Holmes comes fully alive again in these stories and, indeed, from the evidence presented herein, he will never die.

Enjoy.

John Lescroart
May 2019

"What Could Be Better
For the Purpose?"[1]
by Roger Johnson

Arthur Conan Doyle was generally tolerant when his work was parodied. In his reminiscences *Memories and Adventures*, he cheerfully quotes in full "The Adventure of the Two Collaborators", a short and very funny spoof written in 1893 by his friend J.M. Barrie. [2]

He was less amenable to more serious imitations. The French author Maurice Leblanc appropriated Holmes as the only detective worthy to challenge the famous *gentleman-cambrioleur*, Arsène Lupin, but Conan Doyle understandably took exception, and the name was changed to "Herlock Sholmès" – or in some English editions "Holmlock Shears". On a lower literary level, Sherlock Holmes quickly became a hero in the European pulp magazines, where he was given a young assistant named Harry Taxon in place of Dr. Watson. From 1907, innumerable stories appeared on the bookstalls in Germany, France, Denmark, Spain, Poland, and even Croatia. Russia developed its own more intelligent and better written series. None had the approval of Conan Doyle – but he could be generous in his rejection. Consider "The Case of the Man Who Was Wanted".

After Conan Doyle's death in 1930, the family made no proper effort to examine his papers. It wasn't until 1942 that Hesketh Pearson, researching what was intended as *the* authorised biography, discovered among them the typescript of an unpublished Sherlock Holmes story. In 1948, "The Case of the Man Who Was Wanted" was published in *Cosmopolitan*, but upon its British publication the following January the Conan Doyles received a letter from a retired architect named Arthur Whitaker, claiming that he had written the story in 1910 and sent it to Sir Arthur, who had given him ten guineas for the rights to the plot. And despite furious denials and threats of legal action from Sir Arthur's sons, Denis and Adrian, Whitaker easily proved his claim, as he had kept his carbon copy of the typescript and the letter from Conan Doyle. "The Case of the Man Who Was Wanted" is not at all a bad story, written in a fair imitation of the Watson style.

The Conan Doyle brothers' almost fanatical opposition to imitations of their father's work had been demonstrated in 1944, when Ellery Queen's anthology *The Misadventures of Sherlock Holmes* was published in America. That outstanding collection of parody and pastiche – which

18

includes stories by Anthony Boucher, Agatha Christie, S.C. Roberts, Vincent Starrett, and Mark Twain – was short-lived. Denis and Adrian detested the tongue-in-cheek scholarship of the Sherlock Holmes societies, and jealously guarded their legal rights in his characters. After two printings, *The Misadventures of Sherlock Holmes* was withdrawn from circulation.

Ironically, the major contribution to Sherlock Holmes pastiche came in the early 1950's with a series of twelve stories by Adrian Conan Doyle himself, six of them written in collaboration with John Dickson Carr. They appeared in book form in 1954 as *The Exploits of Sherlock Holmes*, and despite the dismissive comment of Edgar W. Smith, head of the Baker Street Irregulars, that they should be called "Sherlock Holmes Exploited", they are about as close to the real thing as any writer has got.

Denis and Adrian's sister Jean outlived them both and achieved far more in her life, becoming head of the Women's Royal Air Force (the first Director to have risen through the ranks), and ADC to the Queen. Her relationship with Holmesian enthusiasts was gracious, courteous, and supportive. As an Honorary Member of The Sherlock Holmes Society of London, she happily attended the Annual Dinners and even took part in pilgrimages to Switzerland. In 1991, she became the first woman to be admitted to the Baker Street Irregulars *with all rights and privileges*. Her investiture, most appropriately, was "A Certain Gracious Lady".

Dame Jean was never entirely happy with Holmesian pastiche, believing that authors should create their own characters. It's a simplistic view of a rather complex phenomenon, but understandable. Now, of course, the afterlives of Holmes, Watson, and the rest have become vastly more complex since the expiry of the original copyrights, everywhere except the United States, in 2000. (Under the USA's unique copyright law, some stories were never protected there, while a few of the late ones will not enter the public domain until the mid-2020s – which has made the situation even more complicated.)

Nevertheless, I fancy that Dame Jean would be pleased with the success of this remarkable series of books. The contents are evidence of worldwide affection and admiration for her father's work, undiminished ninety years after his death. And she would surely approve of the reason for the books' creation and publication: To help support the regeneration – you might say the *rejuvenescence* – of The House That Conan Doyle Built.

Roger Johnson, BSI, ASH
Editor: *The Sherlock Holmes Journal*
January 2020

NOTES

1 – From *The Sign of the Four*, Chapter XII.
2 – Thanks to *Arthur Conan Doyle: A Life in Letters*, edited by Jon Lellenberg, Daniel Stashower and Charles Foley, we know that Barrie was also responsible for the equally neat "My Evening with Sherlock Holmes", published anonymously in 1892.

An Ongoing Legacy
for Sherlock Holmes
by Steve Emecz

Undershaw
Circa 1900

The MX Book of New Sherlock Holmes Stories has now raised over $60,000 for Stepping Stones School for children with learning disabilities and is by far the largest Sherlock Holmes collection in the world – by several measures, stories, authors, pages and positive reviews from the critics. *Publishers Weekly* has been reviewing since Volume VI and we have had a record thirteen straight great reviews. Here are some of their best comments:

> *"This is more catnip for fans of stories faithful to Conan Doyle's originals"* (Part XIII)

> *"This is an essential volume for Sherlock Holmes fans"* (Part XI)

"The imagination of the contributors in coming up with variations on the volume's theme is matched by their ingenious resolutions" (Part VIII)

MX Publishing is a social enterprise – all the staff, including me, are volunteers with day jobs. The collection would not be possible without the creator and editor, David Marcum, who is rightly cited multiple times by *Publishers Weekly* and others as probably the most accomplished Sherlockian editor ever.

In addition to Stepping Stones School, our main program that we support is the Happy Life Children's Home in Kenya. My wife Sharon and I are on our way in December for our seventh Christmas in a row at Happy Life. It's a wonderful project that has saved the lives of over 600 babies. You can read all about the project in the second edition of the book *The Happy Life Story.*

Our support of both of these projects is possible through the publishing of Sherlock Holmes books, which we have now been doing for a decade.

You can find out more information
about the Stepping Stones School at:

www.steppingstones.org.uk

and Happy Life at:

www.happylifechildrenshomes.com

You can find out more about MX Publishing
and reach out to us through our website at:

www.mxpublishing.com

Steve Emecz
August 2019
Twitter: *@steveemecz*
LinkedIn: *https://www.linkedin.com/in/emecz/*

The Doyle Room at Stepping Stones, Undershaw
Partially funded through royalties from
The MX Book of New Sherlock Holmes Stories

A Word From
Stepping Stones
by Lizzie Butler

Undershaw
September 9, 2016
Grand Opening of the Stepping Stones School
(Photograph courtesy of Roger Johnson)

Undershaw continues to develop during this new era as Stepping Stones School. The school is going through a very exciting time of change in 2020, with our student cohort at full capacity of ninety-five students across both our lower school and upper school sites, making daily life here at Undershaw rewarding, exciting and busy.

We really appreciate the support and donations received from MX Publishing and we look forward to another successful year as we fulfil the wants and needs of our students and their families.

"I didn't want to get up in the morning and go to school but now I love school. Everyone accepts each other and we're like a family, we trust, look after and understand each other, I think that's very special. This is now my happy place, where I can be who I am."

– Stepping Stones Student, 2019

Best wishes,

Lizzy Butler
Fundraising Manager, *Stepping Stones,* Undershaw
February 2020

Sherlock Holmes (1854-1957) was born in Yorkshire, England, on 6 January, 1854. In the mid-1870's, he moved to 24 Montague Street, London, where he established himself as the world's first Consulting Detective. After meeting Dr. John H. Watson in early 1881, he and Watson moved to rooms at 221b Baker Street, where his reputation as the world's greatest detective grew for several decades. He was presumed to have died battling noted criminal Professor James Moriarty on 4 May, 1891, but he returned to London on 5 April, 1894, resuming his consulting practice in Baker Street. Retiring to the Sussex coast near Beachy Head in October 1903, he continued to be associated in various private and government investigations while giving the impression of being a reclusive apiarist. He was very involved in the events encompassing World War I, and to a lesser degree those of World War II. He passed away peacefully upon the cliffs above his Sussex home on his 103rd birthday, 6 January, 1957.

Dr. John Hamish Watson (1852-1929) was born in Stranraer, Scotland on 7 August, 1852. In 1878, he took his Doctor of Medicine Degree from the University of London, and later joined the army as a surgeon. Wounded at the Battle of Maiwand in Afghanistan (27 July, 1880), he returned to London late that same year. On New Year's Day, 1881, he was introduced to Sherlock Holmes in the chemical laboratory at Barts. Agreeing to share rooms with Holmes in Baker Street, Watson became invaluable to Holmes's consulting detective practice. Watson was married and widowed three times, and from the late 1880's onward, in addition to his participation in Holmes's investigations and his medical practice, he chronicled Holmes's adventures, with the assistance of his literary agent, Sir Arthur Conan Doyle, in a series of popular narratives, most of which were first published in *The Strand* magazine. Watson's later years were spent preparing a vast number of his notes of Holmes's cases for future publication. Following a final important investigation with Holmes, Watson contracted pneumonia and passed away on 24 July, 1929.

Photos of Sherlock Holmes and Dr. John H. Watson courtesy of Roger Johnson

The MX Book
of
New Sherlock Holmes Stories
Part XIX:
Part XX – 2020 Annual
(1891-1897)

The Sibling
by Jacquelynn Morris
(with apologies to E.A. Poe)

Once upon an evening dreary, while I pondered, not much weary,
Over quaint and enthralling volumes of my favorite lore –
While I read – avoiding sleeping – suddenly there came a peeping,
As of someone softly weeping, weeping at my bedroom door –
"'Tis the cat," I muttered, "howling at my bedroom door –
Only this and nothing more."
Ah, distinctly I recall it was sometime in the Fall;
And each withered leaf to fall left ghostly shapes upon my deck.
Eagerly I read the novel – nestled snugly in my hovel –
Near my bookcase where I revel over tales of crime and suspects,
Of the genius and the missteps of the Master, Great Detective,
Whom adoringly I merely call, "Sherlock."
And the silken woven cadence of each carefully written sentence
Thrilled me – filled me with fantastic wonder as they always did before
And now, to still the beating of my heart, I stood repeating,
"'Tis some feline entreating entrance at my bedroom door –
Some hungry feline begging entrance at my bedroom door; –
This it is and nothing more."
Back to my reading turning, all my soul within me yearning,
To visit once again those treasured days of yore.
Yet again I heard a weeping somewhat louder than before.
"Surely," said I, "that is some feline at my window lattice;
Let me see, then, what that cat is, and its gustatory status –
Let my soul be still a moment and this mystery explore.
Open here I flung the door, when, with many a step and more,
In advanced a stately man from those saintly days of yore;
No acknowledgement made he; not a minute stopped nor stayed he;
But, with dignity and pride, strode through my bedroom door –
Glanced at a bust of Napoleon next to my bedroom door
Glanced, and sat, and nothing more.
Then this gentleman, with sighing, suddenly commenced with crying
While looking as if dying from some deep unspoken pain.
"What has grieved you, sir?" I queried, as his face he sadly buried
In a linen cloth he carried in the pocket of his coat.

"Tell me what thy grievous pain is, reveal what your given name is!"
Said the gentleman, while wincing, "Mycroft Holmes."
"You may know me," he lamented, "from the way I've been presented,
As if somewhat quite demented in those favourite books of yours!"
"All those pages filled with tension or disbelief suspension,
Yet with very little mention of so much that I have done.
Favoring another – Sherlock Holmes, my brother –
As if he could solve a case alone."
I replied, my brow quite furrowed and my eyes so slightly narrowed,
"I have no understanding of this cause you are demanding
That I ponder and abandon all I know.
It is your brother who's the hero and your involvement near to zero."
Mycroft snorted and retorted, "Furthermore . . .
"Every problem Sherlock brought me I explained away directly,
And always quite correctly – as is mentioned most succinctly in a tale
which Watson wrote.
It is said I drove a brougham, yet my brother claims that no-one
Could remove me from the comfort of my favorite armchair –
Accusing that my genius is confined to my armchair."
I pondered this dichotomy; the facts were right in front of me.
"What about Diogenes?" I queried,
"Oh, please," said he, sneering,
"The silence keeps me from hearing all the terms which are endearing
'Bout my sibling evermore.
Just because his name is famous
I've have heard all that I can stomach
Every time I go in public.
I AM the British government, you know."
Wearily he stood as if his legs were made of wood
And he made his way toward my chamber door. Walked slowly out and
through my chamber door.
Painfully he strode and hailed a cab upon the road,
His shoulders stooped and hunched with the burden that he bore.

And now Mycroft, never flitting, still is sitting, still is sitting
In an armchair at the Club Diogenes
And his eyes have all the sorrow of a man whose next tomorrow
Is devoid of recognition for the service he has served.
It will hold no fame nor fortune, but only a mere mention
With all of the attention given to his sibling's name.
Given to his sibling, evermore.

Blood and Gunpowder
by Thomas A. Burns, Jr.

4 May, 1893

I sit at my desk in my Kensington study, wallowing in my grief, as the howling wind drives the cold rain into my windows like tiny pieces of grapeshot. Just last week, my poor Mary's illness reached its climax, and now I will see her no more until Our Lord returns her to me at His Last Judgment. My grief is doubly poignant this day, because it was two years ago that I lost my other dear friend, Sherlock Holmes, the best and wisest man I have ever known, at the hands of the despicable Professor Moriarty. After Mary's death, the pastor told me to remember her not in sickness, but in health, dwelling upon her charm, her vivacity, and the joys of our brief life together. I suspect the same should hold true for Holmes. So, to assuage my sorrow, I choose to take up my pen to chronicle one of our last adventures together, which, had I but known it at the time, was a harbinger of the great tragedy to come.

It was in late April of 1891, in Holmes's sitting room in Baker Street, that he told me of a meeting with the professor some weeks earlier, when the latter had essayed to induce my friend to cease his inquiries into Moriarty's machinations. Of course, Holmes refused, preferring to risk death rather than allow the brand of evil personified by Moriarty to run rampant. Holmes recounted Moriarty's words to him at that fateful meeting.

"You crossed my path on the 4th of January . . . ." said Moriarty.

I well remember where I was on New Year's Day of that year, and that it was I who summoned Holmes to that minacious encounter . . . .

It was a clammy cold day on a beach about a mile from Sangatte, France, where I was engaged in an onerous duty indeed. The son of an old school chum, Kendrick Wood Jr., had accepted a challenge to a pistol duel, which had arisen, as many do, over drink and cards. Young Kenny Wood was engaged in a rubber of whist at the Bagatelle Card Club, imbibing heavily and consequently losing badly, when he had the uncommonly poor judgment to publicly accuse his opponents of cheating. Unfortunately, one of them was the noted journalist and duellist Isadora Persano. A challenge was swiftly issued and accepted. Since dueling has been illegal in England since 1840, and the prosecution of those who cause injury or death during

37

a duel is the rule rather than the exception, the combatants chose France as the venue for their dispute, because the French take a much more tolerant view of defending one's honour than we Britons do.

As an enlightened modern gentleman, I find the practice of dueling abhorrent, and normally, I would have no part in one. However, my friend Kend asked me to be the attending physician at the affair.

"There's no one on earth with whom I would be more comfortable entrusting the life of my only son, Watson," he said.

How could a decent man refuse such a request? Even Mary understood why I must be away on New Year's Day.

So it was that I found myself loitering on the sand at Sangatte, where stark white clouds outlined in gold, backlit by the morning sun, loomed above the meadows of Pas de Calais, the salty freshness of the sea tangy in the air. The Woods, Kend and Kenny, Kenny's second Tommy Babcock, and Persano's second Huston Sipes – they all waited with me for the arrival of Persano on the field of honour, so that the shameful affair could commence.

After some fifteen minutes, Persano had still not made his appearance.

"Watson," Kend called, "perhaps, since you are the only neutral on the field, you might go to Persano's tent to find out what is keeping him."

Two tawny pole marquee tents, erected to shelter the combatants from the weather as they made their preparations for the duel, were situated on the other side of the dune from the field of honour. I made my way to Persano's, stopping outside of the closed flap. Uncomfortable with the idea of simply walking into to another man's tent, I raised my voice, "Persano, it's Dr. Watson. Everyone is waiting for you, old man. Do you require assistance?"

No answer. Heaving a sigh, I drew aside the flap and entered.

Persano was sitting in a canvas chair beside a folding table, staring intently at something that he held in his right hand.

"I say, Persano! Everyone is ready and waiting on the beach. Are you coming?" With all my heart, I hoped he would say no – that he had decided to call the whole thing off.

He did not respond. It did not seem that he heard me. He still stared fixedly at whatever he was holding.

I stepped up behind him, placing a hand on his shoulder. The object he was holding appeared to be a match box. I couldn't see what it contained. But I could see that the hand that held the box was covered in blood! I shook him, calling "Persano! Are you ill?"

As he turned his head to look at me, I saw a red stream trickling lazily from his right ear. When his face came into view, I was horrified to see blood running from his eyes, his nose, and his lips, as well!

"Persano! You're bleeding, man! What the devil is wrong with you?"

He dropped the matchbox onto the sand, and the contents were ejected and bounced along the ground. He brought a bandaged hand to his face, smearing the blood from his nose across his cheek. He looked at his hand stupidly for a moment, then his eyes glowed, and he broke into a smile. His teeth were tinged with pink, with blood red lines between them.

"So I am, so I am! But at least I taught a lesson to that upstart who accused me of being a cheat." He began to laugh in a low, measured tone, and the sound of it chilled me to the bone. He's mad! I thought. He thinks the duel is done!

"I'm a doctor," I told him. "I can help you. Come and lie down. Let me examine you." I reached to take his hands.

He batted my hands aside and attempted to rise, but his knees crumpled so he sprawled onto the ground, face first. With difficulty, I rolled the journalist over. He lips worked – he was trying to speak! I lowered my ear to his mouth. I heard what sounded like "Courtier . . . Paris . . . ." He began to cough, and I hurriedly raised my head lest he spit blood on my face. His mouth was half-open, blood bubbling from his lips as he wheezed and gasped for air. Suddenly, his eyes assumed that fixed gaze that I knew all too well, and his last earthly breath rasped from his lungs, spewing a cloud of tiny red droplets into the air, which settled back onto his face. I didn't need my medical training to tell me that Isadora Persano was stone cold dead.

Since there was nothing more that I or anyone else could do for him, I looked to see what had held his rapt attention in his final moments. A small brownish ball lay in the dirt, its surface festooned with fine, minuscule spines. Closer examination revealed it as some kind of worm, all coiled up into a ball.

Picking it up, I hurriedly dropped it again as a sharp, stinging pain lanced into my thumb. A couple of the spines had embedded themselves in my flesh. Cursing, I retrieved my pocket knife and arduously extracted them. Ruby droplets welled where they had been, and I thrust the hurt finger into my mouth. When I withdrew the digit, I noticed that it still bled. Since the wound was minor, I dismissed it from my mind and hurried to inform my companions about what had transpired.

Coming over the dune, I looked down upon the beach where everyone waited to carry out their sad duties. Kend Woods stood facing his son, his hands on the boy's shoulders, talking to him earnestly. Sipes was ten yards away, his back to the father and son, staring out to sea, assumedly to give them privacy during this difficult time. Joy rose in my heart, due to the news I was about to convey.

"Halloa!" I shouted. "There will be no duel this day!"

"No duel?" Kend Woods said. "What do you mean? Has Persano come to his senses?"

"Hardly," I said. "He is dead."

"What mischief is this?" Sipes said, approaching us. "What has happened?"

I described the scene in Persano's tent, leaving out the details of his madness, and of the worm.

"Why, this is marvellous news," Kend said.

"A man is dead!" said Sipes.

"Yes, he is," said Kend, "and he is not my boy." Sipes glared at him, coals of fire glowing in his eyes.

"We'd best report this to the police in Calais," I said. "Sipes, you can contact those in London who need to know."

We gathered the things from the beach necessary for the conduct of the duel – the pistols, balls and powder, my medical kit. The tents and their contents we would have to leave for later. We walked back to the road where the broughams we had hired awaited us. The drivers congregated, the smoke from their vile French cigarettes forming a heavy cloud in the air.

"*Tu connais le gendarmerie du Caliais?*" I asked them.

"*Oui,*" one replied.

"*Emmenez nous la,*" I ordered.

We boarded the carriages and set off.

The Gendarmarie du Pas de Calais was a three-story white stone edifice with a dark grey slate roof. The drivers pulled the carriages up to the front door, and we all went inside. I had nearly exhausted my meagre French in telling the drivers to bring us here, so I asked the Sergeant, "Is there anyone here who speaks English? We wish to report a death."

After a short wait, a short gentleman in an impeccable grey suit and waistcoat, a monocle dangling from a chain on his vest, arrived. "I am Inspector René Lefébure," he said with a heavy French accent. "What is this death you have to report?" He herded the lot of us into his office. He seemed out of sorts with having to deal with this affair at such an early hour, and his demeanour didn't improve when he discovered we had come to France to engage in a duel. "You will pardon me for saying it, but you should do your killing in your own country, English."

He quizzed us minutely about the circumstances of the duel – what was the insult, who were the participants. When he learned that one of the duellists was the dead man, he said, "So this gentleman expired before the duel could commence? *Mais bien sur*, that was very convenient for the other participant, no?"

The upshot of the interview was that he arrested both of the Woods for suspicion of murder. "I must hurry the investigation to get to the bottom of things, as you say." I thought that he would have liked to arrest Babcock, Sipes, and me as well, but he couldn't come up with sufficient justification, given our limited roles in the affair.

My protestations for naught, we took our leave, but not before I asked the location of the nearest telegraph office, where I sent a wire to Sherlock Holmes: "*Come at once*" it said. I had a difficult time writing it without dripping blood on the form because of my finger.

The wind off the channel that rattled the window glass woke me from a troubled sleep at Auberge du Fenetres sur Mer in Calais. My thumb was still bleeding at bedtime, so I wrapped it in gauze before retiring. My eyes darted to it immediately. I saw a small crimson spot on the surface of the gauze. It was obvious that the needles that pricked me contained some substance that interfered with the clotting of the blood. A shiver ran through me – was I to suffer the same horrible death as Persano?

As I contemplated unwrapping my injured thumb, fearful of what I might find, a knock came on my door.

"Watson! It's me. Open the door."

The sound of Sherlock Holmes's voice was like a stiff drink of mellow brandy, warming my stomach and spreading to my extremities. I pulled on my trousers, for I had no nightshirt or dressing gown, and admitted my friend.

"Your message was urgent, so I caught the first ferry from Dover . . . Hello, man! What the devil is wrong with your hand?"

I told Holmes how I received the injury, as I unwrapped the bandage with much trepidation. When I had it fully undone, I was relieved to see that the wounds were finally beginning to clot.

"Get dressed, old fellow, and allow me to buy your breakfast for you downstairs. You can tell me everything over croissants and coffee, and pray omit no detail, however trivial it may seem."

Holmes was aware of my mission here before I departed London, so I did not dwell upon that. I began my tale at the time I went to Persano's tent. Leaving his food untouched, Holmes sat with his elbows on the table and his chin resting in his hands, taking in every nuance of my story. When I had finished, he asked, "Is the tent still present on the beach?"

"We did not take it down, so it should be."

"Capital!" he exclaimed. "We must examine it at once!"

We went to the local stable where the dueling party had hired drivers the previous day and found a fellow with a dogcart who was willing to take us out there. As was usual during the early stages of an investigation, Holmes was taciturn – I knew better than to ask him for speculation in advance of facts. I simply settled down in my hat and greatcoat to get as much protection from the stiff wind as possible.

Arriving at the duel site, we found the tent still up, but the flap was open and Persano's corpse had been removed, presumably by the gendarmes. Holmes made a sound indicating his disgust as he entered, presumably because of the disturbance to the scene that the local constables had caused.

"We must search thoroughly," he said, "for there might yet be some piece of evidence that the French police failed to destroy."

I remembered the cryptic phrase that Persano has spoken to me just before he died, so I told Holmes about it. "But I don't see how it might be helpful. There must be a thousand courtiers in Paris."

Holmes's only response was a noncommittal grunt.

A short search turned up the matchbox that had held the worm. We continued to explore the tent, looking for the infernal creature that had caused me such grief. I finally found it among the ground litter, and Holmes teased it into the box with the tip of his penknife.

We went outside where the light was better, and Holmes employed his glass to discern the fine details of the worm. "I have never seen its like," he said finally. "I'm no naturalist, but I think it resembles some sort of caterpillar." He closed the box and put it in the pocket of his greatcoat, along with his glass. "It appears, Watson, that the trail in France has grown cold. I think, however, that London may hold answers for us."

Modern transportation is a marvellous thing. Prior to 1820, no passenger ferry service across the English Channel even existed – one had to arrange private passage. But now, the crossing from Dover to Calais was made thrice daily, in the incredible time of ninety minutes. It took us nearly that long to travel by dogcart from Sangatte back to the ferry terminal, with a brief stop at the auberge to pick up my valise and pay the bill. However, we were still able to secure a cabin for the afternoon crossing. The train to London awaited us when we arrived in Dover. We departed Sangatte around noontime, and we were back in Baker Street in time for Mrs. Hudson to provide us a cold supper.

"Your experience with the worm leads me to believe that Persano was deliberately poisoned by person or persons unknown," Holmes opined. "You know how I despise theorizing without facts or evidence, yet some amount of speculation is necessary in their absence if we are to make a start on this crime. Let us assume that it was some journalistic activity on

Persano's part that made him a target for a murderer. If that is the case, we must ascertain what that activity entailed."

"And how do you propose to go about that?" I asked, playing the foil for Holmes's acumen.

"How does a *soupçon* of burglary strike you as an end to your repast?"

"Persano's flat?"

"But of course."

Holmes consulted the London street directory to establish that Persano occupied rooms in Farringdon Street in St. Andrews. We passed a few hours in desultory activities, myself with a copy of the novel *Micah Clarke* sent to me by my literary agent, and Holmes with some samples of cigar ash, the characteristics of which he was considering adding to his monograph on the subject.

Finally, as the bells of St. Marylebone struck eleven, Holmes rose from his work and said, "All good folk should be going to their beds at this hour, so it is time for lawbreakers to go about their nefarious business."

To be circumspect, we had our cab drop us in Fleet Street, and then walked the short distance to Persano's lodgings. We had to pick our way through some pavement work to reach his door, which was difficult for me in the darkness because my leg pained me, but I managed. Holmes made quick work of the lock on the front door while I watched, and then we were inside. The plan of the residence was much the same as 221b – the landlord's apartment on the ground floor and Persano's digs on the first. The stairs stayed mercifully quiet as we ascended, and the lock on the dead journalist's door gave Holmes no more trouble than the one downstairs had. Once inside, we lit a bullseye lantern that Holmes had brought, the light from which had only a small chance of being observed from the street.

Persano's digs comprised just two rooms – a bedroom and a spacious sitting room, made less so because it was crammed with tables, bookshelves, and a massive roll-top desk. Open volumes and papers lay scattered on every flat space – finally, I had the misfortune to encounter someone even more disorderly than Holmes.

Holmes stood, shaking his head. "Nothing is ever easy," he said, surveying the effluvia. "I think that the desk will afford the best chance of discovering something of interest."

The roll-top was closed and locked, so the detective employed his picks for the third time. My heart skipped a beat as it clattered noisily when he raised it. The white beam of the lantern showed a myriad of small drawers in the back, and piles of folders littered the writing surface.

"Why don't you go through the desk drawers, Watson, while I examine the contents of these folders?" Holmes suggested. He cast the light about until he found a candle, which he lit from a match from a box in his pocket before handing it to me. He grabbed an armload of folders and carried them to a nearby table in order to give me room for my work.

Beginning with the topmost one on the left, I opened each of the small drawers in turn, examining the contents in a cursory manner. I suspected that Holmes had assigned me this task just to keep me busy while he went through Persano's papers. Their contents of the drawers comprised the deadwood that a man accumulates after long stay in one place – writing instruments, clips, business cards, *etcetera*. I did discover an ornately carved, pearl-handled, double-barrelled pistol that fit in the palm of my hand. Unfortunately, it hadn't protected its owner from an untimely demise. Another drawer yielded a diverse collection of matchboxes. I mentioned it to Holmes, but received no answer.

I tried to open the first drawer on the right in the pedestal, but it stuck, so I closed the roll top and tried again, after hearing the metallic sound of the pedestal lock as it disengaged. This time the drawer slid out easily. I was just about to reach inside when I caught a glimpse of something in the candlelight that sent a chill up my spine.

"Holmes," I said quietly. "There is something here that you should see."

Holmes approached the desk and directed the lantern beam inside. There, in stark relief in the white light, a bristling tan mass about the size of a cricket ball resided. Worms!

Shuddering, I said, "If the candle hadn't revealed those infernal things, I would have reached into that drawer . . . ."

"Which is doubtless what Persano did, sealing his doom," Holmes opined. "That is likely the source of the worm in Persano's matchbox."

"But why would he carry the thing all the way to France with him? To a duel, of all things?"

"Eliminate the impossible, Watson. He had no use for the worm at the duel. He was not going to throw it at his opponent. Therefore, he had use for it elsewhere."

"And where would that be?"

"Paris. He planned to travel to Paris after the duel was over. A skilled duelist such as Persano would have expected to win, of course."

"He was going to Paris to see a courtier?" I asked, puzzled.

"No, Watson. He was going there to see Monsieur Courtier." He paused, then extended his hand, holding a piece of paper.

"This note informs me that M. Courtier is a noted toxicologist at the Université de Paris," Holmes went on, "known for his work with haemolytic toxins. Persano identified him after he realized he'd been poisoned. He was hoping that Courtier would know how to help him. He took a single caterpillar along to France with him to show it to Courtier."

"Persano showed amazing resilience after he jammed his hand into that ball of worms," I said. "It's amazing that he survived long enough to go to Paris to duel. Why would he even go if he was in such shape? Why didn't he just destroy the caterpillar ball in his desk? I would have stomped the thing into paste on the carpet."

"You must realize, Watson, that Persano had to be a cold fish to be a renowned duelist," Holmes lectured. "When he realized his wound wouldn't stop bleeding, he immediately employed his skills as a researcher to identify someone who might help. He didn't cancel the duel, because that would brand him as a coward. He wasn't expecting a catastrophic, systemic response from his wound."

I shuddered. "It's a wonder that I survived," I said. "I must have received a much smaller dose of venom from the single worm."

"I found something else as well," Holmes said, extending another scrap or paper. It was about three inches by four, and looked like it had been torn from a pocket notebook. The following symbols were scrawled on it in ink:

"What is this codswallop?" I inquired.

"It is Isaac Pitman's shorthand," Holmes replied. "It isn't surprising that a journalist would be familiar with it."

I knew that he was just waiting for me to ask. "And I suppose you can decipher it?"

With a satisfied expression, he said, "It says, '*Porlock, Ten Bells, Spitalfields, 8 p.m., December 27*'."

I was familiar with the Ten Bells, a public house over a century old in the East End, from our investigation of the horrific events of the fall of 1888. "I also know that name," I said. "Porlock."

"You should. You encountered it during the affair at Birlstone three years ago. Almost to the day, in fact."

I remembered, and it seemed if the room had suddenly grown much colder.

"Professor Moriarty! Is he involved in this?"

"I have cautioned you previously that it is a capital mistake to theorize in advance of facts," he said. "However, that is certainly a possibility." He hesitated, then continued, "I have also told you that Porlock defied me to ever trace him among the teeming millions of this great city. To date, I have found no reason to endeavour to do that. That seems to no longer be the case. "

"What do you intend to do?" I asked him.

He smiled thinly. "Destroy these creatures, and then finish searching poor Persano's papers to ascertain a motive for his murder, if I can. Then, if your good wife will allow it, I would be most gratified if you would accompany me to the Ten Bells tomorrow evening."

The following day at my practice was a busy one, as the ailments that people had put off investigating during the Yuletide once again became important considerations. When the last patient had departed, I nipped outside to the jewellers, where I was fortunate to find an inexpensive cameo brooch. I placed the box in my pocket and hurried back home for dinner. After the meal, I presented the trinket to Mary. Of course, she was delighted – cameos were her favourite – but she regarded me with a jaundiced eye.

"I know that we have spent little time together since I returned from France," I said. "I thought that this small bauble might make up for it a bit."

She raised an eyebrow. "And – ?"

She knew me too well. "And Holmes has asked me to accompany him on another excursion this evening."

She glowered, but I could see the corners of her mouth twitching, so I waited for her smile. I knew her well also, you see. It eventually blossomed, and she said, "Oh, you're a child! Be off with you, on your adventure. Don't be too late!"

That is one reason why I loved her so much.

Holmes was hovering impatiently when I arrived in Baker Street, already downstairs with a cab waiting. We were both dressed in somewhat rough garb, as to not stand out. Spitalfields – more particularly, Dorset Street – had a reputation as the most notorious rookery in London and was certainly not a place where a gentleman would go after dark unless he desired less than savoury entertainment. The Ten Bells was only a short distance from Dorset Street, directly across from the Spitalfields Market.

46

In the daytime, the presence of the market made the area more-or-less safe, but after dark, one travelled there at one's peril.

Light from the pub, in a fine old three-storey building, brightly illuminated the adjacent area, but murky shadows loomed just a few feet away. It was a bit warmer this evening than it had been for a few days, but the warmth brought the fog, which was settling over the City like a shroud. We disembarked from the hansom in the lighted area and Holmes paid the driver, who then clattered off as if he couldn't wait to be away.

We passed between the two Corinthian columns at the entry to the pub and Holmes pushed open the double doors. The odours of beer and humanity greeted us as we entered the public room. The place was fairly full, with most of the scattered tables occupied by men of the rougher sort, while ladies of a similar type circulated among them, plying their wares. We elbowed our way into the crowd at the bar, drawing some irritated glances, but no one was sufficiently roused to start an altercation, thank goodness. The publican, clad in a derby hat, tan waistcoat, and a shirt that was once white, asked, "Wot'll it be, gents?"

"Porlock," replied Holmes.

A flicker of annoyance passed over the man's features, quickly replaced by puzzlement.

"We only 'as our own brew 'ere, gents. Ye wants fancy bottles, the Strand is over that way." He pointed toward the exit.

"Tell Porlock that Mr. Smithson is here to see him," Holmes said. "And give us two pints of your strongest while we wait."

"That'll be the *XXXX*," the barman said, picking up a dubiously clean mug and exercising the tap handle. "And ye'll wait till the cows come home. Oi never knew no 'Porlock'." He slapped down two brimming mugs in front of us. "That'll be fourpence, gents."

Holmes paid him, and we retired to a table in a corner.

"The barkeep is lying, of course," Holmes said after sipping his ale. "I expected no less. I must follow him after he closes for the evening, and that will be much easier if I'm alone. Go back to your Mary after we've finished these."

I must confess that I was a bit miffed with him. "If you knew you'd be stonewalled and would have to follow someone, why did you bring me along?"

He smiled. "Because I wanted to drink an ale with my old friend this evening," he said, and I was ashamed.

We left the pub together, and Holmes walked with me to the edge of Spitalfields, where the chances of finding a cruising cab were much improved. "Come to Baker Street after dinner tomorrow," said Holmes,

47

"and I'll tell you the tale of my evening's adventures." I climbed into the cab and watched him vanish into the fog as we clattered off.

The following day, the fourth of January, 1891, was a Sunday. As was our custom, Mary and I attended church, then spent a leisurely afternoon at home, which culminated in a cold supper. I broached the subject of my going out afterwards and she said, "I have been feeling tired of late, John, so I would not be the best company this evening at any rate. Go and see your friend."

So, it was about 7:30 p.m. when I arrived at Baker Street. I entered and found Holmes taking his ease on the sofa with a glass of whisky and soda. He offered me the same and I quickly assented, saying, "Don't get up. I know where everything is. May I freshen yours?"

After I was ensconced in my old chair, he told me of his adventures after I left him in Spitalfields.

"You are aware that I have several places around the City to which I may repair to equip myself with the accoutrements necessary to conduct various clandestine activities," he said. "I established one of these in Whitechapel, near Spitalfields, when we were hunting Saucy Jack, and I went there to procure some beggars' rags. Thus clad, I returned to Commercial Street before closing time and availed myself of the shelter of the Old Market to keep watch on the Ten Bells.

"The publican appeared wary when he exited, but seeing nothing that he didn't expect, his circumspection soon turned to insouciance. I followed him for a few blocks and he approached a corner building. He looked about carefully, but of course he didn't notice me. Then he removed a brick from a stanchion and placed something inside. He replaced the brick and hurried on his way. I saw no need to follow him any longer."

Holmes sipped his whisky-and-soda appreciatively and continued. "Not long thereafter, an urchin arrived and removed the message from the cache. I followed him to a toy shop in Regent Street which was closed at that hour, of course – where he slipped the envelope he'd taken from the mail drop into a postal slot in the door.

"Well, there was nothing for it but to wait it out for the rest of the evening. When the shopkeeper arrived after breakfast, he made no motion to retrieve anything from the floor after opening the door, so it was no difficult deduction that the message had disappeared. Now that part of Regent Street has no back yards, so it was evident that the person who took the note must have entered from a nearby building, or possibly through the sewers. I quickly retreated to another nearby lair, where I keep a number of reference books. A quick check of Kelly's *Postal Directory* revealed that one F. Porlock resided at No. 10 King Street, just behind Regent

48

Street. I was a bit chagrined to realize that I could have found my man just by combing the city directories, but that search would have consumed many days, so it was comforting that the means I had chosen yielded results much more quickly.

'You may imagine the good Mr. Porlock's discomfort when he found me at his door. He is an older gentleman, fifty or so, well-dressed with a prominent nose and the broad brow of the scholar. There is nothing about him to indicate that he's the lackey of a criminal mastermind. Naturally, he feigned ignorance when I mentioned Persano's untimely demise, but when I threatened to inform his master of his duplicity, he gave me a name."

"And that name is?" I asked.

"Courtland Dodd."

"Who is Courtland Dodd?"

Holmes tossed off the last of his drink, then swung his long legs off the sofa prior to standing. Untying the cords of his mouse grey dressing gown, he said, "You will meet him in just a few minutes. I sent him a wire earlier, telling him that I know all about the Persano murder." He turned toward his bedroom door, saying, "I must assume more formal attire before our guest arrives."

As Holmes reappeared, now dressed in sack coat, trousers, collar, and necktie, I heard the downstairs bell announcing our visitor. A moment later, there was a knock on the door.

"Come in, Mrs. Hudson," said Holmes.

The door opened and the landlady said, "Mr. Courtland Dodd to see you, sir."

"Send him up, dear lady."

In a moment, Dodd arrived, dressed in a similar fashion to Holmes and me, carrying a cane and a briefcase. Mrs. Hudson had apparently relieved him of his coat and hat downstairs.

Holmes plucked his evening briar from the mantel, took up the Persian slipper, and began filling it. "Good evening Dr. Dodd. So good of you to come. My condolences on the death of your wife. You have been in Brazil, I perceive."

Dodd, having placed his briefcase and cane on the sofa, was in the act of withdrawing something from his pocket as Holmes spoke. He assumed an irritated expression and said, "You've been prying into my affairs? How dare you?"

'Not at all, sir. The bulge in your jacket pocket tells me your profession, and the groove on your left ring finger from an absent wedding band informs me of your recent bereavement. And that is a fine walking stick of Brazilian cherry and silver, if I am not mistaken. I can also see you've fallen on hard times since your wife passed and have been under a great deal of stress."

Unlike many who have been treated to one of Holmes's little demonstrations, Dodd made no further remarks about the veracity of his deductions. Instead, he fished in his pocket again and withdrew a piece of paper, shaking it open so I could see that it was a telegraph form.

"I would like to know what the meaning of this is," he said, obviously trying to control the tone and the volume of his voice.

"I think that should be quite evident, Doctor." Before Dodd can reply, Holmes turns to me, saying, "Watson, would you please go downstairs and tell Mrs. Hudson to send up tea for three."

Downstairs? "But Holmes . . . ."

"Please, Watson. There's a good fellow."

Trying to refrain from shaking my head, I went to the door and out to the stairs. Two rings on Mrs. Hudson's buzzer meant Bring tea, followed by a number of additional rings to indicate that more persons than Holmes would be served. He obviously wanted me out of the room, so I went to do as he asked.

I re-entered the sitting room to find a scene of chaos!

Holmes stood in his bedroom door, a bull pup levelled at Dodd, who was on the sofa. The doctor was clutching his right hand with his left, and blood was running from the former onto the wrist of the latter. I noticed the Persian slipper was now on the floor, with tobacco strewn around it, and a pair of tongs lying nearby. And there was something else – a round, tan mass about the size of a cricket ball . . . .

"You fiend!" Dodd said to Holmes. "You have killed me!"

Holmes lowered his pistol and placed it in the pocket of his jacket.

"You have no one to blame but yourself for your fate, Doctor," Holmes said. "After watching me fill my pipe, you were going to plant that noxious thing in the slipper to ambush me the next time I wanted a smoke." Dodd shook his head, but Holmes accused, "I saw you do it from my bedroom. It is not my fault that your surprise when I suddenly reappeared to catch you in the act caused you to wound yourself. It's obvious from the splashes of mud on your shoes and gaiters that you've been in Farringdon Street recently. It also provides further evidence of your wife's passing, because I'm certain she would not have let you go out in such a state." Pointing to the ball of worms on the floor, Holmes continued, "And that is ample proof that it was you who murdered Isadora Persano. What I want to know is *why*?"

Dodd glared up at Holmes from his seat on the sofa. "I am a dead man walking, Mr. Holmes. I once saw a Brazilian Indian die from a sting less severe than this one in only two days, blood pouring from every orifice. I

50

have no wish to leave this earth in that manner. If I do as you ask, will you release me so that I might take my own life in a more humane fashion?"

Holmes looked at me, and after a moment, I nodded. "Nothing good would be served by turning this wretch over to the authorities."

"We'll see, Doctor, but if I find you're lying to me . . . ." Holmes cautioned.

"I have no reason to do that, now," Dodd said. "Might I trouble you for a whisky before I begin?"

I gave him a glass with three fingers of single malt, and he took a sip before beginning.

"Some months ago, I had an elderly patient who had a tumour. It was killing her slowly and painfully. Her daughter was caring for her while she wasted away, and it was putting a strain on her marriage. So, I took it upon myself to end the old woman's suffering without informing her daughter. I knew it was for the best for everyone involved."

As a doctor myself, I was horrified by Dodd's confession, but I said nothing.

"For some weeks after the incident, everything was as usual, but then I received a letter in the morning post. It was unsigned, but it informed me that someone was aware of what I had done, and if I did not perform a service for that individual, to be designated at some future date, rumours of my misdeed would be communicated to the woman's family and spread among the medical community. True or not, a scandal such as that could end a physician's career, as well as open him up to investigation by the Crown Prosecutor. So I waited with great trepidation to see what would be required of me to prevent it.

"About a month later, a similar missive arrived. It contained a door key, an address on Farringdon Street, and it directed me to end the life of the person who lived there in the first-floor rooms in the way that I saw fit. It said that if I did this, no more would be asked of me, and that my secret would be safe." He took another sip of his drink, then put the glass down on the low table in front of him so that he could spread his hands in supplication. "What could I do, gentlemen?"

This time I could not help myself. "You could have acted ethically, abiding by your oath, and reported all of this to the authorities."

"Says a man who has never found himself in a similar situation," Dodd retorted, taking another drink. He emptied his glass and held it out for more, but Holmes shook his head.

"Finish your tale, Doctor," he said. "Then you may have another."

"I am somewhat of an amateur naturalist and, as you've deuced, Mr. Holmes, I spent about a decade in Brazil when I was young and foolish, caring for the natives there to fund my scientific studies. I became aware of the venomous caterpillars when I had to attend to the unfortunate Indian whom I mentioned previously. I immediately saw the medical applications of such a potent *haemolysin*, so I brought a crop of the caterpillars with me when I returned to England. The moths are quite simple to rear, requiring only vegetable matter for food and water, so I was able to observe the morphology and development time of the eggs, the larval instars, the *pupae*, and the adults. I have documented all of it in a monograph that will be released upon my death."

"Why wait until your death to publish?" I asked.

"Because I had some difficulties with the medical applications. Some of the patients on whom I tried my preparations did not fare too well. I had heard that that oaf, Courtier, was working on a similar product in Paris, and I had no wish to give him any assistance. I wanted my product to be the first on the market."

"So you chose these worms to carry out the execution of Persano," Holmes prompted.

"They're not worms, they're caterpillars. No one but my dear wife was aware that I possessed these creatures, so I knew I had a means to dispose of the unwanted Mr. Persano that would prove baffling to the police."

My blood lay static in my veins like immobile ice. How could someone who had dedicated his life to ministering to the sick and injured condemn a man to such a cruel and callous death?

I noticed that Holmes had produced the Webley from his jacket and was pointing it at Dodd again. "Go downstairs and summon a constable, would you Watson, so he may remove this vermin from my home."

"No!" Dodd shouted. "You said that you would release me . . . ."

"I said that I would see, then I heard your tale. I only give you the same fate you bestowed on another."

Dodd's face hardened, and he leapt up to rush Holmes, even with the loaded revolver trained on him. But Holmes, understanding what Dodd wanted, did not fire. When the charging doctor neared him, he stepped nimbly aside and lashed out with the heavy gun, catching Dodd on the temple, and sending him sprawling unconscious on the on the floor.

"Go see to that constable, Watson," he said grimly. "I like not the smell in this room."

The next few days were busy ones. Holmes and I went to the Inner Temple to swear out a statement to gain release of the Woods from the French jail, then to Holmes's brother Mycroft to facilitate its transmittal to the gendarmes.

Scotland Yard told us that Dodd died the day after he was arrested. His death was not easy.

Holmes had left Persano's apartment with a sheaf of papers under his arm. He informed me that they were notes, written in Pitman shorthand for a story about a new crime boss who was currently establishing himself in London. No names were named, but Holmes was sure it referred to Professor Moriarty.

"Thus, we have the motive for the murder of Persano," said Holmes. "He did not name the sources for many of his facts, probably keeping them in his head, so it would be useless to turn the notes over to the press. Doubtless the Professor has his sources there as well, so it would just put someone else's life in jeopardy." Holmes's eyes flashed fire as he continued, "I swear to you, Watson, that I will not rest until this pestilence is eradicated from our land, even if it costs my very life!"

I did not realize at the time how prophetic his words were.

The Atelier of Death
by Harry DeMaio

Mrs. Hudson had just cleared away the remains of a very substantial luncheon and I sat back, letting my digestive system work its magic. Holmes had left the room for whatever purpose and I pondered how best to spend the afternoon without the onus of current medical appointments besieging me. I had stopped by for a visit, and to consider whether to take a short sabbatical in order to recover from the violence of our last adventure. My Jezail-induced wound from Afghanistan was bothering me again, and a street fight with a group of Whitechapel toughs hadn't helped it a bit.

I had a small backlog of journals and newssheets beckoning to me, and I was just about to settle in with an early afternoon glass of port when Holmes re-entered the room dressed in his ulster and, somewhat unusual for him, a bowler. He tossed my overcoat and hat in my direction and twirled his stick.

"Come, Watson, the South London Art Gallery will only be open for a few more hours."

"Why should that be of any interest to me? I had just decided on a leisurely afternoon updating myself on local, national, and world events." I shook the newspapers in his direction.

"Then you will be missing the first and only comprehensive exhibition of Vernet family artwork to be seen in London."

"Vernet?"

"You may recall that I have mentioned my grandmother, who was the sister of Vernet, the French artist. There were several generations of painters – Antoine, Joseph, Carle, and Horace, each of whom achieved fame and recognition for their works, beginning in the late seventeenth century. Horace Vernet became quite popular with both the French and the English. By 1825, he had been made an *Officier* of the Legion of Honour, and in 1826, he was elected to the Institut des Beaux-Arts, sitting next to his father, Carle. In 1842, he became a *Commandeur* of the Legion of Honour. This gallery retrospective boasts samples of all their works, from horses to famous battles."

"Famous battles?" My military background bobbed to the surface. "All right, you've convinced me. Let's go see the Vernet collection."

During the long cab ride from Baker Street to Peckham Road, Camberwell, Holmes continued to demonstrate his almost encyclopedic memory of the Vernet family and their "*oeuvres*". When we arrived at The South London Art Gallery, which had just recently opened its doors the previous January, I believe that he had exhausted his well of knowledge. I was simply exhausted.

As we stepped from the growler, we were taken aback by a scene at the gallery doorway. Two uniformed constables from the Metropolitan Police had taken up positions and were directing the public away from the entrance. Holmes recognized one of them and approached. "Good afternoon, Constable James. Has some famous person who requires police protection descended upon the gallery?"

"Oh, Mr. Holmes and Doctor Watson. No, we've a death on our hands. I hadn't realized that Inspector Gregson had called you in. You'll find him in the Director's office."

I asked the constable, "Who is the victim?"

"I don't know, Doctor. I didn't see the body."

One of the gallery guards directed us to the Director's Office. We passed through several exhibition spaces, including the current Vernet offerings, and past a large room behind a curtain set up with easels and platforms. A small space to the side was laid out with tables, chairs, and a sideboard, probably used for taking meals. The remains of a sandwich, a small wine bottle, and a serviette sat on one edge of a table. To the rear was a row of offices, only one of which seemed to be occupied. There were still unfinished areas, as The South London Art Gallery continued to be a work in progress.

The large bulk of Inspector Tobias Gregson filled the entrance of what I took to be the Director's office. He turned, surprised at our appearance, laughed, and shook his head. "I don't know how you do it, Mister Holmes. You have this uncanny ability to arrive at the scene of a crime without being summoned or informed."

"Is it indeed a crime then, Gregson?"

"It would certainly seem so. We have a victim whom we believe succumbed to a dose of poison in a small bottle of wine that she was drinking with her lunch. We haven't yet removed the evidence. How did you know about this incident?"

"We didn't. Horace Vernet was my grand-uncle, and I persuaded Watson to accompany me to this exhibition to view his and his ancestors' work. But this death has certainly piqued my interest."

"It will be piqued even further in just a moment, but first let me introduce the Gallery Director, Professor Charles Montgomery."

The inspector stepped out of the doorway, revealing a room filled with traditional oak office furniture, a window, several bookshelves, two walls full of small paintings, and behind an impressive paper-scattered desk, a small intense-looking individual who stared at us with expressive brown eyes. Gregson did the honors and introduced us.

The professor rose from his perch. He wore a *pince nez* and was dressed in a fashionable grey business suit. A watch fob, from which a small gold medallion swung, traversed his waistcoat. A ruby stickpin secured a cravat of matching grey stripes. All told, he presented the image of a successful businessman rather than an academic.

Montgomery's voice belied his small stature. "Sherlock Holmes and Doctor Watson!" he boomed. "This is indeed an honor. I regret that we are meeting under such sad circumstances."

I replied. "Thank you, Professor Montgomery. This is an impressive establishment. I hope that it's a great success. The public can certainly use another center of the arts besides the National Gallery. You've made great progress in the few weeks that you've been open."

"Yes, we have. I hope this unhappy incident doesn't detract from the general public's interest. Not only have we launched the Vernet exhibit, but we have also initiated our small atelier for budding young artists. We have six participants at the moment, not counting the Principal Master and the models. It has been in session for several months. It began before we formally opened our exhibit spaces to the community at large. Unfortunately, the deceased young lady was one of our first apprentices. She showed excellent promise."

Holmes looked at Gregson. "A young lady?"

The inspector surprisingly grinned. "Yes, and here is the fascinating part: Her name was Vernet – Denise Vernet, from Paris. A member of the Vernet family. She volunteered to assist the Gallery's curators in setting up this exhibit while she improved her painting techniques in the atelier. She's over here on an artistic internship paid for by the French government. We haven't yet checked the veracity of her claims, but Professor Montgomery says he had no reason to doubt her."

"Good Lord, Holmes, she could be a distant relative."

Holmes frowned, "Perhaps, perhaps not. With your agreement. Inspector, I would like to look into this further. Do you have any objection, Professor Montgomery?"

"None whatsoever, Mr. Holmes! Anything that I can do to assist and put this terrible event to rest. I want to reopen the Gallery as soon as possible."

Gregson frowned, "I'm sorry, Professor, but for the moment we must treat the Gallery as the scene of a murder. I will try to keep your atelier active, but we will have to limit public access to the exhibits and the rest of the premises."

Holmes interjected, "Has her next of kin been informed?"

Gregson responded. "She has no relatives here in England. We've wired the French police. We were told that she has an aunt in Paris with whom she normally resides, and to whom she expected to return at the end of her internship. I presume that the aunt and her son will come to claim the body."

"I assume that the corpse has been taken to the morgue. When will you meet with the coroner, Inspector?"

"At six. Please join me there, gentlemen. Meantime, you may wish to examine the scene of her death and the lunch materials before they're packed up and sent to the Yard."

"You're convinced she was poisoned?"

"It certainly appears that way."

"I should like to meet the Principal Master of the atelier," Holmes said to Professor Montgomery.

"The workshop isn't in session at the moment. The Principal Master, Docteur Deland, cancelled the rest of the day's session in view of the tragedy. However, I believe he's still here in the building. Excuse me and I'll seek him out."

Holmes turned to Gregson and me. "While he's searching for the Master, let's look at the scene of her death."

We walked into the small refectory where one of the tables still bore the remains of Miss Vernet's lunch. A chair was overturned and a partially eaten sandwich sat halfway upon a plate. A small glass with a fingerful of red wine stood next to an almost empty half-bottle.

"She was found slumped on the floor by one of the other students. There was a wine stain on her smock and her chin. I am sending the meal back to the Yard for analysis."

Holmes took a small tube and envelope from his ulster pocket. "I should like to take two small samples, if I may."

"I suppose that won't qualify as evidence tampering. Go ahead."

"Was she eating alone?"

"She was at that moment, but several other members of the class had just entered to have their lunches. That's when she was found. They attempted to waken her, but she wasn't breathing. They summoned a gallery guard and the Master. They, in turn, called a local doctor and a constable, who then called me. The doctor confirmed that she was dead."

Professor Montgomery entered the room with a tall, mustachioed man at his side. "Gentlemen, Atelier Master Docteur Deland."

Deland spoke English with a Parisian accent. He had a long shock of dark hair pulled back to his shoulders. A paint-spattered smock covered a velvet jacket. Several paintbrushes peeked out from a pocket. A prodigious multi-colored ascot surrounded his neck. His deep blue eyes glinted and his expressive brows flashed up and down in synchronism with his fluttering hands and arms. "Is it the so-very-celebrated Monsieur Sherlock Holmes that I am addressing? Such a privilege! And you must be Doctor John Watson. You sir! Gregson! I assume you are with Scotland Yard. I am delighted to welcome you to our humble workshop. I hope it will not be humble for long." He grinned. "But I must not make light of the situation. I am *désolé* at the loss of our *chère* Denise – such a wonderful young talent."

"I understand you have six apprentices in the atelier, Docteur," said Holmes.

His face drew down. "Now sadly, only five, Monsieur. But Denise was a special case. She was dedicated to enhancing the name of Vernet – which required no enhancement. In the morning, she would attend the exercises with the other students. In the afternoon, she would take her easel and paints, go into the galleries, and set about studying and duplicating one of the works of the Vernet masters. She wished to perpetuate their styles and techniques. Right now, I can show you her work reproducing *Bridge and Castel Sant' Angelo in Rome* by Claude-Joseph Vernet. Come with me."

We walked out into one of the galleries. Deland pointed to a medium-sized canvas on the wall depicting a bridge spanning the Tiber River, with the Castel Sant' Angelo in the upper left-hand corner. Two fishermen extended their nets in the center of the river all under a grey and moody sky.

"This, of course, is the original by Claude-Joseph Vernet, finished in 1745. Now let me share Denise's incomplete version with you."

He walked to a far wall and pulled open a closet revealing an easel supporting a canvas twice the size of the original, as well as a palette, a shelf of paints, brushes, and tools. The fishermen, their boat, and the castle high on the hill were all in a near finished state and parts of the river and bridge were roughed in. The sky was a brilliant white, which no doubt would be softened, dimensioned, and dulled. The resemblance to the original was startling.

In spite of my lack of artistic training, I ventured, "She was a true talent. What say you, Holmes? Gregson?"

Gregson nodded vigorously. Holmes, who justifiably claimed some authority on the subject of painting, agreed. He took out his glass and studied the brush strokes and color gradations. "Her technique is flawless and quite mature. With all due respect, Docteur, she could be teaching the class."

Deland looked at Montgomery and said, "I agree. I would like to put this on special exhibition just as it is. It will add a poignant special note to the Vernet show."

Holmes spoke up. "May I suggest we determine the cause of Mlle. Vernet's death with more precision before you make such a gesture. If it was an innocent accident, then by all means, proceed. If there was something more ominous involved, you may not wish to bring it to the public's eye."

"Do you suspect foul play, Mister Holmes?"

"As Inspector Gregson and Doctor Watson well know, in a matter of unexplained death, that is always a possibility."

Montgomery agreed to hold off on the special display, and Deland somewhat reluctantly acquiesced. As we were about to turn away, I looked back at the easel and the array of tools and brushes and chuckled. "I say, Holmes, here's an interesting quirk. The lady chewed on her brushes." I pointed to teeth marks on the handles. "I know writers who chew on their pencils. I do myself, but I have never known an artist to do it."

"How many artists do you know, Watson? I believe if we looked in at the atelier, we are likely to find at least one other who does. It is probably an aid to concentration. All artists have their little tics and peculiarities. Isn't that so, Docteur Deland?"

"Ah, *oui*! One of my students chews gum *sans cesse*, and two of them attempt to smoke. I will not allow it. The fumes affect the paint and the other students. They sneak into the refectory in order to satisfy their needs."

"Now, Gregson," said my companion, "I believe it is time we went to the mortuary to view the remains of the unfortunate Mlle. Vernet, her clothing, and immediate possessions. Professor Montgomery, do you wish to join us? Docteur Deland, I would like to meet with the other apprentices tomorrow morning. Will that be possible? Also, can one of you provide me with her home address, and the names of any friends or acquaintances of whom you may be aware."

"Three of the students share living space, Monsieur Holmes. Denise and the two other women in the workshop – Madeleine Fairfax and Lady Selma Wrightship. The men live separately in small rooms near here. I will provide you with their names and addresses."

"Thank you, Docteur."

There is a deadly sameness to mortuaries. The subdued lighting, the near-silence broken only by the sounds of medical procedures, the occasional footsteps and restrained voices, and, of course, the cold. The Camberwell Morgue was no different. Doctor Patterson, the assistant coroner, greeted Inspector Gregson and was somewhat surprised to find he had a small entourage in tow. The policeman made the introductions. I was acknowledged as a fellow member of the medical profession, and Sherlock Holmes's reputation once again stood him in good stead. He was a bit restrained with Professor Montgomery until he realized his relationship to the deceased.

He beckoned us over to a covered slap. He revealed a young woman in her very early twenties. Her hair was black and shoulder length. Her eyes were closed but, upon examination, we noticed blood shot streaks in their whites. The irises were a deep blue. Her mouth was curled into a grimace. Her body was slight and of medium height. Her complexion was pale and reflected an absence of any exposure to the sun. There were smudges of white, brown, and blue paint on her fingers.

"We have only had time to make some preliminary assessments, gentlemen, but there is no sign of physical violence, aside from a cut on her wrist which we assume she sustained when falling from her chair. There is also a very mild bruise on her hip consistent with her fall. Our consensus is she succumbed to some form of internal disorder, either of a natural form or, and this is quite possible, the effects of a poisonous substance. We have tested for the 'Murderer's Five' – arsenic, cyanide, thallium, strychnine, and nightshade – and drawn a blank. Nor did we find any traces of laudanum or opium. We are now searching for something more exotic. Any assistance the Yard – and you too, Mr. Holmes – may be able to give will be gratefully accepted. We've found no significant symptoms of fatal diseases – but again, we are still at the early stages."

"Thank you, Doctor Patterson. I will do some analysis of my own upon the remnants of her lunch, but you haven't given me much hope of success. May we see her clothing and personal items?"

"Certainly! Over here. You can see she has a variety of paint stains on her smock, as well as some spilled wine. She had a painter's stick and knife in her pockets, along with a couple of heavily used brushes. Oddly, there seemed to be tooth marks on several of them."

Montgomery replied, "We noted that back at the atelier. That isn't as uncommon as you may think among artists. They often hold a brush or brushes in their mouth to give them ready access."

Gregson asked the doctor, "Did she have a personal bag?"

"Yes. You may take it with you. It contained two letters, some pound notes and coins, a room key, and several copies of a brochure for the Vernet exhibit at the Art Gallery. There was also a used ticket stub for a French Music Hall review. Oh, and several unopened tubes of oil paint."

"Do you want to look at the bag before we leave, Mr. Holmes? I must take it back to the Yard as evidence."

"Just a brief glimpse, Inspector. Watson, would you please take down the information from the Music Hall ticket. Let's see what the letters say. They are, as expected, short and in French. Both from her aunt, asking after her health and well-being. She mentions a 'Gerard' – perhaps a swain, or maybe a relative. She also mentions a visit from a member of the *Sûreté*. No further explanation. It's as if Miss Vernet would know what that was all about. It's interesting that she carried the letters with her."

I interrupted. "Not unusual if she didn't want her flatmates to have access to her private correspondence. We should examine their rooms and see their living arrangements."

Holmes nodded. "It's on my agenda. Gregson, can you make inquiries with the *Sûreté*! I wonder what that visit was all about. It may be nothing. Professor Montgomery, we'll return to the gallery in the morning if that is satisfactory. I would like to interview the apprentices."

"Certainly, Mister Holmes. I'll alert Docteur Deland. Inspector, I would greatly appreciate your reopening the gallery as soon as you can."

"I believe we may be able to release the public rooms tomorrow, but the atelier, refectory, and offices must remain controlled for the time being. I assume there is a cloak room for the students. We'll need to examine that further as well."

"The release will be most helpful. I guess there is no way of avoiding the press in this matter."

"A mysterious death is like catnip to reporters. I'm afraid that you'll have to issue a statement. The Yard will be its usual reticent self."

"As will I," said Holmes. "Good evening, gentlemen. Thank you, Doctor Patterson. Oh, when will the Coroner's Inquest take place?"

"Probably tomorrow afternoon, as soon as I finish my autopsy."

"Please let us know when and where.

Once back on the street, we bade farewell to the Gallery Director and the Inspector and went in search of a cab. "I believe that Mrs. Hudson is preparing dinner, Holmes. I could use some sustenance and a tipple to restore my frame of mind. This is a sad and mysterious business."

The detective merely grunted.

When we had returned to Baker Street and finished off Mrs. Hudson's roast chicken, I settled into my usual chair armed with a glass of cognac while Holmes withdrew the samples that he had taken from Miss Vernet's lunch and began to analyze them.

"Given Doctor Patterson's prior examination, what do you hope to discover?"

"Probably nothing."

"Do you believe that she was poisoned? And please don't tell me about eliminating the impossible."

"In the absence of facts, I have no belief."

"But perhaps some hope?"

"Nothing in these samples gives me hope. Watson. The wine is untainted and the sandwich remnant is a simple combination of cheese and bread. I must look elsewhere."

"Well, we'll have the students to interview tomorrow.

Next day, having no patient appointments, I accompanied Holmes on the journey back to the art gallery. True to his word, Gregson had removed the constables and allowed the public display areas to be reopened. A few visitors strolled the spaces and set about perusing the gift shop. The inspector once again met us at the director's office.

"Good morning, Professor Montgomery. Will it be possible to speak with the apprentices?"

"Good morning. Yes, Docteur Deland has prepared them to be interviewed. Did you wish to speak to them individually or as a group?"

"Individually, but first I'd like to say a few words to the five of them together. I'd also like to interview the Atelier Master as well."

"I've set aside an office for this purpose," replied Montgomery.

Holmes nodded. "By the way, what is Docteur Deland's given name?"

"Gerard." I raised my eyebrows but Holmes signaled me to silence.

"Thank you. Shall we gather the ducklings? Do you wish to begin the procedure, Inspector?"

"Yes. Let's move into the studio."

The four of us walked into the atelier, where Docteur Deland was holding forth. A semi-draped male model was posed on a platform and the Master was bouncing from easel to easel, commenting, taking a brush and making an alteration, demonstrating how to mix paints on the palette and generally dominating the group. He looked up as we entered and, clapping his hands, said, "Attention, *mes petites*. We have guests: The incomparable Monsieur Sherlock Holmes, his colleague, Doctor Watson, Inspector Gregson from Scotland Yard, and of course you're all familiar with Professeur Montgomery. They are here to inquire into the most unfortunate death of Mademoiselle Vernet. Let us give them our most full cooperation. I shall make the introductions. Ladies first! Gentlemen, this young artist is Miss Madeleine Fairfax. She is a scenic designer at the Garrick Theatre, but aspires to more classical artistry. Lady Selma Wrightship is the daughter of Sir Edward Wrightship of Havelock Hall in

Lincolnshire. She has temporarily moved to London to participate in our apprentice program. Both of these ladies shared rooms with Denise.

"And now, the gentlemen. Our model for today is George Guthrie. He is new to the atelier, and I believe that he never met Mademoiselle Vernet. Is that correct, George?"

The model nodded.

Gregson looked at him and said, "I don't think we need bother you any further, Mister Guthrie. Docteur Deland will summon you back when we have finished our interviews."

"*C'est bon*. Let us proceed. Here are Herr Walter Nagel from Bavaria, Messrs. Algernon Dunphy from London and Willis Griggs from Liverpool. I shall leave it to you gentlemen to organize your interviews."

Holmes interrupted. "We shall also want to speak to you, Docteur. Please make yourself available."

"*Mais, certainment*, Monsieur. I am at your disposal."

"Ladies and gentlemen," said Holmes. "Thank you for your cooperation. We shall try to make this as painless as possible and allow you to return to your artistic labors forthwith. We're endeavoring to identify the cause of Miss Vernet's demise and how it occurred. Any facts that you can provide are more than welcome. I should like to interview each of you separately. Professor Montgomery has allowed us to occupy one of the unused offices. May we begin with you, Miss Fairfax?"

The lady nodded, placed her brushes, pencils, and tools on her easel, and proceeded from the room, glancing back to get directions from Holmes. The office that was made available was equipped with a desk and several chairs. The walls were bare. Gregson and I took up seats near the door. Holmes sat down behind the desk and motioned Miss Fairfax to a chair in front of it. She was a tall, comely young woman with chestnut hair bundled under a flat-crowned hat which she continued to wear inside the building. Her smock, which hid her figure, showed only a few paint spots. I believe she had been sketching in charcoal. Her face was oval and her skin a pale, English-Rose tint. Her eyes were an intense deep blue, and she turned to glance at Gregson and me before casting her attention on Holmes.

"What would you like to know?" she asked. Her voice was cultured, lower than I expected, and without accent.

"You have until now shared rooms with Mademoiselle Vernet and Lady Wrightship?"

"Yes, for the duration of our classes. The session lasts another month. As the Master told you, I am employed at the Garrick as a scene designer and am still working there part-time in the evenings while attending the atelier. As a result, I saw Denise more often in class than at our apartment.

63

She was quite skillful. Since she was making copies of the Vernets, it was difficult to tell how original or creative she might have been, but her technique was excellent. She also did very well with the live subjects in the atelier. She was clearly dedicated to the works of the Vernet family."

"Did she have any male friends or acquaintances here in London?"

"None that I know of. Any relationships of that sort were probably based in Paris. I know that she was anxious to return to her home with her aunt."

"How did she get along with her fellow apprentices?"

"She was cordial, but somewhat reserved. She would often take her lunch alone, but would join the others if they were coming into the refectory."

"Where do the students obtain your lunches?"

"The gallery has a small food shop, but it isn't yet fully stocked or equipped. We stop on the way to the atelier at a little business that's open in the mornings and buy sandwiches and some wine. We keep the bags in the cloakroom."

"So there would be opportunities to tamper with the food."

"Are you implying that one of us could have poisoned her?"

"I am implying nothing. I am just following through to a logical conclusion."

"Well, I certainly did not, and I don't believe that any of the others would either. What motive would we have?"

"It remains to be discovered, Miss Fairfax, if indeed any of you caused her death."

"You're convinced that she died of poison?"

"There is a very high probability, although as of yet, the nature of the substance has not been determined."

"My God!" she cried, her face blanching, "If that's so, we could all be in danger!"

"It isn't clear the poison was inflicted through your lunch items. Are your lunch bags individually identified?"

"No, we just keep them with our outer clothing. They look the same since they come from the same shop. I'm not having any lunch today, thank you very much!"

"In the future, until we discover the type and source of the poison, if any, you may want to keep your lunch bag in your constant view. We aren't accusing you or your co-artists. Others may have had access to Miss Vernet's food. It isn't even clear whether she was poisoned."

"But why kill her? She seemed perfectly harmless."

"We don't know. We have yet to determine a motive, if this indeed was murder."

"Well, you've certainly shaken my peace of mind. Are we finished?"

"Yes, thank you. We hope to have answers shortly. Could you send in Lady Wrightship?"

After she left the room, Holmes turned to Gregson and me and shrugged. "We made little progress there."

Lady Selma Wrightship, the daughter of Sir Edward Wrightship of Havelock Hall in Lincolnshire, sailed into the office, glanced at Gregson and me without acknowledging us, took a seat unbidden at the desk in front of Holmes, and said, "Whatever do you want from me? I barely knew Denise, even if we shared rooms. She made it quite clear that she was only interested in two things: Vernet Art and returning to Paris as soon as she could. We did not socialize, and I'm not sure she that had any kind of a social life at all here in London. She was a skilled artist and made the rest of us look like the rank amateurs that we are – except perhaps Madeleine Fairfax, who works in the theatre. If it wasn't for the Vernet collection, I am sure she would have attended classes at one of the many ateliers in Paris. If, as you seem to believe, she was murdered, I can assure you that I had nothing to do with it. Does that satisfy you?"

She paused for breath. Holmes sat back in his chair and gave her one of his piercing stares, which she returned. She held herself erect in her chair, her flashing dark brown eyes emerging from what was otherwise a rather plain and undistinctive face. Her hair was auburn and piled upon her hatless head. She too wore a smock, but of significantly finer quality than that of Miss Fairfax.

"I'm afraid that it doesn't, Lady Selma. We aren't accusing you of anything, but we are seeking any indicative information that might lead to a further understanding of how and why Mademoiselle Vernet died and at whose hand."

"Do I understand correctly that you haven't identified the cause of her death?"

"We are reasonably certain, as is the coroner, that it was a poison that we have yet to identify."

"Well then, may I recommend that you set about identifying it and let us get on about our business."

With that, she rose and strode out of the room.

I couldn't control my laughter. "I suspect that wasn't our last encounter with Milady Selma."

"Hardly," said Holmes, "but let us allow the lady's lack of good manners to go unnoticed for the nonce, and speak with Herr Walter Nagel. What time is the Coroner's Inquest?"

Gregson, who had been silent during the interviews, replied. "Four o'clock. We'll need an hour to reach the Court. I'm not sure who will be called upon to testify. I'm sure that the apprentices, Professeur Montgomery, and Docteur Deland will be put in the box. I suspect that we will as well. The Coroner has his own bailiffs who are charged with summoning the witnesses. They're probably scurrying about as we're sitting here."

Gregson proved to be remarkably prophetic. A large individual dressed in a blue uniform entered the office carrying a sheaf of papers, which proved to be summonses for the Coroner's Inquest. "Mr. Sherlock Holmes, Doctor John H. Watson, Inspector Tobias Gregson, you are summoned to testify at the London Coroner's Court at four p.m. today regarding the demise of Denise Vernet. No excuse will be allowed and failure to attend will be dealt with severely."

He looked at us with a querulous expression as he passed out the papers. We nodded our acceptance. I wondered how the denizens of the atelier were reacting. I was soon to find out upon the bailiff's exit as Herr Nagel entered carrying his summons.

"Bloody cheek!" he protested. "I thought that I was back in Bavaria. At the command of the Queen, indeed. Oh well, damned little I will be able to tell him. Lady Selma is protesting and threatening to call in the Home Office. Should be entertaining. Well, Herr Holmes, gentlemen, how can I assist?"

"Herr Nagel, as I'm sure you know, we are investigating the nature and circumstances of Mademoiselle's Vernet's death. We understand that you three gentlemen are living in separate accommodations and have had no social contacts with her, other than here at the atelier."

"I cannot speak for my male colleagues, but I certainly have not. I'm not sure I've spoken more than ten words to her during the entire course. I am from Munich, a curator here on a dual mission from the *Bayerisches Nationalmuseum* – the Bavarian National Museum. One is to observe and evaluate the Vernet exhibit with an eye to eventually facilitating a loan. The other is to experience the development process of your new atelier so that we might learn how best to organize one in Munich. The ones in Paris and Berlin are quite mature. We want to live through and witness the initial growing pains. So far, it has been most enlightening, although I cannot claim that Mlle. Vernet's demise has added to my learning experience. Anyway, I am at your disposal."

"We are of the opinion that Mademoiselle Vernet succumbed to poison, although we haven't yet been able to reliably identify the material. The usual deadly suspects have been eliminated, but we can find no other culprit, even among the more exotic substances."

Nagel exploded a booming laugh. "Gentlemen, forgive the reaction of an art curator, but you do realize, do you not, that artists live in a sea of

66

noxious ingredients. Most of our paints contain poisons – some relatively benign, but others highly dangerous. I believe it is the reason that so many painters fall victim to insanity or other dramatic physical reactions, including death. The palette is a toxic swamp. Look there for your poison. Start with some of the more commonplace colors such as Cremnitz white, pigments with cobalt or lead, a variety of greens, as well as thinners and solvents. I'll bet one or more of them killed Denise – especially if she ingested them."

I protested. "How would she ingest a paint?"

"Oh, Doctor, just watch a painter at work. You will see them stirring colors on a palette and then touching their fingers to their mouths or using a paint covered rag to wipe their smocks and then using it to blow their noses. Several of my associates chew on the handles of their brushes. It helps them concentrate. Denise was infamous for that."

Holmes looked at Gregson. "Have we kept her brushes?"

"I'm not sure we have all of them, but several have pronounced teeth marks."

"Have them analyzed immediately! Do you students buy your own brushes, Herr Nagel?"

"Some, but the school also provides a few. You'll have to ask the Docteur."

"Thank you. You have been immensely helpful."

We finished our interviews with Algernon Dunphy from London and Willis Griggs from Liverpool. Both were aspiring amateurs, hoping to come to the attention of a private gallery owner or modern art connoisseur. They had little or no interest in the Vernets and concentrated on the abstract. Both admitted to having met with Miss Vernet, but only in the class sessions. Dunphy claimed he had little interest in French women, especially someone as intense as the mademoiselle. I'm not sure Willis Griggs had interest in any women. He did confirm, however, her habit of chewing on the brush handles. Our last conversation before leaving for lunch and then the Coroner's Court was with Docteur Deland.

He was dressed in what I assumed was his usual modish style. This time red dominated his color scheme. His smock was immaculate. His oversized cravat surrounded his head and shoulders, producing the overall effect of an *avant-garde* fashion plate. A true artistic dandy. (Or was it "fop"?)

"*Mon Dieu*, Monsieur Holmes, the death of Denise Vernet has certainly upset our program. I hope we can return to sanity in short order."

"It is our hope as well, Docteur Deland. I believe your given name is Gerard?"

"*Oui*, that is correct. Gerard Alphonse Deland. Initials *GAD*." He giggled.

"Tell me, Docteur, did you know Denise Vernet in Paris before she joined your studio here in London?"

"*Mais non*, she was a complete stranger when she arrived here at my humble establishment."

"Isn't a bit unusual to accept an apprentice without first having met them?"

"Perhaps, but not when she comes with a strong recommendation from the President of the Académie des Beaux-Arts. As it turns out, she was indeed a remarkable talent."

"What is your experience with the Vernets?"

"Very little. As you may know, my atelier was in business here at the South London Art Gallery before the Vernet exhibit was fully assembled. Professor Montgomery will tell you that the paintings on display came from a variety of private collections and public sources from all over Europe and even the United States."

"So you had no role in curating the exposition?"

"Oh, only some minor consulting, but I am far too busy setting up and managing my own program."

"What is your opinion on how Mademoiselle Vernet died?"

"I share your surmise that it was some form of poison. Probably accidental."

"Why do you say that?"

"I cannot believe that someone would deliberately set out to kill such a gifted artist.

"I'm sure you are aware of the toxic pigments used in many of the paints here at the studio."

"Oh, *oui*, and I have frequently warned the students about them. That may have been the cause of her death. Artists often refuse to be disciplined in their practices. There are so many ways that they can be exposed."

"Is that going to be your testimony at the Coroner's Inquest this afternoon?"

"If I am asked, I will give that opinion, but I would have thought you and the coroner would have already reached a scientific decision on that subject."

"We are carefully winnowing down the options. We aren't yet ready to offer a definitive conclusion. Thank you for your assistance. We shall see you again this afternoon at the Coroner's Court."

Several events took place before Gregson, Holmes, and I assembled for the Inquest. First was lunch, at my insistence. Next was a rapid visit to

68

the office of Mycroft Holmes, followed by a wire to Inspector Georges Villaincourt of the French *Sûreté*'s bureau, specializing in art theft and fraud. We then took an interval to participate in the Inquest. The Coroner received all our testimony, asked a few questions, seemed annoyed at the lack of definitive evidence, and closed the proceedings with a finding of "death by accident or misadventure". Needless to say, neither he nor we were satisfied, but it essentially left the investigation open for further pursuit.

Lunch was hearty and satisfying. Our visit to Mycroft unleashed a series of inquiries with administrators at the Office of the President of the Académie des Beaux-Arts. These in turn triggered a discussion with the *Sûreté*. New information was unfolding rapidly. Henri Gerard, known as Docteur Gerard Deland and other names, was and still is suspected of dealing in art forgeries and altering provenance of existing originals. The Académie President had authorized the *Sûreté* to initiate an investigation into his activities on its behalf and arranged for Denise Vernet – not her real name – to be enrolled in Gerard's newly formed atelier at the South London Art Gallery. She was a skilled Parisian artist and curator who worked part time with the *Sûreté* in their various investigations. Her claim to be a Vernet relative, coupled with her assiduous pursuit of her studies, enabled her to carefully assess the paintings in the exhibition which, in spite of his denials, Gerard helped to provide under different contributor names. There were numerous forgeries amid the genuine Vernets – forgeries that Gerard hoped to foist on unwitting victims.

This was all verified with the arrival of her "aunt" and "brother", both *Sûreté* members, to claim her body. The notes she was carrying about were actually coded messages between the agency and herself. They weren't yet ready to spring the trap on Gerard until "Denise Vernet" could assemble more airtight evidence against him. Fortunately, however, she had developed extensive information that was sufficient to cause the Gallery Director, Professor Montgomery, to prematurely close the Vernet show, much to his extreme chagrin.

Gerard could read the situation and disappeared, enraging his students, and leaving a serious question still unanswered: Did he or did he not kill "Denise Vernet"?

At Gregson's request, the Yard and Holmes both chemically analyzed the brushes used by "Denise Vernet". They discovered, as Herr Nagel had predicted, that the handles were coated in lead white, cobalt green, or cadmium red paints – all of them extremely toxic. They also found teeth marks on all of the brushes tested, providing reliable evidence that "Denise", in spite of her professional experience, participated in her own killing. Her palette bore witness to the profusion of poisonous colors she was using. Was it all an accident, or a carefully engineered attack, taking advantage of her artistic eccentricity? We all believed it was deliberate.

Someone knowledgeable in the deadly effects of the paints and with continued access to her brushes would have needed multiple opportunities to carry off the subtle but effective process of murder. He or she would also require infinite patience, because it wouldn't be clear when the cumulative toxic effect would result in death. Who?

The first item on the agenda was tracking down the missing Gerard. His rooms in Camberwell were abandoned. A belated search by Scotland Yard revealed that he had crossed the Channel to Paris, where he then vanished. He reappeared in an artists' colony in Bordeaux, using yet another name and somewhat altered features. However, the *Sûreté* and Académie des Beaux-Arts, employing their extensive facilities and connections, traced and arrested him. Eventually, he confessed to the attempted fraud in London, but vehemently denied any involvement in murder.

He did his cowardly best to implicate not only the apprentices in the atelier, but also Professor Montgomery. We were hardly convinced but Holmes, in the spirit of redressing the wrong inflicted on his pseudo-relative, decided to pursue the possibilities. Now that the atelier had been disbanded, we had to search out the former apprentices. We divided the efforts.

I rapidly discarded Algernon Dunphy and Willis Griggs as both lacking motive, skill, and opportunity.

Since Professor Montgomery was the victim of Gerard's chicanery and would have benefitted from the lady's work, it was hard for Gregson to see him as her killer. That left the formidable and unpleasant Lady Selma, Herr Nagel, and Miss Fairfax.

Holmes decided not to make the trip to Bavaria. Herr Nagel had shared his knowledge of pigment toxicity with us, and certainly had the skill and knowledge to carry off such a plot, but we searched in vain for motive. He wasn't involved with Gerard's fraud, and had even taken steps as a skilled curator to warn off Professor Montgomery against the Docteur. He had very limited access to "Denise" or her equipment. In short, he wasn't very likely.

I personally would have liked to have seen Lady Selma clapped in irons. Her nasty personality, coupled with the fact that she shared a room with "Denise", certainly gave us sufficient cause to examine her more closely.

However, she provided us with a discovery about Madeleine Fairfax that caused us to change our priorities. Lady Selma revealed most salaciously that Miss Fairfax was seeing "Docteur Deland" – Gerard – on the side. Many of the evenings when she was supposedly working at her position as a set designer at the Garrick Theatre, Madeleine was actually involved with Gerard. Was it strictly romantic, or was she aiding and abetting his fraudulent activities? Could she be a forger? After all, she was a professional artist. Alarm bells began to sound.

We decided that all three of us would visit her at the Garrick Theatre, with Holmes in the lead. We descended upon her in the afternoon on the semi-darkened stage where she was putting the finishing touches to a decorative flat. She was annoyed at being interrupted, evasive and reluctant to talk to us. It was only after Gregson threatened to bring her down to the Yard that she agreed to converse. She took a seat on a small step-ladder and boldly stared down at us.

"Miss Fairfax, can you describe your relationship with Docteur Deland – or should we call him Henri Gerard?"

"I don't recognize that name. Docteur Deland was my instructor at the South London Art Gallery atelier until he disappeared and the atelier folded. That's all that I know about him."

"We have reason to believe that your relationship was both a business one and an intimate one."

"That is sheer nonsense! Who is spreading malicious rumors about me?"

"Someone who was familiar with your comings and goings. When we caught up with him in France, Docteur Deland or Henri Gerard also tried to implicate you in his activities as a counterfeiter and fraud."

"The class suspected he was involved in forgery, but had insufficient proof."

"Well, we do, and we are reasonably certain he wasn't acting alone, and strongly suspect you were his accomplice."

"He's lying and you're wrong. Are you going to take the word of a convicted felon?"

"So you know he is a convicted felon?"

"I'm just assuming that."

"We also believe, based on his testimony, that you conspired in the murder of Denise Vernet. You both believed that she was suspicious of your fraudulent activity and was only waiting for more proof before reporting you to The Gallery Director and the Police. Were you aware that she was in the employ of the French *Sûreté* and Académie des Beaux-Arts, and charged with tracking down forgeries in the Vernet collection?"

Her shocked expression answered that question.

"You had access to her brushes in your shared rooms and coated the handles with toxic pigments when she was out, knowing she would unconsciously chew on them as she worked. It only required a little patience on your part for the deadly paints to do their fatal work."

Gregson moved toward her and said, "Miss Madeleine Fairfax, I am holding you in custody for the willful murder of Mademoiselle Georgette Delacroix, known to you as Denise Vernet."

"No!" She jumped down from the step-ladder and taking up her skirts, ran toward the front of the stage. She turned defiantly back at us as she ran and shouted once again. "No! You won't!" Not seeing where she was going, she tripped over a footlight, lost her balance, and fell from the platform into the orchestra pit. A small scream was followed by a crash, a thump, and then silence. Gregson and I rushed down the stairs leading to the orchestra. She lay motionless with her head at an acute angle. Gregson looked at me and I searched for a pulse or any sign of life. She had broken her neck and died amid the chairs and music stands.

Holmes approached the stage apron and stared down at her lifeless body.

"She is dead, Holmes. Inspector, would you accept her actions as a confession?"

"I believe so, and I think the Coroner will too. Mister Holmes, how did you know she conspired to poison Mademoiselle Vernet's brushes?"

"I didn't until she just told me."

The Adventure of the
Beauty Trap
by Tracy J. Revels

"Watson, tell me what you make of these."

I took the objects that Holmes had thrust at me the moment I entered our formerly shared rooms at Baker Street. I had just concluded a long day of making rounds and wished for nothing more than a glass of brandy to take off the chill before I made my weary way home. I confess that I was in no mood for one of Holmes's little games, but his eyes shone brightly, and he bobbed up and down with his hands held behind him, so full of almost child-like anticipation, that I didn't wish to disappoint him.

"It is a pair of lady's gloves," I said, turning them over in examination. "Rather well worn, of soft leather, with a small tear on the right finger. Perhaps the lady does a good deal of typing. I see that the jet button on the left hand is missing. She is a working woman who must economize, and bought these gloves, which were once very fine, in a second-hand shop. Otherwise – I can tell you nothing."

"For you have learned nothing," Holmes rebuked me, with some impatience. "What lady types with her gloves on? Really, Watson, you can do better than that, I think."

"Not after delivering twins and dealing with a nearly fatal hemorrhage, I cannot," I snapped. "Where's the decanter?"

"Try the sideboard," Holmes chuckled. "I fear that in your attempt to duplicate my methods, you have missed the most obvious fact."

"Which is?"

"The gloves are *here*. They were left behind by a very intriguing lady who, I suspect, will return for them at any moment. I'm quite gratified to see you, for distraught ladies find your presence comforting, and she may be more inclined to be forthcoming with you in the room than if the interview was conducted with me alone."

I wasn't certain that I understood. "But if she has already been here for a consultation – ?"

Holmes waved me to a seat. "She came with her husband. She left the gloves very intentionally, so that she might return for them and a more private chat. Let me tell you of this afternoon's encounter before her arrival. I wonder if you might have made the acquaintance of her husband – Major Albert Winston of the Berkshires."

I nearly spat out my drink. "Bad Bertie is wed? God help the poor woman!"

"Ah, I suspected there would be a reaction. Tell me what you know of him."

"He was famous as a tiger hunter, the greatest marksman in the corps, but also a stickler for discipline, cruel and unforgiving. More than one young soldier died or had his health ruined because he ran afoul of the Major. So, he is back in England and retired, hmm? And with a bride? He was quite the confirmed bachelor when I met him."

"Your assessment agrees with mine," Holmes said. "I took him instantly for a martinet, with no trace of the softer emotions. He is some sixty years of age, and his lady has not passed thirty. It is a tragedy in the making. I felt it even as he spoke, and so I was relieved when I saw the lady remove her gloves and quite discreetly 'lose' them in the cushions of the settee."

"What brings him to you?"

"It seems that his lady – her name is Kathryn, as I recall – has been in the habit of visiting Madame Louvois's Restorative Salon, a 'temple of youth and beauty', where ladies may acquire not only cosmetics and perfume, but take 'Arabian Baths' in 'Waters of Elysium', whatever that might be. She claims that last week, while disrobing in a changing room to prepare for a bath, she placed her pearl earrings in a ceramic bowl – and said earrings were removed when she returned to don her attire. The Major wishes to take the case to the police and thence to court, but his lady is most adamant that the dilemma be solved in some other way, so that her name will not be dragged into the public sphere as a client of Madame Louvois."

I nodded. "It seems reasonable. Women are very secretive about the things they do to maintain or improve their appearance. I assume that the Major's wife is quite hideous. I can't imagine any other sort of female would have him!"

Holmes smiled. "You portray me as a man who is blind to a woman's charms, but I will state with no exaggeration that Major Winston's spouse is one of the most beautiful ladies that I've ever met, and quite beyond the need of any artifice to make her lovely."

"Then why would she – ?"

Holmes held out his hand. A moment later, I heard Mrs. Hudson's stately tread, followed by her soft voice assuring a visitor that Mr. Holmes would be glad to see her.

The lady who entered was as near to feminine perfection as mere mortals could hope to behold. She was tall and regal, with glossy chestnut hair that threw off the light in fiery sparks. Her skin, as pale as milk, quickly turned pink, and her large blue eyes narrowed in fear when she spotted me. Holmes gave a dignified bow.

"Welcome, Madame. Please, don't be alarmed by the addition to the furnishings. I assure you that Doctor Watson is my trusted friend and associate, and a more discreet man you will not find in all of London. For whatever wrong has been done to you, there is no one more determined to see it righted. He is a true chevalier."

I blushed as deeply as the lady at this endorsement. At last she gave a quick nod and hurriedly took a seat on the sofa.

"I'm glad that my little ruse fooled Albert, but not you, Mr. Holmes. There is indeed more to the story than I could tell in his company."

"Forgive me," I blurted, for I was still befuddled by the idea that such a wonderful woman could have been wooed and wed by the fiend I remembered. "I knew your husband briefly in Afghanistan. How did you meet him?"

The lady sniffed. "It was the great tragedy of my life, Doctor. My father served under Major Winston. My dear mother had died when I was a child, and I had been raised by a maiden aunt. I fell in love with a newspaper reporter, Sanford Wells, and when my father returned from the war along with Albert, who had just retired, he disapproved of the match. Sanford tried to win Father over. I thought things were improving when the Major invited Sanford to the barracks, but while he was there a terrible accident occurred. A rifle was discharged during a drill, and Sanford was struck and killed instantly. I was so bereft I hardly knew day from night for months. The entire time, the Major was most solicitous, always inquiring as to my health. When I finally came to myself, I hardly recognized the girl in the mirror, I was so thin and pale. I felt certain that my youth and looks were destroyed – Father implied as much every day. When the Major paid attention to me, and Father said that no other man would ever want me, I felt I had no choice. Albert and I were wed eight months after dear Sanford's death."

"And your marriage has not been a happy one," Holmes said. "Forgive me, Madame, but it takes no great deductive skills to read what is clear upon your face."

"You are correct, sir. If I had only waited longer, and gotten to know Albert better, I would never have married him. He is cold and flint-hearted, tight with his money, and full of criticism. He treats me like a soldier, orders me around, and demands that I obey his commands in silence. It is a miserable existence that I lead. Perhaps it would be more endurable if I had a child, but recently he has grown so distant that even my hopes of motherhood seem dashed. Six months ago, he made a derogatory comment about my complexion, and I began to wonder if he no longer found me attractive. This fear led me to Madame Louvois. I had read her advertisements in the newspaper. Have you ever met her, Mr. Holmes?"

"I have not had that privilege."

"She is short, stout, and goes about her business swathed in oriental robes of the finest silk, yet she has the face and manner of a doting grandmother. When I first consulted her, I met her daughter, who now works in Paris. Miss Louvois was the most elegant and beautiful damsel I had ever seen – her skin glowed with radiance and her hair was wonderous. Everything about her appearance she attributed to her mother's special lotions, tonics, and creams, which are sold for fifteen guineas a bottle."

"Is that not rather expensive?" I asked, thinking of my wife's little collection of toiletries. I had never been presented with such a bill.

"It is, but to have hair and skin like hers! Of course, I knew that Albert wouldn't approve, but I had some savings of my own, and Madame Louvois was generous with credit. Then I became addicted to her 'Arabian Baths'. They helped me relax in a way I never thought possible. Often I would simply drift to sleep and dream that Sanford was alive again." The lady's face turned crimson as she realized what she had admitted. "Please forgive me. I know it is wrong to dream of another man, but I am so unhappy."

Mrs. Winston then took a deep breath and gave a sharp shake of her head, as if coming to some intense resolution.

"This is very difficult to speak of, but I have no one else to whom I can turn. Disaster looms, and perhaps not only for myself, but for a host of other women.

"It was last Saturday. I arrived at Madame Louvois's salon and took my usual treatment. Clarice, the blind attendant, was just handing me my gloves when Madame herself came into the little changing room. She dismissed Clarice quite brusquely, and I was much surprised at the change in her manner, for usually she is rather ingratiating, but now she was brisk and businesslike. She carried a large red book under her arm.

"'I do not wish to be rude,' she said, 'but we must have a settling of accounts. I find myself in some financial difficulty, and I must call in my credit. I believe you owe me some two-hundred pounds for services and merchandise, along with another one-hundred in interest.'

"You can imagine how much this startled me. I made it plain to her that I had no more than a pound on my person, nor could I raise such a sum in a short period. At this, she turned and, to my horror, locked the door of the room.

"'Perhaps we do not understand each other. You will pay me, in cash or jewels, or I will inform your husband of your activities.'

76

"My blood ran cold. Albert had never given me permission to spend so much on beauty treatments, but he had never forbidden me either.

"'You may tell him what you like," I said, 'You led me to believe that I might pay you when I could. I will give you your money, but you will have to wait.'

"A smile slithered across her face. 'Perhaps this will help convince you to settle your debt with alacrity.'

"And then, Mr. Holmes, she slammed the book onto the table before me and opened it wide. I was horrified at what I saw pasted on the page. It was a photograph, of myself, lying upon an opulent bed in a state of complete undress. On one of my visits, I must have been drugged, and then posed in such a degrading manner. To make it even worse, there was a man, also unclad, in the bed beside me. He had a devil's mask over his face. It was . . . unspeakable. I became hysterical, but Madame Louvois remained cruelly calm.

"'I don't think that your husband will be so forgiving once he sees this. Silly girl, do you think it matters if you try to rip it up? I can make a hundred copies and send them wherever I please. Everyone in London will know your disgrace. You will not be able to show your face in the light of day again. Children will cat-call you in the streets. You'll end up a painted strumpet in Whitechapel – or worse. There now, don't cry, it can all be avoided – I will take those pretty pearl earrings of yours for a down payment. Give them to me and we can avoid this unpleasantness for a time. No need to drag anyone's good name through the mud, is there? You certainly join a distinguished company. Look!'

"At that, she began flipping pages. Mr. Holmes, there must have been thirty or more pictures of compromised ladies. And though she was brisk, I recognized a nearly a dozen of them – titled women, professional beauties, even a countess and a Lady-in-Waiting to the Queen herself! My God, what a web this wicked creature has spun, and we are all helpless flies caught in it. I yanked my earrings off and thrust them into her claws. She opened the door and I bolted through it, but there was a man standing in the hallway. He caught me up like a child and carried me through the warrens of her back rooms, into an alleyway, and flung me onto the pavement. Madame Louvois stood at the back door as I climbed to my feet.

"'Do remember this entrance, for you will use it from now on. Bring me cash or jewelry, every Saturday, until your bill is paid in full. If you make any complaint against me, I shall let the world know what larks you have been having.'

"I was barely able to make it home. That very night, while I was still trembling and sick with terror, Albert insisted that we attend a dinner party. The earrings I had given Madame Louvois had been a wedding gift from him and he ordered me to wear them. Had he not barked at me, perhaps I could have thought of some way to explain their absence, but instead I blurted out that I had been robbed at Madame's. He was of course incensed, and it took all I could do to keep him from going to the police that instant. I had read that you could save poor people in trouble, and if there was ever a person in trouble, it is I."

Holmes had listened to the recitation with a dark expression. He now leaned forward, his voice low and firm.

"Madame, could you not tell your husband the truth of what happened? You have done nothing more than perhaps spend money unwisely."

"You do not know him, sir. He has beaten me before, and for far less offenses. No, I would rather throw myself into the Thames than tell him."

"Do you have family you might go to?"

"None. My father died shortly after my wedding, and my aunt passed away last year."

Holmes rose and turned his back to us. My heart went out to the poor woman. I tried to imagine my dear wife being so abused. I looked down and saw that my hands had curled into fists.

"You have almost a week until your next payment is due," Holmes said. "I hope, in that time, to have put Madame Louvois out of business." He turned and raised the lady from her seat. "Have courage as you return to your husband. I will not fail you. And do not forget your gloves."

A few minutes later, when the lady had vanished into the fog, Holmes lit his pipe and shook his head.

"A very bad case. Give me an honest thief or a forthright murderer to a blackmailer. They are the lowest of the sinners. I must put an end to this, and quickly."

"What will you do?"

"I shall burgle Madame Louvois's sanctum. Burning the book will not be enough – I must find where she keeps her camera and the negative plates and shatter them as well. Reason suggests that the filthy studio is on the premises, for it would be difficult to cart unconscious ladies any distance. Everything must be in waiting and used rapidly, though if Madame is as shrewd as I suspect, the plates may be kept under lock and key elsewhere. So little time to work! And I will require a confederate. Assuming a female persona is not beyond my range, but I fear that I would never be convincing enough to gain entrance to the salon's back rooms – nor are the females of my acquaintance the proper clientele for this establishment. Madame Louvios caters only to true ladies, women who can convince her that they have enough money to be properly blackmailed."

"I doubt very seriously that Mrs. Hudson – "

Holmes waved the idea aside. "No, it will require a younger woman, one who is active and intelligent, very observant, with a cool head and splendid resolve. Ah," he said, with a sly smile, "I know just the lady!"

I was not happy with the arrangement. Still, both of them were determined, and I wasn't such a tyrant as to forbid the mission, for I knew that an objection might well cost me the love of my wife and the good will of my friend. I volunteered as well, but Holmes flatly refused with a sharp "You have no talent for dissembling, Watson". Therefore, I spent an afternoon pacing back and forth across the rug in Baker Street. Holmes and Mary returned promptly at four, as promised, but it seemed to me that a year had intervened in just the two hours they were absent.

"Darling," I said, taking my wife into my arms. "Are you all right?"

"John, I was never in danger!" Mary laughed. "All I had to do was sample a few wares and ask to take one of those silly Arabian baths. If anyone was in danger, it was Mr. Holmes."

"I nearly died of boredom and I have certainly lost my dignity," Holmes said. They had portrayed a pair very common in the metropolis: The rich woman and her servant. My wife had been transformed into the mythical Lady Morstan and Holmes into her footman. He was dressed in an old-fashioned livery, complete with brass buttons, a swallowtail coat, and oiled hair, while Mary wore a walking dress of the finest blue silk, set off by bright ruby earrings and a heavy golden chain. I had no idea where Holmes had procured such finery. My wife said she felt like Cinderella at the ball, and I was reminded rather ruefully that neither my medical practice nor my writing career would ever afford the purchase of such an ensemble.

"Mr. Holmes was forbidden to go beyond the outer chamber," Mary said.

Holmes chucked. "Indeed, I was forced to sit in a waiting room along with two other footmen: A blushing young swain, and a rather henpecked husband. Allow me a few minutes to change and we shall discuss what the better detective of our pair has learned."

Once Holmes had disappeared into his bedroom, I clasped Mary's hand. "You did not actually take one of those Arabian baths, did you?"

"Of course not! Mr. Holmes warned me what had happened to his poor client. And even if I were not drugged, I feel sure those rooms must be pierced with Judas holes to give Peeping Toms their thrills."

"How did you find Madame Louvois?"

My wife shuddered. "She could have been any woman's dear old grandmother, all 'dearie' and 'sweet child' in her talk. I can understand why a desperate woman would trust her. Her salon was luxurious once I passed through the curtain, into a realm which she assured me no man was ever allowed to go. There was a magnificent copper basin in the bathing chamber, filled with hot water. A young woman with blind eyes was scattering aromatic leaves over it when I entered. Madame left me with her, instructing her to help me undress. I made the most of the few minutes I had inside – I think I can tell Mr. Holmes the exact dimensions of the room, as I stepped it off with my feet very precisely and peeked behind all the tapestries. It was much smaller than it initially appeared – one of the windows was a fake! He is right, there must be a series of hidden rooms, some kind of labyrinth within that store."

I smiled at Mary's excitement. She would indeed have been gifted for this line of work, had it been the proper occupation for a woman.

"How did you avoid getting into the bath?" I asked.

"I told the girl that I suddenly felt very sick and feared I might vomit. She was most concerned for me." A shadow passed over Mary's face. "She came to me and, before I could stop her, placed her hand on my stomach and asked if I was *enceinte*. I told her I feared that I might be, and she immediately forbid me to take the bath, saying it might be harmful to the little one, and that I should not drink any of Madame's 'restoratives' either. I gave her quite the tip and made a hasty exit!" Mary gestured to a collection of packages that Holmes had placed on his desk. "However, on the way out I made several purchases. Mr. Holmes had told me to pick one of each product. I tried one of the lotions on my hand, but I will thank Mr. Holmes to keep it. Look, dear, it has already given me a rash!"

At that moment, Holmes returned to the room, having washed away the subservient manner of the footman. He handed Mary a pencil and pad and asked her to draw out, to the best of her memory, the chambers behind the red curtain. Again, I was amazed at my wife's talents. I doubt that an architect could have so quickly sketched out a better floor plan.

"There is a central hallway with three 'bathing rooms' on the left and two on the right. I saw the open door of a closet here. It appeared to be filled with extra bottles and boxes of merchandise. I saw stairs leading up at – "

Holmes jerked to his feet. A man had entered the room, unheard and unseen by all of us until that very instant. He was clad in a dark cloak, with his hat pulled over his face and black spectacles shading his eyes. He seemed a ghost, a specter. Holmes straightened, and I saw his expression harden.

"You have a message?" my friend asked. In response, the man extended a gloved hand bearing a small envelope. Holmes seized it and ripped it open, reading the missive tucked within.

"So – eyes are indeed everywhere. A response is expected. Very well . . . I hear and reluctantly obey."

The man inclined his head. In an instant, he had turned and disappeared through the doorway. Mary slid next to me, shivering.

"Holmes? What did that man want of you?" I demanded. "And how the deuce did he get inside – it was like magic."

My friend did not lift his eyes from the paper. "Watson, we are done here. Mrs. Watson, thank you for your assistance."

"But we haven't finished – " Mary objected, gesturing to her half-completed map. Holmes shook his head.

"I fear that we have."

Something in Holmes's expression told me that further questioning would only annoy him. No more answers were forthcoming, as he was deeply and painfully disturbed by the contents of the note. Mary distracted him for a moment in her own charming way, thanking him again for the privilege of wearing such beautiful jewelry, even as she worked to remove the earrings and return them. Holmes tossed the message into the fire, and for just a moment I had a view of it before the flames consumed the expensive paper. I couldn't read the words, but I saw the crest. To this day, I dare not reveal the arms it bore, only to say that the paper had come from one of the highest authorities in the land, a personage whom no loyal citizen could refuse to obey.

As we settled into our carriage, I found my voice again, asking the question that had been on my mind since Holmes had interrupted us.

"Mary, my darling – What you said to the attendant in the bath. Is it – ?"

She touched a gentle hand to my face. "No, John. But we are young yet. Let us not lose hope."

The next day was filled with medical cases that absorbed all my time and energy, so that I could not return to Baker Street. However, Holmes dispatched two items to my house. One was a lovely bouquet of flowers and a further note of thanks to my wife for being a "*brave and observant assistant*". The second was a terse missive to me:

> *Must gamble on past to save future. Come Friday evening at six.*

Knowing Holmes's methods, I followed his instructions to the letter, arriving at Baker Street on Friday evening exactly as the hour struck. I found our old rooms even more hopelessly disheveled than they had been during my residence. Holmes had clearly been spending time with his chemical investigations, based on the number of test tubes and pipettes on display. A few of these experiments must not have been to his liking, as hinted by the mounds of broken glass and stains on the rug. The room was also strewn with newspapers. I picked one up, noting that that it was well out of date. Holmes had been in his shirt sleeves when I walked inside, but he made some efforts to tidy himself and smooth his hair as I worked to clear debris.

"Thank you, Watson. I doubt that Mrs. Hudson would be so obliging with this mess. As you can see, I've been here since you and Mrs. Watson departed. I have eaten very little, but consumed a distressful quantity of tobacco and added to my collection of scars." He held out a hand, and I noted what looked like a spattering of small burns on his fingers. "I have also been wandering in the past, via my archives of *The Times* and other prominent periodicals." He moved to the sofa, opening a place for me to sit. I noted that he shoved aside not only a large collection of newspapers, but a dozen or more notes and telegrams. "I am fortunate to have so many confederates, both in the official and unofficial forces. Mark my word, Watson, someday a historian may prove to be the greatest detective of them all."

Holmes spoke so rapidly that it was clear he was under the sway of some nervous excitement. I forced him to pause.

"You must tell me who that mysterious stranger was. Holmes – I saw the crest. If – "

"It would be better not to speak that name aloud, old friend. I can tell you only this much in safety: Madame Louvois has compromised far more than just the wife of a retired Major. She holds in her filthy hands the lives and reputations of women who are attached to our nation's most powerful men. She could cause a scandal that would do far more than topple a ministry. If she were to ever reveal all that she knows, there would be a rush of titled suicides. They dare not raise a hand against her."

"Holmes, how do you know these things?"

"I can say only that my brother Mycroft doesn't approve of their kow-towing to an obvious criminal, but there is nothing, at the moment, that he can do to change their timidity. Therefore, I must find another way to rescue Mrs. Winston and, perhaps, neutralize the threat of Madame Louvois."

"What did you mean by gambling on the past?"

"Just that I must take a calculated risk. I feel certain that my conclusions are the correct ones, but as I cannot turn back time to walk the scene and apply my methods firsthand, I must – Ah, I hear our guest. On your best behavior, Watson!"

Our door opened and, much to my displeasure, Major Albert Winston stomped inside. He had dramatically aged since I had last beheld him in the passes of Afghanistan, but there remained in his cold eyes, resolute chin, and grizzled side-whiskers much of the heartless officer and breaker of men that I recalled. Holmes attempted a quick introduction, but the Major cut him off, thudding his walking stick against the carpet.

"Yes, I remember you, Watson – second-rate surgeon. Got yourself shot and nearly captured. No great loss to Her Majesty. You call yourself a writer these days, but I've seen nothing in your friend Mr. Holmes to account for the reputation you've given him – he's had nearly a week to come up with those earrings and so far, I haven't seen them! I hope you have something for me today, or I shall be forced to call in the proper authorities."

"You shall do nothing of the kind," Holmes said. "Sit down, Major. I insist. In my home you shall take orders from me."

The Major's brushy eyebrow shot up. Clearly, he was unaccustomed to such a tone, but he settled into the chair as instructed. Holmes stood before the fireplace. Without preamble – and much to my astonishment – Holmes told the Major of his wife's ordeal at the hands of Madame Louvois, omitting only the information that others were compromised and that he had been forbidden to act against the culprit. The Major's expression shifted rapidly from astonishment to rage.

"I fear the earrings will be impossible to recover," Holmes said. "I would advise you to settle your wife's bill, however inconvenient. Wait in patience, for I believe I have a way – though it may take some time – to bring this evil woman to justice without causing further distress and embarrassment to your spouse. Mrs. Winston has been through enough pain already."

"Pain!" the Major roared. "I will show her pain! How dare she spend my money in such a fashion and cavort with other men? She may deceive you, Mr. Holmes, but she cannot fool me! I will show her what it means to cuckold an officer. When I'm done with her, it will take more than some charlatan's face cream to make her lovely again."

He rose from his chair, waving his stick around like a war club. His cragged face turned crimson and angry blood vessels popped in his forehead. Holmes, to my astonishment, seized the cane and pressed its golden nob below the Major's chin, effectively silencing him. When Holmes spoke, his voice was icy with menace.

"You will do no such thing, Major Winston."

The man's eyes blazed with beastly fury. "And how do you propose to stop me?"

"By promising, sir, that if you lay one finger upon your wife, I will let the world know exactly who murdered young Sanford Wells."

A bullet through the heart could not have dropped the Major faster. He collapsed onto the settee, scattering newspapers. Holmes seized one from the floor, pointing to an article circled in red.

"How strange that a bullet which, supposedly fired from a parade ground, tore a wound downward into the body? Or that the caliber of the bullet was not the same caliber as the rifles being used in the drill? And who in the regiment had the greatest reputation as a marksman and tiger hunter – a man known for his patience for sitting in trees and waiting for his victim to appear? It was easy enough to portray Wells as a careless civilian who walked into a dangerous area. But who told him where to stand? None other than the man who invited him to his death, so that he might claim Wells's fiancée."

Never have I seen guilt more clearly written on a human face. The Major had turned ashen as Holmes spoke. He started to struggle for breath as his gnarled hand curled in the bosom of his coat.

"Wells was a young fool," the Major rasped. "He would have ruined her. She would have been penniless. I'd known Kathryn since she was a babe . . . Her father . . . *promised* her to me."

"Do you think that will matter when I bring forth the evidence and the witnesses to your crime?" Holmes asked. The man recoiled, as if being struck with a hammer.

"You . . . you cannot prove . . . ."

"Do you wish to *test* me, Major?"

The man struggled to his feet, swaying like a drunkard. My instinct was to go to his assistance, but a sharp look from Holmes warned me away. The Major shook his head. His words emerged weak and slurred from his blue, quivering lips.

"I will . . . forgive her. This . . . what you know . . . is all . . . forgotten, I trust?"

"That depends on your behavior, Major."

He nodded and wobbled his way toward the door. As it closed, I rushed to Holmes. "He is a sick man. You have given him a tremendous shock."

"Was it any more than he deserved? I opened a correspondence with the officers who investigated the accident. They, it seems, had always been uncomfortable with the affair's conclusion. It was clear to them that Wells was not killed by an inept rifleman on the drill field, but by a sniper hidden on a barracks rooftop. Unfortunately, Wells was unpopular with the regimental commanders for having written pieces critical of their performance in the East. The entire thing was hushed up by powerful people."

"But how did you know it was Major Winston who fired the shot?"

"I did *not* know until he it confessed it, though it stood to reason that he had pulled the trigger. Based on what he gained from the young man's death and his reputation as a marksman, as well as his savage nature, I felt certain he would not have trusted such a delicate business to someone else."

I moved to the window. Holmes's visitor was standing at the kerb, a trembling arm raised in hopes of summoning a cab. Then he let out a cry and toppled to the pavement, his hat rolling away into the street.

Holmes's fingers seized my wrist in an icy grip.

"Let me go!" I snapped, "I must aid him!"

"You? A 'second rate' surgeon?"

"Holmes!"

He released me. My medical oath propelled me down the stairs and out into the street, but my effort was wasted. Even as I pushed through the crowd of idlers and gawkers, ordering them to stand back, I could see from the Major's fixed gaze that my assistance would be in vain. The man had fallen dead not ten paces from our doorstep.

I looked up just in time to see Holmes drop the curtain and step away from the window.

"Have you seen the latest article in 'The War of the Chemists'?" Holmes asked.

A few weeks had passed since the death of Major Winston. By mutual agreement, we had not discussed the case. I was appalled by Holmes's coolness and calculation, by how he showed no remorse for bringing death to the officer. Yet when I considered what Mrs. Winston faced, the brutality her husband would no doubt have inflicted upon her without Holmes's intervention, I felt nothing but relief. How else could justice so long delayed have been otherwise served? How else could the lady have been freed from the monster she had married, or the death of her innocent lover avenged?

"This concerns the concoctions from Madame Louvois's salon?"

Holmes nodded. For several weeks there had been a debate raging in all of the London papers. Some mysterious agent had delivered vials of Madame Louvois's tonics and notions to half-a-dozen of London's most notable chemists, with a request that the samples be analyzed, and the results made public. As soon as one chemist wrote an article condemning the "*noxious confection*" of chemicals, another countered with a more precise measurement of the amounts of dangerous substances within them. Pride pricked, yet a third and a fourth professional weighed in, with the result being that readers were now aware of what these items contained. While some of Madame's potions were nothing more than mixtures of rosewater and oatmeal, others were laced with hydrochloric acid and lead, in amounts that could endanger a fragile woman's health.

"I hear that business has dropped precipitously at the salon," Holmes said. "There was some squawking from the lady, with threats to sue, but nothing has come of it. Be certain that I have retained enough bottles of her vile mixes that if she challenges any one of these learned men, I could come to their aid with fresh supplies." He smiled. "I also hear that some of the local urchins have taken to cat-calling the dame as she makes her way home every night in her carriage. The façade of her Bond Street business was also recently covered in rotten eggs."

"Holmes!"

"Watson, I promise I had nothing to do with the vandalism. But it does not surprise me that, once it was revealed that Madame's 'magic waters' flowed from nothing more enchanted than a tap, she of course became the prey of pranksters. Turn that page and you will see quite the cartoon of her. In fairness, she has only three chins, not twenty. There is even a show about her playing in the music halls: '*Madame LeFraud and the Fountain of Foolishness*' is, I believe, the title."

"Your friends in high places have said nothing?"

"Not yet. You note that I did not disobey their command, at least in the strictest letter of the thing. Yes, Mrs. Hudson?" he said as the door creaked open. "Is it teatime already?"

"No, Mr. Holmes. There was a gentleman downstairs. I told him to come up, that you were in, but then he vanished! I barely turned my head for a second and he was gone, with just these things left behind. Gave me quite a start!"

Holmes shot me a dark look as he retrieved the items that Mrs. Hudson held and offered apologies for her discomfort. He quickly passed me a small jewelry box, and I opened it to find a pair of pearl earrings resting upon blue velvet. Holmes was studying the other items: A note, and a ticket.

"Could your patients spare you for a few days?" Holmes asked.

"Impossible," I said, though I regretted disappointing him. "Are these – ?"

"Mrs. Winston's earrings. Perhaps you could call on her in my stead? No doubt having them returned will help her through any pecuniary

86

difficulties she finds herself in, as it is unlikely that they bear any great sentimental value for her."

"I will. For where is that ticket?"

Holmes had a strange look upon his face. "Paris."

In days to come, when the world is perhaps a better place, there will be no memories of the Paris Morgue. It is a hideous institution, behind Notre Dame Cathedral on the Quai de l'Archeveche, the place where all of Paris's anonymous dead are taken, in hopes that someone can identify them. Unclaimed bodies are displayed in a large window, lying naked upon black marble slabs with only their most private parts covered. The room is kept cold, and the corpses are regularly sprayed with icy water to preserve their appearance for as long as possible. Above each deceased person is a hook, and on it the attire that the unfortunate had been found in is displayed. It is the saddest window in the world, and yet it is also a macabre tourist attraction. One might wait for an hour or more before the gawkers and idlers part enough to permit a closer inspection of the unknown corpses.

Holmes told me how he had stood before that window. Beside him was the man in black.

"She was found in the Seine two days ago," the man said, his voice barely above a whisper. "She had come to Paris to escape the torment in the London streets and take shelter with her daughter, who operates a similar salon on the Rue de la Paix."

"She was a suicide?" Holmes asked.

"No, though that is what the Paris police will claim. I was following her that night, I saw a man confront her. There was the briefest of struggles and she went over the railing."

"You did not pursue him?"

"I was charged only with shadowing her, after I learned where she kept her books and photographic plates, as well as the jewelry she had taken from the ladies she blackmailed."

The man turned and pushed his way through the crowd. Holmes followed him. At last, they reached a bridge, and the man showed Holmes where Madame Louvois had fallen to her fate.

"I could not have saved her even if I had wanted to," the man said to Holmes. "It happened so quickly. But I overheard her killer's words. I have told no one else – not even my superiors. I saved them for you, because I know that you will understand what to make of them."

"They were?"

"*Greedy woman – You have failed the Professor for the last time.*'"

A Case of
Unfinished Business
by Steven Philip Jones

It was that dreadful May of 1891.

My wife Mary did her best for me when I returned alone from Switzerland and took a short leave from my practice. As it was, if not for her well-intended insistence and my own sense of obligation, I would have rejected Mycroft Holmes's request to organize his brother's papers and put 221b Baker Street back in order after the failed fire set by Professor Moriarty's gang. I knew such work would occupy me physically, but not mentally, and therefore delay the process of my moving past the death of Sherlock Holmes.

Even without the attempted arson, Holmes had left our old rooms in more disarray than was his habit. This was understandable considering the circumstances prompting our escape to the Continent, but it did make my chore more difficult than I had supposed. However, after a couple of days' persistence, I had the ship nearly righted again. The one spot I elected to avoid was Holmes's desk. With the exception of retrieving his personal casebook – which Mycroft had informed me that Holmes wanted me to keep per the disposition of his estate – I had no intentions of going through its drawers, believing it was Mycroft's place to attend to his brother's personal most items.

Late in the morning of the third day, Mrs. Hudson stepped into the sitting room to inform me that a visitor was waiting in the foyer.

"Who is it?" I asked.

"A gentleman. He went to your home, only to have Mrs. Watson send him here. He claims that he went to university with you." Mrs. Hudson stepped closer to present me with the visitor's card. "His name is Lot Morrill." Lowering her voice, she confided, "He's an American."

That was true. Morrill was born and raised in the Delaware Valley before his family moved to London a few years prior to him entering college. Where I continued my training to become an army surgeon at the Royal Victoria Hospital after receiving my degree from the University of London, Morrill returned to America, where for a time he worked with Joseph O'Dwyer. The intervening years appeared to have softened Morrill somewhat, adding a paternal patina to his weather-beaten chestnut face, but Morrill was still six feet of brawn with a forty-four inch chest, testaments to a rugged boyhood working on a farm.

I was overjoyed to see Morrill and just as delighted to accept his invitation for an early lunch at Simpson's, which had been a favorite of ours and several of our cronies. As we waited for the waiter to bring the carving meat, Morrill apologized for calling without forewarning me, but I assured him that he couldn't have arrived at a better time. "I've about reached the end of a difficult task and a meal will do wonders for me. Now what's it been? Twelve years?

"About that, although Bart's seems a lifetime ago."

"And I've kept track of you in the Colonies."

Morrill feigned offense. "'The Colonies?' You snob!"

"I'm not! Your work on intubation with O'Dwyer at St. John's Hospital for Sick Children? Revolutionary!"

"Thank you, but I only assisted Joseph. No glory in that. Plenty of satisfaction, though. Speaking of which, I've kept track of you, too." Morrill appeared uncertain how to proceed and at last settled on telling me, "My condolences on Mr. Holmes."

"Thank you." Uncertain how I should proceed, I at last settled on telling Morrill, "He was the best man . . . the wisest man I've ever known."

Sadness creased Morrill's brow, as if he were recalling some dark memory, or my abrupt mourning had somehow upset him. Stumbling a bit for words, he replied, "A very appropriate quote. I'm sure Plato could not have held Socrates in any higher esteem than you did Sherlock Holmes."

"I'm sorry if I dampened the mood."

"Not at all. I'm just getting peckish." For a few moments Morrill looked everywhere else but towards me. "Where's that waiter?"

The cloud over our heads dissipated as we ate, and by the time we finished and walked out onto the Strand once more, Morrill seemed like his old self.

I spied a hansom waiting nearby and waived it over. "What would you say for a tour of our old haunts?"

As the cab drew up beside us, a gangly, bushy-bearded Cockney driver with gray eyes asked, "Where to, gents?"

Morrill beamed. "Well, if you're really up for it, John, I wouldn't mind – "

A familiar voice interrupted from behind. "Doctor Watson!"

Morrill turned. "Who is that? A colleague of yours?"

"In a manner of speaking."

Morrill's previous glumness percolated as he contemplated the small, lean, bulldog-of-a-man with ferret-like face approaching. "Oh, a Scotland Yarder. Rough-looking sort."

"Lestrade is that."

The inspector wasted little time. "Sorry to bother you, Doctor, and if it weren't important – "

"You wouldn't intrude, I'm sure. Inspector Lestrade, allow me to introduce my friend. This is Dr. Lot Morrill."

Both men shook hands and Lestrade asked if I could come with him. "Official business." I began to protest, but he interjected that he had a four-wheeler waiting.

Morrill patted my shoulder. "Go on, John. They must need you."

"I'm sorry. Let me pay for the cab so you can use it."

"I appreciate that, but I'd rather walk. I'm just up the street at Charing Cross Hotel anyway, and the sun feels good."

"Certainly. Dinner tonight?"

"Sure." To Lestrade, "A pleasure, Inspector."

"Same to you, sir. This way, Doctor."

I tipped the cabbie for his time and followed Lestrade. Turning my head, I watched Morrill trudge towards his hotel while the hansom maintained a similar pace as it rambled down the Strand. Then Lestrade was brusquely ushering me into a clarence cab where sat a tall, wiry, unpresupposing fellow dressed in a seersucker suit, waiting for us. He appeared to be in his early thirties, with hair and mustache blonde enough to pass for white. Lestrade said, "Doctor Watson, allow me to introduce my friend. This is Walter Simonson."

Speaking with a slight Swedish accent, Simonson said, "I can't tell you how much I've looked forward to talking with you in person. I only wish that Mr. Holmes could be here, too."

Try as I might I could not recall hearing the stranger's name before. "I'm sorry, but have we corresponded?"

"No, but I did correspond four times with Mr. Holmes using the name Fred Porlock."

It took a second, but then I remembered. "The Birlstone murder! You tried to warn Holmes about it!"

"I did before I tried to warn him off it. Your persistence nearly got me drawn-and-quartered, for all the good that would have done poor Birdy Edwards. From what I hear, he was a bully trap after my own heart."

"Holmes intimated you were working closely with Professor Moriarty."

Lestrade winked at Simonson, who grinned as if sharing some private joke.

"What is it?" I asked.

"Actually I infiltrated Moriarty's organization in '86 for the British government under the aegis of Scotland Yard's Special Branch. The inspector serves as my liaison. There were times, however, when I felt Justice might be better served informing Mr. Holmes rather than my superior about information I learned, but only if he had no idea what I was truly about. But now, Doctor, we need your help."

"My help? Why, certainly."

"Thank you. Before I explain, though, allow me to beg your patience for a few minutes."

We drove in silence until the cab stopped in front of a four-storey house on Wigmore Street, where Simonson rented a suite on the third floor. Lestrade warned me this was the scene of a crime with a body in the sitting room, but I saw no constables as we entered.

The dead man sat in a chair that Simonson confirmed had been turned around to face the suite's entrance. He was a swarthy man in his late fifties with the physique of a person at ease with harsh outdoor living, and even the repose of death couldn't belie a cast to the face that this had been someone best not trifled with. Beside the chair stood a table with a half-filled carafe of brandy and two glasses, one of which had been recently used. Nothing else in the suite appeared disturbed, although I did notice flecks of mud on the carpet around the chair.

"We have no idea who he is," Simonson explained as I examined the body. "We found a garrote, a neddy, concealed knives, and a Colt revolver on him. Things being as they are, we assumed that he was an assassin working for the Professor."

"That certainly sounds sensible, but there is nothing so unnatural as the commonplace. Things are not always what we assume." At first glance the body had every appearance of someone who died somewhat peacefully while asleep. There were no signs of struggle or violence, and every indication suggested the man had only been in the suite a few hours. "It appears as if he was partaking some of your brandy, Mr. Simonson."

"Oh, Walter, please." Simonson bent close to the carafe. "Judging by what's left, my guess is he had two full glasses."

Lestrade snorted in disgust. "That's a nerve. Enjoying a man's spirits while waiting to kill him."

Simonson shrugged. "Better than no one enjoying it at all."

I inspected the used glass. "Perhaps it made him drowsy." Lifted it to my nose. "Smells all right, I suppose." I sniffed again before asking Lestrade why there were no constables outside.

"Unadvisable under the circumstances, but these premises are being watched."

Simonson elaborated, "Expediently apprehending the Moriarty gang takes precedence over proper police protocol."

I said, "That sounds rather drastic, ignoring the fair-play of British law."

"It is, and with cause. The collapse of the Professor's former empire is sending aftershocks through three continents. These past few days have been like going to war. In fact, we are sworn to secrecy regarding this matter."

I set the glass back upon the table. "Is that why I was brought here? So you wouldn't have to call a coroner?"

"Yes, in part. You see, not all of the Professor's associates were willing ones. Moriarty used blackmail and extortion, such as purchasing incriminating debts to manipulate people in high positions of corporate and political power. Now the remains of the Moriarty gang intend to expose them and inflict widespread harm."

Hearing such a scheme sent a definite shudder through me. "The more I learn about the Professor, the more I understand why Holmes would be willing to sacrifice himself to destroy such a man."

"It was Mr. Holmes who informed the government about this plot just before you two left for the Continent, and considerable resources are being dedicated to stymie it, but now my superior needs to see a file Mr. Holmes kept with his casebooks and indexes."

"Oh dear."

"What's wrong, Doctor?" asked Lestrade.

"Holmes kept all that in a large tin box he stored in his bedroom, but it's not there now and I have no clue where he put it.

Simonson waved a hand. "That's all right. Mr. Mycroft has the clue."

"Pardon?"

"Mr. Holmes gave his brother a clue that was to be revealed to you if circumstances dictated."

"What if I don't understand it?"

"There's only one way to find out. The message from Mr. Sherlock Holmes is: '*Not papers. And then my fee.*'"

To this day I am uncertain which I felt first: Relief or annoyance. "Oh, for Heaven's sake."

Lestrade frowned. "That makes no sense at all."

"Actually it makes perfect sense. I've written an unpublished account of one of Holmes's investigations that I titled 'A Case of Identity.' Holmes had read it, and in it I reference an earlier investigation that I call 'A Scandal in Bohemia'. In that one, Holmes requested a photograph of a Miss Adler from the King of Bohemia as a memento."

"Oh, I see now! Holmes wrote where he hid this tin box on the back of that photograph!"

"No. Walter, I must return to Baker Street."

92

Simonson was ready. "Let's go. The four-wheeler is still waiting."

"Just a moment. Once we're there, I must go inside alone. I have my reasons."

"Agreed. Inspector?"

Lestrade bobbed his head.

I thanked them and then said, "Before we do go, Walter, I need you to tell me everything you know about this body."

"I did! I give you my word."

"So you have no idea who put hemlock in your carafe?"

Lestrade took hold of the flask. "What's that?" He inhaled. "Everything smells all right."

"I suppose. Walter, prior to this morning, when were you here last?"

"Yesterday afternoon, and the brandy was fine then or I wouldn't be talking to you now. The body was here when I returned and I immediately contacted Lestrade."

The inspector tapped the carafe. "How can you be sure there's hemlock in here without an analysis?"

"I can't. It could be something similar – say curare. Except that has a bitter taste this man would have noticed if he drank even one glass. On the other hand hemlock contains coniine. Just a tenth of a gram can be fatal, and its effects would have been abetted by brandy's natural inebriant action and ability to depress the motor function of the cranio-spinal axis."

"Fair enough, then. It sounds like a quick and painless death."

"Relatively, yet unpleasant. He probably felt cold, but wouldn't know why, followed by numbness, starting with his extremities. Eventually he wouldn't have been able to move and died alone trapped in that chair. Before paralysis set in, however, it looks like he walked around a bit attempting to warm up. That would explain these dried bits of mud about the floor."

"Actually," Simonson said, "that might have been me when I came back."

"Really? I thought I saw mud on his boots." I took another look and pointed towards the dead man's feet. "Yes. Look here. This mud is the same yellowish brown as what's scattered on the floor. If we can identify where it came from, it might help us identify him."

"Wait a moment please." Simonson scuttled to his bedroom and returned within moments carrying a pair of grubby boots and tweed pants. "I haven't cleaned these yet and you can see they're splattered with the same color mud."

"Where's it from?"

"A Derbyshire mine called Blue John Gap. It's been abandoned for years. Locals claim it's the lair of a beast or creature."

"I've read about that in the *Daily Telegraph*! Fascinating story! Those folktales got stirred up again by a . . . umm . . . Dr. Hardcastle. I recall he passed away from phthisis, which he insisted was aggravated after hunting what he claimed was some primordial monster back into the mine."

"You have a good memory. Hardcastle actually stumbled across an outpost for Moriarty's organization that was playing up the legend in order to scare people away from the mine, going so far as making it appear the thing was nicking sheep whenever there was a full moon."

Lestrade said, "Sounds like an excuse for free mutton to me."

"Waste not, want not. Moriarty's men arranged things to look like Hardcastle treed the monster in the mine, only to have it double-back on him, and then told him to get busy dying or they'd save him the effort."

Another shudder ran through me. "That's outrageous!"

"That was Moriarty's idea of poetic justice, but what comes around goes around. When news about the Professor's death and the search for his associates reached Blue John Gap, Moriarty's men realized they had better leave the country if they were going to save their skins. Fleeing by road or countryside would be dicey, so they opted to commandeer a train that makes runs between Derbyshire and London. They would ride it into London, where they could scatter into the East End and escape England by ship."

"A sound plan."

"Sound enough that when word of it managed to reach London late last night, my superior had no choice but to order me to lead a posse there. We arrived just as Moriarty's men were moving in to seize the train along a deep trench near the mine, and after a brief gun battle they fled back to Blue John Gap to make a last stand. We didn't disappoint them." Simonson held his boots and pants a little higher. "That's where I picked up this mud."

"So this stranger had to have been there, too, except he had more sense than to return to the mine. He must have recognized you and found a way to London to confront you."

"Only to poison himself," said Lestrade. "News about your raid must have gotten back to London, Walter, and another of Moriarty's gang poured hemlock or whatever in this carafe. How could they know about this fellow's intentions? I'd say you had two near-misses this day"

Simonson nodded, nonplussed. "I suppose you're right."

Lestrade's hypothesis generally satisfied me as well, so we left for Baker Street. I was grateful to Simonson and Lestrade for understanding that rummaging through Holmes's things in front of anyone struck me as too severe a violation of his privacy. As for Holmes's clue, in "A Case of

Identity", I erroneously referenced "A Scandal in Bohemia" as "the case of the Irene Adler papers". Holmes had actually been commissioned to retrieve an indelicate photograph taken of the King of Bohemia with Miss Adler. After he had read the manuscript, Holmes had never seemed to tire of chiding me about this slip, although it now occurred to me that there might have been a method behind this needling. The photograph of Miss Adler, given to Holmes, was a reward that my friend had requested on the spur-of-the-moment, whereas the fee the King paid came in the form of a gold snuff-box with a large amethyst on its lid. I was convinced that Holmes had somehow left instructions on how to find the tin box with the file Simonson's superior needed in that snuff-box, but his clue unfortunately didn't seem to include any suggestions as to where he had hidden the gold box.

Since I had thoroughly arranged Holmes's papers and conscientiously put back his belongings, I already knew that the snuff-box wasn't anywhere obvious, like tucked in the tobacco he kept in his Persian slipper or stashed in the coal scuttle with his pipes and cigars. Doing my best to think like my friend, I suspected he would have selected somewhere sensible yet inconspicuous, so I tried exploring places like the pockets of his dressing-gowns – where a snuff box would hardly be out of place – and on the deal table – where it might be lost in plain sight amongst the chemistry equipment, only to come up empty.

The longer I searched, the more frustrating it became.

People's lives depended on me and that weight pressing upon me.

For a fleeting moment, I pondered if Holmes had even left the snuff-box here. He could have left it in Mycroft's care without explaining why. Then realization inspired by simple common sense struck.

Holmes would have known the last place I would search was his desk, where, to any unobservant eye, the snuff box would be just one more *outré* item among many, including the photograph of Irene Adler.

When I found nothing in the first drawer, I opened a second.

"Eureka!"

There it was, along with the photograph of Irene Adler. Holmes had left me a clue.

I opened the snuff box's lid and poked through the powdered tobacco. Feeling nothing, I poured out the tobacco and pried up the bottom.

There was a key! Judging by its appearance, most likely to a bank deposit box.

I bolted down the steps and began to shout for Mrs. Hudson to lock up for me, only to draw up short when I noticed something in the foyer.

"What's wrong, Doctor Watson?" Mrs. Hudson asked. "Are you all right?"

I wasn't, although I tried my best to conceal the fact. "May I ask when you last swept this floor?"

"Why, early this morning."

"And has there been anyone else in here since my American friend?"

"No, sir. Well, that one policeman, Mr. Lestrade, but he's here so often." Mrs. Hudson glanced down and scowled. "Oh, look at that mud on the mat. I'll shake it clean."

"You needn't bother." The events of the past few days came rushing down upon me and nothing seemed to matter any longer.

"Doctor? Are you feeling all right? You seem pale."

"I feel pale. I'm sorry that I startled you, Mrs. Hudson. Would you please lock Mr. Holmes's rooms? I have an appointment."

I gave the key to Simonson and Lestrade, confident their resources would be able to divine the bank box it opened. They had expected me to accompany them, but I begged off under the pretense of getting back to putting Holmes's things in order. Once they were out of sight, I flagged a passing hansom and requested to go to Charing Cross Hotel. Lost in my doldrums, I initially failed to recognize that the driver was the same bearded cabbie from earlier.

Getting Morrill's room number from the front desk, I knocked on my friend's door and called his name.

"Come in, John. It's unlocked."

A wiser man might have been more cautious, but I entered and shut the door behind me with little thought. Daylight was fading outside. The room was growing dark in the gloaming, but I could plainly see Morrill in a high-back upholstered chair, turned towards the door, holding a glass in one hand. His jacket was draped over the back of the chair, and his tie and collar were loose.

"Afternoon," he said. "Or should I say 'Good evening'? Time does fly. I'd offer you a drink, but I'm afraid I just finished the last of it."

I rattled from revulsion and horror. I snatched the glass, but it was empty. "Hemlock?"

"Perceptive. Same old John. You know you gave me quite a turn when you paraphrased Plato this morning. Coincidences like that always pester me. I don't believe in them. I'd rather think everything happens for a reason."

"Well, this isn't going to happen! Not while I can stop it!"

"You know you can't. I'll be dead before you can scrounge anything to use for artificial ventilation, and we both know that's the only way to sustain life until the affects of coniine poisoning wear off. Whatever you could find around here would probably be so inadequate you'd end up

96

killing me anyway, and you don't need that on your conscience. So, please, grant me a final request. Sit down and talk with me one last time."

I was not prepared to give up so easily. "Lot!"

Neither was Morrill. "John."

Faced once more with nothing I could do, I brought a chair beside him and sat, but all I could think to ask was, "Why?"

"You'll find a letter on the bedside table that explains all this. I prepared it just in case." He pointed to an envelope with my name on it. "You can give it to your colleague. Now, did I ever tell you about my family?"

"Only that your father died and your mother remarried."

"That's more than I tell most folks. In a nutshell, my father was a farmer in the Delaware Valley. A good man. Honest. Strong. A Confederate captain named Harsh Washburne killed him near the end of the War. Harsh had taken a fancy to my mother, and she returned the feelings. Only my mother and I knew about the murder, and I never could get myself to hate her enough to take Harsh away from her. Don't ask me why. I can't claim to understand it myself."

"I'm so sorry, Lot. I had no idea."

"It's not really something you confide to someone else, except maybe a priest." Morrill stretched his fingers and legs. "I'm starting to get numb. Best hurry."

My frustration rekindled. "Lot, please! I can – "

"Do nothing, John! You'll do nothing!" Taking a breath to calm himself, Morrill went on. "I presume that Inspector Lestrade of Scotland Yard took you to Simonson's flat?"

My expression served as my answer.

"I'd say it was a coincidence, but – "

"You don't believe in them."

Morrill's expression suggested he might have been having second thoughts about that. "You know, there wouldn't have been an opportunity for any coincidences if I left England this morning. Who would have been the wiser? I could have got away after Simpson's, too, I suppose, but in my heart I knew I could never really escape this, so I paid my call on you." An expression far happier than I would have imagined possible for a dying man spread across Morrill's face. "It's really good to see you again."

"The dead stranger? Is that Washburne?"

"Oh, yes. Like I told you during lunch, my mother died suddenly two weeks ago. Myocardial infarction. Harsh never considered the consequences of that. I was finally free to avenge my father. His murder has been within a hand's reach of my thoughts for most of my life. I couldn't live with myself if I did nothing, but now that I've done it, I still can't live with myself. I'm a doctor. 'Do no harm.'"

I was uncertain how to proceed. "I . . . I don't know what to say."

"You don't have to say anything. That's the wonder of friendship at times like these." Morrill trembled, unable to stop. "I'd ask for a blanket, but it'd do no good."

"Lot, please forgive me, but with recent happenings, I have to ask this."

"'Was I ever part of Moriarty's gang?' Of course you need to ask. For your own peace of mind. But no. That was Harsh. He worked for Moriarty for years. That's why we moved to England."

"As a paid killer?"

Morrill nodded. Talking was obviously becoming more difficult. "And a good one. Give the man his due. Killing came second nature to him. But the War taught him how to lead men. Plan. Execute raids. I suppose he'd have turned that training to crime on his own. Like Frank and Jesse James." A violent shiver forced a momentary pause. "Moriarty paid well. Mother thought I should be grateful to them both. Father could never have paid for my medical education."

"You would have found a way."

"Thank you. That means a lot. Coming from you." Another violent shiver. "Harsh and my mother moved to Matlock. Last winter. So he could run things at Blue John Gap. Then she died. I couldn't get here in time for her funeral. Harsh thought it natural I'd want to visit her grave. That was only one reason I came."

"By the time you arrived, Washburne must have been trying to find a way to get out of the country with his men."

"Yes. He'd decided to steal the train. I thought, 'If he's killed doing that, that's Providence. *'Murmur not at the ways of Providence.'* I went along with him to the Gap this morning. We made plans to meet in Montenegro. I'd avenge my father there, but I told Harsh I'd get him back to America. Instead Harsh came back to the mine. He'd recognized Simonson. Wanted blood. So I helped him get to London. Helped him find Simonson's place. He never thought twice about my helping him. And then . . . when his guard was finally down . . . I poisoned him . . . and watched him die." Morrill's eyes brightened as tears of bewilderment overwhelmed him. "I wish I could say I'm sorry. Why can't I say I'm sorry?"

I placed a hand upon his shoulder. "Because you're not a liar, and, where it really counts, you're still a good man."

Morrill said nothing. He did not move.

"Lot?"

There was no reaction, not even breathing.

"Lot!"

A tear rolled down his cheek of its own volition.

"Oh, Lot. Now you're gone, too."

For the second time in as many weeks a crushing wave of loneliness threatened to drown me.

Night fell by the time I made my way to the lobby to notify the hotel management that one of their guests had committed suicide. Identifying myself as the victim's friend as well as a doctor, I consented to watch the body until the police arrived, as well as keep the matter confidential so as not to upset the other guests.

I honestly have no idea how long it was before Lestrade arrived with a constable to relieve me. He extended condolences as I presented him with Morrill's written confession. "His parents are dead and he has no brothers or sisters. I believe that he was alone in the world, so, unless someone else steps forward, I'll attend to his funeral arrangements."

"Thank you, Doctor Watson. And thank you for earlier today."

"I only hope I was of some assistance."

"You were invaluable." Lestrade tapped the envelope. "If I have any questions after reading this, they can wait until tomorrow."

"I appreciate that, Lestrade."

Outside, I found Simonson paying the cabbie that had brought me to the hotel. As I approached I heard him instruct the man, "Fair warning, make sure you deliver that message." Realizing I had joined them, Simonson turned to me. "Hello. You've caught me in the act of commandeering your cab."

"I don't recall asking him to wait." I appraised the driver. "Weren't you outside Simpson's this afternoon?"

"That I was, sir."

Simonson leaned in to inform me, "His name is John Reeves. I've been assured by my superior that he is a trustworthy chap hired from time to time for simple tasks, such as keeping an eye on certain people."

Reeves smiled a silly smirk at me.

"If you say so, Walter. Why didn't you come up with Lestrade?"

"I'm afraid there's no time. I'm on my way out of the country until all of Moriarty's gang are in a salt box. Orders from my superior. For my own good, he says. This isn't my style, but what choice do I have? *Mea gloria fides* *."

"Yes. Will you be away long?"

"I hope not, but who can ever say how long a war will go on?" Simonson shrugged. "I am sorry about your friend."

"Yes," I sighed. "I've been hearing that a lot lately."

"I'm afraid life is like that sometimes."

"You'd think that I would have learned that in the Army. By the way, Lestrade seemed to suggest you were able to use that key. Hopefully that will speed the war along."

"Hopefully." Simonson's voice was as flat as it had sounded since meeting him.

"I'd be honored if you visit me when you get back."

He brightened. "I'll do that. And I'd be honored if we could share this cab."

"I'd like nothing better."

Reeves asked, "Taking you back to Baker Street then, sir?"

I almost said yes out of reflex, and then realized there was nothing more I really needed do there. "No. No, take me to Paddington." I gave him my address. It was finally time to go home.

"As you say." I joined Simonson in the hansom as the cabbie snapped his reigns and told his horse, "Off with you, Caprice."

* * * * *

May 18, 1891

My dear Watson,

I leave this letter with my brother Mycroft in case events arise that prevent me from seeing you again. By the time you read this, Mycroft should have informed you how I was able to avoid escorting Professor Moriarty into the abyss at the bottom of the Reichenbach Falls. It was a near thing, I promise you, but the lucky opportunity of my "death" proved of invaluable assistance in avoiding the almost certain retribution of Moriarty's most dangerous lieutenants, and it should prove just as invaluable in helping to bring all the Professor's agents to justice.

Mycroft has been my only confident. I can only hope that you will understand what I am doing is with the best of intentions. To include anyone else – even you – would only bring danger to you and Mrs. Watson while increasing the risk of my continued survival. I would not even risk entrusting Mycroft with this letter if recent events had not prevented me from leaving England immediately as had been my plan. That said, I cannot allow you to continue living in ignorance of the trivial part I played in the circumstances leading up to the death of your friend Lot Morrill by his own hand.

If you are angry with me, perhaps you will find some solace in the scolding Mycroft afforded me when he was asked to meet a cab driver named John Reeves in the Stranger's Room at the Diogenes Club, only to discover it was his younger brother. "What in Heaven's name are you thinking?" he said in the closest thing to a holler I have ever heard from him. "You're known here!"

"But Sherlock Holmes isn't here. I'm a cabbie bearing a vital missive." I explained how "Reeves" had been working along the Strand when you chanced to wave me over. You have complimented me more than once in your accounts of our adventures by confessing that I've succeeded in hiding behind a disguise even from you, and I prayed such would be the case at that moment for both our sakes. It did, but I thanked the heavens nevertheless when Lestrade interrupted and you departed with him. When I told this to Mycroft, he attempted to hide his concern that I might have followed after you and Lestrade, but I assured him that had been unnecessary. "I knew their destination as well as you do, so I took the precaution of following Dr. Morrill. His visit to Watson could have been a coincidence, but I felt it wise to verify."

"And did Morrill return to his hotel?"

"Without detour, but for two shillings another cabbie is doing Reeves the favor of watching Charing Cross Hotel in case Morrill leaves. 'An ounce of prevention – '"

Mycroft, as you are aware, possess a greater faculty for observation and deduction in comparison to my own, and, at times, I'm afraid the younger sibling in me delights in taking advantage of this to try his patience. Such was the case that day, but at last he had had enough of it.

"All right, I have no more energy to bandy words. Blast it, you're supposed to be on your way!"

"And abandon a colleague in peril?

"Oh, Sherlock, if that's your important message, I promise you that Dr. Watson is not in peril. I told I will see to that, so you surely don't need to hang about playing guardian angel."

"Actually, I've been playing guardian angel for your right-hand man, Walter Simonson, although he always communicated to me under the nom de plume – '"

"Hush! Even here the walls may have ears!"

I was unaccustomed to my brother showing concern for an underling, but in all candor I had to tell him, "Surely you can see that the time has passed for worrying about that."

I would have never left England if I was not certain Mycroft could keep his promise regarding your safety, so I pray it causes you no pain when I confess that the reason for my delay was to pay back this favor by safeguarding the man who had written to me as Fred Porlock. However, once the inexplicable and sometimes cruel hand of Fate attended to the matter for me through the actions of your friend Morrill, I made my departure as soon as I was assured that Simonson was himself safely away from England.

So now you know that, while I played no part in the deaths of Harsh Washburne or Lot Morrill, I was in the orbit of these events as they played out. As tragic as they were, I was nevertheless grateful for the opportunity they presented me to see you once more, even though I could not personally offer my sincere condolences to you at the time. Please believe I do so now.

As always, I remain very sincerely yours,
Sherlock Holmes

NOTE
* "Fidelity is my glory"

The Case of the
S.S. Bokhara
by Mark Mower

I have mentioned more than once that it was only on a few sporadic occasions that my colleague chose to share with me tantalising details of the many adventures that he had experienced during those three years of his self-imposed exile from May 1891. Even when he did refer to one of his exploits, Holmes would often be reluctant to provide any real details of what had transpired. So it came as something of a surprise when he began to talk about the sinking of a steam passenger ship and his near-death experience off the Pescadores Islands in the Straights of Formosa in October 1892.

"Are you acquainted with Dr. Lowson?" he asked, that particular morning, as we sat together enjoying coffee and cigars within the spacious lounge of a gentlemen's club in Pall Mall.

I looked up from my medical journal, unaware that Holmes had been looking across at the article I was reading. "Only by reputation. He was, of late, a surgeon with the Hong Kong civil service. A friend of mine in the army medical corps is stationed there and speaks very highly of him. You should read this, it's a fascinating article. Lowson debunks some of the medical myths about drowning, based on his own experience of escaping from a sinking ship." *

"Yes, he was lucky to escape the wreck of the *S.S. Bokhara*. A terrible business."

"Then you have read the article?"

"No, no. I met Lowson at the time, for I was also on board the steamer that day."

I stubbed out what remained of my cigar and looked at him aghast. "You were aboard the ship when it sank?"

"Yes, I was working my passage from Shanghai. The ship was carrying a valuable cargo of gold and I had been commissioned to ensure that nothing unexpected happened to it before it could be offloaded in Hong Kong. To my fellow sailors – most of whom were lascars and indentured Chinese deckhands – I was Bill Cartwright, an East End seafarer with an appetite for adventure. In reality, I was working for the Hong Kong and Shanghai Banking Corporation, protecting its consignment of bullion. My brother Mycroft had made the arrangements

103

in an effort to keep me from the clutches of what remained of Professor Moriarty's foot soldiers."

It was an astonishing revelation and I was eager to learn more. "Lowson recounts how the vessel ran into a typhoon on ninth October and never escaped its clutches."

"That is correct. We set sail on the eighth and were due to arrive in Hong Kong on the eleventh. The P&O vessel was carrying one-hundred-and-forty-eight people and one-hundred-fifty tons of cargo. The typhoon hadn't been forecast and hit us hard that first night. It left the ship adrift in the Straits of Formosa. I was below deck, working with others to do what we could to pump out the massive quantities of water which threatened to sink the ship. By the following morning, we had lost all of the lifeboats and most of the deck-house. And while we expected the winds to subside, they continued to worsen throughout the day and into the night, until three enormous waves finally overcame the vessel, flooding the engine rooms, and plunging the ship into darkness. The engineers did what they could to try and fix the steam boilers, but it was too late – with land sighted only a few hundred yards downwind, we struck a reef sometime close to midnight. It ripped open the starboard side, scuppering the steamer within minutes."

I could scarcely believe that Holmes had never sought to relay the story and was gripped by the narrative. "How did you survive?" I asked.

"More by luck than judgement! We were working by the light of tallow dips when one of the quartermasters came below to tell us to make our way up to the bridge, as he feared that the ship would be lost. He brought with him a dozen life-belts. There seemed to be some confusion, with many of the Asian sailors refusing to don the belts. I had no such compunction and alongside the engineers happily took a belt and headed up to the deck. I would say that most of the passengers and crew had done the same by the time the ship began to slide inexorably beneath the waves. The stewards were doing their best to bark out orders, but most of those around me looked paralysed with fear. I took my chances in the water, jumping off the port side as a wave swept across the deck. It carried me some length from the ship, a distance sufficient to prevent me from being sucked down by the maelstrom. It was difficult to make headway, but the life-belt kept me afloat and the prevailing winds ensured that I was pushed unerringly in the direction of Sand Island, which lay less than five-hundred yards from the reef. When I was eventually driven on to the shore, I managed to scramble behind a large rock, which gave me a measure of protection. I then spent the rest of the night helping others who had managed to escape the stricken vessel."

"Is that when you met James Lowson?"

"Yes. He was travelling back from a match at the Shanghai Cricket Club. Of the thirteen cricketers on board, only Lowson and a Lieutenant Markham survived the sinking. Lowson was in a pretty poor state – barefoot, still clad in what remained of his pyjamas, and covered in lacerations. With the help of some of the Lascar sailors who had found their way on to the beach, we carried him to a ruined hut on the uninhabited island, where he slept fitfully for a few hours."

"Lowson hints at a few adventures after reaching the shore. So what happened next?"

Holmes took a sip from his coffee and placed the cup and saucer on a low table to his side. With a solemn look, he continued. "We had further difficulties. There were about twenty of us by the early hours of the next morning, an assorted mix of officers, passengers, and sailors. The hut provided some shelter, but the rough stone floor made any sort of rest nearly impossible. The next day we foraged for any washed-up items that might make our accommodation more bearable, but were then set upon by a band of marauding fishermen who had travelled across to the island to salvage what they could from the wreckage. As they were carrying axes and knives, we had little option but to comply. However, being able to speak a little Mandarin, I was able to persuade them to take us to one of the inhabited islands nearby. There we were well looked after by the locals who fed us and patched up our wounds as best they could."

A question then occurred to me. "Did you continue to maintain the charade that you were Bill Cartwright?"

He chuckled. "Yes, but it proved to be difficult, for a reason I will come onto. I had by this time struck up an acquaintance with Dr. Lowson. In many respects, he reminded me of you – a quiet, resolute fellow with a genuine concern for others. He was proud of his Scottish roots and steadfastly refused to be browbeaten by anyone around him. I found myself talking to him at some length, all the while fearing that I might be revealing too much of my true self. He was still extremely weak and many of his wounds had become inflamed. So much so that I spoke to our hosts in the village and arranged for our party to be transported to the city of Ma Gong, where I believed we would be better able to recuperate. I had two motives for doing so. Firstly, to assist Lowson and the other survivors, and secondly, to make plans for the recovery of the gold from the *Bokhara*."

"I had quite forgotten that part of the story," said I.

"Yes. I too would have forgotten about the gold had the ship been swept away or lost to the depths. But I knew her to be lodged within the relatively shallow waters close to the reef, making the recovery of the bullion a possibility. And I had a local contact I knew I could trust to organise such a salvage operation."

I was at once intrigued. "Really? Who was that?"

"The local mandarin of Ma Gong – an influential official I had once met in London some years before. I assisted him in relocating a small stolen statue, a representation of an ancient sea goddess. He could not have been happier. In conversation with some of the locals, I learned that he was still alive and very much in control of the thriving city. Disregarding any threats to my own safety, I arranged for a short note to be sent, explaining our predicament and requesting his assistance. Luckily, he was only too pleased to help."

I was surprised to hear that Holmes had taken such an approach. "So you didn't send the note as 'Bill Cartwright'?"

"No. The mandarin generally considered himself to be superior to most foreigners. I feared that an unsolicited request from an unknown English seaman might be ignored, or, at worst, construed as lacking in respect for his position. By then, some days had passed since the sinking of the ship and I felt compelled to act for everyone's sake."

"And what was the outcome?"

Holmes beamed. "The official's response was overwhelming and more than a little surreal. We were transported to his palatial home and afforded every luxury. A party was thrown in our honour, attended by local dignitaries. Alongside Lowson, Markham, and the officers from the ship, I was treated to a champagne reception. I had asked the mandarin to keep my identity secret, something which he did with admirable tact, explaining only that I had once assisted him when he visited London. This was enough to convince my colleagues, who were incredulous that I could have engineered such an invitation. In their minds, it also helped to explain why I had been able to speak to the locals in their own tongue."

It was my turn to smile. "Then you were able to maintain the masquerade?"

"Indeed. I found time to speak alone with the man. He said he was very excited to receive my note, as he had believed me to be dead. I realised then that the news of my demise at the Reichenbach Falls had even reached the faraway islands of the Pescadores! Assuring him that I was very much alive, but still fearful of being pursued by international assassins, I placed myself at his mercy and made my requests. The approach seemed to appeal to his vanity. The following day, he arranged for a number of official vessels to make their way to the reef where the *Bokhara* had been dashed. On board were around a dozen local divers who began to work in pairs, descending to where the vessel lay and painstakingly recovering the small chests of gold that were still housed within the hold of the ship.

"The weather favoured the divers' endeavours, and the sea remained calm throughout the two days it took to conclude the work. I had been reluctant to tell the officers of the ship about the salvage operation, but did confide in both Dr. Lowson and Lieutenant Markham in order to put a plan into action. All three of us spent some time on board a sailing junk watching the divers at work. Both men proved invaluable in assisting the locals when any bodies were discovered within the wreck. In short, by the third day, all of the gold had been retrieved and arrangements were made for the bodies to be placed in coffins for the onward passage to Hong Kong."

I ordered fresh coffee from a waiter who entered the lounge at that point. He had clearly heard the closing part of my colleague's narrative and looked at me slightly askance. I tried to reassure him with a gentle nod and a smile. Holmes merely continued with his account.

"There is little to add to the tale beyond that, I'm afraid. Through the intervention of the mandarin, we were picked up by the *Thales*, a vessel run by the Douglas Steamship Company. From there we transferred to the torpedo cruiser *HMS Porpoise* which transported all of the survivors and a large number of coffins to the port of Hong Kong. On board, only Lowson, Markham and I knew that some of these caskets contained the recovered gold."

"Very clever, Holmes – and I imagine that your employers at the bank were delighted with the extraordinary efforts you had gone to in maintaining their assets?

"There was something of a bonus payment, which eventually found its way into the benevolent fund set up for the victims of the *Bokhara*. Of course, I lost the contact with Lowson, moving on within a few days to travel to Colombo. I regretted that I had not been able to reveal my true identity to him, but knew that any such disclosure might place him in further danger beyond all that he had already endured."

I felt I had to interject. "Well, you may feel vindicated by your decision. Only two years later he was to play a lead role in diagnosing the outbreak of the bubonic plague in the Government Civil Hospital in Hong Kong. His work, and that of the other surgeons at the hospital, undoubtedly saved many thousands of lives."

Holmes looked surprised. "I did not know that. Although I still had a few challenges of my own in that year . . . ."

His gaze was fixed upon the mantelpiece and he seemed momentarily to have drifted off into his own recollections. I sought to bring him back. "Well, that was certainly a most remarkable and unexpected tale."

Snapped out of his reverie he gave me a steely look. "Please tell me that you do not plan to write up some romanticised account of this affair.

I fear it would make very dull reading. You would do better to transcribe the singular features surrounding my very next adventure, which featured a most extraordinary blowpipe. Beyond Colombo, I became embroiled in an investigation into the murder of a Tibetan priest at the hands of a Genoese merchant. I will relay the pertinent facts when we are back in Baker Street . . . ."

So saying, he finished his coffee, rose quickly from his seat, and gestured towards the door of the lounge. I was never to learn any more about the unfortunate priest, the merchant or, indeed, the blowpipe. When we reached 221b, Holmes received an urgent telegram from Scotland Yard, inviting him to look into an unusual case of patricide in Walthamstow. He set off immediately, and did not return for two days.

I feel I owe it to my dear friend to set down the case of the *S.S. Bokhara*. While there was no mystery to be uncovered or conundrum to be solved, it helps to fill in another small chapter in that extended period he so often referred to as his "Great Hiatus".

NOTE

* Lowson, James A, "Sensations in Drowning", *Edinburgh Medical Journal*, 13 (1), pp 41-45, January 1903.

The Adventure of the American Opera Singer
by Deanna Baran

There is nothing quite like being away from where one belongs to make one realize the errors of one's absence, and thus it was for me. Whilst in the shadow of the Lama's Himalayan palace, I felt a yearning for the familiar lines of St. Paul's. Upon hearing the sonorous call for prayer from Meccan minarets, I cast my memory back to the noble chimes of Big Ben above Westminster. Taking passage in a *sambuk* across the Red Sea to the Soudan, I couldn't help but think with nostalgia upon the smell of tar and resin permeating the London Docks. Would I not have traded all the exotic merchandise displayed in the *suq* of Khartoum for one stroll through Covent Garden Market, the call of the Baked Potato Man carrying loudly and clearly above the noise? "Taters 'ot! All 'ot!"

But as my absence was neither for sport nor for education, it served a more practical purpose. Roving the Empire and beyond, in sundry disguises, performing tasks that only I was situated to achieve, I humbly acknowledge that neither the years nor the effort were wasted, and my unique talents made differences that few will be destined to comprehend on this side of Eternity, whether due to the natural secrecy of State, or merely to the absence of my faithful Chronicler during the critical periods.

Thus it was during this interval, after my adventures in Mecca (which remain unchronicled due to the first reason), and after a short and interesting visit with the Khalifa in Khartoum (which remains unchronicled due to the second reason), and after the matter of the Cushite Prince and the lost emerald mine of his people (which surely I shall find time to document someday), I found myself in Assouan. It was my intention to make my way via railway ticket up to Cairo, as the swiftest and most direct route possible, but upon telegraphing my intentions to London, I received a response discouraging me in no uncertain terms to avoid that course of action. The presence of enemies anticipating just such a journey made it undesirable at the moment. Rather, I was ordered to join a tourist steamer that had taken berth nearby, for they had been instructed to accommodate my presence with all consideration. In my humble opinion, I would have preferred the mail steamer as a more anonymous and secure method of flight, but perhaps I recognized a gleam of my elder brother's sense of humour with the unnecessary touch of luxury in this unorthodox escape.

Be it as it may, either comedy or timetables, the tourist steamer came promptly to the aid of their countryman as instructed. They were filled to capacity, and I murmured that I would be grateful merely for space on deck. However, it seemed that an American industrialist and his new bride had taken an extra cabin for her maid, next to theirs, but that maid had abruptly left them upon receipt of some emergency telegram, and had taken the railway back to Port Said to tend to the problem. Her quarters, therefore, merely contained the trunks and luggage of her employers, and the American industrialist was informed that the porters would be rearranging his belongings, as there was need for the cabin.

The industrialist was by no means pleased, as he had not been in receipt of instructions from on high commanding *him* to spare no effort in accommodating my presence, and he volubly counter-argued that he had paid for two cabins, and by all that was holy, he would keep two cabins. The captain of the steamer responded by offering Mr. Stepp a refund for the loss of space, as a first class ticket was quite $245. The industrialist responded scornfully that he didn't care about the $245 – *Dash the $245 to perdition!* – It was the cabin he wanted, and he wasn't about to clutter up their honeymoon with a lot of senseless luggage underfoot.

But the captain was master of his domain, and the wealthy industrialist's dollars made no difference in the end. He realized the futility of his argument, no matter that he was in the right, and so he sulked in a deck chair for the remainder of the afternoon, partaking heavily of iced punch and nursing his wounded pride. I, on my part, had little enthusiasm for being assigned such a neighbour in such a way, as it was the exact opposite of the quiet anonymity that I had intended to enjoy. My presence being so volubly discoursed upon to such negative extent did nothing to allow me the pleasure I normally would have felt at the idea embarking upon such a treat – as inferior to the Thames as it may have been.

His wife, however, embarrassed by her husband's disproportionate excitement, hastened to make amends and sought me out to apologize.

"I'm terribly sorry, Mr. – "

"Gray," I said, having informed Whitehall of my intent to discard Sigerson for the temporary duration of this Nilotic interval. "James Gray."

"Darlin' Alfred isn't used to not getting what he wants. He's such a spoilt child," she giggled. "You must forgive him, Mr. Gray."

"I apologize for the inconvenience and the fuss," I said. "Pray believe that any inconvenience to yourselves was the farthest thing from my mind when I came on board."

Mrs. Stepp's default facial expression was the broad, permanently fixed smile characteristic of Western cowboys, readily exhibiting two rows of even, gleaming teeth. She never ceased this affable display, even

110

for the purposes of speech. The words forced themselves through her wide-mouthed grin, as though fearful that, should it cease even momentarily, one might be in doubt of her good nature. At first, I thought she was merely making an extra effort to show there were no hard feelings, despite her husband's bad mood, but after further acquaintance, I found the expression to be unsettlingly ineradicable.

She herself had been once beautiful by Nature, but now relied more upon Art to maintain her looks. I knew little of how women's clothing had evolved during my absence, or what was currently fashionable in America, but to my eye, her costume looked expensive in fabric and line. The industrialist, despite his other faults, spared no expense in the maintenance of his new bride, though I doubted it was a first marriage for either of them. I was more than a little shocked to hear, from the gossip of my fellow passengers, that she was an opera singer from the other side of the Atlantic, and I looked at her with new eyes.

"Oh, yes," she said, when I asked her directly. "Not New York or Boston or those places, mind you. My parents ranched in West Texas, and earned their fortune in the cattle drives. I had always loved singing at church, you see, and did rather well, even if I say so. They indulged my foolishness, and sent me abroad to school to train my voice. Contralto, you understand, so I never got the really good parts. Usually gypsies and nursemaids and princes. Although, of course, you understand I didn't go straight into the opera. I spent several years with traveling groups and stock companies on both sides of the ocean. I traveled all over the place. But I prefer not to remember that far back. Now that I'm married, of course, I don't perform in public anymore at all. Not even a note, so it's not worth even trying to ask, though no one knows the names of any of the contralto songs, anyways. Darlin' Alfred is awfully strict about keeping me all to himself these days, the poor silly man."

It was an opportunity to bring up my fondness for Wagner, which we discussed as the paddle steamer made its way north upstream. It seemed appropriate to discourse upon Erda's emotional arc in *Das Rheingold* and *Siegfried*, seeing that it was, in my opinion, one of the great contralto parts of one of the finest composers of Europe. Mrs. Stepp was an enthusiastic audience, and although she did not seem to have had the fortune to play that particular role or have seen it in person, she did not seem to mind my company. She stayed until her husband came frowning to retrieve her on some pretext, and with that perpetual smile, she said she looked forward to seeing me next opportunity.

I waved until they disappeared round a corner, and then turned my attention to the gray-green waters of the Nile slipping past, the *dahabiyas* sailing in the opposite direction with the wind, the verdant palms and dry

111

sandstone rising beyond, the sunset blazing in the limitless sky – and wondered why Mrs. Stepp would take such trouble to lie to me.

The vessel paused the next morning after breakfast to allow its passengers a second opportunity to revisit Karnak. As I had embarked at Assouan, it was my first time wandering amidst the courts and colonnades. How my chronicler would have waxed descriptive with such fodder for his paragraphs! He would have seen the avenue of criosphinxes and the towering pylons. My eyes took note of how few men exist in this world capable of riding astride donkeys and yet preserving their dignity. He would have commented with sympathy upon the dirt and the rags of the peasants, some of whom had their tents erected against the walls of the temple itself. I found myself thinking fondly of a certain family I'd had dealings with in the Old Nichol. My friend would have had eyes only for the grandeur of the famed colonnades. I observed the passengers sifting through the premises, singly and in groups, and wondered why Stepp, who had been so attentive and solicitous towards his wife over crepes and strawberries this morning, should allow her to explore aimlessly in isolation. Ah, no, there he was, striding towards her from a knot of rascally-looking vendors. He held something in his hand. She exclaimed in approval over the string of faience beads that he presented with a flourish. He fastened them around her neck, managing somehow to work them over her hat without the necessity of her unpinning it from her head. She gave him a spontaneous embrace and they proceeded through the temple complex at a leisurely pace, he gesticulating towards carvings and statuary with his walking-stick, she a few paces behind, peering upwards and nodding agreement. I soon lost sight of them, and turned to follow my own interests.

It was shortly after that a commotion reached my ears. Making my way through the maze of the complex, I found Mrs. Stepp in tears, surrounded by a knot of concerned fellow-tourists.

"Someone tried to kill me!" she sobbed loudly – still wide-mouthed, barely moving her lips. An interesting feat. But her volume was certainly worthy of any stage diva.

"Nonsense," said her husband, embarrassed by all the attention. "Get ahold of yourself."

"Whatever happened?" I asked, approaching.

"We were walking near one of the walls," said Stepp shortly, before she could respond. "A large stone dislodged itself and landed very close to where Mrs. Stepp was walking. Another foot or two, and it would have struck her."

"Someone tried to kill me," she repeated, anguish clearly written upon her features. She shot an accusing look at her husband, as though he were somehow to be held responsible.

"Whoever would want to do that!" exclaimed her husband impatiently. "Come, now, Ethel. Don't make a spectacle. Accidents happen."

A fellow-passenger who had been nearby helpfully pointed out the fallen stone. It was of a significant size. Being struck by such an object, even from a lesser height, would certainly have proven fatal. The temple premises were by no means free of debris, but it was impossible to determine the origins of that particular stone. The stone's flat surface, carved with hieroglyphs, did not correspond with any decaying portion of the nearby wall. Indeed, that particular portion of the premises was in particularly good repair. There was no reason for such a sequence of events to have occurred as indicated, without the deliberate hand of man involved – in which case I found myself wondering if, indeed, someone had designs against the life of the new Mrs. Stepp, or perhaps the industrialist himself.

The signal to return to the steamer was given at midday, and we resumed traveling downstream, north, with the current. There were but a few hours between our departure and our next stop, at Keneh. The sole reason for pausing there was to enable tourists the opportunity to buy clay jugs designed for filtering Nile water. As I had neither an interest in the amusement of a donkey ride to the market, nor an interest in buying pottery once I got there, I remained leaning against the deck rail outside my own door, idly watching the bustle of excursionists preparing to disembark and the doings of the native population around the riverside preparing to receive them.

Quarreling voices rose over the rest of the activity that surrounded our steamer. It was my neighbours, Mr. and Mrs. Stepp. He endeavoured to convince his wife to visit the Keneh market. She was not in the mood to relinquish the safety of the ship. He made a sarcastic remark about cowering in the cabin. She responded frostily that she would feel safest in the open. He sneered at her for drawing such attention to herself and making such *prima donna* displays. Her rejoinder was unprintable.

She sailed haughtily from the cabin and instantly spotted me loitering nearby. "Mr. Gray! Are you not disembarking?" she inquired, still flushed and upset.

"Donkeys do not amuse me," I said truthfully. The next day included four hours astride a donkey, and I did not care to overindulge unnecessarily.

"Then you must sit with me and keep me company," she commanded, and I dutifully fell into step with her as she maneuvered us towards the deck chairs.

Her husband was hardly two paces behind her for this exchange.

"Donkeys don't amuse me, either," he said abruptly. "I think I'll keep you both company."

The three of us made strained, polite conversation for the duration of the excursion. She discussed ranch life amongst the cowboy hands of her parents' ranch. I amused her with tales of an American adventuress who once sang contralto with the Imperial Opera of Warsaw. In the pauses, the three of us drank iced punch. Once or twice, Mrs. Stepp seemed to be on the verge of saying something, then would glance sideways at her husband, purse her lips, and remain silent.

She never had the opportunity to speak freely to me. But it was clear that she was frayed and worried, and with her reticence in the presence of the one man who ought to have been her closest confidante and champion – I perceived the possibility of it being an indication as from what quarter she suspected the source of her troubles. On the other hand, perhaps it merely indicated that their connubial felicity was not as idyllic as the poets' ideal, as so unexpectedly proven by my inadvertent eavesdropping.

The night was quiet, and despite the thin walls, I heard no further argument from my neighbours. Whatever differences they had had had been put aside. In the morning, however, when we mounted our donkeys for the ride through the valley to Abydus, Mrs. Stepp surprised me somewhat by attaching herself to the company of a little French *curé* in our party. Stepp appeared to be annoyed, but he contented himself to keeping on the edges of their amicable conversation, close enough to overhear, but too indifferent to deign to participate. My donkey matched pace with a similarly miserable-looking dirty creature, and thus, through no conscious effort on my part, its rider became my own traveling companion. He was an American professor from some obscure college who had spent years studying ancient Egypt, and was anxious to share the fruits of his observations with anyone who would listen. He explained about the oracle of Bes, the Coptic Monastery, the great Temple of Sethi, and the temple of his son, Rameses II. Having little room in my mental attic for such trivialities, I allowed the earnest enthusiasm of his voice to wash over me, and the sound cast my memories back to certain lecturers encountered during my days at University. The tedium of the uneventful donkey ride allowed the luxury of such unwonted indulgence in nostalgia, and the journey through the valley beneath a limitless sky passed with surprising agreeability.

114

The temples were temples, of course, of which Egypt is full. Evocative, and dusty, and quite Stygian where little excavation had been done. Our tour group scattered and explored like ever so many excited children, and although Mrs. Stepp was initially wary, there were no dreadful accidents as there had been at Karnak, and she soon relaxed. We picnicked amongst the columns of The Temple of Sethos. All through the excursion, she had remained inseparable from the French *curé*'s company, although I observed her husband solicitously kept her plate full with all the choicest tidbits, and maintained her cup full of the iced punch, which was considerably less icy after suffering the rigors of a prolonged donkey ride.

I found it interesting that he did not deign to allow her to be served by the native servants as everyone else, but it was not impossible that it was one of those thoughtful gestures newly-married couples indulge in, especially when one of them feels compelled to be conciliatory. However – and I watched him trot back and forth with her dish – it didn't seem the sort of pacifying gesture that would come naturally to an acerbic millionaire industrialist. Mrs. Stepp, however, did not appear to find it amiss that any man could fail to care to wait upon her, and she accepted the courtesies as her natural due. I stopped counting the dainty honey cakes he pressed upon her after the fifth, and I stopped counting the cups of punch after the eighth. A duller mind than mine could readily predict she was destined for gastric distress from overindulgence in the first, and for a muzzy head after overindulgence in the second, and neither the short trek to the Coptic monastery nor the lengthy journey back to the ship would do anything to help either.

However, we had scarcely concluded our picnic and re-mounted our donkeys for the last mile or two of our journey, to Komes-Sultan and the Coptic monastery just beyond, when her affliction began. Her steps became more than somewhat unbalanced, and she pressed her hand to her forehead, as though beset by dizziness. It soon became clear that this was no ordinary distress, and her fellow-travelers squeezed round about her with great concern.

It was the little French *curé* who had the presence of mind to clear a space around her, to give her room for air. Breathing, however, was only accomplished with much difficulty. There was no doctor in our party – O for my absent chronicler's many talents! – but I moved forward to make what diagnosis I could. It was clear from her respiration that it was not mere intoxication in play. I had seen the pupils of eyes such as hers in many an opium den, and suspected some type of narcotic in play. Due to the timing of her reaction, the most recent dose must have been during the picnic, and there was only one culprit who could be accused of tampering

115

with her food, especially when all the rest of us were unaffected after eating from the common dishes. For a moment, I was grateful that the criminal was as unimaginative as he was, guessing that no one would have the knowledge to label it as anything but an unexpected bout of severe intestinal upheaval. It would have been a different story had he tried to disguise one deliberate poisoning amongst an indiscriminate attack against the entire party!

The little French *curé* murmured in Latin over her, and she squeezed his hand, trying to speak, but no words came out. Her breaths were slow and shallow. Her husband was at her elbow, supporting her, murmuring reassurances for her to rest, not worry, don't try to talk, this would soon pass, she would be better soon. One of the native servants had run off to the Coptic monastery in search of medical assistance.

Although bandits were uncommon in this area, our party was well-guarded by a small escort of armed men. I approached them. "Gentlemen!" I said, pitching my tone into an authoritarian voice accustomed to being obeyed. "I bid you, arrest Mr. Alfred Stepp, for the murder of his wife. He must be detained and the authorities notified."

Stepp's eyes blazed at me as he rose. "You're a fool!" he shouted. "A fool and an interfering meddler! You can't arrest me for the murder of my wife! Not only is she clearly alive – though she's experiencing a bit of distress at the moment – but you're an insolent busybody to talk that type of pointless talk in her very presence while she's suffering!"

"Except for the fact that woman is not your wife," I corrected him. "Did you not hear me? I refer to the murder of your wife. The American opera singer. For this woman has never sung professionally in her life, has never been a trained vocalist. It's physically impossible for a trained vocalist to conduct her discourse in the manner in which this woman converses. A true opera singer trains relentlessly to speak from the diaphragm. It would be painful and unnatural, after all that rigorous training, to speak as this woman does – creating her words in the cavity of her mouth, forcing them through her teeth and her nose!

"All travelers know that the world is full of pretenders. On the other side of the world, away from those who could gainsay, who can say that any man is not a millionaire industrialist? I cannot speak as to the condition of your bank-book, but I would posit that you wooed a wealthy woman to be your wife, with every intention to return from your honeymoon with the tragic news of her sudden death abroad. With your sort, you rarely content yourself with a single scheme. It is frequently a pattern. How many wives have you used so cruelly?"

"You assume much," snarled Stepp through his teeth.

"I assume more," I replied placidly. "I contend that this woman before us is your accomplice. Whatever relation she has to you, I know not, but she loves and trusts you sufficiently to help you in the vilest crimes one human being may commit against another. It is my suggestion that she is, in fact, the errant maid who abruptly abandoned your party, before her fellow-passengers upon the tour had time to make anyone's acquaintance sufficiently to notice the substitution. You rid yourself of your true wife, and disguised her absence by claiming it was the maid who had unexpectedly absented herself. For who notices the departure of a mere servant, or cares to query after the reason?"

"You're a liar!" said Stepp.

"I knew from the moment we spoke that she was lying about being a professional singer," I pressed. "But it was a harmless little fantasy, so I chose not to interfere. How many people present themselves as something they are not, whilst traveling abroad! It would indeed be tedious to reveal every *poseur* for what he is. But I must admit, my interest was sparked after the incident at Karnak, as we made our return-journey to Cairo. That was your first attempt against her life, to my knowledge. I presume you had hired one of the local ruffians to push a rock over the wall. It was only a matter of chance that she escaped with her life.

"And yet you, who raised such a fuss over the matter of the loss of a cabin, should have worked so hard to quiet her down when her life had just been in peril! Why should the one have offended you to such a degree, and why should you have attempted to suppress the other? I suggest to you that you feared having a neighbour next door, who might accidentally overhear some unguarded conversation, and you strove with all your might to discourage my proximity. And I also suggest to you that you wanted the failed attempt to pass from everyone's minds as quickly as possible, and thus you attempted to restrain any excitement to the best of your ability. It almost doesn't bear mentioning that she distinctly said, 'Someone tried to kill *me*' rather than 'Someone tried to kill *you*' or 'Someone tried to kill *us*'. One would normally make concessions for the temperament of a diva, to view the world's events through a rather egotistical lens, but it is still telling that she never considered your life as having been in danger, no matter you were walking together.

"But as my suspicions developed, I noticed a change in this young lady's behaviour. I do not know how long she has been in your company, or under your influence, but she seems to be suffering regret from her choice of actions. That she suffered under emotional strain was undoubtedly certain. Yet was she not on her honeymoon in some exotic locale, the very time when she should have had no cares at all! The very next day after she developed a concern for her own mortality, in fact, she

117

began attaching herself, not to her supposed husband, nor to myself, her casual friend and temporary neighbour, but to the company of this French *curé*. When one's soul is gnawed by guilt and, possibly, contrition, is there not the natural urge to confide? To confess?

"And were you not keenly aware of that? And if she was permitted to divulge her sins, that she would incriminate you as well? The hangman's rope would be a certainty. And thus, you were forced to act yourself. No random tragedies whilst traipsing through crumbling ruins. Instead, I would suggest you be searched. It is my hypothesis that a small bottle or phial will be found upon your person, bearing traces of some sort of strong narcotic. Possibly laudanum. Possibly morphine. Perhaps opium. Something of that nature.

"You introduced it into her food, so that it would take effect before she could cause any further damage with her sudden attack of conscience. My suggestion is the honey cakes, to conceal the bitter taste. When combined with the alcohol of the punch, of which you knew she was especially fond! It was merely a matter of time, and you trusted to our isolation to do the rest. Not as unsuspicious as your original plan, but speed was of the essence. If this woman dies, it will be the second murder to your name, although I have no doubt that, if the proper authorities looked more closely, additional victims shall come to light."

His accomplice had enough strength left in her to make a gesture that confirmed my accusations, in the presence of these countless witnesses. Stepp, of course, was mad with rage. Before anyone could search him, and before anyone could stop him, he produced a phial from his vest pocket, uncorked it, and took a substantial draught of laudanum. He was gone before she was, but she did not last an hour beyond.

I inquired about the situation a few months later, out of idle curiosity. The body of the true opera singer wife was never found and identified, but she was presumed dead. She had actually been an American contralto, well known within certain circles, although not top-tier. However, she had accumulated a tidy fortune during the course of her career, and had married Alfred Stepp after a whirlwind romance. He, on his end, had accumulated the fortunes of four previous wives, which he used to woo this new conquest to a degree that indicated far more affluence than he could lay claim to in reality. However, as he did not intend the marriage to last long enough for this to be discovered, he spent freely. She had converted all of her American real estate and property into gold, which was now jointly theirs, and they had plans to use their combined fortunes to relocate to Paris after a lavish honeymoon spent touring Egypt. Which, of course, she never survived.

The authorities never traced the true identity of the woman who called herself Ethel Stepp, although they had no incentive to try very hard. It was my private suspicion that she had truly been Mrs. Stepp's personal lady's maid, who had been cultivated by the dashing Alfred Stepp to cooperate in the betrayal of her mistress. There was no solid evidence to support that fantasy – no one ever pays attention to servants and their hopes and dreams and loves and hates. It was possible she had an entirely different story that led her to such an unpleasant, anonymous end.

But tragedienne though she was, she was no luminary of the stage.

The Keadby Cross
by David Marcum

"We're closed! Go away!"

The man on the other side of the locked tavern door said something that we couldn't hear, but his expression gave us to understand that he was not pleased. He grabbed the door handle one more time, gave it an angry shake, and turned away, joining and then vanishing into the other passers-by in the street. My eyes stayed drawn to the door and surrounding windows for a moment, looking at the sharply etched scene in the bright morning sunlight while our friend continued to speak.

"They wake up thirsty," said Isaiah Clark, "and take no account of the time. He'll have been drinking until three or four in the morning, and now here it is, not yet ten o'clock, and he's ready to start again." He shook his head with pity. "Poor old sot."

"Wasn't that Alfred Penrith?" asked Holmes.

Clark nodded. "He was of some help to us, if you'll recall."

I remembered the name, and couldn't believe that the man was still alive. He had provided a valuable bit of information during our pursuit of the Whitechapel Killer, and more important, Penrith had later roused himself from an alcoholic stupor when one of the Rippers attempted an ambuscade in Hanbury Street, distracting the man long enough that Holmes was temporarily able obtain the upper hand and send the murderer's blood-stained bayonet clattering onto the pavement. Our attacker had escaped into the warren of allies and passages that surrounded us, eluding even my friend for a time, while I'd remained behind to treat Penrith's wound, a cut along the length of his arm that was fortunately minor. It was then that he remarked that he'd received worse while in the service, and he mentioned a few details of his bravery with Wolesley at Amoaful, and the medal that he'd won there.

As I'd finished binding up the poor vagrant's wound, I had considered that I could have ended up in the same situation as Penrith – wounded in battle, returned to England, and left adrift and without purpose and a head too full of terrible memories. Just weeks after the *Orontes* had put me ashore on the Portsmouth jetty, I was already drifting toward profligacy and starting to pass my empty days with drink, a tendency that had devastated my poor brother, when a chance encounter with an old friend led me to the laboratory at Barts Hospital on New Year's Day, 1881, and thus my introduction to Mr. Sherlock Holmes. He and I had agreed to share a flat in Baker Street, and doing so immediately improved my behavior, decreasing my alcohol consumption in – as I see now in hindsight – what had been an attempt not to give this new acquaintance the impression that I was an incipient drunkard. Then, as I became more involved in his investigations, both my health and my aimlessness improved, each in their own way.

I have no doubt that this chain of my thoughts was apparent to Holmes, who glanced my way with a smile as I came back to myself, still standing by the bar in the Ten Bells in Spitalfields, while the owner, Isaiah Clark, continued to speak.

"There are so many like old Penrith," he said, "and some of us attempt to do what we can. I attend St. Mary's, and while the minister had some initial reservations about the owner of a pub like me actually having a soul, we've come to an accord. I'm in an odd spot, gentleman – something like the eye of the storm. Selling drink all day long, making my living from it, and yet trying to help those who are broken by it. It was through these efforts that I met Father Tim."

He was interrupted by another rattle at the door, this time from a heavy-set man in a long tattered coat and a battered bowler. In spite of his location, standing in the shadowed doorway, I could see that his nose, above a large and shaggy mustache, was oversized, misshapen, and discolored, either from *rosacea*, or chronic abuse of drink, or both. I have no doubt that Holmes could tell that and a dozen other things besides, such as whether the man was a retired Sergeant of Marines, or instead a former eye surgeon who had once served on a whaling ship before losing his practice following an adulterous relationship with the daughter of a friend while his own wife was dying of consumption.

The man looked through the door, rattled it once more, and then drifted away. "Let's go upstairs," said Clark, picking up the metal box that had rested on the bar while he spoke. "They'll never leave us alone down here."

He led us to a back corner of the room and then up the narrow stairwell to the first floor, consisting of a square space the same size as the bar below, identical in both its dismal lack of color and decoration, and presenting the same plain walls and ancient wood flooring. The only difference was that this chamber was empty except for a few rickety tables and chairs, while the downstairs contained the great square bar that filled the center of that room.

Clark led us to one of the tables by the tall front windows looking out onto Christ Church, just across Fournier Street, and then south along Commercial Street. Not far along I could see the corner of Dorset Street, leading to nearby Miller's Court, which will ever be associated with poor

Mary Kelly. I shook my head. All around me, the East End was waking up, and the bright day with its brilliant blue skies might almost make one forget the horrors that had happened here six years earlier. And yet, as soon as Clark resumed his story, I realized that even though the truth of the Ripper murders had been discovered, though only known in its entirety to a few men such as Holmes and myself, the stain would never completely fade from this blighted place.

"I met Father Tim three years ago," said the big man. "He walked in one day, in a black suit and collar, and I didn't need to be you, Mr. Holmes, to see what his calling was, or that he was new at it – his clothes were new, the priest's collar was clean, and his hair was very neatly cut. He looked bright, like a new penny, – nothing about life seemed to have marked him. And yet, when I talked to him, I could see that there was a pain in his eyes – something haunted him. I never did find out anything about him – his past, anyway. He never even shared his last name. That isn't necessarily unusual around here – many men have secrets in Whitechapel and Spitalfields – but I did wonder sometimes. Yet it wasn't my place to ask.

"He explained that he'd rented rooms in New Broad Street, near the station, and that he wanted to help those in need – he said it just like that, without any specifics, and apparently without any kind of plan. I was busy, and I'd seen other do-gooders show up here before, taking a look around for a few days or so with upturned noses before wandering back to where they'd come from, thinking that they'd seen and learned enough in that short time to have a complete understanding of the poor unfortunates, and with material to color a lifetime of sermons. But he stayed, and I saw that he was actually out there amongst those who needed help – finding them shelter, helping them to get home at night, locating food or warm clothing, and most of all, simply talking with them, and listening in return.

"Like so many others around here, we became used to him, and began to trust him. He and I would talk sometimes of a morning – about the same time as we are now, before things get busy – and I soon learned that while he'd discuss people that we knew – those that needed help, or those who might provide it – he was very quiet about his own past. He didn't seem to lack for money, as he always had coins to give to those who needed help, but he didn't spend anything on himself. His black suit seemed to be his only one – I could tell because of a mended rip on the sleeve that was there day-in and day-out – and when that poor coat finally reached the end of its existence, he replaced it with a similar garment from one of the used clothing stalls in Petticoat Lane.

"And so it went, and the days passed, and soon he was as much a part of this little community as any of us. Over time, we became friends, of sorts. I might have been his only one. It was early this year that his

122

landlady brought a message to me, saying that he was sick and asking for me. He didn't seem to want help from any other.

"I went to his rooms, and a plainer sight you've never seen. He had the fever – the Black Formosa Corruption – that was sweeping through the docks then. Possibly you remember it, Doctor? It was before you returned, Mr. Holmes. We hadn't seen it that bad since late '87. In any case, by the time that I arrived, Father Tim was out of his head, raving as the fever took him. I found one of the doctors from the ladies' shelters that would consent to see him, and he gave the landlady and me some medicine, but both she and the doctor seemed afraid to be in the same room with the poor man, so it was up to me to nurse poor Father Tim through the worst of it.

"One night, he was crying out and fighting to climb out of bed, but he was weak as a kitten. He kept calling for Lydia, and apologizing to her – he was weeping and wailing, and just when he'd drop off it would start again. Then the fever broke, and he fell asleep.

"He mended quickly after that, and I didn't mention what he'd said – we all have secrets down here, you know. Within a few weeks he had his strength back, and things resumed as they were, although we were perhaps better friends than before. Possibly that's why, just a couple of weeks ago, he spoke of something that was different from our usual conversations.

"We were sitting right here at this very table. 'I have an item that I wish for you to hold for me,' he said, and then he pushed this very metal box across the table. 'I mean to write a letter to go with it,' he said, 'explaining what it is, but . . . but I just haven't been able to find the courage to do so quite yet.'

"I know that I looked surprised. I generally keep an even expression when dealing with the public downstairs, but I suppose that I'd let down my guard around Father Tim. Something like this was unexpected, and I showed it. He hurried to explain – but he didn't really explain anything.

"'I assure you that there is nothing wrong here,' he said. 'What's in the box belongs to my family – to me. It's simply . . . something from my past that . . . I couldn't leave it behind. I've had it hidden in my room, underneath a floorboard, and in the three years that I've lived there, I've never had any reason to worry about my hiding place being found. But a couple of nights ago, someone went through several rooms in the lodging house. It was one of the other tenants who had become desperate enough to do that, seeking money for drink. I don't believe that he had any idea that my box was hidden there – I haven't taken it out since I first put it under the floor, and one cannot tell that such a hiding place even exists. But since my room was entered, it's been on my mind, and I decided to see about putting it in a safer place. I suppose that I could go to a bank, or leave it with a lawyer, but I'm disinclined to do so. Instead, I thought of you, my friend. You have a safe. Could you keep it there for me? I should really just let it go, but I can't bear it. And soon I'll put a letter with it, so that if should something happen to me, you'll know what it is . . . .'

"He drifted off then, as if lost in his memories. In the meantime, I was naturally curious, but he was my friend, after all, and as you can see, this little box wouldn't take up much room. I agreed, and he looked relieved, and when we finished talking about other things, he went downstairs with me to my office below street level and saw it placed into my safe.

"And I thought no more about it, until two days ago, when he was murdered."

Holmes nodded. "I saw the reports in the press. It seemed like a rather senseless crime of violence – he was struck terribly in the head and found very close to here, I believe."

Clark nodded toward the window. "Just on the other side of the church there, across from the graveyard where the lane opens into Harriot Place – not much more than a mews, really, running through to Fashion Street."

"Is there any idea why he would have been there – in the middle of the night as I recall?"

"No, but it wasn't unusual, either. All of us here use the alleys and cut-throughs to get where we're going, and in Father Tim's case, he could've had business anywhere, checking on someone that needed his help."

"And at any time of day," Holmes added.

"That's right. A lad had taken some food to his father who was working nights at the chocolate and mustard mill on Wentworth, and had come back by way of Brick Lane, and then along Fashion before cutting through Harriot. It was just a random decision on his part, he said, to go that route on his way back home, and if it hadn't been him who found Father Tim, then it would have been someone else soon after, I expect. It may get dark here in the East End, but it never actually goes to sleep."

"I confess that I noted the matter," said Holmes, "but haven't seen anything reported since then."

"Because there hasn't been much to report," said Clark. "I'm surprised that it was in the newspapers at all. Probably they only mentioned it because he was a man of the cloth."

Holmes nodded. "And you don't think that any progress has been made?"

"None at all that I've heard. I spoke to the sergeant that was sent around from the Bishopsgate Station the next morning, but no one has been by since then. But," he added, "the sergeant did mention that a witness had been found – John Llanfair, an old drunk who claims to have heard the attack. He was lying in the cemetery when he heard an argument in the direction of where the body was found. The sergeant was inclined to dismiss this story – he wasn't even sure that old John even knew which day was which – but there was one part of the story that makes it seem true. John mentioned that Father Tim cried out the name 'Lydia' during the argument."

"Did you tell the sergeant that you'd heard that name before – when you were caring for Father Tim earlier this year?"

"I did, and after that he seemed to credit John Llanfair's story just a wee bit more."

Holmes's eyes dropped to the table. "But you didn't tell him about the box?"

"No. Truth be told, at first it didn't occur to me, and then, thinking how Father Tim had acted and his story about his rooms being searched, I decided to ask you about it first, in case there's some connection."

"I see that the little lock has been cut."

Clark nodded. "I felt that I ought to. Father Tim never came back to leave a letter as he'd said he would, but I thought that there might be something inside that would be helpful – the name of a family member, for instance. Someone who might like to know what had happened to him. Instead, I found this . . . ." And drawing the box toward him, he raised the hasp and lifted the hinged lid. It was a small tin box, about six inches square and three deep. From where I was sitting, the interior wasn't visible, but Clark reached in with his thick blunt fingers and pulled out a handful of sparkling fire.

Or so it seemed as the morning light from the high windows beside us lit it up. It was an object in the form of a cross, encrusted with a vast number of gems – at first glance there didn't seem to be any metal showing whatsoever, with every surface faced with some jewel, either large or small. But then I saw that there were some plain surfaces here and there, highly polished, and catching the light as strongly as the stones.

Saying "May I?" Holmes reached for the object. Clark handed it to him and then sat back, as if he had transferred a burden. Holmes looked at it this way and that, and then again with his glass. He held it at different angles to the sunlight and then walked to the window. I noticed that he was careful not to simply hold it up where it would be visible to anyone looking up from the street one floor below. Then, having seen all that he could during that examination, he returned to his seat, handing it to me, saying, "It is most unique, and no doubt worth a fortune – not simply for the jewels themselves, but because of its apparent age and most unique craftsmanship. There is certainly some fascinating story associated with it. Besides the great artistry involved, the metal seems to be platinum, or some related alloy – and as I understand it, platinum is extremely difficult to adapt for this type of purpose. I seem to recall reading something long ago about such an item, and the rumors of a lost process that went into its construction." He shook his head. "The facts elude me for now, but they can be located easily enough."

While he had been speaking, I'd continued to examine the piece, and quite frankly I'd never encountered anything so elaborate, yet perfect in its simplicity. Perhaps that is a contradiction, but seeing it that morning, and recalling still after so many years, I cannot puzzle together a different description. It was in the shape of a Celtic Cross, about five inches long, and covered along the front, back, and sides with jewels. The larger stones were along the main faces of the cross, and there were many smaller stones located along the sides and within the curve of the ring. The stones were arranged in an orderly fashion, and the simple color choices were most pleasing, with rubies running along the main upright and crosspiece, and emeralds around the faces of the ring. Smaller diamonds served to accentuate them, cunningly placed so that when each caught the light, it seemed to reflect back toward the adjacent stones. It was tempting to keep staring at the piece, turning it this way and that as if an even better and more pleasing angle could be found with just one more fractional turn. Sensing that I had looked at it long enough, I returned it to Clark, who held it without the same interest while Holmes turned his attention to both the tin box and the small cut lock beside it. Seemingly there was very little to be found there, for he quickly finished and said, "Nothing useful."

He handed the box to Clark, who replaced the jeweled cross inside. Then he immediately closed the lid and pushed it back across to Holmes. "You'll be needing this, and I have no use for it."

Holmes took the box, saying, "After Father Tim left it with you, did he mention it again? Check on its welfare, or ask to verify that it was still in the safe?"

Clark shook his head. "He did not. I saw him a few times after that, but we only talked about the things that had always passed between us – those in need, and efforts by some of the local churches and their effectiveness."

"And you wish me to locate to whom this object is connected?" asked Holmes.

Clark smiled. "I like how you put that, Mr. Holmes. There's a lot left unsaid when expressing it that way. I don't know why Father Tim had this, or how he came by it, or if it was even completely his, in spite of what he told me. Do you think that he was killed because of it?"

Holmes shook his head. "These are early days. We really don't know anything – but there are a number of threads to take up, and I shouldn't be surprised to know a lot more within just a few hours."

He asked a few more questions, such as where Father Tim's lodgings were located in New Broad Street, the name of the sergeant who had been by the morning following Father Tim's murder, and how to find John Llanfair. Then by mutual accord we stood and adjourned downstairs.

As we descended, Clark asked if we'd like anything to drink, but we declined. We entered the bar, and I was surprised for just a second when the room suddenly darkened. However, I realized that a large dray wagon with barrels of beer was pulling to a stop on Fournier Street just outside the corner doorway of the pub and blocking nearly all of the morning sunlight. Clark seemed apologetic as his attention was now needed elsewhere, but we said our farewells, stepped around the burly horses waiting patiently at the front of the wagon, and then walked across toward the steps of Christ Church, where we could talk relatively uninterrupted.

There was some sort of bazaar taking place on the church's front lawn, and several women looked suspiciously at Holmes as he walked through the displayed clothing without a glance. I nodded and attempted to appear friendly, but after we reached the steps, I glanced back and saw that we were still the subject of glares from several irritated organizers.

"Thoughts?" asked Holmes succinctly.

"Father Tim had a secret past," I speculated. "He showed up without any explanation. His choice of lodgings and clothing were humble. He had no obvious source of income, yet he seemed to have funds available. He was somehow able to pay for food and his rent. And of course there is his possession of this object." I nodded to the box in Holmes's hands.

"Ah, but anyone might seem mysterious under certain circumstances, and no one is obligated to simply provide an explanation about themselves – and in a location such as this, such explanations especially aren't expected. It isn't necessarily sinister that he chose not to share his past – or even his full name. And his possession of this object could be completely legitimate." Only then did he slip the box into the pocket of his Inverness. "As I said, there are several paths to explore, none any better than the others. As it's the closest, I suggest we start where the body was discovered – although I don't expect to find anything useful there."

He was correct. Leaving the bazaar behind, we walked around the front of the church and along the graveyard to the opening of Harriot Place. Holmes then slowly explored along the pavement for several moments, sometimes bent at the waist to see better, but never actually dropping to his knees and crawling as he did in some circumstances. A few times he would lean and touch something with his finger, including one spot about the size of a dinner plate that looked suspiciously like a dried blood stain. Finally he rose and brushed off his hands. "The body was there," he said, indicating the stain. "He was certainly struck down at this spot, for this is where he bled as he died. But there is nothing else that I can see. Let us see if Mr. Llanfair is where Isaiah thought."

We crossed Commercial Street and into the Spitalfields Market, where Llanfair was indeed earning a few coins unloading boxes of produce for one of the stalls. The owner frowned when Holmes asked to borrow him for a couple of minutes, but he became more receptive when a few coins changed hands.

In the end, Holmes paid Llanfair as well, but he had nothing of substance to add to what we'd already heard.

Two nights earlier, the night had been quite fair, with a waxing moon high in the sky. Llanfair had acquired a bottle and made for a spot that had sheltered him before, alongside one of the larger ornate gravestones beside the church. It was there that he'd fallen asleep, and where he'd later awakened to hear an argument nearby, in the direction of Harriot Place. There were two men, he said, and their voices rose for several minutes before the sound of a terrible blow ended the argument – no other words were spoken.

"Did you go to see what had happened?" said Holmes.

The old man shook his head with a shamed expression.

"And you reported to the police that you heard Father Tim say 'Lydia'."

Llanfair shook his head. "That's not right. It was the other voice – the angry-sounding one – that said it. He said it twice, just before I heard the sound – well, it must have been when he did for Father Tim. They showed me the body, and I believe that's what I heard – when his head was crunched in."

The man had nothing else to offer, and we thanked him and left the market, with our next stop being the Bishopsgate Police Station.

We walked down Commercial Street, and then along Dorset Street. I sensed that Holmes had chosen this route specifically, but I was unsure of his motivations. It was almost as if he had decided to do so in order to show that the place had no power to intimidate him, but I rather felt as if we were whistling past the graveyard, as they say in America. We soon passed the narrow entrance to Miller's Court on our right, and my best intention to blithely ignore it quickly failed as I glanced that way, looking into the dim and hellish passage, recalling those terrible events of the early hours of 9 November, 1888, when the Ripper's maddened butchery reached its apex. My physical wounds from that night had healed, but I still carried the scar, and I knew that neither Holmes nor I would ever

128

forget what we had seen in that cursed room, which in itself was only the tiniest piece of the overall catastrophe making up that nightmarish autumn.

Exiting the other end of Dorset Street felt as if we were emerging from a dank crypt, having outpaced creatures in the dark who would have pulled us down like wolves in a dark winter forest. The equally poverty-stricken streets of the remainder of our journey – Raven Row, Artillery Passage, and Widegate Street – seemed almost festive in comparison. Soon we were in the bustling Bishopsgate Road near Liverpool Street Station, and then walking into the stolid Bishopsgate Police Station.

Asking for Sergeant Corby, we were kept waiting in the lobby until a tall man in his thirties appeared from somewhere in the rear of the building. We had worked with Corby before, most recently in the curious affair of the brewer's murder, where Holmes had been trapped with a madman in the lost tunnel running underneath Pall Mall to St. James's Palace. The matter had begun with a rich man's strangling and finished with the recovery of a lost relic – and the sergeant's marriage to the brewer's daughter.

Corby was glad to see us, and after a few questions back-and-forth as to one another's welfare, and with the glad news that his wife was expecting, he led us back to a cramped little office where we could discuss the murdered priest. After confirming what we'd been told about the discovery of the dead man and Llanfair's story, Corby responded to Holmes's question as to the body's current location.

"He's in St. George's Mortuary, in Cannon Street Road. We thought when the body was found that there might be more of an uproar than there was, him being a priest and all, and we wanted to put him out of the way, so to speak. It turns out," he continued, "that there hasn't been much interest at all – which is sad, considering the good works that the man accomplished."

"Has anyone from any of the churches stepped forward to claim an association?"

"No, and in spite of him wearing priest's clothing, I can't find much else to corroborate it. There was nothing related to any formal ministry in his room. There isn't much information about him anywhere. There have been no responses to our inquiries outside of London. I haven't been able to find anyone else who saw or heard anything the night of his murder either, or who knows anything about this 'Lydia'. His room was remarkably empty – no letters or photographs, or even a magazine or newspaper, and there was nothing on the body except for this worn testament." He opened a desk drawer and pulled it out. Holmes took it and looked through it with great care, but finally returned it to the policeman with tight lips. "Nothing," he agreed. "Only a few months old from the looks of it – probably bought to replace another in the same way that he replaced his suit when it wore out."

"From what I've been able to determine," said Corby, shutting the drawer on the small black book, "the man had no enemies, and never had more than a few coins on him at any given time – so there was nothing to steal. Of course we all know that just a few coins that are nearly worthless to some are a treasure to others. Still, it was probably just an encounter with one of the drunks or disturbed men that are everywhere here – either home-grown, or a sailor that has already left port. Something was said, and the killer's temper flared . . . ." His hands, which had been folded on the desk before him, parted as he shrugged. "We really don't have any ideas where to look next." He refolded his hands. "Might I ask your interest?"

"We were approached by his friend, Mr. Clark, the proprietor of the Ten Bells." He didn't mention anything else, leaving that explanation to stand for itself.

That seemed to satisfy Corby, who knew Holmes and understood that my friend would say what he meant and no more. The officer nodded and stood, ending the interview. "Well then. Of course we'll appreciate any information that you find." Thus dismissed, he led us back to the lobby.

Outside, the street had become quite busy with the noon-time traffic. "I noticed that you chose not to share the contents of the tin box with the sergeant."

"It may or may not be a factor in the man's death, and if not, then it doesn't necessarily need to be brought to the attention of the official force. We may be dealing with two different questions."

I indicated that we ought to next examine the dead man's rooms, located just around the corner, and Holmes agreed. We found a rather tidy building, unusual in that particular part of London, and when we spoke to the landlady, Mrs. Carpenter, it was apparent that her strict influence was the reason why. She recognized both of us, stating that she'd been at the funeral of one of the Ripper's victims six years before when we had both been in attendance. She led us up to Father Tim's room, first floor rear, and stood in the doorway with me while Holmes made his examination.

"He knocked on my door three years ago, in the summer, responding to a sign that I'd put in the window just that morning about a room to rent. One of my long-timers, Mrs. Wittering, had passed away from a kidney complaint – we thought it was cancer, but the doctor only gave her some pills. It was terrible to watch her fade, and so fast, putting all her hopes in that useless medicine. No offense intended I'm sure, Dr. Watson."

I nodded and she continued. "Father Tim moved in with not much more than the clothes on his back and started helping with the poor from the first day. I asked which was his church, but he said that he was simply a minister of the streets."

She fell silent as Holmes systematically continued his investigation around the room. She watched with a sharp focus as he crawled along the floors and baseboards and, while still on his knees, lifted the thin and worn mattress, turning it this way and that to see if something might have been concealed within. After finding nothing, he stood and remade the bed before falling to his knees once again, quickly locating the floorboard where the tin box had been concealed. I glanced at Mrs. Carpenter and noticed her surprise when it was revealed, but she withheld comment.

Holmes replaced the flooring and then moved to the rickety deal bureau, looking behind and underneath before opening each drawer and then removing it, checking to see if anything had been hidden behind or concealed within the framework of the piece. He poked through the few items of clothing that were there before he finally reassembled the drawers, asking, "What was Father Tim's last name?"

She seemed surprised, and then she had to think. "Smith, I believe. I think that's what he said when he introduced himself – but really, there was never any need to use it after that. We always just thought of him as Father Tim."

Holmes shut the last drawer and looked around at the rest of the room to see if he'd missed anything. It had a small cot-like bed, a chair and plain table, and the bureau. There were a couple of ratty curtains hanging by the sole window, and the blanket on the bed was worn but clean. There were no decorations in the room whatsoever, and from the fact that Holmes had removed nothing from the bureau or the cavity in the floor, I knew that neither of them had offered anything of importance.

"Did he have any friends?" I asked. "Did anyone help look after him when he was sick earlier this year?"

"Ah, you heard of that? Then you've talked to Mr. Clark of the Ten Bells. He was the poor man's only friend. Other people liked Father Tim, but he never let anyone get too close, if you know what I mean. But Mr. Clark does a lot of work for the poor, and that put him and Father Tim pulling in the same direction more often than not. When Father Tim was so sick, no one wanted to be around him. I confess, I had qualms myself. I have a friend whose brother knew someone at the docks who worked with a man whose cousin died of the Black Formosa Corruption! It sounds dreadful!"

"It is. Was there anyone in the building," I pressed, "with whom he talked? Anyone to spend his spare time of an evening?"

"He didn't really have any spare time," was the answer, "and while he would take evening meals here, he would usually go back into the streets afterwards to help the unfortunates. Up early, out late – that was Father Tim. Day in and day out – except for the days when he'd go away altogether."

"Indeed?" said Holmes. "And when did that happen?"

"Every few weeks, I suppose. Once a month for a few days at a time, actually."

"And was this his habit from the beginning?"

"Oh, no, only since last spring. He came in one afternoon, quite in a hurry and flustered he was, and said that he'd be back in two or three days. He didn't say where he was going, but he returned as he'd promised."

"And what was his mood when he told you that?"

"Hurried, as I said. Maybe a little anxious, as if he was trying to be away as soon as possible."

"Did he tell you every time that he went after that?"

"No, just the first two or three occasions. Not the more recent times."

"This is October. How often did he go away?"

She counted to herself, and then said, "Six. He started in April."

"That covers the six months. Hadn't he gone away this month as well?"

"No, not yet, although now that you mention it, it was just about time for him to go. He always went in the middle of the month – just for a few days. I remember, because it was always soon after that the rent was due, and he'd pay me before he went away. He was never late with that."

I asked her the amount of the rent, and it was quite modest – not surprising in this part of London. Meanwhile, Holmes pinched his lip as if searching for a reason for the priest's behavior, or why it occurred in the middle of the month. Then, seeming to set it aside for the time being, he thanked Mrs. Carpenter and allowed her to take us back to the street, chattering all the while.

"Well," I said as the door shut behind us and we walked up the narrow lane, "the groundwork is laid, and the routine examinations have been made: Talking with a friend, looking at the scene of the murder, questioning both a possible witness and the police, and then examining the dead man's lodgings. I suppose that next we take a look at the body."

"Yes. We progress, Watson – although to what end I'm not yet sure."

As it was farther than we wanted to walk, we finally found an unoccupied hansom in Brick Lane and set off to St. George's, the mortuary where the body had been taken. "What do you expect to find from an examination of the corpse?" I asked.

"Not much, I'm afraid," said Holmes. "This mysterious figure shows up from out of nowhere three years ago in a new priest's suit, and then seems to keep barely any more than that clothes on his back thereafter, replacing them only when necessary. He lives an apparently blameless life, well-known in the community but without any close associations – even Clark wasn't in his total confidence – and then he meets his death violently in an alley across from a graveyard within feet of a major thoroughfare – without explanations or clues. The name 'Lydia' has been mentioned twice, but we have no context, so for now that fact is of no use. His room showed nothing of interest – not a hint of a motive, and nothing about him as a person."

"There was obviously nothing in the bureau. I take it that the cavity hidden beneath the floorboard was empty as well."

"Not even a helpful scrap of paper or a pinch of strange dust."

We grew silent then, each with our own thoughts. I know now what Holmes was considering, but I was thinking about the streets around us, where we had spent so many nights patrolling through the autumn fogs, hoping to prevent additional murders while trying to pick up any threads that might lead us farther along toward a solution to the tangled Ripper killings.

It seemed no time at all before we arrived at St. George's. The fine old church presided over a brutal neighborhood, just a couple of blocks north of the London Docks. The smell of them was in the air – a different scent from the pervasive rot and filth that always hangs over Whitechapel and Spitalfields, even on that clear October morning. Sensing the change, I realized how easy it was to reacquaint myself with those odors without conscious thought. It's the same for a surgeon, who quickly becomes familiar with the mephitises produced by the human body, or for the engineers who maintain the London sewers – or so one of them has told me – in that the offensive vapors of the sanitary pipelines become easier to tolerate with time.

We ignored the main entrance to the church, instead walking to the side in order to approach the small area used as a mortuary. The last time that we'd been here was on the morning of 30 September, 1888, following the murder of Elizabeth Stride in nearby Berner Street. I noticed it in more detail now, as that visit had occurred quite early, and there had been many more things on my mind than cataloging details regarding the building and its surroundings.

The mortuary, too, had its own smells, long familiar to both me and my friend. We identified ourselves to an attendant and were led to the sheet-covered body, one of three or four in a row on slabs at the back of the low-ceilinged room.

Father Tim was in his mid- to late twenties, likely a little over six feet, and thin. In fact, his body, while lanky by nature, was nearly emaciated.

There was a scent of ketosis about him, in addition to the expected early signs of decay.

"Holmes," I murmured. "He's been starving himself."

He simply nodded and continued his examination.

The young man had reddish hair and was clean-shaven. The wound on his head would have been instantly fatal – the left side of his frontal lobe was completely caved in. It could tentatively be assumed that he'd been struck by a right-handed man from the front. The blood had been washed away, and while Holmes would have preferred to examine the injury *in situ*, it was more visible that way.

The dead man's hands were rough, but there were no scars, and the nails were even, with no signs of nervousness, as would be shown if they were bitten down. His feet were quite calloused, as if he did a great deal of walking, and he had the beginnings of a bunion – he hadn't bothered to invest in the proper shoes.

Holmes and I both noted the scar on his lower right side of the young priest's abdomen, and then Holmes moved to an adjacent table, where a basket held the dead man's clothing. I could see that it was the plain and worn black suit as described to us, and Holmes's examination was quick, as there was clearly nothing to find. I could tell that the suit had an unwashed scent about it, as if Father Tim, whose body was itself clean, would bathe and then re-wear the same clothes.

With little left to find, we thanked the attendant and returned to our cab. "The surgical scar showed great skill," I said as we settled ourselves. "Most likely from an appendectomy. Could it indicate that Father Tim came from a comfortable background, with access to proper medical attention and a good doctor?"

"It's possible, although it doesn't firmly establish the fact. Poor men can also obtain medical treatment, even surgery, and a well-stitched scar doesn't have to be placed only by an expensive surgeon. It's indicative, but we can't make any firm conclusions from it."

With that, I didn't see that we had learned all that much, but the proper procedure of examining the body had been carried out, and there was still another avenue to explore. "The cross?" I asked, and Holmes nodded. I wasn't surprised that he directed the cabbie to an address in Hatton Gardens. I briefly considered intruding a thought about finding something to eat, but there would be time enough for that later, after every lead had been explored. We passed through Aldgate and circumnavigated the narrow streets around Barts to end our journey at the residence of Silas Hull, a retired jeweler who owed more than one debt to Holmes.

By then, Hull was not the famous figure that one recalls from the seventies and eighties. He had attached himself in those earlier days to many of the flamboyant figures that were regularly mentioned in the press. This practice had nearly ended with his imprisonment when he was implicated in a string of jewel thefts carried out by the younger son of Lord Byington. When questioned by the police, the arrogant lad had tossed out Hull's name, along with a number of others, in an attempt to confuse the issue. Over the years, Hull had made enemies, as he discovered to his surprise, and when his name was associated with the thieves, however falsely, many were quick to believe the accusations and use them to undercut his position in society. A year or so before this had occurred, Holmes had recovered some stolen objects for Hull, and thus it was because of this that the jeweler sought my friend's help in his time of jeopardy. Hull's innocence was established following a tense confrontation in a Mayfair drawing room. A careless comment by Lord Byington's sister had brought forth the truth, fortunately overheard by Inspector Lestrade, who had allowed himself to be folded and concealed behind a heavy sofa in order to record the confession from the true culprit.

We found Hull in poor health, smoking cigarette after cigarette while his browned fingers turned the cross over and over, muttering all the while. He wheezed and coughed, pulling himself upright each time to find capacity for the breath to do so. He had quite caved in during the months since we'd last seen him, and I feared that he was not long for this world. In truth, he lived another twelve years, never leaving his apartment throughout, before finally setting his bedsheets afire with a carelessly tossed-aside match.

"It is the Keadby Cross," he wheezed almost immediately after his gnarled fingers closed upon it. However, having identified it so easily, he continued to examine it. "Not seen in a generation at least. Where did you find it?"

"There is no doubt then?" asked Holmes, parrying Hull's question.

"None at all," the old man sighed, sounding like a collapsing and leaky bellows. Then he reluctantly he handed it back to Holmes, who replaced it in the tin box, and that into his coat pocket. Lighting a cigarette from the old one that had been smoked to the nub, Hull continued. "It is unknown when it was made, or where. The method of working the platinum is unknown – lost. That kind of thing happens more than you might realize. Only now are we starting to understand how to use platinum in jewelry. This is an ancient process – an ancient piece. The jewels are unusually cut – not a modern method or style at all. They are especially fine and pure. The cross was brought back from the Crusades, but as to its history before? Who knows?"

"And to whom does it belong?" asked Holmes.

135

Hull gave him a curious look. "You don't know? Well, that's interesting. It belongs to the Keadbys, of course. It was Sir Ashton, back in the first Crusade – sometime around 1100 A.D. – who carried it home, and it's been in the family ever since. Or so I thought. The fact that you have it, and didn't know whose it was, is most interesting . . . ."

He left the statement hanging, but Holmes asked another question. "Keadby. Would that be the family from Sparsholt?"

Hull nodded. "It would, it would!"

Holmes frowned, as if that fact provided a darker aspect to the matter.

Hull clearly wanted to know more about the cross, and when it became obvious that no further facts were forthcoming, he tried to interest us in other bits of London gossip in a rather pathetic attempt to keep our attention and lengthen our visit. We stayed and talked for a few more minutes to be polite, but when Hull started slyly delving for the true details of the Hinstock thefts, and what had really happened with Lady Ava's suicide which had so recently been reported in all the newspapers, Holmes stood and thanked the old man for his help. I glanced back at Hull's disappointed visage as the door shut, watching him lighting another cigarette with shaking hands.

Outside, Holmes hailed a cab, giving the address of a club in St. James's. My mouth tightened – I knew that he was seeking further information regarding the Keadbys, and where we were going to obtain it.

As I stepped from the cab, I looked up at the bow window of the club where Langdale Pike spent his days, and saw the languid man watching us. Even from that distance, and with the morning light playing tricks on the glass, his smile at our arrival was obvious.

During my time in the army, and also during certain of Holmes's investigations, I'd had the opportunity to visit the warm climes where reptiles are far more common than Britain. There are some that crawl out on rocks each morning to absorb the sun's warmth, only moving when necessary, to feed or carry out other basic functions before returning to their lairs at night. I didn't know exactly where Pike's lair was located – in his club perhaps, or in a nearby building – but his daily settlement in the bow window, where he gathered those bits of random stories, tales, and tittle-tattle that earned him his bread-and-butter, always reminded me of the actions of those cold-blooded creatures, and I never approached him without feeling the same sort of distaste.

He and Holmes had known each other for many years, and I knew that my friend felt much the same as I did, but Pike was one of the useful tools in Holmes's drawer, and he had his purposes – such as this case, where he almost certainly held some knowledge of the Keadbys.

"Holmes! Watson! It's been too long," said Pike, attempting to right himself from where he'd been sprawled on a purple divan. Thank heavens there were solid and sensible chairs sitting nearby. I imagine that Pike had learned early on to supply them for his informants. "I haven't seen you since you called about that business last June in Whittesley Street. Did matters end satisfactorily? I confess that I've been unable to ferret out exactly what happened next."

"The Duke fled," replied Holmes succinctly. "With his wife's blessing." He leaned forward. "What do you know of the Keadbys of Sparsholt?"

Pike's watery eyes widened, and a wily smile turned up a corner of his mouth. "Now that is an interesting tale. Do you want something to drink?"

We settled for tea which was soon delivered, and Pike tipped something into his from a pocket flask. I sipped mine gratefully, but Holmes pushed his aside. "It's rather a sad story," Pike explained. "The Keadbys were once a great family, but are now down to the very last of them – should he even still be alive. Still a lot of money, though."

Holmes didn't comment, and after a sip, Pike continued. "Five years ago, Sir Brent Keadby died. If you recall, he owned a number of mills in the north, all managed by very competent managers and lawyers, leaving him free to live the life of a country gentleman. He had been widowed for many years, and upon his death, he left behind two children, twins, both in their early twenties: A son Timothy, and a daughter Lydia. These two couldn't have been more different. The boy was always a disappointment to his father – considered weak by the irascible old man, who was well into middle-age before the children were born. Timothy had no interest in business or the family affairs, being instead a scholar of sorts – fascinated by religion, as I recall. He would have been happy to hide away at some university, wandering through the libraries for the rest of his washed-out life. His sister, however, was much more direct about her necessities, and she always got along well with her father, having seemingly inherited his brusque traits. In spite of their differences, the two twins were always close, even though they went along very different paths. Lydia remained in Sparsholt while Timothy went away to school."

"You acted as if one of the twins was still living – 'should he still be alive'," I said. "Yet you also mention both of them in the past tense."

"Yes. About four years ago, not quite a year after Sir Brent died, a man – Stephen Lett – began to pay court to Lydia. His family has something to do with the docks in Southwark, and apparently they met when both were in Portsmouth on unrelated business. You know the type – suave, mysterious, intriguing, and clearly after her fortune. I suspect that she knew it, but it's likely that she saw something useful about him – or so she thought – and she probably believed that she could control him. She should have done a little research. He's at least twenty years older than she was, and he'd had two previous marriages that ended in the unexpected deaths of his wealthy brides. In any event, he moved quickly and married her – it was a nine days' wonder – and took possession of the house in Sparsholt, as well as making himself free with his wife's half of the fortune. From what I heard, she quickly realized that she had opened her door to a scoundrel, but as is always the case, it was too late.

"The marriage was tense from the beginning, as would be expected, and Lett soon resented being trapped in Hampshire for so much of the time. My little birds were quite informative, and they willingly shared, for a few coins here and there, how the arguments escalated when the marital familiarity bred expected contempt. There were rumors of cries in the night, and bruises upon the young lady that weren't really explained by her stories of a sudden clumsiness that had never previously affected her.

"Timothy, who had been pursuing studies in Durham, came home to try and stand up to Lett, and that's where the story becomes a bit more murky. I've had the statements from three people who were there, and they are in agreement, but what they've related to me only tells part of the tale. On the night that Timothy arrived, there was a tremendous row between him and Lett – with a great deal of shouting from the both of them, and Lydia as well, all behind the locked doors of the late Sir Brent's study. It went on for hours, long into the night, but at one point things fell abruptly silent, and eventually the servants went to bed, realizing that the evening's entertainment was at an end.

"The next morning after the fight, the servants were told by their mistress that Master Timothy had departed in the night to return to school. But a few weeks later, one of the maids saw a message Timothy's school in Durham, inquiring as to his whereabouts, as he'd never returned after his visit to Sparsholt. Of course that only fed the fires of rumor. Later, when months went by and no word was ever heard from Timothy, the whispers below stairs ripened into open belief that Lett must have killed young Timothy in the heat of the argument, with his sister's apparent approval, but that seemed to be no more than sensational speculation.

"After Timothy's departure, Lydia seemed to have forgiven her husband for whatever stood between them. And yet, soon after the night of the argument, Lett began to act more agitated. He was seen on a regular basis searching the house for something, but he wouldn't reveal what it was and reacted angrily when any help was offered. Over time, whatever warmth that had reignited between husband and wife cooled, and again there was a pall over the house, while Lett continued to run through his

138

wife's inheritance. She resumed having unusual bruises, making no effort to hide or excuse them, and then she began to drink more heavily. Of Timothy there continued to be no sign at all.

"And so it went, with Lett dividing his time between the Hampshire house and London, until last spring, when Lydia was found dead, apparently stricken by some sort of seizure in the night. Lett was home at the time, and found her. By all accounts, he was most dramatically grief-stricken. A doctor-friend of his quickly certified the cause of death as related to Lydia's ever-increasing alcohol consumption, and she was buried within days. Since then, Lett has spent most of his time carousing with his cronies at Sparsholt, with regular trips to London. Too regular, some would say . . . ."

"What do you mean?" asked Holmes, leaning forward. "Would these trips perhaps be around the middle of the month?"

Pike smiled and crossed his legs. "It would be lunacy to suggest otherwise."

Holmes slapped his knee, a smile on his face. "Of course – the fact that I couldn't recall! For the past six months or so, the full moon has occurred in the middle of the month!"

"Hold on for a moment," I interrupted. "Are you saying that Lett's trips into London are somehow related to the full moon?"

"And why not?" asked Pike. "Lett wouldn't be the first to feel such a pull. By all accounts – and I've heard that this has gone on for a few years – he becomes restless during the week before the full moon, and while his wife was alive, that was the period when the worst of their difficulties took place."

"And you have all of this information from the servants?" I asked.

Pike nodded. "It is well-known where such information may be delivered, and the messengers earn a small bit of financial gratitude."

"It strikes me," I said with a great deal of acid in my tone, "that you are only a few steps sideways from that bloated spider, Milverton. Doesn't he use the same methods?"

Pike's normally indifferent and slightly amused expression darkened in an instant, his lidded eyes flashed, and his voice hardened in a way that I'd never heard before. "The difference between that villain and myself," he said, his normally even-tones harsh and clipped, "is as divided as black and white. I would never use what I learn to injure anyone, and never to inflict pain through blackmail. The information that I gather is used to help in ways that you don't even realize, Doctor. If you only knew what happened to my parents while I was at university, you would never – "

He stopped suddenly, as if his throat had closed, and glanced toward Holmes, who was lost in his own thoughts. Then, by conscious decision, he settled back into the familiar Pike of the bow window, passing the day by watching the world slip by. Only now did I realize that the man whom I had seen all these years might very well be a façade of someone much more capable – and perhaps dangerous. Recalling that he and Holmes had known each other since their college days, and seeing how Pike had looked at Holmes when mentioning the misfortune of his past, I suspected that my friend had in some way assisted the gossip-monger at that time, but I was also aware that it was likely a story that I would never be told.

"In any case," I said to smooth the waters, "I don't disagree with you regarding the effects of the full moon. As any medical man will tell you, there is a demonstrable relation between the moon's phases and agitated behaviors, although some of the theories as to why this occurs are utter nonsense. We simply don't understand enough of the ways of the human mind to provide a full explanation."

Holmes had ignored this last exchange and appeared to be considering how to proceed. After Pike and I fell silent, we sat there for several minutes. Then Holmes spoke. "Watson and I are investigating a murder," he began simply, and then he told what we had seen and heard that morning, how Father Tim was certainly Timothy Keadby, who departed from his family home following the argument with Lett and showed up in London soon after, wearing priest's clothing to which he had no right, and devoting himself to the poor and downtrodden of eastern London. He finished by letting Pike hold the Keadby Cross.

"I would posit that after the argument with Lett concluded," Holmes stated, "Timothy Keadby was so mentally wounded, possibly by his sister's betrayal in taking Lett's side rather than his own, that he fled, convinced that he couldn't return to his former life. However, before he departed, he retrieved the family heirloom from wherever it was kept in the house, feeling that it couldn't fall into Lett's hands. He vanished into the warrens of Whitechapel and Spitalfields, apparently content to remain there."

"And meanwhile," said Pike, "after the suspicious death of his latest wife, Lett, now off the leash, began journeying up to London in the middle of each month – around the time of the full moon – either because of the city's opportunities to satisfy his peculiar tendencies that were absent in Hampshire, or the anonymity to partake of them, or both."

He emptied his teacup and rang for more. "I've gathered reports of some of Lett's activities while he's sojourned here in the capital. The signs of violence that were evident upon his poor wife in the months before her demise have appeared on a number of young women here as well. These unfortunates aren't of a social class to be able to successfully accuse him of anything, and yet they do have a certain amount of protection, and it is

140

only his ability to reward them financially afterwards that has prevented his arrest."

The attentive waiter arrived with another pot of tea, and Pike and I accepted refills. Holmes waved away an attempt to replace his still-full and now-cold first cup.

"I'm glad that you sought me out," said Pike. "I've accumulated quite a dossier on Stephen Lett since he came to my attention, but I didn't yet feel that I had enough to notify anyone. The death of Timothy Keadby – and it is almost certainly him – adds a new layer to the affair. If we can establish that Lett was in London two nights ago when Timothy was murdered – "

" – then we still won't have enough to bring charges against him," finished Holmes. "It is nothing more than a supposition, a coincidence. But perhaps we do have enough of an idea to focus the investigation more intensely, with the result that we can uncover additional facts, and perhaps rattle Lett into making a mistake." And then he added, "I would advise a Council of War with the official force."

And so messages were sent to Sergeant Corby and our old friend Inspector Lestrade. It was decided that Pike's club was as fitting a location as any for a meeting, and while awaiting the arrival of the policemen, we had a late luncheon in the facility's well-appointed dining room. Holmes toyed with his food, as was to be expected, but I enjoyed mine, and found my attitude thawing toward Pike, who related a few facts that I hadn't heard about Milverton the blackmailer. Clearly he was accumulating them with the idea that they would be useful upon some future date when Holmes finally confronted the evil conniver.

We had resettled ourselves in the bow window when the policemen arrived. Holmes explained to Corby that the nature of our findings had necessitated a higher level of authority. Then he outlined our involvement, including both the facts that we had told Pike, and also what we had subsequently learned from him. Corby was stunned that Holmes had identified the priest in such a short amount of time, but Lestrade waved this away, saying that if he continued to work with Mr. Holmes, he would soon get used to it. Then the inspector leaned forward, asking, "What should we do now? I agree that there is almost certainly a direct connection between this Lett and the murdered man, but there is a gap between that and establishing Lett as the killer."

"As Pike mentioned before your arrival," answered Holmes, "we first need to find out whether Lett was in London two nights ago."

"Easy enough," said Lestrade, rising. "I assume that this club has a telephone?"

Pike gave him directions and, while we waited, Corby asked additional questions about the Keadby Cross. This led to the topic of the First Crusade, and Holmes related the curious history of Baldwin of Edessa, the first King of Jerusalem, and his more well-known brother Godfrey, the defender of the Holy Sepulchre, and the curious letter related to both of them that Holmes had once secured from the collection of a Prussian poisoner because of certain damaging facts that it contained which cast dark implications upon the British Crown itself.

Lestrade returned, telling us that, "According to the local constable, who verified the information by way of his brother the station-master, Stephen Lett left on the up-train to London two days ago, was away on the night of the murder, and returned the following morning – that is to say, yesterday. He looked much the worse-for-wear, as he often does following one of his jaunts, but most curiously, he left again this morning on the London train."

Holmes nodded. "Today is the full moon – when he regularly visits the metropolis due to its strange influence upon him."

Lestrade frowned and shook his head. "One of those."

"It would seem so," was Holmes's reply. "But two nights ago he came to London because he was searching for his brother-in-law – and the Keadby Cross."

"That seems to be rather a leap, Mr. Holmes," said Corby.

"Not really," replied Holmes. "Consider: Timothy Keadby began leaving his lodgings in April – around the same time that Lett first began coming to London during the full moon after the death of his wife. It's safe to assume that somehow Timothy saw Lett and wished to lay low in order to avoid him. Possibly he was aware of his brother-in-law's lunar proclivities, or else he asked around and determined when Lett was showing up in London.

"In any case, he was successful at avoiding the man for half-a-year, but somehow Lett finally found him. He didn't just encounter Timothy by chance two nights ago near the cemetery. No, he was in London during a time when he would normally be in Hampshire. It was an intentional trip. He had a good idea about how to find Timothy. They argued, and no doubt Lett demanded the Keadby Cross, which he had sought ever since Timothy liberated it. But Timothy, probably certain that Lett had killed his sister, and yet terrified of the man, refused to turn it over, so Lett killed him. Only through Timothy Keadby's foresight in leaving the cross with a friend are we able to follow along and make sure that justice is served."

We formulated a plan over the next hour or so, with both Holmes and Lestrade slipping away at regular intervals – Lestrade to use the telephone, and Holmes to find and instruct one of his agents. Additionally, a police vehicle was sent to fetch Denholm Waitrose of Barbican, the long-time solicitor to the Keadby family, and when he arrived, he was able to provide valuable insight confirming how Lett had gained the trust of Lydia, and more importantly how Waitrose alone had known of Timothy's residence in London, being the source of the funds that the young man had used to pay for his meagre life.

He explained that when Timothy had originally returned to the family home at Sparsholt with the intention of protecting his sister, he had found that she was completely under Lett's spell. As the argument waxed and waned over several hours, it had become apparent that Lydia had been turned against her brother, body and soul, which broke his heart. Always quite sensitive, he couldn't conceive of returning to what he suddenly saw as an empty existence, duly attending his classes for no apparent purpose, and that very night he came to London, recreating himself as the priest who spent the rest of his life ministering to the unfortunates there. Until we told him, Waitrose hadn't known that young Timothy Keadby was the man murdered in Whitechapel – he was quite upset about it – and he'd also had no idea that the Keadby Cross had been carried away by Timothy when he fled Sparsholt, as no word about it had passed the young man's lips or had reached him by way of Lydia or Lett.

After the lawyer was thanked and dismissed, we debated a few final points, including whether our efforts would result in anything that would lead to Lett's arrest. "I believe," said Holmes, "that he has tasted blood, so to speak, less than forty-eight hours ago, and that he will find it easier to do so again. He is feeling powerful now, and arrogant."

"You speak as if you know this, Holmes," said Pike.

"Watson and I have encountered this man's type before," replied the consulting detective.

"As have I," concurred Lestrade. "If he's as affected by the moon as it sounds, there's a good chance that he'll be looking to kill again tonight."

While the inspector said this, Corby glanced at him, and I was glad to see that, despite his younger years, he was willing to listen and learn.

Finally, with our plans and facts and assumptions in place, we stood, prepared to commence our campaign. Pike shook our hands and gave us to understand that his contributions were limited to what he could provide from his divan, and that he expected to hear the end of the story – hopefully within the next twenty-four hours.

The resources of the officials were able to establish through questioning at Waterloo that Lett had arrived in London on the up-train from Winchester. The cabbie was located who had conveyed him to a small private hotel in Dysart Street, near Finsbury Square, and one of Holmes's Irregulars confirmed with the hotel's owner that Lett stayed there whenever he visited, like clockwork, in the middle of the month for at least the past six months.

The bright blue day had darkened as the hours passed, and by the time we concealed ourselves around Lett's hotel, there was the hint of dampness in the air that indicated fog. I dreaded it, recalling too many nights spent in this same manner, keeping an individual under observation, waiting for hours until he came out and moved around (if he came out at all), and then furtively and frantically following while ever-hoping that the rolling mists wouldn't provide him with cover just long enough to allow him to step out of sight and vanish.

I shrugged deeper into my overcoat, thankful that I had it, and also for my service revolver in my pocket – something that I had learned long ago never to leave behind.

Luckily we didn't have long to wait, as the pull of the full moon, still visible at times through the thickening clouds, exerted its attraction to our quarry. Just after six o'clock, he emerged.

We had circulated a description of Lett, as provided by Denholm Waitrose. Holmes had quietly confirmed it with the hotel manager, so it was easy enough to recognize the tall man who stood for a moment underneath the gas-lamp at the corner. High cheekbones on a thin face, with a rather thick and unpleasant mustache. Even from my position across the way, ostensibly reading a newspaper under the opposite gas-lamp, I could see that his unusual eyes matched their description: Very light, with a great deal of white showing around the pupils. In the dim light, it looked as if his pupils didn't exist at all, and that he was some reanimated lych setting forth in search of prey. I shivered.

He ambled off to the east, and his gait was unsteady, as if he had already been drinking heavily. He passed through Finsbury Market by the stationery works, and then set his steps to a public house on the corner of Vandy Street. Moments later, he was followed inside by Lestrade. My post was in the street, and I found a sheltered doorway in which to tarry for a while.

Lestrade later reported that Lett stood at the bar, tall and moving unnaturally as if he were supported by unseen wires that were being plucked randomly and from different directions. He looked around while consuming two pints in a quick manner before apparently deciding that what he sought wasn't there. He left quickly, and our group followed him as he again headed east – a mixture of plainclothes policemen, Holmes's band of irregulars racing ahead on the side streets, and of course my friend and me.

He walked alternately fast and slow along Market Street, turning into Appold Street just long enough to reach the passage underneath the wide

144

expanse of railway tracks, and then he was soon in White Lion Street, just a few blocks north of the Spitalfields Market. At Commercial Street he turned south, and within moments we were passing by the Ten Bells, where these events had started just that morning. He didn't spare a glance at the pub, but very soon, just after passing Christ Church, he turned into the graveyard, and then stopped at the entrance to Harriot Place, where Timothy Keadby had been murdered two nights before.

While it was entirely possible that Lett could have simply decided to visit the site where his brother-in-law had died, this was highly unlikely. Until that afternoon when Holmes connected the missing Keadby with Father Tim, no one knew the background of the dead man. In my mind, Lett's visitation of this spot proved his guilt.

He didn't pause there for very long. Back into Commercial Street, he crossed and went along Whites Row. The hour was early enough that there were still a number of people on the streets, and he attracted no attention – and more importantly, he didn't notice the crew that was following him. When he reached Bell Lane, he entered another pub, and this time Holmes followed him inside. The sense that I had jumped six years into the past, and the Autumn of Terror in 1888, was becoming rather overwhelming. All that had occurred in those intervening years – my marriage and subsequent widowhood, and Holmes's presumed death and reappearance – might not have happened at all. Here I was, once again tracking a killer through the streets of Whitechapel, the air cool with the approach of winter, and the poverty and despair of the district still as overwhelming as it had ever been. For a moment I wished that it was 1888 once more. I would make a number of different choices, and also provide words of warning for my friend, so that he never even considered approaching the dread ledge above the Falls of Reichenbach.

But I was forced back to the here and now when the pub door slammed open, causing a spill of noise to rush my way as sounds of the raucous crowd inside spilled forth. Stephen Lett was moving once again, and Sherlock Holmes was not far behind.

Our path roamed up and down the streets for the next half-hour. Lett paused when he saw a pair of unfortunate women loitering near Toynbee Hall, as if he wished to approach, but something prevented him from doing so. He visited two more public houses, leaving each soon after entering, before he spotted a solitary woman of the night near the public wash house in Goulston Street. He approached her with confidence, and apparently an agreement was reached quickly, for they set off together, turning into the darkness of Elison Street, and so into a mean little building squatting on the north side.

Once the door had shut, we collected nearby and quickly assigned posts for the various troops, some guarding the front, and some the back. Then Holmes, Lestrade, Corby, and I entered the building.

I had some misgivings about where to look, but immediately after ascending the stairs as quietly as we could to the first floor, we heard a woman's cry, fearful and then immediately silenced. Without hesitation, Holmes approached the doorway and kicked it open.

Thank heavens she was not dead, but it was a very close thing. Lett had the garments at her throat bunched in his left hand while the right held some sort of short-bladed knife – I would later learn that it was originally a specialized instrument used by farriers for popping stones from out of horses' hooves, but the end had been ground and sharpened to make it lethal. The woman was bleeding from a blow to the head, and appeared rather dazed and senseless. As the door slammed open and the four of us crowded in, Lett seemed confused, but also as if his senses had fled. His light eyes appeared to be blank and empty, and I didn't sense that he understood what was happening. Then, as if his compulsion controlled him, he pulled back his hand to accomplish is intention of killing the poor woman.

"Lett!" cried Holmes. "The cross!"

He had pulled the Keadby Cross from his pocket and was holding it before him, approaching the madman slowly. Any thoughts of murder temporarily seemed to slip from Lett's mind as he focused on the jewel-encrusted object, able to catch even the dimmest light in that room and reflect back an unnatural shimmer of winking fire. He let go of the woman's clothing, and she sank to the floor with a moan. If I'd hoped that he would drop the knife as well, I was mistaken. He shifted his grip and stepped toward Holmes, his eyes only on the cross, and reaching for it with his left hand even as his right was extending toward the unarmed detective.

We have argued since then who stopped him first. I maintain that my bullet was obviously faster than Holmes's own actions. And yet, when he pivoted to avoid the thrust of the knife while jamming the end of the cross deeply into Lett's left eye, he moved faster than I could follow. Perhaps it was just a trick of the light, but I didn't realize that he'd done it, until the man cried and pulled back, the five inches of metal still impaled into his eye socket. With a groan he collapsed, his blighted soul having already departed, and it was only later that the two bullet holes were found at his heart. Lestrade, it turned out, had fired his own pistol as well.

When Lett's personal effects were examined the next day, a trove of diaries and hideous souvenirs confirmed that he was a murderer many times over, and that his descent into madness had begun long before his

146

joining with the Keadby family. Details of the deaths of his first two wives, as well as that of Lydia and a number of other unfortunate women, made for disturbing reading – and yet, what was seen in those papers proved to be quite useful in training others in later years to recognize that particular type of madness. One could only wish that such knowledge had been available when hunting the various members of The Ripper Cabal during the autumn of '88.

There hadn't been much time for Lett to record the details of Timothy Keadby's killing, but what little there was seemed to confirm that during one of his trips to London under the influence of the full moon, he'd spotted his missing brother-in-law – and he himself had been spotted in return. He had continued to return to London's East End each month to satisfy his peculiar and escalating impulses, while also seeking Timothy as a means to locate the Keadby Cross, an obsession that only increased with the passage of time. Timothy had clearly left the area during those times, hoping to avoid a further encounter with Lett, but finally on one dark night, the two met. Lett threatened Timothy angrily, eventually striking him down, but without learning the location of that which he sought. This frustration only served further to drive him into insanity.

With none of the Keadby family left, and without any relatives or heirs connected to Stephen Lett, the status of the entire Keadby fortune was suddenly the subject of much discussion throughout London. The facts related to Lett's murder of his brother-in-law, as well as his own dramatic passing, only added fuel to the telling. Eventually Denholm Waitrose, the Keadby family attorney, managed to cut through the complications that threatened to strangle the dispersal of the estate and, working with both Isaiah Clark and – surprisingly – Langdale Pike, a charitable trust was established for the poor of Whitechapel and Spitalfields. Among the first to receive aid was the sad woman who had nearly been killed by Lett, saved only by our intervention. She herself became an advocate for the poor, and served admirably in this role until her death.

The Keadby Cross was gifted to the British Museum, where it vanished into the vaults and hasn't been seen publicly again. And except for this narrative, it's unlikely that anyone has given any thought to it in the two decades that have passed since these events occurred.

The Adventure at
Dead Man's Hole
by Stephen Herczeg

It was a dreary day in mid-October that found Sherlock Holmes and me standing on the northern bank of the Thames. To our backs the great stone walls of the Tower rose up, blocking out what little light there was, casting us into a perpetual twilight and robbing us of any heat that the sun might provide. To our left the mighty north tower of the bridge loomed above us.

Although the bridge's construction had officially finished several months before, there was still a certain amount of work that continued to be done. Shouts rang down from above as the workers went about their business. The clanking of metal and striking of rivets rang out across the slowly moving river as the final construction of the bridge went ahead, heedless of our activities.

The object of our visit lay below, the stinking silt and mud of the riverbed. I could see numerous deep holes in the mud, which could only mean that Lestrade and his men had combed the area for clews before we had been called.

I imagined the fuming anger brewing within Holmes's mind as he surveyed the destitution that was the supposed location of a crime. And it was no surprise when he said, "You would think, Watson, that by now Lestrade would understand not to utterly destroy the evidence of a crime before he calls upon me."

"I do agree, but as I understand it, he wasn't even here when the body was removed, so in his defence he had no control over the matter." My reply met with a solid and angry harrumph, which brought a slight grin to my face.

The body had been found earlier that morning by one of the workers as they arrived for their shift. There had been no surprise or hurry for that matter in recovering the corpse. This area was renowned for trapping anything that floated down the mighty river. The tides of late had ebbed and flowed with remarkable heights as a full moon smiled down on the city at night, bringing with it the waters, but taking them away once morning broke.

In a city of the size and with the vitality of life that London possessed, it was little wonder that numerous cadavers washed up on her banks during the course of a year.

The area was also the daily home to hundreds of workers employed on building the mightiest bridge to ever grace the cityscape. Accidents happened, far too regularly for my liking, which had forced the creation of what came to be known as Dead Man's Hole.

The designers of the bridge had included a small thoroughfare through which pedestrians could quickly circumnavigate the northern tower and gain access to the nearest bank of the Thames. Sadly, as more and more workers succumbed to gravity and other accidents associated with construction on such a large scale, a place needed to be set aside to house the bodies of these unfortunates until they could be collected by the coroner or a mortician. The pylons and footings of the new bridge also provided an unforeseen hazard, whereby they became a catchment area for all and sundry that floated down the river. Many times, that included the corpses of animals and humans. The watchmen who patrolled the shoreline were tasked with releasing animal bodies to the mercy of the river and to ensure that any humans were taken into the Dead Man's Hole to await their fate.

It was to the Hole that Holmes and I had been drawn by an early morning telegram from Inspector Lestrade of Scotland Yard. I was shaken awake by Holmes's entreaties and virtually dragged from my bed chamber and piled into a hansom even before I broke my fast. I think that Holmes had been a little bored of late, and any evidence of a crime worthy of his attention was a singular delight to his mind.

The dour overcast day and chilling breeze did nothing to enliven my spirits, which continued to claw at my conscience with cries for coffee and breakfast.

The hansom had dropped us off near the corner of the Tower, and we'd made our way across the small rutted track that serviced the construction site and towards the North Tower of the bridge.

Lestrade met us, looking almost as tired and worn out as I felt.

"Sorry to bring you out this early, Mr. Holmes," he said, "but this one's got me puzzled."

"I do hope so," said Holmes as we clamoured our way across the mud track and onto the small concourse at the base of the bridge.

The Dead Man's Hole, as I would come to know it, was little more than a covered tunnel, but had been shut off from public access by a series of wooden barricades. I was unsure if they had been there before or were for the benefit of the current occupant.

Inside the temporary room we met with a young man who went by the name of Byron Smith. He introduced himself as the coroner's assistant and shook each of our hands. Dispensing with any small talk, to Holmes's apparent delight, he showed us five lumps lying on the floor covered in stained white sheets.

Smith quickly explained that they had found four bodies in the last three days, three of which were obviously street people that had fallen into the Thames. He pointed to a fourth body and explained it was an unfortunate worker that had fallen from the South Tower rigging just the day before. The last body was the reason for our visit.

Before Smith could unveil it, Holmes turned to Lestrade.

"You haven't explained why this one has you flummoxed," he said.

"No, I haven't," he said, nodding at Smith, who quickly drew back the sheet. "See for yourself."

"Good Lord!" I gasped.

Holmes simply stared at the body, a hand cradling his chin, and murmured to himself.

Before us lay an extremely sorrowful sight. It was difficult to tell the actual age, but it looked at first sight like the body of a young man, or more of a boy, but that would need further confirmation. His skin was sallow and puffed, indicating a prolonged amount of time beneath the surface of the water. It glistened in places from the presence of adipocere, a waxy substance that forms from the fat on bodies in water and protects them from decay. His hair was matted and dark, his eyes closed shut from engorgement. He was completely nude, showing the brutalisation that he had suffered at the hands of the elements. To add to the peculiarity, a thick strand of rope was still tied around his ankles.

I made him to be around five-feet ten-inches tall. His weight was obscured by the bloating, but my instincts told me that he had been between nine and ten stone.

Holmes dropped to his knee to make a closer inspection of the corpse. I stepped closer, mindful of the dim light in the tunnel, and gasped again when I made out the scarring on the body.

"You see it then, Watson?" Holmes said.

"What do you make of it?"

Holmes pointed to the marks on the body's chest. They weren't deep, merely superficial, made possibly with a knife or other sharp-bladed instrument. The edges had been puckered by the exposure to water. A long line ran from the throat to the navel, a smaller line ran across the chest just below the pectorals.

"That looks like a cross, but the horizontal line is too low, it's unsymmetrical," I said.

"Or inverted," Holmes said.

My eyes widened. I had seen that symbology before, but never in this way. It was then I noticed a single deeper wound on the left-hand side,

150

slightly above the horizontal line. It too was puckered, but was certainly not superficial.

"He was stabbed?" I said.

"Indeed he was. These lines were carved before he died. This," Holmes said pointing to the deeper wound, "was what killed him."

I took a deep breath. It was murder then, and not just some poor vagrant who had died of the cold.

I noticed a pattern of cuts on the forehead and pointed to them. "What are those?" I asked.

Holmes pulled out his glass and leaned in closer. I looked around and found a small portable gas lamp nearby. I brought it across and bent down to shed more light on the subject.

"My word," I mumbled in surprise at the strangely intricate pattern.

"Yes," murmured Holmes. "It's a pentagram. Inverted from the traditional wiccan form."

"Witches?" I asked, a hint of unreality in my voice.

"No, nothing like that," Holmes said. I breathed a sigh of relief. Witchcraft in any form was a strange world, especially if some were now delving into ritual sacrifice, as this seemed to indicate.

"This is worse," Holmes finished, before standing up. "This is Satanic."

I almost dropped the lamp in surprise.

"Satanic?" I asked.

Lestrade pitched in, "Satanic?" Even Smith's face dropped in shock.

"I do believe so," said Holmes, "The inverted cross. The inverted pentagram – both symbols of Satanic cults. The deep wound above the heart indicates how this man – " He stopped himself and peered at the corpse for a moment. "How this *boy* died."

"You think he was a boy as well, then?" I asked. He nodded. "My estimation is he was in the water for a good six months."

"I agree," said Holmes, "The level of water absorption, the amount of adipocere, and the lack of overall decay, would suggest that sort of timeline."

Lestrade spoke up. "Do you think he's from London?"

"That is impossible to tell," he said as he dropped down to his knees once again and pointed to marks on the corpse's wrists and neck, and to the rope tied around his feet. "These marks are burns from rope tied around them, just like the type around the feet. They indicate that the corpse was tied and probably weighted to keep it from floating away."

He stood again and turned, gazing off into the distance as if looking through the nearby tiled walls and out across the great river.

"The recent rains and the abnormally high tides have swelled the Thames upriver. Perhaps our friend here resided upstream and his bonds broke, sending him south and towards the sea. I wonder . . . ."

And that was how I found myself observing Holmes as he mud-larked about in the deep, stinking silt of the great river.

We had borrowed long leather waders from the site foreman and long leather gloves. I had to admit to a feeling of foolishness as I stood on the edge of the stone wall that formed the bank of the river. The waders came up to my chest and the gloves covered my hands and forearms. I felt like an out-of-place farmer or steel worker.

Holmes carefully trudged his way across the little area, stopping every so often to plunge his hand deep into the muck and fish around for any clews on offer. His efforts had elicited nothing but more mud. In fact, as I became more bored and my unsated hunger grew I began to question my erstwhile colleague's actions.

Finally, I cried out, "Holmes, what the devil are you searching for?"

He stopped and peered up at me, a familiar look on his face. "Why, I'm searching for clews," he said as if in answer to everything.

"Any clew in particular?" I asked, through my thinly disguised impatience.

At this he gave me his aggrieved look. "Well, we have nothing to tell us of this boy's origins. Is he from London? Is he from farther afield?"

I nodded, I already knew that, but still wondered.

"We have the rope," he began.

Again, I nodded. The rope was made of plain hemp, available in any store.

"To what was it attached?" he said.

At that I shrugged. "Some sort of weight, I imagine."

"Yes, excellent," he said, drawing breath to give me time to reply. When I didn't, he continued. "The body had to have been weighed down at some stage, for at least six months. It was so bloated that it would otherwise simply float on the surface, much like a cork or leaf, and not as subject to the tides. But if weighed down a little, the undercurrent would snatch it and drag it swiftly down river."

I nodded. It made sense – simple physics that I had seen during my own trips to the seaside.

"The weight itself could provide additional information," he said.

"Possibly not," I countered.

"That is also true," he said, a slightly annoyed tone to his voice.

He ducked down and drove his arm up the shoulder into the dirty brown water. He struggled slightly, then peered across to me.

"Watson, I don't suppose that you could assist me," he cried.

152

Not disguising my look of disgust, I moved towards the thin iron railings that acted as a ladder down to the riverbed. I reached the bottom and gingerly stepped off, my foot disappearing into the putrid mud. I stepped towards him amidst the most disgusting *schlooping* noises. Just as I reached him, he stood upright with his prize in hand. He smiled and turned towards me, surprised to find me only a few yards away.

"Never mind now," he said. "I've found it."

I bit my tongue to suppress any remonstration.

It wasn't until mid-morning that we returned to 221b Baker Street. Once she realised that we hadn't eaten, Mrs. Hudson was quick to bring up a sumptuous brunch with coffee. I thanked her effusively over the noise of my grumbling innards and set about demolishing the fare, whilst perusing the morning paper.

A sketch of the latest player on the political scene smiled up at me from the front page. Sir Geoffrey Warrington was a rising star in the ranks of the opposition party. He had previously made a name for himself as an industrialist trading in goods between the Continent and the United Kingdom, and now that he had entered politics, the thinking was that he would soon lead the Liberals into power at the next election in a couple of years' time. I turned the page over to find something less boring to read and soon lost track of time.

Holmes was concentrating on something in his chemical corner. I brought over a small plate of food and a cup of coffee, which he unconsciously ate and drank whilst studying the object of his attention. To me, it was just a bunch of stones, wrapped in a small hessian sack. A short trail of broken rope was attached, but Holmes had verified that it was the same as that which bound the corpse.

"I don't understand what's so fascinating about that," I said.

Holmes grinned. "And that is a little disappointing," he said. "What we have here is evidence."

He carefully emptied the stones onto the table and spread the hessian sack out next to them. He pointed at the sack and said, "This small sack has been cut from a larger open-weave bag and roughly sewn together with hemp twine. This type of hessian is used for the holding of root vegetables rather than grains – hence the open weave. It is still strong, but won't allow the vegetables to escape. The twine is ordinary, which is a shame."

He reached over and picked up one of the stones. It was round and smooth and consisted of a white stone, marked with specks of black and brown.

"This is interesting in two ways. First, it's smooth," he said, rotating the stone between his fingers, "but not perfectly spherical. It was smoothed by nature, rather than the hand of man. I would suggest from a running river."

He picked up his glass and peered closer at the stone itself. "The specks of black and brown rock within the conglomerate indicate that it is a type of white granite – not a very common stone, but one that is well known in particular regions."

He placed the stone down and moved across to the bookcase. He extracted a large volume of Ordnance Maps and plonked it down on the work bench. He flipped to London and placed his index finger on the Thames.

"We can assume that the body came downstream, probably due to the recent rains in the West Country which have filled the local streams and rivers and flushed them into the great river."

He came to the edge of the map near Hounslow, quickly turned the maps, following the river through Slough, up past Maidenhead, eventually stopped and placed his finger on Reading.

"Reading," I said, "Nothing ever happens in Reading. Why do you think this boy is from there?"

"He may not be from there, but that is where his body came from."

He pointed to the River Kennett and traced it up stream.

"The Kennett is one of the fastest flowing rivers that feeds the Thames. It just so happens that the area near Main Lake is home to several quarries that specialise in white granite. One could surmise that the corpse would have been placed into one of the quieter ponds in that area."

"How, exactly?" I asked.

"The poor unfortunate boy has been underwater for at least six months. Therefore, he was placed deep in a quiet body of water." I nodded. "The stones are from a river, probably just picked up from the bank as needed. The hessian material is from a bag used in a more rural area."

I nodded again. It all made sense. "So what now?"

Holmes looked blank for a moment. He stared at me, then his eyes dropped to what remained on his plate. He picked it up and replied, "Food. I think that I need to have a bite to re-invigorate my mind."

I was called away in the early afternoon and didn't return until the evening had settled in. I found Holmes and his brother Mycroft in the sitting room, engaged in a deep debate. Holmes looked across at my entrance with a dour expression on his face. I knew immediately that some new piece of information had come to light in my absence.

"You look exceedingly downcast."

Holmes nodded, as did Mycroft, "Yes, we are. Typically two events occurring on separate days would play no part in the same investigation, but when they transpire within hours of each other, the linkages blaze across my mind like fireworks."

"What's happened?" I asked, looking first at Holmes then at Mycroft, who simply raised his eyebrows and shrugged.

"Mycroft," he said, "has come with a request from a senior member of the House of Lords, Lord Howard Moncrieff."

I searched my memories and reminded myself. "Moncrieff? Isn't he the Earl of Dorchester or some such?" I asked.

Holmes nodded, "Well done, Watson. Precisely."

Still confused I pressed for more information, "And what has happened to him?"

"It seems that Alexander," said Mycroft, "the Moncrieff's teenage son, has vanished. Two days ago."

"But that isn't a long time – especially for a teenager. Perhaps he's run off on some lark for a few days with his friends."

"Perhaps. He disappeared from the school grounds of Pangbourne College. No-one has seen hide nor hair of him since."

The name Pangbourne rang bells within my mind. "Pangbourne College. But that's – " Then it hit home. My eyes widened, "That's just outside of Reading."

"Precisely, Watson, precisely."

"What did he look like?" I asked, my mind on fire.

Holmes held up his hands.

"Calm down, old friend. The body we examined is not Alexander Moncrieff. He is blonde haired, very slightly built, and has crystal blue eyes. Very different from the boy that was pulled from the river. And remember, the Moncrieff boy has only been gone two days, while the other spent six months in the water."

I relaxed but was still very intrigued. "But you think these two are related?"

"I do. At this stage, it is supposition, but the closeness of location, and the age of both, lead me to believe that there may be a connection." He stared at Mycroft for a moment, before saying, "Dear brother, is the Government keeping any files open on the activities of Satanic Cults within England at the moment?"

Mycroft's face remained stoic. "Why do you ask?"

"The boy found in the River had markings that suggest such. He was also killed by a single wound to the heart by a wide-bladed knife. It may have all been a prank gone wrong, but given this second boy's disappearance, I'm leaning towards the conjecture that he was sacrificed, and that there may be more."

"I do not know off-hand if there is anything, but I will make some inquiries. If I find anything, I will return. Until then, what do you plan to do, Sherlock?" asked Mycroft. I could tell he was aching to be gone. His face had shown a hint of disgust at the mention of Satanists, but from experience I knew that he was more than happy for his brother to undertake the more visceral detective side of such an investigation, and would rather hear of the success or failure at a later date rather than be involved in the deliberations.

"In the morning, I feel that Watson and I will away to Reading." He stepped across to his worktable and stared at the maps. "These drawings do not do justice to the physical locations. There should be more data that I can collect that will lead me to a more concrete conclusion. I don't like supposition *per se*, and would rather that my ideas be dashed with evidence than linger in my brain longer than necessary."

"Well, I wish you all the best. Keep me informed. If you find the boy alive, I'm sure the boy's parents will shower you with riches. If not, then at least they shall be at peace."

With that he left.

The constable at Reading Police Station read the letter from Lestrade again, just to make sure that he had our details square in his mind.

He peered up at Holmes, a quizzical look on his face, before he surprised both of us with his next utterance.

"What I'd like to know is, how do two gentlemen from London know about the disappearances?" he asked.

I was shocked. Lestrade had said that Moncrieff hadn't mentioned his vanished son to the police.

"Disappearances?" asked Holmes, placing a heavy inflection on the last syllable. I detected a slight tilt of his right eyebrow as the only evidence of his own surprise.

"Yes," said Constable Corden, eyeing each of us again. "Disappearances."

Holmes continued. "I only mentioned the one body found in the Thames. I don't think that I said anything about any others."

Corden realised he'd made a mistake. He stared at Holmes for a moment, possibly running the conversation back through his mind before nodding.

"So you did," he said finally, "So you did." He reread Lestrade's letter, averting his gaze for a moment before re-locating his confidence. "Well, that's settled then." He looked around. The only other person in the station was a drunk, lying prostate in a cell at the rear of the building. I doubted if the man could hear or even if he would have cared, but Corden leant forward and whispered, "There have been four so far. Regular as clockwork, near the end of the month. All young boys, around mid-teens. Their distraught parents or friends come in. They can't find little Johnny – he's run off or something. I've had no evidence of any foul play, and I'm at my wits' end, but I try to reassure them as best as I can."

He moved across to a nearby desk and brought back a thick file, full of loose papers. He opened it and picked up the top page.

"Neville Borthox: Fourteen, five-foot six-inches tall, dark hair, brown eyes, around ten-stone nine-pounds. Went missing one month ago. Last seen on the Abbey School grounds close to sunset."

I look at Holmes, he shook his head.

"Not our boy," he said.

Corden picked up another sheet.

"Reginald, or Reggie, Hyde-Northam: Fifteen, five-foot eight-inches, nine-stone six-pounds, fair hair, green eyes. Missing for two months. Last known location, Leighton Park Public School."

He flipped to another sheet.

"Clarke Greggson: Thirteen, five-foot two-inches, seven-stone nine-pounds, red hair, green eyes. Missing for almost three months. Last seen at St. Josephs College."

He picked up the final sheet, read his own report and nodded several times, whilst murmuring under his breath.

"I remember this one. Garrison Wainwright: Sixteen, big boy, five-feet ten-inches tall, ten-stone, dark hair, brown eyes. Reported missing four months ago but hadn't been seen for two months before that. Parents thought he'd just run off. Weren't that worried, to be honest."

"Where was he last seen?"

"He was from Farley Field, down south. Out of school. Worked his father's farm. The parents are salt-of-the-Earth types. Not too bright, but hard working. As I said, they weren't worried. He'd run off before. The father's a bit of a drinker and gets a might handy. When he hadn't come home for two months, the mother started to get worried and reported it."

I said, "It sounds like our boy then."

Holmes nodded. He reached into his pocket and brought out the Ordnance Map of the area. He quickly plotted the last known locations of each boy. They were scattered around the area, but even with five points they formed a slight ring around the town of Reading. The location of Pangbourne College was outside the defined area. The Thames ran through the very centre of the ring.

Holmes pointed to a series of ponds and lakes that flanked the River Kennett upstream from its confluence with the Thames near Reading. He peered up at Constable Corden and said, "Could you take us to this area?"

Then, after the officer had walked away, he added, "I'll also send a telegram to Lord Moncrieff. I think that we might need to visit him this afternoon."

The police station had access to a simple cart that they used for carrying several men to situations when required. Corden enlisted one of the junior constables to drive, and the three of us sat in the rear. The station wasn't far from the banks of the river. We crossed a large bridge and continued to follow the southern bank towards the series of lakes that had interested Holmes so much.

The area near the river was lined with deep thickets of trees, the land opening up to farms and fields on the south, with dry stone walls bordering each allotment. The river still ran quite strongly. I could hear the constant bubble as water washed across the small rapids created by the build-up of rocks and stones. It was a totally different sound to the slow languid pace that the Thames achieved even during an exceedingly wet spring.

Holmes had his Ordnance Map open in his lap and was keeping track of where we were in relation to the geographical points of interest marked by the cartographers. To the south I could see the large granite quarry that serviced Reading and provided her with stone and lime for building works.

As we approached a point on the river where it split into two, Holmes called out to the driver, "Take the south fork, please."

We turned and picked our way slowly along the disused rutted track. To our left passed a series of large and small ponds. I glanced at Holmes's map and saw that they were all connected by a network of small streams.

Holmes noticed my interest and said, "This whole area is a major wetland consisting of ponds and lakes, all joined by tiny rivulets that become raging torrents during the wet season."

"I don't understand where you are taking us, though," I said.

Holmes pointed to a small pond at the end of this particular branch of the river.

"Here. From the facts I have at hand, my deductions have led me to this spot."

He looked up from the map and pointed. "In fact, we are here," he said. Corden and I looked in the direction of his finger.

A small calm pond sat at the end of the southern branch of the river. The driver circumnavigated the bank and pulled up on the western side. We stepped out of the cart and onto the muddy ground. Luckily, Holmes had the foresight to insist that we both bring heavy boots. Corden knew the area well and had brought his own from the station.

I peered around. The pond was small, but very still. A tiny inlet on the northern side was the source of water from the larger branch of the river. The water drained on the eastern side, running down that branch until it re-joined further east.

Holmes glanced around for a moment then headed towards the tiny inlet. Corden, the driver, and I hurried after him, struggling to keep up with his rate of stride through the boggy ground.

"A-ha!" he said once we reached the inlet. It was there I saw the object of his attention. The inlet joined the pond to a sharp bend in the river. The bank of the river was littered with masses of round white stones of the same type as we had seen in London.

Holmes studied the area for a moment before peering across the pond. He glanced down at the muddy ground, shaking his head slightly and making *tsk*-ing noises. He gently stepped along the banks of the pond, hunched over and examining the ground as he moved.

Finally, he stood and let out a small triumphant shout.

I walked up next to him, mindful of staying close to his own footsteps and asked, "What have you found?"

He pointed at the sodden ground and I could just make out several of the small round stones, half-pushed into the mud. Several deep holes, which I presumed to be footprints, ran down to the water's edge.

"I assume you detect the presence of bootprints amongst the mud and grasses?" Holmes asked.

I was astonished all the same but had to nod at Holmes's remarkable find. "How?"

Holmes turned to me with a wide grin on his face. "Simple deduction. This little pond is regularly kept filled from the river itself via that inlet. Normally it is as we see it, extremely still. The flow out of the eastern side is the same as the flow from the north. The current runs across the northeastern section of the pond." He pointed to the area before us. "Anything in this area will remain still."

"But the body in London?" I asked.

Holmes turned to Corden. "Constable, when was the last storm?"

Without hesitation, Corden responded, "Five days ago. A mighty storm it was, too. I had to bring the lads out to assist the fire brigade with a few rescues that night. Shocking it was."

"That storm stirred up this little pond somewhat. The river would have flooded, and the current would have disturbed anything lying within these muddy waters. The body we observed was wrenched from its mooring and taken down river on the crest of the torment."

I pointed at the impressions in the mud. "But these are footprints aren't they? Surely, they would have been washed away."

"Which means they are much fresher. Possibly only two or three days old. The ground is still so damp that access without leaving any mark is impossible."

"If they are that fresh, then that means – " I said, realising that someone had possibly left something – or someone – behind.

Holmes's expression turned grave. He nodded. "Yes, Watson, I feel that there is at least one more body in these waters. Somewhere in that direction." He pointed towards the outlet and then turned to Corden. "Constable, did you bring what I asked?"

Corden nodded and trudged back to the cart. He returned quickly with a small four-pronged anchor attached to a long length of rope and handed it to Holmes. "I noticed this anchor at the station. It's used by the canal barges that work the river. The constable was good enough to attach a long length of sturdy rope."

I followed as he made his way to the edge of the water. He unfurled some rope, then swung the anchor around in a wide circle before letting it fly out into the middle of the pond.

The water broke up in a large splash, sending ripples out to all sides of the bank. Holmes waited for the anchor to settle on the bottom then slowly wound the rope back in.

His first try resulted in nothing but an anchor full of dense weed and thick mud. After several more tries in different directions I was about to comment that maybe he was wrong, when the anchor stuck fast.

"I have a bite," he said, as would a fisherman with a live fish on his hook.

He struggled with the rope, slowly dragging in both the anchor and its catch. Bubbles erupted on the surface of the lake as the object at the end of Holmes's rope was dragged towards us.

After a few minutes of a tediously slow battle with his sunken prize, Holmes pointed at the pond surface. A pale white object could be seen through the murk. I didn't need to observe it clearly to know what it was.

Corden, the driver, and I stepped into the water as far as our boots would allow and grabbed at the thing, dragging it up to the bank. I let out an exasperated sigh as we stared at the bloated and sodden body lying on the bank.

Holmes dropped the rope and stepped towards the corpse. It was a boy, of that there was no mistake. His hair was filthy, but even so I could that it was blonde. Two large hessian bags full of stones were tied around his throat and feet. Holmes placed a hand on a shoulder and rolled the body onto its back. The boy was slightly built, possibly around five-foot six-inches in height.

"It's Moncrieff," Holmes said. I nodded.

Corden simply said, "Who?"

"Another boy that went missing a couple of days ago. Son of Lord Moncrieff, up in Pangbourne," I said.

"Oh my," said Corden. "Why didn't they report it to us?"

"They went straight to a higher authority," Holmes said, "Sadly for Alexander here, someone else was trying to do the same thing."

With the boy on his back, we could clearly see a deep wound on the left side of his chest. The two sets of markings on his forehead and chest were the same as those on the body at Dead Man's Hole.

With a slight look of disgust on his face, Holmes pointed out across the water and said, "I think you'll need to drag this pond, Constable. If I'm right, there are at least another three bodies in there."

We were let into the main entrance of Moncrieff House by the butler and shown into a small parlour off to one side of the elaborate foyer. A maid brought tea and scones and, realizing that we hadn't eaten for quite some time, I tucked in while we waited for the Lord and Lady to arrive.

Holmes stood to one side of the room, examining one of the many paintings, but I could tell that his mood was quite grim.

"Would you like a scone?" I asked, holding a small laden plate towards him.

He turned, the darkness on his face. "Yes, thank you," he replied, moving across and taking the plate from me. Just as he took a small bite, we heard movement outside. He set the scone down and prepared to meet our hosts.

Lord Moncrieff entered first. He certainly was a presence with a stout frame, his piggy face sporting a shock of white hair, and with ruddy cheeks and a double chin. He was followed by a diminutive woman who trailed in his wake and was almost unseen behind her larger husband.

"You'd be Holmes then?" Moncrieff said.

Holmes nodded and shook the Lord's proffered hand. "Yes. I hear that you've met my brother."

"Ah, Mycroft. Yes, good man. I assume you have news then, if you're here."

I noticed Lady Elizabeth and offered her my seat. She shuffled across to me and sat down. Her face was a mask of timidity and fear. She stared up at her husband with the haunted look in her eyes of a mother who has lost a child.

"I'm afraid we have nothing concrete at this stage, but a body has been found," Holmes said. Lady Elizabeth let out a gasp and raised a hand to her face.

Lord Moncrieff faltered slightly but caught himself and remained steadfast. "Is it Alexander?" he asked.

"That can only be determined by yourselves, I'm afraid. The poor unfortunate was taken to the Reading Coroner's building. They will need one or both of you to attend and determine whether it is your son."

Moncrieff nodded, his face grave. "An accident?"

"I'm afraid not," Holmes said. "The indications are far worse, but inconclusive. We still have much investigating to do before this can be laid to rest. Which brings me to the main reason that we are here. I understand that your son was last seen at his school. Is that correct?"

Moncrieff's face turned towards anger. "Yes. Damned foolish place. What am I paying for if they just let these boys loose on the local towns?"

Lady Elizabeth looked aghast. "Howard, this isn't the time to be going into that," she said, her eyes bordering on tears, but her heart remaining as stoic as she could.

"I apologise, dear," he said, "but really, this isn't the first time."

"First time for what?" I asked.

Lady Elizabeth peered up at me and said, "There was a boy, two years ago, who left the school one summer's evening and never returned. We heard about it from an acquaintance. It was never reported by the school itself. He was one of Alexander's closest friends. We almost withdrew him because of it."

"And now it's happened to our Alexander," Moncrieff said. "There will be hell to pay when I see that Principal."

He took a deep breath and drew himself up to full height.

"If you'll excuse me, it seems I have a trip to make to Reading," he said and disappeared. "Dear?" echoed back from the nearby hallway.

Lady Elizabeth sprang to her feet, obviously used to being ordered around. She stopped and turned back. "I assume that you were about to ask for permission to talk with the school masters?"

Holmes nodded. "Yes, I was."

"Ask for Mr. Reginald Brown. Alexander liked him." I noticed a tear form and run down her cheek. Her strength was beginning to fade. "Alexander wasn't a strong boy. He inherited my frame and lack of athleticism. He was also a very emotional boy, and easily led. Again, my traits."

She took my hand in her own and stared deep into my eyes. "My husband had always hoped that Alexander would be more like him, but that didn't happen. Still, I think that he loved him. I know my life will never be the same. All I can ask is that you find out what happened. It will never relieve the pain, but it may bring us a little bit of peace."

She released my hand and was gone before I could reply.

162

Holmes stared at the empty doorway, contemplating.

"A trip to the school then," I said.

The main building of Pangbourne College was a towering Georgian edifice built with orange-red brick and grey stone. The window frames and guttering were all white and stood out in stark contrast to the walls.

Holmes and I passed through the main entrance and were greeted by a rather ornate foyer. The school had been refurbished in recent years, possibly due to the input of funds from parents such as the Moncrieffs. A matronly woman with severely tied-back grey hair took our request to see Master Brown and disappeared quickly when we added it was to do with Alexander Moncrieff's disappearance.

Soon we were met by a tall man in his mid-forties with thinning blonde hair. Reginald Brown was an affable man, and I could tell that he held a deep concern for his students' welfare. He plied us with questions of his own to elicit details about Alexander. Holmes gave him several vague answers which either caused him to stomach his unease or told him that no further information would be forthcoming.

Upon hearing that Holmes was a detective, Brown suggested that we should examine the boy's bedroom. The master seemed to brighten at the prospect of watching Holmes at work. I was unsure whether he knew of Holmes's reputation or was merely intrigued. As we walked along the shadowed corridors, Brown stopped a young student passing by and whispered to him. The boy took one look at Holmes and me and scurried off.

We finally stopped at one of the non-descript doors that lined the corridor. Brown turned the knob and ushered us inside. The room was small and brought back remembrances of my own during my time in public school housing. I admit now that those remembrances were not always pleasant.

"Good Lord, these boys," said Brown hurrying over and opening a window. Out of the corner of my eye I noticed Holmes wince in almost physical pain, no doubt imagining the evidence that could be destroyed by such an act.

Brown turned and took a breath of the fresh air flooding the room. "That's better," he said.

Holmes peered around the room. "If you don't mind, sir," he said, looking Brown directly in the eyes. The Master quickly ducked out of the way and joined me near the entrance.

He pointed to the unmade bed on the right and said, "That's Alexander's bed, and his side of the room."

Holmes stood stock still, initially only moving his head for a moment. I could only see the detritus of a teenage boy's life in disarray across the area, but I knew that Holmes was searching deeper.

Finally, he reached forward and picked up an open newspaper from the desk. It took me a moment to form the question internally.

Why would a teenage boy have a copy of the newspaper?

I could make out a black outline surrounding a small square of print on the paper.

"What is that?" I asked as my companion read the page carefully.

He simply ignored me and turned the paper over. A small card dropped from within the pages and fluttered to the floor. Holmes quickly bent and picked it up. A small smile crossed his face.

"Interesting," he said, turning to Brown, "Do you have much interaction with the local girls' school, or is there any interaction between these boys and the fairer sex?"

Browns' face became stern. "Certainly not," he said, a slightly angry tone on his lips, "We have a strict policy on that. There are no organised or even casual activities where students can mix. This school has a strict Catholic philosophy and a matching set of policies."

Holmes nodded.

"Why?" I asked.

He held up the paper. "This is an advertisement regarding a group from the Reading Girls' School," he said. "They want to meet up with boys from the other schools. There's an address to forward an acknowledgement." He held up a card. "This has details regarding the consequent meet-up."

"He was always going on about meeting those girls," said a voice from the doorway. I turned and saw a young boy of about fourteen with a shock of curly red hair and a pasty white face covered in freckles.

"He was supposed to meet up the day that he went missing," the boy continued.

Reginald Brown looked shocked, "Hamish, why didn't you say anything?"

"Alex told me to keep it to myself. He didn't know how long he'd be gone. I didn't want to ruin it for him – it seemed to be important to him."

"Well it may have been very important," said Holmes with a slightly sinister tone. "Did he mention anything further?"

Hamish shook his head. "No. He skipped out in the early evening. Said that he was meeting someone outside the gates, and was heading over to Reading, although he wasn't very specific."

"Did anyone else go with him?"

He shook his head again, "No. No-one else knew anything about these girls. I just thought it was all a joke, but Alex just kept going on about it, always bragging to anyone that would listen. No-one did. No-one thought much of Alex anyway. He was always bragging about something or other. Most people just ignored him when he started talking."

I looked at Brown. He nodded, "It's true. I think that his father was the main problem. Alex tried to be like him, but he was just a braggart with nothing to back it up."

"What do you think?" I asked, looking across at my friend, but his attention was solely on the personal advertisement and the little card. I leaned in and whispered, "Wasn't that the night of the full moon? I was under the impression that was important to these Satanist blackguards."

Holmes lifted one eyebrow and looked at me out of the corner of his eye. I took it to mean be quiet and promptly shut up. After a moment he finally spoke.

"Watson, I think another trip to Reading is in order."

The building that housed the offices of *The Reading Chronicle* were a simple two-story Georgian affair, made of blocks of the same black-specked white granite with which we had become all too familiar.

Holmes and I entered the main entrance, which served as both a reception point and a place for dealing with customer enquiries and requests for advertisements. A young woman of about twenty sat behind the long wooden counter and seemed genuinely pleased at our arrival. It was possible that the day had been rather slow, and any interaction was to be welcomed. A small name plate told us her name to be Bess Frampton.

Holmes produced the copy of *The Chronicle* that we had found in Alexander Moncrieff's room and showed it to the Miss Frampton.

"Good afternoon," Holmes said. "My friend and I are interested in the origins of this personal advertisement,"

Miss Frampton read it thoughtfully and was silent for a moment and then began to nod. "Yes, I know this one. We've had similar requests around the second week of the month for the last six."

"Do you have copies of the others?" Holmes asked.

She nodded and disappeared into the large area behind the counter. I peered through a gap in the frosted glass wall and noticed rows of wooden desks with several people were busily writing. After a few minutes, the young lass returned carrying a bundle of newspapers. She dumped them on the counter and proceeded to open each, laying them out side-by-side.

Holmes and I searched each page for the advertisements and found that they were all of a similar structure, except that the address changed in each.

"It seems as if they are covering their tracks by using a different return address," Holmes said. He thought for a moment before picking up a form and filling it out with his name and our Baker Street address. He pulled out a guinea and placed it on the counter.

"Miss Frampton, if you would be so kind, can you arrange for the delivery of the *Chronicle* to this address?" he said pushing the slip of paper forward, "When the next one of these advertisements appears, and each month onwards until I advise otherwise."

She read the slip and nodded. "I can do that. I'll put it through to deliveries. We already have a few customers in London, but it won't cost a guinea, even if you get the paper every week for a year," she said.

Holmes smiled, "That's fine. You can keep the rest. I don't think that we'll need more than one copy, in any case."

Bess looked delighted and took the guinea from the counter, slipping it into her pocket. "You'll have your paper within a week or two," she said with a wide grin, "if this person is punctual."

"Excellent," Holmes bowed. "And thank you for your service, Miss Frampton."

The following weeks were spent back at 221b Baker Street. Holmes and Mycroft had managed to keep the discovery of the other bodies out of the news. In the meantime, we received two pieces of information that were of the most horrid nature.

The first was that Constable Corden and his men had dragged the little pond off the main part of the River Kennett and sadly found not three but four bodies. Three matched the reported boys, but a fourth was unknown. Each boy had the same markings carved into their foreheads and chests, and had been killed by a single wound to the heart from a wide bladed knife.

The second was that Lord Moncrieff had visited the Reading Coroner and identified his son, Alexander. I could only imagine the grief that had overtaken Lady Elizabeth. I hoped that she had someone to support her, as I didn't believe her husband to be that person.

Early in the week after our return we had received a summons from Mycroft Holmes to meet him in the Stranger's Room at the Diogenes Club, in order to discuss Holmes's findings so far. It was there that my friend explained the five dead boys identified so far and the unknown sixth. Mycroft was appalled by the loss of life.

"Satanism," said Holmes with a dour look on his face.

Mycroft's face was almost as dark as his brother's. "Not good, Sherlock, not good," he said instead, "Britain is too important on the world stage to have this sort of . . . of . . . pagan ritual going on. I would dearly

166

love to put the full force Her Majesty's law on to this matter, if just to help Lord Moncrieff, but it is a purely civil matter. What do you plan to do about it?"

Holmes sipped his coffee and thought for a moment. I knew that he'd been working hard in the background, formulating some plan, but the details hadn't been forthcoming. I was on the edge of my seat, waiting for him to continue.

"I expect the delivery of a newspaper from Reading within the week. In there, I hope to find a personal advertisement calling for boys of a – How should I say it? – a *virginal* aspect, to make contact with the girls from a nearby college. It seems to be a simple fishing exercise, but the catch rate has been rather astonishing."

"I don't follow," Mycroft said.

"It is my belief that these cultists are using the newspaper to find the young boys whom they use as sacrifices in their detestable rituals."

"Why boys?" Mycroft asked.

"From my research," Holmes said, "it seems that virgins feature prominently in the more esoteric and graphic rituals. They believe that the devil requires them to be pure of sin."

I took a sharp intake of breath. It did make sense.

"But why not girls?" Mycroft asked.

"Boys disappearing at that age is less obvious, and not liable to attract as much attention from horrified or distressed fathers."

Mycroft nodded. I was quite disgusted at the thought of what had been going on.

Holmes continued, "When I receive the advertisement, I will answer from an address in Reading. I've already arranged for one of my young cohorts to spend the next fortnight there. He will make the contact and ensure that he becomes the next object of the cult's obsession."

He turned and indicated me. "Watson and I will journey back to Reading and join the young lad. I would hardly allow any harm to come to one of my Irregulars."

Mycroft nodded. "Good, good. You have it in hand. I may be able to provide a tiny bit of assistance, but it will have to be discreet," he said touching an extended forefinger to his nose.

It was early the next month that Holmes's copy of *The Reading Chronicle* finally graced us with its presence. There, as bold as life on the personal pages, was the latest advertisement. It asked for young boys from the local area to meet with the girls of The Reading Girls' School. Those interested were to send a telegram to the listed address, different from the previous six. Holmes read it with a sly smile on his face.

167

"What do you think?" I asked.

"Marvellous," he said. "The exact same format, but a different reply address. The *modus operandi* is perfect to weed out the chaff, but we need to make sure our response attracts their attention."

Holmes disappeared into his room and returned several minutes later, sporting his travelling coat and hat, and carrying a small valise. He handed a small note to me which had an address in Reading written on it.

"Join me in three days' time at that address. By then, I feel that the game will well and truly be afoot." He then promptly left, leaving me slightly aghast.

When I finally set foot at the Reading abode that Holmes had organized, I'll admit that I had been busy with patients and other trivial tasks for the last few days, but throughout my mind raced with questions regarding events that would unfold.

I was greeted at the front door by a young man of around thirteen years, with neatly combed jet-black hair and dark brown eyes that glinted with recognition when they fell upon me. I was taken aback for a moment as the boy drew no remembrances from my mind – that was until he spoke.

"Dr. Watson?" he said.

I stammered slightly, "Aiden?"

When I had seen him previously, he sported torn and dirty street clothes, with a filthy flat cap hiding his mussed and mud-streaked hair. The boy that stood before me was the total antithesis of that. He was remarkably well-appointed and could have passed for any public schoolboy of good upbringing.

"Yes, sir," he replied politely, before bowing slightly and stepping back to allow me in.

I found Holmes in a small reception room. He was dressed very smartly, and I realised that he was affecting the guise of young Aiden's father, or at least guardian.

"Ah, Watson," he said as I entered, before giving Aiden an order to take my coat and valise to the back of the little house. As Aiden left he simply said, "Just in case anyone calls, we must retain the impression that Aiden and I are family and have been here a while."

I nodded and then asked, "What progress have you made?"

Holmes indicated a small chair and I sat, ready to hear all. "We've done very well," he said, "I sent the telegram prior to arriving here in Reading, and young Aiden and I moved straight in. It was only the next morning that a knock on the door revealed an answering telegram. Aiden has been invited to a *soirée* for members of the girls' school and their guests tomorrow night."

"Do we know where?" I asked.

"They're sending a hansom for him tomorrow at six o'clock. We'll follow in our own cart, parked around the corner."

"Good. Do you know anything else?"

"Of course," he said, smiling in that inimitable way of his, telling me almost as much as anything that he would say. "I went to the address and waited to see who, if anyone, of note visited."

"And?"

"It was a small house off the High Street. The only occupants that I could see were a young girl of probably Aiden's age, and a matronly woman that may be her mother – or like me, is posing in that role."

"Interesting. Any idea what they are about?"

"Window dressing," he said, "because it wasn't they who were of interest, but those that visited later in the day. We answered their first telegram with a request for more information. I was present outside when it arrived. The visitation occurred later in the day and proceeded the reply with Aiden's transportation details."

"Who was it?"

"A beautifully appointed black brougham pulled up outside, and a tall man in a dark suit and top hat paid a visit to the two women. By the way he carried himself, I don't believe that he was the owner of the carriage, but rather a servant. I wouldn't be surprised if the same carriage is used to pick up young Aiden tomorrow night." He took a breath before continuing. "I waited until the man had left, then followed the carriage at a good distance, until we left the town and they headed into the countryside. I dropped back and used the dust thrown up by the brougham to track them. After a time, they finally pulled off the road and went up a lane that led to a rather well-maintained manor house."

"Do you know whose?"

"I didn't at the time. They used a side entrance, so I circled around until I found the main gates. The name of the house and the owner were proudly displayed. The house is one you would know – Southcote Manor."

I was puzzled. The name certainly rang a bell. I searched my memories. "You're correct. It seems very familiar," I said.

Before I could find the information, Holmes said, "It's the home of Sir Geoffrey Warrington."

"Good Lord! You don't think that the potential leader of the opposition is involved in this Satanist crowd, do you?"

"I hope not," he said, "but I've sent a telegram off to my brother, who seemed very perturbed by the prospect. We shall have some of that help he promised, tomorrow night."

I snuck my hand into my coat pocket and felt the cold comforting sensation of my service revolver. The fact that we were about to confront a deranged sect that not only worshipped the opposite force of all that is good and wholesome in this world, but one that also had powerful political allies, filled me with the deepest dread.

Several minutes before the allotted time for young Aiden's transport to arrive, Holmes and I left via the rear door and then through the back fence gate into the service alley, and around to the nearby side street where Holmes had parked his hired dogcart. We brought it around and sat almost fifty yards from the front door to keep watch.

The dark black brougham arrived directly on six o'clock. A tall man with the top hat disembarked, knocked on the front door, and a moment later returned with Aiden. The door to the brougham was opened from within, and Aiden's face lit up with a wide smile. I presumed that the young lass was inside.

When the brougham was over a hundred yards away, we fell into the same pace behind it. We turned towards the southwest and I assumed that we were heading towards Southcote Manor. I amused myself by viewing the houses and landmarks that we passed on the way. Most were of Georgian age, with several newly added terraces, along with many grand neo-gothic buildings from a long-ago age.

I noticed that another carriage had fallen into lockstep with us and maintained a distance of fifty yards from our rear. I turned to Holmes and mentioned it, asking whether it might belong to Sir Geoffrey Warrington.

Holmes smiled, "No, but it does belong to Her Majesty's Service. Mycroft has sent us some help. There will probably be more trailing further behind that one."

I took one quick look over my shoulder and studied the cart. It was a large four-wheeler with a pair of well-built men in dark coats in the driver's seats.

After nearly half-an-hour of travelling well into the countryside, Holmes spoke up. "We aren't heading towards Southcote Manor."

When the brougham took a left-hand fork in the road, Holmes pulled the dogcart to the right fork and stopped after fifty yards. Several other carts, including the large four-wheeler, pulled up near us.

Holmes spoke to the driver of the first cart. "Jansen, they've headed towards to the Padworth Quarry," he said. "That's slightly unexpected. We'll need to approach with care and surround it. I suggest sending one group to the western side, while Watson and I and the other group go to the east."

The young plainly clothed man nodded and barked orders at the other carriages. They rumbled off past us. Holmes pulled our cart around and headed down the other trail.

Within a few hundred yards we came to another fork and took the left, I noticed that the right-hand trail dipped as it disappeared amongst the trees. Our track soon opened up and I saw the wide expanse of the quarry lying to our right. Holmes pulled up in a small layby, dropped to the ground, and hurried across to the edge of the pit.

I was shocked at the sight before me.

Down at the bottom of the quarry, in a large open, flat space, a circular area was lined with blazing braziers. The bright full moon bathed the circle of people, their faces hidden by hooded robes. They stood surrounding a central figure dressed in a dark brown robe standing next to a wide flat stone, which had all the hallmarks of an altar. The central figure's hood was thrown back and I recognised him immediately as Sir Geoffrey Warrington.

The black brougham stood off to the side, and as I watched, Sir Geoffrey motioned towards it. Two men quickly broke off and hurried to the carriage. They man-handled the supine from of young Aiden from the carriage across to the altar. There they stripped him and lay him on the large flat stone. Sir Geoffrey drew a large wide bladed dagger from beneath his robes and held it aloft. He began to address the assembly. "Lord Satan, we, your faithful servants, gather beneath the full moon to present to you this poor offering, so that you may bless us with another month of continued success in our endeavours."

I gasped and heard Holmes swear under his breath. Any chance of harm coming to one of his Irregulars was anathema to him. He turned towards Jansen and spoke.

"Get some men down to the entrance!" he hissed and then pointed to the man in the centre of the circle, "I suggest we let the majority of the people escape, as they will want to soon enough, but make sure Sir Geoffrey is detained."

Jansen and his men moved off.

"Why will the other people try to escape?" I asked.

Holmes smiled. "Because of this."

Suddenly, he moved forward and slid and skipped his way down a steep path to the quarry floor. I was taken aback, but quickly joined him. He raced towards the circle of adherents, pulled out his revolver, and fired into the air.

The effect was incredible.

The group scattered like a flock of pigeons, running to-and-fro as if the devil that they had so wished to meet had, in fact, arrived. Holmes ignored them and moved towards Sir Geoffrey. The politician simply stood and eyed Holmes, a grin on his face.

"Drop the knife," said Holmes. "This disgusting play-acting is over."

"You have me at a disservice, sir," said Sir Geoffrey.

"I am Sherlock Holmes."

Sir Geoffrey's smile grew. "Ah, Mycroft's little brother. The detective." He waved the knife before him. "What gives you the right to confront a Member of Parliament embracing his religious freedoms? You aren't the law. You are nothing."

Holmes stepped forward. His face was alight with an anger I had rarely seen. He opened his mouth to speak, but was cut off as Jansen stepped in front of him, a pistol trained on the politician.

"He may not be the law, but I am," Jansen said. "Inspector Michael Jansen, Intelligence Branch, and you are mine now."

It was a dismal day that found Holmes, Mycroft, and me back in the tiny town of Pangbourne for a memorial service. It was a sombre occasion for Lord and Lady Moncrieff to say farewell their son, Alexander.

The rain pattered on the ground as we gave our condolences to the family, who thanked Holmes for both discovering their son's body and his killer. Lord Moncrieff kept his stoic visage as always, but my heart sang for Lady Elizabeth who seemed on the verge of a breakdown.

The three of us moved to a sheltered patch where we could watch the rest of the assembly and speak.

"What of that degenerate, Sir Geoffrey?" I asked, noting my voice was full of disgust.

"He will hang," said Mycroft, "The Prime Minister is adamant of that. He has placed the full force of the Attorney General's Office onto it."

"What of the others?" asked Holmes.

His face soured slightly. "The Security Service is scouring the country for them. Sir Geoffrey has kept his mouth shut, and will probably take their identities to the noose."

"Damn him," I swore.

"Yes," said Holmes. "I think that's what he wanted all along."

"Why would someone in his position do such a thing?" I asked.

"Regardless of any supernatural connotations," said Holmes, "I suppose it was that inner belief in the Devil's works that gave him a level of inner superiority and confidence which enabled him to achieve such a high office. History is replete with many an evil doer that has possessed such an aura, and I'm afraid that it is in the nature of man to bolster his inner worth through such fictitious means."

I nodded and peered out at the rain pattering down as the last of the mourners disappeared from view.

The Elusive Mr. Chester
by Arthur Hall

In many ways, my friend Sherlock Holmes was a creature of habit. Often, in a given set of circumstances, he could be depended upon to act predictably, and during the years of our association I grew quite familiar with his ways. I thought it strange then that he should rise from the breakfast table before consuming the coffee I had just poured, since it was always his custom to remain until we had both finished our meal and he rarely departed from it.

"What is happening out there, that you find so interesting?" I asked, seeing that he had taken up a position near the window that would allow him an oblique view of Baker Street.

"I heard a repeated pattern of footsteps," he replied. "There is little traffic at the moment, so I was easily able to discern that someone was pacing up and down outside our door. It will certainly be a new client, though an indecisive one, who I expect to ring the door-bell in an instant. Mrs. Hudson is nearby, I think, and so the gentleman should be with us shortly."

He was soon proven correct. Our good landlady quickly appeared to clear away the breakfast things, before showing into our rooms a man of medium height and slightly shabby appearance who did indeed appear to be somewhat confused.

"Mr. Sherlock Holmes?" he asked, looking from one to other of us as she withdrew.

"I am he," my friend affirmed. "This is my friend and associate, Doctor John Watson, before whom you may speak as freely as to myself." He subjected the man to a brief scrutiny. "But I see that you are somewhat disturbed. That is why I didn't request our landlady to bring tea. I think a glass of brandy would go much further as a restorative."

At Holmes's bidding, the man removed his hat and sat in the basket chair. I handed him a glass of the spirit and he drank it at once. By the time he placed the empty vessel on a side-table, we were all seated.

"Now," Holmes began after he had allowed our visitor a few moments to collect himself, "pray tell us, when you are ready, how we can be of assistance. It seems likely that it's connected to your rather anxious present state."

"It is indeed, sir." The man nodded his head vigorously. "I am Elias Wynburne, a travelling salesman for Brookman and Turner, the well-known manufacturer of false eyes. It is a strange story that I have to tell, and I confess that I can make neither head nor tail of it."

"Pray begin at the beginning, leaving out not the smallest detail."

As Mr. Wynburne assembled his thoughts, I examined his appearance as Holmes would already have done. That he was married was evident from his wedding ring, and that he was careless in his shaving habits obvious from the numerous small cuts surrounding his rather unkempt handlebar moustache. He had fallen on hard times of late, I deduced, since his clothes, although of good quality, were of a style popular several years earlier and appeared very well-worn. His accent suggested him to be a native of the capital, rather than from the provinces.

"It was Tuesday evening," he recalled. "I had returned from visiting a client in Kent – we frequently sell our wares to soldiers who have lost an eye in battle, you see – and I was quite late reporting back to the office in Kensington. After handing in my order to the clerk, I left the building and, as I'm fortunate enough to live not far away from my place of employment, I walked to my home." He gave an address in Empire Place. "I had crossed the High Street and entered one of the minor roads that eventually lead to my residence when I was set upon.

"A pistol was held hard against my back, and I was warned that I would be shot instantly should I be slow in obeying any of the instructions that I was about to be given. A piece of cloth, which turned out to be a blindfold, was pushed into my hand, and I was instructed to put it over my head. I complied, for the man holding the gun sounded determined and serious, and then I heard a coach draw up. I was ordered to board it, which I did with great difficulty, sustaining numerous prods and a final kick. I felt my way from the floor to a seat, and my abductor said that if I valued my life I would keep still and stay silent. I listened carefully for any sounds which might indicate where I was being taken, but heard nothing unusual. I estimated the journey to take about twenty minutes."

"Excellent," said Holmes, "that you should have maintained such presence of mind."

"When the coach came to rest, I was hurried out and forced along what felt like a stone-flagged path. A door was unlocked and I was pushed through the doorway, or so it seemed, and then the door was slammed behind me. I stood waiting for more instructions, but none came, and there was no sound of my abductor breathing. Nevertheless, it was not until I heard the coach departing that I dared to remove the blindfold, finding myself in an unfamiliar room and quite alone."

"Did you then seize your opportunity to escape?" I enquired.

Our client held up his hands in a gesture of hopelessness. "The locked door was thick and sturdy. I hammered on it with my fists for what seemed an age, without the slightest success. In all that time, I heard no one pass by outside. I had already ascertained that the room had no windows. When I realised that I would have to accept my situation, at least for the time being, I took in my surroundings. A lit candle stood upon the table, and I had been left an ample supply of others. Also, on a shelf above the single armchair, there were several flasks of water, bread, and fruit. In a corner were primitive toilet facilities."

"As if you were intended to be reasonably comfortable," Holmes mused.

"Indeed. I also found a Bible to occupy my mind. I had no way of knowing how long I would be kept there, or if I would be released at all, but I managed to remember to wind my pocket-watch regularly, and so kept track of the time throughout."

"Did not your wife raise the alarm, at your unusual absence?"

"This was my main concern, other than escape. Imagine my surprise then, gentlemen, to find on my eventual return that she had received a telegram notifying her that I had been unexpectedly called away to Liverpool on business."

"Strange, indeed. How did you regain your freedom, finally?"

"Early on Thursday morning, I was roused from my slumber by a strange noise. I was by this time in an unshaven and unkempt condition, and thought at first that I had dreamed of hearing someone outside. I approached the door and listened, without result, but when I turned the handle it opened easily. I was free."

"And there was no one in sight?" my friend asked.

"The place was deserted. The house was part of a row of condemned dwellings."

"Where was this, pray?"

"In a derelict part of Chelsea. I wandered to the end of the street and eventually procured a hansom, which conveyed me to my home."

"Your wife was relieved, no doubt?"

"She seemed mildly surprised when I related the circumstances of my absence. She is used to my business trips, after all."

There was a short silence. I could hear the cries of street merchants through the half-open window. Holmes had adopted a thoughtful expression, but his eyes were suddenly filled with the light of comprehension. "Has anything else occurred since this incident which you would describe as unusual?"

Mr. Wynburne considered for a moment. "I can think of nothing."

"And before the incident?"

"No," he hesitated, "unless you consider the sudden disappearance of my certificate of birth, which I discovered while looking through my

176

papers the night before I was abducted. Could that be what you are thinking of?"

"Something of the sort," Holmes confirmed, his brow clearing.

"I cannot image how that can be connected."

"Perhaps it isn't, but it is at least a possibility."

Mr. Wynburne shook his head hopelessly. "I confess to being all at sea about this."

"You have no explanation of your own, then?" Holmes enquired. "For instance, could this be some sort of practical joke? Is there anyone of your acquaintance who is likely to have arranged such a thing?"

"I know of no one would consider such a senseless jest."

Holmes nodded. "It must be apparent to you that the perpetrator is someone who is familiar with your normal routine. He knew, among other things, where and when to accost you in order to carry out the abduction. Could he be among your friends or colleagues?"

"Any friends that I have I know through my wife, who has always been far more inclined toward social connections than I. As for my colleagues, they are without exception elderly men who would be incapable of such an outrage. I had a dispute with the local butcher some months ago, but it was settled amicably."

"Finally," Holmes asked, "have you consulted the official force on this matter?"

"I have not considered doing so," Mr. Wynburne gave us a puzzled glance. "As there has been no actual crime committed, other than what seems to be a harmless and purposeless prank, I would expect Scotland Yard to dismiss these happenings as unworthy of their attention."

"And there is nothing else you wish to tell us?"

"I have told you all."

Holmes stood up abruptly. "For which I thank you, Mr. Wynburne. I think that we need detain you no longer, and you may expect to hear from us in a day or two. Doctor Watson will show you out. Goodbye, sir."

Our client appeared surprised at Holmes's sudden dismissal, and I did what I could to reassure him as we descended the stairs. I caught the attention of the driver of a passing hansom as we stepped into the street, and Mr. Wynburne was quickly on his way.

I noticed the faint smile on Holmes's lips as I resumed my seat near the fireplace.

"You have, I think, formed a theory to explain this matter."

"In fact, I had arrived at three that would have made things clear, until Mr. Wynburne mentioned the loss of his papers. Now there is but one that fits all of the facts."

"Holmes, something has just occurred to me. I have done you a great disservice."

His smile broadened. "How so, old fellow?"

"I asked no question or made no note of the address in Chelsea where Mr. Wynburne was imprisoned."

"Ha! Do not trouble yourself for a moment longer. I have no intention of visiting the place."

"Are we not to look into this curious business, then?"

"We are indeed."

"But where do we begin?"

"At Empire Place, of course. Tomorrow morning."

We set off for Kensington High Street directly after breakfast. Holmes had indicated that it was necessary for Mr. Wynburne to be away from his home before an investigation could begin, which explained why he declined to proceed immediately after luncheon the previous day.

As the hansom left us, his keen eyes swept our surroundings until they settled upon a collection of market stalls at the end of a row of shops.

"From there we will have an excellent view of the entrance to Empire Place. We will wander through the various stalls until we see Mr. Wynburne leave for his place of work, although fending off some of the vendors hereabouts may prove something of a nuisance."

In less than half-an-hour, our client did indeed pass on the other side of the street. I remembered that he mentioned his custom of walking to his employment, and noted that he looked as confused and unhappy as he had during his visit to Baker Street. When he had vanished from sight, Holmes and I emerged from our concealment.

We entered Empire Place and strode up to the third in a row of terraced houses. He rapped on the door with his cane, and the door was opened almost immediately. The immaculately dressed and heavily rouged woman who stood there wore a welcoming smile that faded instantly as her gaze settled upon us.

"We are so sorry to disturb you, Mrs. Wynburne," said my friend, "but we have an urgent matter to discuss with your husband. It concerns his employment, but beyond that I can reveal nothing to you. May we enter?"

She quickly recovered herself, although she was clearly anxious to dispense with our presence. "Oh, I fear I cannot oblige you, gentlemen. Mr. Wynburne has left for Somerset to conclude a business transaction. When he returns, who shall I say called to see him?"

"There is no need. Doubtlessly we will encounter him at the offices of Brookman and Turner at a later date. Good day, Madam."

"She expected someone already, Holmes," I said when we had regained the High Street. "Her expression made that clear."

"As did her appearance. I have seldom seen a middle-aged woman take so much care for the benefit of her husband, save on occasions when they venture out together in public."

"Are we now to return to Baker Street? A hansom has just left its fare near the emporium across the road."

"Not yet, old fellow. Our next destination is the local Post Office, which I noticed earlier is near the next corner."

The place was crowded, so I elected to wait outside while he completed whatever business he had there. After about twenty minutes, he emerged.

"As I thought, Watson. The first part of my theory is proven."

"You have yet to explain it to me."

He nodded. "With the confirmation of the second part, my case is complete. Then you shall know all."

"How are we to proceed now?"

"Back to Empire Place, I think, though hopefully not for long. I saw a convenient doorway within sight of Mr. Wynburne's house that should keep us hidden."

This doorway, I noticed, was in a position that could not be seen from the Wynburne home. Yet, because of its oblique angle, it was ideal for observing the house. It was set back from the pavement, and we stepped into deep shadow.

"What are looking for, Holmes?"

"For a certain gentleman to either arrive or leave."

"Because he could have arrived while we were at the Post Office, but may not have done?"

"Precisely. In either case I expect my suspicions to be proven."

I saw from my pocket-watch that almost an hour had elapsed, before Mrs. Wynburne appeared on her doorstep and looked cautiously up and down the street. Seemingly satisfied, she stood aside to allow a dark-haired man in a smart morning-suit step out on to the pavement. He turned and gave a little bow, and then strode off after saying something which we were too far away to hear. The door closed before the visitor passed out of our sight.

"Was it he that you expected?" I asked my friend.

"It was."

"And he is Mrs. Wynburne's lover?"

He nodded. "I suspected as much when Mr. Wynburne told us of his experience, and became certain when we visited his wife."

"That then, was the purpose of it? So that you could judge from her appearance?"

"It was. Now I must consult my index to confirm my identification of the man who has just left."

I can recall but one exchange between Holmes and myself during the journey back to Baker Street, as the hansom swayed when the driver took a corner too quickly.

"Holmes, the visit to the Post Office was to confirm the contents of the telegram sent to Mrs. Wynburne to assure her that her husband's absence was due to business, was it not?"

He turned from silently gazing at two men who were in the midst of a drunken dispute outside a tavern.

"There was no telegram."

On arrival at our lodgings he went immediately to the bookshelf. He took a volume of his index and placed it upon the carpet where, on his hands and knees, he quickly turned the pages. It took no more than a minute or two.

"A-ha!" He scrutinized a cutting from a six-month-old newspaper. "We have it, Watson. Two almost identical cases are recorded as having taken place in Sheffield and Bolton. This man has evidently travelled widely in the course of his career. I would speculate that his activities have been even more numerous over the past few years. My case is now complete. All that remains is to telegraph Inspector Lestrade, and for us to find ways to amuse ourselves until tomorrow morning."

With breakfast over, we took up our hats and coats and told our landlady to expect us for luncheon. Baker Street was unusually quiet, with cabbies looking for fares, so it was well before nine o'clock when we resumed our place of concealment in Empire Place.

"As we are here early, we should see Mrs. Wynburne's caller arrive," I remarked.

"Doubtlessly Scotland Yard has a similar intention," Holmes replied. "I have just caught a glimpse of a constable who has stationed himself near a horse trough, further along the street."

Then we waited, he with enforced patience. His eyes glittered with the prospect of concluding the case, and his entire posture resembled a hunting-dog eager to be free of the leash.

After a short time we saw Mr. Wynburne set out, rather later than we expected. Barely half-an-hour passed before the man whom Holmes had described as Mrs. Wynburne's lover appeared, striding along from the direction of the High Street.

He approached the Wynburne's home and knocked softly upon the door. It opened at once to reveal the lady of the house, once more resplendent in a scarlet house-coat and with her face enticingly rouged. He was about to step across the threshold when some animal sense must have warned him, for he paused to look along the street and spied the constable who had begun to walk towards him.

At once he abandoned Mrs. Wynburne and turned away, retracing his steps with increasing speed. The lady was frozen in the act of an embrace, her mouth sagging open in surprise. Then more constables appeared from both directions, so that he was surrounded. He came to a halt, his eyes searching for an escape. They found none.

Holmes and I emerged, for concealment was no longer necessary. At the same moment a familiar figure came into view from the direction of the High Street, and I saw a brief look of surprise cross Holmes's face. I, too, was surprised, for some little time had passed since we had last seen Inspector Gregson.

"You have no chance," he called to the fugitive. "Give up, Chester. There are too many of us for you."

Chester produced a revolver, and replied in a tone edged with hysteria. "Get back, all of you. I will kill as many of you as I have to."

At that Gregson drew his weapon, as did Holmes and I. Chester saw a space between the encircling constables and ran for it, coming to an abrupt halt as they closed in. The hand holding his weapon fell to his side, as he saw that his situation was hopeless. A burly sergeant approached him and took away his pistol, while others gripped his arms and handcuffs were applied.

"Better this way, Chester," Gregson said before his prisoner was led away. "You will meet the hangman soon enough."

The uniformed officers dispersed and Gregson approached us, his flaxen hair blowing in the slight breeze.

"Good morning, gentlemen," he began, and we reciprocated. "Lestrade is occupied with some trivial affair in Northampton, but I saw your message, Mr. Holmes. We have been after Thomas Chester for a long time at the Yard, but he has always escaped us, until now."

"The newspapers were rather harsh on that point," Holmes said.

"Indeed, but this man was clever. In the plain-clothes branch, we came to refer to him as 'The Elusive Mr. Chester', such was his skill at evading capture. I know him of old. This is far from our first encounter. His game is the trifling of the affections of rich ladies, for their money of course. Except that new evidence has recently come to light, and we have discovered that one of his past victims proved difficult for him."

"He murdered her, I imagine," said I, remembering that the hangman had been mentioned.

"Poisoned her," confirmed Gregson. "She died horribly."

"Well then," Holmes said. "You are aware of the present situation, from my telegram. Let us now interview the other participant in this conspiracy. I am certain that Mrs. Wynburne will shed further light on Chester's intentions."

Within the hour, Holmes, with Gregson's permission, had revealed to Mrs. Wynburne all that was known. She sat in her parlour with her head in her hands, not remorseful but sad, only because her plans had failed.

"It would be wisest, I think, to make a clean breast of it," my friend advised.

After a moment of silence, she looked up. Her eyes passed over Holmes, Gregson, and myself before she spoke, her face hard and without tears.

"I married Elias expecting a better life. It is he that is to blame for all that has happened since. He exaggerated his position and his income to me during our courting. When I realised that I had committed myself to an ordinary existence, a life no different to that I had lived until then, my disappointment was unendurable. I knew that, sooner or later, I had to find a way to escape."

"Was he not a good husband, to the best of his ability?" asked Gregson. Holmes gave him a short glance, a sign of his irritation at this interruption.

"He was ordinary, and that I could not bear. I had led what might be called an exciting life before, and this was stagnation."

"Where did you meet Thomas Chester?"

"After a time, I could hardly endure being in the same room as my husband. I sought any distraction, and when a friend suggested I accompany her to an evening embroidery class, I enthusiastically agreed. Some of the other women were brought to the class and met afterwards by their husbands or, occasionally, husbands-to be. Mr. Chester appeared with a much older woman whom he introduced as a friend, but she apparently died soon after. We fell into conversation and eventually progressed from acquaintances to friends, and from there to something much deeper. Eventually it was taken for granted between us that I would leave Elias for a new life with him. One morning, a letter arrived for Elias after he had left for his employment, from a firm of solicitors that I had never heard of. I was curious, and after a while I succumbed to temptation and opened it.

"I was astonished to read that an uncle, whom I knew Elias hadn't seen since childhood, had died, and from the sale of his jewellery concern

182

had left Elias four-thousand pounds. Well gentleman, such a vast sum turned my head, and the next time I saw Thomas I told him about it, adding that this was our chance to be together, and that it was unlikely that we would ever get another like it. I contrived to procure Elias' birth certificate and Thomas saw that he was locked away while we presented ourselves at the solicitors' office. I made certain that my husband had sufficient food and drink during his confinement," she added, as if hoping for clemency.

"Did the impersonation succeed?" enquired Holmes. "If Chester used your husband's papers as proof of his identity, I should be surprised if it did not."

"Oh yes, we were very happy that it was so easy."

"And the money?" asked Gregson.

"That is in an account bearing both our names – that is, Thomas and mine – in the Tradesmans Official Bank."

"I doubt that it is there, by now. At the Yard we have long known Thomas Chester under a variety of names. He is a notorious swindler and an absolute cad. You are the latest of his victims."

Mrs. Wynburne was very still for an instant, and then she began to cry. It was clear that she had never really known the man. After a moment Gregson left the room and called in a constable who had been stationed outside.

"Take her, Campbell," he ordered, and after a few minutes of conversation with us, took his leave.

"My sympathies are with our client," I said to Holmes.

"I regret that he will return from his work to an unhappily altered life," my friend replied with a touch of sadness. "But we have done what we could to explain his curious experience. As for his domestic affairs, it is beyond us to assist, for these can usually be settled only by the parties involved. You see, Watson, once again, what I have managed to avoid, due to my maintained distance from the weaker sex."

The Adventure of
Old Black Duffel
by Will Murray

"It is an ever-changing world, is it not, my dear Watson?"

We were strolling along the Strand when my friend Sherlock Holmes chanced to make that remark. I didn't think it apropos of anything in particular. We had been taking the air after sharing a substantial meal in a new restaurant, the Aviary. As is often the case, we rambled along in silence, Holmes mentally ruminating on I know not what. Thus I observed a respectful silence.

More than once, my friend has vouchsafed that comfort with his silent companionship was one of my most endearing traits. I don't think that anyone else I could possibly encounter would share that opinion, but as it happened, many years of being on intimate terns with Holmes had inured me to his prolonged spells of introspection.

This conversation – if I may call something so one-sided – took place in the late autumn of the year 1894. The trees were almost bare. Winter was creeping close. I wore a muffler against its chill advance.

"I suppose that it is," I replied.

"London grows old, yet she renews herself in perpetuity. This is not the Londinium of our distant ancestors. Parts of it aren't even the London of our grandparents. Yet other quarters would be very familiar to them. Consider the new Tower Bridge. Is it not a wonder? Some future generation may know of it only through photographs and the recollections of the aged. A newer Tower Bridge may stand in its place, greater than the proud structure we presently admire. For one imagines that, a few centuries hence, it must be pulled down to make room for its inevitable successor."

"The Thames is quite different now than it was in our youth."

"How well I recall. It was filthy, an abomination."

Holmes lapsed into a period of silence, which I didn't trouble. I noticed that he seemed to pay scant attention to those passing by, and yet I suspected that he missed nothing. Many times he has upbraided me – if I may employ so strong a term – at the failures of my powers of observation. His were superlative. If I believed in such things, I would catalog them as supernatural.

Had I dared to use such a preposterous term to describe Holmes's rare abilities, he would have heaped such scorn upon me that I would have been ashamed to call him my friend – at least until such a time as his justifiable ire had subsided.

"That poor woman," he muttered at one point.

"The one with the towering auburn hair?"

"The very same," replied Holmes.

"She doesn't seem to my eye to be poor. I would class her as comfortably well off."

"I am not referring to the obvious, Watson. Not to her dress, nor her shoes. Nor the way her hair is arranged. I was referring to her eyes."

"I didn't note their color."

"A charming russet hue. Rather, the irises were. The whites of her eyes held the faintest traces of green. A very distressing thing to see in a young woman still in her prime."

"My word! I didn't see."

"But I did. I don't have to tell you that the green coloration of the eyeball is a symptom of advancing kidney disease."

"Kidney failure. Very sad. I doubt that woman will live to be a matron."

"Nor do I. The green was quite pronounced."

Such was the powers of observation possessed by Holmes that I, despite my line of work, failed to diagnose the condition in a passerby. But he spotted it easily, no doubt at a glance. Another man might have admired the woman's figure, the color of her hair, and other feminine attributes. Like a hawk, Holmes's gaze went directly to the most salient feature.

We continued our stroll. Once or twice, Holmes made remarks after glancing at this person or that, deducing their occupation, and at one point, announcing a passing man's home address.

"How the devil could you deduce such a specific thing?" I demanded.

"A letter poking out of his coat. It displayed a street number of considerable digits, along with the initial of the street. Few London streets boast such a number, and the initial completed the revelation."

"I did perceive that he had an envelope sticking out of his coat pocket," I pointed out.

"Hardly a revelatory fact," said Holmes.

He wasn't smoking his pipe. His brow wasn't furrowed. And I hadn't heard from him any mention of a case all week. Yet he didn't seem to be bored. When Sherlock Holmes didn't have a mystery to solve, he often lapsed into boredom. This didn't appear to be the case.

"I imagine that since you are between mysteries, practicing your observational skills keeps them sharp."

"I don't practice them," he retorted. "They are ever-active. I don't even think of using them or not using them. Observing to me is second nature. It would be more difficult to ignore the data my senses pick out than otherwise." Rounding a turn, he added, "And I am not in fact between mysteries. I am at the very beginning of a new undertaking."

"Oh?"

"Have you not heard of the resourceful footpad who has become the scourge of the East End?"

"I have read in *The Evening Standard* that there has been an increase in assaults and robberies. No doubt the onset of winter compels the criminal class to take advantage of the plentitude of pedestrians before the first snowfall."

"I don't think it is that, although I don't doubt that your theory might not carry some weight. I think there is another reason for the increase. Nor do I believe that most of these outrages are the work of various individuals. More than once, the perpetrator has been described as wearing a duffel coat with the hood pulled up."

"Since the Royal Navy issues such coats, and any number of them are discarded each year," I observed, "this doesn't strike me as a very individual item of attire."

"In principle, I agree with you. But this duffel coat is unique in one respect: It has been dyed black as a raven's wing. The naval issue is, as you know, camel-colored."

"I see," said I. "That *does* alter matters. Do you think this footpad is a Royal Navy man?"

"I will not rule it out. But I am inclined to think that a British tar would have more respect for his convoy coat than would someone who plucked one off a trash heap where it had been discarded."

"I gather you have no suspects."

"On the contrary. I have scores of them. Too many to winnow them down to any two or three known police characters. That is the rub, Watson. The crimes are finite, but growing every week. Of suspects, I am blessed with an abundance."

"Have you made any progress?"

"Physically, no. Mentally, some. An insufficient amount, but I'm at liberty to label it as progress. 'Old Black Duffel', as Scotland Yard has dubbed him, has twice escaped across the Thames, from one section of the city to another. On two occasions, he has disappeared up Kidney Stairs and onto Narrow Street in Limehouse."

"Suggesting that he dwells there."

"Possibly. Between the foreign element and the generally disreputable environment, Limehouse is an excellent section in which to become lost. But it's a place to begin. I don't have a high expectation of success based upon this one line of inquiry – but a start is a start."

"I quite agree. How will you proceed?"

"Old Black Duffel has already provided me with a glimmer of the patterns governing his brain-box. He prefers to commit his crimes on the southern side of the Thames and escape to the opposite bank, traversing the reaches between facing watermans' stairs which lie in a straight line from one another. If I seek him out on the northern bank, perhaps he will pick me out of the throng as a tempting target and attempt to make off with my wallet."

"My word, do you mean to *bait* him?"

"Once it is practical to do so. But first I must get the lay of the land – reconnoiter his haunts, as it were. You will wish me luck, Watson."

"Of course I do. Do you mean to start tonight?"

Coming to the Charing Cross Station, Holmes paused and said, "You have it exactly. We must part here, for where I am bound, a decent and well-dressed fellow such as yourself shouldn't venture, even in the company of a capable person such as myself. I will be in touch."

With that, Holmes disappeared from my sight, leaving me to walk back to Baker Street myself.

I didn't fear for his safety. I knew him too well to doubt his ability to handle himself under difficult circumstances. And yet I couldn't but feel a sense of unease. Holmes didn't normally go about armed, but he did have his single-stick. I hoped that it would prove sufficiently stout.

As I walked back to our common quarters, I made a greater effort to observe those whom I passed on the street. My observations produced only the most meager and routine conclusions, most of which lacked conviction. However, I did observe a fellow who showed signs of emphysema, or some other lung condition. His fingernails displayed a telltale blush tinge. Of course, this was precisely in my line. Understanding its medical significance, I resolved to mention it to Holmes at the next opportunity. I didn't think it would impress him, but hope does spring eternal.

I did not see Sherlock Holmes again for several days

He failed to return to Baker Street to sleep, nor did he post any letters that would keep me apprised of his progress, if any.

I began to fear for his well-being. I followed the newspapers closely in that difficult interim, learning that Old Black Duffel had struck again, in Wapping this time, and again in Southwark. In neither case was anyone seriously injured. But still I fretted for his life.

Late one evening, my friend returned to Baker Street and resumed his armchair by the fireplace. I had already gone to bed. But the fragrance of his tobacco smoke wafted to my nostrils, awakening my senses. I threw off the bed covers, donned a dressing gown, and found him puffing away in his usual ruminative manner.

"My word, Holmes!" I exclaimed. "Where on earth have you been all this time?"

"Good evening, Watson. Sorry to rouse you from your rest. As to your question, I have been plying the Thames day and night. For I have taken to toiling as an unlicensed waterman. By day, I've fallen in with the members of that rather downtrodden class. By night, I prowled in search of Old Black Duffel, but without success. He is quite an elusive fellow. If I was Southwark, he struck in Wapping. When I went to Wapping, he materialized in Southwark. It was as if he anticipated my movements."

"Have you learned nothing of this phantom?"

"I learned that the lot of a waterman isn't as jolly as the song of a century-gone-by would have it. The steam boats and the trains have stolen much of their commerce. They loiter about the crumbling old waterman's stairs along the embankments, virtually idle, ferrying such the flotsam-and-jetsam of life that fortune brings to them. Where once they didn't lack customers, now they wait half the day for a farthing fare."

"But nothing of your quarry, I take it?"

"You take it perfectly. I had hoped to ingratiate myself into the watermen's trade, but there were so many of them that I haven't yet encountered any who have seen Old Black Duffel closely enough to describe his features."

"But surely some of these men have."

Holmes puffed away for a moment. Then he said, "Certainly. Between the licensed fellows of the Company of Watermen and Lightermen and his unlicensed rival, I have made many acquaintances. But their sheer numbers far exceed my energy, as well as my patience."

By this time, I had settled into my customary seat, facing Holmes.

"You aren't giving up? That doesn't sound like you."

"No, my dear Watson. Although I am weary, I'm not inclined to give up. But I must contrive a fresh line of inquiry if I'm to get anywhere. Old Black Duffel has continued his depredations, eluding Scotland Yard and, for the moment, confounding me."

"This is rather novel. I had half-expected you to return with the matter entirely resolved."

"I, too, harbored higher hopes than the meager fruits that I lay before you. I'm coming to think that Old Black Duffel is a clever chap. But how clever, I cannot say. His methods are simple. He strikes on one side the town, seeks out the nearest river stairs where he accosts a waiting waterman, of which there is an ample supply, day or night, and allows himself to be sculled across to the river stairs opposite the scene of his crime. Afterward, he disappears into the night."

"One would think a waterman would report him to the nearest constable."

"A licensed waterman surely would. But an unlicensed one might not, for they are a wretched group, poaching upon guild men, and caring nothing for society at large. I'm inclined to believe Old Black Duffel prefers the unlicensed variety to any other."

"This is regrettable," I said. "You appear to have nothing more than with which you started – namely, a description of a coat."

"I have no more nor any less than what Scotland Yard currently possesses. Reports of a skulking black duffel coat, occupant unknown."

"What will you do next?"

Instead of replying directly, Holmes offered, "Let me suggest that you seek restful slumber, Watson. By the time I finish my pipe, I intend to do the same, for I'm at a dead end. I don't deny it. But I will allow my black shag to lull me into a frame in mind in which my brain will cease turning its gears and permit sleep. Tomorrow is a new day. I intend to make use of it, but at the moment I sit before you, unqualifiedly flummoxed."

With a sympathetic good night, I sought out my bed, and was soon fast asleep.

Holmes wasn't to be found at breakfast. Nor did I see him the rest of the morning. His bed was neat, and appeared not to have been slept in. I didn't know what to make of that. And since it was a splendid day, I strolled about the city for several hours, enjoying the fresh air.

Only then did I remember that I neglected to inform Holmes of my observation of the man with the bluish fingernails. No doubt the opportunity would arise soon enough.

I next laid eyes upon Holmes at the supper hour. He came trudging up the steps without his usual spritely spring. From the deathly sound of his tread, I inferred that he had made little or no progress.

"Good evening," I said in greeting. "I was just about to go out for a bite to eat. Would you care to join me?"

"I would not," said Holmes in a disagreeable tone, doffing his raglan overcoat.

"No progress, I gather?"

"If you gathered this from my tone of voice, you are correct," he snapped.

"In truth, I concluded this fact from the sound of your footsteps trudging up the stairs. They struck my ears as disconsolate. When you are on the hunt, your step is more lively."

Holmes sank into his familiar armchair. "It would appear that my ways are rubbing off on you. My congratulations."

"Since my appetite isn't yet at its peak, I'm prepared to join you as you consider matters."

Holmes reached for his pipe, and then took the Persian slipper, into which was stuffed a supply of shag tobacco. "Let me not dissuade you from your supper. Such progress as I have made is the progress of the man approaching a fork in the road, only to discover even more forks beyond the one he must select."

"The problem multiplies?"

"The problem splinters like broken glass. I have more data than I possessed one day ago, but like a stained glass window that has fallen to the floor, I no longer hold a recognizable picture in hand, but instead the profoundly shattered remnants of one."

I sat down, knowing that when Holmes stood at an impasse such as this one, only two things were helpful. One was the silence of his own thoughts, and the other a stirring of his deductive powers through conversation. I don't give myself very much credit for assisting my good friend in solving any of the unusual crimes that interest him, but as Holmes himself has said many times, I am something akin to a sounding board whose own observation and insights allow him to turn over a problem in his mind so that he eventually perceives all facets of it, much in the manner a jeweler rotates a gem he is cutting so that all surfaces present themselves to his attention.

"The problem with observation, Watson, is that so few practice it in a scientific manner. People observe what they happen to observe, nothing more and often less. Yet when impressed, they will expand upon their observations after the fact, filling in the glaring gaps with imagination and premature conclusions. I have been to Scotland Yard. I spent the better part of the day conferring with Inspector Lestrade. He has gotten nowhere. And he has led me to the identical empty destination."

"Surely the unwitting watermen and unfortunate victims provided some useful data," I offered.

"Pah! Useful if it weren't so contradictory. One victim claims that Old Black Duffel has dirty white hair, another says he is grey-haired. Yet another insists it is merely greying."

"In the dark, such distinctions are mere the tricks of light and shadow."

"Unquestionably. The bounder hasn't been clearly seen. He no doubt contrived that this be so. He walks about hunched, with his lower face buried in the collar of his duffel coat. During each foray, he keeps his hood pulled over his head, yet is observed to wear different hats, all as black as roosting ravens. Once it was a gambler's hat. On another occasion, it was a so-called pocket cap, which can be crushed and pocketed or discarded. Between the hood and the hats, his visible hair makes little impression."

"Odd that he would wear the same coat, but change hats so frequently."

"Old Black Duffel hasn't worn the same hat whilst committing the robberies he has perpetrated. Lestrade informs me that on each occasion, he has discarded his hat on the side of the river to which he fled. Unfortunately, the hat size is meaningless, since it is invariably worn over the hood. No doubt it is at least a half-size larger than what the phantom would wear in broad daylight, and hence of no further use to him."

"Peculiar, that. His coat is the most distinctive item of his apparel, and therefore the most incriminating."

"Inasmuch as duffel coats are rarely dyed black, this particular coat has been made so for professional reasons. Conceivably, the thief doesn't wish to abandon his most useful item of apparel."

"I quite concur."

"According to Lestrade," continued Holmes, "every victim agrees on a few points. The thief is an aged man of middling height and weight. He wears a unique black duffel coat. Some report that he has flaring nostrils, while others say they are merely distended from the exertion of his deeds. No one can speak authoritatively as to his eye color, for none have seen his eyes clearly."

"The only certainties appear to be that he is over sixty and lives on the northern bank of the Thames," I remarked.

Holmes made a sound deep inside his throat of derision. It now occurred to him to begin filling his pipe.

"Perhaps, perhaps not. I don't draw any strong conclusion from his method of operation. This is what is so baffling to me. I have handfuls of observational data from the victims and witnesses, but I cannot sort them into anything sensible. I don't know which I can safely discard and what I may retain as factual. Without a stronger foundation of facts, I cannot reason this out. Therefore, action is necessary. The brain has its uses. Reason is a tool. But sometimes men must use their more primitive skills to achieve their objectives."

"What do you propose?"

Holmes filled his pipe. He was looking at it as if not sure what to make of it. I have rarely seen him so distracted.

"I propose that we find ourselves a hospitable restaurant and dine well. After which I'm going to the East Side, where I will stride about and present myself as a potential victim."

"Do you think this wise?"

"Hardly, but I'm a desperate man. I've beaten my brains out against this riddle for nearly a week now. It is time for action. If you have a mind to, you may assist me. You will be my shadow, walking a block or two before or behind me. If he strikes, I will strike back. But if I fail, you will follow him as best you can. Between us, we might capture the bloke."

"It's chancy, but he hasn't committed violence as yet."

"Keep your revolver in readiness, Watson."

"Should you not have it?"

"I carry my own pocket piece, but I prefer to use my stick. The revolver is a tool of last resort. You will be our first resort, as well as my last, should I fall victim, my own weapon unfired."

"I wouldn't mind reversing our roles, as it were," I suggested.

"Not for a minute, Watson! This is my affair, and I prefer to act the central part in it."

"Since your mind appears to be made up, I won't attempt to dissuade you further."

Laying his pipe aside unlit, Holmes stood up and said, "Let us go about our business then."

We departed Baker Street and found a restaurant that we both agreed was substantial as well as economical. We ate our separate repasts, Holmes driving through his meal like a coachman taking a late-night fare homeward. I was more leisurely, for I understood the value of proper eating in regards to sound digestion.

Whilst we dined, I thought to remark on one puzzling point. "This is a lot of bother to go through, since you appear to have no client, and remuneration is therefore lacking."

"I consider keeping London safe to be in my own personal interest, my dear Watson," Holmes stated. "Inasmuch as I dwell within its confines, I'm not disinclined to contribute to its upkeep in my own way. Civic duty and all that."

"Well stated, Holmes."

When we were done, we made our way to Bermondsey, where we separated, Holmes walking ahead of me while I loitered for a few minutes before falling behind. Over dinner he had explained his reasoning for this choice.

Old Black Duffel appeared to be a creature of the London Docks, and Limehouse in particular. He had struck across the river at Southwark Park and Grand Surrey Docks, retreating to Shadwell and London Docks. Scotland Yard was laying for him. Undercover men were about, watching the waterman's stairs. But the footpad had yet to do any robbing in Bermondsey, across the river from Wapping. This, deduced Holmes, was his likeliest hunting ground if he stayed true to form and wished to elude the police, who were being pressed by newspaper clamor.

The gas-lamps were illuminated by the time Holmes struck out for the congeries of tenement-choked streets that made up Bermondsey in the shadow of Tower Bridge. The leather trade was quite active here, so the parish was usually awash with tanners, leather-dressers, fell mongers, and the like. Longshore labourers, coal porters, bricklayers, costermongers and others added to the ever-shifting human tide. But as the hour was growing late, these examples were little in evidence.

I did my best to keep my friend within view as he wended his way through the darkened byways. The usual nocturnal inhabitants swirled around us – mudlarks, mariners, and stevedores. I kept a watchful eye as I moved from each oasis of gaslight to the intervening pools of shadow.

I observed that Holmes rambled about in approximate circles, keeping close to the river bank – for I understood that Old Black Duffel never struck except where a set of waterman's stairs were convenient for a quick escape.

Holmes turned onto Marygold Street and was briefly lost to view until I hurried up to the corner and made my turn.

When I caught up with him, I saw a remarkable thing. Although he had dressed modestly, he made no effort to disguise himself. Yet the more he walked along, the more subtly he altered his gait, decreasing the swing of his arms as he moved. He appeared to have lost a few inches in height, and his shoulders became slumped, his head hanging forward as if heavy with workaday fatigue.

Up until that point, I hadn't noticed what he had been doing. Having momentarily lost sight of him, upon catching up I would have mistaken him for another fellow, had it not been for the severe cut of this coat.

It has been said that the world lost a great actor when Holmes bent his considerable talents to detection.

As I was marveling over this artful transformation, which was still taking place before my eyes, albeit slowly, from out of a cobbled alley directly ahead, a shadowy figure stepped.

This figure was short and squat, and he came up from behind Holmes on mincing steps. I didn't see the blackthorn cane in his hand until it lifted. With a start, I realized that Holmes was about to be struck a cruel and cowardly blow upon the head.

"Watch out!" I shouted.

It was unnecessary, for Holmes was already turning, his own stick lifting. And for a moment two stout canes banged and clashed against one another as Holmes fought to beat off his attacker.

In the dark, I made out the fact that the man wore a bulky black duffel coat, the hood raised. A hat of some sort sat atop his hunched head.

I rushed ahead. Out of my coat pocket came my revolver.

The battle raged on. Not a word was spoken. Old Black Duffel – for this assailant could only be he – was giving a good account of himself. But he was soon overmastered by the towering strength of Sherlock Holmes.

The hat was knocked off the assailant's head. With his return sweep, Holmes struck the cane from his hand.

At this point, he broke and ran. I lifted my revolver into the air and fired a single shot. I don't know if, in his terror, Old Black Duffel simply didn't hear it, or if he didn't care. Escape was all that was on his maddened mind.

Holmes and I raced after him, I shouting for the beggar to halt, and Holmes blowing on his police whistle.

These actions only impelled the man to pump his legs more strenuously.

We were in the vicinity of Fountain Stairs. Down them he plunged.

The bulky fellow reached the bottom before we could gain the top. A heated exchange of voices came from below. I could make nothing sensible of it.

When I reached the top step, I could spy Old Black Duffel hunched in a skiff being rowed away by a waterman, his head down, chin tucked into his coat collar, the greater portion of his head enveloped by the bucket hood of his bulky black coat.

His voice rose up in warning. "If you dare to follow, I will shoot this man! Do not tempt me."

The waterman, an elderly fellow with sparse hair, cried out, "Please, sir! He is armed. It is my life if you disobey."

We watched as the oarsman rowed strenuously, with Old Black Duffel keeping his eye on us both.

I demanded, "Holmes, dare we follow?"

Holmes shook his head gravely. "I wouldn't risk it. This is a stalemate. We must respect the danger to the poor waterman."

Whilst we stood at the top of Fountain Stairs, waiting for a constable to arrive, we watched pensively as the poor waterman conveyed his unwanted passenger across the turbid waters of the Outer Pool to the muddy foreshore of Wapping.

There, he was let off. The devil scuttled up Wapping Old Stairs and was quickly lost from sight.

A policeman finally arrived, demanding, "What's the row?"

When Holmes identified himself, he was given all due respect accorded to the greatest consulting detective in London.

"We nearly bagged Old Black Duffel. He got away in that skiff."

The constable didn't have to hear all of it. His whistle skirled, and he shouted for the bewildered waterman to return for us.

This took some minutes, during which Holmes went back to the street and returned with Old Black Duffel's hat.

It was a gambler's hat, black and made of leather. A stylish thing in its extreme way, yet no proper gentleman would be found wearing one on the West Side.

Holmes was examining it as I was relating the events of the evening to the constable.

"A pity you didn't shoot him," the man said. "But it is understandable."

When the skiff bumped the bottom of Fountain Stairs, we were there to meet it and quickly climbed aboard.

"Take us across," the constable instructed.

"And give us your story as you row," added Holmes.

"Well, sir, you saw the whole thing, I take it. I was mindin' my lawful business, waitin' for a fare and the bloke descended upon me. He presented a derringer. An ugly little thing, black as if carved from coal. He showed me both barrels, and I didn't fancy either of them discharging into my entrails, so naturally I did as demanded. I have been on the river all of my adult life, and I wasn't ready to surrender it just yet."

"What does the fellow look like?" demanded the constable.

Holmes gave the answer to that question. "Round faced, not much above the age of sixty. Hair very grey. Clipped salt-and-pepper mustache. The eyes were pale blue. I will be happy to draw you a picture, Constable, when opportunity affords."

Addressing the waterman, the constable asked, "Can you add anything to that description?"

"I would say that the eyes were light grey, not blue."

"I disagree," said Holmes. "But that is the problem with individual powers of observation. No two persons see the same thing in the same way. And there are individuals who possess irises which appear grey or blue, depending on how the light strikes them."

There wasn't much more to the story than that.

We reached the opposite river stairs, bounded up to the top step, and looked about.

No sign of Old Black Duffel could be seen among the throng of dockers, street boys, and other river inhabitants.

"Vanished!" muttered the policeman.

"Not exactly," returned Holmes. "Observe where I point."

Up the way, peeping out from an ashcan was one sleeve of the black duffel coat. We hurried up to it. Holmes lifted the lid, and the constable removed the threadbare item, now smeared with greyish coal ash.

"It appears that we harried him into abandoning his prized garment," I proclaimed.

"There can be no doubt that this is the same coat," said the constable.

Holmes inspected the garment. "None whatever. Observe the lining. Tartan. Royal Navy coats are lined plainly. This is a common coat, not a convoy coat which has been dyed black. Our man has no connection to the British Navy. We will turn the coat and the hat over to Inspector Lestrade. Perhaps he can make something more of it."

The constable availed himself of his whistle, and before long two of his fellows showed up. Once apprised of the situation, the trio dispersed in three directions, seeking the coatless man, armed only with the most vague of descriptions and his approximate hat size.

We went here and there, Holmes having observed where the police hadn't that in disposing of his coat, the rogue had disturbed some of the ash and stepped unawares in the residue that had leaked onto the cobblestones. We followed the trail of flaky ash for almost a block when at last all trace petered out.

An hour had almost elapsed. All concerned reluctantly concluded that there was nothing more to be discovered. Old Black Duffel had disappeared into whatever disreputable warren had welcomed him.

"This is Wapping," murmured one constable. "There are many gambling houses, spirit cellars, and other such unsavory establishments that would welcome such a man. We've looked about, but wherever he has gone, the edifice has swallowed him entirely."

Holmes said, "Very well. Give Inspector Lestrade my regards. Perhaps we all have better hunting tomorrow." He walked back to the river stairs and we descended to the bottom step, where the gurgling Thames lapped against the stone. A different waterman was standing on the little jetty, his punt tied up there.

"Take us across," Holmes directed.

"Of course, sir."

We got in and the fellow began pulling at his oars. Engaging him in conversation, Holmes asked, "How is your business, fellow?"

"Mighty poor. If you're workin' below the bridge, a bloke is lucky to make ten shillings. But when winter comes it will be far worse. I don't speak just for myself, but for my brothers on the river. The steamships and the railways, as well as changin' times, have all but done us in. When I was younger, this was a good trade to apprentice in. No more. It would've been better to become a scavenger or a mummer."

196

"I hear the same from others of your guild. I imagine it is harder on a man of your years."

"Neither harder nor softer, sir. Us old 'uns have been puttin' their pennies aside for many years yet. It is the young 'uns just startin' out that struggle most. They never had the good times. If you saved, you can press onward. If you didn't, I imagine your future is bleak."

"Are you licensed, my good man?"

"I am, sir. But many aren't. They steal from us who are. But what is a man to do? All one needs to be an able waterman is a boat and a brace of oars. In my youthful days, I wore the dark blue jacket and white ducks of my trade, as well as pumps so polished they turned fair heads, they did. I cannot afford such things anymore, for I have children to feed."

He pointed to his checked shirt and the black silk neckerchief tied in a sailor's knot about his throat. "This is all the uniform I can afford now. Most scullers don't bother with even that much. It's rare to see the round glazed hat of old. But these are the times we swim in."

When we reached the northern bank, Holmes paid the man and asked, almost as an afterthought, "Do you know the other watermen who ply this reach?"

"Most, but not all."

"The man who took us across in the last hour might be familiar to you."

Holmes gave an accurate description of the fellow, but after scratching his head, the waterman said, "I don't know the bloke. I doubt if he has a license. I know all the licensed scullers by face and by name. I know their boats as well as I know my shoes. He must be in the way of a scalawag. Do you understand?"

"I do," said replied Holmes. "Good evening, and thank you."

Holmes strode about the neighborhood, looking in the alley out of which Old Black Duffel had emerged, but found nothing of interest.

Standing in this ill-lit court, I remarked, "Apparently we have struck a dead end as blind as this very cul-de-sac."

"Not entirely, for I have seen the bounder's face. And tonight I'll make a sketch of it and see that Lestrade has it by morning. Although we haven't captured the phantom, we have made the first progress that I can measure."

"No doubt he will lay low for a period of time."

"I would expect so."

"And when he resurfaces, if he does, he'll be wearing a different coat."

"But the same face, Watson. The same face."

Over breakfast the next morning, Holmes wasn't in a talkative mood. Evidently he had slept, albeit fitfully. More than once, I had heard pacing in the sitting room. The odor of his tobacco smoke was fresh in the air when I awoke.

I permitted a certain interval of silence to pass while we consumed our eggs, scones, and tea. Then I ventured to remark, "Have you finished your drawing?"

"I have, but it doesn't satisfy me."

From the pocket of his dressing gown he removed a folded sheet of paper and laid it down on the table.

Sketched in sure-handed detail was the face of a man. His hair was concealed by a black hood, but his features were executed with the distinctness of an etching. The clipped mustache was rendered so that it was unmistakably of the salt-and-pepper variety.

"I didn't see the man's features as well as you did," I remarked, "but I would say that it is a credible likeness."

"It is the spitting image. Make no mistake about that – the spitting image. Yet for reasons I cannot fully articulate, it doesn't satisfy me."

"I wouldn't be so hard on yourself. A pen-and-ink sketch isn't the same as a camera study."

Holmes didn't reply. He continued eating.

The morning paper was at hand, and I opened it, seeking respite from Holmes's rather fuming silence.

"Good heavens!" I exclaimed.

"What is it?"

"Old Black Duffel struck again last night. Or should I say, quite early this morning. In Southwark, this time. A waterman carried him across the river to Queen's Stairs at Tower Wharf, where he made his escape."

"Would you hand me that?"

I did so. Holmes took the paper and read the account.

"According to this," he mused, "he's still up to his familiar tricks. He accosted a docker who was coming home drunk from a public house, relieving him of his wallet. Remarkable!"

"He isn't easily dissuaded from his self-appointed rounds."

"I wonder where he acquired another duffel coat dyed black so quickly?"

"It would be nearly impossible for him to do so, it seems to me. Therefore, one can only conclude that the old boy owns more than one such coat."

"The hat he wore this time was a derby. It was found on the other side of the river after he made his escape."

"Strange that he should change hats, but retain the same coat style of coat. What it offers in the way of concealment would seem to be a hindrance, insofar as his breathless escapes are concerned."

"Yet he has made them each time," mused Holmes, "effortlessly and apparently flawlessly."

"Except that you have clearly seen his face."

"Yes, I knocked his hat off his head at my first opportunity."

Holmes dwindled again into a sullen silence.

After I resumed my breakfast, I remembered something. "Do you recall the passing woman with the greenish eyes?"

"I do."

"After we parted that very night, I happened to notice a man striding along and, applying your own edict of observing closely, chanced to see that his fingernails were unusually blue."

Holmes frowned. "No doubt he suffers from some affliction of the lungs, or possibly the heart."

"Exactly. Oxygen isn't getting to his fingertips as it should. I passed by him rather quickly. But not so quickly that I failed to see that one telling thing."

Holmes's frown increased slightly. A notch formed between his bushy eyebrows.

"Tell me, Watson," he said dryly, "what was the color of his hair?"

"I didn't take note of that. He wore a top hat."

"I see. Did you happen to glance at his face? Did his eyes reveal their color?"

"In those brief moments, I had only time to study his hands. I couldn't tell you anything about his face or features."

"What type of coat did he wear? Surely, you spotted that?"

Feeling deflated, I allowed, "I confess that I didn't. Nor do I clearly recall."

"Therefore, Watson, you are deficient in the art of observation. You observed one thing closely and it so captivated your attention that you failed to apprehend any other details, other than the subject was a man who is well dressed."

"As a doctor, I would naturally observe things that are in my line."

"True enough. But as an observer, one must perceive as many things as possible, commit them to memory, and draw as many conclusions as possible from the data acquired. The eye must be quick. The mind even quicker. One must see and one must catalog, and most importantly one must retain all that one perceives. For what good is observation if the memory is faulty?"

"I fear that despite your example, my dear Holmes, I am still a mere amateur in the game of observation. With practice, I may improve."

"No doubt you will, no doubt you will." His voice was distracted, and I could tell that his mind was on the matter of Old Black Duffel even as his attention was struggling to get through his breakfast. When baffled, Holmes's appetite was thin. I imagine that he anticipated a long day ahead of him, or he would have skipped it all together.

"As a medical man," I said with a trace of defensiveness, "I would naturally pay more attention to the morbid than the fashionable. One can hardly diagnose a man's condition from the cut of his coat, any more than one can tell very much from the duffel coat discarded so urgently."

"On the contrary. One can tell a great many things from a coat. A man's height. Conceivably his weight. Certainly his sense of fashion is evident in what he wears, from which one can readily deduce his station in life."

"Not in this instance, Holmes. Surely the man has affected the dark duffel coat in order to skulk about, and for no other reason."

Something appeared to click in Holmes's brain. I didn't think he had heard my last remark, but evidently he did. For a sharp light spring into his keen eyes.

"Watson, you are a godsend. I have the key!"

"I beg your pardon?"

He stood up abruptly, his breakfast forgotten. He folded the sketch of Old Black Duffel and placed it into his dressing gown.

"I must be off and hasten to share my theory with Inspector Lestrade."

"Do you have a theory?"

"When you noticed the man's fingers but failed to observe his coat, you were demonstrating a principal known to all who practice the arcane art of stage magic."

I struggled to respond.

"Misdirection, Watson! Misdirection is the key!"

And with no more explanation than that cryptic refrain, Holmes dashed to his room, dressed for the day, and left for Scotland Yard, leaving me in a most profound quandary.

I couldn't imagine what he was talking about.

Twilight was upon the city as I was walking homeward for the day. Turning towards Baker Street, I was startled by a hansom cab pulling up to the kerbstone. Out of it stepped Sherlock Holmes.

"Watson! Ask no questions. Join me."

I did as my friend requested, climbing in ahead of him. The driver was soon off and running.

"May I inquire where we are bound?"

"I have had an interesting afternoon with Lestrade. I believe that I've worked out a great many things that were previously obscured."

"This is good news. Congratulations!"

"It may be some time yet before true congratulations can be accepted, but we're once more on the scent-trail."

"Jolly good. Knowing the blighter's face should make the battle so much easier."

"I wish that were true, but it is only partially true. Perhaps half-true. Perhaps only a third true."

"I don't follow these strange constructions of yours."

"If we're successful, all will be revealed. And the shadowy footpad will be ours."

We were let off in Rotherhithe at Cockolds Point, where Inspector Lestrade appeared to be waiting for us. Dusk was gathering. Evening would soon be upon us.

"Good evening to you both," Lestrade greeted. "Dr. Watson, Are you ready?"

"As ready as I imagine I will ever be. But Holmes hasn't explained precisely what I should be ready for."

"All about us, constables are strolling about in disguise. Mr. Holmes will select a path, and I understand that you will select another."

"If you're willing," said Holmes. "Previously, the bait was sparse. Now it will be plentiful."

"I see. I suppose that I shouldn't refuse. But I don't have my pistol."

"You may not need it, for I don't intend to stray very far from your path. You see, having been waylaid once, I expect that I will be avoided henceforth."

At this point we separated, Holmes admonishing me to keep near to Pageant Stairs and Horse Ferry Stairs.

Knowing that my friend was close at hand, I set out on my way. I walked at a slower pace than is my wont, and circled about is if I had lost my way, a gentleman from the West Side slumming through this East Side labyrinth.

Holmes was a canny man. He left a little to chance. On this evening, his plan appeared to be sound – but that didn't mean that it was foolproof.

As I traversed Rotherhithe Street, I approached Pageant Stairs. Below its steep incline, watermen and lightermen were pushing their boats about the slate river. Darkness lay upon the Thames like a blanket of sable.

It was ebb tide. The mudlarks and scavengers were out, digging away at the exposed mud of the shore in search of dropped coins and other minor salvage. I paid them no heed. They were as eternal as the ravens at The Tower of London.

Looking out at the sluggishly flowing river, I saw a small punt approach – a waterman with his fare.

In the dark, I could make nothing of them, but one sat hunched in the bow of the boat, swathed in shadow. He held his head down, as if it was raining. Perhaps it was the chill that caused him to do so.

As the waterman feathered his oars to bring his boat alongside the bottom of the stairs without undo jarring, the passenger stepped off without a word or even to pay his fare.

Up the steps he came, his spring purposeful.

As he walked, he took a hat out from a commodious coat pocket, and blocking the crown properly, placed it up on his head. It was a gamblers hat. His coat was a black, bulky affair and the hood was up.

That was when I realized the truth.

Mounting the steps came Old Black Duffel himself!

I stepped away, feigning nonchalance.

As the fellow reached the top step, I said to him, "Good evening." I kept my voice level.

"It will be a good evening if all goes well," the fellow said thinly.

"All seldom goes well, especially in this part of the city at this hour."

The man halted, and stared at me. The brim of his hat threw his features into deep shadow.

"Queer thing to say."

"But truthful," I returned.

"Do I know you?"

"I doubt it. I'm rarely in Rotherhithe."

Curiosity causing his head to cock like that of a dog as he approached me.

"Slumming, are you?"

I started at him closely, expecting to behold the features sketched by Holmes from memory. But to my surprise and relief, this old fellow bore no resemblance to the man so sought by Holmes and Scotland Yard. His upper lip was cleanly shaven. The clipped mustache of the other night was wholly absent. Of course, mustaches are easily shorn.

My failure to reply caused him concern.

"Do you know me?" he demanded.

"I scarcely think so," I said curtly. "Good night to you. Have a pleasant evening."

With that, I turned on my heel, and began to walk briskly. I didn't care for the men's tone of voice. Nor was I any longer certain that I had correctly identified him.

With a scuffling of leather heels, he caught up with me and blocked my way.

"I will trouble you for your wallet, sir."

Ordinarily, I would resist. But I knew that Holmes was nearby.

"This is rather rough, sir!"

"I'm a rough sort of fellow. Now your billfold. Hand it over."

Reaching into my coat, I produced the item and tendered it to the fellow.

He was quick off the mark, I'll give him that. Down the river stairs he raced and into the boat bobbing below he jumped.

I heard him shout, "Haste! I'm returning to Limehouse."

I couldn't see if Old Black Duffel produced his pocket pistol, but the waterman didn't give an argument. He dropped upon his bench and took up his oars. Soon, he was pushing across the sluggish currents of Limehouse Reach.

"Holmes!" I cried out. "Holmes!"

He came out of the shadows from a direction I didn't expect.

"He has my wallet!" I told him, pointing down the stairs.

"I know. I saw it all, Watson. You did well."

Holmes raced down the stairs. Upon reaching the bottom, he called to the waterman to turn around.

Back came the piteous reply. "I cannot, sir! That would mean my end."

"It will mean jail for you if you don't return after you have dropped off your passenger," warned Holmes.

"I understand, sir."

In the darkness, Old Black Duffel was hectoring the poor waterman to pull harder, ever harder.

By this time, I had joined my friend at the bottom of the river stairs.

"If they were only another waterman about," I said. "We could give chase."

"Chase may not be necessary. All has been thought out well in advance."

Soon, the boat was all but lost to our view. But across the dark current, we could hear its bow grate against Kidney Stairs.

Hearing that sound, Holmes lifted his pistol and fired two shots into the air.

"A signal?" I cried.

"Yes. Watson. A signal to our allies."

Before long, the waterman returned and bumped his craft into the bottom of the stairs at our feet.

We leapt aboard with Holmes exhorting the man to return to the opposite bank. "That was him. Did you see his features clearly?"

"I did, sir. He was round of face and with red cheeks. His nose cut exceedingly narrow. Like the back fin of a shark, it was. I would know him anywhere."

I said nothing. The bounder who accosted me didn't lay claim to either description, but in the darkness, such mistakes were commonly made by the unobservant, as Holmes would no doubt remind me.

The waterman got us across in excellent time.

Down Kidney Stairs came Inspector Lestrade, saying, "My men are following him. He shall not get away this time."

"Excellent!" said Holmes. "This waterman got a good look at him."

Inspector Lestrade addressed the fellow. "You must come with us as a witness. Strictly a matter of form, you understand."

"If I must," the man said hesitantly.

He stood up in his boat, and stepped off.

We three pounded up Kidney Stairs. When we reached the top, I saw the waterman's face clearly in the gaslight.

"Upon my word!"

"What is it?" the waterman demanded, startled by my outburst.

Holmes interrupted. "Time enough for conversation later. Let us see what the constables have accomplished."

We strolled up gaslit Narrow Street with its Georgian terraced houses and dust-heaps. A uniformed constable came to meet us, the black gambler's hat in hand.

"An undercover man is right behind the blighter. He'll blow his whistle at the appropriate moment."

The waterman quavered, "Sirs, is there danger for me here?"

"I imagine so," admitted Holmes. "But as a good citizen I trust that you'll put aside all considerations of personal risk, for we are on the trail of Old Black Duffel, the scourge of the Thames."

"I don't feel comfortable, sir, for I'm up in years. I don't wish to squander any of my remaining time on earth."

"Buck up!" encouraged Holmes. "This is Inspector Lestrade of Scotland Yard, and I'm Sherlock Holmes. This is Doctor Watson. Together, we'll see that no harm comes to you. But it's essential that you aid us in identifying the man who stole the doctor's wallet."

"Can *he* not identify him?"

Lestrade said, "Two witnesses are more material than one. Especially under these circumstances."

We walked along. It wasn't many blocks farther when a police whistle resounded. We picked up our pace and hurried in its direction.

The undercover man waved to us and pointed to a plain door that led to a basement of a decrepit building.

"He went down there, sir. It is gambling den of known disrepute."

"Sound your whistle again, constable."

The piercing whistle brought additional reinforcements. One constable was deputed to hold the frightened waterman in safety while the rest of us went down the creaking and rickety stairs into such a foul den of perdition as I have never before seen.

As we descended, I whispered to Holmes, "That waterman looked familiar to me."

"Thank you, Watson," Holmes returned.

I didn't immediately understand his reply.

Three constables surged into the smoky gambling den and announced themselves to the shiftless Chinese, English bully boys, and polyglot harridans who congregated there.

"We seek a wanted man. Once we have him in hand, our business for the evening will be concluded."

Holmes raised his drawing for all to see, adding, "This is the man in question. If he is on the premises, he should present himself and submit to arrest forthwith."

Holmes went among the riffraff, displaying the drawing and receiving muttering responses to the effect that no one present had ever laid eyes upon such an individual.

"He is Old Black Duffel himself," Lestrade announced. "He was seen entering this establishment. Once we have him, our business here will be concluded."

The constables failed to find their man, but they did locate a black duffel coat. It was hanging from a hook amid a flock of others, conspicuously buried between varied items of apparel.

"Who is the owner of this?" demanded Inspector Lestrade.

No one claimed the coat.

Drawing close to me, Holmes made his voice very low. "Watson, point out the man who accosted you."

I confessed to being very puzzled. But I did as my friend requested. I went among the group, and soon found him.

Out from a pocket of the red-faced bounder's waistcoat came a small black derringer.

"I'm not afraid to use this!" he cried out.

Lestrade was firm and without fear. "You have two bullets to expend. And we are many."

Producing his own revolver, Holmes pointed out, "There are six shells in my cylinder. I don't believe the numbers are in your favor tonight."

Old Black Duffel was having none of it. "Nevertheless, you will let me go free, or some of you will die. Now make a path. I'm a desperate man. Do not underestimate me."

The crowd in the gambler's den didn't seem very agitated by the sight of the small black derringer. No one made any outcry. Nor did anyone drop to the floor in fear.

I took a step back from the man, and bumped into the edge of a round table. Reaching back, I found a stout mug of beer. This I grasped.

The man's eyes were on the door leading up and out and he directed the blunt barrels of his derringer on the uniformed men. He was very intent upon escape.

Hence, as he move past me, it didn't register on him that I was swinging the mug downward, knocking the derringer from his fist, and incidentally but fortuitously stinging his eyes with a flying wave of beer.

His empty hands clapped over his eyes in blinkered surprise.

"Well done, Watson! Well done!" cried Holmes as the constables descended upon the shocked man.

"I will trouble you for my wallet when you are no longer engaged in resisting arrest," I said casually.

Handcuffs in place, the man was hauled to his feet and stood before Lestrade and Holmes.

"If you don't need my wallet as evidence," I said firmly, "I would like it back."

Lestrade's questing hand found the wallet and surrendered it to me.

"But I don't understand," I said, studying the man. "This isn't the robber you drew."

"Let's take our prisoner out into the fresh air, Lestrade," suggested Holmes. "We'll sort things out under cleaner light."

The prisoner was taken to the sidewalk, and his vociferations were coarse and repugnant.

Turning to me, Holmes asked, "Watson, did you not say something about the waterman being familiar to you?"

"In a vague way, yes."

"Perhaps this will assist your memory."

Holmes held up the drawing of the man who had accosted him previously. Except for the absence of a recently-removed clipped mustache, the likeness was sound.

"There is your answer."

Lestrade said, "Consider yourself to be under arrest." Handcuffs were placed on the waterman's wrists. He made no resistance. Shock made his face pale and his expression momentarily vacant, slackening his lean jaw.

"What is this?" he managed. "Am I not a witness?"

Holmes asserted, "I believe the correct term is *accomplice*."

The prisoners were taken away forthwith. Lestrade addressed Holmes, saying, "Your theory was correct, Mr. Holmes. Congratulations. You have done it again."

"Thank you, Inspector. It was quite a chase, but in the end the hounds won the day, whilst the foxes now stand to pay the penalty for being the wretched curs that they truly are."

On the ride back to Baker Street, Holmes divulged the remaining pieces of the puzzle.

"You see," he was saying. "Misdirection was the key to everything. I had thought that the differing descriptions could be laid at the failure of ordinary persons to note and recall items of description faithfully. While this is demonstrably true, it wasn't necessarily the answer. When you mentioned your failure to recall the coat worn by the man with the blue fingernails, it was as if my brain was a photographic darkroom that had been illuminated by a candle.

"Heretofore, we had assumed that our footpad wore a black duffel coat to assist in his nocturnal operations. That he was an aged man seemed beyond question. But it dawned on me that when Old Black Duffel disposed of his coat, yet reappeared within hours wearing another, I knew that there were two coats, not one. Two coats suggested two rogues. The uncommon black duffel coat had to be replaced, because it was the key to their misdirection. In reality, it proved to be their undoing."

"I see now. One man rowed the other to the scene of the crime and then brought him back to his safe harbor in Limehouse, or some waterside stretch convenient to it. But Holmes, the waterman of the other night is neither of these criminals."

"And here I came to another conclusion: If there were two rogues playing the part of Old Black Duffel, why not three, or four, or more?"

"It is a ring of thieves!" I cried.

"More correctly, it is a clutch of starving watermen who banded together in a joint scheme. Unable to make a living by day, they turned the disadvantages of their dying profession into the illicit advantages of a common cause. All were older, and most were destitute and unlicensed. Virtually anonymous, they were able to operate with impunity, wearing different hats, but the same jacket. In all reports, the bucket hood was raised, concealing much of the guilty party's head even after the hat was abandoned."

"No doubt the idle watermen plying the river served as spies, frustrating the police investigation."

"As well as my own. In gaining the confidence of certain scullers, I inadvertently betrayed the fact that I was on their scent. Small wonder Old Black Duffel never struck where I toiled. He was advised of my whereabouts."

"But what about the others? There are thousands of unlicensed watermen plying the Thames. We have no idea how many number this ring."

"Small matter. I will draw another sketch for Scotland Yard. The waterman who slipped away the other evening will be picked up before long. I imagine Lestrade and his men will extract much useful information from their prisoners. That is work best suited for them. We have achieved our goal. The ring is smashed. Their ways are known. No more will they glide across the mighty Thames in search of meager fares and greater plunder."

"Well done," I said heartily. "But I remain unclear on one point: How did you know to come to Rotherhithe on this very night?"

"Even though he was not a single individual, Old Black Duffel showed that he was a creature of habit. Invariably, he came 'round to Limehouse. I imagined that meant that one of the footpads who took on the dark mantle lived there."

"I see. Each man retreated to his own personal stamping ground at the conclusion of a foray."

"Precisely. It was only a matter of time before the inhabitant of Limehouse took his turn. If it didn't occur tonight, the man's turn would soon arrive. I was prepared to stalk Rotherhithe until it did."

"Ah, so patience won this day, as much as did scientific observation."

"The salient lesson here, Watson, is that observation without discernment is only a half-measure. One can recognize a shilling at a distance, but if the distance is too great, it is difficult to impossible to tell whether one is looking at the face of the coin, or its reverse."

"Remarkable what alterations the passing years bring about," I mused. "A group of aging idlers down on their luck banded together to make an unsavory living. Desperation motivated them. Once they were jolly young watermen in their polished pumps, white ducks and black hats. And now – "

"And now they are bound for prison . . . ."

The Blood-Spattered Bridge
by Gayle Lange Puhl

The letter that started us on one of our most dangerous cases was dated November 1st. It arrived the day after, from Kent, in the afternoon post. Sherlock Holmes lifted it from the stack of letters and circulars that Mrs. Hudson had delivered a few moments before. He slit the flap with the tiny silver dagger from his desk. The miniature weapon had been a gift from King d'Forrest, a former client that had asked Holmes's assistance with a case involving three lost companions and a malevolent old woman. Holmes perused the missive swiftly, then leaned back in his armchair and read it again. I stirred up the fire with the poker and then settled back into the basket chair with my copy of *The Lancet*. It had been a slow, late autumn day, cold and overcast, and I was in need of some diversion. I had always found reading my favorite medical journal to be relaxing.

Holmes tossed the letter across to me. "What do you think of this, Watson?" he drawled. He picked out a pipe from the several on the table beside him and began to fill it from his pouch.

I tried to emulate my friend's methods. "It is a letter written on inexpensive paper. The message is written in blue ink, with a fine nib, and so closely composed in a cursive style that the meaning is almost lost among the curlicues and flourishes. It is signed Mrs. Tobias Ogden and I think I see mention of – " I squinted at the note. " – a husband and a bridge. Otherwise, I can make nothing of it." I handed the letter back.

"Not too badly done," he smiled. I brightened and laid down my magazine.

"You have grasped the major outline of the letter," said my friend, "but missed all the important details. The style of cursive writing is noteworthy, however," "With copperplate written out in this old-fashioned way, the author could not be anyone under the age of sixty. You recall my little monograph on autographs and calligraphies spanning the last three-hundred years that was published in *Graphic Studies* last year."

My dear Mr. Holmes, (he read aloud)

> *Please excuse my writing to you directly like this, without an introduction, but I feel that my need is great and will not stand delay. My name is Mary Ogden and I am the wife of Tobias Ogden, former coachman of the Duke of Morris. After*

decades of faithful service, my husband and I were, by the good-will and grace of the Duke, retired to a small corner of his estate in Kent.

My husband refused a pension, feeling still capable of work, so the Duke set him to see to the care and repair of a small stone arched bridge just outside the village of Livermoore. A bridge, first of wood and later of stone, has spanned the White River at that spot since the Romans were here. There is a road which skirts Livermoore on the way to the city of Moncaster, but using the bridge and crossing the Duke's estate saves several miles, so the bridge is very popular.

The population of the village is a mixture of estate workers, small shop owners, and people who work in the city of Moncaster, but prefer country living. The principal features of the place are the church, the village hall, the public house, and the school.

Starting two weeks ago, my Tobias and I were awakened every night for seven nights by the sound of thundering hooves pounding over the bridge and the squeal of a horse. When I mentioned it to a woman friend after services at church that next Sunday, she told me of a story going the rounds in Livermoore.

It seems that an old legend, the Spirit of Dan Rounders, has been revived. He was a soldier, late of Edward the First's army, back in the 1200's. He came back from the first Crusade and wooed a maiden of the village. She rejected him and he went mad. He killed her, her parents, and two neighbors who had been attracted by their cries. He stole the mayor's prize black horse and fled Livermoore by way of the west road going over the bridge. No one knew what became of him after that. The signs that Dan Rounders was abroad were the sound of hooves and the cry of a horse late on moonless nights. It had been moonless the week that we heard the noises.

Ben Walker, an estate worker, said that he had seen the ghost of Dan Rounder racing through the streets that same night that we first heard the disturbance. Two other men said they saw the apparition on different nights. It was the talk of Livermoore.

Tobias and I don't believe adding to such gossip, so we agreed to avoid such talk. We had nearly forgotten the story until an incident happened last night.

210

We heard the sound of hooves and the horse's squeal after midnight. When Tobias went out to inspect the bridge this morning, he found an odd thing. Across the roadway and parapet of the far end of the bridge were large splashes in red – blood. It was extensive and still dripping. We called the constable and the doctor. No accidents or injured persons were reported in the area. The policeman was baffled.

At the same time the local town clerk disappeared. The council are checking the town books right now. But what bothers me the most is the source of that blood. I fear that some outlying farmer or poor animal is lying wounded out in the fields and it breaks my heart.

My husband and I agreed that I should write to you about these things. Please, Mr. Holmes, would you lose no time to come out here and investigate? Thank you.

Mrs. Tobias Ogden
White River Bridge
Livermoore, Kent

"What do you think of that, Doctor?" Holmes peered at me through a thick cloud of tobacco smoke.

"The woman sounds sincere," I replied. "Something strange is happening at the White River Bridge. Will you answer her letter?"

"We shall do better than that," said my friend. "If you would be pleased to accompany me, we can leave by the first train to Moncaster, Kent, in the morning. All that blood bothers me too."

So it was that Sherlock Holmes and I found ourselves stepping off the 9:23 to Moncaster on November 3rd, warmly clad for the country and clutching our grips. We asked about transportation to our destination and were directed to the cab stand. A short trip brought us to the village of Livermoore.

After leaving our bags at The Four in Hand, which was both an inn and the local public house, Holmes and I walked the few blocks to the Livermoore Police Station. Unfortunately, since it was early November, the beautiful gardens famous in Kent's summer were long past their prime. Blasted plants and bare tree limbs were visible everywhere. Even the scarlet and yellow bushes set along the stone garden walls lining the pavement of the High Street appeared bedraggled and neglected, their branches whipped bare by the autumnal gusts. The sky hung above us, heavy with grey thick clouds, and the cold wind swirled around our coattails.

On the way to the police station, Holmes insisted we take the High Street. We passed gracious old stone and brick buildings, erected very much in picturesque styles, with doors opening directly to the pavement. There was an ironmonger's, a flower shop, a tiny but quaint tea shop, a butcher, a livery stable, a green grocer's, a notions shop, a dressmaker's establishment, a doctor's office, and two bakeries. The crowd on the pavement was sparse, but there always seemed to be someone around as we strolled along to our destination. In the street, small puddles gathered between the cobblestones, evidence of a recent shower.

The Livermoore Police Station was a thin, narrow edifice, squeezed in between the village hall and another flat-faced building that sold farming supplies. It was constructed of yellow Portland stone, its windows topped with thick grey lintels. We climbed the steps to the entrance and found the sergeant-on-duty at his desk in the lobby.

Holmes introduced himself to Sergeant Pratt, who received us with an offer of hot coffee. He was a robust man of middle years, nearly as tall as the detective, with close-cropped hair and a ruddy complexion. He ushered us into chairs in his office down the corridor from the entrance. Another man, his constable, took over the front desk as we walked away.

Sergeant Pratt took Holmes's card with a skeptical air. "I have heard of you, Mr. Holmes," he said, "but I admit that I think the claims made about your exploits may have been exaggerated. Telling a man's travels by the dirt on his shoes and the stains on his sleeve!" He chuckled and smiled at us.

I huffed into my moustache. Holmes smiled at the officer. "My biographer Dr. Watson does have a tendency to romanticize my cases, and I have often taken him to task for it. However, I'm willing to put on a demonstration for your benefit. Your shoes, for example, tell me that you bicycle a great deal, no doubt in the course of your official duties. You store the machine in the cloakroom to the right. Your haircut was chosen to disguise the fact you're going bald, as did your father, who was also a Livermoore policeman before you."

Sergeant Pratt stared at my friend in amazement. "How did you know?" he gasped. "It is all true! Both Constable Comstock and I use bicycles in the performance of our duties. Livermoore is a small village and the cost of a carriage must be justified in the expense book."

The detective shook his head. "I've told Watson that I should never explain my methods – that doing so takes away the wonderful effect created and reduces me to the mortal man I really am. My reasoning was simple. Many rural policemen cover their territories by bicycle. Therefore

212

I looked to your shoes for the tell-tale scuff on the inner sole that touches the petal cover. I also see the wrinkles on your pant leg caused by the clip worn to keep the cloth from fouling in the gears.

"The street outside has several rain puddles and the tyre marks of your bicycle are plainly visible on the flagstones of your station hallway, turning to the right and disappearing behind the door marked "*Cloaks*". I know that it was your bicycle because of the faint splashes of mud upon your cuffs. On the wall behind your head is a group photograph of a line of men posed before the steps of this very building. The style of clothing is that of nearly thirty years ago. The uniformed man receiving a citation from the mayor, distinguished by his badge of office, bears a strong resemblance to yourself. He is bald. Therefore I deduce he is a close relative, even your father, who also served Livermoore in decades past. Was it on the occasion of his retirement?"

Pratt stared at Holmes as a man bewildered. "Well, I have never seen the like! It's witchcraft, it is! I am very impressed. You are a man to watch, Mr. Holmes. What brings you to Livermoore, and how may I help?"

Holmes explained about Mrs. Ogden and her letter. Before interviewing the woman and her husband, he wanted to learn what the local police thought about the case.

"The whole thing is very strange. Ben Walker has been talking for days about the dark horseman that he saw. Two other men, Paul Booker and Jerald Peabody, saw the same thing, but at different times. It was always late at night, after midnight. The horse was black, and the rider wore a shapeless hat and a dark cloak. Not a very good description, I'm afraid.

"Frankly, if it weren't for the reports of Mr. and Mrs. Ogden, we might be tempted to dismiss the story altogether. Dan Rounder is a local legend around here and usually told to frighten the children. Young men might be up to mischief, but the Ogdens are quite a respectable, settled couple. They were adamant about what they heard. And of course, there was the blood."

"Ah, yes, the blood," said my friend. "What can you tell me about that?"

"There was a lot of it – likely several quarts, I'd say. It was found the morning after the last reports of the sighting of Dan Rounder by Peabody and Booker. They staggered into the bar of The Four in Hand just at closing time, downed several drinks, and told everyone there that they had just seen the apparition gallop out of town on the west road, which went over the bridge. The village had been on edge about the sightings for a few weeks, so no one was eager to rush out and see what happened to the ghost.

The next morning, Tobias Ogden walked into town with the report of the blood.

"I had Constable Comstock fetch Doctor Mainstead and we went out to the bridge, followed by half of the population of Livermoore. Comstock was tasked in keeping back the crowd while the doctor and I examined the scene.

"We found much blood, but no sign of a body. A complete search was made of the fields for over a mile beyond the bridge, but nothing was discovered except for a few tufts of grass torn up along the road's verge and tossed aside. There doesn't seem to be anything else that we can do. There have been no reports of sightings or sounds of the spirit of Dan Rounder since."

"No unusual activities in the village lately? No uptick in break-ins or such?"

"Well, the town clerk didn't show up for work that morning. Claude Penn is his name. He was seen the night before, but in the morning the only sign of him was a note slipped under his landlady's door saying he'd decided to emigrate to America, and that she should hold his things until he sent for them. Had three days left on his rent, too."

"What did the village think of that?" I asked.

"I tell you, the first thing the mayor did was have someone come in and go over the books! They're at it now, at the hall, but word is they won't be done for several days. It is hard to believe such a thing about Claude Penn, though. He was always such a mousey sort of man."

"What did he look like?" I asked.

"Short, just shy of forty, with a round, bespeckled face. Blond hair worn a little long. Always with a book in his pocket. Very easy not to notice." Pratt felt the coffee pot, but it was cold.

Holmes rose to his feet and I followed him. He thanked the sergeant for his help, and then asked how to get to both the clerk's residence and the Ogdens' home by the White River bridge. As he drew on his gloves and turned to the door, he inquired casually, "Was Mr. Penn a good horseman, then?"

Sergeant Pratt could not hold back his laughter. "Why, Claude Penn lived here five years and nobody ever saw him near a horse, much less astride one. I believe that the man was afraid of them. Didn't get along with dogs, either. Tolerated the landlady's cat, she said, but wouldn't let it in his room."

With another chuckle, the sergeant closed the door of the police station behind us.

Ten minutes' walk from the outskirts of Livermoore brought us in sight of the hump-backed bridge and its cottage off to the side of the road. The White River burbled along on the left, the cold water steaming slightly in the chill air. The sizable bridge was ahead, spanning the water as it flowed to the right, and the Ogdens' cottage stood about fifty feet to the river's side. The cottage was built of stone, and the dry vines on its walls only hinted at the glorious garden that must have surrounded it earlier in the year. Dried dead leaves piled up in the corners and skittered across the brown grasses. Far away in a field, a man was bent over some twisted branches, digging with a grubbing fork. A knock at the door brought both Ogdens to us. Tobias Ogden was a tall, dignified man with grey hair and knotted fingers, dressed in rough trousers and a dark workman's shirt. His wife's hair was white and tightly curled. She wasn't quite as tall as her husband, instead being rounder, garbed in a simple blue dress covered with a white apron. They invited us in and soon tea and biscuits were served on the gingham tablecloth of the kitchen.

Mrs. Ogden retold the story contained in her letter. Her husband, who seemed content to let his wife take the lead in the conversation, said little, but corroborated everything that she said. After a few minutes, Holmes expressed a desire to see the bridge itself. We were soon standing on the flagstones of its arch and Holmes whipped out his magnifying lens. The old couple watched from their window for a while, and then left us to ourselves.

I expected him to begin with the dried substance splashed over the roadway and the stone sides of the span. Instead, he started at the other end, toward the village, with a close examination of the dirt road. He fell to his knees, crawling over the path and over the grass lining both sides, and only after he'd finished with that did he approach the bridge.

Again he examined every inch of his subject. I stood silently to one side as he crept, climbed, scrambled, and laid flat upon his face to run his lens over the hump-backed bridge. He even extended his search to the roadbed beyond, sifting through the mud and gravel of the road. Finally, he concentrated on the blood that covered the rough stones of the bridge's sides.

The liquid was dried now. Holmes removed his gloves, ran his hand over it, picked at it with his fingernail, and even licked his thumb and rubbed it on one of the spots. Each time he would check the results with his lens. Finally, after what seemed to be hours, he rose to his feet, thrust his magnifying glass into his pocket, and pulled on his warm gloves.

"The day is advancing, Watson, and I've finished here. Let us return to The Four in Hand and seek out some lunch. I have a busy afternoon planned and you shall be a great help. Wave goodbye to our clients and let us be gone, Doctor."

An hour later, with a good ploughman's lunch supplied by the bar of The Four in Hand inside us, Holmes and I found ourselves on the doorstep of Claude Penn's rooming house. A farm wagon rattled by. It was a stolid brick building, with starched lace curtains at the windows and a pot of aspidistra in the parlor window that shouted "Respectable!" louder than the curtains.

Holmes took off his hat and nudged me to do the same. At his knock the door was opened by a worn little housemaid. Upon Holmes's inquiry for Mrs. Clements, we were ushered into a front room so spotless that the very furniture appeared to squeak in protest. Colourful wallpaper framed a cast-iron fireplace stoked with a small coal fire.

After a few moments the landlady came in. Mrs. Clements was one of those High Church-attending, middle-aged women who gave the air of having come up in the world through her own determined efforts and was now resolved to hold her independence and her respectability in equal measure. Her manner changed from distant but pleasant regard to a barely-disguised eagerness to gossip when she learned that we weren't interested in renting rooms, but instead in the doings of her absent tenant. A mention of Sergeant Pratt appeared to encourage her cooperation.

"Well, I'm not one to pry," she said archly. The maid brought in tea and she poured three cups with a regal air that went oddly with the parrot-printed wallpaper and the aspidistra. "I believe in giving my guests their privacy, but there are certain . . . uh, *things* that a boarding house owner finds out over the course of time. After all, Claude Penn has lived here for five years.

"Mail? Oh, he received letters occasionally – not just tradesmen's bills, you understand, but real letters. At least, he did for the first four years. From Birmingham, where he came from. From family, if one could trust the names and addresses on the back flaps. Not that I ever pried, you understand, but there they would be, visible on the paper. But then I noticed the letters stopped. He did get one last one, heavy paper and a strange-sounding name on the back flap. He went away for a couple of weeks after that, last December, but never said a word about his traveling when he got back, for much as I hinted and gave him plenty of chances. He is close, is Claude Penn.

"He works as a clerk at the village hall. There were never any bad reports about him that I heard, but that's not to say there might not have been some strange goings on. Always dressed well. Why, two new suits in five years! I don't know how he could wear them out, just sitting at a desk all day. He did start sending his shirts out to launder a few months ago. He said I didn't do them well enough for him! Tried one washerwoman, but she ruined them and he had to go out and buy new ones. Ha! Ha! Sometimes I wondered how he could afford it. Well, they are checking the village books, so we may have an answer to that pretty soon. Keeps himself to himself, but that could mean he has something to hide. You can't trust the quiet ones, you know. Go along nicely for years and then murder their wife and children with an axe and run off with the barmaid.

"Married? Not that I ever knew. I only rent to respectable single people, men on the third floor and women on the second. The only time they mix is during meals and in the big parlor after dinner. No, I never noticed Mr. Penn giving any extra attention to any other woman in the house. I have three ladies with me just now, Mrs. Bailey and Mrs. Hind, both elderly widows, and Miss Bradley-Knowles, who was the sister of Sir Arthur Bradley-Knowles, the former MP of our district. She kept house for him, but when he died, she heard about my establishment and was glad to get a suite here, second-floor front. Always pays her rent on time, and doesn't niggle over extras, either."

With a little difficulty, Holmes got her off the fascinating subject of the estimable Miss Bradley-Knowles and back to her missing boarder, Claude Penn.

"Pastimes? No, he read a lot. The room is full of books, and he took walks, but there was never . . . well, there is that one thing . . . ."

"Yes?" Holmes said encouragingly.

"Last year, in February, a bunch of young people decided to form a sort of amateur theatrical group. Not a lot to do in Livermoore in the winter, I suppose, and he was urged to join it, although he was probably fifteen years older than them, if he was a day. He got them a place to rehearse in the village hall, and wrangled the use of the main room for the shows, so I guess they wanted him in for that. He got a part in the cast, too. They did *Merry Wives of Windsor* last fall, and he was one of the husbands, I don't remember which one. Miss Bradley-Knowles wasn't quite sure that the town clerk being in a play was respectable, but she enjoyed it enough when we went to see one performance.

"He told me he was going to be in the next play, too. I asked him why he was staying out late so many nights."

"What was the name of that play?" asked Holmes.

"It is an old one, something I remember from the days when my husband was still alive. *Murder in the Red Barn*, it was. He got the part of the old father. Came down one evening all decked out with a bald cap and false whiskers. Looked quite the sight, but that was what he had to wear, I guess. It certainly gave us something to talk about after he left to meet the others."

217

"Do you know who else is in this group?"

"Silly bunch of youngsters, if you ask me. Alice Bowditch, whose husband should have known better than to let her make a spectacle of herself, and her best friend, Rosie Windom, who was always a little wild, and those boys from The Four in Hand – Ben Walker and the Peabody lad and three or four others. I suppose Claude Penn is a sort of steadying influence on them, he being so much older."

Holmes asked her if we could examine her tenant's room and she consented, after a show of reluctance. Holmes reminded her that we were working with the police and that helped her to decide. Mumbling that his rent week was about to expire anyway, she led the way up the stairs to his door on the third floor. Unwillingly she left us there after unlocking it, and we waited until we heard her footsteps descend the steps all the way to the ground floor before entering.

There was nothing remarkable about his furnished room except for the table situated in one corner. A large mirror hung over it, and the surface was littered with grease paint, false hair, and other tools of the theatre. A plain chair sat before the mirror and a row of hooks on the wall next to it held costumes and hats that went with the position of elderly father in the play *Murder in the Red Barn*.

Holmes went over the entire room, of course, but paid particular attention to the table's contents. He found the script, much marked with notes, and sat in the chair to read it.

That took some time and finally I had to strike a match to light a candle against the darkness of the November afternoon. Holmes started out of his concentration as I did so and rose, laying the sheaf of paper on the table. He glanced out the window at the dusky street.

"Watson, I had no idea it was getting so late. Let us get back to the pub. It is nearly time for tea, and you must be hungry."

I was hungry and followed him willingly. To my surprise, however, after leaving Mrs. Clement's boarding house, he turned not left to The Four in Hand, but right to the road leading to White River Bridge. He ignored my inquiry so I simply followed, surmising that something in Claude Penn's room had given him a clue that I had missed and he was now pursuing at the cost of my dinner.

The sun behind the clouds had set before we left Mrs. Clement's, and we had no lantern. We passed only a few people on our way. The Livermoore street lamps were sufficient for our purposes until we got beyond the village limits, but then we had only the half-light of a waning moon to guide us. Around us was silence, broken only by the sound of dried leaves rustling in the never-ending breeze and our boots crunching on the gravel of the road. After a brisk walk, we came through the darkness

218

to the bridge, seeing the candle-glow from the Ogdens' kitchen gleaming to one side. Holmes didn't go to knock on the front door, but instead headed for the span instead.

My friend stepped to the far end where the spilled blood still clung to the rock walls of the parapet. He motioned for me to hold open an envelope that he handed to me from his pocket and knelt to scrape some flakes of red into it with a penknife from his pocket. This took several minutes. We were crouched together at this task when I felt a sudden, hard blow between my shoulder blades. I staggered forward and dropped the envelope. A second later I saw Holmes jerk sideways and fall to the ground. In an instant the two of us were grappling with a crowd of unknown men armed with clubs or staves.

We were unprepared and unarmed. It proved to be an uneven fight. I believe I got in a few good blows, but the struggle ended with both Holmes and me being lifted up and dumped over the side into the river. We landed with a splash and floated under the arch and downstream.

What moonlight there was glittered on the rushing water and cast ragged black shadows from the skeletonized shrubbery lining the river banks. The water was shockingly cold and struggled to drag me down into its dark depths by my soaked wool coat and thick country boots. I fought to keep my head above water as I flailed about, searching for Holmes.

I choked on the freezing water as it forced itself down my throat and splashed over my head. I despaired of finding Holmes as the minutes passed and my energy was sapped away by the cold water and my exertions. It seemed like as if was trapped in an increasingly vain attempt to survive. A realization of my own mortality seized my spirit and I began to panic. With my last desperate surge of strength, I flung out an arm and touched a yielding surface. I grabbed at it but my freezing hand slipped.

Instantly I felt Holmes's strong fingers grip my coat sleeve and draw me close to him. Kicking and splashing, gasping words of encouragement in my ear, my friend struggled to reach the river's edge. Sputtering and dripping wet, he grabbed roots of bushes growing there and we helped each other climb out, digging our heels into the muddy bank and snatching at any dead vegetation that we could reach. The attack had happened so swiftly that we hadn't had a chance to cry out. Now, as we stood shivering on the bank, we could hear footsteps and see in the moonlight a huddle of figures running back toward Livermoore.

Holmes made a motion as if to follow them, but I, mindful of pneumonia, held his sleeve and started for the nearby Ogden cottage. Luckily we had emerged on the correct side of the water. Two astonished people opened the door to our frenzied knocking, and in a few moments we were sitting in matching rockers close to the Ogdens' kitchen fire, being plied with blankets, hot drinks, and cries of dismay.

After listening to our story, Tobias Ogden disappeared to alert Sergeant Pratt. Mrs. Ogden wrapped us in wool blankets and dried what clothing of ours that she could by the fire. She kept our coffee cups full, even adding a splash of something from a jug stored in one of the cupboards. I supervised as she brought out some hot water and clean gauze and dressed the cuts and bruises that we'd acquired during the fight and our attempted drowning.

The policeman and his constable, a short fireplug of a man, showed up in a carriage with Mr. Ogden not long after we dragged ourselves from the river. They listened impassively as Holmes recited the facts. In the middle of it, Pratt dispatched Constable Comstock to retrieve the envelope that I had dropped on the bridge. The constable returned with it, dirty and trampled from being underfoot during the fight. Apparently the mysterious men hadn't thought it important enough to destroy or carry away after our dunking. Holmes checked the contents and put it in the pocket of his coat. The constable also handed Holmes the little pen knife with which he'd been scraping at the stones when we were attacked.

Pratt's face was grave at the end of my friend's tale and he shook his head solemnly.

"This has gone far beyond a joke now, Mr. Holmes. The legend of Dan Rounder and a mysterious horse galloping through village streets at midnight is one thing, but a physical attack on peaceful men is another."

"I don't think our attackers viewed us as peaceful, Sergeant," said Holmes. "I believe that we have been watched ever since we arrived in Livermoore, and by tonight our rowdy friends decided we were posing a threat to them. This attack was a message for us to drop our investigation and leave the village."

"Shall you?"

"Of course not. There are too many unanswered questions. Who were the men who attacked us? Are they the same people responsible for the blood splashed on the bridge? Where did they get such a quantity? How does Dan Rounder's story come into it? What happened to Claude Penn? Is he connected with our attacks, and how? Is there money missing from the village accounts? If so, who took it and where did it go? No, Sergeant. I'm more determined than ever to clear up these mysteries before I see London town again. I think this object will help me."

He opened his hand and handed a tiny item to the sergeant. I was seated too far away to see what it was, but Pratt turned it over in his hand and gave it back to the detective.

"Well, it is more than we had before, Mr. Holmes."

"I see that our stockings are dry now, and our shirts nearly so. We must not impose upon the Ogdens' hospitality any longer. It's getting late, and Doctor Watson has missed his dinner."

At that, Mrs. Ogden protested that it would be a shame for her to let us leave with empty stomachs. We told her it wasn't necessary, but in ten minutes a nice little supper was laid out, featuring cheeses, cold ham, and homemade bread. More coffee was brewed and the entire company tucked in. I admit that I was grateful and did my best to uphold the honour of London in my appreciation of the country cooking that Kent and Mrs. Ogden could supply.

Sergeant Pratt and Constable Comstock dropped us off at the local inn before midnight. As we made our soggy way through the lobby to the staircase leading to our rooms, a man with black eyes and a scraggly beard thrust his head through the door that led to The Four in Hand public bar. He watched us enter with a grimace on his face and called back into the bar, "Looks like someone went for a swim!"

A voice answered, "Who would be that stupid in this weather?"

The answer came. "London people!"

Holmes gave him a piercing glance.

With that, the man disappeared into the bar. There was a burst of laughter and I heard some ribald comments from the crowd within. We proceeded to our rooms and Holmes bade me goodbye until the morning. I warned him to keep his bandages clean and told him that I would redress them in the morning.

I came down for breakfast to find my friend picking at a plate of eggs and ham. He had ordered for me and I ate mine hungrily. Holmes was silent until I had finished and redressed his wounds. I had attended to myself earlier. The cuts and scrapes that we had received were healing nicely. As I lingered over my coffee, he told me that he had contracted a slight cold from our adventure the night before.

"Then you must go straight to bed!" I exclaimed. "You do look flushed and tired. You must rest. I will order you a brandy at once."

Holmes waved a hand. "I will rest today, Doctor," he said. "But I prefer to sit quietly downstairs, not in my room. The fireplace doesn't draw well and the wind rattles the window. They stock the London papers here and the bar will supply all that I need in the matter of hot drinks and food. I promise you that I'll remain still and not excite myself. Meanwhile, I want you to go to the village hall and ask the mayor about Claude Penn. You know – his reputation in the workplace, impressions of the man, perhaps get a report on the examination of the financial books. Then talk to his tailor and his laundress. Find out everything you can about him, including his financial history if possible."

I was flattered to find that Holmes was relying on me to discover so much about the missing clerk, but I was concerned about leaving him alone for so long. He scoffed at my worries and waved me out The Four in Hand door. I left him sitting at a small table in an alcove of the public bar, well-supplied with newspapers, cigarettes, and a hot toddy.

I had escaped the chill that had sickened Holmes, and I was glad he could spend his day indoors by the fire. The weather had grown more windy, and the temperature had dropped by several degrees, so I clutched my overcoat to me as I hurried down the cobblestone street toward the police station. At Holmes's suggestion, I was calling on Sergeant Pratt to add his official influence to my errand.

For the rest of the morning, the sergeant and I spoke to others who knew Claude Penn in Livermoore. That included the mayor, the auditors, and several of his fellow office workers. No one questioned that he had chosen to depart, and no irregularities had been found in the books. The mayor, one Garrison Whitney, spoke favourably about Penn, but under the current circumstances would admit to no final conclusion as to his character. The clerk was regarded as friendly and efficient among his fellow workers. He came across as a loner who was always ready for a night out or a frolic but never volunteered, always waiting to be asked.

We proceeded to the Livermoore haberdashery and talked to the young woman who sold him his socks and handkerchiefs. She giggled a bit about his choices, declaring he "was a bit of a dandy" and always fussed about his ties and gloves, requiring "the best in the shop". Her employer, the tailor, confirmed that in the past five years he had ordered two new suits but emphasized that he always paid his bill promptly and in full, unlike others in town that he could name. In fact, there was a handsome broadcloth suit waiting to be finished for him right now, and what was the man to do now that he was missing?

We left the tailor to his problem and sought out the laundress, Mrs. Beech, in a little cottage on the edge of town. She was a late middle-aged, big, red-faced woman, out back in her yard, surrounded by her bubbling laundry cauldrons, clothes lines, and flapping sheets and hand towels, assisted by her equally red-faced daughter. A couple of young urchins, future laundresses both, tumbled about at her feet as she lifted her head from the steam and the linen to answer our questions.

She was proud of her work. Did the gentleman desire some washing done? No? The London gentleman doesn't need to give her anything but, thank you sir, much appreciated. She was glad to answer questions, especially as Sergeant Pratt said it would help the police. She and all her family were honest people, to be sure. Yes, she did Mr. Penn's shirts and small clothes. Yes, he engaged her last winter, right after Twelfth Night. No, she hadn't worked for him before that. Who had recommended her? Why, she didn't know. He just showed up one morning with a bundle of things. Who else did she work for? Why, the mayor himself sent his washing to her. Also the doctor, the priest, all the tablecloths and sheets of The Four in Hand, and half the shopkeepers in town. Who had done Mr. Penn's shirts before? That was her rival, Mrs. Newton, in Hastings Lane, a silly old woman more likely to lose buttons and tear the cloth than do a good job. Her only virtue was she was cheap. Didn't care how much she charged, because the old biddy drank it all anyways. Oh, thank you again, sir, and maybe she would take her daughter and the babies out for a treat on Sunday.

Our trip to visit Mrs. Newton in Hastings Lane was wasted time. Sergeant Pratt and I found her passed out by drink at her kitchen table. She made no coherent sense to anything that we asked her, and we finally gave up and left her to her bottle.

In High Street, the sergeant and I called on the president of the Livermoore Bank, Mr. Hawkins. On behalf of police business, he brought out Claude Penn's accounts. What I discovered seemed to put a whole new complexion on the case.

Sergeant Pratt left me as we passed the police station and I hurried to tell my news to Holmes. I found him much improved, sitting by the fire in his bedroom upstairs, newspaper stuffed into the cracks around his rattling window.

He had ordered sandwiches and hot tea against my return, and I sat down to eat my lunch as I reported on my investigations. Holmes listened with interest, asking questions at intervals, and I finally came to my last bit of information.

"Last December Claude Penn's uncle, his mother's brother, died and left him a tidy inheritance. The chief feature was a brewery, along with several rental properties, including two shops and four flats in the city of Birmingham. There were no other relatives. Penn traveled up to the city for the funeral and to consult with the lawyers. That was the trip he refused to tell his landlady about.

"He received checks from the Birmingham lawyers and opened an account at the Livermoore bank in January. There has been a lot of activity in his account. According to the records, he has been using most of his new-found wealth to support the theatre company. That included an order of cheap jewelry for *The Merry Wives of Windsor*. Strangely enough, two months later there was a charge to the same Moncaster jewelry shop for a real silver and garnet pendant, and later for a woman's gold ring."

"You have done very well, Watson," said Holmes. I glowed in the warmth of his rare praise. "I, too, have spent a fruitful day. Sequestered in the bar of The Four in Hand, I made a study of the local inhabitants. I even managed to be told the legend of Dan Rounder and his ghostly horse several times. By a generous dispersion of shillings and pence, alcohol has assisted in my enquiries, and I believe that I now have all the threads of this case into my hands."

"You have solved it?"

"Yes. If you have finished your food, Watson, would you be so kind as to go and ask Sergeant Pratt and Constable Comstock to be here tonight at eight?"

"Both of them?"

"Yes. Our strength may well lie in numbers."

My errand soon completed, I rejoined Holmes and insisted that he lie down to rest. I took my own advice and came down at six o'clock to find him again sitting up and eager for our guests to arrive. I recognized the signs. Having solved the case using his unique powers, he was now impatient for the final act, the confronting and apprehension of the plotters, and the clearing up of any such questions that may remain. He refused to reply to my comments, but concentrated on a small collection of bowls and jars on the table of his room. A small spirit lamp was extinguished as I entered, and Holmes sat brooding over the results of his experiment until the arrival of the local constabulary.

Sergeant Pratt entered first, a telegram clutched in one hand. Constable Comstock slipped in behind him and stood silently by the door. Pratt advanced and thrust the opened telegram toward Holmes.

"This changes the case, Mr. Holmes. Now it is murder most likely, and someone shall swing for it."

Holmes read the message and handed it to me. It was sent by the Chief Constable of Kent, advising Sergeant Pratt that a drowned man had been found miles down the White River, and asking for assistance in identifying the body. The description of the man fitted the Livermoore village clerk. One detail mentioned was that the poor victim's skull had been cracked before death.

The village clock outside the window chimed eight. Holmes arose. "It is time."

He led us down the stairs and into the public bar. Three or four men stood there, and a large group of diners were seated at one side. A door on the back wall gave entry into a private room. Apparently it had been hired for the evening for a "*Reserved*" sign hung by a tack from the panel.

224

Holmes strode purposefully to it and opened the door. He entered, the policemen and I right behind him, and interrupted the party within. A bearded man, vaguely familiar to me, was sitting at a table with several others. He was laughing when we entered, but at the sight of Holmes and Sergeant Pratt, the smile vanished from his lips and he motioned the others with him to hush.

He was the same man who had taunted Holmes and me for coming back to the inn wet from our adventure the night before. Sergeant Pratt whispered that he was Ben Walker, the man who had made the first report of the return of the Spirit of Dan Rounders and his ghostly black horse. He was dressed in a rough tweed suit and gaiters, such as groundskeepers wear, his black hair flopping into his grey eyes, and his thin nose slicing his blotched face in half. With a twisted mouth and disfiguring whiskers, he looked far gone to drink, even at this hour. The others at his table were nearly as intoxicated. Mugs and glasses crowded the table before them. It was obvious that they had been sitting there for some time.

I now noticed that two of the group were women. They both sat with another man between them on a sofa set against one wall, near to the fire. Sergeant Pratt addressed each person with familiarity, pointing them out to Holmes as I stood with Constable Comstock against the door. It was the only exit.

The names of the room's occupants were given to us. Ben Walker's companions included Jerald Peabody and Paul Booker, who also had reported the appearance of the Spirit of Dan Rounder. Another man, Peter Glass, scowled at us. On the sofa, Bernard Bowditch sat between his wife, Alice, and Rosie Windom. We had intruded into what appeared to be a meeting of the core of the Livermoore theatre company.

Holmes stepped forward. "I have been investigating the blood-stained bridge outside of town," he began. Walker and the other men seated at the table looked at each other and hissed a few words to the others. Holmes paid them no heed.

"As a result of that, I have also been looking into the disappearance of the village clerk, Claude Penn." Paul Booker opened his mouth, but a fierce glare from Walker made him shut it.

"I'm going to tell you what happened that night," stated Holmes, "and any of you can correct me where I go wrong." The people all shifted in their chairs and Mr. Bowditch spoke up. He ignored Holmes and addressed Pratt.

"I don't understand, Sergeant. What has the disappearance of Claude Penn have to do with either me or my wife?"

"Mr. Holmes is going to tell us a story, sir," replied Pratt. "Surely listening to a story is a harmless enough activity. If anyone objects, they can leave, but that would only insure further investigation of that person in the future."

Alice Bowditch whispered in her husband's ear and he lapsed into silence.

"Claude Penn was the village clerk of Livermoore," continued Holmes. "He lived a quiet life, more from circumstances than from choice, for he was shy. Last December, he learned that his uncle in Birmingham had died and left him a considerable fortune. He didn't tell his landlady and made only a few changes in his habits, but somehow word got out about his money. Suddenly he was invited to join a merry group of younger people to form a local theatre troupe. He agreed, and soon found himself not only one of the cast, but also the chief financier of the theatre activities.

"He found the attention agreeable, but as time went on things slowly turned sour. Expenses were more than he thought necessary. Rosie Windom encouraged his attentions at first, but as he grew more serious she began to draw back. He noticed that Ben Walker seemed to be against their relationship. He started to think that Walker was poisoning Miss Windom's mind against him, just as Walker was demanding more and more money for sets, props, and costumes."

"How do you know this?" I asked.

"I gathered the last bits of information that I needed while apparently nursing my cold in the bar at The Four in Hand," said Holmes. "Sorry, Watson, but I am afraid my cold would have never responded to your nostrums, seeing as it was quite imaginary."

"I'm not surprised," I said wryly. It wasn't the first time that I had been duped by my friend about his state of health for the sake of a case.

"Perhaps Claude Penn decided that the costs of the theatre were too high for him to sustain. Perhaps the cooling relationship with Miss Windom had something to do with his thinking. He had given her a silver and garnet pendant which she had accepted, but when he offered her marriage and showed her the ring, she turned him down. Is that the pendant Mr. Penn gave you, Miss Windom – the one you are wearing around your neck right now?"

Rosie Windom raised her hand to clutch the glittery ornament resting on her bosom. Mutely she nodded, her eyes fixed on Holmes as would a snake on the flute wielded by an Indian charmer.

"After he was refused by Miss Windom, Claude Penn told Ben Walker that he planned to withdraw all support from the theatre company. He even planned to move to Birmingham to better attend to his affairs there. Walker convinced him to support one more play, the aptly named *Murder in the Red Barn*. It is a melodrama about a young woman who is murdered by her perfidious lover, who then hides her body in an old barn. The case is only solved when her mother dreams that the girl appeared before her and directed her mother to her burial place.

"Penn still questioned every bill for the production. That was a threat to Walker, who had been padding the expense accounts from the beginning and keeping the excess for himself. He devised a plan.

"He would frighten Claude Penn so badly that the man would leave the village and never return. He would be so scared that he wouldn't even return to question the money lost in the theatre business. Walker convinced two of his friends, Mr. Booker and Mr. Peabody, to help spread a rumour that Dan Rounder and his ghostly horse had been seen in Livermoore. After weeks of increasing tension, Walker and his friends kidnapped Penn on the night of October 31st and brought him to the White River bridge. There they beat him, tossed a bucket of fake blood as called for in the play over him, and threw him into the water."

Walker, Peabody, Booker, and Glass began to object loudly. They struggled to rise from the table, but I drew my revolver and showed it to them. Lulled by our bucolic surroundings, I had neglected to have it with me before the attack at the bridge. Now I carried it everywhere. Constable Comstock stepped forward, his truncheon at the ready. The commotion faded away as the men recognized their dilemma.

"When Dr. Watson and I showed up, my name was recognized and we were put under continuous watch. Soon it was obvious that we were on the trail of the blood splashed on the stone bridge and the disappearance of Claude Penn. These men thought that they had successfully driven Claude Penn away.

"They decided to use the same methods on Dr. Watson and me. The night was dark. They sneaked up on us from behind, and attacked so suddenly that we couldn't defend ourselves. Throwing us over the parapet was the same method that they'd used for Penn. They felt secure that we would fold our tents and steal away after such treatment. Fortunately we were able to escape the river's grip and seek help."

Ben Walker sneered at Holmes. "A very exciting tale, Mr. London Detective, but you can't prove it. You never got a good look at your attackers."

"No, but I was able to tear this button off a coat while I was being beaten. I believe it belongs to you, Mr. Peabody." Holmes stretched out his hand and opened it to reveal a brass button, embossed with a pine tree. Our eyes shifted from the button to the man's brown coat. A bit of thread hung from the place where there was a missing button. All the other buttons on his coat were embossed with a matching pine tree.

"Earlier today, Sergeant Pratt received a telegram from the Chief Constable of Kent announcing that a drowned body had been recovered miles down the White River from Livermoore. It has been identified as Claude Penn. It was discovered that someone had cracked his skull before he went into the water. He is dead."

Peabody's eyes shifted from the dangling thread of his coat to Holmes's open palm where the embossed button lay to Ben Walker's twisted, angry face. His own visage was drained of blood. He leaped to his feet, almost crashing his chair into the fireplace, and yelled, "Penn is dead? Penn is dead?"

"Yes," Holmes replied.

Peabody raised a shaking finger to Ben Walker. "He made me do it! We were only going to scare him! It's all Ben Walker's fault! He said it was only going to be a bit of fun! He carried the heaviest stick!"

"Shut up, you fool, or we will all hang!"

Ben Walker lurched across the table at Peabody. The policemen were ready. In a few minutes everyone was secured, including Bowditch and the two women. The confessions came quickly. Holmes was proven correct in every detail. Rosie Windom sobbed her heart out, telling how Walker had pressured her to lead Penn on, then to cut him off after he proposed to her. Walker, with violence, had made her refuse him. Soon after Penn had announced that he was leaving Livermoore. The other men blamed Walker as the mastermind of the whole scheme of beating and scaring the clerk, and denied any knowledge of the money Walker had stolen from the victim.

Ben Walker, once restrained, slumped in his chair, mumbling threats against everyone, including Holmes. Bernard and Alice Bowditch escaped the accusations. Everyone agreed that those two weren't involved in the scam or the attack. They had really joined only to indulge in play-acting. Ben Walker admitted that Rosie Windom had only been a pawn in his plan. Those three were allowed to go free.

With the help of the innkeeper, who had sufficient reasons to stay on Sergeant Pratt's good side, the villains were transported to the police station and the Chief Constable was notified.

The next morning, Holmes and I met the sergeant at the station as we prepared to board the train to London. Although he had spent the night taking statements from everyone involved, Sergeant Pratt still had a few questions for my friend.

Pratt held open the door and leaned into our compartment from the platform as we settled our bags and found seats.

"Mr. Holmes, grabbing that button was quick thinking. How could you have solved the case without it? That was excellent luck."

"Luck had nothing to do with it, Sergeant Pratt. It was all observation and logical thinking. I knew when I first examined the blood on the bridge that it was fake, made from a formula popular in the theatre. I have some experience in that line. Connecting the blood with the Livermoore theatrical company was simple. When we went back there, I was looking for the *real* blood that the *fake* blood had been thrown over to hide. Where is the best place to hide a leaf? In a forest. So it was with the blood of Claude Penn's head wound. I later isolated the human cells from the dyed syrup in my room at The Four in Hand. I slipped out to a local physician's office when I was thought to be asleep, and he kindly allowed me to make use of his microscope. I was able to identify the blood cells in the dyed syrup.

"Since I noticed that we'd been followed ever since we arrived in Livermoore, I was half-prepared for the attack. Cutting off the button with the penknife in my hand was but the work of a moment. I also took note of several points of interest in the garb and faces of the gang, but that knowledge proved unnecessary once Peabody broke down. However, I would take prompt action in securing that heavy stick Peabody mentioned. Check it for hair and blood."

"I already have," said Pratt. "It was hidden in a woodpile behind Walker's house. There was a tweed thread caught in a splinter that matches Walker's sleeve."

"Then it was just a matter of allowing the suspects to gather so that arresting them would be convenient for you and Constable Comstock. If you ever get to London, sir, please drop by for a drink. I would like to introduce you to some gentlemen we know at Scotland Yard."

With those parting words, Holmes pulled shut the first-class carriage door, the whistle blew, and our train slowly steamed out of the station.

The Tomorrow Man
by S.F. Bennett

Readers of the cases that Sherlock Holmes permitted to be shared with a wider audience may wonder why so few of these merited mention in the press of the day.

If so, it was not due to lack of interest on the part of Fleet Street, which on the contrary was considerable, but rather through my companion's determination to control his public exposure, for the sake of his profession and the reputation of his clients. This moratorium extended as far as my own writings and it was only with the coming of a new century, when his hand had slackened on the rein, that I was given some freedom to select those investigations which I believed best demonstrated his particular skills.

There are times, however, in every man's life, when his deeds become coal to feed the fire of the public's interest. It may well be remembered for Holmes this day came in the spring of 1896 when every newspaper in the land borne that deathly headline: *Sherlock Holmes Shot*.

The uproar that surrounded such an announcement can only be imagined by those who were not witness to the events of that day. Only now, with the passing of time, is it possible to elaborate on the particular details of this case. In so doing, it may be that I leave myself open to charges of peddling preposterous nonsense. I am bound, however, to report the facts exactly as they happened. Embellishment, in any case, would be superfluous.

So it was that a balmy morning in the April of that year found me returning to Baker Street in high spirits. Holmes had been called away on a matter concerning a famed recluse on the Continent. As my attendance was not desired by the client, I had elected to take myself down to the South Coast. A change, as they say, does wonder for the soul, although I must admit the sight of familiar faces and locations transformed by age from the images of my memory served only to remind me how quickly time passes. Invigorated by sea air, however, I had been determined not to be burdened by the past, and as a consequence found myself homeward bound in a better frame of mind than when I had arrived.

If there was one cloud casting its shadow on that momentous day, it was that I was returning without an old friend: My father's watch. Somewhere between Baker Street and Southsea, we had become parted.

For days, I grieved for its loss. Now, arriving home, I had accepted what could not be changed and resolved to find myself a suitable replacement.

Holmes had arrived at our quarters shortly before me, and I found him sprawled on the sofa, still in his travelling clothes, a newspaper draped over his face, and apparently in a state of supreme physical and mental exhaustion. Any rising fears that this presaged the news of an unsuccessful conclusion to his last case were soon quelled.

"The lamentable state of the railways is enough to give any man a headache," Holmes grumbled. "I had the misfortune to find myself sharing a carriage on the train from Dover with a group of fellows returning to their *alma mater* for Founder's Day. I will not deny that certain elements of the conversation carried interest, but there is only so much one can tolerate of tales of pranks, rugby matches, and eccentric schoolmasters before one's enthusiasm begins to pall."

"Could you not have moved?"

"There was not another seat to be had on the train, so the conductor informed me," he replied, rising to stretch his back. "I had no intention of standing, so I was very much between Scylla and Charybdis. The only thing to be said in favour of the experience is that the journey was not extended by unnecessary delays." He came to rest by the window. "Ah, here is a fellow who would agree with me. See here, friend Watson, does our visitor not bear the look of the man harassed beyond endurance by the deficiencies of modern-day travel?"

I joined him to see a stocky man of middling years on the opposite side of the street in a heavy overcoat and yellow scarf. Unkempt hair stuck out from under his hat at all angles, a ragged brindled beard hung down to his chest, whilst a straggling moustache clung to his face like ivy to a castle wall.

"How do you know he is coming here?" I queried.

No sooner had I spoken than the man crossed the road and marched up to our door.

"It is not difficult to say that a fellow who walks with such a determined step does so with a purpose," Holmes said. "There is the barber's shop at the end of the road, and it is not too great a stretch of the imagination to say matters of personal grooming are not our visitor's chief concern. He has a newspaper under his arm, so the newsagent is not his destination."

"He could have been passing through Baker Street on his way to somewhere else."

Holmes turned from the window. "Then he would have taken a cab. For a man of his generous proportions, excessive walking is not to his liking. Given the armour he has donned despite the warmth of the day, I

231

should also say he has an aversion even to the slightest chill. Yes, Mrs. Hudson?"

At his call, our landlady entered. "There's a gentleman to see you, Mr. Holmes. A Mr. Smith. I've told him you've only just arrived from your travels, but he's insistent, sir."

"Then show him up, Mrs. Hudson. For what is the purpose of our existence if not to be at the beck and call of our fellow man?"

A minute later, our visitor was ushered into the room, bringing with him the mingled odours of stale tobacco and a mustiness associated with rooms that have been long unaired. No shrinking violet, he strode up to Holmes and shook his hand with gusto. It may have been an idle fancy, but on seeing this, I had the first twinges of uneasiness about him. There was something about his supreme confidence which did not sit well with our usual experience. Holmes's clients displayed a range of emotions at their initial introduction, varying from the nervous and embarrassed to the distressed and wretched. Uncertainty bringing them to our door in the first place, it was rare for anyone to display the level of over-familiarity that distinguished this man from previous visitors.

"A pleasure, sir." He promptly took a seat on the sofa and plucked his hat from his head. "I do not have much time, Mr. Holmes. Therefore, I shall be brief."

Holmes shot me a look of wry amusement. "Brevity is always to be preferred."

"No tea, thank you," said Smith, holding up his hand. "Nor anything stronger. The offer is appreciated, but unnecessary, Dr. Watson."

My jaw fell open. Given the state of the man, with trickles of sweat running down his temples and dappled throughout his bedraggled whiskers, I had been about to offer some form of refreshment. It was almost as though he had read my mind.

"Nor will I remove my coat," said Smith, directing the statement to Holmes, who seemed equalled intrigued by our visitor's perspicacity. "I have my reasons, which are pertinent to my case."

"As you wish, Mr. *Smith*," said Holmes, taking his accustomed seat by the fireplace. The emphasis he placed on the name made our visitor glance over at him. "We have entertained princes and dukes, popes and archbishops. I feel we may be trusted with your name."

"Very well," said Smith hesitantly. "My name is Regis Teyton. It will mean nothing to you, Mr. Holmes, because in this place I am not known."

"We hope soon to rectify that situation," said my friend with a smile.

"The story I am about to tell you will seem fantastical, I dare say."

"There is little I have not heard." Holmes took up his pipe and closed his eyes in readiness for the tale to come. "I am fairly proof against surprise at this stage in my life."

"The facts then, as difficult as they may be." Teyton took a deep steadying breath before continuing. "I am not of your time. I have come from ten years hence to meet you today."

Holmes abruptly opened his eyes. I paused in my note-taking and glanced across at the man, expecting to find some trace of humour in his expression. If anything, he appeared more deadly serious than ever.

"From whence I have come," Teyton continued, "time travel is a reality, as real as the ships that sail in our skies and the automobiles that have displaced the horse from our streets. Unlike those advances, however, it is accessible only to the trusted few. It was discovered very soon after the initial experiments that the technology is a dangerous one and has limitations. We cannot travel into the distant past. If you ask me, sir, whether I have met King Henry VIII or stood on the field of battle at Agincourt, I must disappoint you. A point of travel must have a beginning and an end, and as a consequence we can only travel to those periods in which the technology existed."

"I see." Holmes returned his pipe to the table with care and regarded our visitor gravely. "Which begs the question, how are you here, Mr. Teyton?"

"You may recall that a story was written in 1895 concerning such a machine."

Holmes looked across at me enquiringly. "Dr. Watson is well versed in sensational literature."

"I read it," I replied. "But it was a fantasy – a work of fiction."

"Presented as fiction, yes," said Teyton, "but based on fact. A workable device capable of creating a corridor between the present and past was created in 1891."

"Perhaps you would care to explain how the author came by the information," asked Holmes.

"It was considered expedient to provide him with certain concepts. As a species, *homo sapiens* is suspicious of change. It is a survival characteristic. Your century, sir, was one of unprecedented innovation. Ideas that came without ancestry met with the most resistance. Therefore, in the case of the time device, it was thought best to prepare the way. Icarus may have flown too high, yet, by the very act, so was the idea of flight seeded in the public awareness. One may be fearful of the practicalities, but one does not question that it is possible. Thus it is so with time travel."

"Ingenious," said Holmes thoughtfully. "Then why have you come to me? If it is to promote your 'concept', then I am afraid you have had a wasted journey. I am no lapdog of government."

"You misunderstand, sir," said Teyton hurriedly. "I have come because I am in need of your assistance." His eyes took on a haunted look. "My time has seen half the world consumed by war. The dead outnumber the living. It begins in the summer of 1898 and now knows no end. Brother turns on brother, and those who were once our gallant allies are now our enemies. For those that are left behind, disease and pestilence are their constant companions."

I caught Holmes's eye as I listened to this dire prediction. He shook his head in a cautionary gesture to say nothing.

"Although it is forbidden," our visitor continued gravely, "I have been able to trace the line of cause and effect through time to a single act, which will happen tomorrow. From this will set in motion a series of consequences which will lead to uprisings on several fronts. War will be the result."

Teyton paused, as if waiting for us to ask the inevitable question. As the silence persisted, I became impressed with the sensation that the world was collectively holding its breath.

"What is this act?" I asked.

His dark eyes moved to rest on mine. When he spoke, there was a strain in his voice.

"It is the murder of Sherlock Holmes."

I confess I had no reply to this. I sat there, my amazement turning to alarm as without warning our visitor drew a pistol from his pocket and levelled it at my friend. Holmes eyed it with interest, but said nothing.

"Twelve times have I been here," said Teyton unsteadily. "Twelve times have we had this conversation. Twelve times have we failed to prevent your murder. We have changed the location, we have removed you from the country, we have attempted to apprehend those responsible: Nothing alters the events. Twelve times, Mr. Holmes." The revolver trembled in his grasp and he had to use his other hand to steady it. "Time is not on our side. So that the world is not plunged into chaos, I must do what I have tried to prevent. I must kill you and let the responsibility fall upon myself."

Holmes drew a deep breath and rose from his chair. As if Teyton had suggested nothing more sinister than afternoon tea at the Savoy, he took up a cigarette and lit it. Seeing my expression, a small shake of his head was enough to keep me from springing from my seat to wrestle the weapon from the man's hand.

234

"Tell me, for my own curiosity you understand," Holmes said, unconcernedly. "How will our deaths solve this problem? I take it you are not including Doctor Watson in this scheme?"

"No. There must be a witness to say that I have done this thing. At the time, the police were never able to solve your murder."

Holmes permitted himself a small laugh. "That does not surprise me. It has long been my contention that Scotland Yard's finest couldn't detect a murder were it to happen under their very noses. But please, Mr. Teyton, do continue. Believe me when I say you have my full and undivided attention."

Pronounced beads of sweat were glistening on Teyton's brow. Several times he had to adjust his grip on the revolver when it threatened to slip from his grasp.

"With no one to blame," he said, his voice betraying his nervousness, "rumour will be rife. Several anarchist groups will claim responsibility. The press will speculate on some criminal motive – that your great nemesis, Professor Moriarty, has spawned imitators. Others will say you have been assassinated to protect the highest in the land. This contagion will spread, until one government will fall to blaming another. Then will follow other deaths and we shall know war." Teyton swallowed with difficulty. "I cannot permit that to happen. For what I must do, you must forgive me."

To my surprise, Holmes gave a short chuckle. "Whilst I have some sympathy with the notion of the noble sacrifice, we are surely not yet at that point. Come, sir, put aside your pistol. It is too early in the day for gunplay and our landlady has an aversion to loud noises. I am sure, Mr. Teyton, if we put our heads together, we may make some sense out of this affair without resorting to violence."

He approached Teyton with confidence, his hand extended. I held my breath, expecting the worst. But slowly, almost gratefully, I saw the light of reason come to Teyton's wide eyes and he placed the revolver in Holmes's hand.

"Better," said Holmes, stowing the gun safely in his pocket. "Nothing is more destructive to the optimum functioning of the mental faculties than the added complication of weaponry." He rubbed his hands briskly together as though he was relishing the challenge. "Now, the details of my murder, if you please, Mr. Teyton. There is a popular belief that thirteen is unlucky for some, but we must prove the exception that disproves the rule."

"It occurs tomorrow at midday in the forecourt of the British Museum. You are shot."

"At close or long range?"

"It was never established."

"Dear me, the investigation must have been a poor one indeed. Why was I there? That at the very least must have been known."

"I am afraid not. You told no one the reason for your presence."

"I fear I begin to see the limits of my behaviour. What else can you tell me?"

Teyton shook his head. "That is all. No one was ever arrested. You see now why speculation has been our greatest enemy."

"Well, it is precious little." Holmes seemed almost disappointed. "What we have is a place, a method, and a time." He tapped his finger against his lips. "You say we have attempted to elude my murderers? Have we allowed the scenario to play out?"

"Why, no."

"Then that is the course of action we must pursue!"

I could contain myself no longer. "Holmes, this is intolerable!"

"Watson, from what Mr. Teyton says, and since I cannot outrun this thing, then it's surely time to grasp the nettle and face it."

At the mention of his name, Teyton rose unsteadily to his feet. "I fear my time grows short," said he. "I must leave soon or remain forever. Before I go, however, I have this to give to you, Doctor Watson."

He fished a bundle wrapped in a handkerchief from his pocket. As he reverentially peeled back the fabric, he allowed me to see the precious contents. I caught my breath when I beheld my old watch.

"Good heavens!" I declared, taking it up and inspecting it.

Indeed it was my property, from the initials on the back to the correct hallmarks inside the case, along with the pawnbroker's marks and the small chip on the enamel of the face, which I had added several years ago. This battered specimen was unmistakeably mine.

"How did you come by it?" I asked.

"You gave it to me, Doctor," said Teyton. "That is to say, you *will* give it to me before I set out on this mission. You said you would have doubts as to my story and that I was to give you this as proof of my sincerity."

"Upon my word, I thought it lost!"

"It was. And I give it back to you, so that you might give it to me several years hence to return it to you now."

"Good heavens," I breathed, vaguely aware that I was repeating myself, but being otherwise lost for words.

"I must depart," said Teyton, pressing his hat firmly on his head. "I know you will have me followed, Mr. Holmes, but I should caution against it. Beneath my coat is the apparatus by which I am able to travel through time. Rest assured, however good your spies, they will never see me reach my destination." He managed a wan smile. "Take care, sir. The fate of the world is in your hands."

"A weighty responsibility indeed!" said Holmes. With a flourish, he ushered our guest towards the door. "I shall do my utmost to prevent tomorrow's misadventure, and if I fail, then you have my blessing to return and shoot me for the dullard I most certainly am."

He shut the door and turned to me, his hands thrust deeply into his pockets. "Well, Watson, what do you make of it?"

"The man threatened your life, Holmes."

"With this?" He took the revolver from his pocket and threw it onto the table. "It has been a while since I have seen a pinfire revolver of this type. A Lefaucheux 1858, unless I am much mistaken. This particular model fell out of favour with the French Navy over twenty years ago." A tight smile enlivened his stern features. "One would hope the weapons of the future would be more advanced. You will notice that the hinged gate on the barrel is not completely closed and the cartridge already discharged. A mere prop then. The mark of an amateur, Watson!" If he seemed greatly amused by the episode, I was less impressed. "And there he goes," said he, taking up position by the window.

I looked down at the street where our recent visitor was climbing into a four-wheeler. Out of the corner of my eye, I saw Holmes raise his hand. Several vagabonds playing knucklebones on the pavement opposite immediately abandoned their game and scrambled after the cab. As it turned a corner at the end of the road, one of them managed to jump onto the back suspension and, so clinging on, vanished from our sight.

"Shouldn't you have followed him yourself?" I suggested.

"It would be an exercise in futility," said Holmes, pushing himself off the wall. "I have no doubt the trail Mr. Teyton leaves will run cold since he appears to know my methods. We have other avenues to pursue."

"Surely you do not place any credibility in this fantastical story?"

"You are the 'Doubting Thomas', Watson, if your future self is to be believed. That is your watch, I take it?"

I nodded.

"Then what is your opinion of the case? Get down to details and what do you have?"

"That someone plans to kill you tomorrow."

"And how might such a person come by this information?"

"Because he intends to do it."

Holmes shook his head. "He could have shot me just now. Why wait another day?"

I gave it due consideration. "Because he knows who is going to do it and when."

"Precisely." Holmes rocked on his feet, his chin upon his chest, lost in thought. "We know everything and yet we know nothing. Are you familiar with Meno's Paradox, Watson? If we know all, then enquiry is unnecessary. If we know nothing, then enquiry is impossible. What shall we choose? The unnecessary or the impossible?"

"The impossible must surely be Teyton's story."

"Teyton will keep." He seemed to come to a decision, for there was new determination in his voice. "A visit to brother Mycroft is in order. Into your coat, Watson. The Diogenes awaits!"

We took a cab to Pall Mall and found the usually sedate club to be a hive of activity. Several carts laden with building materials were halted outside whilst their owners debated loudly and enthusiastically who should give way to the other. A gentleman in overalls with a brush in his hand touched his cap as we approached the main entrance and cautioned us not to touch the door frame on account of the wet paint. Inside, the floor and furnishings were sheeted, and it was under the watchful and curious eye of several men on ladders who were employed in painting the ceiling that we picked our way through the maze of their assorted debris and made our way upstairs.

Mycroft Holmes was ensconced in one of the members' private chambers and it took some persuading to get him to relinquish his sanctuary to join us in the Stranger's Room. He entered, florid and flustered, and slammed the door on the chaos that was taking place outside in the corridor.

"That a group of men with such refined needs could cause this much damage defies belief!" he declared. "I fear you find us in a state of disarray, Doctor. The annual refurbishment is upon us and we must endure."

"You could leave," Holmes suggested. "It is only a week, after all."

His brother gave him a withering look. "Don't be impertinent. Now, what is it you want, Sherlock? I am supposed to be convalescing on the instructions of my physician."

It answered my question as to what he was doing at his club in the middle of the day. "I am sorry to hear that," I said. "I trust it is nothing too serious."

"See, Sherlock," said Mycroft Holmes, with a gesture in my direction. "*This* is the normal response to a declaration of illness. The doctor here has the good grace not to doubt the diagnosis. You are too long in the tooth for me to hope that this association might teach you better manners." He bestowed upon me a generous smile. "A temporary condition, I assure you, but one cannot be too careful where one's health is concerned."

As if to illustrate his point, he gave a delicate cough. Holmes glanced across at me with an air of exasperation.

"Well, Sherlock?" said his brother. "Speak plainly and succinctly. I am not a well man."

Holmes smiled. "Who is visiting the British Museum tomorrow at noon?"

Mycroft Holmes had been helping himself to a pinch of snuff. He paused and regarded his brother warily over the open box before setting it aside. "That is highly privileged information. How did you come by it?"

"Tell me who it is and I shall reciprocate."

His brother pursed his lips. "*Outis*."

"Ah, yes, nobody. Really, Mycroft, that will not do." He glanced in my direction and must have seen my confused expression, for I confess the direction of their conversation was baffling. "*Outis*, Watson, a name used by Odysseus, when he defeated Polyphemus. The word means 'nobody' in Greek, so that when the dying Cyclops called for help by declaring 'nobody is killing me', no one came to his assistance." He turned back to his brother. "Who is *Outis*?"

Mycroft Holmes sighed. "This information must not leave this room. It certainly must not find its way into one of those insufferable accounts of those cases of yours, Sherlock." Having obtained his assurance, he continued. "The eldest son of certain of the crowned heads of Europe wishes, against the inclination of his father, to strengthen the bonds between his country and ours. His visit here has been undertaken in the greatest secrecy and so it has been maintained. If the prince has one vice, however, it is a taste for history. He has expressed a wish to see the Rosetta Stone. Naturally, we wish to accommodate him. To close the British Museum would be to attract unwarranted interest, and the prince has said that he requires no special treatment. He wishes to be treated as any other visitor, without pomp or circumstance."

"Very egalitarian of him, no doubt."

"Sarcasm does not suit you," said Mycroft Holmes censoriously. "In this case, it has, to some extent, worked in our favour. It has limited the people who needed to be informed – the director of the Museum, for instance. The prince will attend tomorrow incognito in the company of his advisor and several Scotland Yard detectives. As far as anyone else knows, he will be in his rooms dealing with his correspondence."

"Someone knows differently," said Holmes. "The visit must be cancelled."

"Impossible."

"There will be an attempt on the prince's life."

Mycroft Holmes turned an unfriendly eye on his brother. "Your source?"

"A client, who wishes to remain anonymous for obvious reasons."

"You trust this fellow?"

Holmes glanced across at me. "He was most persuasive."

Mycroft Holmes rocked back and forth in his seat until he had gained enough momentum to propel himself upright. "To cancel would be to insult the prince. His wish must be accommodated. But . . . ." He drew a long breath. "The consequences should he be assassinated on British soil are appalling to contemplate. You must investigate, brother, and if it is in your power to prevent this, then every resource is at your disposal."

"That is most generous. However, discretion being the better part of valour, I can do what needs to be done faster alone."

"Unthinkable!"

"Mycroft," Holmes said calmly, "you have a spy in your midst. One of the men accompanying the prince tomorrow is an obvious candidate. I would prefer that they did not know."

"This client of yours," said his brother. "Have you considered whether he is involved?"

"It has."

"I see. Well, Sherlock, it appears we are all in your hands. It is a great responsibility you take upon yourself." He held his brother's gaze. "That responsibility is not one to be undertaken lightly. You do understand the price that may be demanded to prevent this?"

"I do."

His brother nodded. "Then you have my sanction, if not my blessing. Go on with you, Sherlock. You have tried my patience enough for one day."

So bidden, we left. Outside, I hailed a cab. Holmes appeared reluctant to join me.

"It would be better that you go home, my dear fellow," said he.

"But, Holmes, if I can help in any way – "

"I would not have you involved, Watson. Nothing is assured, and I could not rest easy in my mind knowing that I had been the means and cause of your demise."

"If you think that concerns me for one moment – "

"Staunch fellow that you are," Holmes interrupted me, "I fear that this is one case that I must investigate alone." He tapped his cane impatiently on the pavement. "I shall see you back at Baker Street."

I watched him go, a stern figure in black cutting through the milling crowds, with no small feeling of concern chipping at my soul. As much I resented being dismissed in such a peremptory fashion, I was determined to prove my worth to the investigation. Despite Holmes's insistence to the contrary, I was certain the answer lay with Teyton. Accordingly, I didn't spend the afternoon in idleness. I scoured the records at Somerset House,

I searched trade and telephone directories – yet no trace of the man could I find. It was as though he had never existed – certainly that was the opinion of the boys set upon his trail, who reported back that their quarry had inexplicably "vanished into thin air" from his cab somewhere in the vicinity of Piccadilly Circus. So it was that by the time Holmes returned, I had precious little to show for my efforts.

"That is because you are looking in the wrong place." He threw a copy of *The Times* on the table before me. "In this morning's notices, you will observe the announcement of the appointment of the new canon to the stall of Teyton Regis in Salisbury Cathedral. It isn't difficult to imagine our guest lighting upon the name whilst perusing his newspaper, no doubt whilst he was waiting for us."

"He knew the hour of our return?"

"Naturally. His entrance was timed to perfection. Had you consulted Mrs. Hudson, you would have discovered that an inspector from the gas company called here two days ago to inspect the meter: Our Mr. Teyton, unless I am much mistaken. Amongst the information he gleaned from our landlady was the location and duration of your impromptu holiday. I dare say that was also when he took your watch. A lucky find! It added credibility to his deception." Holmes gave me a sideways glance. "You did leave here in haste the morning of your departure?"

I was forced to admit he was correct. I had been late for my train.

"And, in so doing, left your watch behind. Well, well, another mystery is solved."

"But, Holmes, to have planned in such detail."

"Suggests a man with something to lose, but with a conscience. He fears discovery, more from us than the conspirators, from which we may deduce that they are not immediately at hand. That may help our friend, Watson, but not us." He pounced upon his Persian slipper and supplied his pipe with a quantity of tobacco. "The result of my investigation has been much the same as yours. The three detectives who will accompany the prince were amongst several suggested by the Commissioner of Police himself as men of the greatest integrity. Oh, he didn't know the purpose of the request, and the final choice lay with the prince's personal advisor. The detectives themselves will not know their destination until they arrive tomorrow. The prince's advisor – let us call him 'the Baron' for the sake of propriety – has been with him for fifteen years, and has his confidence in all matters."

"What of the location?"

Holmes sucked thoughtfully on his pipe. "Is open on all sides, save the museum steps, which may as easily provide concealment for an assassin behind the columns, as do the rooms that face onto the courtyard."

241

He sighed. "I have no choice but to attend tomorrow, if the prince's life is to be preserved."

"Holmes, you cannot."

"It is my duty."

"Then I shall accompany you."

"No," he said firmly. "You will be on the milk train to Cornwall, as far away from London as is possible. There is your ticket." He fished it from his pocket and passed it to me. "It is likely to be a bloody business, Watson. I don't want you anywhere near the British Museum."

I faced him across the table. "It seems to me that is where I am most needed."

"On the contrary, my dear fellow. If there is to be a shooting, the last place you should be is by my side, lest the assassin miss his target. No, my mind is made up," said he, holding up his hand to silence my protest. "You may not fear the consequences of your promised assistance, but I do."

He would brook no argument. Accordingly, I set out early next morning after passing a restless night. What Holmes did not know, however, was that it had been my intention to alight several stations along the line and retrace my journey back to London. Five minutes to twelve found me at the British Museum, my hat pulled low over my brow and a scarf concealing my face as I hid behind my newspaper, trying to spot any potential assassins in the crowds of people.

It was uncommonly busy that day, not just with visitors and families, but also with the usual street sellers supplying tea and toffee-apples, an organ grinder surrounded by children more intent on dancing than learning, and an elderly bespectacled programme seller plying his wares to any who would part with a few pennies for his wealth of knowledge.

In the midst of this general melee, I fear that my position by the gate was not well-chosen. Having failed to account for the many departing as well as arriving, I almost missed the prince's party. Three men whom I took to be the detectives accompanied two other men, whose bearing betrayed their otherwise common or garden clothing. Of Holmes I had seen no trace. That he was there, however, I was certain. I watched the group enter and tried to follow at a discreet distance, only to find myself being near knocked from my feet when a giggling boy collided with me and sent me into a spin.

By the time I collected myself, the royal party was nearly to the museum steps. Once inside, I felt sure the danger would be past, but suddenly from the right I saw the programme seller drop his leaflets and run headlong towards them. Before I could raise the alarm, he had hurled himself at the group of men. Even as I started in their direction, I was already too late. Above the babble of voices, there came the sound of a shot, then another, then the screams of women and the sharp trill of a police whistle. My heart was in my mouth as I attempted to push through the huddle of people pressing around the prince's group. From what little I could glimpse between them, a figure lay on the ground surrounded by a widening pool of blood.

In that terrible moment, all my fears were made flesh. I struggled in vain to find a way through. My cries that I was a doctor went unheeded. The morbid masses refused to yield, preferring instead to watch a man die before their very eyes. In spite of my efforts, I couldn't sway them and it took the iron grip of a hand around my wrist to haul me away. I was about to remonstrate with this individual when I found myself looking into the troubled face of Inspector Lestrade. If he was present, then it must have been at Holmes's instigation.

"I can't let you go in there, Doctor Watson," Lestrade insisted, tightening his hold as I attempted to prise his fingers away.

"If Holmes is injured – "

"It's too late, sir. I have my orders. You have to leave!"

I pulled free of his grasp. With one last valiant attempt, I threw myself into the fray only to hear a call from Lestrade to one of the constables. Something heavy landed across my shoulders and I knew no more.

I came to on the museum steps, propped up against a column. A constable stood at my side, a censorious look upon his face. My head ached and the world was blurred. From what little I could discern, the crowd had thinned and the place of curious onlookers was taken by several constables. From this group, a single figure detached itself and headed in my direction. The closer he came, the more I could make out a severe profile now shorn of applied whiskers and round spectacles. By the time he eased himself down at my side, I was certain I was in the company of my old friend once again.

"Well, Watson, you do not disappoint," said Holmes brightly. "I expected you to try something like this. It is fortunate for us both that I had Lestrade on sentry duty."

I stared at him, studying every detail of his face to be sure that he was no fanciful vision. "I thought you had been shot," I said.

"You would not be wrong." He turned slightly and I saw a stain darkening the sleeve of his battered tweed coat. "No, my dear fellow, it is a flesh wound, nothing more. Yours is the graver injury. I fear my instructions were carried out too zealously. When I told Lestrade to prevent you from interfering, I didn't expect him to order you to be struck down. Constable, tea for Doctor Watson, if you would."

Grudgingly, the sentinel detached himself from my side and went on his way.

"I thought . . . ." I faltered, trying to grasp the elusive memory. "I was certain that I saw someone on the ground."

"You were not wrong," said Holmes briskly. "One of the detectives, Chief Inspector Roger Ingleby. Who better placed to carry out an assassination than a man in the prince's company who comes ready armed with a revolver?" He sighed with no little frustration. "His record was an exemplary one – on paper. No doubt on further investigation we shall find evidence of a motive that carries enough weight to warrant the sacrifice of his own life."

"But to kill, Holmes! What grudge could he hold against the prince?"

His gaze wandered back to the gathering around the fallen man. "I would wager the grudge was not his. He merely named his price. The Baron, I fancy, was his financier. The man appears to owe his loyalty more to the father than the son. Even in his own country, the prince has his enemies who fear his liberal ideas. I dare say it will come as some surprise to His Highness to learn such people are closer to home than he realised."

"How did you know the Baron was involved?" I asked.

"I had had the group under observation for some time when I noticed him take a step away from the prince. That was my cue to act. I attempted to wrestle the gun from Ingleby, only to get shot for my efforts. It was the Baron's own pistol that ended Ingleby's life. You may call it quick-thinking – I call it preparation. No witnesses, you see," he added ruefully. "A pity. Ingleby could have confirmed the details of the case."

"Is the prince safe?"

"As much as he can be with the Baron at his side. I shall have to spend the afternoon attempting to convince His Royal Highness otherwise." He rose wearily, wincing slightly as he held his arm at an awkward angle. "Go home, my dear fellow. The less you're involved in this sorry affair, the better. I looked into the Baron's eyes after he shot Ingleby. He knows, Watson, that I am aware of his involvement. It is enough that one of us has made an enemy this day."

"What of your arm?"

He did not look back as he headed down the steps. "A mere graze. It will keep."

I spent a tiresome afternoon nursing a sore head. Holmes returned late into the evening, his entrance akin to a thunderbolt from a clear sky. The door was thrown open, the bang reverberating through the whole house. First his hat and then his gloves were thrown in disgust onto the nearest chair.

"The prince will not see reason!" he declared hotly. "The Baron has his claws into him and will not so easily be shaken free. One may admire loyalty, but to persist in the face of all arguments to the contrary is foolishness of the highest order!"

With his hands thrust deep into his pockets, he prowled about the room like a caged beast, wearing his ills openly for all to see. It took patience and gentle persuasion on my part to convince him to allow me to dress his wound, and it was with the greatest reluctance that he finally relented and removed his coat.

"He has convinced His Highness this was the work of the British government attempting to hide behind the cover of anarchists," he explained while I worked. "Who can blame him? The detective who tried to kill him came with the highest recommendation. The details of his visit were known to very few. Add to that the advantage of the Baron's years of devoted service, and you can see why our poor efforts fell on stony ground."

He gave a snarl of frustration and thumped his hand on the desk, dislodging the bandage I was attempting to fasten about his upper arm.

"You should have seen his face, Watson," he said, still broiling with indignation. "The confidence of the man is galling. He believes he has won. It could not have worked out better had the prince died. Any goodwill the visit has fostered is in tatters and the prince will leave tomorrow in high dudgeon. For the sake of all concerned, the newspapers will run a story that I was shot whilst foiling an attempt on my own life. Whitewash and balderdash! Well, we shall see," he added, his eyes glinted with renewed determination. "Teyton may yet provide us with answers."

"Then we must find him."

Holmes said nothing as I completed my ministrations. No sooner had I finished than he was on his feet, swiftly gathering up the morning's newspapers and spreading them across the table.

"May I be of assistance?" I ventured.

"I am looking for something quite particular," he said, studying our creased copy of *The Daily Telegraph* intently. "I'm afraid I shall be poor company this evening. Tomorrow, I trust, will bring better news."

I took this as my invitation to leave. A little after seven o'clock the next morning, I found myself being shaken awake. The eager light in Holmes's eyes told me his research had been productive. Less than half-an-hour later, we were in a cab heading east.

"An interesting man, our Mr. Teyton," Holmes began as we travelled. "An amateur actor, whose talents have yet to be appreciated by the press. He takes *The London Record* and is fond of sensational literature. If he has one fault, it is in underestimating people – in this case, Mrs. Hudson. Do you know, Watson, our landlady has a remarkable ability to draw the smallest detail of people's lives from them without ever alerting them that they are being interrogated? I would like to think that I have taught her this skill, but I fear it is innate."

I could not resist smiling at his remark. "Are you saying she is a hopeless busybody?"

"On the contrary, she exhibits a genuine interest, which people find irresistible. Our Mr. Teyton told her a great deal about himself when he came to Baker Street in his guise as a gas inspector. He is to marry in three weeks' time and his prospective father-in-law is a pawnbroker. Teyton's error came in assuming she wouldn't tell me of his visit. He also neglected to don a disguise. Thus, we have a clear description. He is a fresh-faced man of five-and-twenty, fair-haired and slim – quite the opposite to his appearance when he came to us with fanciful tales of time travel."

"And *The London Record*?"

Holmes drew yesterday's newspaper from his pocket. "A curious publication that I doubt will be long in circulation. It is devoted entirely to news about the theatre and other various amusements. See here in the announcements, a piece about the Teyton Regis appointment. It warranted a mention because the previous incumbent became a man of the cloth late in life after a promising career on the London stage."

"Many people have an interest in the theatre, Holmes."

"How many read reviews of amateur productions unless they have some vested interest? On the same page as our theatrical clergyman, Watson, there are two columns devoted to the critic's opinion of local theatre, some more favourable than others. Observe this review of *The Man Who Returned*, currently being performed at a church hall in Shoreditch. A farcical melodrama, by all accounts, about a man who returns after a lengthy absence and adopts one disguise after another in an attempt to test the affection of his fiancée. The critic is fairly scathing overall, but reserves the worst of his bile for the actor in the leading role, one Reginald Talbot. He writes: 'If ever a man was born to be a gas inspector, it is surely Mr. Talbot, for he excels at little else'."

"Then this Reginald Talbot must surely be our Regis Teyton," said I.

"The coincidence of the initial letters would suggest you are correct. Ah, here we are. Ho, cabby, here will do!"

Holmes rapped on the roof of the cab and we came to a halt. Shoreditch High Street had the usual array of shops, with the steeple of a fine church rising at one end and the towers of a music hall at the other, but it was to the back alleys that Holmes directed us, where the red-brick buildings sagged against each other like drunken sailors. A single shop situated next to a public house boasted the three gold spheres of the pawnbroker's profession along with the owner's name, Bickerstaff, on a sign above the door. As we entered, Holmes indicated a poster in the window advertising *The Man Who Returned*, and I gathered we had found the location of the prospective father-in-law's business.

Inside, the shop was packed to overflowing with an assortment of old clothes, gimcrack ornaments, and other tawdry trinkets. Behind the counter, a rotund, red-faced man greeted us with an unctuous smile.

"Now, sirs, what may I be doing for you?" said he.

"It was the younger gentleman to whom I spoke when last I was here," said Holmes. "Is he available?"

"Certainly, sir." He pushed aside a curtain and yelled into the back room. "Reginald, come out here now. There's a customer for you!"

A thin smile touched the corners of Holmes's mouth when a young fair-haired man appeared from behind the curtain. He came to an abrupt halt when he saw us, his look of dismay mingled with alarm alerting me that Holmes's instincts had been correct. It took him a moment to gather his wits before coming over to us.

"How may I be of assistance?" he said in a voice that betrayed his nervousness.

"I am looking for a book about a time machine," said Holmes nonchalantly. "You have one there on your shelf, Mr. Talbot. Or do you prefer Teyton?"

The young man quailed. "I don't know what you are talking about."

"Then perhaps we should take up the matter with Mr. Bickerstaff."

"No!" Talbot gestured to us to step aside, away from the older man. "For the love of God, do not expose me, Mr. Holmes," he said lowering his voice.

"Be honest with me and I shall do what I can for you. A man has died and I have suffered a blood-letting. Now tell me how you came by the information."

"By chance, you have my word!"

"We shall be the judge of that."

Talbot swallowed heavily and cast a wary glance at Bickerstaff, who was busy with another customer. "The public house next door has rooms to let. The walls are uncommonly thin, and it isn't unusual to hear the conversations of the guests in our upper rooms. Well, last week, I was doing an inventory of our stock and the hour became so late that I was obliged to spend the night here. As I was going to sleep, I overheard people in the room next to mine. There was talk of murder, Mr. Holmes – of a death on yesterday's date at the British Museum at midday. 'He will be there,' I heard one of them saying.

"There was another voice too, an older man from the sound of it. I heard something about a death ten years before, of the man's godchild run down by a carriage that didn't stop on a foreign street. The older man cried bitterly when he heard it. He said he would have vengeance, but the other man said there would be none, for the murderer was a powerful man who would never come to justice. If he would have his revenge, then he must do it himself. 'As he has taken a child from me,' said the older man, 'so I shall take his child from him'.

"What was I to do, Mr. Holmes?" Talbot wrung his hands nervously. "I couldn't go to the police, for they would surely think me an accomplice. I am to marry in several weeks' time. What was I to tell my fiancée, the sweetest girl that ever drew breath, should I be arrested?"

"You could have said nothing," said my companion.

"Aye," said Talbot, "perhaps I should. For what had been done to this man, it might have seemed like justice. But to take another's life for the sins of the father didn't sit well with me. I've studied the accounts of your cases, sir. I believed you would give me a fair hearing. When I first came to Baker Street, it had been my intention to tell you all. But when I found that you weren't at home, my nerve failed me. I devised a plan whereby I could tell you what I knew without revealing my identity. I am something of an amateur actor and I had a number of costumes to hand. I considered the idea of telling you that I had received the information at a séance, but you are a man of science. I knew you would be sceptical. I thought the idea of a time traveller might be more convincing as a way of explaining how I came by the information."

"That, and this weapon." Holmes placed the pinfire revolver on the counter. "I would refrain from pointing a gun at people in the future, Mr. Talbot, unless you intend to use it. Others are less observant than me. Replace it in your father-in-law's stock before he misses it."

"He has. I shall say it was misplaced." The young man's voice became strained. "What will you do, Mr. Holmes? Will there be charges? For the theft of your watch, Doctor Watson, I apologise. It was borrowed, I swear upon my mother's grave. I thought that you might believe me if I had proof."

"A grand scheme, no doubt," said Holmes. "Fuelled by the fantasies of literature and cultivated by your theatrical imagination. I could have wished for more candour from the outset."

The young man nodded unhappily. "I read that a man died. Was it the man I heard crying that night?"

"I believe so. If it is any consolation, Mr. Talbot, the gentleman's fate was sealed from the moment the perpetrators of this crime approached him."

Talbot started. "There was but a single perpetrator, surely. I bumped into him coming out of the public house the next morning. He dropped his cigarette case and I saw his initials: *E.V.*"

"Now this is most interesting," said Holmes. "How do you know it was the same man?"

"Because he cursed me for my carelessness and I recognised his voice. He had an accent, black eyes, and a thin black moustache."

Holmes considered for a moment. "If it is the same man of whom I am thinking, then you have been most wise to exercise caution. Had he been aware that you had overheard him, you would now be dead." Talbot's eyes widened in alarm. "But you may rest assured this will go no further. Nothing is to be gained from your exposure."

"God bless you, sir!" Talbot exclaimed, causing Bickerstaff to glance over at him.

"There is one thing," said my companion as he turned to leave. "Had the critic of *The London Record* seen your performance at Baker Street, his review would have been very different. It is but one man's opinion, after all."

Holmes kept his peace until we were in a cab and homeward bound. "I fear that I owe an apology to the spirit of the late Chief Inspector Ingleby. Nothing so base a motive as money, Watson, but revenge! What lies were told to him, I wonder, to provoke such a response? Was the prince's father blamed for the death of the child? You see now why Ingleby had to die."

I nodded solemnly. "Who is this '*E.V.*'?"

A frown settled on my companion's brow. "He is known only as Victor. And yes, he is an agent of the prince's country. Do you see their plan? To kill two birds with one stone, so to speak. To rid themselves of the troublesome prince and implicate the British government in his murder – to harden his father's heart against us forever."

"Can we not find this man?" I asked.

"Victor will have left the country by now. He found his mark in Ingleby and worked on him. From there, it was a simple case of the Baron choosing his name from the list of detectives provided unwittingly by the Commissioner. Remember, he had influence with the prince to choose the time and location of the assassination. It was elegant in its simplicity, as the best of plans usually are."

"Then what will you do?"

"I shall lay what little we know before the prince and appeal to his good judgement. But what hope is there without solid evidence? If only we had Ingleby!" Holmes sighed and sat back in his seat, his gaze turning to the view of the busy street from the cab window. "I cannot help but feel, my dear fellow, that if there is a failing anywhere in this case, it is in my inability to save the man."

He fell into a brown study and I left him to his thoughts. As we pulled up at Baker Street, I saw the familiar figure of Lestrade on our doorstep. From the hurried manner in which he ran up to our cab, I gathered his visit was one of urgency.

"Good to see you, Doctor Watson," said he. "I trust you've recovered after yesterday's events. I apologise for that, by the way. These young constables don't know their own strength."

"No harm done," I replied.

Lestrade turned to my companion. "I need to speak with you, Mr. Holmes."

"Won't you come inside?" said he. "The street is hardly the place – "

Lestrade cut him short. "It won't wait. This was handed in to Scotland Yard this morning." From an inner pocket, he drew forth a folded letter. "It's from Ingleby. I've removed the name of the recipient. They prefer to remain anonymous. You'll see why."

He waited while Holmes read the letter and then passed it over to me. In Ingleby's own hand, it related an account of what had happened and the reasons for his attempted crime, exactly as Talbot had told us.

"If this is true, Mr. Holmes, Ingleby was used and deceived by these people," said Lestrade earnestly.

"I believe that he was."

The inspector stared hard at him. "Roger Ingleby was one of us. He was ten years an inspector before I ever got my promotion. He was respected."

"The death of his godchild was not in the official record."

"Of course not!" Lestrade's eyes were blazing. "Oh, we all knew. That little girl was the grandchild of his boyhood friend. He swore to look after her when her grandfather died out in India, and he did his best to keep his word, even when the family went to live abroad. Crushed beneath the wheels of a coach-and-four, she was, in front of her parents. Her death put her mother in an asylum and drove the father to suicide. It broke Ingleby. He never found out who was responsible, though by the Lord Harry he did his best to find out. Gone for days he was, never with a word to any of us. He should have been disciplined, but nothing was ever put on record because he was a good detective and needed the job as much as we needed him. After ten years, we thought he'd come to terms with it. And now this."

He shook his head, part of out of sorrow, part of out frustration.

"If I take this to my superiors, it will never see the light of day. But you, Mr. Holmes, and your brother might make good use of it."

"Rest assured, Lestrade," said Holmes, "this may make the difference."

"It had better do so," the inspector returned. "Because if Ingleby is branded a traitor, there's not a man in Scotland Yard who won't swear before God to the contents of that letter."

"That would be unwise," Holmes said carefully.

"Then make it count. Because they won't silence all of us."

With that, he stalked away. Holmes watched him go before glancing in my direction.

"Such is the burden of responsibility, Watson," he observed. "I will show this to the prince. If we can persuade him this was the act of a desperate man before he leaves these shores, we may rescue our reputation. I shall then devote myself to doing the same for Ingleby. He deserves that much."

Holmes was true to his word. The prince was indeed swayed by the contents of the letter, although he denied his father's involvement in the death of the child. Soon after his return to his own country, the Baron was dismissed from service. The man reportedly took his own life by drinking poison added to a brandy decanter – a questionable means of suicide, as Holmes noted, for adding it to his glass alone would have guaranteed the result. Nor did the elusive Victor survive long, for the bloated corpse of the agent was discovered by railway tracks in rural Carpathia. At Holmes's instigation, the landlord of the Shoreditch public house was able to identify Victor as the man who had rented a room and had had a visitor that night, a police detective who he recognised from the newspapers as Ingleby. It was evidence enough for an amendment to the official account, where it was recorded that Chief Inspector Roger Ingleby had been killed whilst on duty.

It was, as Holmes later remarked, justice of a kind.

The Sweet Science
of Bruising
by Kevin P. Thornton

Sherlock Holmes had been restless this past fortnight. He had finished a case of some simplicity but great import to the realm, and another of no substantial effect on same that had nevertheless been interesting enough to tax him for two days.

Since then, although he had resolved some conundra, they had been by his standards trifling. There were three cases, not one of which held his attention for more than a peremptory period. In two of them he had scribbled a solution on the supplicating missives and sent the manservants scurrying, while the third, a missing child in Bexhill-on-Sea, he had solved in an afternoon, again without leaving the confines of 221b Baker Street.

As was usual when his mind was not occupied, he manifested his frustration in either pent-up pacing or abject lethargy. I preferred the former. As his doctor as well as his friend, I worried that the latter was self-medicated, so although his prowling was irksome, it was also the more desirable. Meanwhile I prayed for a case to come his way.

As if in answer to my wishes, Holmes stopped and peered out onto the street.

"Watson," he said. "Come here if you will, and tell me what you make of this."

I looked out the front window. There was a man coming down the road towards our door, and what an astonishing man he was. He towered over everyone else by at least six inches, and he walked like someone with liquor in his stream. He was dressed in dishevelled evening wear, with his tie undone and jacket hanging at an angle. He had a black cravat raised over his face as if a mask, and as he walked towards our door pedestrians scurried out of his way.

"Why, he is a scoundrel, and he appears to be drunk," I said. "If he is indeed coming here, he has something terrible in his heart. Maybe he wears the mask to rob us." I made to retrieve my handgun, but Holmes stayed me with a wave of his hand.

"He is nothing of the sort, Watson, and you will find that out for yourself when Mrs. Hudson shows him in, for though he is big, I suspect he is a gentle man."

And so it proved. Our visitor blocked the light in the doorwell, standing behind our landlady, but there was no sense of danger. Indeed, he seemed deferential, even awed by his surroundings.

"Thank you, Mrs. Hudson. You may let Mister Jeb Cracken in. He has, I believe, business with me."

A look of astonishment slowly dawned on the giant's face. "You know me?" he said.

"We have never met," said Holmes, "but you are a notably distinguishable man. I can tell that you are a caring and careful person, that you were on the undercard in the prize fights at Lord Pomeroy's gardens last night, that you lost, and that something weighs heavily on your mind. Whom did you fight, and for how long were you knocked out?"

The look on Cracken's face was childlike in its reverence. "Jem Mace was right," he said. "He told me there was none smarter in all of London, and if I needed help you were the man to see. How did you know all that about me? Every word of it is true."

"Your dress, the evening wear, indicates you were in the company of so-called 'gentlemen' from last night until this morning, yet the way you wear it suggests you find no comfort in such clothing. A footman then, or a personal guard maybe? In your walk you appeared to be listing a little, yet it would be most unusual for a servant to be drunk in the middle of an errand. I suspect, sir, that you have had this feeling before. You are therefore a pugilist. The concussions that come from prizefighting wear on a body after a while, and the effects take longer and longer to go away. As to your caring sensibilities, you wear that cravat over your face not to instill fear, but to prevent it. I suspect you lost heavily and you are bruised and cut. You feared that you would scare people, so you tried to cover up, not realizing that the act of masking yourself makes you look just as menacing. All is clear to me. I observe and deduce." As usual it was simple, once he explained it.

"So Jem Mace sent you to me? How is he?" Without waiting for an answer, Holmes turned to me. "Mace may be the best prizefighter ever over the last forty years. He won a world title under the Queensberry Rules as well as in bare-knuckle, and I have heard he returns to America soon to fight Donovan, once more for a world title, even though he has long seen the back of his sixtieth birthday." He gestured towards the chair near the fireplace. "Please, Mister Cracken, sit down and unmask." The prizefighter did so. Even seated he seemed to fill the room. Standing he must have been near six-and-a-half feet tall and an eighth-of-a-ton by my estimation, some two-hundred-and-eighty pounds.

It was patent why he felt the need to wear the cravat. That Jeb Cracken had lost his fight was obvious by the damage done to him. His eyes were puffy, his nose broken for what may have been the tenth or even hundredth time, and there were welts and cuts all over his face.

"It's not as bad as it looks," said Cracken. "On any other day I'd have taken him. Billy Welty and I have fought many times before and usually I have the measure of him. But I slipped in the fourth round and hit my nut hard on the cobblestones. My head wasn't clear for the next five or six rounds and Billy laid into me. I kept on going, but he had me down-and-out in the twenty-seventh."

"Twenty-seventh?" I said. "Holmes this is insane. We must report this to the police. Mister Cracken was concussed in the fourth round and yet fought on for . . . . ." I paused, temporarily losing my ability to do simple mathematics.

"Twenty-three more rounds," said Holmes, "each round lasting until a knockdown, which typically can take anything from a few seconds to some moments, although I once saw a round last thirty-two minutes, when I was learning this noble art. In answer to your unasked question, Watson, Mister Cracken likely fought on for another sixty to ninety minutes while concussed. I'm surprised the damage isn't worse, but as you can see from the scarring, he is used to such treatment."

"Even so, what manner of man is this Billy Welty that he can cause such damage?"

"Billy Welty is two inches shy of six feet tall, and may on a good day weigh one-hundred-eighty pounds. As do so many, Watson you have equated size and strength with skill. Mister Cracken here may be the largest and most menacing prizefighter in England, but he is very slow, and in truth I don't think his heart was ever in it."

The giant's face saddened. "You're right, Mister Holmes. I come from a poor background, and the more I grew, the more I was pushed into the fighting life. At first it was easy. My size and strength saw me win often and well. I've always had trouble against the quick 'uns, though. They can dance 'round me, and by the time I found out it was too late. This was my life and there was no getting away from it. I always wanted to be a farmer, to be out in the country with the animals, but the road from the docks of Liverpool don't lead out that way."

All through this, the giant sat passively and I tried to tend to his wounds. For all the damage inflicted to him, I felt as useful as King Canute trying to hold back the tide.

Holmes, unusually so, was patient, waiting for me to finish before he continued.

"Now," he said, "How may I help you?"

"Well Mister Holmes, it's the strangest thing," Jeb Cracken said. "You seem to know a bit about the fighting game. A lot of the time it's been illegal, and even though there are now rules in place to make it right, the Marquis of Queensberry's paper and all that, the real money is still to be made in bareknuckle boxing. There's toffs that like to sponsor such fights for their friends, and there is gambling that wins and loses fortunes and reputations. The fights I was at last night, and there were four of them, started after supper and went on until three in the morning. Lord Pomeroy, him who set it all up, has one every month or so. He invites his friends over – there must have been two-hundred men there in his gardens last evening – and a good fighter can take home a year's wages if the crowd take a fancy to him." Cracken paused for a moment and tried to smile through his battered face. "It's been a while since I was on the rich end of the stakes, Mister Holmes, but I does what I can and I make a living, such as it is. A man my size is always a draw, and there was a time when Hec Nancarrow, the Cornish Giant, stood toe-to-toe with me for forty-seven rounds and we both never gave an inch. I won that one, but that was ten years and three-hundred fights ago. He's dead now, and I've slowed down a bit, but by heck we gave the crowds their value that night."

"And your problem?" said Holmes. "Why did Jem Mace send you to me?"

"Ah well. Often at these events, when there's been drink taken, one of the young toffs always fancies a go at one of the fighters. None of the lads mind too much – it always means some more money in the pocket, and in among us fighters we have some rules. Don't hurt them too much, and let them look good for a minute or two before putting an end to it. I can't tell you the number of young rakes I have sparred against who are now sitting in the House of Lords."

"There are some might say that you may have even knocked some sense into them," said Holmes, "though it is doubtful, given their provenance. Her Majesty's government survives despite the nobility, not because of them. But come now Mister Cracken, get to the nub of the story."

"About three weeks ago," said Cracken, "I was at the Duke of Cleveland's event when I was asked to stand against one of the guests. When he stripped off, I knew I was in for a fight. He was lean and muscled, and he moved like he knew what he was doing, unlike most of them. He was sharp and hit me a couple of times, and I don't mind admitting he 'urt me a bit. I figured to lay 'im out before I forgot me place and did him some harm, so I clapped him on the side of the ear and put him down. Only he got back up again, and there was a look in his face I hadn't seen before. He was enjoying himself, and he seemed to want to be hit again. Anyway, as I said, he had some skills, but when he got up off the floor, he held his guard differently."

"His guard?" I asked.

"The way a fighter holds his hands and arms up to defend against his opponent," said Holmes. "Failure to do so is normally the sign of a losing battle. The boxer is fatigued, typically"

"Aye, but he weren't tired," said Cracken. "He wanted to be punished. So I did something I've never done before, Mister Holmes. I let him hit me and I went down as if he's knocked me cold."

"Your instincts were right," said Holmes. "For whatever reason, this young rake wanted you to hit him. You were in a no-win position."

"But that's not all that was strange," said Cracken. "As I was lying there pretending to be glassed, he stood over me screaming at me to get up and fight. He had to be dragged away by his friends. Since then, the word has gone 'round, and none of the other fighters will touch him. He's too good to just fend off, and the danger is he'll come up against someone who will react to his punches by doing him some real damage, and that way still leads to gaol. And then there was this." He reached into his jacket and pulled out an envelope, handing it to Holmes.

Holmes perused it quickly

"My word," he said, "this is indeed interesting." He handed it to me. It was a solicitor's notification that James Everett Runcie, Esquire, intended to pursue a suit of defamation against Jebediah Cracken.

"But what does he hope to achieve?" I said.

"I don't know," said Cracken gloomily. "It's not like I have any money. I can't even afford to defend meself. I went to go see him, hoping he'd talk to me. At first, I was kept waiting by his butler, but then he came out as if he was going somewhere, saw me, and invited me in."

"Interesting," said Holmes.

"Yes, but get this," said Cracken. "He offered to drop his suit if I agreed to fight him in a proper bareknuckle fight, winner take all, for five-hundred Guineas."

"That is a considerable sum of money," I said.

"More than I've ever seen," said Cracken. "I have to tell you, Mister Holmes, with that kind of money I could retire for good. I was tempted, I really was, but I asked him for a couple of days to think about it. Then I talked it over with Jem Mace last night after the fights, and he reckoned I should come and see you."

"I'm glad you did," said Holmes. "This promises to be an interesting little puzzle." He guided Cracken to the door. "I ask you to present yourself here in two days' time at the dusking of the day, and I believe that I shall have a solution for you."

After our visitor had departed, Holmes sat back and lit a pipe. The room became clouded and fumed, as if in a pea-soup fog created by an insane scientist. I felt sure I would succumb to the rank odour, and yet I waited. If there was any action to be taken, I didn't want to miss out.

Holmes murmured to himself every now and then. He consulted his filing system twice, grimacing at the first and unveiling a satisfied "A-ha!" the second. He also looked in the *Who's Who*. "Ah yes" he said. "The oldest child of the fourth son of the Earl of Ness. His father went into trade and made his money in rubber plantations, and James Everett Runcie, Esquire, is therefore a very wealthy man, who lists as his interests *inter alia*, sports, and boxing."

"He is far enough away from the Earldom that he can afford some frippery in his *Who's Who* entry," I said. "Listing boxing as an interest when the sport is mostly illegal is his way of cocking a snoot at the Establishment."

"Indeed," said Holmes. "And sports is a code word for being a betting man. So why does he want to die?"

He paused for a second and I tried to keep up with his rationalizations. As usual, he was several steps ahead of the rest of the world.

"Watson!" he said, startling me. "Do you still have the newspaper from last Wednesday? Not *The Times*. That new ha-penny one, *The Daily Mail*. I know you keep them in the forlorn hope that you'll catch up with your reading."

I went to my room to fetch the newspaper. Holmes opened it and perused the columns. He stopped and read an article with interest.

"This may be the answer," he said. "I must send a telegram. Then I need to go and see . . . Watson, you must come with me, if you will. He seems to like you, and his mood will be elevated by your company. It is tedious to pander to him, but it will make our quest quicker."

"Who are we going to see?"

"Mycroft."

I grabbed my coat and hat, as well as the newspaper that Holmes had found so interesting, and followed him down the stairs.

In the cab, I read the article. It was of the new sort of gossip journalism, and I wasn't sure if I approved or if I would even continue taking it. I didn't approve of such sordid reporting.

The story was about who among the rich and famous were seen either leaving for the Continent or returning, and with whom. Without any substantive facts, it managed to infer much that seemed salacious. Among those noted, James Everett Runcie, Esquire, was seen to be travelling back alone, on the same train from the coast as the famous surgeon, Sir Joseph Lister, Baronet.

"I fail to see what conclusions you may have drawn from this article," I said.

"I have concluded nothing, Watson. I merely see possibilities. This new type of newspaper reportage, as tasteless as it seems, crafts a fine suggestive line in its work. I need to check on a singular fact with my brother, and await the answer to my telegram before I help Mister Cracken out of this legal mess in which he is mired."

We waited in the Stranger's Room of the Diogenes Club, the only room where conversation was permitted.

Mycroft came in with an impatient look on his face. "Sherlock, with what trifle do you need help today? Doctor Watson, as always it is good to see you. Are you keeping my brother away from depravity?"

"Your brother has always had the highest standards of moral probity," I said, then stopped, as I realized I was being gently joshed.

"Has he?" said Mycroft, permitting himself the ghost of a smile. "Then he is lucky to have you as a friend."

"Indeed," said Holmes. "What can you tell me about the travels of James Everett Runcie, Esquire, the grandson of the Earl of Ness?"

"We are aware of his sojourns on the Continent," said Mycroft. "He came back from his second trip to Wurzburg last week, having made the same journey six weeks prior. The Earl of Ness has caused us concern in the past with his leanings towards the Kaiser. He was married to Wilhelm's second cousin, so we like to know what he and his family are up to."

"Even though the German Emperor is the Queen's grandson and therefore above suspicion," observed Holmes.

"No one is above suspicion," said Mycroft. "Nevertheless, we are always interested when a member of the Ness clan takes sudden and abrupt trips into the heart of the German Empire. The Earl is divisive in his opinions of the world situation, loathes our own Royal family, and has been known to suggest that a Teutonic influence at Court would better serve our nation. Although he hasn't quite fomented the idea of a revolution, he would, it appears, be in favour of one."

"And are you still interested in the Earl's grandson?"

"No," said Mycroft. "Runcie's visits to Germany have nothing to do with either politics or espionage."

We were interrupted by a servant wearing a grave look and carrying a silver salver covered with a silk cloth. He whispered to Mycroft, who frowned and retrieved an envelope underneath. "Really, Sherlock, this is too much. Now you are having telegram messages sent to my club?"

Holmes snatched it from his brother, tearing it open. "Thank you for your help dear brother, but Watson and I must away. Sir Joseph Lister lives over near Regent's Park. We need to prevail upon the great man to see us before we visit young Runcie and put an end to Jeb Cracken's legal woes."

I picked up the discarded telegram and read it. It was from the ticket master's office at Victoria Station, and it said that Lister and Runcie had travelled on the same boat train to Germany on two separate occasions. Holmes had made something of this information. For the life of me, I could not.

Lister was home and receiving visitors. His ideas on anti-sepsis had revolutionized medicine and saved incalculable lives, and he was only now receiving his due and the gratitude of the nation after years in the scientific wilderness.

"Sir Joseph," said Holmes. "Thank you for permitting us to disturb you. I read your seminal work, *Antiseptic Principle of the Practice of Surgery*, shortly after it was published, and it had an influence on the work that I do today. It galvanized my studies, sir, to know that you were out there seeing beyond the obvious, and it is a tragedy that it took so long for your theories to be put into common practice."

Lister seemed to study Holmes for any signs of gushing insincerity. Finding none, he said, "Read it when it came out eh? You were likely just a boy then?"

"I was," said Holmes. "Now sir, you have been to Wurzburg twice recently. Without breaking your doctor-patient confidentiality, I beg to ask you only one question. Is there any hope for him?"

Lister paused, measuring his answer. "No," he said.

"Then thank you for your time."

Holmes wanted to walk to Runcie House. I refused. My friend is secretive at the best of times. He would be impossible to question as he passed down Regent Street. Once ensconced in the cab, I looked straight at him.

"I have never been more confused in any of your cases. You seem to know what is going on, but your leaps of logic have confounded me yet again. Pray tell me what you have concluded."

"Patience, Watson. All will be revealed. My conclusions are based on a supposition that needs to be verified, although I can see no other rational explanation. I will leave you with this until we get there. The Runcie family and the Lairds of Ness are a long line of proud warriors and tribal Lords, originating in the highlands of Scotland. Why then do you think young Runcie is so insistent on fighting Jeb Cracken in a bareknuckle contest?"

I was no nearer an answer when we arrived.

James Everett Runcie, Esquire, was not receiving visitors when we called. Holmes gave the doorman our cards and mentioned that we were representing Jebediah Cracken, and we were let in.

Runcie was a fine specimen of all that was the best of British nobility. Tall, lean, and well-muscled, he looked as if he would be at home either bowling from the pavilion end at Lord's or leading a charge of cavalry at Waterloo.

"I have heard of you, Holmes. You are well thought of in the fisticuffs world as well as for your ability to solve the unsolvable. I'm surprised you are here on Cracken's behalf. Surely it is a simple matter. I wish to fight him, for him to give me his best, toe-to-toe, and I shan't take no for an answer."

"Money has a power that those without it can scarcely realize," said Holmes. "It allows you to place a poor fighter in an invidious position where he can see no clear way out. I hope we can resolve this as gentlemen. If not, I will advise Mister Cracken to wait it out until nature takes its course. You are dying, sir, for there can be no other reason for your actions. At first I thought your behaviour and your travels linked to the beliefs in subversion espoused by your grandfather. It was only when I matched the research being done at the University in Wurzburg to all the possible explanations that I was left with only one solution."

"And that was?" said Runcie. He attempted to be insouciant, but he didn't manage.

"You are dying, and for whatever reason – probably your Highland bloodline – you wish to die in battle. You don't have time on your side or else you would do what many of your foolish forebears have done in the past, lead from the front in a suicidal charge with all guns blazing." As he said this Runcie's demeanour crumpled, and he sat down in a large wingback armchair.

"How did you know? Lister gave me away, did he not? He should have respected our confidentiality."

"Your surgeon said nothing of substance, merely confirming what I had surmised. The facts are thus: Your ailment presented itself mayhap as headaches that would not dissipate, followed possibly by dizziness, and maybe even an occasional loss of balance. You are wealthy, so you consulted the best surgeon in the land, Sir Joseph Lister. He couldn't help, as there was nothing to see, but he mentioned that there was a radical new science at Wurzburg that may enable him to make a better diagnosis. You both travelled together, but separately, to Germany where Professor Wilhelm Röntgen, no doubt for a large donation, agreed to take one of his photos of the inside of your head."

260

"All of what you say is true," said Runcie. "Röntgen calls them *X-ray pictures*, and they can see past the skin and bone, right into the heart of the matter. There is a large and aggressive growth at the base of my brain. Lister was not confident it could be operated on – there was too much danger that I would be left in a vegetative state. Röntgen suggested we come back in a month. He had some small hope that the X-rays, as he called them, may in themselves be the cure. So we came home and then returned three weeks later."

"And it was worse," said Holmes.

"Much worse. The tumour, for that was what they called it, was growing, and invading my brain. Not only was it inoperable, but the nature of the beast meant it likely that I would lose all sense, all control of body and functions, and the abilities to speak, hear, see, and eat."

"It will be an aggressive and miserable death," said Holmes, and I winced at his bedside manner. Runcie, however was not put off.

"You understand," he said. "The certainty of losing everything, of losing my very self, was too much. I couldn't bear the thought of ending my days as a dribbling, mewling fool, so I sought an alternative. I thought of suicide, but my beliefs do not allow such actions, and the shame on the family would be too terrible. Similarly, a faked accident would not rest with my conscience. How could I go to my Maker with such a stain on my soul?"

"So you blackmailed Jebediah Cracken," said Holmes. Runcie started to protest, but Holmes interrupted him. "You have chosen to die at another's hand, without thought of the consequences."

"It will be a fair fight," said Runcie.

"It will not," said Holmes. "Jeb Cracken is a professional fighter. You won't hurt him, or put him to the ground. What I think you will do is annoy him, deliberately to the point where he takes the bout seriously. Will you lower your guard a little to make his options obvious? I suspect one punch from him at the base of your skull will do it. You will die the death you seek, but what of your opponent? What do you think will happen to him, the poor man from the streets of Liverpool? He will be found guilty of murdering a toff and strung up on the scaffold before your body is even cold. What will your Maker make of you then?"

"I hadn't thought of him," said Runcie. "Oh dear Lord, what a fool I have been! What must I do? Help me Holmes, please. I have been so selfish."

"You should pay Cracken the same amount you offered him, and stay away from local prizefighters. Though the word is out among them, for five-hundred Guineas, you will find someone willing to do your dirty work."

"I will do that immediately – the money is meaningless anyway. And I will pay you for your time as well, so he does not have to. Will you deliver the money to him, please?

"I shall take your note to the bank immediately, and help him to use it carefully."

Runcie went away to make arrangements. Holmes walked over to the writing table and sealed a note in an envelope. He gave it to Runcie on his return.

"Your fear clouded your judgement," said Holmes. "I understand more than you can possibly imagine. When you live as I choose, using the grey matter inside one's head to make sense of the nonsensical – well, your concern is one I share, perhaps more than most."

He handed him the envelope. "Open this only when we have left, commit it to memory, and if you choose to act on the information do so quickly, while you still can."

We never spoke more about the case that day. What was the point?

Cracken, two days later, was delighted. He tried to refuse the money and only accepted it after Holmes mentioned a farm in Herefordshire looking for a trainee shepherd. "The money will help you to live better than the pittance the farmer will pay," he said. "It's time to find out if life in the countryside suits you."

It was about a fortnight later when the matter was finally concluded. *The Times* (I had given up on the tawdry *Daily Mail*) reported the strange incident of the death of James Everett Runcie, Esquire – grandson of the Earl of Ness – on the Marseilles docks. He had been beaten badly and the local police suspected that a robbery that had gone wrong. I placed the article in front of Holmes.

"This is your doing, is it not? That note you gave him."

Holmes glanced at it. "Do not trouble your conscience, Watson. It is for the best. In my recent travels, I came across some dark, dank clubs on the Mediterranean shorefront, where the fighting is tough, the money pitiful, and the rules non-existent. I suggested to Runcie that he would have a chance to win some bouts, and if he had money he would find opponents."

"You sent him to his death."

"I pre-empted the time and cause."

"And did he have a chance?"

"I don't know. I have never seen him fight. Jeb Cracken thought he was good for a toff. At least he went with a clear conscience in the knowledge that he would not endanger his eventual meeting with his maker. He died *compos mentis*, which is all he wished for – all any of us can wish for."

"I wonder how Jeb Cracken is doing on the farm," I said.

"My cousin says he has a broad back, a willingness to learn, and a delicate touch with animals and the milkmaids."

"Your cousin? Holmes I had no idea. That was very kind, what you did for him."

"Jebediah Cracken is a good man who deserves his happiness. And so too, in his own way, did James Everett Runcie, Esquire."

The Mystery of
Sherlock Holmes
by Christopher Todd

Our paths in life are often marked out for us at birth. One's class, one's family, one's father's profession dictates the direction of one's life. It is rare that a person determines his own way in the world. Such a person is usually gifted with a great talent and the will to develop it, and in doing so, he may inspire others to follow their call. An example of the first kind of person was my friend Sherlock Holmes. And he, in turn, helped me find my way.

I was always one for making up tales of adventure – brave knights slaying dragons, pirates burying treasure, heroes saving maidens from horrible fiends. As soon as I learned to write, I committed them to paper. But early on I realized that I wouldn't be permitted to make a living as a scribbler of stories. My father worked to put me through medical school. Still, my taste for adventure led me to become an army surgeon. A Jezail bullet put an end to that. Yet it also put me on a trajectory to meet the person who would help me discover my destiny: To chronicle the life of the most remarkable man I have ever met, the pioneer of a new science destined to save the lives of many as well as cut short many careers of evil.

The cases that I recorded were true. To protect the lives and reputations of men and women (and governments), names and dates and identifying details were changed. This also protected Holmes's livelihood, since few would have come to him if they thought their tragedies would appear in the next issue of *The Strand*. Some tales of necessity were embargoed for a time and some have never been published. But it is the nature of the writer to record everything of note. And the story I'm about to set down is one that shall not see the light of day while my friend lives, though it is the key to the greatest mystery of his career.

It was a typical London day – which is to say, it was gray and rained sporadically. I read while Holmes alternated between working with his chemicals, scratching on his violin, and smoking prodigiously. His divided attention told me he had come to a point in his current investigation beyond which he could not venture without more data. It was a nasty business that involved a man of unsavory repute named Royce. I was trying to deduce if Holmes was waiting for a telegram, the latest newspapers, or a visit from one of the detectives from Scotland Yard, when a commotion downstairs answered my question. Loud protestations from Mrs. Hudson were succeeded by a stampede of small feet and shrill voices charging up the steps to our rooms. The door burst open and in poured a platoon of street Arabs, wet from the weather and covered in mud to boot. Holmes arose from his chair and in a few long strides came to staunch the tide of tiny boys with our agitated landlady bringing up the rear.

"My apologies, Mrs. Hudson. I will see to it this behavior is not repeated," he said with an appropriately contrite face, all the while closing the door on her. Turning to the children, Holmes said sternly, "I have told you before, there is no need for all of you to come and make work for Mrs. Hudson. Wiggins can rep – " He stopped and ran his eyes over the mob he ironically called the Baker Street Irregulars. "Where is Wiggins?"

The boys fell silent. Holmes shifted his hawk-like gaze to one child named Alfie, who functioned as second-in-command. "He isn't watching our suspect on his own, is he?"

"No, sir," said Alfie, barely audible.

My experience with the families of patients caused me to blurt out, "Has he been injured?" a second before Holmes began to ask the same question.

"Yes, sir," said Alfie, even more quietly.

All color drained from Holmes's face. "Was it an accident, or did Royce do this?" Holmes asked in an uncharacteristically husky voice.

"No, sir. It was his da." Holmes was silent for what seemed like an eternity.

"Where is Wiggins?" I said, to break the uncomfortable quiet as much as to get an answer.

"Gosh!" another boy said. If Wiggins were at the Great Ormond Street Hospital for sick children, his injuries must be great indeed.

"Watson . . . ." Holmes said.

"I have it," I replied, retrieving my medical bag from the table next to my chair.

"Boys . . . ." Holmes began. Then he paused. I believe that I was witnessing a rare moment of indecision on my friend's part. And just as suddenly it was over. "Come with me. And leave your boots outside the door. Except you, O'Connor," he said, indicating Alfie. These instructions engendered a great deal of fuss, followed by the curiously loud footfalls that children make when descending staircases. As I shrugged on my coat, I heard Holmes downstairs say something unprecedented. "Mrs. Hudson, I wonder if I may ask a great favor of you. The weather is inclement and these children are doing an important job for me. Can you find it in you to feed them before they leave? My dinner and Watson's can be used. We shall be out this evening. And may we first have a sandwich for young O'Connor here? He will be joining us."

As I came down the stairs, his coat over my arm, I was surprised to meet Holmes bounding back up. He neatly twisted his body to let me pass, relieved me of his coat, and proceeded back into our rooms. A moment later he came down again, more slowly, adjusting his garments. Soon we were out on the street, hailing a cab.

As we rode to the children's hospital, Holmes questioned Alfie. "How did this happen?"

Talking with his mouth half-full of meat and bread, Alfie said, "We was headed to your flat when we hear some'un call Wiggins by name. We turn and it's his da, worse for drink. 'Where you off to, eh?' 'e says.

"'Mum sent me for sumpin,' says Wiggins.

"'For wha'? Where? Ain't nothin' in that direction. 'Cept that 'Olmes feller! Is you workin' for 'im today?'

"Wiggins says nothin'. But his da says, 'You are, ain't cha? He pays you good, don't he? You come back after and give it to your da, you hear?'

"Wiggins turns and goes, but his da says, 'You bring me them coins, boy? You hear me?' Wiggins keeps walkin'. 'You 'ear me? Answer me, boy!' You can hear 'e's getting mad. Wiggins pays 'im no mind and we walk faster. '*You 'ear me?*' 'e hollers and we jumps cuz he's right be'ind us. Wiggins starts to scarper, and next thing you know 'is da 'as got 'im by the arm and is shakin' 'im. '*Don't you run from me, boy! You answer me! Yer givin' me that money, ain't you?*'

"Wiggins says, 'Mum needs that money! We ain't et in two days! Yer just gonna throw it away at the pub!'' And Wiggins' da just picks 'im up and 'its 'im and shakes 'im and slams 'im up against the wall. 'E trows 'im to the pavement and kicks 'im. Three times. Den 'e storms off. Wiggins is a right mess. Limp as a doll. A lady comes runnin' up and calls a cab and takes 'im to 'ospital. And I gets the rest of the Irregulars and we comes to you."

Anyone else observing Holmes would think that he listened to this recital without emotion. But I have known him long enough to see beneath the mask. I read it in the rising colour of his cheeks, the white, tight line of his lips, and the clenched jaw. And in the even more piercing look in his eyes I spied something I rarely saw in this man of logic: Cold fury.

I thus hesitated before asking a question once more prompted by my experience as a physician: "Has Wiggins' father ever done this before?"

"'Course. 'E whomps 'im regular. 'E's 'is da." The boy seemed surprised at my query – not that it was inconceivable, but that I, an intelligent adult, could be ignorant of something so commonplace. The other person in that cab who showed surprise was Holmes. Again the signs were subtle: The slight lift of the eyebrows, the nearly imperceptible slackening of the jaw. It was as close to open-mouthed amazement as I have ever seen on his countenance. Then his eyes dropped from the boy's face and focused on the middle distance between them. He spent the rest of the cab ride lost in thought.

Just as we approached the hospital, Holmes pulled himself out of his reverie and questioned Alfie closely concerning the revelations that he and Wiggins had been bringing Holmes about the Royce case. As we stopped at the kerb, Holmes said, "Watson, I wish to hear your medical assessment of Wiggins' condition and his chances for recovery later this evening. I want him to have the best of care. To that end . . ." Here he withdrew his purse and filled my hand with a generous amount of coins. ". . . you are to use these to ensure he receives the finest treatment."

"Holmes!" I protested. "Surely you don't think that I must bribe the doctors and nurses to do their duties!"

"Not everyone has your noble dedication to your profession, Watson. Nevertheless, these are not bribes. I am not unknown to certain members of the staff. Matron Garland was once a beneficiary of my talents. See that you talk to her. Give her this money and tell her that Sherlock Holmes has a particular interest in the boy's well-being. "

"I take it you aren't going in with us to see Wiggins."

"Other matters demand my attentions," he said. His face was expressionless. The mask was back in place.

Alfie and I entered the hospital. I am used to the smell of such places, but the combined odours of body fluids and excretions and chemicals struck me as particularly pungent. The high pitch of the crying and wails of pain reminded me that the patients here were far younger than those that I usually saw. I found a young man pushing a child in an invalid's chair, and he directed me in turn to a person who could help me locate Wiggins.

The ward sister led us down the line of beds to the one occupied by Wiggins, although "occupy" seems too expansive a term for the small figure lying there. He barely reached the bottom half of the bed's length. I had seen the boy on numerous occasions, and yet his face was so swollen and disfigured that I had to trust the nurse's identification of him. From the side of my eye, I saw Alfie's face go pale and his frame begin to wobble. I put an arm around his shoulder lest he topple, but before I could ask her, the sister fetched a chair and helped the shaken boy onto it. I urged Alfie to lean forward and put his head between his knees and breathe. Once I was certain that he wouldn't faint, I proceeded to examine Wiggins. His body was a mass of contusions, and some weren't fresh. I saw scars on his back and arms and legs such as I had only seen on soldiers who had been captured by the enemy and tortured.

"He has been cruelly used," said a woman of some years standing at the foot of the bed. Such was my concentration on the boy that I hadn't heard her approach. I turned and said, "Matron Garland, I presume."

"Doctor Watson, is it not?" the matron responded. "Mr. Holmes's description was quite accurate – as one would expect." Her eyes returned to the pitiful child in the bed. "We're doing all we can. His recovery . . . if he recovers . . . is in God's hands now."

"And yours," I said. "Speaking of which . . . If I may?" I took her hands with one of mine and poured the coins Holmes had given me into them.

Rather than taking affront, as I had feared, she looked at them and said, "The tithe is rather larger than usual."

"Tithe? What do you mean?" I said, baffled.

"That's what he calls it. Mr. Holmes often deposits such sums with us. For the upkeep of this ward. The governors of the hospital wanted to put up a plaque, but he wouldn't have it."

For the first time I actually looked at the tiny patients in their beds lining the walls. I detected signs of malnutrition, ill use, accidents from working in factories, and even, I was startled to realize, signs of drug use. I had seen these in Holmes, whom I had finally weaned from his unhealthy use of stimulants and soporifics. I had heard that poor women, having to work long hours, and with no one to watch their children, would administer laudanum to them to keep them out of trouble during the day. I never thought of the long-term effects they would have on the little ones. The children in this ward were all obviously from the most wretched classes and, astonishingly, I was hearing of my friend's efforts to help them for the first time.

"I see that he is as reluctant to let this be known privately as he is publicly," Matron Garland said, observing me. "Considering his interest in them, it's odd that he has never married or had children of his own."

Recovering myself, I began to act as a professional again. I asked her about the child's exact injuries, vital signs, and plan of treatment. She also led me to the physician-on-call and I talked with him. I returned to the ward to collect Alfie, only to find him missing. The sister told me that he was in the chapel. I made my way there. I must confess that the sight of the Byzantine splendour of St. Christopher's Chapel recalled to me my childhood in Scotland, serving as a choirboy. There were two or three women in there, praying no doubt for their children, and there was one man who seemed utterly bereft. Spotting Alfie kneeling in a pew, head bowed, hands clasped, I hesitated to interrupt. Though I rarely attended church these days, my hand stole into my doctor's bag and closed around the rosary my mother gave me upon my graduation from medical school. I said a brief yet fervent prayer for Wiggins and then a vow. I went to Alfie and laid my hand on his shoulder. He looked up. "Matron said 'e's in God's

268

hands. I told 'Im to fix 'im."

I nodded and we left. As we passed the alms box, I dug into my purse and matched Holmes's contribution.

While we waited for an available hansom cab, I asked the boy where Wiggins lived. He told me, but then said, "But Wiggins' mum won't be there. She's on the job. And his da' will be at the pub."

"You know which one?" I asked.

"Ten Bells," he answered. We had our driver take us there with all alacrity.

We disembarked in a squalid section of Spitalfields. It was dusk, and the miasma that gripped London was making landmarks indistinct. Yet the dirty windows of the Ten Bells pub, positioned on a street corner, were beacons in the spreading gloom, and we crossed the busy road and slipped inside. The pub was crowded and I realized that Alfie might not be able to see the elder Wiggins through the mob. But the boy took my hand and wove us through the knot of humanity to Wiggins' customary spot at the bar.

"That's 'im," he said. He stood at a safe distance and nodded at a bull of a man. Wiggins Senior was a barrel-chested, red-faced giant, who appeared to be on the verge of bursting the seams of his shabby clothing. By their style, I supposed that he had acquired them when he was a much younger, less-corpulent man. Wiggins was presently talking to an elderly gentleman hunched over his pint, one who looked to be rather worse for drink than his Falstaffian companion.

I stood for a minute contemplating my next move. I wasn't afraid to confront this bully, despite his size, but I didn't want to make a scene in a room full of drunken louts. Finally I turned to Alfie, gave him a few coins, including a sovereign which I admonished him to give to Wiggins' mother. As he slipped out between the forest of legs, I turned and squared my shoulders – only to see Wiggins and the smaller man move towards the door.

I pushed through the crowd but my quarry was out on the street before I could make the door. Just as I tried to exit, a large party of men and women poured into the establishment, delaying me further. When I stepped out into the street, the two men were gone.

My eyes darted to all possible routes from the spot. But it was my ear which pinpointed their location. I heard the distinct grunt of a man as he is punched in the solar plexis, followed by a pained gasping for air. I ran to an alley a few doors from the pub. As I rounded the building, I saw the bulk of Wiggins looming over his felled companion, who was trying to regain his knees while protecting his abdomen. "You were very free wit' yer money in the Bells. You look like you could spare some fer me. Just 'and it over."

"Please," the old man's reedy voice wheezed. He struggled to rise and his left hand fumbled for purchase on the lapel of Wiggins' coat. I was about to step in when the old man rammed his right hand into the underside of Wiggins jaw. The bull's head snapped back as the old man, as if pulled by the momentum of his punch, rose to an astonishing height of over six feet. Wiggins staggered back against the wall, shook his head, and then charged at his taller but thinner adversary. They collided and Wiggins wrapped his hands around his wiry opponent, picked him up and slammed him against the other wall. The pinioned man slipped one arm out of the larger man's embrace and drove his palm into the underside of his attacker's nose. Wiggins howled and his hands went to his nose which bled profusely. The slender man took a moment to catch the breath that had been squeezed out of him. Wiggins' right hand went to his pocket, to grab his handkerchief and staunch the nose bleed, I supposed. But instead he withdrew a knife.

He charged, intending to skewer the thin man, when his adversary shot out one of his long legs, kicked the knife from Wiggins' hand, and pivoting in place in an almost balletic fashion, turned out of the big man's way, while simultaneously bringing his elbow to bear on the back of his foe's head. Wiggins rocketed headlong into the alley wall, making impact face-first. He toppled to the ground and lay there, stunned.

Holmes (of course it was he) walked to the spot where the knife had landed, picked it up, and looked at it with a professional interest. "Nasty," he said, and then took it and laid it a few feet from Wiggins' limp hand. He nudged the prone man with his foot until a moan and a flickering of his eyes showed that he had regained his senses.

"William Wiggins, you are a brute and a bully. You are used to exercising your physical powers on those weaker than yourself. You are everything that I despise in a human being. Fortunately, you are also stupid. You didn't observe how I nursed my one drink while buying you round after round. And you brought a knife to a fight, whereas I . . . ." and here Holmes withdrew his pistol, "have brought a gun. You are a violent man and you deserve a violent death. I very much doubt anyone will miss you or wonder long whom of the many people who have come to harm at your hands delivered the *coup de gras*." He thumbed the hammer of the pistol back. I heard the click.

"*Holmes!*" I shouted. My friend's head snapped around towards me. His look was uncanny in its complete lack of expression.

"Watson, I regret that you came to see this. Pray return to our lodgings. I will join you after I put down this rabid dog." His tone was as cold as stone.

270

"He is a man, Holmes!"

"Is he? Only the lowest of animals devours its young. Why does he deserve any better than a rat? Perhaps it would be better to drop him in the Thames as one would an inconvenient bag of cats." Again, someone unfamiliar with Holmes would be forgiven for missing the increasingly clipped articulation that signaled rising anger.

"Holmes!"

"The sins of the fathers are visited upon their children. Most of the miscreants I have encountered in my career have come from homes rife with violence and disorder. I am tired of treating the symptoms rather than dealing with the cause. This man is a cancer. What would you do, Doctor?"

"He is a man. And my oath is to 'First, do no harm'."

"Is it harm to remove the one who causes harm? When I attacked the speckled band, I knew it would probably precipitate Roylott's death. All that I'm doing here is stepping up and taking the needed action myself." Now his rage was obvious. His voice was rising, getting more intense.

"He was a violent men, whose violence rebounded on him. You are not a violent man. You use your powers to stop them."

"My powers! My powers! He *beat* him, Watson! He beat him often! And I didn't see it! I missed it! I missed it! I shall not let him do it again!" He stood over the moaning man and pointed the gun at his ruined face.

"*Holmes*! You are *out of control!*"

Holmes froze. He stood as still as a statue, poised over the now-whimpering soul, the pistol inches from the man's head. The tableau held for what seemed an eternity.

"Quite right," said Holmes. He straightened up. Stepping over Wiggins, he walked toward me. He pocketed the pistol. "Watson, see to this man." Continuing past me to the entrance of the alley, he fished out of another pocket a police whistle. As I bent to check the blubbering man, Holmes gave several sharp trills. Then he returned, wiping makeup from his face. He looked around the alley, picking up the white wig that had come off during the fight, and the other bits of his disguise. Then he came back to where I was working. "Will he live?" he asked.

"He's lost and probably swallowed three teeth. His nose is broken. His cheek as well and possibly his jaw. I must get him to hospital."

"You shall." Turning to Wiggins, Holmes said, "Mark my words. If your son dies, Dr. Watson's ministrations will be for naught."

Holmes returned to the alley entrance. In minutes two constables showed up.

"I am Sherlock Holmes. The man being treated by my colleague attacked me. I'm afraid it did not go well for him. Dr. Watson feels the man requires greater medical attention than he can provide here. I think,

271

in view of the man's violent rages, he needs to be guarded. And then taken to gaol when he is released from hospital. I will be by later to explain."

The constables nodded and one ran off to get an ambulance. I accompanied Wiggins to hospital and gave an accurate but edited account of how he received his injuries to the doctor taking charge of him. When I returned to our rooms on Baker Street, I found Holmes sitting in his chair. Not smoking, not reading, not fidgeting with his incessant energy, but simply sitting. And waiting for me, evidently.

He waited until I hung up my coat and hat and sat in my usual chair. Then he began to speak. And I dared not interrupt him.

"Watson, I know that you have questions, as you do after all of our adventures. And I know that your questions in this matter would be of such a personal nature, that, out of friendship, you might hesitate to ask. What you witnessed was an aberration, a symptom of something that is disturbed, and as a physician, you seek a diagnosis, an explanation. I believe that I owe you one.

"You have called me a 'thinking machine' in your narratives, and I have not asked that descriptor be removed, for in fact, it is what I wish that I were. And it is what – at my best – I am. Emotions are corrosive to logic, as we have seen this night. But I have seen them do this before, and I speak from personal experience.

"Having met my brother and observed our interactions, you may be forgiven for assuming that our family was not a demonstrative one. You would be wrong. While my father could be distant, my mother was much endowed with the softer emotions, and my early childhood was a very warm and happy one. Indeed, had it not been, had it been the like of the children with whom we spent much of today, I might not be the person you know. Considering my other gifts, I could see myself as becoming a criminal to rival Professor Moriarty.

"Yet that early happiness was not fated to last, for my mother became so ill when I was eight that she was sent to a sanitarium. I did not see her again for a long time. But that wasn't what led me to adopt the facade of the cold calculating man with whom you share rooms. I was devastated. And my grief was exacerbated when my father sent me away to boarding school. My brother had been going to one for years, but to me the experience was akin to losing both parents in a single year.

"Worse, due to the difference in our ages, I wasn't sent to the same one that Mycroft attended. I was utterly miserable at boarding school. Not only was I missing my family, but schoolchildren are often harsh to those who are different. Though I hadn't yet constructed the system by which I logically go from observation to conclusion, I frequently made small deductions about my classmates and shared them, often to their discomfort and shame. Moreover, I was not then very tall, nor able to physically defend myself, and thus I was often bullied.

"The one bright spot in that place, besides my studies, was the schoolmaster's daughter, Miss Moira. She took me under her wing, as was her wont with the less popular boys. She invited us to tea and fed us with cakes and biscuits and listened to us as we related our enthusiasms to her. There were four of us that year: Robbie, Gene, Teddy, and myself. They were not my intellectual equals, and I would probably never have been friends with them were it not for Miss Moira. My hours with them, and especially with her, were the brightest in that dark time.

"Again, it seemed that fate would deny me even that refuge from my grief. After a few months, Gene took ill. He underwent the most painful seizures. Miss Moira threw herself into caring for him, but it seemed that her ministrations were for naught. The doctor was called for, but before he could arrive, Gene died, horribly. We were all of us shocked. It cast a pall over that term. And it made Teddy, Robbie, and I draw closer to each other and to Miss Moira.

"Then Teddy took ill. The malady that had taken Gene from us had seized him as well. His face looked tight and his limbs went rigid. Miss Moira once more did what she could, the doctor was called earlier than he had been for Gene, but Teddy died even as his foot was upon the stair. The whole school was horrified. Miss Moira was prostrate with grief for weeks. Robbie and I visited her and tried to cheer her up, despite our own grief over Teddy.

"The rest of that year we were spared any more horrors. After the summer holidays, during which time I was still not allowed to see my mother, I returned to school and was glad to see Robbie, but especially to see and bask in the glow of Miss Moira. She had regained her joy and charm and seemed to live only for our high teas together.

"I had started to play with the idea of going into medicine, to find the cause and cure of the things which had deprived me of mother and friends. I began to take books on medicine and pharmacology from the school library and peruse them in my spare time.

"Then death came for Robbie. He complained of a metallic taste in his mouth and seeing flashes of light. He became restless, and his calf muscles stiffened and he took to bed. Recognizing the symptoms of the same disease that had taken Gene and Teddy, I ran for Miss Moira. She came at once and tried to comfort the stricken child in vain. I told to send for the doctor and she agreed. But I heard her tell the servant to fetch the doctor in the neighboring town. Concerned that he wouldn't make it in time, I asked why she hadn't sent for the local doctor. She said he had been unable to diagnose the boys and that she had heard the other town's doctor was better. Unfortunately, Robbie died before this new doctor came and he was as clueless as to the cause as the previous one.

"Two developments followed. First, I was drawn into greater intimacy with Miss Moira, though our teas were somber affairs. Nevertheless, she found it within herself to be even more charming, more winning than before. I was a little amazed that she could act as if nothing had happened. I envied her emotional equilibrium.

"The second development was that I dove into my medical researches with a greater fervor. I was determined to identify and eliminate this natural evil which had caused so much suffering. One day when I was scouring the appendices of the Pharmacology text, I came upon a list of toxic chemicals. As I read lists of symptoms, a cluster of them seized my attention. The symptoms my friends had displayed were all there. With growing excitement, I ran from my room to Miss Moira's and showed her the page. Her face failed to display any of the emotions one might expect from receiving such news: Horror, unbelief, sadness, or even my excitement at solving the puzzle. Barely glancing at the page, she turned her gaze to me and it was the coldest examination I have ever endured.

"'I don't see anything here that need concern you. Those boys died of disease, Sherlock.'

"Suddenly and out of nowhere, her face grew animated and joyful and she said, 'But you are a very clever boy and I am sure you will work it out. You will be a marvelous doctor someday, I'm sure. Let us turn from this morbid subject and have ourselves a special tea, right now.'

"She led me to her parlor and my usual chair and went to put on some tea. While she bustled and filled the air with cheery talk, I tried to make sense of what I had just seen. I knew that the chemical I had discovered must be the one used to poison my friends. But how? And who? And why? What good would the deaths of three small children do anyone?

"She came into the room with the familiar tray and the familiar teapot, cloaked in the familiar tea cosy and the familiar plate of biscuits. She poured me a cup and then herself. She gave me a biscuit, which I held absent-mindedly, for I was too lost in thought.

"'Sherlock!' she said rather loudly. I emerged from my reverie. 'That is the third time I've called your name. Aren't you going to eat your biscuit? I made it specially for you.'

"I looked at the biscuit in my hand rather dispassionately. And then I saw it. Her thumbmark. Whenever she had us four to tea, she would listen to us and find something to commend in what one of us said and reward that boy with a special biscuit she had made just for him. And we could know that it was special because she had pressed her thumb into the still warm biscuit. It was, she said, her signature. And a wave of nausea overcame me as I remembered that before each of my friend's deaths, they had been the lucky recipient of that biscuit.

"I don't know how long I stared at that biscuit, but after what felt like an eon, Miss Moira said, 'Eat the biscuit, Sherlock.' I looked at her and noticed something I hadn't before. Her lips were smiling but her eyes were not. They were as round and cold as an adder's. 'I made it for you alone, Sherlock. There's no one left but you.' She said it as sweetly as any woman ever had.

"I will remember this moment until my dying day, Watson. I looked from her to the biscuit to her again. My mind was awhirl with emotion: Fear, shock, horror. And yet, overwhelming all of them, as well as my rational mind, was a desire to do what she said. I wanted to please her. No, that's not quite accurate. I didn't want to *disappoint* her. The woman had been like a second mother to me, and I didn't want to make her unhappy. Knowing with certainty that I was going to die, I raised the biscuit to my lips.

"A great disturbance came from without and below. There were hurried footsteps on the stairs and the door to the parlor burst open. In bounded a man I had never seen before, along with a very agitated constable and Mycroft. His eyes swept the room, looked over the plate of biscuits, and the one in my hand. He looked at me sharply.

"'This is the one,' I said and handed it to him. He pulled out his handkerchief, took it, and turned to the stranger. Then he thought, turned back to Miss Moira, and he took one of her hands and ascertained that it did fit in the depression in the biscuit. He then gave both biscuit and handkerchief to the man that I had deduced was a chemist of sorts. Turning to Miss Moira, he said, 'This is Professor Wiltshire, my chemistry tutor. He will verify that this sweet is laced with strychnine. Constable Taylor will take custody of you, Miss, and I my brother.'

"Mycroft had deduced the situation by piecing together the clues found in my very detailed letters to him. Somehow, despite his adolescence, he had convinced his chemistry tutor of his conclusions, and with his help they were able to get the constable to act against a woman of good repute in that town. Fortunately, he did so a day before I discovered the same information about strychnine, or they wouldn't have be able to get to me in time.

"I will not bore you with the details of the inquest, Watson. It turned out that Miss Moira had fraudulently taken out insurance on us. Suffice it to say, she was found guilty of three homicides and hanged."

It was all I could do to stammer, "How awful for you, Holmes!"

"Indeed. More awful were the emotions that coursed through me over the following days and months. Renewed grief, horror. Bad dreams and deep depression. But worst of all was the guilt.

"You were guilty of nothing! That woman did it all. And you were a child."

"I was guilty of letting my emotions cloud my judgment, Watson. I realize that I didn't then have my specialized knowledge and my refined skills at systematic deduction. I know now what I didn't know as a boy: That I couldn't have saved my friends then.

"But I almost ate that biscuit, knowing full well that it would spell my death, simply to please a woman who had offered me the affection I craved. Based on that fact, I knew that I must eliminate emotion from my thinking. You have occasionally made the observation that I distrust women. That isn't quite correct. I don't trust *myself* around them. I'm not indifferent to the fairer sex, Watson. I am as susceptible as any man. So I keep them at a distance. The cost of not doing so, as I have seen, would be too high.

"I must add, however, that thanks to that . . . *incident*, I did find a purpose for my talents, a direction for my life. My interests turned from curing the illnesses that harm the body to those that harm society. I use my gifts for observation and deductive logic to expose deceit and to oppose the violent."

Here Holmes paused for a few moments. "But I realize today that penchant to harm others resides in us all, however much we strive against it. I would have succumbed tonight, Watson, had you not stopped me. I am grateful to you for that. And I regret that I've shown you that I'm not the paragon of logic and virtue you have portrayed me to the world."

"I never took you for a saint, Holmes. That said, you do strive more than most of us, and you have turned a deep personal tragedy into a great boon for others. Not just for your clients but for many children, not as fortunate as you were. You are a good man, Holmes. You are a beacon to the world, all the more for having encountered such darkness."

"Thank – " Holmes's voice caught. When he mastered himself, he stood and, so softly I scarcely heard it, said, "Thank you, my friend." He walked to his room and shut the door. Sensing his need for privacy, I collected my hat and coat and went for a walk.

We never spoke of it again. Not when we gave evidence against William Wiggins for his assault on Holmes, and the other crimes my friend was able to trace to him. Not when Holmes managed to get the recovered Billy Wiggins employment with Mrs. Hudson. Not even when we occasionally crossed paths at Great Ormond Street Hospital, where I began to volunteer my time. And of course, I couldn't publish it. Yet scribbler that I am, I felt I must document this pivotal story in the life of my friend.

There was one last time the subject came up, albeit obliquely. After his retirement, I was visiting Holmes at his cottage in the Sussex Downs. We spent a long day of catching up on the news of our now separate lives, concluding with an excellent supper served by his housekeeper. As she served us our pudding, we somehow ventured onto the case of Charles Augustus Milverton, during which Holmes managed to get himself engaged to the blackmailer's maid. Holmes was a marvelous actor, able to change his appearance and demeanor in extraordinary ways. Nevertheless, I was always amazed at this feat, his wooing of a woman who actually had another beau at the time. "How did you pull that one off?" I asked.

"Acting is more than externals like costuming, makeup, and words. To be convincing, one must use the imagination to put oneself into the mind and situation of the role one's playing. I simply imagined how I should conduct myself were I to act on my desire for a romantic companion."

"It must have been a great feat of the imagination, since you have never, as far as I know, had such feelings," I said, chiding him as only a friend of forty-odd years could.

"You forget 'The Woman'," he said.

Even knowing his regard for the woman who outwitted him early in his career, I was astounded to hear him confess that his feelings were more than respect for a clever opponent. "Irene Adler? But what of your history with women?"

The housekeeper, entering with our coffee, froze and listened.

"My 'distrust' of the fair sex, you mean? In the case of Miss Adler, I never had any reason to wonder if she was up to no good," he said, lighting his pipe. "I knew it."

I stared at him for a long moment as he drew on his pipe and waved the match to extinguish it. When he looked up, I saw the twinkle in his eye and the shadow of a smile. And I began to laugh. And he laughed. And the housekeeper set down the coffee pot, and left the room, shaking her head at us both.

The Elusive Mr. Phillimore
by Matthew J. Elliott

T*his script has never been published in text form, and was initially performed as a radio drama on May 27, 2012. The broadcast was Episode No. 105 of* The Further Adventures of Sherlock Holmes, *one of the recurring series featured on the nationally syndicated* Imagination Theatre. *Founded by Jim French, the company produced over one-thousand multi-series episodes, including nearly one-hundred-and-forty Sherlock Holmes pastiches. In addition, Imagination Theatre also recorded the entire Holmes Canon, featured as* The Classic Adventures of Sherlock Holmes, *the only version with all episodes to have been written by the same writer, Matthew J. Elliott, and with the same two actors, John Patrick Lowrie and Lawrence Albert, portraying Holmes and Watson, respectively.*

This script is protected by copyright.

CHARACTERS
- SHERLOCK HOLMES
- DR. JOHN H. WATSON
- MYCROFT HOLMES
- INSPECTOR LESTRADE
- MRS. HUDSON
- ROBERT DENBY – Nervous, shifty public servant, 30's.
- JOSHUA BURNABY – Sullen professional criminal, 40's.
- WAXFLATTER

SOUND EFFECT: OPENING SEQUENCE, BIG BEN, STREET SOUNDS

ANNOUNCER: *The Further Adventures of Sherlock Holmes . . .*

MUSIC: *DANSE MACABRE* (UP AND UNDER)

WATSON: My name is Dr. John H. Watson, and I was privileged to share the adventures of Sherlock Holmes. When, one morning during the summer of 1896, we were visited by an unimposing gentleman going by the name of Mr. Robert Denby, I had no notion that we were about to find ourselves involved one of the most important and baffling cases of our career . . . .

<u>MUSIC: OUT</u>

DENBY: It is . . . very difficult for me, Mr. Holmes. I'm unable to provide you with any specifics, but I'm afraid my life may be in danger.

HOLMES: Please elucidate, Mr. Denby.

DENBY: I told you, I can't be certain –

HOLMES: I do not deal with cases of persecution mania, sir. I require information. If you are unable to supply it, then I must wish you a good day. No doubt my friend Watson can refer you to one of the many specialists on Harley Street.

WATSON: Holmes, I think we should at least hear the gentleman out.

HOLMES: (PEEVED) If you say so, Watson. (TO DENBY) Proceed, Mr. Denby.

DENBY: He's tried to enter my home on several occasions. The first time he said he was an Inspector of Plumbing for London County Council. The next day, he claimed he was raising a subscription list for a charity hospital. Both times, he looked completely different, but I'm certain it was the same man!

HOLMES: Someone in disguise?

DENBY: I know it sounds ridiculous.

WATSON: Less than you'd imagine, Mr. Denby. Mr. Holmes himself has often made use of that particular art during the course of an investigation.

HOLMES: Quite. Do you believe you could identify this gentleman if you were to see his face undisguised?

DENBY: Under the whiskers, the spectacles . . . Honestly, Mr. Holmes, I doubt it.

HOLMES: (TUTS) Unfortunate.

DENBY: It's my job to be observant, but not when it comes to faces.

WATSON: What *is* your job?

DENBY: I'm a civil servant. I hold a position at the Foreign Office.

WATSON: Really? Then perhaps you know Mr. Holmes's brother?

DENBY: As a matter of fact, I do, Dr. Watson.

HOLMES: (INTERRUPTING) Yes, yes. Returning to the matter at hand, this unknown gentleman is desirous of gaining entrance to your property, it seems?

DENBY: I have a suspicion he might already have done so, Mr. Holmes. I am a very light sleeper, you see, and I was awakened in the early hours, convinced that I was not alone in the house.

HOLMES: You heard a noise?

DENBY: No, sir, but one has a sense . . . .

HOLMES: I'd prefer something more substantial than intuition. Did you confront an intruder?

DENBY: No, but . . . I am a tidy man, sir, very tidy, but when I came downstairs to investigate – well, it seemed to me almost *too* tidy.

HOLMES: Mr. Denby, this is intolerable! You have had two callers who may well turn out to be entirely genuine, and a mere suspicion that your home has been entered . . . I am more and more inclined to favour my original suggestion of paranoid delusion.

WATSON: Why would anyone want to break into your home, sir? Not to harm you, clearly. They could have done so when they called at your door. Do you have any valuables?

DENBY: Not a civil servant's pay, Doctor. It's a complete mystery to me. But one, I'm afraid, that Mr. Holmes has no interest in investigating.

HOLMES: On the contrary, Mr. Denby, my practice has been rather quiet of late. My mind needs a case, and I shall be delighted to look at the problem you've set before me.

WATSON: (SURPRISED) You shall?

HOLMES: Return to your home, and I'll call upon you there this evening. Until then, good day.

DENBY: Uh, Mr. Holmes – I haven't given you my address.

HOLMES: Of course. How remiss of me. It is?

DENBY: 14 Kensington Gardens Square, Bayswater.

SOUND EFFECT: A KNOCK ON THE DOOR

WATSON: Come in, Mrs. Hudson.

SOUND EFFECT: THE DOOR OPENS

MRS. HUDSON: Sorry for interrupting, Doctor.

DENBY: I shall show myself out.

WATSON: Goodbye, Mr. Denby.

DENBY: (DEPARTING) Dr. Watson.

SOUND EFFECT: HE LEAVES

HOLMES: Something I can do for you, Mrs. Hudson?

MRS. HUDSON: How many meals should I cancel, Mr. Holmes?

HOLMES: Cancel?

WATSON: She does have a point, you know. Food is the last thing on your mind when you have a client.

MRS. HUDSON: And as I heard you tell the gentleman you'd take his case, I expect you'll be too busy to eat from now on. Elementary, Mr. Holmes.

HOLMES: Elementary, but quite incorrect. We shall be dining at the usual hour, Mrs. Hudson.

MRS. HUDSON: (SLIGHTLY BAFFLED) Very well, sir.

WATSON: Are you sure you're quite well, Holmes?

HOLMES: Well? Yes, quite well, I think. Why do you ask?

WATSON: You said you were going to call on Denby this evening.

HOLMES: Indeed I did.

WATSON: Furthermore, you forgot to ask his address.

HOLMES: So it would appear.

WATSON: And you never forget anything. So what's going on, Holmes? Have you changed your mind about this investigation?

HOLMES: The investigation is complete. No further effort on my part is required.

WATSON: Denby was lying? About the callers, the intruder?

HOLMES: By no means. In fact, I'm entirely satisfied that he was telling the truth. But as it happens, I already know the name of the man who's menacing him.

WATSON: And it is?

HOLMES: Sherlock Holmes.

WATSON: (DISBELIEF) *You're* the one . . . ?

HOLMES: Yes. I must say, I'm rather dispirited that he picked up on my presence in his home. I thought I'd done an excellent job of hiding any signs of my intrusion. Yet it seems I did *too* good a job.

MRS. HUDSON: What a tangled web you weave, sir.

HOLMES: Mrs. Hudson, is there a particular reason why you are still hovering in the doorway? I understood you were anxious to start work on dinner.

MRS. HUDSON: This telegram arrived for you, Mr. Holmes.

HOLMES: Ah!

SOUND EFFECT: HE RIPS OPEN THE TELEGRAM, UNFOLDS IT

WATSON: Holmes, why are you spying on this Denby fellow when you have no client?

HOLMES: Who says I have no client?

WATSON: You did, just a moment ago. And I happen to know that the only time you've been outside in the last few weeks was – Ah! When you visited your brother at the Diogenes Club. You're doing this as a favor to him.

HOLMES: Flawless deduction, Watson.

WATSON: But why? Apart from the obvious fact that they're both employed by the government, what connects Denby to Mycroft Holmes?

HOLMES: Perhaps Mycroft will have the opportunity to explain to you in person.

WATSON: He sent you the telegram?

HOLMES: Asking me to meet him at his Whitehall office. It would be nothing short of treasonous to refuse such an invitation. (TO MRS. HUDSON) Mrs. Hudson –

MRS. HUDSON: (WEARY) Dinner is canceled, I know, I know . . . .

MUSIC: STING

MYCROFT: We find ourselves in a pretty mess, Sherlock.

HOLMES: On the contrary, brother, my reputation is quite secure.

MYCROFT: Oh, really? I am informed that Robert Denby called upon you at Baker Street this morning.

WATSON: Mr. Holmes, are you spying on Denby – or on us?

HOLMES: Both.

MYCROFT: That is neither here nor there.

HOLMES: Your agents, my dear Mycroft, are here, there, and everywhere. Why you don't entrust *them* with this business, I can't imagine.

MYCROFT: Spies only observe, they do not deduce. For that, I need a detective.

WATSON: Perhaps if someone could explain to me just what is going on . . . .

MYCROFT: You mean you haven't told him?

HOLMES: I thought it would be better coming from you, Mycroft. Doubtless, the good doctor would be fascinated to know how his income tax is spent.

MYCROFT: Is he secure, Sherlock?

HOLMES: As the Bank of England.

WATSON: You trusted me during the Bruce-Partington affair, Mr. Holmes. I gather this matter concerns national security also. Relating to the F.O., since that's where Denby is employed.

MYCROFT: You know, he's nothing like as slow-witted as you'd been leading me to believe, Sherlock. (TO WATSON) You're quite correct, Doctor. Documents relating to troop movements have been stolen from the Foreign Office.

WATSON: And you suspect Robert Denby?

HOLMES: Denby was one of two suspects, Watson. The other is a gentleman by the name of James Phillimore.

WATSON: You've questioned them both, I take it?

MYCROFT: We have not. To do so would be to alert the guilty party of our suspicions. I only became aware of the theft when I entered the office shared by Denby and Phillimore in order to make some minor adjustment to the document, and found the safe empty.

WATSON: You have the combination of the safe, Mr. Holmes?

MYCROFT: I have the combination of every safe in Whitehall, Doctor.

WATSON: And Denby and Phillimore were absent at the time, no doubt. Wouldn't it have been simpler to make copies rather than steal them?

HOLMES: They are far too detailed for it to be done before the papers are delivered into the hands of our generals. Whoever took them must have done so knowing that their theft would inevitably be discovered. Once that occurred, they could no longer stay in England.

WATSON: The reward the thief was offered must have been considerable, then.

MYCROFT: £40,000 is the usual sum for such an act of treachery, I understand.

WATSON: Good Lord. And so you enlisted your brother?

MYCROFT: And Scotland Yard. This is still a criminal matter, and an arrest will hopefully be made.

HOLMES: I suggested that our friend Lestrade investigate Phillimore. It meant taking him off his gold smuggling case, but he's having little success with it, anyway. I, meanwhile, attempted to search for the documents at Robert Denby's home.

WATSON: Why did you favor Denby, Holmes?

HOLMES: Pigeon feathers.

WATSON: Pigeon feathers?

HOLMES: I found them under his desk as I examined the office. They obviously became detached from his clothing.

WATSON: I don't see any obvious connection between pigeon feathers and troop movements.

HOLMES: One feather showed signs of having something tied around it. The notion of using carrier pigeons to relay messages, rather than entrusting them to more conventional means, appealed to me greatly.

WATSON: And did you find any evidence of these messages?

HOLMES: Nor even of the pigeons, Watson. Of course, it could be that the birds are kept by the other party in the correspondence.

MYCROFT: It could also be that the messages are unrelated to the theft of the papers – some vulgar affair, perhaps, or chess moves in a long-distance competition.

HOLMES: And *you* criticize *me* for having too much imagination.

MYCROFT: Nevertheless, Denby's presence at Baker Street shows that you were recognized.

HOLMES: Impossible.

WATSON: But your involvement was perhaps suspected, Holmes. A natural assumption, given that Denby works for your brother. Perhaps he called on us not to consult you, but to warn you off.

HOLMES: In a rather roundabout fashion.

MYCROFT: I wouldn't have thought he possessed that much cunning.

HOLMES: Nor would I, from your description of him, brother. It seems you underestimated him.

MYCROFT: Impossible!

SOUND EFFECT: A KNOCK AT THE DOOR

WATSON: You're expecting someone else, Mr. Holmes?

HOLMES: Lestrade. His footsteps have a rhythm as identifiable as fingerprints.

MYCROFT: Enter.

SOUND EFFECT: THE DOOR OPENS AND LESTRADE ENTERS

LESTRADE: Mr. Holmes, Dr. Watson. (A BEAT) Mr. Holmes.

MYCROFT: Inspector, my brother has nothing positive to report. I hope you have better news for us.

LESTRADE: Not . . . exactly, sir.

WATSON: You were watching James Phillimore, yes?

LESTRADE: Watching him . . . . Yes, I was watching him, Doctor. Right up until the moment he . . . vanished.

HOLMES: He eluded you.

LESTRADE: Not eluded, Mr. Holmes. He vanished. In front of my eyes.

MUSIC: STING

HOLMES: People do not simply vanish, Lestrade.

LESTRADE: Well, this fellow did. He just went back into his house to fetch his umbrella, and never returned.

HOLMES: That is not, strictly, in front of your eyes, Lestrade.

LESTRADE: Be that as it may, Mr. Holmes, he's gone.

WATSON: Through another door, perhaps.

LESTRADE: Impossible. My officers had the place surrounded.

287

MYCROFT: Explain yourself, man. And kindly omit the hyperbole.

LESTRADE: Yes, sir, I'll certainly . . . do that thing you said. Well, I positioned myself in the bushes in front of Phillimore's house, and I was preparing myself for a long wait, when a furniture removal wagon turned up, followed by a hansom.

WATSON: Phillimore was preparing to flee.

HOLMES: Not exactly flee, Watson. He could hardly move with rapidity, if he was taking his furniture with him. (TO LESTRADE) Did you note the name of the firm, Lestrade?

LESTRADE: It was written on the side of the wagon – Magrana Removals.

WATSON: "Magrana"? Romany name, do you suppose?

MYCROFT: (SNORTS IN DISGUST) Pfui!

LESTRADE: The driver and the removal men entered the house, but I decided to act only if Phillimore himself made to leave.

WATSON: A sound decision, Inspector.

LESTRADE: Thank you, Doctor.

HOLMES: Details, Lestrade, details.

LESTRADE: Well, twenty minutes or so passed, the removal men appeared and started loading the van with various items – rugs, a large box, probably containing ornaments, paintings . . . .

MYCROFT: And it never occurred to you that one of them might have been James Phillimore in disguise?

LESTRADE: It did not. I followed him home from his office, and I got a good look at him. Neither of the removal men matched his frame or height. And besides, Phillimore was right there in the doorway, overseeing the whole thing.

HOLMES: You're sure it was him?

LESTRADE: Quite sure, Mr. Holmes. I heard him chatting to colleagues as he left the office, and I recognized his voice when he spoke to the workmen. And before you ask, it wasn't someone impersonating him, I'm certain of it.

HOLMES: I don't doubt it. And just what did he say?

LESTRADE: He told the removal men to go on ahead. "I'll follow behind in the cab," he said. "But it looks like it might rain – I'll just go in and get my umbrella."

WATSON: Rain? There hasn't been a drop all week.

HOLMES: But an Englishman is never fully dressed without his umbrella, Watson. I'll warrant he never returned.

LESTRADE: That's right, Mr. Holmes. A few moments later, the cabbie reappeared scratching his head. When it became clear something was wrong, I emerged from the bushes and questioned the fellow. He said he'd been told to wait in the morning room 'til Phillimore was ready for him. He began to think his fare wasn't coming back, so he went looking for him. Seems like Phillimore walked back into his home and just vanished.

WATSON: I know you dismissed the notion of impersonation before, Inspector, but there's no possibility the driver could have been Phillimore himself, is there?

LESTRADE: My first thought, Doctor. But though there was a superficial resemblance from a distance, the driver had a full head of hair – and, yes, I made sure it wasn't a wig. But the voice was entirely different, and if it had been Phillimore, which it wasn't, we're still short one person.

WATSON: If he didn't leave the house, then he's obviously hiding in some secret room. You must remember the case of the Norwood Builder!

LESTRADE: There's no secret room, Doctor. I'm as certain of that as I am that Phillimore's your traitor. Why else would he flee?

WATSON: The matter seems quite beyond conjecture.

MYCROFT and HOLMES: (SIMULTANEOUSLY) Commonplace.

HOLMES: Lestrade, you took the number of the cab, of course.

LESTRADE: 2603.

HOLMES: I should like to speak to the driver.

LESTRADE: I've already spoken to him, Mr. Holmes. I can promise you, he's got nothing to more tell us.

HOLMES: Nevertheless.

LESTRADE: (RELUCTANTLY) As you wish, Mr. Holmes . . . .

HOLMES: One final question, Lestrade: Was Phillimore wearing his hat when he saw off the removal wagon?

LESTRADE: Naturally, Mr. Holmes. He was out of doors.

HOLMES: Naturally. Well, let's be off. Mycroft, I shall report to you in due course.

MYCROFT: Those papers must be recovered! Your country is depending on you, Sherlock. (TO WATSON, AS AN AFTERTHOUGHT) And you too, Dr. Watson.

WATSON: Thank you, Mr. Holmes.

MUSIC: BRIDGE

SOUND EFFECT: A BUSY LONDON STREET

WAXFLATTER: Waxflatter is my name, sir. Nigel Waxflatter.

WATSON: Oh, Lord. You again. (TO HOLMES) Holmes, you remember this fellow?

HOLMES: Indeed.

LESTRADE: You're not the cabbie!

WAXFLATTER: To my shame, I admit that I am. But my true profession is the stage. This is merely a temporary position.

WATSON: It's been temporary for almost ten years, then.

WAXFLATTER: Is it my fault if London theater managers fail to recognize real talent?

LESTRADE: What's going on here? How do you two know this person?

HOLMES: Mr. Waxflatter was of material assistance to us in the Lesterson case, Inspector. And I suspect he will be of use to us now also, by telling us the name of the man to whom he loaned his cab earlier today.

LESTRADE: Well?

WAXFLATTER: I never actually learned the fellow's name. I encountered him at the Swan and Cygnets on Percy Street in Shepherd's Bush. Cab driving can be thirsty work, you know. On long journeys, I often regale my passengers with a performance of Shakespeare's sonnets.

WATSON: How fortunate for them.

WAXFLATTER: The gentleman at the public house offered me a, er, certain financial inducement to let him have the use of my vehicle. And Euripides, of course.

WATSON: Euripides?

WAXFLATTER: My horse.

LESTRADE: You didn't ask why, I suppose?

WAXFLATTER: I believe he may have provided some explanation, but I must admit, I wasn't really paying attention. You see, it occurred to me that this brief respite would provide me with the opportunity to audition for the revival of *Shadow of Death* at the Orpheum on

291

Beacon Street. I consider myself ideally suited to the role of the corpse.

WATSON: The corpse.

LESTRADE: Enough with this tomfoolery! I want a description of this man.

HOLMES: You already have a description of him, Lestrade. He was the man you met at Phillimore's house. *And* we know where to look for him – the Swan and Cygnets on Percy Street.

WATSON: Then that's where we should go next. (TO WAXFLATTER) Goodbye, Mr. Waxflatter. Best of luck with the play. Or is it bad luck to say "Good luck"?

WAXFLATTER: It's immaterial, I'm afraid, sir. You see, I was deemed unsuitable for the part.

LESTRADE: Of a corpse? Bloody actors . . . .

SOUND EFFECT: A ROWDY DRINKING ESTABLISHMENT. PLENTY OF HEARTY SOUNDS (BACKGROUND)

MUSIC: PERIOD-APPROPRIATE MUSIC ON A PIANO

LESTRADE: What makes you so certain the fellow will come back to this place, Mr. Holmes?

HOLMES: I'm not certain at all, Lestrade. But we simply have no other avenue of investigation.

WATSON: What about Magrana's Removals?

HOLMES: If all else fails, Watson, but I'm in no doubt that the firm will turn out to be entirely fictitious.

LESTRADE: How do you work *that* out?

HOLMES: Given that the name is an anagram of the word "anagram" itself, I think it more than likely.

292

LESTRADE: *"Magra . . ."* *"Anag . . ."* Has anybody got a pencil?

WATSON: And this man – presumably he'll be able to tell us how Phillimore managed his vanishing act?

HOLMES: Oh, Watson, surely that's perfectly obvious.

LESTRADE: It is? How did he walk back into the house and just disappear?

HOLMES: He never did, Lestrade.

LESTRADE: What are you talking about? I saw him.

HOLMES: You saw the cab driver disguised as Phillimore.

LESTRADE: We went over this, Holmes. Phillimore was bald, the driver wasn't.

HOLMES: But the man you saw wore a hat. You were some distance away, and you admitted that there was a resemblance between the two men.

WATSON: The inspector also said that their voices were quite different.

LESTRADE: Exactly. How could I have heard Phillimore if it wasn't him?

HOLMES: The voice you heard belonged to Phillimore. He was hidden in the box you saw the workmen carry out.

LESTRADE: Oh, my Lord! Then I watched him escape.

HOLMES: Because your attention was on the wrong man. Once Phillimore was safely aboard the wagon, he called out that he needed his umbrella. The driver went back into the house, returned Phillimore's clothes to the cupboard where he found them, and reappeared in his cabbie's garb, looking suitably confused.

WATSON: By which time, the real Phillimore was already long gone in the wagon. It certainly sounds as though you had the wrong man when you went after Denby.

293

HOLMES: (DRY) Thank you, Watson.

WATSON: I simply mean, Holmes, that Phillimore obviously knew he'd be watched.

HOLMES: As did Denby, if we interpret his visit to Baker Street as a warning rather than a plea for assistance. Curious . . . .

LESTRADE: I think I see the fellow, Mr. Holmes – sitting in his own, over there.

HOLMES: Perhaps we should introduce ourselves, gentlemen.

SOUND EFFECT: FADE THROUGH TO ANOTHER PART OF THE TAVERN

BURNABY: And what business do you three think you have with me, then?

LESTRADE: You've got a short memory, my friend. I bumped into you in Highgate this afternoon, don't you remember?

BURNABY: Highgate? Not sure I've ever been to Highgate. Are you thinking of someone else?

WATSON: What's your name, sir?

BURNABY: My name is my own, *sir*. I don't give it away without assurances.

HOLMES: The gentleman's name is Joshua Burnaby.

BURNABY: I don't know who that is.

HOLMES: I don't doubt that Inspector Lestrade recalls the names of most of the men he's arrested over the years, but my interest in criminal matters is somewhat broader.

BURNABY: Don't know what you're talking about, mister.

HOLMES: You once held the position of Paymaster-Lieutenant on one of Her Majesty's warships, I believe. But after you were court-martialled for misappropriation of funds, you have never again attempted anything remotely law-abiding. You've turned your hand to many trades over the years, all of them disreputable: Forgery, debt collection . . . recently, you were a supplier of marked cards and other cheating paraphernalia for gamblers.

BURNABY: You're thinking of someone else. That's not me.

LESTRADE: This is getting us nowhere.

WATSON: You might be a criminal, Burnaby, but are you a traitor?

BURNABY: Got a match, mister?

WATSON: Phillimore probably chose you because of your physical similarity to him, but did he tell you why he needed you to create a diversion? He's betraying his country, selling our secrets to a foreign government. If he's caught, he'll hang for treason, and you'll likely hang with him, unless you help us.

BURNABY: (AS CALM AS EVER) Got a match?

WATSON: (AGGRAVATED) Here!

BURNABY: Ta.

SOUND EFFECT: HE STRIKES A MATCH

BURNABY: Treason, you say?

WATSON: That's right.

BURNABY: That's something to think about. (WITH PIPE IN HIS MOUTH) Yeah, that's definitely something to thi – Ow! (NO PIPE) Bloody Hell!

LESTRADE: What? What is it?

BURNABY: (TRIES TO SPEAK, BUT IT'S LIKE HIS MOUTH IS OUT OF CONTROL)

MUSIC: OUT

BURNABY: (HE BABBLES, DESPARATE TO TALK. HE CONTINUES UNDER THE DIALOGUE, GROWING EVER MORE AGITATED.)

WATSON: What's happening to him?

HOLMES: He's been poisoned!

LESTRADE: How?

HOLMES: Stay away from his pipe, Lestrade. There's a thorn lodged in the stem, Burnaby. Cut his lip on it! (TO WATSON) Watson, can you do anything?

WATSON: Not without knowing the type of poison. We have to get him to a hospital, if there's time.

LESTRADE: (URGENTLY) Burnaby? Burnaby, listen to me! Where is James Phillimore? Can you tell us? Where is he, Burnaby?

BURNABY: (UNDER LESTRADE'S LINE, HIS BREATHING BECOMES FASTER BEFORE CUTTING OUT ALTOGETHER)

WATSON: It's no good, Lestrade. He's dead.

LESTRADE: Damn it! Phillimore killed him before he could tell us anything.

HOLMES: Then why didn't he do so straight away? Something's wrong here.

LESTRADE: You don't have to tell me, Mr. Holmes! What are we going to do now?

HOLMES: There's only one possibility left to us – to search Phillimore's home, and hope to discover some clue to his whereabouts. Fortune may still be with us.

<u>MUSIC: BRIDGE</u>

MYCROFT: Burned to the ground?

HOLMES: To all intents and purposes, Mycroft. Whatever evidence might have been in the house, it's lost to us now.

MYCROFT: Why on Earth would Phillimore take such a risk?

HOLMES: He didn't. The matches used to start the blaze were manufactured by the Phoebus Match Company. When I examined Phillimore's office, I noticed that he favored a Raphael's Hygienic.

MYCROFT: Really, Sherlock! The things you waste your time on.

HOLMES: I did, however, find Phoebus matches in Robert Denby's ashtray.

MYCROFT: Denby?

HOLMES: It would appear that both men were in it together – Denby contacted the representatives of the Imperial German Government via carrier pigeon, while Phillimore took the documents overseas. I have my doubts as to whether he ever intended to return, in order to give Denby his half of the blood money.

MYCROFT: Denby must be interrogated at once.

HOLMES: Impossible, I'm afraid, brother. He died shortly after Lestrade arrested him.

MYCROFT: Poisoned like the Burnaby fellow, no doubt.

HOLMES: As a matter of fact, his death was accidental. He seemed perfectly well as Lestrade put him in his cell – if a trifle agitated. Disoriented, perhaps.

MYCROFT: (FIRM, DEMANDING) What happened, Sherlock?

297

HOLMES: Watson tells me he's seen something like it before. Apparently, it's perfectly possible for a person to walk away from a fire apparently unharmed, only to succumb to smoke inhalation some hours later.

MYCROFT: Smoke inhalation?

HOLMES: The presence of blood and soot in Denby's mucus confirm the doctor's diagnosis. No doubt he was following his colleague's instructions in destroying the house. In that sense, one might argue, Phillimore is perhaps partially guilty.

MYCROFT: Well, perhaps Phillimore can be traced through the poison on the thorn that killed Burnaby.

HOLMES: I've already identified it as the venom of the diamond-backed rattlesnake.

MYCROFT: Rattlesnake? Then he might be in America.

HOLMES: He might be almost anywhere, Mycroft. The snake was imported by a firm based in Chinatown. They supply rare and exotic creatures to zoos.

MYCROFT: The Chinese! They're involved?

HOLMES: They are not. It seems that gold was being smuggled into England inside cases containing dangerous animals, thereby evading customs. Burnaby was responsible for selling the gold, but he was evidently less than honest with his cohorts, and paid the price for his treachery.

MYCROFT: You are telling me that Burnaby's death has nothing to do with Phillimore's actions?

HOLMES: It may be frustrating, brother, but at least take comfort in the knowledge that Lestrade has succeeded in clearing up his smuggling case.

MYCROFT: That is no comfort, Sherlock! Phillimore has the report of our troop movements, and now there is no way of finding him!

HOLMES: No way whatever. May I suggest that you have your agents overseas let it be known that you have deliberately allowed falsified reports to be stolen in an attempt to misinform our enemies.

MYCROFT: (THOUGHTFUL) It might, at least, give us time to draw up a new set of plans. But it's hardly satisfactory.

HOLMES: I entirely agree. It would appear that, through a happy mixture of cunning and good fortune, James Phillimore has eluded us.

MUSIC: BRIDGE

SOUND EFFECT: LONDON STREET (BACKGROUND). IT'S RAINING.

WATSON: You told him, then?

HOLMES: I did.

WATSON: What was his reaction?

HOLMES: Stoical, as ever. But he is displeased.

WATSON: Surely not with you, Holmes.

HOLMES: In the past, Mycroft has placed his trust in me, but I think it will be quite some time before he would wish to do so again. A pity. Mycroft represents my last link with – (HE STOPS HIMSELF) With former times.

WATSON: But you did everything possible.

HOLMES: Everything but succeed, Watson. Everything but that.

SOUND EFFECT: OUT

MUSIC: *DANSE MACABRE*

The Murders in the
Maharajah's Railway Carriage
by Charles Veley and Anna Elliott

There were eighteen of us at Victoria Station that winter morning, waiting on the platform for the arrival of the maharajah's train. Nasik, a fat, middle-aged official from the Colonial Office, stood beside me. He had been sulking, pouting, and uncomfortable ever since we had arrived. Now he said, "Your plan had better work, Mr. Holmes."

Holmes appeared not to notice. He stood closest to the outside of the station. The thin sole of his leather shoe rested on the flat surface of the nearest rail, sensitive to any vibrations that would signal the approach of the train. The air was frigid. I followed Holmes's gaze down the empty track, my eyes stinging from the coal smoke of two other trains waiting to depart. More smoke hung in clouds above us, with thin black wisps escaping at the edge of the curved roof high overhead.

The maharajah we awaited was the ruler of a small state in the western region of India. His Highness and his retinue were bringing an enormous diamond, said to be more magnificent than the great Kohinoor given to Queen Victoria by another maharajah earlier in her reign. This priceless new gift for Her Majesty was called The Star of the Orient, and the arrangements for its delivery had been planned for nearly a year. Telegraph reports had confirmed the diamond's safe passage through its ocean voyage from India to Constantinople, its subsequent railway journey to the Belgian port of Ostend, and its brief voyage across the Channel to Dover.

Sir Edward Bradford, Commissioner of the Metropolitan Police, was with us on the platform, maintaining a calm and steadfast expression on his white-mustached face. The empty left sleeve of his uniform bore witness to an encounter with a tigress during his service in India more than a decade ago. As commissioner, Sir Edward had given approval to Holmes's plan for the final journey of the diamond within London. Like Holmes, he made no acknowledgement of Nasik's churlish remark.

Holmes took his foot off the rail and said, "The train is coming,"

Sir Edward turned to his men, twelve Metropolitan Police musicians who carried weapons as well as their instruments. "Remember, no one gets off the maharajah's carriage until the others are emptied and the crowd dispersed," he said. "Then you begin your music, and march to extend yourselves along the length of the maharajah's carriage. The rest of us greet the maharajah and his retinue as they exit from the front. Constables Wallace and Sharp will step up to the rear platform and give the signal to Inspector Lestrade to open the rear door."

We waited. The locomotive entered the station, belching coal smoke and pulling five carriages, the last of which I knew to be the maharajah's. Steam clouds issued from the squealing brakes of the locomotive.

But then, without explanation, Holmes was running towards the last carriage. Before it had stopped, Holmes swung himself up onto the rear platform. "Lestrade!" he called, pounding on the reinforced glass of the rear window. His voice was barely distinguishable over the shriek and hiss of the train finally coming to a halt. He was shaking the door handle. Then he drew his revolver and smashed the glass. He called out, "Commissioner! No one is to leave the train! Watson! I need you here!"

I ran forwards. As Holmes pulled open the rear door of the carriage, I clambered up to the platform.

"Lestrade needs help," Holmes said, beckoning me inside as he stepped into the carriage.

The horrific scene is etched upon my memory. Nearly blocking the doorway, the little inspector lay spread-eagled on the carriage floor, wide-eyed, lips moving wordlessly, bleeding from a great gash on the outside of his thigh. Further inside the compartment, a huge Indian man in an unfamiliar uniform lay on one side of an open metal safe, head lolling sideways at a grotesque angle, a bullet hole ringed by the scorch of gunpowder in the center of his forehead. On his back at the other side of the safe lay a young blond-haired man, also in uniform, this one the red parade dress garb of the British military. At the center of the chest of the blond-haired man was the ornate handle of a curved dagger. The weapon had been plunged deeply into its victim, very nearly up to the hilt.

I immediately dropped to my knees beside Lestrade. Holmes crouched down, closely inspecting the dagger in the young man's chest. I saw him remove a small twist of material with the tips of his fingers.

"You have something?" I asked over my shoulder.

He said nothing, but I thought the material appeared to be a small tuft of blue fiber, as though the murderer had accidentally torn some article of his clothing on the weapon before employing it for its deadly purpose.

Behind me I heard the voice of Sir Edward. "The diamond?"

"Gone," Holmes replied. "Search everyone."

Then he was stepping over the two other shapes on the floor, pushing through to the rest of the carriage and the remainder of the train.

Lestrade's eyes fluttered, in the way I remembered all too well from dying men I had lost in Afghanistan. "Stay with me, Lestrade," I said. "Stay with me." I pulled off my necktie to fashion a tourniquet. I slipped the fabric underneath Lestrade's leg and made a knot, drawing the ends tight. On the floor I saw a walking stick. I twisted it into the knot of my necktie and turned it like a lever to tighten the band of fabric.

Lestrade groaned at the increased pressure, which was a good sign. He was trying to say something. "Do not exert yourself," I said.

I heard a woman's voice from within the train, coming closer, tight with fear and worry. "Parker? Are you all right?"

In the doorway stood a young blonde-haired woman. Golden curls framed her lovely blue-eyed face. Our eyes met.

"Go back!" I told her. "Don't look!"

But I am sure she saw the bodies as she turned away. Her eyes widened in horror. Then she collapsed.

"You have failed me."

The maharajah's bald head glistened with perspiration as he looked down the table at Commissioner Bradford and Holmes, who sat with me at the opposite end. The Indian potentate's large dark eyes shone with outrage. Even the pointed tips of his long black mustache seemed to quiver.

We were in Sir Edward's conference room on the first floor of Scotland Yard. With Sir Edward, Holmes, and me at the table were the colonial official, Nasik, and the maharajah. We were to interview the maharajah and Miss Clarissa Sheffield, the golden-haired young woman who had been with the maharajah in one of his two personal carriages. Sir Edward's men would question those in the maharajah's second personal carriage, as well as the conductor assigned to that section of the train. The police would also interview the forty-five other passengers and staff who had been in the other carriages. Lestrade, unconscious, had been taken to nearby St. Thomas Hospital, on the other side of Westminster Bridge. Holmes and I planned to look in on him as soon as we completed our interviews. I knew that he had lost a great deal of blood and the prospects for his recovery were by no means assured.

The maharajah continued, withdrawing an ornate gold cigarette case and equally ornate gold matchbox from his waistcoat pocket. "My magnificent, priceless diamond travels safely over the course of two months. More than two-thousand miles. Then it reaches England. A mere two hours later, under the guard of your police detective, according to the procedure devised by Scotland Yard and sanctioned by the great Sherlock Holmes, my prize possession, one of the most valuable gems in the world, is stolen."

"We are working diligently to determine what happened," said the commissioner.

The maharajah continued, ignoring the remark, striking a match and lighting his cigarette with a dead-steady hand. "Akbar Singh, my trusted security man, has been murdered. Also slain is Parker Sheffield, Queen's Commander and Palace Resident, who has overseen my relations with the Crown since the time I became ruler of Badora State, eleven years ago. Your man from Scotland Yard was to complete the triumvirate of guards, over a locked safe, inside a locked compartment. But that was evidently not enough. Your plan has failed. *You* have failed."

"Inspector Lestrade is incapacitated," said Sir Edward. "But he may yet provide us with useful information."

"On the contrary, from what I have been told, Inspector Lestrade may be the perpetrator of this outrage. I should trust nothing that he says."

"Preposterous," said Nasik, the Colonial Office man. "Slanderous."

Holmes leaned forward. "Gentlemen, if you will permit, we might keep an open mind, considering the situation. Your Highness, would you kindly tell us why you believe Inspector Lestrade to be . . . at fault?"

"Because I know Singh and I know Parker Sheffield, and both of them are most reliable. Neither would be a party to such an outrage. They are . . . were loyal to me."

"But how did Inspector Lestrade – *perpetrate*, I believe was the word you used – the outrage?"

"Quite simply. He shot Singh with his police revolver."

"There was no revolver found on Lestrade," said Sir Edward. "Nor in the compartment."

"Recall that the window was open. Here is what I believe happened after the shot, which would not have been heard in our portion of the carriage due to the noise of the train. My man Sheffield reacted, knocked the revolver away from Lestrade, and grasped the only weapon he could find, the ceremonial curved Gurkha knife that Singh always carried. He succeeded in wounding Lestrade, but Lestrade got the better of him in the struggle and killed him. Then, with both his opponents dead, Lestrade opened the safe – taking the key from Singh's pocket – and extracted the diamond, passing it out the open window to his accomplice. At the same time, he might easily have also disposed of the revolver. But then, due to his wound, he collapsed."

Holmes considered, steepling his fingertips together in the meditative posture he sometimes adopts at such moments. Then he said, "It is certainly a hypothesis that bears consideration. There may be others, however, and we must examine such possibilities as may present themselves."

"All very well," said the maharajah, "But the fact remains that tomorrow at noon I am to present my diamond to Queen Victoria. Will you have recovered it in time?"

"We shall do all that we can," said Holmes. "But would you please – for the moment – set aside your suspicions of Inspector Lestrade and the deductions you have just related? I should like to concentrate on what you saw, directly, while you were on the train after it departed the Dover station."

"I saw nothing suspicious on the train from the time we left Dover. However, others in my party may have seen something. You should talk to them."

"Your party occupied two railway carriages."

"Yes. Ten of my people were in the carriage directly forward of the one where I was seated. My three wives, their maidservants, my cook and his assistant, my valet, my personal physician. Yes. Ten."

"And in the carriage where you were seated?"

"There was only my assistant, Miss Sheffield."

"Why were the others not in that carriage?"

"I was planning to rehearse my speech for the ceremonial presentation tomorrow. I do not like to have my servants as an audience for such a rehearsal."

"Did anyone enter your carriage?"

"Only the conductor who brought me my chai."

"When did you drink it?" Holmes asked.

"Just after we departed Dover."

"Did you eat or drink anything in Dover?"

"We had a light breakfast in my carriage. My cook prepared it. Your man Lestrade joined us, before he and Singh and Sheffield took up their positions in the secured compartment."

"The four of you verified that the jewel was in the safe before the train departed Dover?"

"We did. It was."

"And you followed procedure afterwards?"

"After Singh locked the safe, I locked the secure rear compartment with the three guardians inside, pocketed the key, and then took my seat in the forward section."

"And the key was still in your pocket when the train reached London?"

"Undisturbed."

"And after the train got underway, did you rehearse your speech?"

"I did. Miss Sheffield listened. She may have taken notes."

"You were awake until the train reached London?"

"I may have dozed off. That happens sometimes."

Holmes nodded. "You appeared to have been dozing when I pushed open the door from the compartment and crashed into your passenger section to sound the alarm."

"What of it?"

"I merely point out that you cannot provide further help as a direct witness as to who went into the secure compartment, or how they might have gained access. Unless someone had made a duplicate key?"

The maharaja's lips pressed together in an expression of disbelief. "That is surely unlikely."

"Perhaps." Holmes regarded the maharaja a moment, then asked, "Have you in your possession any garments made of blue wool?"

The other man blinked in surprise at the question. "That is surely an odd thing to ask. But no." He gave a shudder. "I cannot abide your English habit of wearing wool close to the skin. As a fabric it is so rough and coarse. No, all my garments are hand-sewn by my personal tailor in my own country and made of silk or the finest cotton."

"No matter." Holmes made a dismissive gesture, waving the issue aside. "Then might you assist us from a different perspective?" he asked. "Your own first instincts may be of great value. Who comes to mind as a suspect? Not merely for the execution of the theft, which could have readily been the work of a paid mercenary. But who would pay for such a crime? And let us assume the primary motive for the theft was not the diamond itself. Otherwise it might have been stolen at any time since you acquired it. The larger question is, therefore: Who would have wished to prevent you from presenting The Star of the Orient to Her Majesty?"

A flicker of respect came into the maharajah's eyes. "My predecessor, Malhar Rao, is in exile," he said, and then continued, "but it is known to me that he hopes to mount a rebellion and regain power."

"We'll never let him do that," said Nasik, the Colonial Office man. "Malhar Rao was removed from office for attempting to murder the British resident. Dirty sneak bribed his servants to put arsenic and diamond dust in our man's sherbet, of all things. We're watching him where he's exiled in Bombay, and we will keep him bottled up there."

"But the theft could have been arranged from afar," the maharajah said. "Just as he paid others to attempt murder by poison, so too he could pay others to spoil the presentation to the Queen."

"We will look into that aspect of the case," Sir Edward said.

"I should like to see the file on Mr. Rao," Holmes said. "Also the files on the two victims, Singh and Sheffield."

"I trust you will have more success than you have enjoyed today," the maharajah said. He stood up. "Now, gentlemen, I am fatigued and wish to go to my hotel."

"Who killed my brother?"

Miss Sheffield slapped the table with her small, white-gloved hand, surprising us all as she sat in the chair the maharajah had most recently occupied. Something in the young woman's voice made me feel her urgency and her deep hurt. Her blue eyes were wide and imploring, not filled with horror as when I had first seen her. The tilt of her well-shaped chin and the furrow of concern in her lovely brow evidenced her need more eloquently than any words might have done. "He must have justice," Miss Sheffield went on. "He gave his life serving your two governments, protecting a cold, lifeless gem."

Sir Edward attempted a benign smile. "We are doing everything – "

Miss Sheffield ignored the commissioner. "I know what to expect from officials. I have submitted to the indignity of a search, as has His Highness and all other members of his party. I hope for better treatment from you, Mr. Holmes. What can you tell me? Please?"

"Might I ask first, Miss Sheffield, the same question I asked His Highness. Did you drink tea on the journey?"

"I did. We usually do. His Highness and I."

"And were you awake at all times?"

"I may have dozed off."

"What comes to your mind when you consider who might have done this awful thing? Did your brother have enemies?"

"I know of no enemies," she said. "I came to visit him last year, and that was when I met His Highness and had the honor of being selected as his assistant. I never heard anyone speak ill of my brother."

"Were you aware that his predecessor, the previous British resident in the palace, had been poisoned?"

"Of course. But His Highness is the polar opposite of the former ruler. There was never a hint of danger to my brother." She paused. "Now, I have answered your question, Mr. Holmes. What can you tell me of the circumstances surrounding my brother's death?"

"Do you recall seeing me in the corridor of the maharajah's carriage?"

"Yes. You ran past me and told the maharajah – His Highness – that no one was to leave the train. Then you yourself continued, into the next carriage, where the others in our party were seated. I thought just then that something dreadful had happened."

"Had you seen anyone else coming from the rear compartment, where the diamond had been kept?"

306

"I already told the commissioner here. No one."

"But you had dozed off, you said?"

She shook her head. "I am a light sleeper. I doubt that someone would have passed me."

"What did you do after I passed you in the carriage?"

"I feared for my brother's safety, and so I ran back to the rear compartment. I saw Dr. Watson. And – "

She broke off, closing her eyes as if trying to suppress the memory.

"Did you notice that two of the windows in the carriage were open?"

"Why, no. I didn't. I was fixated on – I don't want to think about that. And then I fainted."

"Well, two of the windows in the compartment were indeed open," Holmes said. "One on either side. As the train pulled into the station, I observed the open window on the platform side."

"I wondered what prompted you to break with procedure and immediately board the train." said Sir Edward.

Holmes nodded. "Orders were to keep the windows of the compartment shut. Even under normal conditions, they are shut prior to entering the station, to keep out the soot. I suggest that one of the windows was opened and a canister with incapacitating gas was inserted. The window was then closed. When the gas had done its work, the perpetrator re-opened the window and climbed into the compartment. The man must have been an acrobatic individual, to accomplish this while on a moving train. So that is my first hope – that you may know someone with such physical capabilities. There are a number of most proficient acrobats in India, I believe."

I stared at Holmes. It was unlike him to create such an elaborate theory so early in the case, when the facts were still being established. But I did not interrupt, and neither did the commissioner.

Miss Sheffield shook her head. "I have nothing to do with acrobats. And why would someone use poison gas?"

"To overpower three men would require assistance. The compartment was locked, and no one saw anyone enter it from the corridor. Therefore, someone must have entered from outside. But such entry would have been so easily prevented by the three men guarding the diamond that something else must have been used."

"So you suspect poison gas?" asked Sir Edward.

"Traces may be found on the clothing, though they will be obscured, no doubt, by the soot that came in at the station through the open windows."

"My men can look for marks to show that the intruder gained entry from outside."

"Those were obscured by the soot accumulating within the station. I examined the exterior of the carriage myself."

The commissioner nodded. "So the acrobatic person incapacitated three men with poison gas. How did he get into the locked safe?"

Holmes replied quickly. "If he knew Singh held the key, he could easily have removed it from Singh's pocket."

"But why would he spare Lestrade?"

"Possibly the train had come too close to the station for him to complete the task."

"We shall search the tracks," Sir Edward said. "Someone may have seen the man making his escape."

Miss Sheffield appeared mollified. "A brilliant reconstruction, Mr. Holmes. I should think you would believe it, Commissioner," she said. "Particularly when the alternate theory proposed by my employer is so damaging to the reputation of the Metropolitan Police."

Sir Edward looked as though he were about to speak in Lestrade's defense, but Holmes interrupted smoothly. "I wonder if there is one last favor we might beg of you. I have collected a dozen or more items from the floor of the train carriages. Nothing bloody or gruesome, I assure you," he added in response to Miss Sheffield's look of alarm. "Many may in fact be detritus from previous train occupants and have nothing to do with the case at hand. But I wonder whether you might cast your eye over them and tell me whether any are familiar to you?"

Miss Sheffield looked uncertain, but nodded. "Certainly. If you believe that it will help."

"Capital." Holmes rose and from the top of a nearby book case took down a tray of the sort used for serving meals in the dining car of a train. "Here we are, then."

He set the tray down on the table in front of Miss Sheffield, who peered at the items with curiosity.

They were: A brass button that looked as though it might have been torn off a train conductor's uniform, the stub of a cigar, a pair of knitting needles, a scrap of newspaper, much spattered with grease, as though it had been used to wrap up someone's dinner of fish and chips, a baby's silver rattle – and the tuft of blue fiber that Holmes had found on the murder weapon.

I watched Miss Sheffield's face closely as her gaze lingered on the final item, but she showed no trace of recognition or alarm, only shook her head. "I don't recognize anything here." She touched the pair of knitting needles. "Perhaps one of the maharaja's wives was crocheting some lace? But no – I don't recognize anything in particular."

"No matter." Holmes removed the tray again. "I thank you for the effort."

At that moment came a knock at the door. A tall sergeant entered. "A note for you, Commissioner."

Sir Edward opened the note and read it aloud:

> *We have the diamond. Deliver one-hundred-thousand pounds in Bank of England notes to ransom it. Miss Sheffield and Dr. Watson are to deliver the notes in a tan satchel to the Red Dragon Inn at midnight tonight coming unaccompanied in a cab. In the event that payment is not satisfactory or that they are followed, they will both meet the fate of the three men in the train, and the maharajah will die*

Holmes was the first to speak, breaking the silence that followed. "Those are certainly clear instructions." He sounded entirely unperturbed, as though he had been expecting something of this nature to occur. Knowing Holmes, he very likely had.

He rose from the table. "I have some preparations to make. But in the meantime, Sir Edward – " He drew a card from his pocket and scribbled a few words on the back before passing it to the commissioner. " – if you would continue with the questioning of the train's occupants, including the maharaja's wives? I believe that you will find the line of inquiry I have outlined productive."

I couldn't see what Holmes had written, but Sir Edward's eyebrows rose when he read the scrawled words, as though their content surprised him.

Then he nodded. "Very well, Mr. Holmes, it shall be done as you suggest. And I hope that our trust in you may not prove misplaced."

"I am terribly frightened, Dr. Watson."

Miss Sheffield sat close to me in the cab, her golden curls covered by a plain felt hat, and mostly hidden in the shadow. We were passing a street lamp and its yellow glow flickered in her blue eyes.

"I've visited the Red Dragon Inn before and lived to tell about it," I said. "On police business, of course." I smiled to reassure her, comforted by the heft of the Webley revolver in my inside coat pocket.

"I really have no idea why that note had my name on it," she said. "I wish that it hadn't."

"I understand," I said. Then an impulse seized me, and I added, "No, actually I do *not* understand. Why should you place yourself in danger?"

"I might ask you the same question, Dr. Watson. You are in equal danger."

"But I am – "

She interrupted. "You are going to say that because you are a man, you have no choice but to bravely advance into the fray, because your country needs you."

Her charming smile warmed my heart. "Something of the sort, I suppose."

"Well then, how is it hard to believe that I should want to help my country as well, even though I am a woman? I was raised to expect no special favors from anyone, even though my father is a retired general and extremely wealthy. Although not in the military myself, I have inherited his courage. I can be strong and brave when it is necessary – though I don't have to enjoy it."

"Are you doing this to help the maharajah?"

She shook her head. "He is a dreadfully demanding employer. He has letters to dictate at all hours. Invitation lists to consider. Things like that. Wakes me up, I believe, just to show his control over me. As if I were one of his servants, always at his beck and call. My brother tried to influence him, but to no avail." She spoke softly, as though she were confessing, eyes downcast. "You will understand why I hope to remain in England after this is over. Though I know the maharajah will miss me. He has valued my services very highly." Then she looked up. "Who is paying the ransom that you are carrying in that satchel?"

"Lloyd's Insurance Company."

She nodded with satisfaction. "I thought so. They have already been paid more than a hundred-thousand pounds as their premium, and if the diamond is not returned, they will have to pay ten times this amount to the maharajah. One million pounds sterling. I was the one who suggested that he take out the policy before we began the journey, so you see, he has good reason to value my services."

Something puzzled me. "Why," I asked, "is he so intent to recover the diamond, when he will be made whole by the insurance?"

"It is a matter of prestige. If he goes home with the thanks of his queen, with the story of being face-to-face, ruler-to-ruler, receiving her gratitude – that is worth far more to the maharajah than one-million pounds. And though I don't care tuppence for the maharajah's prestige, I do care for the reputation of my own country, which will suffer if the loss of the diamond is made public. So I am here. Besides, my brother died protecting that diamond."

"You are a brave woman, Miss Sheffield."

"Kind of you to say so." She paused and then she appeared to remember something. "Have you had news of the third man, the British policeman? You were helping him in the carriage. You must have saved his life."

"I applied a tourniquet to staunch the bleeding."

"Fortunate that you, a medical man, were on hand when he needed you. Was he in pain?"

"I cannot tell. He was incapacitated."

"I hope that he'll recover and provide some clue."

"As do I. Lestrade is a friend. We've been on numerous cases together."

"It must have been painful for you when you visited him in hospital, to see him in such a state. Will you go again?"

"I hope to see him when we have completed this – delivery mission," I said. "On my way home."

"I trust that you find him recovered." She gave a polite smile. "Now, what ought I to know about The Red Dragon Inn?"

I was reluctant to describe the Inn to Miss Sheffield, for it was a vile opium den where sailors and unfortunates of the city go to forget their troubles, sometimes for days at a time, with steadily increasing costs and surrender to the hold of the drug. I had seen men and women whose bodies had shriveled to husks, lying on hard wooden pallets, oblivious to the damage they were inflicting upon themselves. The interior of the Red Dragon Inn was no fit sight for a lady.

"I hope you need know nothing at all about the Inn," I said. "I hope to simply make the transfer outside the premises, exchanging the ransom money for the diamond."

"Then I hope the same," she said.

We arrived at the Inn soon after. As we stepped down from the cab, the cold, dark Thames, illuminated only by the running lights of a few small vessels, was behind us. Ahead of us was the Inn, a decrepit wooden structure, one in a row of several tumbledown shops, its sagging roof only dimly illuminated by a single exterior gas lamp.

"Wait here, cabby," I said.

For answer, the man whipped up his horse. The cab clattered away to disappear into the fog.

I hefted the tan satchel in my right hand. With my left hand I patted my top coat pocket, to reassure myself that my Webley was still in place.

Miss Sheffield shivered, hugging herself and tucking her chin into her chest. She was whispering to herself. "I hope that my brother is watching," she said. "I hope he appreciates – "

"*Don't move!*"

The command came harsh and cold, a hiss from the alleyway beside one of the other shops. "Don't call out."

The shadowy figure stepped forward, barely visible in the gloom. He pointed to the Red Dragon. "None in there'll take notice."

The voice was that of a Cockney man. He approached, stopping about an arm's length away from where we stood. He was shabbily dressed, a flat cap above his slab-like face. The sort of man readily hired to do a job, be paid, and forget the transaction. "Now, hand over the satchel."

I did so. "Now, hand over the diamond," I said.

"Not so fast," the man went on. "Step this way, Miss Sheffield."

She shuddered. I had a glimpse of movement of her hat and curls and wide frightened eyes.

"Do no such thing," I said.

Behind me I felt something small and hard pressing into my spine. The man in front of me said, "You want to be a cripple, that's up to you. Now, Miss Sheffield. Into the carriage."

She moved, hesitant, walking slowly with the first man but with her eyes on me, as if asking permission. Finally, she climbed into the carriage.

"She is our hostage," said the man. "You can get her back, here, midnight tomorrow, along with the diamond. You come alone with another hundred-thousand pounds ransom money. If all is in order she will be here. If not, she dies. You can remember that?"

I nodded.

"She will be inside the Red Dragon Inn. She may be a bit sleepy."

I was calculating my movement. The slab-faced man was closing the carriage door behind Miss Sheffield. The man at my back was breathing faster. I could feel the pressure of his gun barrel at the center of my spine. Mentally I rehearsed my moves. *Spin away from the gun while drawing my Webley –*

Then came a cracking great blow at the side of my skull. I saw stars, and then darkness.

"I heard the conversation," Holmes said.

We were side by side in a dog-cart, Holmes driving. I was slowly coming to my senses.

"I knew that keeping you alive was worth another hundred-thousand pounds to them," Holmes continued. "Nevertheless, I would have stopped them if needed. They are a pair of cheap hirelings. If we're fortunate, the commissioner's men will be able to follow them to their employer. I should like to know where that ransom money was to be taken."

"And to rescue Miss Sheffield."

"Of course, Watson."

312

Something in his tone made me feel petulant. "The instructions said no one was to follow Miss Sheffield and me."

Holmes shook his head. "I didn't follow. I came ahead. I was behind the Red Dragon and heard everything. My revolver was aimed at the man who put Miss Sheffield into the carriage. Do you still have your Webley?"

I patted my overcoat pocket. "I do."

"That is fortunate. You may need it."

"Are we going to see Lestrade at the hospital before we go home to Baker Street?"

Holmes shook his head. "That would be a dangerous mistake, for we are being followed. As yet our adversaries don't know where Lestrade is being held, but if they were to see us visit St. Thomas's, they would assuredly make the connection and take action to ensure that he doesn't survive to tell what he knows."

I felt a moment's relief. "When I was in the cab with Miss Sheffield, I very nearly said the name of the hospital within the hearing of the driver."

"But you did not?"

"I only said that I hoped to visit Lestrade after I had delivered the ransom."

"That may explain why we're being followed," he said. "I've arranged for us to change carriages before we proceed to our next destination."

"Not Baker Street?"

"We are going to Sheffield House, in Clapham Common."

"It is two in the morning, Holmes!"

"Nevertheless, we must rouse General Sheffield and his household. I hope we aren't too late to prevent another tragedy."

Holmes would say no more. After a detour into a warehouse and a change to a hansom cab, and a seemingly interminable ride in the cold night air, we finally reached Sheffield House. The General's residence was positioned at the end of a short drive that extended into Clapham Common, isolated from other residences in the area. By day the common was a grand open parkland, but at this hour, barely five a.m. according to my watch, it appeared a vast dark emptiness, darker even than the Thames, for it was without boat lights or reflections on the waves. There was no light on the gravel drive, but the lamps on our cab were sufficient for us to make our way to the house.

Holmes rapped the oaken door sharply with the brass handle of his walking stick. After we had waited for several minutes in the dark, the door was finally answered by an old servant. Then the lights went on as other servants appeared. Holmes was most insistent. "You must rouse your

313

master," he said. "Tell him Mr. Sherlock Holmes is downstairs and has news that cannot wait until morning."

General Sheffield, in his fifties with iron-gray hair and luxuriant gray muttonchop side-whiskers, soon descended the main staircase. He strode with a military bearing even in his dressing gown, which he had wrapped tightly around his ramrod-slim frame.

We moved to the drawing room. The old servant who had greeted us had lit the fire. The glow from its yellow flame danced across the general's resolute jaw and steely eyes.

"Well, Mr. Holmes?" he asked.

"You know of the tragic end of your son, General Sheffield," Holmes said. "I regret to inform you that a similar fate may befall your daughter. She has been abducted. Dr. Watson here was with her, and I observed the incident from a short distance away, though I was unable to prevent it. Dr. Watson, would you please elaborate?"

I recounted my tale, and Holmes completed it, saying that an enclosed cab had been waiting alongside the Inn, and that Miss Sheffield, now a hostage, had been placed into it before driving off with the two abductors, one driving and the other with her inside the cab.

I had to credit General Sheffield's military discipline. His face tightened with anxiety while I was speaking, but by the time Holmes had concluded, he had himself once more firmly in hand, his expression steady, if grim.

"So, you have come about the ransom," he said.

"No, General. We have come about your own safety."

"Mine?" The man appeared completely taken by surprise.

"You are a widower, and your son would have been your heir. Your daughter is next in line, is that correct?"

The general nodded.

"With both of them gone, to whom would the estate pass?"

"A preposterous question for Commissioner Bradford to ask me earlier today, and even more preposterous for you to ask me at four o'clock in the morning, Mr. Holmes. But I'll answer it for you all the same. As I told the commissioner, my fortune would go into a charitable trust, now being run for the benefit of poor people who have immigrated here. The institution, in the Limehouse District, is called the Strangers' Home for Asiatics, Africans, and South Sea Islanders. I don't see, however, that anyone would wish to kill me to benefit a trust. That's why I made my will in that manner."

Holmes said, "Yet there are those who might accede to a position within the charitable trust and wish to have control over your wealth for their own purposes."

314

"You have some indication of corruption in the trust?"

"It's very possible. And the possible elimination of both your children would give your death an outcome far different from the result it would have had twenty-four hours ago."

He appeared thoughtful. "When my daughter left for India to join her brother, I realized that dangers might overtake them. The lives that they had chosen placed them at greater risk than if they had remained here. But that is the way with children. One of life's paradoxes. One cannot entirely ensure their safety without harming them."

Holmes nodded.

"This morning's news has caused me to think I may have erred – gone too far in my insistence on children's independence," the general went on. "I've always thought my wealth would be a corrosive curse for them rather than a blessing. My children never had access to it. Each of them had a first-rate education, university courses – even for my daughter – but beyond that I forced them to make their own way in the world. My son took the queen's shilling and then rose to a position in the Colonial Office. My daughter followed. Best thing for both of them. I thought. Now I am not so sure."

"You have a country estate near Oxford, I believe?"

"Yes. Not far from the university where both my children had tutors."

"Could you go there at once?"

The older man stared at Holmes in astonishment. "Why the urgency?"

Holmes was about to reply when from behind us we heard a crash. We whirled.

One of the two tall French doors overlooking the Common had been broken, a tangle of wood frame and broken glass. Inside the room, on her knees, mud-spattered and gasping, was a woman.

Miss Sheffield.

"Oh, Father!" she cried. "Rao's men are outside! They're trying to kill me!"

Instinctively, I moved forwards to assist Miss Sheffield, but Holmes's hands clamped onto my upper arm in a grip of steel, pulling me back and away. His voice was at my ear, low and urgent.

"You must leave by the front door. Move around between the house and the open space of the common, where you can see the broken window and Miss Sheffield. Stay silent in the shadows. A murderer will emerge from the darkness and approach that broken window. He may try to enter this room. You must wait for him and take him from behind before he kills the general. If ever you have trusted me, trust me now and move!"

I obeyed.

Outside the drawing-room were the manservant who had admitted us and two women in dressing gowns. All three stared at me. I held my finger to my lips. Then I had another thought. "Miss Sheffield has come in from outside," I said. "She should have brandy, a hot water bottle, soap and hot towels, and a dressing gown."

Then I departed. Keeping to Holmes's instructions, I stayed as close to the wall of the house as possible, between shrubs and garden mulch, wending my way among the plants and trees, keeping watch for a dark figure. My hand went to my Webley, and this time I drew the weapon out, so as to be ready. Turning the corner to view the rear of the estate, I saw that the grounds were landscaped with large shrubs and wide stone steps, leading down to the common park area. The darkness there was absolute, although in the east I fancied that I could detect some lightning on the horizon. Dawn would come soon.

Closer to the house there was a puddle of light from the broken French window, but only enough for me to see the steps and a few feet beyond. I tried to position myself so that I could see the people inside: Holmes and Miss Sheffield and her father, and perhaps servants bringing Miss Sheffield the assistance that I had requested. But I could not, for my main objective, as Holmes had ordered, was to keep watch on the area leading up to the house. I crouched behind a large bush close to the steps and waited, my revolver at the ready.

As I watched, my thoughts whirled. How had Miss Sheffield escaped her captors? Was the murderer that I awaited the slab-faced man, in pursuit? Or did Holmes have some other reason for expecting an attack? And if one came, would there be only one attacker, as Holmes evidently surmised? If more than one, my ability to defend would be seriously impeded. But with the advantage of surprise, I thought, I might overcome the numerical odds.

I waited. My hand on my revolver was firm. The voices from the drawing-room were audible, but too far away for me to understand anything of what was being said. Around me the sighing of the wind, the creak of the tree boughs, seemed magnified, ominous somehow, as though portents of some approaching agent of doom. The skittering of a night creature – a fox, perhaps, or a feral cat – emanated from the bush on the far side of the steps. I drew in my breath, but I did not move.

Then my heart began to race as beyond the bush I saw a shadowy figure, very nearly motionless, slowly emerge from a clump of plantings on the other side of the stone steps. He crouched low, and then rose up, his silhouette now outlined against the dark gray sky of the eastern horizon. From the silhouette, I thought he was a broad-shouldered man, wearing a top hat and a cape. He took a cautious step forward and I realized that he held something in his hand.

A rifle.

With two quick strides he was at the top of the wide garden steps, facing towards the broken French window and the drawing-room. He stood for only a moment and then he knelt.

He drew the bolt of his rifle.

He was about to raise the weapon to his shoulder when I charged.

I ran at him full tilt, my own weapon in hand. Knowing that he would be no use to us if he were dead, however, I was determined to overpower my opponent without killing him.

I hit him at full speed, leaping and diving in a rugby tackle, driving into him with my shoulder, all my weight and force behind the blow. I heard the rifle clatter down the stone steps, knocked away by my first impact. The would-be assassin and I hit the ground together. He was a bulky fellow and fit, and he struck out at me, but I got the better of him and soon had him pinned, face down, his arm twisted behind his back. He lay motionless, the wind knocked out of him.

"Don't move or I shall break your arm," I said.

He said nothing.

Then from above where we lay at the foot of the steps, I heard the clatter of a carriage coming to a stop on the gravel drive. I looked up and saw a flood of uniformed constables jumping out, followed by Sir Edward Bradford.

"My men lost the carriage with Miss Sheffield," he said, "so we came here as Holmes instructed. Who have you got there, Dr. Watson?"

I lifted the man's head, turning his body.

I saw the outraged face of the Maharajah of Badora.

"I was pursuing one of Rao's men," said the maharajah.

We were in the drawing-room with the general, Miss Sheffield, and Holmes, along with Commissioner Bradford and four robust constables.

"I thought that he had gone in here," the maharajah continued. "I had followed the carriage from the Red Dragon. They stopped on the other side of the common. I saw Miss Sheffield escape and followed her. I'm sure that Rao's men are outside, somewhere near the house. You must apprehend them at once!"

"We shall do no such thing," Holmes said. "Lestrade has regained consciousness in the hospital. He has told all that he knows."

I was watching Miss Sheffield at that moment. She glanced at me. Our eyes met. Then she looked away.

317

"Whatever Lestrade said cannot be trusted," said the maharajah. "As I pointed out earlier this afternoon – "

"You took pains to incriminate him," said Holmes, "hoping to sow disbelief if he lived and told his story."

"I tell you, he is a murderer! You are covering up for him."

"No. *You* are a murderer, *Your Highness.*" Holmes spat out the honorific in a contemptuous hiss, and then continued, "As is Miss Sheffield."

"How dare you!" she exclaimed.

The maharajah's expression darkened. "Commissioner, General, you must put a stop to this outrage!"

But Holmes held up his hand, and the other men waited. "Shall I recount what actually happened?" Holmes asked. "You both entered the secure compartment, using the maharajah's key. The maharajah picked up Sheffield's walking stick and struck Lestrade on the back of the head on the pretext that Lestrade was a traitor. Using a Gurkha knife, Miss Sheffield wounded Lestrade to make it appear that there had been a struggle. Then she stabbed her brother, just as you, Maharajah, were shooting Akbar Singh with your own revolver. You took his key from his body and opened the safe. You removed the diamond, opened the windows, and disposed of the revolver. You left the compartment and relocked the door, resuming your comfortable seats and pretending to doze. Behind you two men were dead and one man was dying."

"Preposterous," said the maharajah. "I was not pretending. I was asleep in my seat until we reached London and you awakened me."

"As was I," said Miss Sheffield. "And the inspector could not possibly have told you such a story. By your own description of the events, he was unconscious when the other two men were killed."

"But your own actions have betrayed you, Miss Sheffield," Holmes said. "Dr. Watson told me you stared in horror when you first saw the carnage in the secured compartment, just before you fainted. Though the faint was a pretense, the horror was real – when you realized that Lestrade, whom you had thought had already bled to death, was still alive, and had seen both you and the maharajah."

"You have only his word against ours."

"We have more than that, Miss Sheffield. You had your knitting with you on the train. When presented with the needles that were found on the floor of the train, you spoke of someone using them to 'crochet lace' rather than to knit. It was a clumsy effort to distance yourself from them, to make it appear as though you didn't even know the correct terminology or what they might be used for, and it attracted my attention to you from the outset. When questioned, all three of the maharajah's wives told Sir Edward that you were knitting a long blue scarf for your return to a cold climate, and none of them could confirm that Singh habitually carried a Gurkha knife. You brought the knife with you on the train. You held it within the scarf, first to conceal it in order to get close to your brother, and then to shield yourself from his blood. Wisps of blue wool from the scarf remained on the hilt of the Gurkha knife. I noticed them when I first inspected his wound. And now the blue scarf is gone."

"I tell you, I had no such scarf!" Miss Sheffield's voice rose.

"It was blue, the wives said. They thought you wanted to match the color of your eyes."

"They are lying."

Holmes went on, his tone inexorable. "We must also consider the position of the blade that killed your brother, Miss Sheffield. The murderer did not thrust the blade all the way to the hilt. Was it some womanly emotion, some vestigial humanity, that made you hesitate to plunge in the knife to its full length? Was it compassion at the final moment, when you looked into your brother's face as you killed him? Or was it revulsion?"

"I deny it," Miss Sheffield said. She turned to the General. "Father, are you going to let him speak to me in this way?"

A curious expression etched the General's face: Dawning horror mingled with disbelief. Or rather, the desperate wish that he might find reason to doubt Holmes's words. He opened his mouth, then closed it again before clearing his throat.

"You will need evidence, Mr. Holmes, to back up such claims as these."

It was far from a ringing proclamation of his daughter's innocence – a fact which I could see registered in the brief flash of something hard and ugly that crossed Miss Sheffield's blue gaze.

Holmes kept his gaze trained on her. "We will find your blue scarf alongside the train track, stained with your brother's blood. A British jury may find it persuasive evidence at your trial for murder."

"Rubbish. Why should I kill my brother?"

"To inherit the Sheffield estate."

"A remote possibility. My father is here, and quite alive."

"But you arranged for his removal. That event would have occurred here, and a room full of servants would have sworn that you were innocent, being ministered to in this room just after your desperate escape from your supposed abductors. You would have said that they intended to kill *you*."

For a moment, Miss Sheffield stared at Holmes in silence. Then she said, "You cannot prove it."

Holmes turned to the General. He gestured to indicate the maharajah's rifle, now in the hands of one of the constables. "Sir, the maharajah was about to fire that rifle when Dr. Watson stopped him. The rifle was aimed at you."

General Sheffield stared at his daughter. "Is this true, Clarissa? This is how you honor your father?"

At these words, there came a transformation in the manner and appearance of Miss Sheffield. Her expression hardened, her features suddenly resembling the cold, resolute face of the general.

"You withheld everything from me!" she cried, her eyes blazing. "I had to work for that scaly creature – " She indicated the maharajah. " – in that beastly sweaty climate, and you thought that was just perfectly fine, that your own daughter should be sent off to be forgotten in the Indian jungles and treated like a slave. Well, you were wrong. I wanted what was rightly mine. I wanted what I deserved. And if it weren't for this interfering creature – " She pointed at Holmes. " – I would have had it!"

The general's gaze grew cold and distant, staring out the shattered French window, towards the darkness of the great parkland that lay beyond. "You are dead to me," he said.

Miss Sheffield made no acknowledgement. She still held her head high as the constables led her away.

Holmes then walked over to stand beside the maharajah. "Might I trouble you for a cigarette, Your Highness? It has been a long and trying day for both of us."

As if by reflex, the maharajah drew his ornate gold cigarette case from his pocket. Then he hesitated.

Holmes's hand shot out and grasped the case, wresting it from the maharajah's fingers. "And your matches, Your Highness, if you please."

A moment later, Holmes held the ornate gold matchbox. He opened the lid and spilled the matches onto the nearby table. Then he pressed with both thumbs at the end of the case. There was a click. He held the case delicately between one fingertip and thumb, upending it onto the heel of his other hand. Then he pulled the case up and away with a flourish, as a waiter at an expensive restaurant would unveil the featured dish for an evening's feast.

Something glittered in Holmes's open palm.

"Gentlemen," he said. "The Star of the Orient."

Holmes turned to the maharajah. "You very nearly defrauded the Lloyds Insurance Company of one-million pounds, not to mention an additional one-hundred-thousand pounds in ransom money. To fulfill your bargain with your clever assistant, all that remained for you to accomplish was the death of General Sheffield so that she could receive the inheritance that she craved. It would have been a clear shot, into a lighted room, through a large window, already smashed wide open by Miss Sheffield. Was it she who proposed the plan?"

The maharajah folded his arms across his chest. "I am a sovereign," he said. "I am a prince of the realm. I have diplomatic immunity."

"That will be up to the Colonial Office to decide," said Sir Edward.

The commissioner took The Star of the Orient from Holmes and turned to his two remaining constables. "Please escort His Highness to Whitehall. I shall inform the palace that there will be no need of a presentation ceremony."

Soon Holmes and I were with Sir Edward in his police carriage, on our way home. It was just past seven o'clock. A pale winter sun had risen, casting faint shadows across the roadway ahead.

The commissioner asked, "What made you suspect them, Mr. Holmes?"

Holmes said, "The simplest explanation of the facts was that the two parties who had access to the secured compartment did indeed utilize that access while giving alibis to each other. But both parties embellished their alibis with more elaborate explanations – talking of rehearsing a speech, drowsiness possibly induced by drinking tea, and even accusing Lestrade of the crime. Then Miss Sheffield made no challenge to my absurd theory of the acrobatic intruder on the railway carriage, even though the carriage windows open from the inside, and the windows, while large, cannot be raised high enough to admit an intruder. When she said my theory was brilliant, it was plain that she was not sincere and that she wished us to take the inquiry down a blind alley. Therefore, she was concealing some other motive. My suspicion was confirmed when I learned she had been knitting a blue scarf while on the train."

The commissioner nodded. "One more question: How did you know that Inspector Lestrade had regained consciousness? I myself did not hear the news until just before I left my office to come here."

Holmes blinked and drew in his breath. "I'm delighted to hear such welcome news, Commissioner," he said. "I didn't know that Lestrade had recovered until this very moment."

Then he gave one of his small smiles. "Watson, I propose we stop at St. Thomas Hospital on our return to Baker Street. An account of the case will no doubt brighten the new day for the Good Inspector."

NOTES

1. The story of the diamond at the center of this adventure was inspired by the history of The Star of the South, an enormous diamond owned during the late Nineteenth Century by the Maharajah of Baroda. The predecessor to that maharajah was indeed removed from office for attempting to poison the British resident with arsenic and diamond dust. There is no record, however, of this diamond ever being offered to Queen Victoria. It was eventually bought by Cartier in 2002.
2. The compartmentalized design of the railway carriage described in the story is based on the kitchen-dining car with separated smoking compartment then in use by The Wagonlit Company for the journey from Constantinople to Paris and Ostend. The route would soon become famous as that of The Orient Express.
3. The character of Commissioner Bradford in this story is based on Sir Edward Bradford, who indeed lost his left arm to a tigress during his military service in India. In London, Sir Edward served as Commissioner of the Metropolitan Police between 1890 and 1903.

The Ransomed Miracle
by I.A. Watson

The ransom note was written in squared block capitals on cheap common stationary, delivered in a plain envelope by third post. It read:

> *IF YOU WISH TO SEE THE CHILD ALIVE THEN YOU WILL VOTE AGAINST THE WORKMAN'S COMPENSATION ACT.*
>
> *INSTRUCTIONS WILL FOLLOW TO PAY £2000 AFTER THE VOTE.*

Holmes examined the letter with his magnifying lens, held the paper up to the light, then smelled the correspondence.

"Well?" Inspector Farmer asked anxiously.

"You must be patient," Inspector Bradstreet advised the local officer. "Mr. Holmes has his methods and takes his time. He cannot be rushed."

I covered my hand with my mouth to hide the amused quirk of my lips at the Scotland Yard man's words. Bradstreet was one of the old-school policemen who had started out running in Bow Street. I was amused to hear him speaking so familiarly of the consulting detective to whom the Metropolitan Police so reluctantly but persistently resorted.

There was little else to be amused about. Eighteen-month-old Samuel Deverill was missing from his cot, abducted by night from a locked and sealed house. His life was feared for. The ransom note had been delivered in the time between Bradstreet convincing the Somerset constabulary to send for Holmes and our arrival by train at St. Ethelreda's Manor [1] in sleepy Quantoxhead, Somerset.

"Will Mr. Deverill accede to the demands?" I had asked the investigators in charge of the case when they had produced the message.

"Deverill is so distraught that it is hard to know what he will do," Farmer responded. "As a Member of Parliament, he must be above such pressure, whatever the threats. He cannot go against his party and its whip [2] without serious consequences, especially on so controversial and marginal a vote as for the Workman's Compensation Act. [3] It would break him. But so would losing the boy."

Holmes had declined to speak to the desperate MP and his wife until he had examined the primary evidence. We now stood in the empty nursery while Holmes evaluated the ransom document.

Since Bradstreet was taking my customary role of keeping the local police inspector in check while Holmes worked, I took the opportunity of looking round the neat bedroom from which young Samuel had been snatched. The chamber was one of three south-facing rooms on the first floor, above the dining room. It had two Georgian windows of the type that shuttered at night, and they had been sealed and locked at the time the child was found missing. The main furniture apart from the barred crib from which Samuel had vanished were a nursemaid's bed, a pair of chests of drawers, a wardrobe filled with child's clothes and toys, a rocking chair, and a large rocking horse.

I drifted over to inspect those internal shutters. They folded back concertina-fashion into the deep recesses at each side of the windows. When closed, there was a bar that swivelled down to secure them in place, with a small hasp through which a padlock was threaded to prevent the bar being lifted. No burglar who somehow jimmied the window-sash could even reach the lock, and the keys for the padlock remained with the family butler who secured the house every night.

From the window, I had a fine view over the snow-frosted landscape, across the fields and woodland that formed part of the estate and to the start of the Quantock Hills. Westward past the trees I could glimpse the bleak silver strand of the Bristol Channel.

I checked the chimney as best I could. At this time of year a small fire still blazed in the grate. Just above the upper level of the hearth was a "pigeon trap", a metal grill fastened across the broad chimney to prevent stray birds from intruding. I did not need to be Sherlock Holmes to see the depth of soot crusting the bolts that held the ironwork in place to know that it hadn't been opened in the recent past.

Nor need I search the wardrobe or other containers. Enthusiastic searchers had already pulled out every toy and garment, hunting for the missing boy. Contents were roughly scattered over the carpet. I suspected that the nursemaid would not appreciate how clumsy officers of the law had rifled and then casually tossed aside the intimate contents of her private linen drawer.

There was but one door, out onto the landing above the main entrance hall. All the family and guest rooms of the upper floor opened onto this one balcony, except for two box rooms that were accessed via the servants' stair that extended to attics where the house's domestics slept. That layout was significant too. The butler locked the intervening door to the back stairs at night, suggesting that no member of the household staff except the nursemaid should have access to the main part of the mansion after lights-out.

The nursery door had a rim lock on the inside, but it hadn't been fastened at the time the kidnapping was discovered. Why would such a precaution be considered necessary?

Holmes stirred from his examination. "The man who wrote this note," he announced without preamble, "was right-handed, of some but limited education, probably of around thirty years of age. He may be known to the family. The stationary was purchased recently, especially for the purpose of sending this message. The ink-type is cheap and common, but note that amongst its uses is the filling of inkwells in public venues such as Post Offices. The message was written shortly before it was sealed into the envelope. The envelope was addressed after the letter was placed inside."

Bradstreet's brows rose. "Come now, Mr. Holmes. You will have to explain how you might possibly make such assumptions!"

"Not assumptions," I assured the Scotland Yard officer.

"Hardly," Holmes agreed. "Must I show you what is quite obvious to anyone who takes the time to view the letter with an analytical care? Very well. The writing on the note is by metal-tipped ink pen, the old-fashioned sort requiring one to continually dip it into a reservoir. It has a broad nib that cants, depending on whether it is held left or right handedly. Determining which it was is child's play."

Farmer looked suspicious of such conclusions. Bradstreet rather resembled a fellow to whom the obvious had now been pointed out to him after he had missed it.

Holmes continued his lecture. "The use of capitals, possibly intended to disguise a hand that might otherwise be recognised, is also valuable in determining the age and education of the writer. The choice of how to render the capitals *A*, *G*, *K*, *N*, *M*, and *Y* are all telling. Examples of all of those characters appear in the letter before us. Fashions of writing vary, but for most people they are set from the time they first learned their *A-B-C*'s, and from those variations one may glean an inkling of the age of the author – or at least the age at which he was taught his letters. Female writers tend to different pressures on the pen than male ones and are often taught a more flowing, 'feminine' hand."

Bradstreet might have cut in, but Holmes hadn't finished. "Professional secretaries and clerks become more precise in their execution of script over time. Regular writers become somewhat sloppier as constant repetition makes handwriting less neat. On this letter, I see signs of a man taught literacy some score or more years ago who has written in pen since then with less frequency than one would expect if he were a more educated fellow."

"And the other guesses?" Farmer pressed. "About the Post Office and such?"

"Hardly guesses, Inspector. The recent purchase of the envelope is indicated by its faint odour of lilacs. It has been shelved or racked beside scented stationary, suggesting it was on sale somewhere. The scent would have faded if it had been long separated from it shelf-mates. The use of cheap standard ink of the kind put out as a courtesy to members of the public who need to use one of the pens chained to a shop desk suggests but does not prove the note was written at a Post Office – probably the Central Taunton branch indicated by the letter's postal mark.

"That the letter was posted immediately may be proved by examining the traces of ink from folding the paper before it had been adequately blotted and allowed to dry. There is a particular imprint where pressure was placed upon the envelope to stick on the stamp, and lesser signs where the pen pressed onto the envelope when the address was written while the note was folded inside. We might possibly infer that the writer was in haste to prepare and send his note to catch the third post. Enquiries at Taunton might establish a description of someone who rushed at the last minute to get a newly-written letter into the mail sack."

"We will . . . we'll see to that immediately," Inspector Farmer promised, astonished at this sudden lead in his investigation. He hastened from the room to pass on instructions.

Holmes turned his gaze upon the cot. In particular he was interested in two grooves rubbed into the varnish around the base of the box between two of the vertical bars. "What do you make of these?" he asked Bradstreet and me.

The twin marks were scarcely visible, each a minor scrape on the curved bevel of the wooden tray that held the cot mattress. They were about an inch apart, up near where the child's head would have settled. "I confess I'm baffled," I told Holmes.

"Some kind of . . . of . . . ." Bradstreet attempted, but he too could think of nothing that would explain the abrasions.

Holmes declined to offer any help to satisfy our curiosity. Instead, he cast about the room, pausing once to examine the carpet beside the maid's bed and a second time to look at the sad tangle that had been left when the constabulary had emptied out the contents of the nursemaid's knitting basket. Finally he looked at the hearth much as I had done, except he also took the rake and pulled some ash from under the firegrate.

"List the members of the household and then summarise events as they have been established," he told Bradstreet, while he fixed a jeweller's lens to his eye to inspect the fireplace cinders. "Be precise about times."

The Scotland Yard inspector referred to his notebook. "Let's see. The family consists of Mr. and Mrs. Deverill, Mrs. Deverill's widowed mother Mrs. Swift, the missing boy Samuel who is not yet two, and a nine-year-old sister Veronica. Additionally there are seven staff: A butler and his wife the cook, a footman-driver, two general maids, a page, and Miss Clementine, the nursemaid who sleeps here in the nursery with her charge. Mr. Deverill is the local Member of Parliament, a coming man in his party."

"They are all present and accounted for?" I checked. After all, someone must have unlocked the house to allow the child to be extracted.

"All are here and being questioned. As to times, young Master Samuel was put to bed around six-fifteen last night. He was somewhat colicky and was given a spoon of watered brandy to settle him. Miss Clementine remained with him as he slept, keeping watch from her chair. She did not leave the room before she retired at around nine-forty p.m., and she slept soundly until she was suddenly woken at around twenty-past-four this morning."

I noticed that there was a carriage clock on the mantel, so presumably the nursemaid's attestations about time would be accurate.

"Mistress Veronica was sent to bed at seven-thirty. Her grandmother went up and read to her, leaving her tucked up at ten-past-eight. The adult family met in the small lounge for a light supper at eight-thirty and then retired by nine-fifteen. It is Mr. Deverill's custom to retire early when he is in the country unless he is entertaining. Sleddow, the butler, locked up the house and put out the light by nine-fifty."

"Was he alone or assisted?" Holmes demanded.

"Alone. He is also the only key-holder, apart from a set that is locked in an escritoire drawer in Mr. Deverill's bedroom."

"How secure is the house?" I wondered. "Could a burglar enter without a key?"

Trust a Scotland Yard man to have checked for that, at least. "All the windows were shuttered and locked. Evidently the wind comes in fiercely off the Bristol Channel and the house is draughty unless it is properly sealed. There are three external doors, all of which were bolted as well as locked. The chute into the coal cellar has an internal padlock. I don't say but that a skilled burglar couldn't break his way into St. Ethelreda's Manor, but he could not do so without leaving traces of a forced entry."

That point made, Bradstreet continued his history. "Miss Clementine was woken by some noise. At first she thought it was 'Little Sam' coughing. She rose to check that the child was alright, uncovering a night-light that she keeps burning for such a purpose. That was when she discovered that he was not in his cot."

327

"What did she do?" I asked.

"At first she hoped that either Mrs. Deverill or Mrs. Swift had come into the nursery and taken the child to sleep with them for some reason. She therefore looked in first upon the old lady, and on finding her sound asleep she ventured to disturb her employers. Mrs. Deverill was alarmed to hear that the boy had vanished. A quick check was made that Veronica had not for some reason taken her baby brother to sleep with her, in vain. At this point the alarm was sounded – that is, the dinner gong that warns of fire or emergency – and the whole household assembled."

"I imagine so." I could well picture the spreading panic as family and staff searched the premises trying to understand where the missing child had gone. What greater nightmare is there than this?

"The house was found to be secure." Bradstreet paused to add, "That's what makes it certain to be an inside job, of course. Only one of the occupants of the house could have snatched the child, unbolted and unlocked a door or window to hand him out, and then sealed it again as if nothing had happened."

Holmes was less interested in the detective's conclusions than in his facts. "Times and events," he scolded Bradstreet.

"Yes, well . . . By ten-to-five it was clear that the boy had been taken. Mr. Deverill raised the alarm with his field labourers and grounds staff, who live in a row of cottages down the hill there. He had them start searching the grounds and gardens, and he sent off a man for the local constable, and also a rider to Taunton to summon a police inspector. He was . . . well, they remembered the Road Hill House tragedy."

The Scotland Yard veteran's voice dropped as he mentioned one of the Detective Branch's earliest and darkest cases. I wasn't familiar with the events he remembered, being a tender seven years of age at the time they occurred.

Holmes, that very compendium of crime, saw my confusion and enlightened me. "On the night of 29th June, 1860, four-year-old Francis 'Saville' Kent vanished from a room where he slept with his nursemaid in a locked house. After a desperate search, his body was recovered from the cesspit of an outhouse privy. He had been stabbed and his throat was cut so deep as to almost behead him. The atrocity was reported by the press and garnered national interest and revulsion. An inspector of the then-new Detective Branch at Scotland Yard was dispatched to investigate. He uncovered a number of unsavoury things regarding members of the household, including adultery and abuse, but eventually concluded that the culprit was the boy's sixteen-year-old half-sister, Constance."

"No!" I gasped. "Surely not!"

"That was what the general public said then, too," Bradstreet told me bitterly. "A common policeman imputing such wickedness on a sweet young lady of quality? There was public uproar and the case was dismissed. The detective was broken, his reputation lost. But five years later, Constance Kent's priest confessor convinced her to come forward and own up to her crimes."

"Yes," Holmes said heavily, but did not elucidate. [4]

I could see why the present circumstances at St. Ethelreda's Manor might raise ghosts for a senior Scotland Yard man of Bradstreet's vintage. "Has the outhouse been checked?" I asked hesitantly.

"It has," Inspector Farmer confirmed, returning to the nursery. "I've had men in waders down there sluicing it out since this morning. Never have constables been so relieved to grope around in such foetid slurry and find nothing."

Holmes rose from the hearth and stalked out to the landing. "The room can tell us nothing more, Watson," he called to me. "Let us see what we shall learn from the people!"

"That family tree is not quite right," Mrs. Swift advised me as I tried to take notes. "Little Samuel is actually the son of Edward's older brother, not . . . Oh, give me your paper here. Look!"

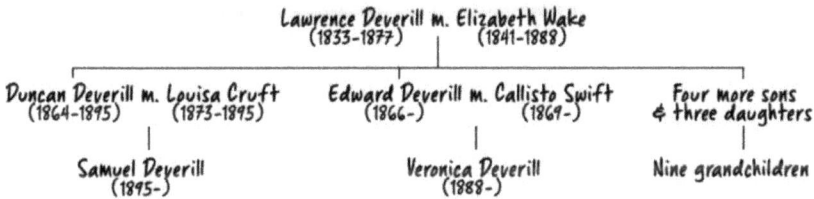

Lawrence Deverill m. Elizabeth Wake
(1833-1877) | (1841-1888)

Duncan Deverill m. Louisa Cruft | Edward Deverill m. Callisto Swift | Four more sons
(1864-1895) (1873-1895) | (1866-) (1869-) | & three daughters

Samuel Deverill | Veronica Deverill | Nine grandchildren
(1895-) | (1888-)

"You see? Duncan was the older brother, married to Louisa Cruft of those Crufts – you know, the Hampshire shipping people. Poor Duncan! He died of one of those horrid tropical diseases while he was visiting his Caribbean holdings. He never even knew that his wife back home was pregnant. And Louisa took the news of his death very badly. She became sick, and she didn't survive more than half-an-hour after childbirth. So Edward and my Cally, they adopted poor Samuel and made him their own."

"Samuel and Veronica are cousins by birth but siblings in law," I understood.

"That's right. She is very fond of him. You have no idea how upset she is about all this."

"You have the room next to the nursery," Holmes said to the old woman. "Did you hear or see anything unusual last night, before you were woken by the alarum?"

"I have trouble sleeping," Mrs. Swift confided, "and so the doctor has prescribed me a little medication. One spoonful puts me right out and it takes an earthquake to wake me. Or, last night, Cally shaking me to ask if I knew where Little Sam was."

"You didn't hear the nursemaid looking in first to see if the child was with you?"

"I'm also getting a little deaf. I wish I could tell you anything useful, Mr. Holmes, but really . . . all I can do is plead with you to find these monsters who have taken Sam!"

"It is a nightmare. A nightmare!" the Right Honourable Edward Deverill MP told us when Holmes interviewed him. His hand shook, almost spilling the whisky in his glass. "What am I to do?"

"You may begin by answering my questions clearly and precisely," my friend told him. "Begin with what you saw and heard last night."

"I saw nothing, heard nothing!" Deverill cried in anguish. "I saw Sam being taken up to bed. He was fussing and irritable and I was . . . I was pleased to have some peace and quiet! Lord . . . ! And then I knew naught until I was woken by Susan in the middle of the night."

"You had no inkling that the boy might be at risk?"

"No. Who would do such a . . . ?" The MP paused. "I should have known, of course. Samuel is rich in his own right. Richer than me."

"He is adopted, your brother's son," I observed.

"Yes. Of course we took him in, made him our own. But from his mother's legacy he will one day be a rich man." Deverill hesitated before daring to add, "If only we can get him back."

"The ransom note asked for a massive sum," Holmes mentioned. "Do you have two-thousand pounds available to meet the demand?"

"Of course not. My resources are quite tied up – in commerce, in land, in property. If I liquidated them all, I would still struggle to meet the amount, and it would take months."

"You said that Samuel also had some wealth," I noted. "Perhaps that is what the kidnapper is depending upon?"

"Then he is grievously in error. When Duncan married, his bride's family settled upon the newlyweds an income for life, a very substantial bequest and an annual bursary to support a daughter of the wealthy Crufts. In the event of her decease, the legacy passed to any extant issue – Samuel. But until Sam comes to majority, he cannot dispose of any assets from the bequest or draw more than the stipulated annual income."

"You are his guardian and trustee?"

"Indeed. But I cannot dispose of his estate, even to meet a ransom demand."

"And if the child dies?" Holmes enquired ruthlessly with no regard for Deverill's feelings.

"Then the bequest lapses. The estate, all entailments, revert to the Crufts."

Holmes allowed that revelation to sit, and now asked, "How vital is your support of the Workman's Compensation Bill likely to be?" [5]

Deverill dropped his head into his hands and used language unbecoming a member of the House of Commons. "If I don't toe the party line, there will be hell to pay! The Whip will come down on me like the Hammer of God. I'll be done, cast out, if this vote fails because of me. And it may be that marginal!"

"Do you believe this abduction to be political in nature, Holmes?" I asked worriedly. Tempers were running high about the issues, with thundering leaders in the national newspapers and demonstrations in the capital. It was not too hard to imagine some radical or reactionary deciding to force the issue by threatening an infant.

"It seems to be," the great detective answered. "However, my enquiries have far from run their course."

It was some time before Mrs. Deverill was calm enough to speak to us. "My angel! My sweet Sammy!" she moaned through her tears. "What has become of him?"

"That is what we endeavour to discover," Holmes told her severely. "The most useful practical thing you could do would be to render your testimony."

I offered a gentler persuasion, and between us Holmes and I drew out her account of the night before. The only new information was that Mrs. Deverill was accustomed to walking around the house before bed, checking on the security of the doors and windows. "You hear such terrible things about burglars and beggars," she told us. "Edward thought me silly to worry so, but . . . look!"

Also of interest was the almost-vicious way in which the lady of the house assigned blame on Miss Clementine. "If Samuel were to be discovered this minute, I would still want her out of my house!" Mrs. Deverill declared. "Gone without references! How could she have slept through my angel being stolen? No – this is too much, too far! She must go!"

"This is too far?" I repeated. "It is not the first time that you have found fault with the nursemaid?"

"We have had significant trouble finding a reliable girl. This will be the third such person I have had to dismiss."

"What faults did you find?" I wondered.

Mrs. Deverill stiffened defensively. "I'm sure that is a domestic matter of no concern to your investigation," she assured us.

"I would prefer to decide that for myself," Holmes interjected, interested now.

"Impertinence and overfamiliarity," the lady of the house declared, then clarified that she was referring to the nursemaids, not to our questioning. "Polly, the first, came with excellent testimonials, but proved to not know her place in a respectable household. Emma was the second and I had suspicions about her honesty."

"I cannot assist you in the matter of your missing child if you offer me evasions and untruths, Mrs. Deverill," Holmes insisted sternly. "The facts, if you please!"

Callisto Deverill blanched at his challenge, but it is very difficult to resist the penetrating gaze of Sherlock Holmes. "Polly was being overfamiliar with Edward," she reluctantly admitted. "Or he with her," she added bitterly. "I dismissed her in favour of a less attractive nursemaid."

"Ah." I understood the lady's reluctance to explain the circumstances. "And Emma?"

"Less attractive evidently does not mean unattractive," Mrs. Deverill spat.

"But you have no reason to suspect Susan Clementine?"

"I have no evidence of any irregularity. But that does not mean that my husband has not succumbed to his weakness. In any case, the girl has proved unreliable in the one thing she is here for, caring for Sammy. My angel is lost! Lost!"

It took some time for us to calm Mrs. Deverill again enough to continue with the interview. At last Holmes was able to ask, "You mentioned your habit of walking the house before retiring. Did you also visit the nursery last night to look in on Samuel?"

"Of course I did. My angel was unwell yesterday, suffering from colic. I had the doctor to him in the afternoon. I went up to check that Little Sam was settled at last."

"And was he?" I enquired.

"He was fast asleep, curled in his crib. Susan was sat beside him in the rocking chair, knitting. She had the impertinence to lift a finger to her lips to entreat me to silence so as not to disturb my angel – as if a mother does not know such a thing! I watched him breathe for a while, tucked under his sheets in his little frilled cap and gown, and then went to bed. And then . . . we were woken by . . . by . . . ."

332

She became distraught again, and had little else to offer Holmes's investigation.

Miss Clementine was an attractive young woman in her mid-twenties. I could understand why Mrs. Deverill might harbour suspicions about her husband around so neat and bright a person. But this nursemaid was a few years more mature than the previous incumbents and struck me as less naive and susceptible to seduction. She had also borne up tolerably well to the interrogations of Inspectors Farmer and Bradstreet.

"Must I tell my story again?" she asked us with a hint of weariness. "Well, if it helps. I brought Sammy up to the nursery just after the hall clock had chimed the quarter-hour after six. I gave him the teaspoonful of brandy-and-water that Dr. Finland had prescribed and settled the lad in his cot. I sang to him for a short while, but he was soon asleep. Then I settled down to watch over him, occupying myself with some knitting. After Mrs. Deverill's customary visit I got ready for bed and retired – that would be around ten-past-ten, shortly after Mr. Sleddow had come around and locked up. I had already closed the window shutters, of course, but he brings the padlocks that fasten them tight overnight. I read a little and was asleep by ten-thirty."

"This is your regular routine?" checked Holmes.

"With small variances depending upon Sammy's moods, yes. Except for Tuesdays, which is my half-day, when one of the housemaids looks after him until I come back on duty."

"You were woken at four-twenty," Holmes prompted his witness.

"Or a minute or two before. I thought I heard a cough. I may have been dreaming."

"The child's cough?"

"I assumed so at the time. Who else would it be?"

"It might have been a member of the family," Holmes suggested.

Miss Clementine's mouth tightened. "I have previously made it clear to Mr. Deverill that night-time visits are not part of my duties," she told us curtly.

"I'm sorry that you had to make such a statement," I told her. It was a problem too common in certain affluent households.

"It was just a matter of being firm. I gather that previous staff have lacked such resolution. You will note that Mr. Sleddow customarily locks the door to the servants' stair at night. But Mr. Deverill also has a set of keys."

"Might anyone else of the staff have access to the keys?" Holmes wondered.

Miss Clementine considered the matter. "Well, Mrs. Sleddow would presumably be able to get to Mr. Sleddow's bunch, but I don't know that any of the others could. If Mr. Deverill was visiting the servants' rooms and had his keys with him, then I suppose that might possibly allow a wax imprint to be made, but I do not think that probable."

Holmes had more questions for the nursemaid: Whether she had observed anyone taking a special interest in Little Samuel while he was promenaded in his carriage, whether anyone had attempted to strike up a conversation about the household or its routine, how much was generally known about the child's legacy . . . and what she was knitting last night when Mrs. Deverill had visited.

Miss Clementine seemed as puzzled as I was at that last enquiry. "It was a cardigan jumper for my sister's child," she answered. "You will see the remains of it over the nursery floor, all dropped stitches and pulls after the police cast it aside in their searches. I'm . . . not sure how that helps your investigation."

"I was trying to understand why you would burn a quantity of cotton-wool and eiderdown in your hearth yesterday," my friend revealed to her. "I found the ash. Neither of those things are components of an infant's jumper."

The nursemaid's eyes widened in surprise, "But how could you know . . . ? But then, you are the famous consulting detective of Dr. Watson's accounts. Well, if you must know, I suffer from extremely heavy monthly discharges." [6] She blushed. "The cotton wool and down were contents of my hygiene bags."

Holmes was unembarrassed by his interrogation. "Thank you, Miss Clementine. That is a very helpful explanation."

"Do you think you will be able to find Little Sam?" the nursemaid asked anxiously.

"Holmes is rarely thwarted," I assured her, but she seemed little comforted.

Sleddow was a short, stooped man who had been in service to Mr. Deverill senior and to Mr. Duncan Deverill before coming to work for Mr. Edward Deverill after the older brother's demise. More properly, he had remained in service at St. Ethelreda's Manor when the property had passed to young Samuel Deverill.

"I noticed nothing unusual when I locked up, sirs," he assured us. "Everything went just as always. The house was quiet until Mr. Deverill rang the dinner gong to summon assistance."

"Who responded first?" Holmes wanted to know. "Details, man, details!"

Sleddow considered the question. "It took me a moment to get my boots on," he confessed. "By the time I got to the servant's stair with Mrs. Sleddow, the rest of the staff were on their way down – excepting Miss Clementine of course, who sleeps in the nursery. We passed through the connecting door and all entered the hall together. Mr. and Mrs. Deverill were already there with Susan. Mrs. Swift was attending upon Miss Veronica in her room, making certain that she was alright."

"A thorough search was made of the house then?" I expected.

"Very thorough, sir. The footman and I even climbed into the attics and unlocked the cellars. Mrs. Deverill had us turn out every closet and trunk, even the old cobwebbed packing cases in the wine cellar. We couldn't understand how young Master Samuel could have left the manor, you see. Not without an abductor leaving footprints."

Holmes looked up sharply. "There was snow on the ground. You looked for traces of passage?"

"Yessir. Me and Mr. Deverill, we were the first to walk the perimeter of the property while the farmhands were being summoned. It had snowed lightly in the night, just enough to frost the ground, but we were leaving treads right enough. We didn't see any sign of other prints, such as a burglar might leave, whatever way they got into or out of the place."

"You are certain you saw no tracks?"

"Not at front door, back door, terrace door, or under any of the windows. The coal hatch was frosted over. For that matter, now I think on it, so were the joints of the window sashes. It should have been obvious if any were opened, if anyone had passed through them."

Holmes cradled his fingers and stared at them for a few moments. Then he returned to his questions. "You served in this house when it belonged to Mr. Duncan Deverill and his wife. Has the establishment changed much since then?"

"Not substantially," the butler judged. "The present Mr. and Mrs. Deverill were frequent guests, being as he was standing for election hereabouts. When Mr. Duncan Deverill went on his Caribbean business voyage and Mrs. Duncan Deverill discovered that she was with child, and later when word came of her husband's illness and passing, Mrs. Edward Deverill stayed to keep her company in her confinement."

"She was present during the tragedy of the childbirth, then?"

"Yessir. The midwife said there was nothing could be done to save the lady. It is a miracle that the boy survived. That was the words they used – miracle child. An angel blessed on us in time of tragedy."

"Samuel was not expected to live, then?" I surmised.

335

"The prognosis was always that it would be a difficult birth, and Mrs. Deverill's declining health and morale were additional complicating factors."

"What would have happened to the Cruft legacy settled upon Claire Deverill had Samuel not survived?" Holmes probed.

"I believe the balance of the assets would have reverted to the Cruft estate, sir. There was some loose talk of it both above and below stairs as Mrs. Deverill's time of delivery approached and her life was in balance. But then Master Samuel survived – a miracle!"

"And if the boy dies now?" the detective continued ruthlessly.

"I believe the legacy still reverts to the Crufts," Sleddow admitted.

I glanced over at Holmes. Here was another motive for kidnap – or worse. Some member of those Hamptonshire Crufts might do very well out of the demise of the missing infant.

My friend had other concerns to raise with the butler, though. "There have been some staff difficulties during Mr. Edward Deverill's ownership of St. Ethelreda's," he noted. "Miss Clementine is the third children's nurse in eighteen months."

Sleddow blanched. "Those were matters outside the scope of this investigation, sir."

"I'll define the scope of my investigation, Mr. Sleddow," Sherlock Holmes warned him. "You are aware of your master's nocturnal wanderings?"

"I can't discuss such things, sir."

"A politician must appear beyond reproach," I recognised, "but a child's life may be at stake here. That must count for something. Come, Sleddow. Get your priorities straight, man!"

It took us a while to winkle the sordid facts out of the butler, but at last he admitted the liaisons between master and maids. "That's why I started locking the servants' door," he confessed.

"But Deverill has a spare key," I pointed out.

"Yessir," the butler replied dispiritedly. "I believe however that the master's bunch is now kept in the bedroom escritoire – to which only Mrs. Deverill keeps a key."

"What happens in case of fire?" Holmes enquired. "If all the exits are sealed, how could anyone escape?"

"When the gong is sounded twice together we are all expected to assemble in the hall. If the clamour is instead continuous, I am to get the staff out by opening the rear external door at the base of the servants' stair, and then come round to unlock the other doors from outside."

"So there is scant chance of Mr. Deverill unsealing the servants' interior door last night?" I recognised. "What of duplicate keys?"

336

Sleddow could say nothing of any such facsimile. He was reluctant to discuss details of his master's nocturnal perambulations. My hopes of a breakthrough in the investigation diminished.

But Sherlock Holmes seemed satisfied with the interview.

Constable Whatley had been the first police officer on the scene, being the local man based in nearby Quantoxhead. He opened up his pocket notebook, flipped to the relevant page, and outlined his actions.

"I was knocked up at 6:12 by John Claridge, sirs, 'im being one of the farm 'ands at St. Ethelreda's, sent down to summon aid. I proceeded with him up to the manor, arriving at 6:24, by which time there was quite a search going on for the missing tyke – Master Samuel Deverill, that is. I interviewed Mr. Deverill and the nursemaid and took a look at the nursery myself, conducting a quick search."

It seemed that Whatley had been responsible for the damage to Miss Clementine's jumper-cardigan-in-progress. Holmes asked some clarifying questions about the scene. "Was the fire lit? Were the cot-sheets in place, or had they been removed?"

Whatley frowned to remember. "There was a bit of a fire – mostly embers, like it 'ad burned down over the night. It 'adn't been banked up again, if that's what you mean. And the crib? It was all neat and tidy as you please, like they'd made it ready for the baby to be put back in when they found 'im."

That seemed odd. A distraught nursemaid on finding her charge missing would hardly halt to make up his bed, and at the time the police constable had arrived, the search for the missing Sammy was still in full halloo. Did that indicate that the abductor had paused to smooth down the quilts as he took the boy away?

"You interviewed Deverill and Miss Clementine," Holmes observed. "No, don't bother trying to report that. Give me your notebook and let me read the account you recorded at the time. Hmm, I see that the nursemaid was somewhat distressed."

"Quite naturally, sir," Whatley pointed out. "Especially being as Mrs. Deverill as much as accused her of allowing the child to be taken, or of being part of the plot. I know that Inspector Farmer is something of that opinion too."

The constable stifled a yawn and looked embarrassed. He had been on the scene from the time he had been called in the small hours up till almost noon, and had then been ordered back to be interviewed by Holmes. He could scarcely have had three hours sleep in between.

"You cycled some distance along the road past the manor," Holmes read from the policeman's notes. "You were looking for the 'Peggles Camp'."

"Oh yes. Them Peggly Gypsies is well-known for stealing away babies," Whatley informed us. "Beggars and tinkers and puppet-show men, out for what they can get and no better than they should be! They'd moved on from where they'd been squatting when I got there – run off in the night, like as. I don't doubt but what the Inspector'll 'ave the whole county force out looking for them."

"I don't doubt it either," Holmes agreed. "Nor do I imagine he will have any explanation as to how the missing boy picked a window lock, flew out of his nursery, fastened the shutters behind him, then ran away to join the Romanys. But it won't stop him wasting time and manpower on the matter. Tell me, were there any traces of the Gypsies' passage in the snow? Or had they already packed up and left before that?"

The policeman had to allow that there was no sign that camp had been struck after dusk.

"Were there any other tracks on the road past the manor?" I wondered. "Before all the circus of the search spread that far, I mean?"

"Nothing I noticed, Doctor, but it was still dark when I rode out." Whatley stifled another yawn.

We let him retire to his interrupted repose.

"I hold that it was the nursemaid," Farmer insisted. "How could anyone creep into her room and abduct an infant – a colicky infant who had cried for much of the day, at that – without awakening a girl sleeping less than ten feet away? She was in the pay of the abductors, you mark my words, and when we investigate her, we shall uncover it!"

Holmes had already sent off a slew of telegrams, including those that might check Miss Clementine's references and establish her character. He frowned slightly at the local inspector's hasty conclusion.

"It's not necessarily her," Bradstreet argued. "This is political. It's not just about money, it's about perverting the course of Parliament. There are powerful concerns out there that have set themselves against the Workplace Compensation Act, and some of them have plenty of money and fewer scruples than they should. In London we encounter professional cracksmen and housebreakers who can sneak into anywhere, seemingly by magic. I expect that Mr. Holmes can think of half-a-dozen specialists who might infiltrate St. Ethelreda's Manor without ever betraying their intrusion and be away with the babe. As for the bairn not waking, he had been given brandy to help him slumber."

"If it is political, then that same money could have been used to suborn a domestic," Farmer countered. "We know that any of them might have wandered the house if they had obtained keys at any time in the past eighteen months. That is all that was required to extract young Samuel. We shall be looking carefully at the two dismissed nursemaids also, for either of them might have a grudge that could be exploited and might also have taken key-copies for their own use."

"Neither of you has explained how the child could be taken without leaving footprints in the snow," I reminded them. "Evidently the light fall began about half-past-nine, just before the house was secured, and continued until after everyone was asleep."

"The child might still be in the house," Bradstreet mentioned ominously. "An old place like this, there might well be a priest hole [7] or other secret place. If the boy isn't traced soon, I shall insist that we rip off the wainscoting and search for such a hidden chamber."

Holmes had also conducted a measured survey for such things and was satisfied that no such lost room existed.

"If your kidnappers are so professional, then why demand so unrealistic a sum?" Farmer challenged the Scotland Yard man. "Why seek an amount so large that it cannot be raised? That smacks of an amateur effort, say from a servant with a grudge."

"Or the ransom is a distraction," I suggested. "Remember that there is a fiduciary motive for the poor boy's death. The note might be to make us believe we are dealing with an abduction, when we are actually facing a heinous murder."

Holmes shifted in his chair. I perceived that he was not entirely in agreement with my assessment.

"It is the better part of a day since Little Sammy's loss was discovered," despaired Farmer. "He might be anywhere by now."

"It is snowing again," Bradstreet added gloomily. "If the boy has been hidden somewhere in the nearby countryside, a sick child exposed to the elements . . . ."

"We can only hope for more correspondence from the abductors," I suggested. "If they set a time and place to receive the money they demand, then we might set a trap."

"But first Mr. Deverill must throw his vote in the House the day after tomorrow," Bradstreet objected.

"We should put Susan Clementine in a cell until she talks," Farmer recommended.

"We should wait patiently until I receive answers to my enquiries," Holmes interrupted us. "All that should be done had been set in motion.

Only one thing remains. Watson and I must interview Miss Veronica Deverill."

"Do you understand what is happening?" I asked Veronica carefully.

The pigtailed girl sat on a cushion in the bay window of her bedroom, surrounded by her toys and doll's house and an elaborate doll's crib complete with porcelain baby. She regarded us solemnly and nodded.

"Tell us," I urged her, to make sure.

"Little Sammy has run away," she confided. "Everyone is looking for him. I don't suppose he packed any lunch."

"Run away," I repeated. "But he is too small to walk."

"That makes no difference," the child told me. "Golly couldn't walk, but he ran away."

"Golly?" I asked, puzzled.

Veronica pointed to her toybox and then to a bookshelf where two colourful illustrated volumes held pride of place: *The Adventures of Two Dutch Dolls and a Golliwogg* and *The Golliwogg's Bicycle Club* by Bertha and Florence Upton. I recognised the works. They were the latest popular children's books and the main character in them, a clever black-faced fellow with frizzy hair and red lips, had become the soft toy of choice. Every household that could afford it now contained a "Gollywogg", and those of limited means created homemade knitted or sewn versions of the same. [8] "Golly came last Christmas," Veronica explained, and then sadly added, "but he went away again a few days ago. Susan says it is because he is to have more adventures, and I shall read about them when his new book comes out."

"When your toy left, by what means did he depart?" Holmes asked the little girl.

"I don't know," Veronica puzzled. "He crept out at night. Like Sammy."

"It is quite possible that he did," Sherlock Holmes assured her. "Thank you for your invaluable assistance, my dear."

We spent the night at St. Ethelreda's Manor, and the morning post brought a handful of replies to Holmes's enquiries. He browsed through them over breakfast at the subdued family table. Mr. and Mrs. Deverill were not present, and Mrs. Swift ate silently and departed. Bradstreet was evidently a late riser, but then he had worked into the night with the search parties, and had even chased Whatley's gypsies.

I read the envelopes as best I could, but only one had a return address printed on it, correspondence from the National Bureau of Births, Deaths, and Marriages at Somerset House. Another came in embossed stationary

340

from a legal firm. A third bore the stamp of Sedgemoor Cottage Hospital, Bridgewater.

"I have received some useful data from a variety of sources," Holmes assured me. "I now fully understand the provisions of the Cruft bequest. I have confirmation of the governing trustees and benefactors of a number of local hospitals. I have testimonials from Miss Clementine's previous employers. I have a statement from the family's doctor in general practice. These, with the notes in P.C. Whatley's journal and the evidence of Miss Veronica Deverill, should prove sufficient to untangle this affair."

"You can recover the boy? Find the kidnapper?"

Holmes nodded and returned to his ham and Scotch eggs. He preferred not to say more until he could gather the family together with the officers who had called us in.

I tried to swallow a bite of breakfast but in truth my appetite was soured by my concern for the missing child. I knew if anyone might solve the mystery it would be my friend, but I felt sick and anxious.

"It is one thing to abduct a full-grown man," I muttered, "but a quite different thing to take a helpless child."

Holmes laid his plate aside. "My dear Watson! Your heart does you credit. Whenever I am in danger of forgetting the human element of our adventures, you are able to remind me of the true consequences beyond the intellectual puzzle."

"A workman as assiduous as yourself must sometimes be myopic," I assured him. "That is why he sometimes requires a companion to remind him of the wider world."

"And so you do, Doctor. But you are also a medical man. You know that sometimes to heal a wound, there must be cutting and blood, pain and loss for a greater gain. I fear that this case might require such a surgery."

I felt my stomach tighten. "But the boy is alive?"

"I have every reason to hope so, though I fear that restoring him to his mother will be a costly and unhappy task."

"See young Sammy safe and well, Holmes. Every decent parent would require that over any price or consequence."

Holmes turned to retrieve his breakfast. "You are my compass as well as my Boswell, Watson. I shall endeavour not to let you down – or Master Samuel."

An hour later, Holmes's assembly convened in the library. Deverill looked exhausted, as if the very hounds of Hell haunted him. Well he might, given the choice between his son and his honour, between political ruin or being turned out of his home. "I have tried to raise the sum demanded in the ransom," he informed us, "but even if I go to the Jews, I cannot raise so much in any sort of time."

Mrs. Deverill cast a despairing look at him. Her mother gripped her hand and squeezed it.

"We have questioned all the staff again," Farmer promised the family. "Even the workers in the cottages. We are seeking the gypsies who were camped nearby, but so far without any luck. They seem to have disappeared."

"I have spoken with my colleagues and superiors in the Detective Branch," Bradstreet informed us. "Suspicion is growing that there is a political motive behind all of this – maybe even a foreign power."

P.C. Whatley, obviously out of his depth and extremely uncomfortable about it, tried to blend into the wallpaper.

Also present at Holmes's request were Miss Clementine and Mr. Sleddow. The butler looked gloomy and resigned. The nursemaid was pale-faced and tense, as well she might be after the ordeal of interrogation to which she had been put. I worried that history might repeat itself and that a domestic might be scapegoated, as evidently first happened at the horrible murder at Road Hill House all those years before.

"It is time to draw back the veil on this sorry sequence of events," Holmes told us all. "I doubt that afterwards any of you will be very satisfied with the outcome, but the truth will out."

"Then the boy is . . . dead?" Farmer ventured.

Holmes was not to be rushed to his revelation. "We must go back some eighteen months to September 25th, 1895, the time of Master Samuel Deverill's birth," he began. "Mrs. Louisa Deverill, *née* Cruft, was weak and ill, devastated by her recent widowhood and the difficulties of her pregnancy. The prognosis was pessimistic. You looked over the medical notes, Watson?"

"I did," I confirmed. "It was thought, and rightly so, that Mrs. Deverill might not survive childbirth. Without going into obstetric detail, there was good reason to fear that both mother and infant might perish. For that reason a Caesarean operation was considered, despite the significant risks that would entail. However, Mrs. Deverill went into labour early before such a plan might be effected."

"A doctor and midwife from Sedgemoor Cottage Hospital attended at the birth here at St. Ethelreda's Manor," Mrs. Callisto Deverill stated.

Holmes nodded. "Quite so. Here is the certificate of birth for young Samuel, written and signed in the same hand as the certificate of death for his mother. You will see that the times are less than an hour apart."

"I don't see what this . . . ." began Farmer, but Bradstreet shushed him to silence.

342

Holmes produced another birth certificate. "At the same time that Mrs. Deverill went into premature labour here, Sedgemoor Hospital was tending to the charity case of a Miss Agnes Potter, who was likewise entering into the final stages of labour. She gave birth to a sickly baby boy who lived only minutes." The detective looked over at Mrs. Swift. "You are a patroness of Sedgemoor, I believe," he said to the old woman. "Edward Deverill is now on the board of trustees."

"That's right," the MP replied before his mother-in-law could speak.

"Within four hours of the healthy Miss Potter birthing an illegitimate son who did not live, the sickly Mrs. Deverill produced a miracle child who was healthy and whole despite the traumas of his nativity," Holmes observed. "The same two medical professionals signed all the relevant certification."

"What are you suggesting?" asked Mrs. Swift coldly.

Bradstreet could snatch a motive as well as any Scotland Yard man. "If the Deverill boy had not lived, the Cruft fortune would be lost. But an heir was provided, and so he and his fortune fell under the control of his uncle, the foster-father who adopted him and enjoys all the advantages of young Samuel's fortune."

"I do not care for your insinuations, Inspector!" Deverill thundered.

His tirade was interrupted when Holmes slammed down more papers on the table. "An examination of the banking accounts of the doctors and midwife involved will doubtless prove of profit, as will taking testimony from various staff at the cottage hospital at the time. But let us move on now to the question of Master Samuel's ransom."

The Right Honourable Edward Deverill managed to restrain his fury long enough to hear who was levering him to his political destruction.

"You see the received ransom letter here before you," Holmes told the assembly in the library. "I shared my analysis of it with the inspectors upon my arrival yesterday. In brief, it was written by someone of limited education who does not regularly write with a pen, and who knew little enough of the Cruft bequest to assume that so vast a sum might be available to redeem the child. Of course, nothing in the note offers any sort of proof that the writer actually has Samuel in his possession."

"What?" I gasped. "You mean the demand is a hoax?"

"Somebody who was aware of the boy's disappearance decided that there was a chance to make some money, Watson."

"Or to gain a political advantage," Bradstreet insisted.

"No, Inspector. That demand was by way of another subterfuge, to mask a purely financial motive. I doubt that the writer even understood the full implications of that instruction. But we can confirm that with the letter-writer, who is in this room."

Holmes's words caused consternation and speculation, even before the great detective pointed one long, sensitive finger at the corpse-pale P.C. Whatley.

"Of all the people familiar with the crisis, few left the scene or gave up the search in time to post a letter in Taunton to catch the afternoon delivery. Few are more accustomed to filling in a notebook in pencil than in using pen and ink. The message was in capitals for fear that the officers in the case might recognise their subordinate's normal script."

"No!" Whatley cried. "You're wrong! I never – !"

"A check on stationers in Taunton and at the Post Office itself should verify your presence there," Holmes told the fellow inexorably. "For myself, the dozen minute signs of guilt you are betraying now are enough to confirm your actions. However, I shall leave it to Inspector Farmer to undertake proper enquiries."

"Seb Whatley, step outside," the local inspector said in dark, wrathful tones. He saw the unfortunate, stricken constable into the hands of the other policemen in the house before returning to join the shocked throng in the library.

"If the note was not from the kidnapper, then who did take Samuel?" Mrs. Deverill almost wailed. "And how?"

"For that information we must thank Miss Veronica," Holmes revealed. "It was she who told me about the disappearance of a beloved and treasured stuffed toy some days past. I can now tell you what happened to the missing Gollywogg."

"Golly?" Miss Clementine sounded puzzled. "What has he to do with it?"

"He was required as an alibi," Holmes explained. "Or rather, he was required to donate a substantial mass of cotton wool and internal stuffing to fill out a mannequin sewn into the shape and size of the sleeping Samuel. When the puppet was dressed in the frills of the boy's night attire, he might look quite realistic, especially if someone was to operate a pair of canes under the quilts to give him the appearance of breathing. Of course, such canes might rub a mark on the varnish of the cot as they were manipulated under cover of moving knitting needles.

The nursemaid went deathly still. She swallowed hard. "Well," she said, "you are as clever as I feared, Mr. Holmes."

"I don't understand at all!" Mr. Deverill objected. "You mean that Susan abducted my son?"

"No!" the young woman protested. "I never."

"She means," Holmes explained, "that she instead *retrieved* her son. This is not the Susan Clementine to whom her references referred. That lady is actually working for the Hunter family in Birmingham, entirely unaware that someone has borrowed her identity for an adventure. Before us is Miss Agnes Potter, mother of the child who was substituted at birth for the stillborn Samuel."

"By George!" muttered Bradstreet.

Miss Clementine's – Miss Potter's – eyes flashed defiantly. "They stole my baby from me. Gave me chloroform for the pain, for an easy birth they said, and when I woke they told me that my boy was dead. They showed me his little mangled corpse. It took me a long time to find out what had really happened, where my true child had gone."

Mrs. Swift trembled and looked away. Mr. Deverill looked at his wife aghast. "Callisto . . . what have you done?"

"She tried to save you, Edward," Mrs. Swift answered for her daughter. "To save your career. To set you up in Parliament as you wished. To free you from debt and ruin. Did you never suspect?"

"You stole my baby to grab your money!" Miss Potter accused the family she had infiltrated.

"And you came to get him back," declared Holmes. "The infant was sedated with Mrs. Swift's borrowed sleeping draught and lowered from the nursery window to an accomplice before night fell, before ever the shutters were locked, before the snow fell to betray any traces of a visit. The marionette was placed in the crib so that Mrs. Deverill could attest to the child being there after all was locked up. Thereafter you need only dispose of the puppet in the hearth and all evidence of it was gone. You straightened up any trace of the apparatus when you made the bed. Then all that remained was for you to 'wake' and discover the boy was gone. By then the 'puppet-show men' – the supposed-Gypsies – were well away, taking your son to refuge with . . . a sister? The one to whom you were to send the child's jumper you prepared?"

"I'll say nothing of that," the false nursemaid told us defiantly.

"You need not," I suggested. "If Holmes is right about the boy's true parentage – and Holmes does not make errors of that kind – then you are his legal guardian. You might have gone to court and claimed him without this charade."

"With what proof?" Miss Potter demanded. "Me, a disgraced unwed mother, a poor nobody, with no money for a brief, all but a Gypsy and a tramp, against the rich and powerful Deverills and Crufts? What chance do any of you think that I would have had?"

"There is fraud here, and I don't know what other charges, as well as that fool Whatley's crimes," Bradstreet considered. "This will give the Chief Constable of Somerset a proper headache, and make my report to my superiors rather complex too."

Inspector Farmer winced at the account he would need to render. "Who do I arrest, then?" he wondered.

Sherlock Holmes declined to comment. "The boy is safe and well?" he asked Miss Potter.

"And loved," she replied. "I'll not give him up."

Holmes rose. "Then the rest is beyond the ambit of the detective sciences. Come, Watson. We shall catch the 12:59 train to London!"

NOTES

1 – St. Ethelreda (*Æthelthryth*, Audrey) was an East Anglian princess who managed to remain a virgin despite two marriages and the fierce pursuit of her ruthless and amorous second husband. Her chastity was evidently considered miraculous. The village and parish of West Quantoxhead was also called St. Audries after the saint.

2 – A whip is a voting instruction issued by a British political party to its elected members, usually requiring obedient support to some significant policy issue. Defying the whip can lead to censure or even exile from the party. Political parties also appoint elected members as enforcers, also called Whips, under a Chief Whip, whose job it is to ensure that other members "toe the party line" when a whip instruction is issued.

3 – Liberal Unionist Samuel Chamberlain's *Workman's Compensation Act* 1897 replaced the *Employer's Liability Act* 1880, changing the burden of proof for labourers injured at work so that a worker need only prove that he had been hurt on the job. It was controversial in some quarters because of fears that it might lead to employers been overwhelmed with liability claims and because it was an unfunded mandate on the private sector.

4 – The Hill House Murder was amongst the first to be widely reported as the investigation was ongoing, in an era where newspapers were first becoming powerful. Many readers wrote back to the broadsheets expounding their own theories about the case or commenting on Inspector Jack Whicher's investigation. Some literary commentators have suggested that these events created or illustrated the thirst for the genre of detective fiction that began only eight years later with *The Moonstone*. Wilkie Collins' ground-breaking mystery novel is itself set in an isolated country house with a family laden with secrets, where a working-class policeman faces difficulties because of a social gulf with his "betters".

Constance Kent's confession led to a spirited debate in the Houses of Parliament over the confidentiality of the confessional, and to claims that she was covering up for the true murderer, either her father or brother. She was eventually condemned to death but had her sentence commuted to life and served a twenty-year prison sentence. She was released from custody in 1885 at the age of forty-one and moved to Tasmania under another name. She worked as a nurse and ended up as matron of the Pierce Memorial Nurses' Home at East Maitland, New South Wales. She died at the age of one-hundred, lauded for her charitable works, good deeds, and community service.

5 – The imminence of a vote on this bill indicates that this case takes place in the first half of March 1897, just before "The Adventure of the Devil's Foot".

6 – Sherlockians familiar with Dr Watson's notes as managed by his literary agent, Sir Arthur Conan Doyle, will observe that mention of such delicate feminine issues would have been instantly red-lined by *The Strand* editor George Newnes. Whilst medical men such as Watson and Doyle might not

347

shy from mention of such bodily functions and the necessary but unspoken hygiene they required, and a nursemaid might be more practical and candid about such matters than most people, the inclusion of such a comment in our present account is a sure indicator of this story being drawn from that wealth of unpublished dispatch-box cases which were never submitted to the Victorian editor's pen.

7 – During the sixteenth-century persecution of Catholics in England, when harbouring a Catholic clergyman was considered treason and incurred a death penalty, many rich houses were equipped with small hidden rooms in which a visiting priest and religious items could be concealed from searching Protestant soldiers.

8 – American cartoonist and author Florence Kate Upton (1873–1922) published her first and second Gollywogg books in 1895 and 1896 respectively, and went on to write and illustrate eleven more entries to the series. Her character caught on quickly in Britain. The knitted and stuffed dolls with their exaggerated Negro characteristics were the most desired stocking-filler of the late nineteenth century, at a time long before concerns of racism or blackface much affected popular opinion.

Upton did not copyright or trademark her creation. The term "golliwog" quickly became a general class of toy rather than one particular character of one particular author. The prolific Enid Blyton published three books about golliwogs and added the character to her popular *Noddy* series. Robertson's jam company adopted the golliwog as their mascot. In the middle of the twentieth century, only the teddy bear topped the gollywog for cuddly toy sales.

It is only in recent years that the golliwog's popularity had declined as racial sensitivity has waxed. A 2018 *YouGov* poll in the UK recorded 20% of respondents felt that sale of golliwogs was racist, versus 63% who felt it was acceptable. Many young people do not now know about the toy, and the term "wog" is used offensively as a term of racial abuse.

The Adventure of the
Unkind Turn
by Robert Perret

It was that precious, fleeting moment in spring when the air of London was fragrant with the scent of flowers and grass rather than the bouquet of the Thames and the streets below, and thus it was that I had thrown open the windows of Baker Street, allowing Holmes and me to hear the arrival of Mr. Conrad Blevins well before he rapped upon our door. Indeed, we could hear the man rehearsing his forthcoming interview.

"What do you make of that?" I asked. "Is there some charade afoot?"

"Anyone of a duplicitous nature would have been well-rehearsed before reaching our doorstep," Holmes said, his head slightly tilted as he listened to the monologue below. "No, I rather suspect the gentleman simply prefers to take the lead."

"At this rate, you'll have solved the thing before he makes it up the stairs."

Holmes waved dismissively and turned back towards his chemistry bench. He had been working on recreating a solution that would fabricate an instant patina upon silver without actually destroying the precious metal beneath. When Mrs. Hudson discovered the fate of her wedding set she would be most displeased, I suspected. The knock came at last and soon Mr. Blevins stood before us, looking between the two of us in hopes of finding Holmes.

After a few moments, I stepped forward and extended my hand, "Doctor Watson at your service."

Blevins stepped around me. "Then you are Mr. Holmes, I take it?"

"I'm afraid that I'm previously engaged," Holmes said without looking up. "Good day."

"Why, you haven't even heard me out, sir!"

"Always beware of open windows," Holmes replied.

I gestured towards the offending portico as Blevins sputtered.

"I understood you to be a gentleman, Mr. Holmes. It seems I was misinformed."

"Grievously," Holmes smiled to himself.

"There is no justice to be had in London," Blevins said, stepping around me again and thrusting his hat upon his head.

"There no justice to be had at the card table," Holmes said.

349

Blevins spun on his heels. "What do you know of it? Cards are a matter of honor at the St. James, and yet a scoundrel like Nigel Pike is free to pick our pockets."

"This is very serious, indeed," Holmes said, sitting upright suddenly.

"What?" Blevins asked, echoing my own thoughts.

"I shall look into this little affair, after all," Holmes said. "The St. James Club, you said?"

"I'd rather you kept out of my business, now," Blevins said.

"That is entirely up to you," Holmes replied. "Whether I recover your chits, in particular, is of no concern to me."

"But you just said it was very serious!"

"I said the situation was serious, not your part in it," Holmes replied. "Leave your card with Watson. If your gaming losses happen to be recovered, he will get word to you".

Blevins angrily thrust his card at me before stomping down the stairs.

"You could be a bit more sociable than that, Holmes, even if you did not intend to take the case."

"The man was pompous and insufferable and I wanted no illusions that we are beholden to him."

"That's a bit of a quick judgment, even for you," I said.

"If he had the common courtesy to shake your hand, he might have received a different reception."

"It hardly matters."

"In any eventuality, I was sincere in my apathy towards his gambling losses."

"But something piqued your interest."

"Nigel Pike."

"The man picking Mr. Blevins pocket?"

"Hardly," Holmes said. "Nigel Pike has been dead for the last twenty-five years."

"The name is not so uncommon. A coincidence, perhaps?"

"In isolation, perhaps. But in combination with the St. James Club, it would be an awful coincidence."

"You knew Nigel Pike, then?" It was rare to see Holmes become agitated.

"Only as one of Mycroft's school peers. It would be too much to say that my brother ever had chums."

"And yet you seem greatly affected," I said.

"I was myself only just graduated, not quite yet at university when Nigel Pike died. I hadn't yet set upon detective work, and yet the case still occupies my mind. I had not been so adjacent to a death before. If only I had applied myself at the time . . . Of course, there was no way of knowing what would happen to him." Holmes slipped but momentarily into a fugue. "What matters at present is that Mr. Blevins has been visited by a ghost. How are you at whist, Watson?"

"I can't say we played much whist in the barracks."

Holmes sighed. "So be it. Is your charcoal suit pressed?"

"More or less."

"Put it on then. We are off to the Mule Club."

"But Blevins said he was pilfered at the St. James."

"Yes, but Nigel Pike was a member at the Mule. I doubt very much that any record of him exists outside of that place, save perhaps in the Pike family Bible, but I hesitate to poke at any old grief unnecessarily."

After I had donned my funeral suit and Holmes had slipped into a silk three-piece that I'd never seen before, we were soon deposited at the Mule Club, the kind of teetering hovel tucked away in a London back alley that only the exceedingly rich or the exceedingly poor enjoy. Indeed, the roof sagged so much I rather feared that closing the door too hard might bring the whole place down upon us. The stone was black with centuries of tobacco smoke. By all appearances the place was a tatty tavern, with a couple of poor fellows slouched over their drinks and a weary barkeep keeping a pained eye upon us. Without hesitation Holmes moved forward, disappearing into the shadowy recess next to the hearth. I tipped my hat to the tavern keeper as I passed, and as I stepped into the dark I found that what appeared to be a continuous wall, in fact, hid a small passage within the grime and low light. Sidestepping through and doing my very best not to press my clean suit against the walls, I suddenly found myself in an opulent chamber, with rich oak paneling and gas chandeliers. The ceiling rose far above my head, which led me to suspect that we had passed into the building behind the one we had entered from the street. Holmes was waiting impatiently and dropped his coat and hat into my arms as I approached.

A stern major-domo had appeared when Holmes turned around again.

"My apologies, sir, but this is a private club," the man said.

"My personal friend Conrad Blevins assured me that this was the establishment in London for gentlemen looking for an honest game of skill," Holmes said.

"There is no member by that name."

"Ah, Conrad. Another fine jape, I see," Holmes chuckled. "Nonetheless, I am here and ready for a rubber."

"Our groom can ferry you to another establishment. Perhaps the Army-Navy Club?"

"I have an appetite for meatier fare," Holmes said, producing a thick stack of fifty-pound notes from his pocket. "Do you not accept the Queen's currency here?"

"I really must insist . . . ." the major-domo began.

"Now, now, Carter," a man in a velvet club jacket came sweeping in. "The gentleman came all this way. Let us be hospitable. Come this way, Mr . . . ?"

"Andover," Holmes said. "Father sent me to London on some tiring business and I simply must find a way to shake off the boredom."

"Certainly, certainly. My name is Jonathan Elmwood, and I would be honored to have you as my guest this evening." He escorted Holmes to one of the gaming tables.

As I went to follow, Carter seized my arm. "Mr. Andover's servant may wait over there." He gestured to a spare wooden door at the far side of the chamber. Opening it, I found myself in a spartan room, not so run-down as the pub out front, but a far cry from the club within. I took a seat at the plain oak table that represented the only major feature of the room and strained my ears to hear what was happening outside. Jovial chuckles seeping under the door told me that Holmes was playing losing hands to ingratiate himself with the men. When a servant came bustling through the opposing door, I nearly fell from my chair.

He paused to render a stern appraisal. Apparently finding me satisfactory, he nodded to the door through which he had just passed. "Head on through." He then disappeared out into the club. Gathering myself, I did as he suggested and found myself in a rather homey space. The air was heavy with the rich scent of stew, and each door I passed was adorned with a cheery needlepoint depicting what was presumably the occupant's name. At the end of the hall, I heard the swell and bark of contented conversation. As I made my way along I soon found a small kitchen in which a groom lulled idly at a table while two girls in maid's uniformed tittered at each other. The groom was the first to see me.

"Behave yourselves, ladies," he said. "We have company."

I doffed my hat and introduced myself as Mug Sewell, manservant to Mr. Jonathan Elmwood.

"None of that here, my friend," the groom said. "My name is Norris. This here is Evy and Coraline."

The girls curtseyed deeply and then fell into hysterics.

"Join us," Norris, said. "It'll be hours until that lot are done."

"You all work here, at the Mule Club?"

"That's right," Coraline said. "Your master will be told not to bring you round again. This lot likes to keep it – well – *friendly*. Amongst their own, anyway."

"Of course no one is saying you couldn't come back for a visit on your own," Evy cooed. "Servant's door is just off the alley on Knightsbridge."

"Not through that horrible pub?" I asked.

"Oi!" Norris said. "My brother runs that pub! Horrible is too nice a word for it!"

They all burst out laughing again.

"Makes them feel real totty to pass through the slums and into opulence," Evy said.

"And the coppers won't bother to poke around in a place like that."

"I heard old King Henry was racing horsecarts in there back in his day and plowed right through the wall. To save face they all pretended the thing was intentional, bought the shack he'd barreled into, and turned that into their secret entrance. I mean, right up these stairs is the hotel. They could walk in right through the front door if they wanted."

A bell hung upon the wall jangled. Caroline and Evy played a quick game of odds-and-evens, and from the way Evy groaned I took it that she was the loser. With great pathos, she made her way up the stairs.

"Be glad you weren't born unto the fairer sex, gents," Coraline said. "I'd shovel horse leavings or split rocks all day before being a maid if I had the choice."

"It can't be as bad as all that," Norris said.

The same bell now jangled again but in bursts of two.

"It's worse than you boys can imagine," she said, taking a bag with her as she went.

"They aren't . . . being imposed upon?" I asked.

Norris laughed. "Not to worry, friend. It's an old folk home up there with the long-term residents. Besides, I wouldn't let them come to any harm. They're like sisters to me, and don't you forget it."

He jabbed me with a gnarled finger.

"I certainly have no designs," I stammered.

"More's the pity, that," he laughed. "Life is short and bitter. Besides, I think Caroline likes the looks of you."

"It seemed to me Miss Evy was the flirtatious one."

"She gets really subtle when she gets ideas," Norris said. "She's giving you the wink-and-giggle that gets the codgers to dote on her."

"I see," I said.

"Take no offense, friend. It's how the poor girl makes her way in this world." Norris leaned back and reached into a cabinet, pulling back a bottle that gave off the sweet smell of a well-aged whisky. "To new friends!" he said, taking a swig and then offering the bottle to me. I saluted the man and took a sip. It tasted of smoke and caramel and felt thick on my tongue. I found another sip before I passed the bottle back.

"Not too bad, am I right?" Norris said. "The gentlemen can't be bothered to account for their liquor, so reserves of quality find their way into appreciative hands."

The door banged open and the man who had sent me here appeared. "Norris, I hope you aren't drunk. Elmwood finds his pockets empty and he needs you to replenish his purse."

"Is there a bank open at this hour?" I wondered.

"Course not," the new man said.

"Don't let Mr. Franks's sour disposition get to you," Norris said. "He has unfulfilled ambitions and we all suffer for it."

"Mr. VanDerDyke, like many of his peers, keeps a small stash in a lockbox at the train station, which is, of course, always open."

"I'll be back before the gentleman has cause to complain," Norris said. "Help yourself to some stew. It's naught but table scraps, but consider the table and then sample the scraps." Norris laughed and was gone.

Franks, for all his chilly demeanor, ladled out two bowls of stew and placed one before me as he sat down.

"The Mule Club doesn't have a lot to recommend it as an employer, but we are likely the best-fed staff."

"Is it always like this?" I asked, sampling the truly excellent stew. "It does seem a bit out-of-hand."

"It has been like this as long as I've been here, which is most of my life. The whole affair just trundles along with no one at the rein. The proprietor, Giles Wulver, went mad with grief, you see. Lost a son and lost all interest in the ways of the world. Still lives on the top floor of the hotel, all alone. I guess his friends kept patronizing the place out of charity, paying up on their tabs and what-not, even when there was no collector calling. Some accountant somewhere keeps the payroll going, though we haven't seen a raise in all that time. That's why we've taken up living here and eating their food."

"And drinking their spirits," I said.

"Yes," Franks said. "Well, some do. We all find our little compensations,"

The bell over the main door rang.

"Duty calls," Franks said. "Norris can see your gentleman home if you have other obligations."

"I'll finish my supper, at least, and see where we stand then."

"Ta," Franks nodded before lifting his silver tray again and vanishing down the hall. I waited until I heard the door close, drank down the rest of my bowl, and got to work. Quickly I surveyed each of the staff rooms,

354

which, as Holmes predicted, were unlocked, because of course the staff had master keys. Norris's was unmistakable, and little better-kept than a stable, with pungent clothes strewn about and half-a-dozen empty bottles standing guard. The next room belonged to Carter, the major-domo, and stood in stark contrast. His leather-bound furniture and richly appointed walls were very much akin to the gaming room outside.

Caroline's room had a feminine grace to it, smelling of lilac and adorned with delicate laces. I opened Evy's door expecting to find a tawdry boudoir, but her small space had a country feel to it, freshly scrubbed and practical at every turn. I didn't have Holmes's perceptive eye, but I had yet to discover anything that pointed to serious criminal activity. I introduced myself to the domiciles of another half-dozen people that I had yet to meet with similarly unremarkable results. It was only when I came to Franks's quarters that my suspicions were roused, for unlike the all the other rooms, this one had the stale, musty aura of a room not in use. Indeed, running my finger along his pillow won me a ring of cottony dust. Just then I heard footsteps outside.

"Mr. Sewell?" came Evy's voice. "Mr. Sewell, are you here? That's a shame. I thought we were in for some fun tonight."

"Now, now, girl, you'll scare all the good ones away with your silliness and then where will you be?" Caroline said.

"Oh, he was one of the good ones, was he?"

I could hear them cackling as they passed and then were gone. I held my ear to the door and waited for a few moments. Hearing nothing I risked stepping outside again. Finding myself alone, I hurried through the back and up the stairs to the lobby of the hotel above. A man who could have been Carter's brother was at the reception desk.

"Are you a guest, sir?" he asked.

"No. Well, that is, I am here on behalf of a prospective guest," I managed.

"Is that so?"

"Yes, my employer is playing at cards downstairs, and I think he will be wanting a room."

The man gave me a searching look.

"Mr. Carter recommended it," I said.

"If you have Carter's approval then you must be alright," he said. "The gentleman's name?"

"Andover. Reginald Andover," I said. "And I am Mr. Sewell."

"Here is Mr. Andover's key," he said pointedly. "One floor up and to the right. Servant's stairs are just back there," he pointed from whence I had just come.

"Thank you," I said, taking the key and retreating. Securing a room had not been part of the plan, but something strange was going on.

I returned to the stairs and made my way up. The first floor held the room that we had been assigned. I presumed all the short term guests were lodged thus. Earlier, the maids had been summoned to the second floor, likely the home of the long-term residents. Continuing up to the third floor, only one spare light was lit at the far end of the hall. There was the unmistakable musk of abandonment. I was able to climb one more half-flight, but at the turning, there was a locked gate. I idly tried the room key, which of course was ineffective. Holmes would have to return with his lock-picks, I thought. Fearing being caught out of place, I quickly returned to the first floor and opened the door to our assigned room. It looked very much the part of a room twenty years out of date. The bedspread put me in mind of my parents, and the wallpaper had faded unto a ghost of itself. I went to the window and looked out at Knightsbridge, the evening bustle in full swing.

"Will you be staying with your master?" came a voice behind me.

I turned to find Coraline hugging a folded sets of linens and I fancied there was a blush upon her cheeks.

"Always," I replied. "He can hardly get on without me."

"They are all like that, aren't they?" she asked. She stepped forward to look out the window. "So much happens out there." She sighed.

"Might I be of assistance?" I asked, gesturing for her bundle.

"I've yet to meet the man who can dress a bed properly," she said. "You see if you can work that window open. It is dreadfully musty in here. We don't get many visitors. I brought fresh sheets, knowing that the ones already present will be stale with age."

"It is most kind of you," I said.

"It is no bother," Coraline said. "Besides, it leaves Evy to suffer the whims of Madame Beauregard and the others."

In the evening light, for just a moment as she swept a hand across the duvet to smooth it, I caught a glimpse of Mary. "Is it really so bad, here? I'm sure Mr. Andover could secure another placement for you."

"Worry not for me, Mr. Sewell. As much as we girls grouse, it is light labor here. I wouldn't mind if a few more charming fellows such as yourself passed through, but it is truly more than I could hope for from life."

My collar was suddenly warm. "I had best send word of our accommodations to Mr. Andover."

"You'd best let Franks do it," she said. "He doesn't like for anybody else to be seen by the gentlemen."

"I thought no one was particularly in charge."

356

"No one is in charge, particularly, but he does become a bother when cross, and if he wants to take on more work he is welcome to it. Care to escort a lady home?"

I stammered and she smiled as she took my arm and led me back down to the kitchen. Norris and Evy were playing at some sort of game that involved flipping a wine cork, but they paused for a moment to give us lecherous grins as we entered.

"Hush," Coraline said under her breath as she passed them and ladled out two bowls of stew. She sat at the table and gestured for me to take the chair next to her.

"That is most kind," I said, "but I have already eaten one bowl and I do not wish to take advantage."

"Have you ever tasted a soup so fine?" Coraline asked. "And you never will anywhere else," she continued without waiting for an answer. "Don't be foolish."

So I sat.

"Be careful, Mr. Sewell," Evy said. "You might develop a hunger for something you can only get here."

Caroline gave Evy a swift kick under the table. I kept my mouth full and became supremely interest in the game the two were playing. "Where is Franks?"

"Wherever he goes when he isn't snuffling after the guests," Norris said.

"Perhaps you will have to go to your master, after all," Coraline said.

"Does Franks disappear often?" I asked.

"I wouldn't say he disappears, but he keeps to himself mostly."

Carter burst in then, casting a suspicious eye around the kitchen. "You are wanted, Sewell. As for the rest of you, make yourselves useful for once." With that, Carter spun on his polished heel and was gone.

Norris blew a raspberry.

"Poor Mr. Carter," Evy said. "His father was Mr. Wulver's valet, and he had hopes of holding the same position."

"What did happen to Mr. Wulver's son?" I asked, trying not to look too interested.

"Sewell!" Carter cried from the doorway.

"You'd better go," Caroline said.

With no small reluctance, I stood and made my way past a glaring Mr. Carter and into the game room, which had largely emptied out, although Jonathan Elmwood sat at the bar nursing a drink and a grudge, from the looks he was giving Holmes.

"I was just making headway," I whispered.

"Me as well, I'm afraid. I did everything within my power to lose, but there's just no helping some people."

"The whole game broke up because you won a hand or two?"

"Only one, in fact, but I had created an illusion of being a dunce at cards so convincing that the others kept chasing the bet in order to be the one to take my money, which they perceived as a sure thing. Despite my best efforts, I couldn't help but manage a small slam. I'm afraid that our welcome has worn thin."

"Well, send round champagne and caviar for breakfast then, because we're staying the night."

"Dreadful," Holmes replied.

"There is an eccentric hermit locked away on the top floor, and a footman whom his fellows can never quite account for."

"That's a bit better," Holmes replied.

"The bar is now closed, Mr. Andover," Carter chided from the doorway.

"Good evening to you, gentlemen," Holmes said and gestured across the hall. We found stairs with brightly polished rails and deep carpet runners. Up we went and up again to the first floor. I showed Holmes to the room and explained what I had found. We watched the hands on my watch slowly promenade around the face to give time for the occupants of the hotel to settle. At last, we ventured out into the hallway. Rough snoring from two doors down let us know that we weren't alone. I led Holmes the other way and up the servant's stairs. As we passed the second floor there was a surprising cacophony of a wheezing cough from one room, a muffled argument from another, and what I presumed was a phonograph recording coming from a third. Evy exited from the coughing room and my mind spun with excuses I might give, but thankfully she passed directly across to another room.

Up we went to the darkened third floor, and eagerly I began the ascent to the gate that barred the forth. A moment had passed before I realized Holmes wasn't with me. Instead, he was pawing his way down the abandoned floor, and his furtive manner made me wonder what he might have observed that I had missed. He put his eye to the keyhole of the door at the far end and then leaped back as if scalded. I began to move towards him but the door was suddenly flung open. Holmes had compacted himself in the shadows, and so I endeavored to do the same. Franks came barreling through, so distracted that he took note of neither of his secret observers. When his footsteps had disappeared at the bottom of the stairs, I ran to Holmes's side.

"Are you quite alright?" I asked.

358

"Merely startled," Holmes chuckled. "A rare occurrence, as you know. The man placed his hand upon the knob just as I had peered inside."

"That is Franks, the wandering footman."

"Let us see what he has been up to," Holmes said. He gave the knob a perfunctory twist but found it locked. To my surprise, he reached not for his picks but rather fumbled at the base of the dark lamp opposite. A moment later he had produced a golden key, which turned perfectly in the lock. "However did you know of that key?" I asked.

"Nigel Pike couldn't be bothered with such trivialities," Holmes said, stepping inside. "I saw him resort to this spare on three occasions.

"This was Nigel Pike's room?" I asked.

"And it has hardly changed," Holmes said. "Save for this crude trunk."

Indeed there was a trunk, roughly tacked together and lacking the finish one found in the rest of the hotel. Now Holmes did, at last, produce a pick and quickly released the lock. Inside must have been nearly eight-thousand pounds in notes.

"Our footman proves quite industrious," Holmes said. He quickly rifled the bills. "And practical as well. No keepsakes or mementos."

He turned then to the wardrobe, which held three fine, if dated, suits, and a pair of well-worn brogues. Holmes closed it up and turned to the nightstand. Here the drawer was stuffed full of coins, and no less than five beautiful watches that put my old timepiece to shame.

"Any chance these things belonged to Nigel Pike?"

"Like all scions, Nigel didn't bother with cash, but rather put everything on his father's accounts. Besides, surely a common squatter would have managed to spend this treasure already, had he but stumbled across it. No, these are the savings of Mr. Franks. Ah, Mr. Blevins's watch," Holmes dangled one of the timepieces between his fingers. "A trophy, I suppose."

"So Franks is our cardsharp?"

"So it would seem," Holmes said with an air of lingering dissatisfaction. "Why bother with all this? Franks could make a living at the gaming table."

"Old habits die hard, perhaps?"

Holmes made a quick pass at the room, returning everything to its place as if we had never been there.

"To the fourth floor, then?"

"Not just yet," Holmes replied. "We are playing a delicate game now, against a master of his craft." Even as we hurried back to our room, Holmes peered over steepled fingers.

359

I was awakened by a gentle knocking at the door.

"Mary?" my sleep-addled mind called out.

"I've never seen a valet wake so late after his master," Caroline said, stepping into the room, but discreetly keeping her eyes fixed upon the far wall. "I'm afraid that Mr. Andover departed several hours ago, and Mr. Carter – the junior one, that is – demands that you vacate the room."

"Sore feelings remain after last night's rubber, eh?"

"Not at all. Mr. Andover paid for a champagne breakfast for the whole hotel, even the staff! Such a considerate man. I can see why you are so fond of him. I'm sure that Mr. Elmwood is having a club jacket tailored for Mr. Andover as we speak. At least that means I might see more of you." Her eyes flickered to me briefly. "In any eventuality, as Mr. Andover has checked out, Mr. Carter is insistent that propriety is observed. I volunteered to convey the message, of course. I hope that I was a more pleasant Mercury than Carter himself would have been." With that, she disappeared, leaving only the scent of lavender behind.

"That was a sour trick," I groused to Holmes when I found him gazing into the hearth back at Baker Street.

"Come, Watson, there will be other breakfasts. You had your turn at interviewing the staff and I wanted mine."

"And you've solved the case, I presume?"

"A few things were clarified by that Norris chap. An old hack always has tales to tell."

"Any that bear repeating?"

Holmes chuckled. "Tonight we play at the St. James, where I hope to finesse Mr. Franks."

After a rather plain breakfast of toast and old sausage, I left to make my rounds, thumping a few rheumatic backs and proscribing salve for a rather severe rash. All the while, the scent of lavender clung to my coat.

When I returned, Holmes has resumed the role of Reginald Andover, going so far as to have procured a Manchester tie. Someone, Mrs. Hudson I presumed, had pressed my charcoal wood suit and I retired to slip into it. Upon my dresser lay an Oxford tie, a diamond tie pin, and three rings each worth more than I cared to imagine. Returning to the study, Holmes produced a jar and applied a russet-colored dressing to my hair.

"Tonight, you are Mr. Hawthorne," Holmes said.

"It isn't much of a disguise. Franks will recognize me, surely."

The corner of Holmes's mouth pulled upwards but he said nothing. Outside a rather gaudy landau waited, and thus we were conveyed to the St. James, a far cry from the Mule Club. Behind delicately wrought iron fences rose the stout brick edifice, adorned with pristine white crenulations. The man at the gate reflexively open it and bowed when he saw our ostentatious cart coming. Holmes tossed him a shilling as we passed.

"Where the Mule Club is a secret hideout for overgrown boys, the St. James is a stage on which to promenade," Holmes explained.

When we came to a stop a man weighed down in buttons and epaulets stepped forward. "Good evening, sir. Are we expecting you?"

"But of course, my good man," Holmes said, taking a great step down and clapping the doorman on the shoulder. "Reginald Andover of Manchester. All the arrangements have been made, I presume?"

The man bowed. "Indeed, Mr. Andover. Right this way. Your man can stay with the carriage."

"Ah, a simple misunderstanding," Holmes said. "Mr. Hawthorne is not in my employ but rather a business acquaintance. I'm surprised that you don't know of him. I understood that he is an important personage in London. Are you not a member here, Mr. Hawthorne?"

"I haven't time for this nonsense," I bristled, reeling a bit from the sudden change in my role.

"One night surely won't be the end of you," Holmes said, ushering me in past the doorman.

"A bit of warning wouldn't have gone amiss," I whispered.

"I don't think we will enjoy the same latitude here that was afforded us last night," Holmes replied. "I want you standing ready, and you can't do that from the carriage house. You're playing with Mr. Blevins' money, so bet freely. I plan to make it up in any eventuality."

Here the gaming room took pride of place, well-lit by large windows and attended by half-a-dozen staff in white. Holmes pressed something into the hands of the major-domo and they whispered briefly before we were led to a table. Blevins was already seated, chomping on a cigarillo and clearly flushed with more than a few drinks. Holmes made introductions as if we had never met. Blevins came closer to cordiality.

"I understand we are to be partners tonight, Doctor – er, Mr. Hawthorne, was it?"

"Is that so?"

"Quite," Holmes said. "There is a certain player of exceptional ability here whom I wish to put to the test."

As if conjured, Franks appeared and seemed startled to see Holmes. After a moment he seemed to regain his composure and sat.

"Good evening, Mr. Pike," Holmes said. "My name is Reginald Andover and I requested that you be seated at my table tonight. I hope you don't mind."

"Not at all," Franks replied, "but I'm not certain why I have been so favored."

"I fancy myself a serious gambler, Mr. Pike," Holmes said. "Amateur play bores me, so I inquired after the very best players at St. James. Your name came up time and again."

Sweat beaded upon Franks's brow. "I didn't realize that I had garnered such a reputation."

"The name Nigel Pike is becoming famous," Holmes said.

"Or infamous," Blevins grumbled.

"Perhaps this isn't the right table for me, tonight," Franks said, beginning to rise.

"Mr. Pike, you simply cannot begrudge Mr. Blevins's right to try at getting even. We are all gentlemen here."

Franks collapsed into his chair. "Fine, I suppose."

With that, a deck was provided and the cards were dealt. I have only the most rudimentary understanding of the game, so I can only state that Blevins was most unhappy to have me as a partner, and Franks and Holmes were fencing against each other via the subtleties of card play. Nonetheless, they easily took grand slams in the first two hands. On the third hand of the rubber our luck took a sudden turn for the better, and Franks became quite agitated.

"Cheats!" he suddenly cried. "Conniving scoundrels!"

Holmes smiled.

The major-domo hurried over. "Is there a problem here?"

"Andover here is passing tricks to his friends!" Franks declared.

"Oh my, that is a very serious allegation," the major-domo said. "I hope you can support it."

"Mr. Andover was a buffoon at cards last night, yet tonight he plays with a keen alacrity that I've never witnessed before. And his partner, whose red tint has begun to run at the brow I might add, now plays the early hands worse than a child and then has a sudden turn of luck. I defy you to find an innocent explanation for that!"

"Where was it that you saw me play last night?" Holmes asked.

"At the Mule Club, of course!"

"And if we were to ask Mr. Carter at the Mule Club, we would discover that Mr. Nigel Pike was a guest last night as well?"

"Do you deny that you were at the Mule Club last night, intentionally boffing tricks to make yourself seem a lesser player?"

"I do not deny it," Holmes said. "Nor do I deny that you saw me there, but I do deny that Nigel Pike had anything to do with it."

"What is this nonsense?" Blevins complained.

"Quite simply, this man's suit is borrowed, his membership is borrowed, and worst of all *his name* is *borrowed*."

"Outrageous!" Franks declared. "I don't have to sit here just to be accused! If this is how the St. James allows its members to be treated, I shall take my custom elsewhere."

"Now, now, Mr. Franks, let us not make a scene," Holmes said. "We can settle this affair like gentlemen, I should think."

"You've a sharp eye, Mr. Andover," Franks said. "I've been at this for a year and none have caught on yet."

"Eight-thousand pounds in a year is no small testament to your abilities," Holmes replied.

Franks seemed to swoon for a moment. "What do you mean, eight-thousand pounds?"

"That is the amount held in your chest, is it not? Maybe another two-hundred pounds in bits and baubles?"

"You don't understand, Mr. Andover! Might we speak in private?"

"You'll do no such thing!" Blevins shouted. "We'll have the truth and we'll have it now!"

Two-dozen eyes were upon Franks now. His mouth fluttered but no words came out.

Holmes sighed. "You observe the players at the Mule Club, where you work as a dogsbody, and then, knowing their quirks, play against them here at the St. James, with great success."

"That's right," Franks said.

"So he is a cheat, after all," Blevins crowed.

"Thus far nothing Mr. Franks has done is illegal," Holmes said. "Any of your opponents can, and likely do, gather the same intelligence by actually playing against you."

"Precisely. He's getting the advantage of learning how I play without risking a penny!"

"Which makes Mr. Franks the smartest player in the room," Holmes said.

"But he lied about his name!" Blevins continued. "That's a crime, isn't it?"

"It is likely against St James club policy," Holmes said.

"That's right," the major-domo chimed in. "I'm afraid you aren't welcome here anymore, Mr. Pike – er, Franks."

"There's not much left in it for me anyway," Franks sighed.

"What was in it for you in the first place?" I asked. "You are clearly an excellent card player, whatever small advantage spying may have given you. Why not do it under your own name?"

363

"I have no desire to spend my life at a gaming table," Franks said. "I've wasted too much time there already. It's mere chance that I have an aptitude for it."

"How does Nigel Pike come into it?" Holmes asked. "Mere chance, again? I think not. You came into the Wulver household when Sidney Wulver and Nigel Pike died. Why? Not as a proxy for Sidney, surely. There is no evidence that Giles Wulver is even aware of you. Someone else brought you in, correct?"

"I've been at the Mule Club as long as I remember," Franks said.

"It would be a senior staff member, and I doubt either of the Carter brothers would be so charitable."

"What does it matter?" Franks said. "I'm sure this has done for my employment there as well."

"I think you'll get by all right on the eight-thousand pounds in your trunk," Holmes said.

"What!" Blevins objected. "You'll let him keep the dividends of his deceptions?"

"Until someone can prove that he did in fact cheat, his winnings are as legitimate as anyone else's," Holmes said. "Now, I think Mr. Norris drinks for the same reason that he sheltered you."

"Leave the old man out of it!" Franks said. "Anything I might have done is on my own."

"Were you there when Pike and Wulver died?" Holmes asked.

Franks turned away sharply.

"You would have been but a small child," Holmes said.

"In my mother's arms," Franks spat. "That's where Norris found me. In her cold arms."

That image rested heavy upon the room for a moment.

"The police never even took a look," Franks said. "My mother was in a potter's field before the sun rose. Sidney Wulver and Nigel Pike were just gone like nothing had ever happened. No one was held accountable. No one paid the price."

"So you decided to make them pay," Holmes said.

"I came of age in the house of my mother's killers," Franks said. "Mrs. Wulver died of grief, and that was something. Mr. Wulver lived in torment, and that was something better."

"The Pikes never recovered either, if it means anything to you," Holmes said. "They are friends of my family."

"But everyone else just walked away. The Chief Inspector who put a stop to any paperwork, the Coroner who disposed of the bodies, even the liveryman who made the carriage disappear." With that, he turned a sour eye on Conrad Blevins.

"That was twenty-five years ago," Blevins said. "All I did was put a carriage on a boat."

"You sold it overseas," Franks said. "And used the money to start your own hack company, earning you the riches you enjoy today. Did you see the blood? Did you care?"

"I wasn't in a position to ask questions back then," Blevins said.

"So you are having your revenge by ruining them at the gaming table?" I asked.

"Thick as thieves, they are. They were Wulver's cronies before, which is how they were elected to cover the whole thing up."

"I know that you see me as a villain," Blevins said. "I'm just a man like any other. All I did was drive a carriage less than a mile."

"And all Hockney did was send the patrolmen away, and all Elmwood did was find the open grave, and all Sidney Wulver did was pull the trigger."

"They were just boys, drunk and playing stupid boys' games of honor. They tried to take your mother to a hospital. They could have left her in the street."

"We might have been better off," Franks said. "She might have survived the errant bullet she took in their ridiculous duel. But then they drove the carriage into the river."

"In a blind panic!" Blevins said. "And they drowned for their troubles."

"They drowned because they were drunken jackanapes, and they got away with it because their parent's station placed them above justice."

"Earthly justice, perhaps," Holmes said.

"I've had to live with it every day, an innocent child doomed to a life of torment. Where is the justice in that?"

"Where was it to end?" I asked.

"When each man responsible was in a pauper's grave, like my mother."

"That is not what she would have wanted for you," I said. "You can walk away now. Start a new life at the expense of these men. Make that your revenge."

"It isn't enough," Franks spat, before leaping at Blevins.

Holmes easily pinned Franks to the table with one arm. "If you would, Watson."

I locked my arm around Franks's right shoulder and Holmes took the left. We marched the poor man out as Blevins screamed about justice and reparations. Franks was making no small spectacle of himself in the street so Holmes took a vial from his pocket, uncorked it, and held his hand to Franks's face. The crazed man sputtered beneath Holmes's iron grip but soon weakened and finally slumped into our arms. Holmes hailed a passing cab and we were soon away.

"Dare I ask what you have given the poor soul?" I asked.

"I keep chloroform at the ready in support of my lepidopterology studies," Holmes said. "He'll have stomach complaints in the morning, but at least he shall awaken a free man."

It was some weeks later that Mr. Norris paid a call on us at Baker Street. He shook his head at me when he entered and chuckled. From his pockets, he pulled two well-worn issues of *The Strand*. "The girls are wanting your autograph, Doctor Watson."

"I hope there are no hard feelings," I said as I scrawled my signature.

"Miss Evy has made sure that everyone in London knows that she met you," Norris said. "Miss Caroline has been a bit more circumspect about it, but I think she has made her peace with it. There will be another fine gentleman coming along soon, I'm sure."

"To what do we owe the honor of this visit?" Holmes asked.

"I just wanted to know if you've heard word from Johnny. Mr. Franks, I mean."

"He is dear to you, isn't he?" I asked.

"Like a son, of a sort," Norris said. "I raised him as well as I could, under the circumstances."

"It doesn't seem to have soothed your conscience," Holmes observed.

"I don't suppose anything will do that," Norris said.

"What's all this, then?" I wondered.

Holmes left a moment for Norris to answer. Finding only silence, he continued. "Posh lads like Wulver and Pike don't drive their own carriages. They have people to do that."

"You were driving that night?" I asked Norris.

"To my eternal shame. They practically rolled me out of bed in their frantic state. They had just shot poor Miss Franks on accident, as they fired a pair of dueling pistols in the street after some minor disagreement over cards. I was half-asleep and had the two of them screaming in my ears, and then we carried the poor girl to the carriage. I suppose you fellows must be used to stumbling upon violent death, but it was a bit of a shock to me. I muddled along in a bit of a stupor, and the boys were each yelling different commands and we were going down back streets with no lamps. The horse took a bad step on some missing stones and went mad, poor thing. I couldn't rein her in before we pitched over the bank. Young Wulver was caught up in the tack and Mr. Pike was floating motionless inside the carriage, blood pouring from his head. I pried the door open to free them and there was something splashing about inside. The infant Johnny Franks, it was, swaddled around his mother's chest.

"I pulled the babe free and tucked him inside my own coat. He never made a peep that night, nor hardly ever after. By the time I saw him safe to shore, the carriage was submerged completely. Giles Wulver had sent his man Blevins out to find the boys, and it was just then that he came upon us. I told him of what had transpired and then made my sorry way back to the Hotel Atelier. I thought the police would come for the baby, and then me. But no one ever came. There were no funerals or anything. Giles Wulver simply disappeared into his suite. Blevins's personal effects were gone a few days later, and it would be years before I saw him again, this time as a member of the St. James Club as I ferried the Mule Club men around. I don't think he even recognized me.

"Back then there was a housekeeper and half-a-dozen maids, for the hotel was still at full capacity. Johnny never wanted for attention, and he came of age as a natural denizen of the club. It was all fine until one night when old Elmwood and Madame Beauregard was in their cups and arguing about who was most dear to Wulver, when Elmwood told of the night he buried a woman for his friend. Franks overheard it all and began to ask questions. I thought I owed it to the boy to give him the truth. I regret it every day. He turned hard against me – against everyone really. I thought with some time he would return to his old ways, but I guess he threw himself into his revenge plot instead. He's a good boy, Mr. Holmes."

"A clever one, at any rate," Holmes said. "And of no harm to anyone else. Which is why he awoke upon a steamer headed across the Atlantic, rather than in a cell."

"Can't you tell me where he has gone?" Norris asked.

"I can tell you only that he arrived safely at the Port of New Orleans," Holmes said. "As did his trunk. I asked the Pinkerton's to keep watch. Perhaps you shall hear from him someday, perhaps not. Whether or not the boy thinks kindly of you, I believe that you should think kindly of yourself, Mr. Norris."

After the groom left, Holmes sank heavily into his chair. "What a peculiar little drama unfolded right before me, and I never observed any of it," he said at last.

"How could anyone have known?" I replied. "I think you have more than made up for it over the years."

"Perhaps," Holmes said. He sat listening to the sounds of Baker Street below for the rest of the evening.

367

The Perplexing *X*'ing
by Sonia Fetherston

My longtime friend, Mr. Sherlock Holmes, is not a pious man. He is not an habitual church-goer, nor does he count men of the cloth among his close circle. Yet never suppose that my friend is uninterested in religion. Indeed, I have often heard him refer to his great brain, and his deductive powers, as being "God-given". He has performed several discreet favours for a certain prince of the church, as well as for the Holy See itself. Holmes once served as the personal representative of two Coptic Patriarchs for the purpose of negotiating the return of a stolen relic, the value of which was said to be beyond price. On one occasion he disguised himself in the garb an aged ecclesiastic, a costume which allowed him to elude Professor Moriarty. And Holmes is the only Englishman I know who ever spent a week as a guest of the Head Lama in Tibet. So it should not come as a surprise that my friend agreed to take the case of one of the most singular religious persons ever to appeal for our help.

According to my notes, this particular adventure unfolded one Tuesday evening during the spring of 1897. A rainstorm was splashing across the city, and we could hear the wind whistling like a passer-by frightened of a dark burial ground. Under the lamps outside in Baker Street, a lone man struggled to keep his umbrella aloft against the chilly raindrops. We, on the other hand, were warm and dry in our cosy sitting room. Mrs. Hudson gathered the remains of our supper onto her tray, gently tut-tutting over Holmes's uneaten meal. As his friend and sometimes-physician, I was alert to this early sign of *ennui*. My suspicions were seemingly confirmed when I observed Holmes, a few moments later, standing before the fireplace, his right hand twitching reflexively and his eyes raking a nearby table where rested the black case containing his favourite syringe. I gently cleared my throat. "A little violin music just now would be a treat. Will you play?"

He cast an annoyed look in my direction. "Your powers of observation improve, Watson, but as usual your conclusion landed wide." Then he shook his head ruefully. "Yes, I am bored. Yes, a distraction would be welcome. But you are sufficiently acquainted with me to know that when I am working I eat very little so that my blood can pass over my stomach and race instead to my brain. As for the thing which interests me upon the table, it is not my needle but that wire beneath it, which arrived this afternoon." His sinewy arm reached across and he seized a yellow telegram from under the needle case. "Read it yourself."

Must urgently consult you regarding a perplexing matter. Shall arrive in Baker Street to-night at 9 o'clock.

L. Binney

I looked across at my friend. "Holmes, you have a case!"

As if in answer the downstairs bell rang, then almost immediately rang again. "Ah!" Holmes sighed. "One ring means a little something to while away an evening. Two rings promises brainwork." He vaulted into his habitual chair, and arranged his long limbs. Within a minute our door opened half way, and to our surprise our friend Stanley Hopkins peered around the edge, his shoulders glittering with raindrops. Hopkins was a Scotland Yard inspector who had associated with us on several recent cases. Like Holmes, he was an admirer of science, and of following facts to wherever they might lead. He frequently expressed awe at my friend's methods and he sought to apply them in his own work, though with varying degrees of success. Holmes thought Hopkins was capable and talented, and he took what might be considered a fatherly interest in the young man. "Care for a visitor?" Hopkins twinkled.

"Most certainly you are welcome," I replied, rising from my place at the table to greet him.

"Would you mind two visitors: Myself and one other?" he asked, and the door swung open to reveal a slender woman of about thirty years who stood beside Hopkins. Her dark eyes darted around our sitting room, taking it in with equal parts intelligence and curiosity. A mass of rich, brown curls threatened to explode from beneath her remarkable hat. It was an enormous, round black bonnet, lined with tight, ruched pleats, and secured at the side with a huge satin bow.

"Dr. Watson, Mr. Holmes, may I present Major Louise Binney, an officer in the Salvation Army?" Hopkins announced. "She came to me with what she described as a 'perplexation'. It seemed the sort of thing which might appeal to you, Mr. Holmes, so I suggested that she wire you in advance of our arrival."

"A lady Major?" I ejaculated, not entirely sure what to make of this development. "Good heavens, ma'am, you outrank me! I was in Her Majesty's service myself, regular Army, though a mere surgeon." I glanced at the black, belted tunic she wore over her full skirt, its stiff collar standing at attention, epaulettes on her shoulders, along with other insignia which bore the unmistakable mark of a commissioned officer.

"How do you do, Dr. Watson," she said with a slight nod. If her appearance was brisk and military-like, her voice was low and musical. "Yes, I'm a Major. You may know that the Salvation Army is a church, founded right here in England. We officers are ordained ministers, while our lay members are called soldiers. General William Booth established the Salvation Army shortly before I was born. [1] Offering one's heart to God and one's hand to mankind is a rigourous calling, so General Booth drew inspiration from the discipline of the regular Army. We wear uniforms as a witness of our service." Both of her gloved hands rose to her high collar, where, on either side of her chin, were two round pins, each bearing the letter *S*. "We are *Saved*," she said, touching first the pin on the left and then its counterpart opposite, "so that we might *Serve*."

"Sit beside the fire, Major," Holmes invited. "Watson will fetch you a glass of sherry, and some whisky for Hopkins."

"Liquor? No," the Major shook her head. "Salvationists thirst only for the word of our Lord. We abstain from alcohol."

"I see." Holmes held up his pipe. "Would you object if I were to smoke? I find that it concentrates and refines the deductive faculties."

"I prefer that you do not, sir," she quietly replied, and he obliged by placing his old briar in a small dish on the table at his side. He turned his gaze on her.

"Then pray tell me how I can assist you," he said quietly. "Save what you've just revealed about your rank and beliefs, the only the other obvious facts are that you are a single woman, an ardent cornet-player, are preparing to undertake a journey to America, and studied Paul's *Epistle to the Corinthians* just prior to coming here. Beyond that, I know nothing whatever about you."

"Why, Mr. Holmes!" she exclaimed. "How on earth did you – ?"

"May I?" I interjected, handing the whisky to Hopkins and motioning him to a chair. I drew my own seat nearer the fire and settled there. "I have had the pleasure of associating with my friend on a number of cases, and am somewhat acquainted with his methods. Beneath your left glove there is no outline of a wedding ring. Your cheek muscles are high and rounded, indicative of blowing into a horn such as those I've seen Salvationists use in street corner services. A cornet is smaller than a trumpet, so it is better suited to a woman's hands. The edge of a steamship ticket, second class, is protruding from your pocket. I can just make out the word '*Hoboken*'. If I'm not mistaken, that is the port immediately west of New York City. As for your evening's reading material, I am in the dark as much as you are."

Holmes smiled and lifted his chin a bit, with that self-satisfied air he sometimes exhibited. "There is a nearly imperceptible dusting of gold on your skirt, where rested the gilt edge of a book. Since you are an ordained minister, a Bible is the sort of book you might choose. From the slimness of the imprint, it could only be a New Testament. You had it open slightly past the mid-point, I perceive, which suggests *Corinthians*. Child's play."

"How easy it is!" said she, folding her hands on her lap. "There is no mystery, then, save for the one I bring to you."

"Tell me more about yourself," Holmes invited, "and then pray let me know how I might help."

"When I was a babe, Mr. Holmes, my own mother was dying of consumption, and so she left me at the Army's foundling home in Spitalfields. There I spent my early years. 'Mrs. General' – General Booth's dear wife, Catherine – frequently worked in the home, and she was always kind to me. She taught me to sew, and to read, and to speak properly. From her I learned to trust the Lord in all things. I would often play with her own daughter, Eva. As a young girl I longed to be just like the Booths! When I reached my teen years, I preached on street corners, and laboured for our Lord in blighted neighbourhoods. Eva and I were what they called 'Sallie Slum Sisters', visiting the sick, helping women and children, and advocating temperance. We studied, and eventually we became officers, beginning our ascent through the ranks. Now Eva is a Colonel and commander of our Marylebone Centre, while I command the Whitechapel Corps."

"Quite enthralling," he said, waving his hand while staring at the ceiling. "Is there some specific way in which I may I assist you?"

"Perhaps I can explain," Hopkins interjected. "I find it helps me to restate a case." I silently blessed him – he knew as well as I the dangers of a bored Sherlock Holmes. Hopkins thrust his hand into his pocket and extracted his notebook. Turning the pages, he began to recite the facts which were known to him.

"The Salvation Army is fortunate to have several generous friends who supply against its needs. One such individual was the late Mrs. Thomas Peppercorn who, with her husband, built a prosperous watch and clock shop in Peter Street, just north of the Gloucester Road. For many years, Mr. Peppercorn was both shopkeeper and repairman, while Mrs. Peppercorn kept the inventory and ledger books. She also was an ardent volunteer and financial helper of the Salvation Army.

"The couple were childless. Having no son or daughter to succeed them, the problem became: What to do with the business? When Mr. Peppercorn died a little more than two years ago, his wife sought to continue their work. She hired a Mr. Edward Spool, who has some skill in repairing timepieces. Mrs. Peppercorn also added a bookkeeper to take over many of her own duties. His name is Tim O'Donnell. He is a

Salvation Army soldier – a member of the congregation at the Whitechapel Corps – whom Mrs. Peppercorn met in the soup kitchen during her volunteer service."

"We found him living rough, on the streets," Major Binney said. "A tall man with a pronounced curve in his spine, so he has a crooked appearance. His temperament is a bit coarse at times. Excitable, according to his Irish ways. But I believe his faith is genuine. His skills are good. He helps us a few hours each week with our church finances."

"How did he go from keeping ledgers to living on the streets, and back again?" Holmes enquired.

"He lost his previous position due to drink," she said very simply. "Several years ago, General William Booth published a book, *In Darkest England*. Perhaps you've read it? It contains personal stories of some of the men and women with whom we are privileged to work . . . even to save. Many suffer from the effects of drink. The General estimated there are at present one-million people in England who are completely under the domination of alcohol. It is a wicked, ruinous thing, as Tim learned. He lost his livelihood and friends."

"The Sallies cleaned him up and converted him," Hopkins added.

"Now Mr. O'Donnell is a decent, God-fearing man," Major Binney said.

"You trust him?" I asked her. "You don't worry that he will lapse and drink again?"

She was pragmatic. "There's always a chance, Doctor. And there is always forgiveness."

Hopkins looked at his notes once more and continued. "Mrs. Peppercorn finally wearied of her business responsibilities and sold her shop to Spool last summer. He retained O'Donnell as bookkeeper and Mrs. Peppercorn settled into retirement. She lived with her maid and cook. Mrs. Peppercorn's charitable instincts kept bringing her back to the Salvation Army. She continued as a volunteer in the organization's Whitechapel Corps. Mrs. Peppercorn survived her husband by about eighteen months."

"She was Promoted to Glory ten weeks ago," Major Binney said.

"Promoted to Glory?" Holmes exclaimed.

"That is how we Sallies refer to death," she replied.

"Upon her passing," Hopkins resumed, "Mrs. Peppercorn's estate, approaching four-thousand pounds, was to be transferred as a gift to the Salvation Army. The money came from the sale of the Peppercorn's business, and from the auction some days ago of Mrs. Peppercorn's house and its contents." He paused and drew a single sheet of paper from his notebook. "Here is the Salvation Army's copy of the will, signed by Mrs. Peppercorn on the twenty-third of November of last year." Hopkins handed it across to Holmes. "That is the lady's signature, witnessed by two men employed by her solicitor, Mr. George Besbury-Dubbs."

Holmes scanned the document quickly, then handed it to me. "It seems straightforward. enough," he remarked. "Thirty pounds apiece to her housemaid and cook, then the remainder shall go to the Salvation Army. I am not seeing a 'perplexation' clause, Major Binney."

"Indeed, there is one," our uniformed guest offered. "Mrs. Peppercorn loved the Salvation Army. She often said that we inspired all that was good in her. She worked shoulder-to-shoulder with us, serving soup, distributing bricks of soap, and reading the Gospel aloud in our day room. Could you love the unloved, Mr. Holmes? She most assuredly did. She told me several times over the years that in due course her estate would come to us in order to help the poor. That's why her abrupt change of heart makes no sense. You see, there is a second will."

Holmes suddenly leaned forward like a hound catching a scent on a breeze.

"Dated?"

"The twenty-sixth of November last year."

"Where?"

"At her solicitor's chambers, same as this previous will."

"Witnessed?"

"By the same two who witnessed the first signing three days earlier."

"The benefactors being?"

"Gifts of thirty pounds apiece were made to her servants. But Mr. Spool is now the sole beneficiary of the remainder. The new will goes on to state that '*not one penny*' is to go to the Salvation Army!"

"Legally done?

Our Salvationist visitor shrugged her slim shoulders. "Well, that's the thing, Mr. Holmes." She regarded him quietly for several seconds. "The newer will, the one which eliminates the Salvation Army, was properly drawn up by her solicitor and duly witnessed. That second document, however, was signed with an *X*."

This development sent an immediate shiver through me. "But why?" I asked. "Why would a perfectly literate woman sign her will with an *X*?"

"My dear Watson, you shimmer with pure intelligence. Why, indeed?" Holmes purred. "That her own hand made the *X* cannot be doubted – there were witnesses to her having done so. Yet we know Mrs. Peppercorn to be literate from her business duties, and from her Gospel readings at the Whitechapel Corps. By her previous will we can see that the lady was perfectly capable of signing her full name. Her ability to read and write are facts. So is her unexplained *X* on this second version: It is another fact. And yet – and yet – It is, Major Binney, just as you say. It's a *perplex*."

"It is inexplicable!" she cried. "The Mrs. Peppercorn I knew for many years would *never* cut the Salvation Army from her will, and if by some chance she did, she would never write into that will the vindictive words that '*not one penny*' should come to us. To do so would be cruel, and she was not a cruel woman. Why, on the day before she was Promoted to Glory, Mrs. Peppercorn stopped in at the Corps. She told me how much she loved the Salvation Army. She said that she considered Salvationists to be her family, and that I was like a daughter to her. Then she gave me a present, a clock which Mr. Peppercorn himself built. Her great heart gave out the next morning and I never saw her again."

As she spoke, Hopkins extracted a second paper from between the pages of his notebook. It was a true copy of the second will, which he explained was provided by Mrs. Peppercorn's solicitor to the Salvation Army when that organization came forward to claim its inheritance. We handed it amongst ourselves for a moment, silently reading the pitiless words the Major had described, and examining the X near the bottom.

"It does not rise to a police matter," Hopkins asserted. "It is rather a matter for a probate court – or perhaps better, a tangle for you to unravel, Mr. Holmes."

"In the morning I shall undertake to learn more," Holmes said with finality. "I shall look into this matter for you, Major Binney, and offer my expert opinion."

"You have just answered my prayers," Major Binney declared, much moved. "You, and the Lord who works through you. But Mr. Holmes," she continued, "I'm afraid I have but little money to pay you for your services."

"Having and solving your puzzle are payment enough," he told her. "Consider it my contribution to your ministry."

"My gratitude is boundless, sir!"

We said goodbye and they returned to the rainy street, where their hansom waited. "What do you make of her, Watson?" Holmes asked, lighting his neglected pipe.

"An extraordinary woman," I replied.

"An extraordinary client," he corrected. "A client is to me a merely a problem-bearer, a means to an end, an escape from the perils of boredom. Major Binney's perplex helps fill the empty hours, and because it is unusual – the mystery of the X, the giver who suddenly withdraws a gift – it should keep my mind nicely occupied for a day or two."

"Have you any theories?"

374

"No theories as yet," he replied. "I do, however, have a working hypothesis that has to do with the *X*. Rather, with the precise *nature* of the letter. Consider that an *X* consists of two contrasting impulses that meet in a crossing point, then continue on their separate ways. When we find that intersection, we will find the facts necessary to solve Major Binney's perplexing problem."

"We?"

"If you would be so good, Watson? I find a chronicler to be handy, but a friend and able companion is invaluable."

Here was his heart! I've sometimes called Sherlock Holmes a thinking machine, or an automaton – an orphan-like being devoid of emotion. Yet there were times when the mask slipped and he revealed human feelings. "I will be honoured to assist you in any possible way," I told him.

"Thank you, my dear Watson."

Next morning, as we finished our ham, boiled eggs, and toast, the stately figure of Mrs. Hudson glided in, a fresh pot of tea in one hand and a salver bearing a calling card in the other. "A gentleman to see you, Mr. Holmes," she reported.

"I'm expecting him," Holmes replied, brushing a crumb from his lapel. "Show him up, if you please." As she went to the door and began her descent down the steps, he stood and crossed to our hearth, where he proceeded to jab at the glowing coals with a poker. "There's a chill in the air," he said. "Today's weather is almost colder than the heart that changed that will."

"You believe it to be altered, or possibly forged?" I enquired.

"No, I didn't say that – the lady's mark was made and properly witnessed, so it's not a case of was it changed. Rather, it is a case of why that change occurred. We stand on the brink of learning more." The poker clattered to the floor, as Holmes suddenly turned around. "Do come in and be seated, Mr. Besbury-Dubbs."

Mrs. Peppercorn's solicitor was a short, slight, startled-looking man of middle years. His eyebrows rode high on his creased forehead, a condition perhaps aided by a hairline in full retreat. He handed Mrs. Hudson his hat and overcoat, revealing attire a baronet might choose for a Sunday in the park: An impeccable gray wool suit, enlivened by a jaunty, striped silver-and-red tie that was pinned at his throat with a large pearl. "Of course I've heard your name, Mr. Holmes. It was the talk of the Temple when we read Dr. Watson's account of the marriage of our colleague, Godfrey Norton, to that American." [2] His voice was high and reedy. "If I remember correctly, you played a role in that drama – or was it a comedy?" He seated himself and chuckled. "Imagine my surprise when

I received a telegram from that same Sherlock Holmes, asking me to call at Baker Street this morning. How might I be of service, sir? Perhaps you wish to consult me regarding legalities because you yourself are to marry?"

"Ha!" barked my friend, as he subsided into his usual chair, elbows on its arms, and long fingers steepled before him. "That is more likely to be the eventual fate of our resident ladies' man, Dr. Watson!"

"I lost my wife several years ago," I explained, wistfully, to our visitor.

"No, Mr. Besbury-Dubbs, I wish to consult you about something even more perplexing than Dr. Watson's love life," Holmes continued. "It is an estate in which you were instrumental. In November of last year you prepared a will for a Mrs. Thomas Peppercorn."

"I did, sir."

"And she signed it?"

"She did indeed, sir" the solicitor agreed. "I saw her sign it, as did two of my clerks who served as witnesses to the act. She affixed her signature to the document in my own chambers. She took the original, and we retained two signed copies of her will in our office safe, as is our usual practice."

"The Salvation Army was the primary beneficiary of that will?"

"It certainly was," the little solicitor replied. "She was very generous to them. As I recall she did 'give, devise, and bequeath' the vast majority of her estate to that organization."

"Just a moment," I interrupted. "I have always wondered why wills use those three words together: 'Give, devise, and bequeath'. They mean the same thing, so they simply repeat themselves."

"So one might think," Mr. Besbury-Dubbs explained. "Though there is an actual difference. In legal terms, to 'devise' is to make a gift of real property, such as land, or a house. To 'bequeath' is to leave behind one's personal property, such as jewelry, china, or a book collection. Both devising and bequeathing constitute an act of giving. Use of the different words dates back nearly a thousand years when it was necessary to include Anglo-Saxon, French, and Latin in our English legal documents so that there could be no misunderstanding of intent."

"I suppose that 'will' and 'testament' are different words, too?"

"Under the law, yes," he told us, "though they are now normally combined for the sake of convenience. However, in times past they could exist as two separate documents, with the will standing for real property and the testament for personal effects. The words '*last* will and testament' indicate that it was to be the will-and-testament maker's final word on the subject."

Holmes cleared his throat to let us know that my lesson in the legal lexicon had come to an end. "Several days after the first will was signed, did you not prepare a second will for Mrs. Peppercorn?"

"I did."

"But she did not sign the second will. Rather, she marked it with an *X*."

Mr. Besbury-Dubbs nodded in the affirmative. "The second will was marked with her *X*. I saw her place her mark on it, as did the same witnesses, my two clerks. As before, we gave her the original, retained her *X*'d copies in our safe, and presented another *X*'d copy to Mr. Edward Spool, to whom she had recently sold her business and who was now to be the main beneficiary of her estate. He accompanied her to my chambers."

"How did she appear?" Holmes enquired. "Her bearing and demeanor? Was she sensible and businesslike, or did she seem upset in any way?"

"Now that you mention it, Mrs. Peppercorn was rather introspective. She read through the changes, and so did Mr. Spool. Truth be told, it was he who put forward that 'not one penny' should go to the Sallies. At first she was reluctant to sign. She complained to us that her hand hurt, and that she couldn't possibly hold the pen properly. She asked to set the second will aside to sign at a later date. At Spool's insistence she finally placed her mark on the document, the *X* of which you spoke. The *X* is perfectly legal, just like a signature, as long as it is properly witnessed. It was. She then departed."

"But why proceed with the *X*, given that her hand would eventually recover and she could come back, as you say, at a later date?" Holmes mused. "What was so important about that will that she had to get the thing done, rather than come back another day?"

"Ah!" The little solicitor's brows inched higher than ever. "I'll wager you are wondering why she marked the second will with an *X*, when both the first and the third wills were inscribed with her full name?"

Had he fired a ship's cannon across Holmes's deal table he could not have startled us more. "Mr. Besbury-Dubbs!" Holmes exclaimed. "I am all attention. Pray tell me about this third will." My friend leaned back into his chair and closed his eyes, a satisfied smile playing across his lips.

"Two days after affixing her *X*, Mrs. Peppercorn returned to my chambers, alone. She desired me to make a third will. That one was intended to cut out Mr. Spool and reinstate the Salvation Army as the primary beneficiary. At her insistence I had it drawn up in a hurry, while she waited, and she signed it with her full name. Her hand certainly did not hurt that day! My two clerks witnessed it, as before, so the thing was legally done. She directed that no copies were to be made. She took the

377

one and only version of that third will away with her. That was the end of it."

"How very curious," Holmes said. "And if I am not mistaken, that third will, signed and witnessed as it was, would supersede the second will?"

"Indeed, if it can be produced. Unfortunately, I do not know where it is, so I cannot present it to the court."

"And if I can recover that third will, and bring it to you?"

"It can proceed to a judge, and much joy to the Salvation Army."

Once the little solicitor left us, Holmes reached for his hat and overcoat and made for the door. "Hurry into your things, Watson. Not a moment to lose! We have an appointment with a lady and we must not keep her waiting." In a moment we were seated in a cab, flying through the fog that had settled on the Marylebone Road, making our way toward Bayswater. At ten o'clock Holmes was rapping with his stick on the door of a townhouse located on a quiet side street. Large pots planted with bright red geraniums stood at either side of the shiny black door, their spicy scent filling the air. We were admitted by a butler of perfunctory habits who guided us into a sitting room and told us to wait. "Mrs. Rosalind Baugh is the pre-eminent expert in the field of handwriting analysis," Holmes explained to me. "As respected in her particular field as – " He was cut short when the eminent expert herself stepped into the room.

On first glance, Mrs. Baugh appeared delicate. Even with a rope of thick, white hair coiled atop her head, she was small of stature and thin almost to the point of frailty. She appeared to be near the age of sixty, her face being gently lined, yet her complexion retained the colour which I believe is called Healthy English: Clear and pale, with a delicate pink tint. Her morning gown was indigo, with a rich froth of lace and ribbons at the throat and wrists. As she stepped across the room to greet us, I noticed that her movements were energetic. "Mr. Sherlock Holmes! I've had your telegram, sir!" she cried in a cheerful, girlish voice. "And Dr. Watson! This is indeed an honour, one author to another. Do you know that on one occasion a little treatise of mine appeared in the same edition of *The Strand* as your own account of one of Mr. Holmes's cases? It's delightful to finally meet you both!" Her hands fluttered as she spoke, like twin white moths.

She paid us the compliment of asking us to sign a large autograph album, though we quickly realized she was less interested in having souvenirs of ourselves, and more interested in collecting written specimens of us for study. She carefully fitted a silver pince-nez to her face and peered at our names. "Ah, Mr. Holmes, your capital 'S' will never be surpassed!" she exclaimed, studying the page we had inscribed. "The position of the letter reveals prodigality devoid of pretension. Your upslope indicates a certain clearness of mind, while the shoulders of the subsequent letters affirm an absolute rectitude of character. And Dr. Watson, see how the angular bases of the vowels in your name reveal your intuitive nature. The looping capital 'W" of your second name asserts kindliness and initiative. These are fine attributes for a physician."

"You are able to infer all of that from our signatures?" I asked.

"Of course I can," she insisted. "Handwriting reflects the personality and condition of the writer: His intelligence, his character, his emotions, his tendencies. A determined person writes with a masterful hand. A happy person writes with a lilting hand. One who is ill writes with a weakened hand. The writing of a troubled person loses energy as each letter and line escape his pen. Writers who are in the throes of passion – joy, anger, grief, and the like – betray those sensations to a skilled graphologist. Graphology is superior to its sister pursuits of phrenology and palmistry. The seeker need not submit his head or hand to a practitioner, merely a sample of his writing. The expert scrutiny of handwriting is much more reliable than trying to understand an individual through observation, or even interview."

"Indeed?" Holmes said, with a trace of asperity, as if his ability to "read" a visitor was on par with a mere parlour trick. Holmes was the keenest observer of humans and human nature that I have ever encountered but, as noted elsewhere in my accounts of his cases, egotism was also a strong factor in his singular nature. I wondered whether Mrs. Baugh had discerned this as well from his signature, and was attempting a little jest at his expense.

"Graphology is an exact science, Mr. Holmes," she continued. "Though its roots are ancient, it was the Italians who, three-hundred years ago, refined it to the extent that it became possible for them to detect spies and enemies from writing samples. But it was the French, of course, who introduced romance into graphology – practitioners in the household of Louis *Quatorze* were able to discern the true intent behind notes sent between men and women of the Royal Court." She waggled her raised index finger at us. "Sprightly, Mr. Holmes, sprightly!"

His face assumed a solemn aspect. "Well, I mean to test the limits of your abilities, Madam. Can you, for instance, make meaningful conclusions from a single letter of the alphabet?" He drew the will, signed with the *X*, from his pocket and handed it to her.

Mrs. Baugh dropped into a chair and bent her head over the document. "A very commonplace Copperplate," she began, then looked at

Holmes with a shrewd expression. "But you have no interest in the clerk who copied this document, have you? Neither do I. But see this X at the end? That is quite interesting." She reached for a large magnifying lens which lay atop her chairside table, then concentrated the full force of her attention on the single letter. Holmes and I stood patiently before her. And then she lifted her head, her eyes set thoughtfully on the window opposite.

"One prefers to have a paragraph, so as to compare the penmanship against itself. A signature is next best, as writing one's own name is such a personal and revelatory thing." Mrs. Baugh gently shook her head and turned to my companion. "But a single letter, composed of two lines intersecting at roughly the mid-point! You either flatter me, Mr. Holmes, or you come to tease me, asking me to interpret such a little thing!"

To my astonishment Holmes dropped to one knee before her seated figure, and looked directly into her clear blue eyes. "In my career, my dear Mrs. Baugh, I have found that it is often the little things which are the most important." An encouraging look played across his features. "Tell me something most important about that little X."

She studied it half a minute more and then rose from her chair, offering her hand to my friend and bringing him to a standing position. "The letter X is widely considered to be the most eccentric in the English language, Mr. Holmes," she began, handing the will back to him. "It is a letter rarely used, and therefore brimming with evocation. We shall begin with the downstroke on the left, which travels diagonally to the lower right position. You may have observed it was made first. It is not straight, but contains a hint of a jag. So slight is that jag that one must scrutinize it under a powerful lens, as I did, in order to see it. Think of a river, Mr. Holmes. Rivers always take as their course the route of least resistance – that is why they are crooked. I find it is the same with people. This downstroke was made by a person who is seeking an easy way, the easiest available means to an end, and so the hand has twitched ever so slightly. On the right is the second line of the X. It commences on the upper side and moves diagonally toward the lower left. It extends slightly higher than its counterpart, hinting strongly at dissimulation. Candor, you see, is invariably indicated by a certain evenness of each stroke – in other words, for an honest person the lines would be equal. Therefore, this X was made by an individual who is trying to deviate, or to trick. Taken together, these two strokes confirm that the X-writer is insincere. She – for the mark contains other characteristics that lead one to conclude it was made by a woman – was being dishonest."

"Mrs. Baugh, you are a wonder," Holmes said, and he bent to gently kiss her hand.

We hurried to a lane in West London, near a small park of that name, where the Peppercorns had lived. As Hopkins told us the previous evening, their home had just been sold. A wagon sat before it laden with rugs, tables, and other household goods. A driver tying down the last of the home's contents directed us to a door at the back. After a moment a thin, careworn woman appeared and admitted us. At my companion's enquiry she told us her name was Florrie Budd, housemaid. It seemed the cook, Mrs. Hixson, had already departed for a new situation, while Florrie was left to see to the emptying the house. "I go to my cousin the day after to-morrow," Florrie said. "She's housekeeper of a hotel in Scarborough, and I'm to work with her."

"And you leave here with thirty pounds in your pocket," Holmes commented.

"Mrs. Peppercorn were good to me," Florrie confirmed. "I were housemaid to her and Mr. Peppercorn going on fifteen years." Her face crumpled and tears spilled down her cheeks, which she mopped with the corner of her apron. Holmes steered her toward an old stool, settling her onto it. He patted her arm gently. His manner was invariably kind in situations such as this. "Pray compose yourself, Florrie," he said to her. "Tell me, was Mrs. Peppercorn generous with others, too?"

"With Mrs. Hixson, same as me," Florrie said.

"How about with the Salvation Army?" Holmes asked.

"Oh, yes sir, she loved the Sallies!" Florrie told us. "But there was questions later."

"What kind of questions, Florrie?"

"Mr. O'Donnell come by one day. He has a temper, that one. He were shouting, and Mrs. Peppercorn began to cry."

Holmes glanced over at me, then back at the maid. "He was shouting at Mrs. Peppercorn? Why?"

"No sir, not at her," Florrie said. "He were shouting about Mr. Spool – that's the man that has the Peppercorn's clock shop now. He said Mrs. Peppercorn were careless, and she must do as Mr. Spool wants. Do it. Make it right."

I spoke up. "Tell me, Florrie, did Mrs. Peppercorn leave behind any papers – anything official-looking? Anything that might have come from her solicitor's office? A will, perhaps?"

"Oh yes, sir," she replied. "A lot of papers, in her desk. I can't read. I don't know what they was. But I put 'em in boxes."

I leaned toward her. "Where are those boxes?"

"The dustman took 'em. Ten days ago, likely," she said. "Those papers are gone. And the last of the furniture goes today."

"But is the desk still here? It's possible you overlooked something."

381

"Maybe I did. Maybe the desk is in the wagon."

Holmes and I sprinted out and around the house. The wagon-driver was about to leave, but after Holmes parted with a half-a-crown he was willing to wait. We climbed on the back and moved some dining chairs aside. There, under a square drugget, was Mrs. Peppercorn's desk. We quickly opened its drawers, even checking for false bottoms and tapping for concealed panels, but to no avail. Florrie had done her job well. There was no sign of any will: First, second, or third. Defeated, we climbed down and the wagon went on its way.

We were still brushing the dust from our knees and hands when Holmes turned to me, wearing a bemused expression. "But for the intervention of 'Mrs. General' Booth, our friend Louise Binney might well have had a life like Florrie's," he observed. "They are similar in age, and it's probable their backgrounds are much the same. Thanks to the Salvation Army, today Louise is a high-ranking officer. Florrie didn't have that advantage, so she remains in a lowly state. Notwithstanding, they have hard work in common."

The sun was labouring to break through a fog that lingered into the afternoon. Holmes and I stopped at a stall for sandwiches and tea, then pressed on to the Peppercorn's former place of business. We stood on the pavement across from the shop, trying our best to look like two acquaintances who'd met there by chance. From the corners of our eyes we each stole quick glances across the street. In a large front window we could see a jumble of clocks and watches displayed for the benefit of passersby. Over the door protruded the round face of a real clock, its skeletal workings throbbing with each passing second. Presently, I felt Holmes's hand on my wrist. "I say, Watson," he said with quiet urgency. "The pocket watch that belonged to your brother – the one I once examined and told you of his having descended into poverty and drink. Have it with you?" [3]

I clapped my hand to my pocket. "I do."

"May I?" He held out his hand, and I gave it to him. I observed, dumbfounded, as he seized the stem and wound it forcefully until the spring snapped. He broke it! "Alas, Watson, your watch needs attention," said he, returned it to me. "See if they'll tend to the injury while you wait. Now off you go to learn a great deal."

"Learn a great deal about what, Holmes?" I asked with annoyance.

He snarled impatiently. "You know my methods. Put them to use! What is particularly noteworthy about the shop? Its contents? Its workers? Its condition? Is it prosperous, or fallen on hard times? What of Spool himself? His appearance and character? Data, Watson – bring me data!"

I suppressed the urge to tell him to do it himself. I remembered the solicitor, Besbury-Dubbs, and how that individual was already well-versed, as a result of my published accounts, on the subject of Sherlock Holmes. My friend was well-known and might be recognized, whereas I was merely his invisible chronicler, his "Boswell", his interpreter, his companion. No one knew me. I shrugged and waited for the traffic to lighten so that I could cross the street.

The bell over the door tinkled a welcome as I entered the shop. It was small, though neat and attractively arranged. After being in the chilly street it felt warm and cheery. A sharp tang of oil and metal hung in the air, and underneath it, from somewhere in the unseen back of the shop, came the smell of coffee. A portly man in shirtsleeves, wearing thick glasses, peered at me across the counter. I'd interrupted his work – the dismantled gears of a large clock lay spread on a piece of cloth before him. He was of middle years, medium height, with dark hair and beard after the Van Dyke style. He took off the glasses and reached for his coat. Drawing it on, the man greeted me and asked how he could help me.

"I say, is Mr. Peppercorn in?" I enquired. "My pocket watch has stopped, and he has always looked after it beautifully."

"I'm very sorry to say that Mr. Peppercorn died two years ago," the man replied. "I'm Mr. Spool, and this establishment is now my own. I've a skilled hand with watches. Perhaps I may be of assistance?"

I handed over my watch. He removed the crystal and face, and peered inside. "Why, it's just the spring needs replacing. I've three others ahead of you. Will you leave your watch overnight and return for it to-morrow? Four pence for the repair, and no charge for cleaning." He smiled – here was a pleasant, capable man at home in his establishment.

"All right. If you would be so kind as to prepare a ticket so that I might claim it?" I said to him. "My name's Hudson. And perhaps I might have some of that coffee I smell? Just the thing to warm me up before I return to the cold and damp outside."

"Of course! Just you wait."

As I hoped, he pulled back a curtain and vanished into the rear of his shop. As he did so I had a glimpse of a little stove, cups on a table, a whisky bottle, and a plate with a half-eaten meal, and then the curtain fell. I quickly seized my chance, and, in a paroxysm of activity, I darted behind the counter. I scrutinized that morning's post, as well as several bills which were opened. I memorized names on a couple of accounts that were past due. Heart pounding, I had just resumed my former position when I heard an angry unpleasantness from behind the curtain.

"We are in this together." This was Spool!

"We are not." It was a harsh, accented voice I didn't know.

"I'll inform them you're clutching a bottle again." Spool again. "You'll be ruined."

"That's blackmail, you cur," the mysterious voice replied with a snarl.

"You're finished here. Out, and never come back!" Spool hissed.

The curtain flew aside and a man I'd never before seen – a tall man with a twisted spine matching the description Major Binney had given us for Tim O'Donnell, the Sallie soldier and bookkeeper – stalked out. Though dressed in shabby clothes, he placed a smart Salvation Army cap on his head and looked over his shoulder to the back room. "I took another drink or two, but there is healing for that," he declared. "No such cure for the likes of you, Spool!" He departed, slamming the door so hard the bell dropped to the floor.

After a few seconds of silence the curtain twitched again, and a smiling Spool came out with a cup of coffee in his hand. He was unruffled, though his colour was high. "Here you are, sir. Now about a ticket so you may claim the watch . . . ."

"Thank you kindly, but I have pressing business elsewhere," I told him. I snatched my broken watch from the counter, returned it to my pocket and hurried out the door. O'Donnell was nowhere in sight, and neither was Sherlock Holmes. After several minutes of searching, I gave up and went back to Baker Street.

Holmes was already there when I returned, and to my amazement he was seated before our fire with none other than Tim O'Donnell. They were deep in conversation. It seemed Holmes, too, had recognized the man by his malformed spine and had persuaded the bookkeeper to accompany him. According to O'Donnell, Spool was perpetually short of cash – he'd bought the business from Mrs. Peppercorn, but he was in trouble because of his many other expenses. "That accounts for the past-due bills I saw," I told them.

"There are several more like it," O'Donnell confirmed. "Spool has to raise cash, and do it quickly. He remembered Mrs. Peppercorn – she was an old woman, and her heart was failing. Clearly, she didn't have much time left. That's how he came up with a plan to frighten her into making him her heir.

"He began to leave bottles of whisky in the back room," our visitor continued. "I wasn't able to withstand the temptation. When I started drinking again, he threatened to blackmail me, saying he would go to the Sallies and get me sacked. I risked losing my position at the shop, and at the Salvation Army, if I didn't support his unfounded claims." Spool confronted Mrs. Peppercorn with the old ledgers she'd kept for many years. He maintained that she'd exaggerated the shop's value, thereby cheating him. She hadn't, but in order to bolster his complaint he produced O'Donnell to support the accusations. "I had to lie to protect myself. I told Mrs. Peppercorn there were problems with her books, that she must do as Spool said, and repay him. I did that, and I am ashamed. I even caused her to weep!"

"So we were informed," Holmes commented.

Spool threatened the widow with legal action if she didn't re-write her will, leaving him the portion previously set aside for the Salvation Army. According to O'Donnell, the words, *"not one penny"* were suggested by Spool as a sort of cock-a-doodle.

"So, Mr. O'Donnell, you are the *X*," Holmes exclaimed. "He represents the crossroads of this case, Watson, where Spool's greed intersected with Mrs. Peppercorn's intentions. No wonder Mrs. Peppercorn told her solicitor that her hand hurt. The second will was made under grave duress, after the warning of a professional bookkeeper. Marking it with an *X* was the only avenue of protest she had."

"And Spool seemed like such a nice, jovial man," I said.

"We want the third will so that Spool cannot profit from his scheme," Holmes concluded. "Unless the third version is produced, the *X*'d will is the one that the court must accept. Mrs. Peppercorn's money will be released to Spool."

O'Donnell said in future that we could find him at the Whitechapel Corps, and he left us with his promise to give the police a full statement. "He will give evidence against Spool. For that the judge will show Mr. O'Donnell a measure of mercy," Holmes predicted after our visitor was gone. "Maybe that's more than he deserves, but I think that O'Donnell has taken this valuable lesson to heart. Major Binney will forgive him. She's already told us there is forgiveness for drunkards." He looked at me and shook his head. "You still think Spool is 'nice'? You must learn a lesson, too. *'O villain, villain, smiling, damned villain!'*"

"Shakespeare, I suppose?" I queried, and my friend nodded.

A half-hour later we were on our way again, stopping only so that Holmes could send Hopkins an urgent telegram explaining what had transpired, and requesting that he come immediately to the Whitechapel Corps. Our cabby deftly navigated the East End with its pungent, badly congested streets. The inspector was waiting when we arrived. We found the Corps to be a much-repaired old building not far from the Liverpool Street Station. It consisted of a large, clean central room with a kitchen and a couple of offices at the rear. Here was where daily bowls of soup were given out to hungry persons of all ages. Here also was where poor souls could find refuge from the elements. Here, too, was where noontime Christian services took place, amid considerable singing, shaking of timbrels, and preaching. I never heard Louise Binney preach, but if her kind manner was any indication, then I am certain her sermons were less about brimstone and more about practical goodness. She was Christianity with its sleeves rolled up.

When we arrived it was nearly half-past-six, already growing dark outside. Inside, we found Major Binney handing around mugs of sweet tea and pieces of buttered bread to the ragged mass of humanity huddled on benches placed throughout the room. Though she noted our arrival, she continued to push her tea cart until it was empty, then turned it over to a young associate and stepped forward to greet us. We shook hands and she motioned us into her small office located behind the kitchen. It felt chilly. The tiny grate was empty, as coal would have been an extravagance for this woman who placed the comfort of others before herself. A folded military-style cot was tilted against one wall. On her writing table lay a battered silver cornet, an oil lamp, a neat stack of correspondence, a tray for a fountain pen, her gilt-edged New Testament, and a chipped saucer containing several pennies and some postage stamps. Holmes, Hopkins, and I sat shoulder-to-shoulder on a short bench placed against the wall. Major Binney settled on a hard chair in front of her table. She untied the bow at the side of her chin and lifted the stiff round bonnet from her head. "Please excuse the informality," she told us. "It has been a tiring day. I helped deliver two babies, one of whom won't survive this night. Then I ministered for several hours outside an opium den near the river. Afterward, I nearly came to blows with the Devil himself in Aldgate. I must admit, though, that I'm happy."

She listened solemnly as Holmes explained about the three wills, and how Mrs. Baugh suspected the *X*-mark was made under duress. He finished by relating our adventures: The visit with Florrie, the sacrifice of my pocket watch, and O'Donnell's shame. Hopkins added that the will with the *X*, the version which left "*not one penny*" to the Salvation Army, would necessarily be accepted into probate court, as no trace of the third will could be found.

"I'm terribly sorry for Mrs. Peppercorn," the Major finally stated. "She must have been frightened by the spectre of two angry men claiming she'd cheated Mr. Spool. No wonder she looked so sad when I last saw her."

"But why didn't she come to the police for assistance?" Hopkins asked. "We could have helped her."

"Put yourself in her place," Holmes advised. "The police would have questioned her. Beyond that, she faced the prospect of arrest because of

Spool's accusations. Mrs. Peppercorn was old and alone, in failing health, and, as the Major has noted, she was likely very frightened."

"At this very moment my men are bringing in Spool for questioning," Hopkins said.

"Will he be charged?" I asked.

"Interfering with a witness – O'Donnell – at present," Hopkins replied. "If we had that third will, I could easily add fraud and attempted theft."

"Well, I'm most grateful for your having shed a lot of light on my case, Mr. Holmes," Major Binney said. "I'm appreciative of Dr. Watson's help, too. I'm so glad that Inspector Hopkins arranged for me to meet you. You've been very gracious toward me and my church."

Just for a moment, the only sound in the room was the steady ticking of a small mahogany mantel clock located above the fireplace. Holmes turned toward it.

"Is that by chance the clock Mrs. Peppercorn gave you the day before she was, as you say, 'Promoted to Glory'?"

"Why, yes, Mr. Holmes, it is." She rose, took it in her hands and placed it on her table.

Holmes regarded it curiously. "Of all things: The clockmaker's clock is not very good at keeping time. See? It's thirty-five minutes behind. May I?" He reached across, released the latch on the back, and opened the small door that provided access to the clock's movement. Wedged inside, amid three pulsating brass wheels, there was a slip of white paper. He extracted it, and unfolded it on the table. "Major, I believe this is the *final* last will and testament of Mrs. Thomas Peppercorn: Behold the third will."

And so it was. The document, dated the 28th of November last, stated Mrs. Peppercorn's clear intent to revoke all previous wills and leave her entire estate to the Salvation Army, less thirty pounds each to her cook and maid. It was signed, not with an *X*, but with the full signature of Mrs. Thomas Peppercorn. Rosalind Baugh had been correct: The will signed with the *X* was completed under stressful conditions, against Mrs. Peppercorn's wishes, but done to prevent Mr. Spool from further harassing her. This third will was dated two days after the will with the *X*. Clearly, Mrs. Peppercorn left this final will with those she trusted most: The Salvationists, and Major Binney in particular.

Hopkins reached for the will. "At first light, I will stand before a judge in company with Mr. Besbury-Dubbs," he told us. "If the circumstances are bit irregular, this will is perfectly legal. The Salvation Army will inherit after all."

"No more perplexes," Holmes said.

Major Binney smiled her thanks to us, and for an officer of superior rank I thought she blushed quite prettily. Then she insisted on giving me the clock in honour of my broken pocket watch.

"You've found that will at a fortuitous time, Mr. Holmes," said she. "Eva Booth and I have just received orders to leave in two days' time for America. Our schedule is moved up! Eva has been promoted to Brigadier. She will become the Salvation Army's commander for the Eastern United States. I am to be a Colonel and her second in command!" We congratulated her and then rose to go. As we filed out through the kitchen, I happened to glance back over my shoulder – a gold sovereign glinted atop the pennies and stamps in her chipped saucer! The sight of it must have caused me to stumble, for Holmes's strong hand steadied my shoulder and directed me through the central room and outside.

Our uniformed friend remained with us on the pavement as Hopkins hailed a cab. A misty evening rain was falling, and a single gas lamp illuminated the wet cobblestones and damp passersby. At that moment, Holmes and I saw an inebriate topple into the watery gutter, and to our horror he suddenly vomited on himself. We looked on in amazement as Major – now Colonel – Binney knelt beside him and with her own clean linen gently wiped his chin and breast. The cabby called down to her. "Miss, I wouldn't do that for a million pounds!"

She looked up at him, the raindrops sparkling on her face and hair. "Neither would I," she replied. "But I'd do it for love." She helped the drunken man to his feet, watched him toddle away, and went back inside her Corps as we three departed for our supper in Baker Street.

I settled into the cab between my friends, cradling the clock in my hands. "A most remarkable client," I stated.

"No," Holmes corrected me. "A most remarkable woman."

NOTES

1 – Booth founded the Salvation Army in 1865.
2 – Norton married Irene Adler in "A Scandal in Bohemia".
3 – *The Sign of the Four*.

The Case of the
Short-Sighted Clown
by Susan Knight

Despite it being near midsummer, the morning was dull enough, and I had settled down in my slippers and smoking jacket to peruse the newspapers and generally not bestir myself. I skimmed past reports of the preparations for our dear Queen's Diamond Jubilee celebrations, loitered briefly over news of the publication of a novel entitled *Dracula* by one Bram Stoker that looked diverting enough if somewhat sensational, noted the continuing search for Lord Tonbridge in connection with the murder of his wife's personal maid, and observed with a degree of disappointment, being a Surrey supporter, that Lancashire was likely to win this year's County Cricket Championships.

One article, however, particularly caught my attention, and required a deeper study. It concerned horrifying news from Assam of an earthquake that had claimed fifteen-hundred dead. Following my military service in that part of the world, I have always taken a special interest in the Indian sub-continent. Indeed, I have friends and colleagues still living there and was now hoping that they had survived the disaster.

While I was scanning the news to find further details, Holmes, already dressed to go out, burst into the room. I read action on his face.

"Ah, Watson," he said. "You're here. Capital. I see there is nothing of great moment to detain you and would be delighted if you would join me on an expedition as soon as you can get dressed."

I groaned. Unless this was a case of overriding interest, I would much rather have stayed home with my newspapers. But Holmes persisted.

"We will be detained overnight, so bring the usual necessaries with you."

I groaned some more.

"An overnight expedition," I asked. "Where to?"

"To the seaside, my dear friend," he replied, eyes gleaming. "The seaside and the circus."

I was aghast.

"Seaside! Circus! Holmes, you cannot be serious."

"I assure you that I am most serious, Watson. I have always, you know, wished to revisit Sanger's Circus, ·after it so sadly moved out of London. You recall, do you not, the Amphitheatre that used to stand by

Westminster Bridge. What a place that was! What shows they put on there!"

To say that I was taken aback is hardly to give justice to the amazement with which I received this speech. Never before in all the years I had been acquainted with the great detective had he expressed any notion so frivolous.

He continued, one might even say merrily, rubbing his hands, "Sanger's now has a permanent base in Ramsgate, and I find I have an overwhelming desire to witness again this company which, by-the-bye, is reputed to be much admired by none other than Queen Victoria herself."

I am afraid I was still gaping at my friend and could not bring myself to utter a word in reply.

"You look surprised, Watson, and yet is it not true that recently the two of us have exerted our mental and physical capabilities to the extreme, and dearly need a rest."

This was a reference to our trip to Cornwall two months earlier, when Holmes was supposed be recovering from a bout of nervous exhaustion. Instead we found ourselves caught up in yet another fiendish crime, written up as "The Devil's Foot", resulting in a near-death experience for the both of us.

He now continued. "Are we not due some diversion? Are we not due some fun? And by the seaside too. A much more civilised seaside, I might add, than Mount's Bay."

My mouth dropped open still further. Fun at the seaside was the very last thing that I associated with my friend.

"Come, come," he went on, amused by my stupefaction. "Unless you pull yourself together, Watson, we shall miss the train, and that would be a great pity."

Thus it was that, very shortly after, we were in a cab making with all speed for Charing Cross Station. I could see that Holmes was absorbed in thought, a smile occasionally playing over his thin lips. He was to astonish me further that day – I knew it.

We arrived just in time for the train and found a carriage to ourselves. Soon we left the city behind and rumbled into the garden of England that is the county of Kent. The landscape before my eyes was of rolling fields dotted with farms and oast houses where, as I understand the procedure, hops for local ales are laid out to dry. The round brick structures, with their conical roofs and white chimneys, form a most attractive sight. I tried to call Holmes's attention to them but he seemed more interested in his pipe, and I soon gave up and returned to my newspaper and the deadly events in Assam.

On arrival at Ramsgate, we immediately took rooms in the Railway Hotel, a somewhat down-at-heel establishment but, as Holmes remarked, "Convenient for our purposes." We left our bags and walked the short distance to the centre of the town. I had never before had occasion to visit this once-fashionable resort and was struck immediately by the faded elegance of the Georgian buildings that lined its crescents, the pleasant walks beneath cliffs so white they might rival those of Dover, and a sandy beach which almost made me regret that I had omitted to pack my bathing attire. However, it seemed that the fun we were to have in this place resided not in any of these delights, but in the Amphitheatre that housed Sanger's Circus – the next performance of which, as we ascertained, was to take place at six o'clock that evening. We purchased our tickets and then, not having eaten a morsel since Mrs. Hudson's admittedly substantial breakfast, found ourselves a tavern that served a decent mutton pie and local ale, and feasted most satisfactorily.

"I fear," Holmes remarked, spooning up his gravy with something resembling a relish unusual for him, occasioned perhaps by the fresh sea air, "that this new amphitheatre will bear a feeble enough resemblance to that splendid edifice in Lambeth. However, it will serve, Watson. It will serve."

Yes, but for what, I wondered. I had started harbouring dark suspicions regarding our presence in this town. Holmes had the look about him that I recognised so well – the look that signalled that the chase was on. But when I quizzed him, he simply repeated, "It will be fun, Watson. Just you wait and see."

Before six o'clock, we duly presented ourselves at the Amphitheatre and were shown to a box with crimson drapes. I had never visited the famed Lambeth establishment, and so was not disappointed by this one, while Holmes pronounced himself to be well-enough satisfied. We had a splendid view out over the stage and, although I am not a frequenter of such entertainments, the excitement of the crowd pouring into the galleries around us transferred itself to me and I soon found myself agog with anticipation. I looked across at Holmes, who seemed to share my emotions, his eyes shining, his long nose twitching, like a foxhound at the hunt.

What can I say of the ensuing performance? How we the audience all exclaimed at those sleek Arabian horses speeding around the ring, mounted by acrobats who leapt and somersaulted from one to the next in the most death-defying ways, or at the lady who posed as Britannia with at her feet a lion as tame-seeming as a puss cat, caressing his fur, letting him lick her hand (I have seen lions in the wild and know of what bloody ferocity they are capable – he could have bitten off her hand in a trice), or the wire walkers and trapeze artists flying above our heads in defiance of Mr. Newton's Law of Gravity. How we laughed at the knock-about clowns, with their red noses and grotesque make-up, trying in vain to best the white-face in his motley costume and pointed hat, their worst efforts rebounding back on them, constantly getting themselves drenched with water, kicked on the backside, or slapped about the head.

The next act thrilled me even beyond all the preceding. I have, of course, seen elephants in both Africa and Asia, and was not so amazed as my neighbours at the agility and intelligence of these magnificent beasts, even when they performed a charming little dance or lifted young ladies high in the air with their trunks. Yet even I could not suppress a gasp when one of the young ladies laid herself down under the raised foot of the biggest elephant of all. In a second she could have been crushed to death. I glanced around at Holmes to judge his reaction – but he was nowhere to be seen. How long he had been gone I could not even say, I had been staring so hard at the performers all the while.

Knowing my friend, I understood that he must have good reasons which would became apparent in the due course of time, and so I sat back again to enjoy the show. First came the jugglers, tossing a seemingly infinite number of balls into the air or spinning plates on slim poles held in their mouths. Then a fire eater and a sword swallower. As a medical man, I was particularly interested in the physical issues relating to the latter two acts. For the sword swallower, I reasoned that once past the pharynx and oesophageal sphincter, the rapier could be lowered straight down into the stomach, though progressing, it must be said, dangerously close to the aorta, the heart, and the lungs. And how to control the gag reflex? It was certainly an amazing feat.

As for the fire eater, whose act consisted in taking some inflammable spirit into his mouth and igniting it so that a massive flame spurted out, dragon-like, I was just trying to judge how this was possible without inflicting severe burns on the mouth and throat, recalling those natives I had observed in India who thought nothing of walking over red hot coals, when the clowns tumbled in again. There seemed to be more of them now, all vying to persecute the white-face, who, lordly as ever, frustrated their every attempt. They kept trying to whisk off his face a gigantic pair of green spectacles and sometimes even succeeded, leaving white-face to chase the thief around the ring, until he managed to grab the scamp by the scruff of his neck, kicking him on the backside so that he cannoned across the ring, and then with exaggerated dignity replacing the spectacles on his own nose. It was most comical. Next, one of the clowns urged another through mime to swallow a sword. We roared with laughter as the reluctant sword swallower kept hesitating, while the first flapped his arms like a chicken.

Then the horses returned, and the clowns tried most hilariously to emulate the leaps and bounds of the acrobats, their apparent clumsiness almost requiring even more skill than that of the tumblers themselves. Indeed, it appeared inevitable at any moment that one or other clown would be crushed beneath those racing hooves as they swung perilously under the belly of the beasts. One daredevil with a most villainous painted visage even managed to clamber on top of a horse's back and stood balancing there for some seconds, waving, it seemed, right at me, until he leapt off again and tumbled over the sawdust of the ring. How we cheered! How we applauded!

At last the show was over and still no sign of Holmes. I lingered in the hope of seeing him amidst the diminishing throng but without success. Wherever could he be? Then I had a sudden fearful thought. What if his enemies had followed him here and abducted him under my very nose? Colonel Moran was capable of anything. I blamed myself. I should have kept watch instead of letting myself be distracted by the show. It was with trepidation, therefore, that I hurried back to the Railway Hotel.

There, to my great relief, tempered with no little annoyance, I found my friend comfortably reclining in the snug, calmly smoking his pipe, a mug of ale at his elbow.

"What kept you, Watson?" he enquired.

"Where were you?" I countered, not mentioning my worries concerning his safety, which no doubt he would have found foolish.

"My apologies. I bumped into an old acquaintance and quite lost track of time," he said. "I trust you enjoyed the rest of the show."

"Indeed, I did." I started to regale him with an account of the acts. "I cannot see," I said, "how the fire eater avoids getting terrible burns on his mouth."

"Come, come, you as a doctor should understand the basic science of the trick. When the man closes his mouth, the oxygen that stokes the fire is cut off and it goes out."

"Yes, but it is still very dangerous," I couldn't help but add. "I'm sure there must be some terrible accidents."

"No doubt, if the practitioner doesn't take the correct precautions. But tell me, did you not enjoy the clowns the most?"

"The clowns?" I replied. "Indeed they were very comical, but I think the elephants were the best."

"Pah, elephants!" Holmes exclaimed, and would have said more on the subject, had a noisy crowd not just then entered the public bar.

"Why," I said, glancing through the glass partition. "Aren't these circus folk?"

"I believe some of them are staying here," Holmes drawled.

My suspicions that this was not the simple excursion Holmes had claimed it to be were renewed and I peered more closely at my friend.

"Holmes," I said, "there is a rim of white on your face and something in your hair. Allow me."

I stepped forward and brushed at his head, picking up one or two of the flakes and examining them.

"Sawdust!" I exclaimed.

"Oh, Watson, I fear you have found me out. Now at last I may retire and leave the detecting to you."

"But I don't understand."

"You still do not see. Ah, my friend, my friend." He sighed, then, "Walter!" calling to the group in the bar. "Walter, a moment if you please."

An elderly man detached himself from his party and joined us in the snug. Holmes was smiling broadly, as was this new arrival.

"Watson, meet Walter, the old acquaintance of whom I was just now speaking."

"So did you enjoy yourself, Mr. Holmes?" the man asked. "Looked like it anyway. Like old times it were. If ever you wants a job . . . . "

"Do not tempt me, Walter," Holmes laughed. "And pray, let me buy you a mug of the best Kentish ale. It is the least I can do."

"I won't say no to that, Mr. Holmes," replied the old man. "Indeed and I won't."

I looked from one to the other, totally mystified.

"Poor Watson," said Holmes. "Let me put you out of your misery. You see, one summer when I was a lad of fourteen, Walter and his troupe came to the town where I was holidaying with my parents and brother Mycroft. Every night I crept out in secret to mix with the circus folk."

"Indeed, Dr. Watson," the old man said, "we thought that when we left town, young master Sherlock would come along with us for certain."

Again I found myself gaping in astonishment. I suppose I had never thought of Holmes as a boy, or if I did, it would have been as a studious solitary lad, never one making merry with the circus.

"I sometimes regret, Walter," my friend went on, "that I did not do that very thing. How differently my life would have turned out."

"You had a natural talent, Mr. Holmes. Well, you proved that tonight, didn't you."

Suddenly I realised what had been right under my nose.

"That was *you* in the ring – the clown on horseback!" I exclaimed. "That was you, Holmes, was it not?" Now I understood the greasepaint on his face, the sawdust in his hair.

"Did you see me wave at you?" Holmes chuckled.

"You could have been killed."

"I admit, I am not as flexible as I was at age fourteen, and yet I acquitted myself not too badly, though I am perhaps a little bruised."

"So was it for that, so you could play stupid tricks, and worry me half to death, that you dragged me to Ramsgate?" I asked, my anger rising.

Holmes became suddenly serious,

"No, my dear friend, not for that. Not at all."

The door of the snug opened then and a young man entered, muffled as if against sharp mid-winter chills, when it was nearer mid-summer and still a balmy evening. The newcomer was wearing thick eyeglasses which flashed at the sight of us and he seemed about to withdraw again, when Walter called out to him, "Joey, don't go yet. Join us, please."

"Yes, Joey," said Holmes. "The ale is on me tonight. I insist on treating you."

The man hesitated, then shrugged and sat himself in a chair at a slight distance from the rest of us, away from the lamplight, while Holmes signalled to the potboy to refill our mugs and bring a new one for our guest.

"You recognise Joey of course, Watson," said Holmes.

"Should I?" I replied, looking at the man. Did I imagine it or did he recoil from my gaze?

"Perhaps not without his white-face," Holmes smiled.

"Ah, the clown, the *auguste*," I said. The other seemed to relax. "It was a great show," I added.

He nodded in recognisance.

"A good name for a clown, Joey," Holmes went on. "After Joey Grimaldi, perhaps."

"Indeed." A low voice from our guest.

Walter meanwhile was casting searching glances from one man to the other. A strange tension had arisen. Something was up. I didn't have to wait very long to learn what it was.

The potboy brought our mugs of ale and Holmes raised his to the newcomer.

"Your very good health, my Lord," he said.

The other started up, spilling his ale as he made for the door.

"Stop, sir, stop!" cried Holmes. "I mean you no harm! I am sorry to have frightened you."

What was this? I gazed in astonishment at the man, no white-face now needed, his face the colour of Ramsgate's chalk cliffs.

"Please to sit again, my Lord, and take my mug of ale. Your need is greater than mine."

That title again.

"I assure you that, without your whiskers, you are almost unrecognisable," Holmes went on. "Only for Walter's sharp eyes, and my own corroboration when I saw you back stage."

I tried to put whiskers on the shaved face. A sudden inspiration hit me.

"Lord Tonbridge!" I exclaimed.

"Hush, Watson," Holmes chided.

This was the man wanted for the murder of his wife's maid! I had seen his likeness in the paper that very morning.

"Walter sent me a telegram last night," Holmes continued. "He didn't wish to alert the police at once, to give you a chance to explain yourself."

"I am innocent," his Lordship whispered.

"And yet you have run away – gone into hiding."

"A foolish panic, I admit. But believe me I never harmed Marianna."

"It is said that you mistook the maid for your wife, whom you hate."

"I do not hate my wife."

"You were heard threatening her that afternoon."

Lord Tonbridge put his head in his hands in despair. "The evidence is against me, I know. But however far Lydia drove me, I would never have hurt her, never have killed her."

Holmes considered the man. "I am prepared to believe you," he said at last, "and I will try and help prove it. But in God's name, man, whyever take refuge in a circus, publicly on display to the whole world."

His Lordship explained that his first plan had been to flee to the Continent where he could have disappeared forever. But on arrival in the port of Dover, he had caught sight of a poster for Sanger's, with a grinning clown face on it.

"Since I was a boy," he said, "I have had a yen for the circus."

I glanced at Holmes, who was nodding with understanding.

"I thought it would be the perfect disguise," his Lordship went on. "As a clown in heavy make- up. And as you say, clean-shaven for the first time since I started to grow a beard. Who would recognise Lord Tonbridge, or even dream that the white-face could be he?" He turned to Walter. "And yet you recognised me."

Walter smiled. "I am like one of our elephants, your Lordship," he said. "I never forget. Not a face, anyway. Just like with Mr. Holmes here, I remembered how you came to see the circus as a young lad. Night after night, you crept to the tent and asked me about the clowns, the animals. Of course, what you really wanted was to catch sight of young Rosa, our little trapeze artiste."

"Rosa, yes. I often wonder whatever happened to her." His Lordship's voice softened at the memory.

"She married Victor, the strong man, and had a litter of babies," Walter said. "I think they're up north, York way, these days."

"I'm glad she's happy," his Lordship remarked a little sadly.

"Anyway," Holmes interrupted, perhaps impatient with the notes of sentiment and nostalgia that had crept into the conversation, "we need a plan if we are to help you. I propose returning to London forthwith to interview all the witnesses, examine the murder scene, and see what emerges. I assume that her Ladyship is staying in the capital."

"Yes, she will be at our town house in Piccadilly. Lydia hates the countryside. But on what pretext will you visit her? My wife will hardly relish your presence if she knows that you're trying to clear my name."

Holmes gave him a sharp look. "Is that a fact? Interesting! Well, I will not tell her that, of course. Quite the opposite. She will think that I'm on her side. But first, please give me an account of the evening of the murder, as well as you can remember it."

"That's the problem, Mr. Holmes. I remember very little."

"Come, come, sir, that will not do. You remember little Rosa from fifteen years ago. You must remember what happened less than two weeks since."

"Well, now," his Lordship reflected. "I had been at my club, my usual refuge from the unpleasantness of the domestic scene. And had perhaps, as was my wont, partaken rather too lavishly of wine and brandy. To numb my senses, you understand."

My God, I thought – the poor gentleman, driven to drink.

"Hmm," said Holmes. "But I understand it was *before* you went out that you had been heard threatening Lady Tonbridge."

"She goaded me unmercifully, Mr. Holmes. I may have said some foolish things, but I almost feel that she put the words into my mouth. I remember at a certain moment she raised her voice and cried out, 'Don't strike me again, you brute!' when all I had done was to lay a hand upon her arm."

"I see. And it was for that reason you went to the club?"

"Indeed, the house has become intolerable to me." He paused. "No, I did not murder Marianna thinking it was my wife. I cannot imagine who might have done such a deed. I can only think it was an interloper come to rob us – it is well known that my wife has many valuable jewels. Perhaps the poor maid interrupted the thief and bore the fatal consequences." His Lordship peered hopefully at us through those thick glasses.

"Perhaps, perhaps," Holmes said. "And yet . . . ."

"It was madness to run away, I know that now. Everyone thinks that it proves my guilt." Despair rang in his voice.

I decided to speak. "If you are innocent, Holmes will prove it."

"If?" the young man turned on me, suddenly imperious. "If? There are no 'if's' about it, Dr. Watson."

"Well, well," Holmes said, peaceably, "Let us try to collect some facts. You can start by telling me who was present in the house on the day in question?"

Tonbridge took off his glasses and squeezed his eyes shut, as if trying to reconstruct the scene in his head.

"Her Ladyship was there of course, and the servants . . . Well, our son James, but he is only four. His nanny, Rogers . . . Ah, I remember now. The lawyer, Mr. Shanks, was briefly at the house. Lydia had asked him to call. Something to do with a piece of property she inherited from her late godmother." He furrowed his brow in thought. "Miss Overton, the dressmaker came around as well, to fit yet another shockingly expensive robe for her Ladyship, which she will probably only ever wear the once. That was the reason for our row, in fact. The ruinously costly way of life that Lydia insists upon." He shook his head. "That is all, I think. Oh, Hobbes, the butler, informed me that the young man poor Marianna was seeing had been lurking in the kitchen at one time, against all the rules of the house."

Holmes sighed. "The young man's name?"

"I do not know it." Spoken with the dismissive arrogance of a man who hardly could be expected to be aware of the identity of one of his servant's followers.

"You are sure that is all, then?" There was a sardonic tone to Holmes's query.

"Yes – No, Lydia's brother had called in earlier, but like most of the others, I think he had left by the evening."

"Her brother?"

"Yes, Cedric. Cedric Crane. Her twin. He's an all-too-frequent visitor, I'm afraid."

"You don't like him?"

"Not at all. He's a wastrel and a parasite who can do no wrong in Lydia's eyes. Indeed, I had just announced a few days before that I would be stopping the allowance that Lydia insisted I bestow upon him. She was not at all pleased, but, Mr. Holmes, Cedric just fritters it all away – clothes, gaming, indulgences of all kinds. I told them for his own sake he should get himself some employment. Earn his keep."

Holmes considered this then asked, "No one else?"

"Not that I know of. At least, I don't think so – "

Holmes banged his hand on the table and we all jumped.

"Really, your Lordship. This will not do at all. Not at all. First you tell me no one was in the house, and now it seems a whole menagerie was present at one time or another."

"I apologise, Mr. Holmes. I do, indeed," replied the chastened gentleman. "I am most grateful for your interest and help. But at the time of poor Marianna's murder . . . well, as I said, all of these visitors had left."

"So you know the time of her death, then?" Holmes fixed a piercing gaze on the young man.

"I . . . I assumed . . . I mean . . . ."

"We make no assumptions. We only deal in hard facts." Then Holmes relented. "My dear fellow, you have gone through a great deal. I am sorry if I sound harsh. I assure you, Dr. Watson and I will do our very best to get to the bottom of the matter. But it is still not clear to me exactly why you should be suspected to the extent that you felt the need to take flight."

"Oh," replied his Lordship. "Well, because I found her."

"No more than that?"

Tonbridge looked discomforted. "It didn't look good, Mr. Holmes. As I told you, I had returned late from my club and went to my study, where I'm afraid that I partook of more brandy." He looked up as if expecting some rebuke. A weak man after all, I thought, easily put down. "I dozed off and . . . well . . . it would not be the first time that I have woken up in the study, sometimes spending the whole night upon the couch"

"Not this time."

"No, some noise disturbed me. I cannot say what it was. In my confused state, I simply wished to return to my bed. I left the study and almost stumbled over Marianna . . . ." His voice broke at the memory. "It was quite dark, you know."

"The body was not there when you came back from the club."

"Oh no. That would be impossible. She was lying right by the door. I would swear on the Bible that she wasn't there earlier. I should have had to have step over her to gain access to the room, and I did not."

With great delicacy, Holmes raised his hands and joined the fingers of each, closing his eyes as if praying. He was clearly deep in thought, envisaging the scene.

"Was the body cold?" he asked at last.

"Good Lord, man, I didn't touch her! I could not. And how could she be cold? I wasn't asleep for more than an hour."

"What then?" asked Holmes. "You raised the alarm?"

"I didn't have time. The next thing that I knew, my wife was standing at the head of the stairs, staring down at me. Then she started screaming. Hobbes the butler arrived soon after, and the other servants. I cannot recall exactly. It is all such a horrible blur. I heard Lydia cry out, 'Murderer! He has killed her!' Mr. Holmes . . . the way they all looked at me . . . ." The young gentleman broke down entirely.

"Calm yourself, sir," Holmes said sternly. "We need your clearest recollections. Tell me, were you wearing your eyeglasses at the time?"

"Of course, I am almost blind without them."

"And yet you performed perfectly well at the circus. I didn't see you wearing them then. Apart from the sham ones, of course."

"I can explain that," said Walter, who had been sitting quietly the while, as had I. "Surely you observed how the other clowns led him around and put him in the right place?"

"I did, but I thought it was part of the act."

"It is a strange thing, though," said Tonbridge, "and I have only just thought of it. Before I left for the club that night, I couldn't find my eyeglasses anywhere. They weren't where I thought that I'd left them, and I had to leave without them."

"And yet you found them on your return."

"No, indeed. They were still missing. Luckily I keep a spare pair at the club."

"A-ha!" Holmes said smiling and rubbing his hands. "Excellent. Excellent."

We all regarded him in amazement. How was this important?

"Well, your Lordship," Holmes continued. "Watson and I will take our leave of you. I hope to be able to give you some good news very soon."

And with that, we bade a somewhat surprised Walter and Lord Tonbridge a very good night and adjourned to our respective bedrooms.

"It is indeed a most interesting case, Watson, though not so complex after all," said Holmes as we journeyed back to London the following morning, having first sent a wire to Lady Tonbridge requesting an interview. "Things are starting to fall into place. I merely need to confirm my suspicions."

"Do you?" I asked. "It seems a complete puzzle to me. I was racking my brains all night. Do you think – maybe a lovers' tiff that went wrong? Who knows what sort of a ruffian Marianna had taken up with? Or perhaps indeed, as his Lordship suggested, it was some thief who broke in after the jewels and was surprised by the maid. In fact," I warmed to the thought, "the lover and the thief could be one and the same person."

"The mysterious interloper. Ah yes, indeed. It might well be, although the supposed thief got nothing for his pains. No jewels were found to be missing. So what do you think? Perhaps his Lordship murdered her, after all. That swift flight wouldn't seem to be the act of an innocent man. And you have of course noted that without his eyeglasses he can hardly see anything. In the dark, he might well have mistook the maid for the wife he pretends not to loathe."

"But he said he was wearing eyeglasses."

"Watson, Watson . . . Have you met a murderer yet who told you the truth?"

Was Holmes serious? His words troubled me and, as we sped towards London, I sat staring at my hands, hoping it was the lover or the interloper because I should not like his Lordship to be guilty after all.

"But Watson," Holmes interrupted my thoughts. "you are missing the oast houses. Are they not a most pleasing sight?"

With all haste that very afternoon – so not, as Holmes said, to give Lady Tonbridge time to refuse our request – we arrived at the town house in Piccadilly. A dignified elderly butler I took to be Hobbes showed us into a splendidly appointed room that looked out through golden drapes at the bustling thoroughfare. A pale Chinese carpet partly covered a polished wooden floor. Delicate furnishings reflected an excellent if expensive taste. In particular, a chaise longue in the rococo style caught my eye – surely an antique. The delicious perfume in the air could be traced to a lavish display of mixed flowers standing in a Murano red-glass vase on a side table.

Her Ladyship joined us soon and received us graciously enough.

Lady Lydia Tonbridge proved to be an imposing young woman in her middle-twenties. Tall, in a fine dress of pearl grey silk and sparkling with some of those notorious jewels, her almost-white blonde hair raised in a lavish chignon, she was at the same time painfully thin and pale, those diamonds adorning a neck that was bony and scrawny. As for her bosom, it barely existed – she could have passed for a boy. Were she my patient, I should have prescribed a hearty diet of roast beef, mutton stew with dumplings, and plenty of rice puddings.

"You sent word that you have news of my husband?" she said, regarding us with slate grey eyes. "I hope he isn't planning to return here soon and finish the job."

A coarse-enough expression, I thought.

"You are convinced then that he is guilty of the crime and that you were the intended victim?"

"What other explanation could there be? So where is he, Mr. Holmes?"

"I have it on good authority that he planned to flee to the Continent and may now be in France."

"Ah, I suspected as much. Good riddance to the coward. Although of course," she added in a cold tone, "it would be preferable if he had been captured by the police, brought to trial, and hanged."

Good Lord, what a woman! What a wife!

"It is kind of you, of course," she added, "to come in person to set my mind at rest, and yet it seems an unnecessary journey. A letter would have sufficed."

Holmes put on his most charming smile, a smile that I often thought could charm a snake. "I was hoping," he said silkily, "that I might prevail on your Ladyship to indulge myself and Dr. Watson in a project on which we are engaged."

Her Ladyship regarded us quizzically.

"You may know," Holmes continued, "that I have some small interest in crime."

She bowed in acknowledgement.

"It just so happens that Dr. Watson and I are writing a monograph on notorious murders of the decade – "

Are we, indeed? First that I heard of it.

" – and I would like to include an account of the murder of your maid. Sad to say, the public love to read about the nobility when they have been found to be up to no good."

"So true, Mr. Holmes. So true . . . Alas, poor Marianna." Her Ladyship pressed a lacy handkerchief to her eyes. "If only I had not given her my old dress and shawl, Ralph might not have mistook her. But then – Oh God! It could have been me! I could have been the one so cruelly strangled to death. Horrible! Horrible!" She sank, quite overcome, onto the chaise longue.

At that moment, the door swung open and an exceedingly thin and fair young man entered, followed by a small child and a motherly looking person whom I took to be the nanny.

"Oh, my deepest apologies, Lydia," he exclaimed, looking askance at us. "I didn't know that you had company." The young man was so identical to her Ladyship that I judged him to be the twin brother. "I was just bringing Lord Tonbridge to see his dear mamma. He wouldn't stay away."

Lord Tonbridge – and the child's father not yet dead! I couldn't help but notice the boy's reluctance to run to his dear mamma, and how he was watching us all with wide eyes, clutching on to his nanny's skirts betimes, as if hoping they would envelop him.

402

"Cedric," said Lady Tonbridge, quite recovered from her previous emotion, "this is Mr. Sherlock Holmes and Dr . . . er . . . er. . . ."

"Dr. Watson!" The young man strode forward and clasped each of us by the hand. He looked effete, a dandy, dressed in a pale suit with a flowered silk waistcoat, his jacket sporting a carnation in its buttonhole in the style of the followers of poor Mr. Wilde. Yet his grip was strong. "My dear sirs, I am most honoured to make your acquaintance. Cedric Crane, younger brother by a whole ten minutes of my dearest Lydia." He smiled, though his eyes were as flinty as hers. "I have long followed Mr. Holmes's illustrious career through your most excellent accounts, Doctor."

He was perhaps a little too enthusiastic, and his hand a little too wet.

"But to what do we owe this most delightful visit?" he went on.

Lady Tonbridge explained.

"Lord Tonbridge in France," he exclaimed. "Then you have nothing more to fear, Lydia."

"Just so long as he stays there, of course," her Ladyship said drily.

"And now Mr. Holmes," Crane went on, "you wish to see the scene of the crime, to write about it. Capital! I shall show you myself."

"Thank you," said Holmes gravely. I was sure, knowing his methods, that he wouldn't wish to be encumbered by the presence of such an overbearing young man. But how politely was he to extricate himself?

We left her Ladyship with her son, Holmes bending first to sniff at the fragrant flowers, shaking his head in an uncharacteristic appreciation of the blooms. As we quitted the room, I heard Lady Tonbridge mutter, "Rogers, I am not able for this now. Please take James to the nursery or out to the park or somewhere – anywhere, out of my sight."

A loving mother, indeed!

Holmes examined the study and the hallway outside in minute detail, with Crane and myself looking on, though what could be found there so long after the event was quite beyond me.

"Marianna was lying where exactly?" Holmes asked.

"Oh well," Crane said. "By the door, I think. I cannot say exactly. I wasn't present, you know."

"Then you weren't staying here that night?"

"No. Why would I?"

"Well, being so close to your sister . . . ."

"Would that I had been here, Mr. Holmes!" he burst out. "I might have prevented this foul deed."

"How could you have done that?"

"Well . . . ."

"You weren't to know that it would happen, were you?"

403

"No, of course not. But Ralph – Lord Tonbridge – had threatened Lydia earlier that day. He had struck her, you know."

"All the more reason, I should have thought, to stay and keep watch."

"Well, I didn't." Crane sounded petulant.

Holmes then asked to speak to the butler.

"Hobbes?"

"I understand that the butler was one of the first on the scene – after your sister, of course, but I really don't wish to trouble her further."

"Ah yes, yes. Hobbes. I'll fetch him." And Crane wandered off down the hallway.

"Watson, rid me of this boy, please. I don't wish him present while I talk to the butler."

"How am I to do that?"

"You must think of something."

An instruction I did not relish. When Crane returned with the butler, all I could devise was a request that he take me below stairs to talk to the servants to see if they had any evidence to provide.

"To give a full picture to our readers, you know," I added lamely.

Crane gave me a sharp look, which I returned with a blank one. Let him think me a fool. At any rate, it worked for, without demur, he led me down to the kitchen where I kept him with me for as long as I could, asking stupid questions of the cook and scullery maid, who had seen and heard nothing at all.

Meanwhile, Holmes was free to speak to Hobbes, and later gave me an account of what transpired. It seemed that the butler had been roused from his slumbers by her Ladyship's scream. It being about two o'clock of the morning, it took him several minutes to reach the sorry scene.

"Were the lights on?" Holmes asked.

"No," Hobbes replied, "but her Ladyship was holding a candle, which provided sufficient illumination."

"It was lucky she was up and about at the relevant time."

The butler bowed his head but made no reply to that.

"So what exactly did you see?"

"Her Ladyship was at the top of the stairs, sir, while his Lordship, seeming frozen with shock, was standing over poor prostrate Marianna." Hobbes shook his head at the memory.

"Was his Lordship wearing his eye-glasses?"

"His eyeglasses, sir? I'm sure I could not say."

"And yet, I suppose you are used to seeing him with his eyeglasses." Hobbes nodded. "So it might have struck you particularly if he was *not* wearing them."

"Yes, sir. I suppose that is very possible."

404

Holmes then asked what the butler did next and learnt that he had examined the body, to make sure life had left the poor girl. Something, I recalled, that his Lordship had been too fastidious to do.

"Was she warm or cold?" Holmes queried.

"Oh sir, she was colder rather than warm," Hobbes replied. "And already going stiff, you know. I thought that very odd, sir, if the murder had only just taken place."

"So do you think his Lordship did it?"

Hobbes paused, shocked perhaps at the brutality of the question, and then replied, "To be honest, no, sir. It is not in master's character to be violent. I have known him since the man was a boy, and a gentler person you could not hope to meet."

"Yet he threatened her Ladyship earlier," Holmes persisted. "He struck her."

"So they say, sir. So they say." (He laid heavy emphasis on the word "they".)

"If not his Lordship, Hobbes, then who do you think might have done the deed?"

The butler replied that he couldn't imagine. Marianna was a sweet girl with no enemies.

"Her young man perhaps?"

Hobbes was aghast. "Robin? Never! He adored her. They had an understanding, sir."

"Do you think it could have been an interloper, then?"

Hobbes raised his eyes to Holmes' face and looked him straight in the eye. "It depends what you mean by that, sir."

"A thief."

"Thieves come in different shapes and sizes, sir."

"What do you mean by that, Hobbes?"

The butler just shook his head, faithful retainer that he was, and would say no more.

"If someone wanted to conceal a body for a short time, where could they hide it?"

The new question made Hobbes start.

"Somewhere near enough to the study?" Holmes persisted.

After some thought, Hobbes suggested a recess under the stairwell, ever plunged in dark shadow. He indicated the place to Holmes, who looked but indeed could see very little.

It was at that moment that, unable to stay Cedric Crane's impatience any longer, I came up from the kitchen, the young man striding ahead of me.

"A lamp, Hobbes, if you please," Holmes was saying.

"A lamp?" Crane asked.

"Mr. Holmes wishes to look more closely under the stairs," Hobbes explained and set off to fetch a light.

"Under the stairs. Good heavens, man, why?"

"I think the body was perhaps concealed there before it was moved."

"Moved?" Crane's tone was suddenly shrill. "How can that be? Why would Ralph have strangled the woman and then moved her to his study door."

"Why, indeed. To incriminate himself perhaps."

The young man gaped.

"Or perhaps he was planning to carry her out of the house, but was interrupted by her Ladyship."

"Yes, perhaps, so. Indeed."

"No," Holmes shook his head. "No, I do not think so." He smiled, fixing that snake-like gaze upon the young man.

Crane froze. Then exploded.

"This is quite absurd, Holmes. I refuse to take part in this farce. I know your methods, oh yes. I know what you are up to." Cedric Crane's pallid face was now turning red with rage. "Leave this house immediately. Go, I insist upon it."

"I am sorry. Is it your place to give orders here?"

"Lydia will back me up. Lydia! Lydia!" Crane raced off to fetch his sister.

Meanwhile, Hobbes returned with the lamp. Taking it from him, Holmes proceeded to the understairs. I followed him but as far as I could see, the lamp revealed nothing but dust.

Several servants, curious at the noise, including those with whom I had spoken in the kitchen, had come to see what was going on, withdrawing behind half-open doors when their angry mistress burst on to the scene.

"Mr. Holmes, what is this? Doctor . . . whoever you are. Whatever is going on? You presume too much on my good nature, sir."

"He says that Ralph moved the body" Crane babbled. "Have you ever heard anything so absurd? Ha ha ha!"

"No, no, no. Not Lord Tonbridge," said Holmes, emerging from the recess. "He moved no one. He did nothing. The one who moved her was the one who wanted it believed that his Lordship murdered the maid. The cold-hearted devil who murdered her himself."

"Who?" asked Hobbes. "Who did it? What did you find?"

Holmes opened his hand. A few crushed petals lay there. "Hobbes, is his Lordship in the habit of wearing a flower in his buttonhole?"

"No, sir. I have never seen him wear such a thing."

We all looked at Crane, at his carnation. And he, panic-stricken, stared back as us. Then turned on his sister.

"It was all *her* idea! Lydia's idea. I never wanted to go through with it. Never – "

She struck his face so hard that even I flinched. "Fool!" she screeched. "Can you not see it is a trick? I saw Holmes take that flower just now from the vase. After two weeks, petals would not be so fresh." And she struck him again.

"Indeed, your Ladyship," Holmes said, "and yet I think the point is proved."

A few days later we found ourselves in the same lovely room where Lady Tonbridge had first received us. This time we were sitting with her husband, who was dandling his little boy, James, on his knee. From time to time he kissed the boy's head. I suppose he had thought never to see his son again.

"The plan," Holmes explained, "went somewhat awry when you fled the scene so quickly. The pair had expected that you would be arrested, charged, and perhaps, as Lady Tonbridge herself hoped, hanged for murder."

Lestrade, who was now in charge of the case, had reported back to us that, while Lady Tonbridge maintained a cold silence, Cedric was leaking like a bucket, as the inspector so colourfully put it. The pair had carefully concocted evidence against Lord Tonbridge, using the servants to confirm bad blood between husband and wife, particularly in the light of the staged "attack" earlier in the day, when Lady Tonbridge had made sure that everyone would hear her cry out, "Do not strike me again, you brute!" Not realising that his Lordship had a replacement set at his club, as Cedric further revealed, they had stolen and disposed of his Lordship's eyeglasses. Without them, the claim he had mistaken his victim would prove much more persuasive.

"Fiendish, fiendish." Lord Tonbridge stroked his son's hair.

That day, too, it seemed that Marianna had been lured by Lady Tonbridge to dress up in her clothes. The poor girl, according to Hobbes, had been delighted with the cast-offs. She had announced how she could cut a fine dash when next out with her beau. Alas, the poor girl never had the opportunity, strangled by Cedric and unceremoniously dumped under the stairs for some hours – *rigor mortis* having already started to set in – until Tonbridge returned from his club. As was his Lordship's habit, he went straight to his study. The noise he subsequently heard there was perhaps the body being moved into position, or perhaps just a sound intended to arouse him from his slumbers, with her Ladyship already waiting at the top of the stairs for him to emerge.

"I do not understand," his Lordship said. "Did Lydia hate me so much that she was willing to sacrifice an innocent to get rid of me?"

"I doubt if Lady Tonbridge has passion in her for that much hate," Holmes said. "Indifference to the lives of others, certainly. Her passion was greed, pure and simple. You were curtailing her spending. You cut off the allowance to her beloved twin."

"Yet, she had wealth in her own right. The inheritance from her godmother."

"Ah yes," said Holmes, "I have spoken to Mr. Shanks, the lawyer, on that very subject and have discovered that the inheritance Lady Tonbridge was expecting turned out to be a paltry sum after all. With you out of the way and the next Lord Tonbridge," here he indicated the child, "many years from his majority, she and Cedric could get their hands on the family money and indulge their extravagancies to their hearts' content – until the money all ran out, of course."

Lord Tonbridge shook his head. "Money truly is the root of evil. Speaking of which," he added, smiling wanly as he took an envelope from his breast pocket, pressing it into Holmes's hand. "Please accept this, with my deepest gratitude."

Glancing at the contents, Holmes remarked. "Too much, my Lord. Far too much."

"It can never be too much," Tonbridge replied, again kissing the top of his son's head. "And yet, there is after all one thing I regret: Never again to don the motley or whiten my face. Never again to enjoy the comradeship of the circus."

"I am sure," Holmes smiled, "that Walter, who indulged me with a turn in the ring, would certainly not begrudge it you, your Lordship, once in a while."

We all laughed at that, but I noticed a somewhat wistful expression cross Holmes's face. Was he perhaps wondering what his life would have been if, as a boy that time, he really had run away with the circus?

About the Contributors

The MX Book of New Sherlock Holmes Stories
Part XX – 2020 Annual (1891-1897)

Deanna Baran lives in a remote part of Texas where cowboys may still be seen in their natural habitat. A librarian and former museum curator, she writes in between cups of tea, playing *Go*, and trading postcards with people around the world.

S.F. Bennett has, at various times, been an actor, a lecturer, a journalist, a historian, an author and a potter. Whilst some of those things still apply, she has always been an avid collector, concentrating mainly on ephemera and other related items concerning Sherlock Holmes and British science-fiction of the 1970's. To date, she has written articles on aspects of The Canon for *The Baker Street Journal*, *The Sherlock Holmes Journal*, and *The Torr*, the journal of *The Sherlock Holmes Society of the West Country*. When not collecting, she can be found writing science-fiction and mystery stories, and has contributed to several anthologies of new Sherlock Holmes pastiches. Her first novel was *The Secret Diary of Mycroft Holmes: The Thoughts and Reminiscences of Sherlock Holmes's Elder Brother, 1880-1888* (2017). She is also the author of *A Study in Postcards: Sherlock Holmes in the Golden Age of the Picture Postcard* (*Sherlock Holmes Society of London*, 2019).

Brian Belanger is a publisher and editor, but is best known for his freelance illustration and cover design work. His distinctive style can be seen on several MX Publishing covers, including *Silent Meridian* by Elizabeth Crowen, *Sherlock Holmes and the Menacing Melbournian* by Allan Mitchell, *Sherlock Holmes and A Quantity of Debt* by David Marcum, *Welcome to Undershaw* by Luke Benjamen Kuhns, and many more. Brian is the co-founder of Belanger Books LLC, where he illustrates the popular *MacDougall Twins with Sherlock Holmes* young reader series (#1 bestsellers on Amazon.com UK). A prolific creator, he also designs t-shirts, mugs, stickers, and other merchandise on his personal art site: *www.redbubble.com/people/zhahadun*.

Thomas A. Burns, Jr. is the author of the *Natalie McMasters Mysteries*. He was born and grew up in New Jersey, attended Xavier High School in Manhattan, earned B.S degrees in Zoology and Microbiology at Michigan State University, and a M.S. in Microbiology at North Carolina State University. He currently resides in Wendell, North Carolina. As a kid, Tom started reading mysteries with The Hardy Boys, Ken Holt and Rick Brant, and graduated to the classic stories by authors such as A. Conan Doyle, Dorothy Sayers, John Dickson Carr, Erle Stanley Gardner, and Rex Stout, to name a few. Tom has written fiction as a hobby all of his life, starting with The Man from U.N.C.L.E. stories in marble-backed copybooks in grade school. He built a career as technical, science, and medical writer and editor for nearly thirty years in industry and government. Now that he's truly on his own as a novelist, he's excited to publish his own mystery series, as well as to contribute stories about his second-most-favorite detective, Sherlock Holmes, to *The MX anthology of New Sherlock Holmes Stories*.

Lizzy Butler has been the Fundraising, Community, and Events Manager at the Stepping Stones School, located in Hyndhead, Surrey, since early 2019.

Harry DeMaio is a *nom de plume* of Harry B. DeMaio, successful author of several books on Information Security and Business Networks, as well as the twelve-volume *Casebooks of Octavius Bear*. He is also a published author for Belanger Books and *The MX Sherlock Holmes* series edited by David Marcum. A retired business executive, former consultant, information security specialist, pilot, disk jockey, and graduate school adjunct professor, he whiles away his time traveling and writing preposterous books, articles, and stories. He has appeared on many radio and TV shows and is an accomplished, frequent public speaker. Former New York City natives, he and his extremely patient and helpful wife, Virginia, and their Bichon Frisé, Woof, live in Cincinnati (and several other parallel universes.) They have two sons living in Scottsdale, Arizona and Cortlandt Manor, New York, both of whom are quite successful and quite normal, thus putting the lie to the theory that insanity is hereditary. His e-mail is *hdemaio@zoomtown.com* You can also find him on Facebook. His website is *www.octaviusbearslair.com* His books are available on Amazon, Barnes and Noble, directly from MX Publishing, and at other fine bookstores.

Sir Arthur Conan Doyle (1859-1930) *Holmes Chronicler Emeritus.* If not for him, this anthology would not exist. Author, physician, patriot, sportsman, spiritualist, husband and father, and advocate for the oppressed. He is remembered and honored for the purposes of this collection by being the man who introduced Sherlock Holmes to the world. Through fifty-six Holmes short stories, four novels, and additional Apocryphal entries, Doyle revolutionized mystery stories and also greatly influenced and improved police forensic methods and techniques for the betterment of all. *Steel True Blade Straight.*

Anna Elliott is an author of historical fiction and fantasy. Her first series, *The Twilight of Avalon* trilogy, is a retelling of the Trystan and Isolde legend. She wrote her second series, *The Pride and Prejudice Chronicles*, chiefly to satisfy her own curiosity about what might have happened to Elizabeth Bennet, Mr. Darcy, and all the other wonderful cast of characters after the official end of Jane Austen's classic work. She enjoys stories about strong women, and loves exploring the multitude of ways women can find their unique strengths. She was delighted to lend a hand with the "Sherlock and Lucy" series, and this story, firstly because she loves Sherlock Holmes as much as her father, co-author Charles Veley, does, and second because it almost never happens that someone with a dilemma shouts, "Quick, we need an author of historical fiction!" Anna lives in the Washington, D.C .area with her husband and three children.

Matthew J. Elliott is the author of *Big Trouble in Mother Russia* (2016), the official sequel to the cult movie *Big Trouble in Little China, Lost in Time and Space: An Unofficial Guide to the Uncharted Journeys of Doctor Who* (2014), *Sherlock Holmes on the Air* (2012), *Sherlock Holmes in Pursuit* (2013), *The Immortals: An Unauthorized Guide to* Sherlock *and* Elementary (2013), and *The Throne Eternal* (2014). His articles, fiction, and reviews have appeared in the magazines *Scarlet Street, Total DVD, SHERLOCK,* and *Sherlock Holmes Mystery Magazine,* and the collections *The Game's Afoot, Curious Incidents 2, Gaslight Grimoire, The Mammoth Book of Best British Crime 8,* and *The MX Book of New Sherlock Holmes Stories – Part III: 1896-1929.* He has scripted over 260 radio plays, including episodes of *Doctor Who, The Further Adventures of Sherlock Holmes, The Twilight Zone, The New Adventures of Mickey Spillane's Mike Hammer, Fangoria's Dreadtime Stories,* and award-winning adaptations of *The Hound of the Baskervilles* and *The War of the Worlds.* He is the only radio dramatist to adapt all sixty original stories from The Canon for the series *The Classic Adventures of Sherlock Holmes.* Matthew is a writer and performer on *RiffTrax.com,* the online comedy experience from the creators of cult sci-fi TV series *Mystery Science Theater 3000* (*MST3K* to the initiated). He's also written a few comic books.

Steve Emecz's main field is technology, in which he has been working for about twenty years. Steve is a regular trade show speaker on the subject of eCommerce, and his tech career has taken him to more than fifty countries – so he's no stranger to planes and airports. He wrote two novels (one a bestseller) in the 1990's, and a screenplay in 2001. Shortly after, he set up MX Publishing, specialising in NLP books. In 2008, MX published its first Sherlock Holmes book, and MX has gone on to become the largest specialist Holmes publisher in the world. MX is a social enterprise and supports three main causes. The first is Happy Life, a children's rescue project in Nairobi, Kenya, where he and his wife, Sharon, spend every Christmas at the rescue centre in Kasarani. In 2014, they wrote a short book about the project, *The Happy Life Story*. The second is the Stepping Stones School, of which Steve is a patron. Stepping Stones is located at Undershaw, Sir Arthur Conan Doyle's former home. Steve has been a mentor for the World Food Programme for the last several years, supporting their innovation bootcamps and giving 1-2-1 mentoring to several projects.

Sonia Fetherston BSI is a member of the illustrious *Baker Street Irregulars.* For almost thirty years, she's been a frequent contributor to Sherlockian anthologies, including Calabash Press's acclaimed *Case Files* series, and Wildside Press's *About* series. Sonia's byline often appears in the pages of *The Baker Street Journal, The Journal* of the *Sherlock Holmes Society of London, Canadian Holmes*, and the Sydney Passengers' *Log*. Her work earned her the coveted Morley-Montgomery Award from the *Baker Street Irregulars*, and the Derek Murdoch Memorial Award from *The Bootmakers of Toronto*. Sonia is author of *Prince of the Realm: The Most Irregular James Bliss Austin* (BSI Press, 2014). She's at work on another biography for the BSI, this time about Julian Wolff.

Mark A. Gagen BSI is co-founder of Wessex Press, sponsor of the popular *From Gillette to Brett* conferences, and publisher of *The Sherlock Holmes Reference Library* and many other fine Sherlockian titles. A life-long Holmes enthusiast, he is a member of *The Baker Street Irregulars* and *The Illustrious Clients of Indianapolis*. A graphic artist by profession, his work is often seen on the covers of *The Baker Street Journal* and various BSI books.

John Atkinson Grimshaw (1836-1893) was born in Leeds, England. His amazing paintings, usually featuring twilight or night scenes illuminated by gas-lamps or moonlight, are easily recognizable, and are often used on the covers of books about The Great Detective to set the mood, as shadowy figures move in the distance through misty mysterious settings and over rain-slicked streets.

Arthur Hall was born in Aston, Birmingham, UK, in 1944. He discovered his interest in writing during his schooldays, along with a love of fictional adventure and suspense. His first novel, *Sole Contact,* was an espionage story about an ultra-secret government department known as "Sector Three", and was followed, to date, by three sequels. Other works include five Sherlock Holmes novels, *The Demon of the Dusk, The One Hundred Percent Society, The Secret Assassin, The Phantom Killer*, and *In Pursuit of the Dead*, as well as a collection of short stories, and a modern detective novel. He lives in the West Midlands, United Kingdom.

Stephen Herczeg is an IT Geek, writer, actor, and film-maker based in Canberra Australia. He has been writing for over twenty years and has completed a couple of dodgy novels, sixteen feature-length screenplays, and numerous short stories and scripts. Stephen was very successful in 2017's International Horror Hotel screenplay competition, with his scripts *TITAN* winning the Sci-Fi category and *Dark are the Woods* placing second in the horror category. His work has featured in *Sproutlings – A Compendium of Little Fictions* from Hunter Anthologies, the *Hells Bells* Christmas horror anthology published by the Australasian Horror Writers Association, and the *Below the Stairs, Trickster's Treats, Shades of Santa, Behind the Mask,* and *Beyond the Infinite* anthologies from OzHorror.Con, *The Body Horror Book, Anemone Enemy,* and *Petrified Punks* from Oscillate Wildly Press, and *Sherlock Holmes In the Realms of H.G. Wells* and *Sherlock Holmes: Adventures Beyond the Canon* from Belanger Books.

Steven Philip Jones has written over sixty graphic novels and comic books including the horror series *Lovecraftian, Curious Cases of Sherlock Holmes,* the original series *Nightlinger, Street Heroes 2005,* adaptations of *Dracula,* several H. P. Lovecraft stories, and the 1985 film *Re-animator.* Steven is also the author of several novels and nonfiction books including *The Clive Cussler Adventures: A Critical Review, Comics Writing: Communicating With Comic Book , King of Harlem, Bushwackers, The House With the Witch's Hat, Talisman: The Knightmare Knife,* and *Henrietta Hex: Shadows From the Past.* Steven's other writing credits include a number of scripts for radio dramas that have been broadcast internationally. A graduate of the University of Iowa, Steven has a Bachelor of Arts in Journalism and Religion, and was accepted into Iowa's Writer's Workshop – M.F.A. program.

Roger Johnson BSI, ASH is a retired librarian, now working as a volunteer assistant at the Essex Police Museum. In his spare time, he is commissioning editor of *The Sherlock Holmes Journal,* an occasional lecturer, and a frequent contributor to *The Writings about the Writings.* His sole work of Holmesian pastiche was published in 1997 in Mike Ashley's anthology *The Mammoth Book of New Sherlock Holmes Adventures,* and he has the greatest respect for the many authors who have contributed new tales to the present mighty trilogy. Like his wife, Jean Upton, he is a member of both *The Baker Street Irregulars* and *The Adventuresses of Sherlock Holmes.*

Susan Knight's most recent collection of short stories, *Mrs Hudson Investigates,* was issued by MX Publishing in November 2019. She is the author of two other non-Sherlockian, story collections, as well as three novels, a book of non-fiction, and several plays. She lives in Dublin where she teaches Creative Writing. She is currently working on a new Mrs Hudson novel set in Ireland.

John Lescroart is a New York Times bestselling author known for his series of legal and crime thriller novels featuring the characters Dismas Hardy, Abe Glitsky, and Wyatt Hunt. His novels have sold more than ten-million copies, have been translated into twenty-two languages in more than seventy-five countries, and eighteen of his books have been on *The New York Times* bestseller list. Libraries Unlimited has included him in its publication "The 100 Most Popular Thriller and Suspense Authors". Lescroart was born in Houston, Texas, and graduated from Junípero Serra High School in San Mateo, California (Class of 1966). He earned a B.A. in English with Honors at UC Berkeley in 1970. Before becoming a full-time writer in 1994, Lescroart was a self-described "Jack of all trades", who worked as a word processor for law firms as well as a bartender, moving man, house painter, editor, advertising director, computer programmer, and fundraising executive. Through his twenties, he was also a full-time singer-songwriter-guitarist, and performed under the name Johnny Capo, with Johnny Capo and his Real Good Band. In addition to nearly thirty novels, Lescroart has written several screenplays, and he is an original founding member of the group *International Thriller Writers*. John's blog at *JohnLescroart.com* is updated regularly with writing tips, insights on his books, recipes, recommendations, book give-aways, and more! Please also find John on Twitter and Facebook.

David Marcum plays *The Game* with deadly seriousness. He first discovered Sherlock Holmes in 1975 at the age of ten, and since that time, he has collected, read, and chronologicized literally thousands of traditional Holmes pastiches in the form of novels, short stories, radio and television episodes, movies and scripts, comics, fan-fiction, and unpublished manuscripts. He is the author of over sixty Sherlockian pastiches, some published in anthologies and magazines such as *The Strand*, and others collected in his own books, *The Papers of Sherlock Holmes*, *Sherlock Holmes and A Quantity of Debt*, and *Sherlock Holmes – Tangled Skeins*. He has edited fifty books, including several dozen traditional Sherlockian anthologies, such as the ongoing series *The MX Book of New Sherlock Holmes Stories*, which he created in 2015. This collection is now up to 21 volumes, with several more in preparation. He was responsible for bringing back August Derleth's Solar Pons for a new generation, first with his collection of authorized Pons stories, *The Papers of Solar Pons*, and then by editing the reissued authorized versions of the original Pons books. He is now doing the same for the adventures of Dr. Thorndyke. He has contributed numerous essays to various publications, and is a member of a number of Sherlockian groups and Scions. He is a licensed Civil Engineer, living in Tennessee with his wife and son. His irregular Sherlockian blog, *A Seventeen Step Program*, addresses various topics related to his favorite book friends (as his son used to call them when he was small), and can be found at *http://17stepprogram.blogspot.com/* Since the age of nineteen, he has worn a deerstalker as his regular-and-only hat. In 2013, he and his deerstalker were finally able make his first trip-of-a-lifetime Holmes Pilgrimage to England, with return Pilgrimages in 2015 and 2016, where you may have spotted him. If you ever run into him and his deerstalker out and about, feel free to say hello!

Jacquelynn Morris, ASH, BSI, JHWS, is a member of several Sherlock Holmes societies in the Mid-Atlantic area of the U.S.A., but her home group is Watson's Tin Box in Maryland. She is the founder of *A Scintillation of Scions*, an annual Sherlock Holmes symposium. She has been published in the BSI Manuscript Series, *The Wrong Passage*, as well as in *About Sixty* and *About Being a Sherlockian* (Wildside Press). Jacquelynn was the U.S. liaison for the Undershaw Preservation Trust for several years, until Undershaw was purchased to become part of Stepping Stones School.

Mark Mower is a member of the *Crime Writers' Association, The Sherlock Holmes Society of London*, and *The Solar Pons Society of London*. He writes true crime stories and fictional mysteries. His first two volumes of Holmes pastiches were entitled *A Farewell to Baker Street* and *Sherlock Holmes: The Baker Street Case-Files* (both with MX Publishing) and, to date, he has contributed chapters to six parts of the ongoing *The MX Book of New Sherlock Holmes Stories*. He has also had stories in two anthologies by Belanger Books: *Holmes Away From Home: Adventures from the Great Hiatus – Volume II – 1893-1894* (2016) and *Sherlock Holmes: Before Baker Street* (2017). More are bound to follow. Mark's non-fiction works include *Bloody British History: Norwich* (The History Press, 2014), *Suffolk Murders* (The History Press, 2011) and *Zeppelin Over Suffolk* (Pen & Sword Books, 2008).

Will Murray is the author of over seventy novels, including forty *Destroyer* novels and seven posthumous *Doc Savage* collaborations with Lester Dent, under the name Kenneth

Robeson, for Bantam Books in the 1990's. Since 2011, he has written a number of additional Doc Savage adventures for Altus Press, two of which co-starred The Shadow, as well as a solo Pat Savage novel. His 2015 Tarzan novel, *Return to Pal-Ul-Don*, was followed by *King Kong vs. Tarzan* in 2016. Murray has written short stories featuring such classic characters as Batman, Superman, Wonder Woman, Spider-Man, Ant-Man, the Hulk, Honey West, the Spider, the Avenger, the Green Hornet, the Phantom, and Cthulhu. A previous Murray Sherlock Holmes story appeared in Moonstone's *Sherlock Holmes: The Crossovers Casebook*, and another in *Sherlock Holmes and Doctor Was Not*, involving H. P. Lovecraft's Dr. Herbert West. Additionally, his Sherlock Holmes stories have appeared in *The MX Book of New Sherlock Holmes Stories*. His most recent book is *Tarzan, Conqueror of Mars*.

Sidney Paget (1860-1908), a few of whose illustrations are used within this anthology, was born in London, and like his two older brothers, became a famed illustrator and painter. He completed over three-hundred-and-fifty drawings for the Sherlock Holmes stories that were first published in *The Strand* magazine, defining Holmes's image forever after in the public mind.

Robert Perret is a writer, librarian, and devout Sherlockian living on the Palouse. His Sherlockian publications include "The Canaries of Clee Hills Mine" in *An Improbable Truth: The Paranormal Adventures of Sherlock Holmes*, "For King and Country" in *The Science of Deduction*, and "How Hope Learned the Trick" in *NonBinary Review*. He considers himself to be a pan-Sherlockian and a one-man Scion out on the lonely moors of Idaho. Robert has recently authored a yet-unpublished scholarly article tentatively entitled "A Study in Scholarship: The Case of the *Baker Street Journal*". His is the author of *Dead ringers: Sherlock Holmes Stories* (2019). More information is available at *www.robertperret.com*

Gayle Lange Puhl has been a Sherlockian since Christmas of 1965. She has had articles published in *The Devon County Chronicle*, *The Baker Street Journal*, and *The Serpentine Muse*, plus her local newspaper. She has created Sherlockian jewelry, a 2006 calendar entitled "If Watson Wrote For TV", and has painted a limited series of Holmes-related nesting dolls. She co-founded the scion *Friends of the Great Grimpen Mire* and the Janesville, Wisconsin-based *The Original Tree Worshipers*. In January 2016, she was awarded the "Outstanding Creative Writer" award by the Janesville Art Alliance for her first book *Sherlock Holmes and the Folk Tale Mysteries*. She is semi-retired and lives in Evansville, Wisconsin. Ms. Puhl has one daughter, Gayla, and four grandchildren.

Tracy J. Revels, a Sherlockian from the age of eleven, is a professor of history at Wofford College in Spartanburg, South Carolina. She is a member of *The Survivors of the Gloria Scott* and *The Studious Scarlets Society*, and is a past recipient of the Beacon Society Award. Almost every semester, she teaches a class that covers The Canon, either to college students or to senior citizens. She is also the author of three supernatural Sherlockian pastiches with MX (*Shadowfall*, *Shadowblood*, and *Shadowwraith*), and a regular contributor to her scion's newsletter. She also has some notoriety as an author of very silly skits: For proof, see "The Adventure of the Adversarial Adventuress" and "Occupy Baker Street" on YouTube. When not studying Sherlock, she can be found researching the history of her native state, and has written books on Florida in the Civil War and on the development of Florida's tourism industry.

Vincent Starrett (1886–1974) was a Canadian-born American writer, newspaperman, and bibliophile. Born in Canada, his father moved the family to Chicago in 1889. In 1907, he began working for the *Chicago Daily News* as reporter, feature writer, and columnist. In 1920, he wrote the Sherlock Holmes pastiche "The Adventure of the Unique 'Hamlet'", and his most famous work, *The Private Life of Sherlock Holmes*, was published in 1933. He wrote the book column, "Books Alive", for *The Chicago Tribune*, which ran for twenty-five years before retiring it in 1967. Starrett was one of the founders of *The Hounds of the Baskerville* (*sic*), a Chicago scion of *The Baker Street Irregulars*.

Kevin P. Thornton is a seven-time Arthur Ellis Award Nominee. He is a former director of the local Heritage Society and Library, and he has been a soldier in Africa, a contractor for the Canadian Military in Afghanistan, a newspaper and magazine columnist, a Director of both the *Crime Writers of Canada* and the *Writers' Guild of Alberta*, a founding member of *Northword Literary Magazine*, and is either a current or former member of *The Mystery Writers of America*, *The Crime Writers Association*, *The Calgary Crime Writers*, *The International Thriller Writers*, *The International Association of Crime Writers*, *The Keys* – a Catholic Writers group founded by Monsignor Knox and G.K. Chesterton – as well as, somewhat inexplicably, *The Mesdames of Mayhem* and *Sisters in Crime*. If you ask, he will join. Born in Kenya, Kevin has lived or worked in South Africa, Dubai, England, Afghanistan, New Zealand, Ontario, and now Northern Alberta. He lives on his wits and his wit, and is doing better than expected. He is not one to willingly split infinitives, and while never pedantic, is on occasion known to be ever so slightly punctilious.

Christopher Todd has been a nurse for four decades, was a radio production director and copywriter for twenty years, and has been an ordained Episcopal priest for eighteen years, as well as an interim Lutheran pastor and jail chaplain for eight years. He has been a Sherlockian since he was twelve, was a member of *The Noble Bachelors of St. Louis*, has been published in *The Baker Street Journal* and cited three times in *The World Bibliography of Sherlock Holmes and Dr. Watson*. His numerous careers and widespread interests color his blog at *preacherofthenight.blogspot.com*. He lives in the Florida Keys with his wife and is indoctrinating his grandkids in his faith and in Sherlock Holmes, possibly in that order.

Charles Veley has loved Sherlock Holmes since boyhood. As a father, he read the entire Canon to his then-ten-year-old daughter at evening story time. Now, this very same daughter, grown up to become acclaimed historical novelist Anna Elliott, has worked with him to develop new adventures in the *Sherlock Holmes and Lucy James Mystery Series*. Charles is also a fan of Gilbert & Sullivan, and wrote *The Pirates of Finance*, a new musical in the G&S tradition that won an award at the New York Musical Theatre Festival in 2013. Other than the Sherlock and Lucy series, all of the books on his Amazon Author Page were written when he was a full-time author during the late Seventies and early Eighties. He currently works for United Technologies Corporation, where his main focus is on creating sustainability and value for the company's large real estate development projects.

I.A. Watson is a novelist and jobbing writer from Yorkshire who cut his teeth on writing Sherlock Holmes stories and has even won an award for one. His works include Holmes and Houdini, Labours of Hercules, St. George and the Dragon Volumes 1 and 2, and Women of Myth, and the non-fiction essay book Where Stories Dwell. He pens short detective stories as a means of avoiding writing things that pay better. A full list of his sixty-plus published works appears at:
http://www.chillwater.org.uk/writing/iawatsonhome.htm

*The following contributors appear
in the companion volumes:*
The MX Book of New Sherlock Holmes Stories
Part XIX – 2020 Annual (1882-1890)
Part XXI – 2020 Annual (1898-1923)

Ian Ableson is an ecologist by training and a writer by choice. When not reading or writing, he can reliably be found scowling at a clipboard while ankle-deep in a marsh somewhere in Michigan. His love for the stories of Arthur Conan Doyle started when his grandfather gave him a copy of *The Original Illustrated Sherlock Holmes* when he was in high school, and he's proud to have been able to contribute to the continuation of the tales of Sherlock Holmes and Dr. Watson.

Hugh Ashton was born in the U.K., and moved to Japan in 1988, where he remained until 2016, living with his wife Yoshiko in the historic city of Kamakura, a little to the south of Yokohama. He and Yoshiko have now moved to Lichfield, a small cathedral city in the Midlands of the U.K., the birthplace of Samuel Johnson, and one-time home of Erasmus Darwin. In the past, he has worked in the technology and financial services industries, which have provided him with material for some of his books set in the 21st century. He currently works as a writer: Novelist, freelance editor, and copywriter, (his work for large Japanese corporations has appeared in international business journals), and journalist, as well as producing industry reports on various aspects of the financial services industry. Recently, however, his lifelong interest in Sherlock Holmes has developed into an acclaimed series of adventures featuring the world's most famous detective, written in the style of the originals. In addition to these, he has also published historical and alternate historical novels, short stories, and thrillers. Together with artist Andy Boerger, he has produced the *Sherlock Ferret* series of stories for children, featuring the world's cutest detective.

Derrick Belanger is an educator and also the author of the #1 bestselling book in its category, *Sherlock Holmes: The Adventure of the Peculiar Provenance*, which was in the top 200 bestselling books on Amazon. He also is the author of *The MacDougall Twins with Sherlock Holmes* books, and he edited the Sir Arthur Conan Doyle horror anthology *A Study in Terror: Sir Arthur Conan Doyle's Revolutionary Stories of Fear and the Supernatural*. Mr. Belanger co-owns the publishing company Belanger Books, which released the Sherlock Holmes anthologies *Beyond Watson, Holmes Away From Home: Adventures from the Great Hiatus* Volumes 1 and 2, *Sherlock Holmes: Before Baker Street*, and *Sherlock Holmes: Adventures in the Realms of H.G. Wells* Volumes I and 2. Derrick resides in Colorado and continues compiling unpublished works by Dr. John H. Watson.

Andrew Bryant was born in Bridgend, Wales, and now lives in Burlington, Ontario. His previous publications include *Poetry Toronto, Prism International, Existere, On Spec, The Dalhousie Review*, and *The Toronto Star*. His first Holmes story was published in *The MX Book of New Sherlock Holmes Stories - Part XIII*, with the second in *Part XVI*. The two stories in this collection are the third and fourth. Andrew's interest in Holmes stems from watching the Basil Rathbone and Nigel Bruce films as a child, followed by collecting The Canon, and a fascinating visit to 221B Baker Street.

Bob Byrne was a columnist for *Sherlock Magazine* and has contributed to *Sherlock Holmes Mystery Magazine* and the Sherlock Holmes short story collection *Curious*

418

Incidents. He publishes two free online newsletters: *Baker Street Essays* and *The Solar Pons Gazette*, both of which can be found at *www.SolarPons.com*, the only website dedicated to August Derleth's successor to the Great Detective. Bob's column, *The Public Life of Sherlock Holmes*, appears every Monday morning at *www.BlackGate.com* and explores Holmes, hard boiled, and other mystery matters, and whatever other topics come to mind by the deadline. His mystery-themed blog is *Almost Holmes*.

Nick Cardillo has been a devotee of Sherlock Holmes since the age of six. His first published short story, "The Adventure of the Traveling Corpse" appeared in *The MX Book of New Sherlock Holmes Stories – Part VI: 2017 Annual*, and he has written subsequent stories for both MX Publishing and Belanger Books. In 2018, Nick completed his first anthology of new Sherlock Holmes adventures entitled *The Feats of Sherlock Holmes*. Nick is a fan of The Golden Age of Detective Fiction, Hammer Horror, and Doctor Who. He writes film reviews and analyses at *Sacred-Celluloid.blogspot.com*. He is a student at Susquehanna University in Selinsgrove, PA.

Chris Chan is a writer, educator, and historian. He works as a researcher and "International Goodwill Ambassador" for Agatha Christie Ltd. His true crime articles, reviews, and short fiction have appeared (or will soon appear) in *The Strand*, *The Wisconsin Magazine of History*, *Mystery Weekly*, *Gilbert!*, *Nerd HQ*, Akashic Books' *Mondays are Murder* web series, *The Baker Street Journal*, and *Sherlock Holmes Mystery Magazine*.

Leslie Charteris was born in Singapore on May 12th, 1907. With his mother and brother, he moved to England in 1919 and attended Rossall School in Lancashire before moving on to Cambridge University to study law. His studies there came to a halt when a publisher accepted his first novel. His third one, entitled *Meet the Tiger*, was written when he was twenty years old and published in September 1928. It introduced the world to Simon Templar, *aka* The Saint. He continued to write about The Saint until 1983 when the last book, *Salvage for The Saint*, was published. The books, which have been translated into over thirty languages, number nearly a hundred and have sold over forty-million copies around the world. They've inspired, to date, fifteen feature films, three television series, ten radio series, and a comic strip that was written by Charteris and syndicated around the world for over a decade. He enjoyed travelling, but settled for long periods in Hollywood, Florida, and finally in Surrey, England. He was awarded the Cartier Diamond Dagger by the *Crime Writers' Association* in 1992, in recognition of a lifetime of achievement. He died the following year.

Craig Stephen Copland confesses that he discovered Sherlock Holmes when, sometime in the muddled early 1960's, he pinched his older brother's copy of the immortal stories and was forever afterward thoroughly hooked. He is very grateful to his high school English teachers in Toronto who inculcated in him a love of literature and writing, and even inspired him to be an English major at the University of Toronto. There he was blessed to sit at the feet of both Northrup Frye and Marshall McLuhan, and other great literary professors, who led him to believe that he was called to be a high school English teacher. It was his good fortune to come to his pecuniary senses, abandon that goal, and pursue a varied professional career that took him to over one-hundred countries and endless adventures. He considers himself to have been and to continue to be one of the luckiest men on God's good earth. A few years back he took a step in the direction of Sherlockian studies and joined the *Sherlock Holmes Society of Canada* – also known as *The Toronto Bootmakers*. In May of 2014, this esteemed group of scholars announced a contest for the writing of a new Sherlock Holmes mystery. Although he had never tried his hand at fiction before, Craig entered and was pleasantly surprised to be selected as one of the winners. Having enjoyed the experience, he decided to write more of the same, and is now on a mission to write a new Sherlock Holmes mystery that is related to and inspired by each of the sixty stories in the original Canon. He currently lives and writes in Toronto and Dubai, and looks forward to finally settling down when he turns ninety.

Ian Dickerson was just nine years old when he discovered The Saint. Shortly after that, he discovered Sherlock Holmes. The Saint won, for a while anyway. He struck up a friendship with The Saint's creator, Leslie Charteris, and his family. With their permission, he spent six weeks studying the Leslie Charteris collection at Boston University and went on to write, direct, and produce documentaries on the making of *The Saint* and *Return of The Saint,* which have been released on DVD. He oversaw the recent reprints of almost fifty of the original Saint books in both the US and UK, and was a co-producer on the 2017 TV movie of *The Saint*. When he discovered that Charteris had written Sherlock Holmes stories as well – well, there was the excuse he needed to revisit The Canon. He's consequently written and edited three books on Holmes' radio adventures. For the sake of what little sanity he has, Ian has also written about a wide range of subjects, none of which come with a halo, including talking mashed potatoes, Lord Grade, and satellite links. Ian lives in Hampshire with his wife and two children. And an awful lot of books by Leslie Charteris. Not quite so many by Conan Doyle, though.

David Friend lives in Wales, Great Britain, where he divides his time between watching old detective films and thinking about old detective films. Now thirty, he's been scribbling out stories for twenty years and hopes, some day, to write something half-decent. Most of what he pens is set in an old-timey world of non-stop adventure with debonair sleuths, kick-ass damsels, criminal masterminds, and narrow escapes, and he wishes he could live there.

Tim Gambrell lives in Exeter, Devon, with his wife, two young sons, three cats, and now only four chickens. He has previously contributed two stories to *The MX Book of New Sherlock Holmes Stories*: "The Yellow Star of Cairo" in Vol. XIII, and "The Haunting of Bottomly's Grandmother" in Vol. XVI. He also contributed a story to *Sherlock Holmes and Dr Watson: The Early Adventures*, Vol. III, from Belanger Books, and has a further tale in Vol. II of the forthcoming collection *Sherlock Holmes and The Occult Detectives*, also from Belanger Books. Outside of the world of Holmes, Tim has written extensively for Doctor Who spin-off ranges. His books include two linked novels from Candy Jar Books: *Lethbridge-Stewart: The Laughing Gnome – Lucy Wilson & The Bledoe Cadets*, and *The Lucy Wilson Mysteries: The Brigadier and The Bledoe Cadets* (both 2019), and *Lethbridge-Stewart: Bloodlines – An Ordinary Man* (Candy Jar, 2020, written with Andy Frankham-Allen). He's also written a novella, *The Way of The Bry'hunee* (2019) for the Erimem range from Thebes Publishing. Tim's short fiction includes stories in *Lethbridge-Stewart: The HAVOC Files 3* (Candy Jar, 2017, revised edition 2020), *Bernice Summerfield: True Stories* (Big Finish, 2017) and *Relics . . . An Anthology* (Red Ted Books, 2018), plus a number of charity anthologies.

Jayantika Ganguly BSI is the General Secretary and Editor of the *Sherlock Holmes Society of India*, a member of the *Sherlock Holmes Society of London,* and the *Czech Sherlock Holmes Society*. She is the author of *The Holmes Sutra* (MX 2014). She is a corporate lawyer working with one of the Big Six law firms.

Dick Gillman is an English writer and acrylic artist living in Brittany, France with his wife Alex, Truffle, their Black Labrador, and Jean-Claude, their Breton cat. During his retirement from teaching, he has written over twenty Sherlock Holmes short stories which are published as both e-books and paperbacks. His contribution to the superb MX Sherlock Holmes collection, published in October 2015, was entitled "The Man on Westminster Bridge" and had the privilege of being chosen as the anchor story in *The MX Book of New Sherlock Holmes Stories – Part II (1890-1895)*.

Denis Green was born in London, England in April 1905. He grew up mostly in London's Savoy Theatre where his father, Richard Green, was a principal in many Gilbert and Sullivan productions, A Flying Officer with RAF until 1924, he then spent four years managing a tea estate in North India before making his stage debut in *Hamlet* with Leslie Howard in 1928. He made his first visit to America in 1931 and established a respectable stage career before appearing in films – including minor roles in the first two Rathbone and Bruce Holmes films – and developing a career in front of and behind the microphone during the golden age of radio. Green and Leslie Charteris met in 1938 and struck up a lifelong friendship. Always busy, be it on stage, radio, film or television, Green passed away at the age of fifty in New York.

Arthur Hall – *In addition to a story in this volume, Arthur also has stories in Parts XIX and XXI*

Paula Hammond has written over sixty fiction and non-fiction books, as well as short stories, comics, poetry, and scripts for educational DVD's. When not glued to the keyboard, she can usually be found prowling round second-hand books shops or hunkered down in a hide, soaking up the joys of the natural world.

Christopher James was born in 1975 in Paisley, Scotland. Educated at Newcastle and UEA, he was a winner of the UK's National Poetry Competition in 2008. He has written two full length Sherlock Holmes novels, *The Adventure of the Ruby Elephant* and *The Jeweller of Florence*, both published by MX, and is working on a third.

John Lawrence served for thirty-eight years as a staff member in the U.S. House of Representatives, the last eight as Chief of Staff to Speaker Nancy Pelosi (2005-2013). He has been a Visiting Professor at the University of California's Washington Center since 2013. He is the author of *The Class of '74: Congress After Watergate and the Roots of Partisanship* (2018), and has a Ph.D. in history from the University of California (Berkeley).

David L. Leal PhD is Professor of Government and Mexican American Studies at the University of Texas at Austin. He is also an Associate Member of Nuffield College at the University of Oxford and a Senior Fellow of the Hoover Institution at Stanford University. His research interests include the political implications of demographic change in the United States, and he has published dozens of academic journal articles and edited nine books on these and other topics. He has taught classes on Immigration Politics, Latino Politics, Politics and Religion, Mexican American Public Policy Studies, and Introduction to American Government. In the spring of 2019, he taught British Politics and Government, which had the good fortune (if that is the right word) of taking place parallel with so many Brexit developments. He is also the author of three articles in *The Baker Street Journal* as well as letters to the editor of the *TLS: The Times Literary Supplement, Sherlock Holmes Journal*, and *The Baker Street Journal*. As a member of the British Studies Program at UT-

Austin, he has given several talks on Sherlockian and Wodehousian topics. He most recently wrote a chapter, "Arthur Conan Doyle and Spiritualism," for the program's latest book in its *Adventures with Britannia* series (Harry Ransom Center/IB Tauris/Bloomsbury). He is the founder and Warden of "MA, PhD, Etc," the BSI professional scion society for higher education, and he is a member of *The Fourth Garrideb*, *The Sherlock Holmes Society of London*, *The Clients of Adrian Mulliner*, and *His Last Bow (Tie)*.

Michael Mallory is the Derringer-winning author of the "Amelia Watson" (The Second Mrs. Watson) series and "Dave Beauchamp" mystery series, and more than one-hundred-twenty-five short stories. An entertainment journalist by day, he has written eight nonfiction books on pop culture and more than six-hundred newspaper and magazine articles. Based in Los Angeles, Mike is also an occasional actor on television.

David Marcum – *In addition to a story in this volume, David also has stories in Parts XIV and XV*

Steve Mason has been the Third Mate (President) of *The Crew of the Barque* Lone Star scion society in Dallas/Fort Worth for over seven years. He is also the Chair of the Communications Committee for *The Beacon Society*, a national educational scion society. With Joe Fay and Rusty Mason, he produces the *Baker Street Elementary* comic strip each week, the first adventures of Sherlock Holmes and John Watson.

James Moffett is a Masters graduate in Professional Writing, with a specialisation in novel and non-fiction writing. He also has an extensive background in media studies. James began developing a passion for writing when contributing to his University's student magazine. His interest in the literary character of Sherlock Holmes was deep-rooted in his youth. He released his first publication of eight interconnected short stories titled *The Trials of Sherlock Holmes* in 2017, along with previous contributions to *The MX Book of New Sherlock Holmes Stories*.

Mark Mower – *In addition to a story in this volume, Mark also has a story in Part XXI*

Will Murray – *In addition to a story in this volume, Will also has stories in Part XIX*

Richard K. Radek, the author of *The Sequestered Adventures of Sherlock Holmes* series, is a native of Evanston, Illinois (USA), and a graduate of Northern Illinois University. He is a prominent arbitrator, certified educator, and author of many legal articles and awards. A long time student of The Canon, Mr. Radek writes traditional, period-authentic Holmes adventures, faithful to the style and chronology of the original Doyle tales. One hallmark of his work is the accuracy of the historical detail Mr. Radek instills in the plots, persona, and settings of his Holmes stories. Another is the wit and wry humor woven in and interspersed. The result is a body of work that can be appreciated by the entire spectrum of Holmes aficionados, from the novice only just learning about Sherlock who wants an entertaining story, to the most discriminating experts who can appreciate the many, sometimes subtle, Holmesian insights Mr. Radek hides in the stories. In the main, Mr. Radek's tales are great fun to read.

Roger Riccard of Los Angeles, California, U.S.A., is a descendant of the Roses of Kilravock in Highland Scotland. He is the author of two previous Sherlock Holmes novels, *The Case of the Poisoned Lilly* and *The Case of the Twain Papers*, a series of short stories in two volumes, *Sherlock Holmes: Adventures for the Twelve Days of Christmas* and *Further Adventures for the Twelve Days of Christmas*, and the new series *A Sherlock Holmes Alphabet of Cases,* all of which are published by Baker Street Studios. He has another novel and a non-fiction Holmes reference work in various stages of completion. He became a Sherlock Holmes enthusiast as a teenager (many, many years ago), and, like all fans of The Great Detective, yearned for more stories after reading The Canon over and over. It was the Granada Television performances of Jeremy Brett and Edward Hardwicke, and the encouragement of his wife, Rosilyn, that at last inspired him to write his own Holmes adventures, using the Granada actor portrayals as his guide. He has been called "The best pastiche writer since Val Andrews" by the *Sherlockian E-Times.*

Jane Rubino is the author of A Jersey Shore mystery series, featuring a Jane Austen-loving amateur sleuth and a Sherlock Holmes-quoting detective, *Knight Errant, Lady Vernon and Her Daughter*, (a novel-length adaptation of Jane Austen's novella *Lady Susan*, co-authored with her daughter Caitlen Rubino-Bradway, *What Would Austen Do?*, also co-authored with her daughter, a short story in the anthology *Jane Austen Made Me Do It, The Rucastles' Pawn, The Copper Beeches from Violet Turner's POV*, and, of course, there's the Sherlockian novel in the drawer – who doesn't have one? Jane lives on a barrier island at the New Jersey shore.

Geri Schear is a novelist and short story writer. Her work has been published in literary journals in the U.S. and Ireland. Her first novel, *A Biased Judgement: The Diaries of Sherlock Holmes 1897* was released to critical acclaim in 2014. The sequel, *Sherlock Holmes and the Other Woman* was published in 2015, and *Return to Reichenbach* in 2016. She lives in Kells, Ireland.

Brenda Seabrooke's stories have been published in sixteen reviews, journals, and anthologies. She has received grants from the National Endowment for the Arts and Emerson College's Robbie Macauley Award. She is the author of twenty-three books for young readers including *Scones and Bones on Baker Street: Sherlock's (maybe!) Dog and the Dirt Dilemma*, and *The Rascal in the Castle: Sherlock's (possible!) Dog and the Queen's Revenge*. Brenda states: "It was fun to write from Dr. Watson's point of view and not have to worry about fleas, smelly pits, ralphing, or scratching at inopportune times."

Matthew Simmonds hails from Bedford, in the South East of England, and has been a confirmed devotee of Sir Arthur Conan Doyle's most famous creation since first watching Jeremy Brett's incomparable portrayal of the world's first consulting detective, on a Tuesday evening in April, 1984, while curled up on the sofa with his father. He has written numerous short stories, and his first novel, *Sherlock Holmes: The Adventure of The Pigtail Twist*, was published in 2018. A sequel is nearly complete, which he hopes to publish in the near future. Matthew currently co-owns Harrison & Simmonds, the fifth-generation family business, a renowned County tobacconist, pipe, and gift shop on Bedford High Street.

Robert V. Stapleton was born and brought up in Leeds, Yorkshire, England, and studied at Durham University. After working in various parts of the country as an Anglican parish priest, he is now retired and lives with his wife in North Yorkshire. As a member of his local writing group, he now has time to develop his other life as a writer of adventure stories. He has recently had a number of short stories published, and he is hoping to have a couple of completed novels published at some time in the future.

Joseph W. Svec III is retired from Oceanography, Satellite Test Engineering, and college teaching. He has lived on a forty-foot cruising sailboat, on a ranch in the Sierra Nevada Foothills, in a country rose-garden cottage, and currently lives in the shadow of a castle with his childhood sweetheart and several long coated German shepherds. He enjoys writing, gardening, creating dioramas, world travel, and enjoying time with his sweetheart.

Kevin P. Thornton – *In addition to a story in this volume, Kevin also has a story in Part XIX*

Thomas A. (Tom) Turley was born in Virginia, grew up in Tennessee, and lives now in Montgomery, Alabama. He and his wife Paula have two grown children and one beautiful granddaughter. Although Tom has a Ph.D. in British history, he spent most of his career as an archivist with the State of Alabama. Approaching retirement, he returned to a youthful hobby: Writing fiction. Tom's first story, "The Devil's Claw", appeared in *The Book of Villains*, a 2011 Main Street Rag anthology. His pastiche "Sherlock Holmes and the Adventure of the Tainted Canister" (2014) is available as an e-book and an audiobook from MX Publishing. It was also published in *The Art of Sherlock Holmes – USA Edition 1* (2019), in company with a painting by artist Angela Fegan. Three of Tom's stories, "A Scandal in Serbia", "A Ghost from Christmas Past", and "The Solitary Violinist" have appeared in MX Publishing's ongoing anthology of traditional pastiches (Parts VI, VII, and XVIII). The latter two were praised by *Publishers Weekly* in its reviews of the relevant MX volumes. "Ghost" was also included in *The Art of Sherlock Holmes, West Palm Beach Edition* (2019), paired with a painting by artist Nune Asatryan. Tom's latest short story, "A Game of Skittles", appears in MX Publishing' spring 2020 anthology, *Part XIX*. Later this year, Tom should complete a collection of historical pastiches entitled *Sherlock Holmes and the Crowned Heads of Europe*. The first story chronologically, "Sherlock Holmes and the Case of the Dying Emperor", is already available from MX Publishing as an e-book. Set in Berlin in 1888, during the brief reign of Emperor Frederick III (son-in-law of Queen Victoria and father of the notorious "Kaiser Bill"), it inaugurates Sherlock Holmes's espionage campaign against the German Empire, which ended only in August 1914 with "His Last Bow". When completed, *Sherlock Holmes and the Crowned Heads of Europe* will also include "A Scandal in Serbia" and two new stories on the last dynastic tragedies that befell the House of Habsburg. Tom's non-literary interests include hiking, ship modeling, classical music, and University of Tennessee athletics (not a popular pursuit in Alabama!). Interested readers can contact him through MX Publishing or his Goodreads and Amazon author's pages.

D.J. Tyrer is the person behind Atlantean Publishing, was placed second in the Writing Magazine "Local Reporter" competition, and has been widely published in anthologies and magazines around the world, such as *Disturbance* (Laurel Highlands), *Mysteries of Suspense* (Zimbell House), *History and Mystery, Oh My!* (Mystery & Horror LLC), and *Love 'Em, Shoot 'Em* (Wolfsinger), and issues of *Awesome Tales*, and in addition, has a novella available in paperback and on the Kindle, *The Yellow House* (Dunhams Manor) and a comic horror e-novelette, *A Trip to the Middle of the World*, available from Alban Lake through Infinite Realms Bookstore.
His website is: *https://djtyrer.blogspot.co.uk/*
The Atlantean Publishing website is at *https://atlanteanpublishing.wordpress.com/*

Peter Coe Verbica grew up on a commercial cattle ranch in Northern California, where he learned the value of a strong work ethic. He works for the Wealth Management Group of a global investment bank, and is an Adjunct Professor in the Economics Department at

SJSU. He is the author of numerous books, including *Left at the Gate and Other Poems, Hard-Won Cowboy Wisdom (Not Necessarily in Order of Importance), A Key to the Grove and Other Poems,* and *The Missing Tales of Sherlock Holmes (as Compiled by Peter Coe Verbica, JD).* Mr. Verbica obtained a JD from Santa Clara University School of Law, an MS from Massachusetts Institute of Technology, and a BA in English from Santa Clara University. He is the co-inventor on a number of patents, has served as a Managing Member of three venture capital firms, and the CFO of one of the portfolio companies. He is an unabashed advocate of cowboy culture and enjoys creative writing, hiking, and tennis. He is married with four daughters. For more information, or to contact the author, please go to *www.hardwoncowboywisdom.com.*

Matthew White is an up-and-coming author from Richmond, Virginia in the USA. He has been a passionate devotee of Sherlock Holmes since childhood. He can be reached at *matthewwhite.writer@gmail.com.*

Sean Wright BSI makes his home in Santa Clarita, a charming city at the entrance of the high desert in Southern California. For sixteen years, features and articles under his byline appeared in *The Tidings* – now *The Angelus News* – publications of the Roman Catholic Archdiocese of Los Angeles. Continuing his education in 2007, Mr. Wright graduated *summa cum laude* from Grand Canyon University, attaining a Bachelor of Arts degree in Christian Studies. He then attained a Master of Arts degree, also in Christian Studies. Once active in the entertainment industry, in an abortive attempt to revive dramatic radio in 1976 with his beloved mentor the late Daws Butler directing, Mr. Wright co-produced and wrote the syndicated *New Radio Adventures of Sherlock Holmes* starring the late Edward Mulhare as the Great Detective. Mr. Wright has written for several television quiz shows and remains proud of his work for *The Quiz Kid's Challenge* and the popular TV quiz show *Jeopardy!* for which The Academy of Television Arts and Sciences honored him in 1985 with an Emmy nomination in the field of writing. Honored with membership in *The Baker Street Irregulars* as "The Manor House Case" after founding *The Non-Canonical Calabashes, The Sherlock Holmes Society of Los Angeles* in 1970, Mr. Wright has written for *The Baker Street Journal* and *Mystery Magazine.* Since 1971, he has conducted lectures on Sherlock Holmes's influence on literature and cinema for libraries, colleges, and private organizations, including MENSA. Mr. Wright's whimsical *Sherlock Holmes Cookbook* (Drake) created with John Farrell BSI, was published in 1976 and a mystery novel, *Enter the Lion: a Posthumous Memoir of Mycroft Holmes* (Hawthorne), "edited" with Michael Hodel BSI, followed in 1979. As director general of The Plot Thickens Mystery Company, Mr. Wright originated hosting "mystery parties" in homes, restaurants, and offices, as well as producing and directing the very first "Mystery Train" tours on Amtrak beginning in 1982.

Lightning Source UK Ltd.
Milton Keynes UK
UKHW011436140520
363261UK00001B/36

9 781787 055667